The Path of the Hawk

Ballas swung an uppercut into the first guard's jaw, clashing his teeth together. A second guard swept a knife at Ballas's face, but the Hawk seized his wrist and twisted and pulled, flinging the guard over the balustrade. Then something cracked against the back of his skull. Sparks blossomed in the Hawk's vision, drifting and glittering. Stumbling, Ballas turned as a cudgel swept forward and cracked his eyebrow. Roaring, Ballas grabbed the guard's tunic and, shifting his weight, brought his boot down on the man's knee. The joint broke loose, detaching with a muted *pop*, and the guard fell, yowling. A fourth guard remained, clutching a short-sword. He looked very frightened, very confused. He had entered the bed-chamber with three companions, spurred on by a hunger for glory. Now, he was alone.

The Path of the Hawk

Ian Graham

www.orbitbooks.net

ORBIT

First published in Great Britain in 2016 by Orbit

1 3 5 7 9 10 8 6 4 2

A CIP catalogue record for this book is available from the British Library.

ISBN 978-0-356-50693-7

Typeset in Garamond by Palimpsest Book Production Limited, Falkirk, Stirlingshire
Printed and bound in Great Britain by CPI Group (UK) Ltd, Croydon CR0 4YY

Papers used by Orbit are from well-managed forests and other responsible sources.

MIX
Paper from
responsible sources
FSC
www.fsc.org FSC® C104740

Orbit
An imprint of
Little, Brown Book Group
Carmelite House
50 Victoria Embankment
London EC4Y 0DZ

An Hachette UK Company
www.hachette.co.uk

www.orbitbooks.net

For Harriet

PART ONE

PROLOGUE

The crows are to blame.

Thronging the cluster-reeds, flapping and cawing, they are frightening the fish. The silver trout are hiding somewhere under the surface, maybe tucked in the gloom of the overhanging riverbank, perhaps cloistered in the weeds sprouting from the riverbed.

Wherever they are, they refuse to show themselves. The boy has tried various types of bait, from maggots to sweetcorn, and still they lie low, fearful of the dark birds.

Yes; the crows are spoiling everything.

Laying the rod on the grass, the boy troops along the riverbank.

It is a hot day, the sun warm on his bare shoulders, the sky clear. The previous night, he had dreamt of a day such as this. Standing on the riverbank, he had fished the river, catching trout after trout. In fact, he fished as no man had fished before: each time he cast off, a trout had snapped up the bait as soon as the hook was on the water. No pause, no delay. Just cast, snap and a slow reeling in. It had happened again and again, until his catch lay in a waist-high heap, scales gleaming pink-silver.

Of course, dreams are not prophecies, but theatre stages on which a fellow's wishes and fears are enacted. But he likes to think they contained a grain of truth, a hint of premonition.

So it was that, when he woke and went to breakfast, he said to his mother, 'How many trout do you want for supper?'

'You are going to the river? Take care, then,' she had said.

'But how many? One, two, half a dozen?'

She pretended to think. 'One will be enough.'

'I will get two,' he said. 'There is no reason we should starve.'

At this rate, he will not catch anything. Except sunburn. Striding toward the cluster-reeds, fifty paces away, he waves his arms and shouts.

'Aiy, you lot – get lost! Go on, back to your nests, you toe-rags!'

The crows are unperturbed. He is not surprised: they are stubborn creatures, difficult to frighten. Few things alarm them – certainly not his cries and gestures, nor the grinning scarecrows in Farmer Heatle's wheatfields, nor the local customs of sprinkling crowblood and powdered cats' bones into the soil where crops grow.

Drawing closer, he spots a cloud of flies hovering over the reeds.

Small wonder the crows have not fled. Something dead is trapped amongst the thin stalks. A drowned dog, perhaps. Or a sheep drifted down from Bulkin's Weir. It hardly matters. As long as the dead thing remains, the crows will not go away. Whatever it is, the boy will have to move it. An unpleasant task, no doubt. Most likely, the thing will be rotten, maggoty and foul-smelling enough to make a rat vomit. It might well fall to pieces in his hands, too. But that is of no odds. If need be, he will cleanse himself in the river.

Ten paces away, he spots a patch of colour in the reeds. A flash of scarlet. The colour of death, of mutilation. Then something flashes gold, catching the sunlight.

Intrigued, the boy picks up his pace. Five yards away, and the crows bundle off, settling on the ground a little further downstream.

The boy halts at the reeds. Looks down.

It is a man. Or rather, a man's corpse, trapped where the reeds sink into the water.

The boy has seen only one dead body before. His grandmother's, lodged snugly in an open casket on her burial day, preened and powdered, radiating tranquil acceptance. The fellow in the reeds is in his seventh decade, his grandmother's age, more or less – but there the similarities *end. He does not appear contented. He looks as though he would scream, were it possible. Decaying, his flesh slithers off his skull in greasy clods whilst that which remains bears traces of monstrous ill-treatment. His nose has been sliced off, as have his lips. His teeth are shattered and his tongue, lolling from his mouth, has been halved lengthwise to resemble a serpent's. Embedded in his eyeballs, there are darning needles, glittering; all that remains of his sheared-off ears are gill-like furrows.*

The corpse wears scarlet robes. This is important, thinks the boy. Important, too, is the pendant around his neck, a gold triangle on a fine-linked chain. Both garb and adornment signify something, although he cannot say what.

Something stirs in the corpse's mouth. Something sleek, trembling in the darkness.

A bubble rises, popping on the surface. Then a trout slithers out, slopping over the man's cheekbone and plunging into the water.

The boy yells and this time, the crows skirl away, shrieking toward the wheatfields.

By noon, the riverbank teems with Papal Wardens. The law-keepers are impressive in their black tunics and helms, and their sheathed swords give the boy a tiny buzz of excitement. They are important men, engaged in important business. Stitched on their tunics are elongated red triangles, similar to the corpse's pendant. The boy's father has explained what the insignia represents and the boy understands that the corpse is not that of any old man, but one of the most powerful individuals in Druine.

'Aye, he vanished a month ago. Snatched off Grimlarren Moor, his guards slain. Gone without a trace,' says a Warden, his grizzled face thoughtful. 'No ransom was issued, so we wondered why he had been taken. I suppose we have our answer now.'

Hands on hips, the boy's father stands close to the Warden. 'Blessed Master Helligraine,' he murmurs, shaking his head. 'Is that it, then? He was kidnapped purely to what — suffer?'

'To be punished,' confirms the Warden. 'There are many heathens in Druine, deluded souls who do not tread the true path. Mercifully, they hold no sway – all they can do is lash out like idiots, making stupid gestures like this.' He pats the side of a cart. The Master's corpse lies on the back, hidden under a tarpaulin. Its journey from the river was not uneventful: rotten from flesh to bone-marrow, it had shed a hand, and a foot, and entrails had leaked from its belly, slopping onto the grass. 'It was revenge, born of frustration. You ever seen a hen-pecked man kick his dog, for he dares not square up to his wife? This is the same thing, more or less.'

'They say Helligraine was a good man.'

'One of the finest to ever walk the corridors of the Sacros,' says the Warden. 'He will be in Paradise now. The Four will have led him through the Forest, and he will be reaping the rewards of a life well lived.'

Evening comes and the boy sits at the table in the kitchen, taking his evening meal. As soon as the Wardens were gone, his father had throttled the plumpest chicken, which his mother served with onion gravy and potatoes flavoured with mint. Now, they talk about the corpse, for there is little else they can think of.

The boy says, 'He was a good man. One of the finest to walk the corridors of the Sacros.'

His father and mother look at him.

The boy blinks. 'That is what you said, Father. And the Warden.'

'It is not wise to speak truthfully in the company of those men,' says his father, laying his knife upon his plate. 'Utter an ill word about the Masters, and you will be hanged. And all words, the honest ones, about those scarlet-clad weasels are ill. To a man, they are filthy, corrupt, greedy pieces of dung. They set taxes, declare wars and force us to live under the cruellest laws imaginable. I'll give you an example. You know what they believe, don't you?'

'About the Pilgrims?'

'Yes. Tell me.'

The boy glances uneasily at his mother. 'Thousands of years ago, four men were told by the creator-god to walk through Druine and as they went, they healed the sick and told people how they ought to live. Then they met on the top of a mountain called Scarrendestin. That is what the triangle on the Warden's clothes means. It is supposed to be the mountain.'

'Go on,' says his father.

'On top of the mountain, they Melded, which means they joined together to become a single holy being. Now, when folk die, they are sent to the Eltheryn Forest, which is a horrible place, full of demons. But if you are a good person, the Four protect you, and lead you to Paradise.'

'You can see it is all nonsense, can't you?'

The boy hesitates. 'Is it?'

'It is horsesh—' Catching himself, the boy's father grunts. 'It is horse manure, from top to bottom. A fairytale, nothing more. But if you do not believe it, or pretend to, the Masters will have you killed. And before they kill you, they will torture you. Do you remember how Helligraine was all chopped up?'

The boy nodded. He doubted he would ever forget.

'The Masters will do worse, far worse. So even though you and I know they talk nonsense, we must keep it to ourselves. You understand?'

'Yes, Father.'

The boy's father pats him on the hand. 'Good lad,' he says, picking up the knife and skewering a lump of chicken.

7

CHAPTER ONE

And so to Druine . . .

I will keep this entry brief, for I have written extensively on this subject elsewhere.

I was born and bred in Druine, such was my misfortune. It would take several volumes to describe everything detestable about this crumbling, bankrupt country, so I shall point out only its most striking flaws.

It is governed by the Pilgrim Church in general, and the Blessed Masters in particular, twenty-seven clergymen who reside in the Esklarion Sacros in the country's capital city, Soriterath. My feelings concerning religious leadership are well known, but can be summarised thus: when dealing with practical matters – that is, everything required for the smooth running of a country – one must not put one's faith in faith. By all means, entertain yourselves privately with thoughts of gods, demons, faeries and hobgoblins, but do not rely upon such fictions to guide you in matters of state. When a hospital must be built, or taxes set, or laws laid down and enforced, you must be led by common sense, nothing else.

Of course, this runs contrary to the principles of Druine. There, *The Book of the Pilgrims* is the cornerstone of civilisation, a collection of folktales and myths, transfigured into an allegedly historical chronicle of divine events occurring two millennia ago. We all know – and have been bored tearful

8

by – the story of the four men who climbed a mountain and became the Four.

As mythologies go, the tale is exceptional only in that it is prodigiously uninteresting. Whilst it is common for religions to pillage old stories, changing them here and there and proclaiming them as their own, it is rare for any creed to choose the most tedious, implausible and insultingly banal as the basis for their beliefs. One would swear that the Church had been created as part of a wager, struck up by giggling drunkards in a tavern, to pass the time between cock-fights.

Yet the Church must be praised in one regard: in the Penance Oak, it created a symbol recognisable throughout the globe. Like the best symbols, it is essentially simple: a gigantic oak tree, upon whose branches are nailed the heads of those who have committed the sin of sorcery. It catches the eye and inhabits the mind; whilst everything else created by the Church ought to be forgotten, this image alone deserves to persist . . .

Extracted from *A Guide to the Nations* by
Cavielle Shaelus

When did it begin? wondered General Standaire, commander of the Hawks.

It was impossible to be certain; it had crept up on him, by imperceptible degrees, this tendency to dwell upon the past. No one could deny he had spent his life well, enlisting in the Druinese army at twenty-two, and serving loyally for the next thirty-four years. He had risen through the ranks as swiftly as an arrow launched skywards; he had fought in countless countries, gaining countless decorations. Most importantly, a quarter-century ago, he founded the Hawks, the Druinese military's elite regiment.

The Hawks were not a conventional fighting unit. They

were never found upon battlefields; they existed not within the crimson uproar of outright war, but the dark crevices of intrigue. Spying, sabotage, assassinations, and other less definable practices, were their meat and drink. Subtle, secretive, as intangible as a shadow's shadow, they were a vital cog in the machinery of the Church; and whilst the commonfolk knew of the Hawks by reputation, none knew exactly what they did, or how they did it. The regiment was a living mystery, as enigmatic – and feared – as any entity in folklore or superstition.

The Hawks were barracked at the Roost, far out on Kelledin Moor. It was there, two days earlier, a Papal Messenger had arrived with a letter addressed to Standaire. It read:

General
  Meet me where the marble ships sail to and fro, an hour
  before dawn, in two days' time.
  Secrecy is all.

Although the document lacked a signature, it bore the distinctive red seal of High Office, indicating it had been written by a Blessed Master. The missing signature aside, the letter was strange for a couple of reasons.

First, a Papal Summons always entailed a meeting in the Esklarion Sacros, the holy building where the Masters conducted business. Why, then, was Standaire ordered to meet the letter's author a mile and a half away, at a war memorial in a seldom-trodden quarter of the city?

Second, and surely related to the first, there was the matter of secrecy. Meet *me*, the letter said, implying it had been written by a single Master, acting alone – one who did not want his scarlet-clad brethren to know about the summons.

During the long ride from the Roost, the general asked

himself, *Why?* over and over, without reaching a satisfactory conclusion.

Now, he would find out soon enough.

He stood in a small city square. Alleyways extended into darkness on all sides, cutting between grim little shops with boarded-over windows, moss-tufted stonework and fungus-speckled eaves. The war memorial suffered from the same neglect. A marble block, six feet high and ten along, it was sullied by patches of dark grey mould. Although he was not a sentimental man, Standaire began wiping away the mould with his sleeve, slowly revealing the frieze beneath.

As he worked, he recalled the events commemorated by the memorial. Thirty years ago, a fleet of battleships dropped anchor on the south-eastern coast of Druine. They hailed from Vohoria, an island nation fifty miles across the Saelfus Ocean. The Vohorin soldiers disembarked and an invasion began. Although the Vohorin forces were small, just some ten thousand men, they made good progress for the first week, venturing fifty miles inland, defeating regiment after regiment of the defending Druinese. Stationed a hundred and fifty miles away, Standaire, then a mere foot soldier, did not see battle. But like everyone else, he heard the rumours: the Vohorin were so unexpectedly successful because they were employing sorcery. After every battle, only charred corpses remained of the Druinese combatants, and the men had perished not on the battlefield, but in their encampments as they took their nightly rest. Initially it was thought the Vohorin had used some clever fire-spreading device, explosives perhaps, but the few survivors reported something quite different: the men simply burst aflame as they stood talking, or lay sleeping. Eventually, the magic was traced back to a sorcerer named Jurel Kraike, an aide to the Vohorin Emperor Grivillus. Upon Kraike's assassination, the Vohorin, knowing they stood no chance of victory – they were too heavily outnumbered – fled back to their homeland . . .

And the Needful Scourge began.

Rubbing away the last blotch of mould, Standaire contemplated the frieze. It was split into three parts. The first showed the Druinese warships chasing the enemy back to Vohoria, the second Vohoria's destruction, the third the warships' homeward journey, their triumphal flags flying from the mast-tops.

Rendered in stone, it looked like a simple, hygienic operation. But Standaire knew different: he had been there, after all.

The Church-decreed objectives of the Scourge were clear: slaughter every man, woman and child, torch every building, grind salt into every square inch of soil. Do not destroy Vohoria; *obliterate* it.

And they had done so. For three years, the Vohorin streets frothed with blood, and the sky hung black with smoke. Standaire, along with countless others, ceased to be a soldier, becoming instead a mechanism of destruction. The Church promised that the carnage was not sinful; on the contrary, it was a holy act, one so profound it purified the soul, and those soldiers who died in Vohoria would gain immediate entry to Paradise. After all, Kraike's sorcery was so obscene in its effects, so contrary to laws both holy and natural, it could only be of demonic origin; to fight the Vohorin, the Church claimed, was to fight evil itself.

Yes, Standaire had played his part. He had fought, and fought well; he had killed, and not once had he disgraced himself by showing mercy.

Once Vohoria had fallen, he had sailed back to Druine. The atmosphere aboard the warships was strange, he recalled. The soldiers were dazed, as if they had woken from a dream – or a long nightmarish hallucination. As they coasted over sunlit

12

blue water, they could not connect themselves with their deeds in Vohoria: immersed in constant violence, in butchery and near-barbarism, they had become different people, animals of a sort. Some were stricken with guilt; others were merely numb. As for Standaire – he harboured no extraordinary feelings either way. He had done his duty, that was all.

At the time, he paid it no thought. Now, in his fifty-sixth year, he brooded on it, as he did many things. He was getting old, not for a man, but for a soldier. How long could he continue serving the Church? How long, until he was let out to pasture? And when the time came, what would remain of him? The army had filled every hollow atom of his existence for most of his adult life. Was there a civilian Standaire, waiting to emerge? One who occupied himself with— with what? Standaire had no idea how ordinary people passed the time. Did they lounge in taverns all day? Go to the theatre? Keep a garden? He supposed they must do; there was little else in life, once one's work had ended. But none of this appealed to him. More, the mere thought of such gentle idleness revolted him.

He glanced at the various alleys, seeking movement. Nothing, except rats and the occasional stray cat.

He was not the same man who sailed to Vohoria. For a while, it had seemed he belonged to that peculiar breed of man who remained youthful almost until the point of death. But three years ago, his age started to show. His chestnut hair grew grey; creases appeared on his face, arriving as suddenly as fissures threading the ground after an earthquake. His hard, sinuous strength was diminishing; his movements were slow, and every morning he woke to find his body sleep-stiffened, his muscles sore and joints cracking. Worse, he was plagued by weariness, a constant fatigue that sleep could not cure. He fought against it, but it was always there, the unavoidable heaviness of mortality.

'Dwelling on past glories, General?'

Standaire blinked, and looked away from the memorial. A stooped figure emerged from an alley, clad in a long woollen coat, despite the night's warmth. Sweeping back its hood, it revealed a face older than old – a relic of sagging, rumpled skin, the scalp hairless, the eyes shadowed. Hunch-shouldered and hook-nosed, Blessed Master Faltriste resembled a preybird, a scraggly vulture skulking on a branch in some heat-blasted wasteland.

'Your holiness,' said Standaire, bowing.

'Are you well, General?'

'I am well enough. And yourself?'

'I am unravelling, one thread at a time. But I am glad you are here. Let us be seated.'

They sat upon a wooden bench next to the memorial. Faltriste was silent, staring emptily ahead. Then, 'I apologise for the unorthodox nature of your summons, General. I was not sure if you would answer. My message carried the whiff of intrigue, did it not?'

'It did, your holiness.'

'But you have spoken of it to no one?'

'Not a soul.'

'You are a good man, General.'

Standaire caught the tang of wine on Faltriste's breath. Was he drunk? No, the general did not think so. But he seemed troubled, and perhaps supped a goblet or two to steady his nerves.

'I must be back inside the Sacros before dawn.' Faltriste looked at the sky. 'So I will be brief. If I begin to ramble, you must slap me across the face.' A faint smile, tinged with sadness. 'Do you recognise the difference between the Church and its custodians? You understand that the Church is an institution dedicated to implementing the Four's will yet men like myself,

14

the Masters, are merely servants of that higher cause? And we are not the Church, only the means by which it exists?'

Standaire said he did.

'And if someone within the Sacros were to act against the Church, you would do what was needed?'

'It would be my duty,' said Standaire. 'Is there such a person?'

'There is *always* such a person. Normally, they are capable of causing little damage before they are exposed. But in this instance . . .' He coughed; the wine-tang grew stronger. 'You will recall that nearly a year ago, Blessed Master Helligraine was abducted from Grimlarren Moor whilst riding to the Theosophical Library at Graenletter. His guards were killed; he disappeared. We searched high and low for him; assuming he had been taken by bandits, or rebels, we waited for a ransom demand. None came. Then, a month later, his corpse was found in Blackstyre River.'

'It was a dark day for the Church,' said Standaire.

'The darkest in living memory,' confirmed Faltriste. 'Helligraine was the holiest man to ever tread the Sacros corridors. Devout, intelligent, compassionate – he deserved his scarlet robes more than anyone. Of course, the populace learned of his disappearance; such things cannot be kept secret. But certain details were kept secret, secret even from *you*, General.'

He gazed at his hands, interlaced upon his lap.

'No one outside the Sacros knew Helligraine would be crossing Grimlarren on that day, at that hour. Originally, he planned to make the journey by boat, mooring at Linklatre in the evening then sailing on to Graenletter the next morning. The night before he departed, however, the Church Elementalist predicted storms and Helligraine, never fond of sea-travel, decided to travel overland, on horseback. This change of plan occurred at the last moment; no one knew of it, except the other Masters. Even Helligraine's guards were kept in the dark, until they set forth. So, we must ask: Who could have informed Helligraine's kidnappers of these new plans?'

'An aide, perhaps?'

Faltriste shook his head. 'They did not know, not until Helligraine had departed. Too late, certainly, to arrange the ambush. Who else, do you think, General?'

There was only one real possibility. Quietly, Standaire said, 'You suspect a Master?'

'We are but men,' said Faltriste, sadly, as if identifying a fact that had blighted the Church since its inception, two thousand years ago. 'Beneath our holy attire, we are prey to vices like anyone else. Greed, ambition, arrogance . . . We struggle and sometimes we fall short. I believe I know who betrayed Helligraine. But I shall not name him. Not until the hour is ripe. One must proceed warily, you see. It is not unknown for a Master to die prematurely, even in the safety of the Sacros.'

'You fear assassination?'

'That is why I am meeting you in secret, General. None of my fellow Masters know I am here, and it must remain that way, until I am ready to make my move.' Something caught Faltriste's eye. A tatter of cobweb, clinging to his shoulder. He brushed it away.

'You came out by the tunnels?' asked Standaire, referring to the warren of passageways running beneath the Sacros. Constructed several hundred years ago, they emerged in various parts of the city, escape routes in case the Sacros was besieged by rebels.

'It was the only way.' Faltriste drew a breath. 'It is ironic, General, that if Helligraine were here, he would have resolved this awful business as swiftly as a rat vanishing down a drainpipe. He had the most astonishing mind. Instinctive, analytical — it would be easy to envy him, if he were not such a gracious

16

soul. I pray that his current circumstances have not diminished his mental powers.'

Current circumstances? An odd phrase to use about a dead man.

Spotting Standaire's confusion, Faltriste said, 'And now we get to the heart of the matter. Helligraine is still alive, and I want you and your Hawks to find him.'

Standaire blinked, slowly. 'The corpse in Blackstyre River . . .'

'. . . was not Helligraine's,' said Faltriste. 'It wore Helligraine's holy attire, and was of similar proportions to the absent Master. There were other superficial similarities – hair colour, and so forth. But the one thing that could have proved it was truly Helligraine, its face, was both mutilated and water-rotted.' He shrugged his thin shoulders. 'Nonetheless, we assumed it was he. I suppose we had given him up for dead, and were waiting for the proof. Expectations colour our perceptions, do they not?

'When Helligraine was invested as a Master, he was required to confess his sins. In his days before piety, he had led a lively, adventurous life, laden with physical dangers. He suffered various injuries, broken bones in particular, and these were recorded by the priest who took his confession.

'As you will know, General, a damaged bone tends to heal imperfectly; it *overheals*, so to speak: more bone matter is produced than is strictly needed to repair the break, as if the bone is strengthening itself against another identical injury. Two weeks ago, I received information suggesting the dead man in the river was not Helligraine. So I ventured to the Sacros ossuary and inspected the bones in the casket bearing Helligraine's name. Yes, they bore traces of numerous breaks sustained during life, but these were the result of the sort of mishaps common amongst working men of any complexion. Certainly, none corresponded to those described in Helligraine's confession. Make no mistake: Helligraine's breaks were distinctive. A snapped femur sustained by falling from a mountain in Keltuska; a splintered forearm acquired in a tavern-brawl in Geldaste . . . As I say, Helligraine's life had been inordinately lively before he took his vows. And that life, it seemed, was continuing, for the bones in the casket were not the Master's. The corpse in the river was a decoy, a ruse.'

'And the other Masters know nothing of this?'

'It is a truth known only to you and me – oh, and one other. But I will speak of him in good time.' He was silent for several moments, watching a rat scurrying out of the alley. 'There are other details you must know,' he said. 'One in particular.'

He turned his face to Standaire.

'I do not believe Helligraine was kidnapped because he is a Master. He was taken because of who he *used* to be, before he adopted the holy life.

'In his younger days, Helligraine was a sinner. His crime was, shall we say, *errant scholarship*. He wrote forbidden texts, works considered antithetical to the Church's teachings. Not only that, he attacked the Church itself, denouncing it in treatises of the most venomous nature. All this occurred before his conversion, of course; and that conversion was brought on by a holy experience, a divine visitation . . .' He laughed noiselessly, eyes bright. 'Sadly, I am not permitted to speak of it, although it is quite a tale. Nonetheless, Helligraine became a man of the cloth and like many who have seen the light, he loathed the man he had once been. It is often the way with reformed sinners: they gaze upon their former selves as embodiments of wickedness. It keeps them from regressing into their old habits, their abandoned wickedness. And yet . . . yet I fear this is what has befallen Helligraine. He has regressed, in deed, although not in spirit. He has been *forced* to take up his quill again, and write as he once wrote.

'New forbidden texts have appeared on the Dark Market, bearing the hallmarks of Helligraine's writing style. Certain turns of phrase, various dramatic flourishes, a tone of contemptuous indignation – they are consistent with his work during his dissolute days.' He looked keenly at Standaire. 'Understand me, General. Helligraine is not producing these works willingly. His kidnappers have plunged him into servitude; they have compelled him to toil as a slave-scribe. Goodness knows what they must have done to break his spirit, for he would not have reprised his old profession unless he was in grave danger – or, indeed, suffering unspeakable torments. I have no doubt he has been tortured, abused, ill-treated in every imaginable way. He often said he would rather die than speak badly of the Church, or the Four. And yet he is doing so, in the most appalling fashion.'

Faltriste closed his eyes.

'I cannot imagine how he must be feeling. Every word must be an agony, every phrase an excruciation worthy of the Forest. The poor man, the poor, poor man . . .' His eyes flicked open, glittering with resolve. He clenched his fists, and for a moment the tatty vulture vanished, replaced by a threadbare but strong-hearted eagle. 'You must find him, General. Find him, yes, then take him to safety.'

'Druine is a large country,' said Standaire. 'I would not know where to start.'

'Oh, it will not be difficult. Are you familiar with the methods employed by Scholars of Outrage?'

Scholars of Outrage were the Church's hunters of forbidden texts. Feared throughout Druine, they tracked down those who were guilty of buying, selling, writing and producing outlawed books. Fiercely dedicated to their work, they had a reputation for mercilessness, even cruelty. 'I am aware of their duties,' said Standaire. 'But I do not know how they go about their business.'

19

'Often, they are content to apprehend the lesser miscreants, the text-vendors and collectors,' said Faltriste. 'But they also pursue those who print the outlawed works. To do so, they interrogate someone who owns a certain text, demanding to know where he obtained it. Once they have acquired this information, they visit the supplier, and ask the same question. Then they move on to the next person, and so on, until they have traced the text back to whoever printed it to begin with. These men, the printers, are the ones who truly profit from the Dark Market.

'If Helligraine is being used as a slave-scribe – and I am certain he is – it is likely he is imprisoned close to the place where his books are printed. Find it, General, and you will be a cat's whisker away from the Master himself.'

Standaire immediately saw a problem. 'It is my understanding that once a Dark text reaches the Market, copies are made by *other* printers, keen to make some money of their own. And these printers may have nothing to do with Helligraine. What is to say we will not embark on a wild goose chase?'

'The first editions of Helligraine's work, those produced by his captors, bear certain typographical flaws,' said Faltriste. 'The top is missing from every capital A and the letter y, like the unlucky mouse in the fairy story, lacks its tail. Find the printing press which uses this faulty type, and you will find Helligraine, too.'

He pulled a folded parchment from inside his coat.

'This,' he said, handing the document to Standaire, 'contains the name and address of a man who owns a first edition. Go to him; ensure that he reveals all you need to know. I have also written down the address of Leptus Quarvis, a retired Scholar of Outrage. A good man, he is the only other soul who knows of this terrible business. You must take Helligraine to his dwelling place, once you have set him free. He will know what

20

to do next. Oh,' added Faltriste, 'I nearly forgot: the text you need is called *The Loss*.' A pause. 'It does not bear Helligraine's name, but that of his former self. It is a name guaranteed to kindle interest, and earn a good deal of money for text-sellers throughout Druine.'

He looked intently at Standaire.

'Once, before he trod the sunlit road, Helligraine was Cavielle Shaelus.'

For a split instant, Standaire felt as if he was falling. Cavielle Shaelus – the incomparable scholar, the reckless adventurer, the thorn in the Church's side. The writer of countless forbidden texts, mocking the Church and those faithful to it. Yes, Cavielle Shaelus, who had been hunted by every Scholar of Outrage and Papal Warden in Druine, yet evaded them all.

Standaire exhaled, slowly.

'I see the name means something to you,' said Faltriste, wryly.

'How could it not? Everyone has heard of him, one way or another.'

'He takes no pride in his old name. In fact, it sickens him. His conversion was absolute,' Faltriste went on. 'His years of sin are far behind him. He came to us years ago, after undergoing a mystical experience strong enough to change the alignment of his heart. Once we determined the experience was genuine, we had no choice but to let him join our ranks. Not as a Master, you understand. Not straight away. He served many years as a priest in a remote parish, and several more as a Scholar of Outrage, before he was granted the scarlet.' Suddenly he looked up. A faint bluish tint infiltrated the night-darkened sky. A lone bird sang somewhere close by.

'Sweet mercy, dawn is coming. How swiftly the sun seems to rise, when one is old. General, I must return to the Sacros.'

21

He got stiffly to his feet. The eagle had been replaced by the vulture; the Master looked worn out, half crippled by age and responsibility.

'Find Helligraine and take him to Quarvis,' he repeated. 'On no account deliver him to the Sacros, no matter how much he wishes to return. He will not be safe there.'

Standaire stood. 'Permit me to walk you to the tunnels.'

'No, General. I wish to enjoy this brief spell of freedom alone.' He glanced at Standaire. 'The Sacros is much like a prison,' he said, sadly. 'That is something the commonfolk cannot understand. They imagine we dwell in luxury, and take our duties lightly. It is not so. We all suffer, in our own ways. Good luck, General.'

Faltriste shuffled off into the alley from which he had emerged, vanishing into darkness. Standaire stood still, listening to the Master's boots scuffing on the paving stones. When they drifted out of earshot, he turned, and walked back the way he had come.

A short time later, he reached Justice Square. To his right, the red-stone bulk of the Esklarion Sacros loomed, as colossal and imposing as a mountain. Which was precisely the desired effect: two hundred and seventy-three feet tall, shaped like a flat-topped pyramid, it was a symbolic structure, representing Scarrendestin, the holy mountain, where the Pilgrims Melded into the Four. At each corner of the base, a tall tower speared skywards – one tower for each Pilgrim. The Sacros was designed to kindle feelings of pious wonder. Here was the celestial spark made tangible, the essence of the unseen ever-after manifested in stone. Undoubtedly, it affected many citizens in the desired way: it was easy to mistake physical grandeur for proof of divine authority. For others, though, it stoked the fires of resentment. Druine was crumbling; from north to south, east to west, the nation was sliding into decay, disrepair. The bony-fingered spectres of death, disease and poverty prowled the land, and when the afflicted gazed upon the Sacros, they felt only bitterness.

There it is, the home of the Blessed Masters. In their grand bedrooms, they sleep warmly, whilst we shiver in the gutter. In their great halls, they feast on delicacies, whilst we gnaw rotting meat from old bones. And those ancient fools are cared for when they sicken, whilst we suffer alone, weeping, puking, wrapping our sores in dirty bandages . . .

To an extent, it was true. The Masters led lives of comparative luxury, whereas hardship was the lot of the common man. Yet Standaire was loyal to the Church. How could he be anything else? As a soldier and a Hawk, he had travelled widely, visiting lands where different forms of governance prevailed. Tyranny, monarchy, oligarchy – he had seen them all, and come to the conclusion that they were worse than the Church's form of rule in one vital respect: they could not create an enduring stability. A people who lived with a despot's boot upon their neck, or languished under the control of someone whose power was an accident of birth, nursed a singularly vicious type of resentment, so extreme it propelled them toward revolution. When such uprisings were thwarted, it was done brutally, and the rulers, fearing a repeat, treated their subjects with renewed severity. On the rare occasions the uprisings were successful, the methods used were barbarous and, having proven their worth, were employed in day-to-day governance: in effect, one tyrant was traded for another. For all its flaws, the Church had never suffered a genuine attack from the people. In its centuries-long rule, there had been domestic peace, of a ragged kind, and whilst the citizens simmered with grievances, they never boiled over into outright rebellion.

Halfway across the square, Standaire halted.

Ahead, the Penance Oak sprouted from a gap in the paving

23

stones. According to the Church, it was seeded by an acorn blown from the Eltheryn Forest into the corporeal world and, whether or not the claim was true, the great tree *did* possess an unearthly quality. Ancient, clad in craggy black bark, its branches as glossily dark as molten tar, it was unlike any other example of its species Standaire had ever seen. It was vast, the trunk as wide as a barn door, the upper branches groping some forty or fifty feet into the air. In its own way, it was more impressive than the Sacros, for that was contrived by the minds of men, but it had developed organically, at once obeying the laws of nature and stretching them to their limits.

It was also a place of punishment.

This morning, there were three heads nailed to the branches, each held in place by an iron spike driven through the forehead. Two were rotting, the flesh tumbling from their skulls in greasy, fly-speckled lumps; from their size, and the long hair dangling from scalps that had slithered askew from the bony pate beneath, Standaire guessed they had belonged to girls, adolescents perhaps, a year or two away from full womanhood. Their mouths hung open, their swollen, blueish-green tongues lolled, and their eyes were missing, plucked from their sockets by the magpies that gathered at the Oak every dawn. Like all those mounted on the Oak, the girls were being punished for practising the magical arts. Their heads were nailed side by side, indicating they had been co-conspirators in their forbidden activity; although there was no public notice describing the precise nature of their crimes, Standaire suspected they were trivial. Concocting a love potion, perhaps. Or casting some minor maleficium on an enemy. Nothing worth dying for.

Its flesh intact, its eyes still glassily staring, the third head was a newcomer to the Oak. It belonged to an old man, with a neat short-cropped beard; even though his facial muscles were slackened by death, he wore an expression of gentle kindness. What, then, was his story? Again, the general's imagination made a suggestion: he was a healer of some description. Such men were popular throughout Druine. Their services were cheaper than those of a physician and, it was said, not always as ineffective.

He thought about Helligraine. Once, when he was Cavielle Shaelus, the Church had desired more than anything to display his head upon the Oak, not because he was a magicker in any true sense, but because he had written texts that occasionally contained occult content. He had been hunted throughout Druine, and beyond; as his reputation grew amongst the commonfolk, who were beguiled by his adventurous spirit and frequent attacks upon the Church, he was denounced from every pulpit in the land. And yet, in the end, he had gone to the Church and, incredibly, the Church embraced him.

Standaire had encountered Helligraine numerous times, during summons to the Sacros. He and the Master had spoken on several occasions and although they had discussed nothing of any consequence, he had been struck by the old man's lively, fast-sparking mind, and the intense goodness that radiated from him like light from the sun. It stretched credulity to believe he had once been the Church's prime enemy. But maybe it was really no surprise. The general had heard that converts often embodied their faith to a higher degree than those who had always believed; aware of the perils of sin, they embraced the holy life with an urgency lacking in those who knew no different.

Faltriste had spoken of a mystical experience. Standaire was curious. It was not unusual for a heretic to turn believer after a vision, a flash of insight. But for the Church to not merely forgive such a man, but to grant him a priesthood and, in time, elevate him to the highest rank? What had Helligraine's experience consisted of? What *could* it consist of, to deserve such exceptional treatment?

It did not matter. Standaire began walking. He had work to do, and a great distance to travel.

CHAPTER TWO

Whilst there have been many writers of forbidden texts, only one has gained any degree of fame. Ostensibly, Cavielle Shaelus's notoriety was peculiar, for his works were unintelligible to the common man. His subjects were lofty: lost civilisations, metaphysics and arcana – all intriguing in themselves, but beyond the understanding (and interest) of ordinary folk. He became known to every household because of his opposition, in action as well as word, to the Pilgrim Church. It was much less his anti-clerical writings that earned his reputation than his knack for evading the servants of the Church who hunted him, doggedly, throughout his career. He became a symbol for resistance, even entering into the parlance of the day. If one committed a daring act, no matter how petty, one could claim to have 'pulled a Shaelus'. Likewise, a particularly horrific sight was said to be 'enough to make Shaelus wince', a reference to the man's numerous, often bloody adventures, hunting relics overseas. Indeed, it was his reckless nature that caught the imagination as much as anything and, it seems, fired the passions of women throughout Druine; as nothing was known about his physical appearance, it was common for men to claim to be the errant scholar, whilst seducing the fairer sex. Apparently, it was an effective technique, so much so that Shaelus wrote, 'My name has supplanted powdered bull's horn as my homeland's favourite aphrodisiac. Many ugly, artless men have employed it to their advantage, beguiling members of the gentler sex who, in ordinary circumstances, would cringe from their touch. Well, good luck to them, I say! And may their mistresses, as is customary, scream all the proper blasphemies upon reaching gratification.'

It is true that Shaelus's tone was often flippant and, furthermore, he was often accused of exaggeration. Indeed, his first book, an account of his journey through the derelict gardens of Dalzerte weeks before they were destroyed by the Salandier barbarians, nearly shattered his reputation before it was formed. In the first place, few could believe he had visited such an inhospitable region; in the second, the adventures he described stretched plausibility to breaking point. Even I, an admirer, am doubtful whether he walked the 'cracked, weed-draggled paths' as he claimed. But what of it? Excess was merely one aspect of his extraordinary character, and no one can deny that in general, his intentions were serious, whether he was railing against the Church, or describing the lives and philosophies of those who inhabited strange and ancient cultures. Indeed, it was this latter fascination that earned much opprobrium from the Church, for Shaelus demonstrated that there were other ways to lead one's life, and do so happily, without embracing papal dogma. Furthermore, he committed a deed unforgivable in the eyes of the Masters: harnessing his incredible knowledge, and extraordinary analytical powers, he proved that the Church's treasured beliefs – the Four, the Melding – were not merely myths, but myths plundered and adapted from stories already extant amongst various peoples throughout the Globe, many of them heathen. Shaelus cared nothing for the Church's ire, nor the unsettling effect of his studies upon the commonfolk; he said, 'It is my duty – my divine purpose, were the idea not so laughable – to dispel the darkness upon which the Church relies for so much of its power.'

28

Shaelus did indeed enlighten – but obscurity followed incandescence. This man, whose life had been writ large for so long, simply vanished. Some believed he perished on an expedition overseas, whilst others insist that he retired, his work done. Who can say? It is known for certain, however, that he evaded the Church until the very last. Had he been captured, the Masters would have made a great song and dance; his execution would have been a festival, and a symbolic proof that one opposes the forces of light at one's peril. No sinner can escape his crimes, they would say. This is what becomes of those who oppose the Four's will, and the will of its earthbound emissaries.

As I say, they did not capture him, and if he owes the Church a debt of blood, it remains unpaid.

Extract from *The Book of Black Fame – A Catalogue of Sins, Sinners and Errancy* by Shenter Racken

Standaire rode over Kelledin Moor.

The day was punishingly hot. Sun-yellowed grass sagged in the heat and black-bodied flies hovered in throbbing, drifting clouds. Here and there, moss-patched blocks of limestone simmered, hot enough to fry bacon upon. Standaire could not recall a summer of such relentless heat. For months the sky had glared a hard, remorseless blue, unblemished by cloud. Druine was baking, as if locked inside some colossal kiln.

The Roost rose into view – a jumble of low greystone buildings, shimmering in the heat. This was the barracks where the Hawks resided. Drawing closer, Standaire could make out a row of archery targets and hear arrowheads thunking into the packed straw behind the scoring charts. Further off, several groups of Hawks were practising swordplay, wooden swords clattering, whilst more still rehearsed unarmed-combat moves, their groans and grunts drifting lazily through the dry, drowsy air.

Standaire cantered into the stableyard. Several Hawks were cleaning the cobbles.

'You want her settling, sir?' asked Jeilek. Propping his broom against the wall, he approached, a short, stocky man brimming with restless energy. Standaire liked him; he was a stout, trustworthy soul. But he would play no part in the mission to find Helligraine.

'See she is fed, watered and curry-combed.' Dismounting, Standaire handed Jeilek the reins. 'Where is Hawk Ekkerlin?'

'The library, sir,' replied Jeilek, patting the neck of Standaire's chestnut mare. He had a fondness for horses, as, it seemed, did all the Hawks. No matter how diverse their backgrounds, how varied their temperaments, nearly every man in the regiment held the animals in high regard. It was a strange phenomenon, one Standaire could not explain, even though he was not exempt.

'And Hawk Ballas?'

Jeilek shrugged. 'I have no idea, sir. You might try the gym.'

Leaving the stableyard, Standaire visited the gymnasium, a low-roofed outbuilding fifty paces from the roped-off fighting squares. Inside, a dozen or so Hawks hefted weights, groaning and growling, tendons ridging from their necks, veins jutting from their muscles.

Standaire had adopted a scientific approach to the physical conditioning of the regiment. Consulting the finest anatomists in Druine, he determined which exercises would be of greatest benefit to men needing to combine strength with speed and stamina. Too much of one quality generally existed to the detriment of the others; strong men were usually slow and cumbersome, whilst those who were swift tended to be lacking in brawn. But there were exceptions, he admitted – oddities who defied the usual principles.

'Anhaga Ballas?' Standaire scanned the gymnasium.

'Haven't set eyes on him since breakfast,' said a Hawk called Farandrike, sitting on a bench, hands white with chalkdust.

Departing, Standaire visited the dormitory, lined with wood-framed beds. Again, there was no sign of Hawk Ballas.

At last, he went to the library. Here, there were bookcases stuffed with treatises relevant to every aspect of a Hawk's trade: sea-craft, lock-picking, poisoning, interrogation methods . . . A Hawk's mind was crammed with practical information. By and large, they were not an intellectual breed. They seldom read for pleasure; they studied only that which might prove useful. But once again, there were exceptions.

Hawk Ekkerlin sat at a desk, her chestnut hair in a ponytail, a raft of texts spread out before her, her sun-browned face thoughtful, her dark eyes flitting back and forth. As she read, she made notes on a blank parchment, the quill zig-zagging at a furious rate. A Hawk for three years, she bore the hallmarks of service: a pale scar arced across her left cheek, whilst a thin hairless strip in her right eyebrow was testimony to a knife-cut she suffered in the Milvanian swamps. She was solidly built, her shoulders as broad as a lightweight pugilist's; her hands were large, though not unwieldy, the knuckles calloused from hours working at the punching bag.

She did not hear Standaire enter.

'Hawk Ekkerlin.'

She glanced up. 'General.' Rising, she laid down the quill. 'You have returned.'

'We have work to do. Where is Hawk Ballas?'

'Running, sir.'

'Another black mood?'

'Yes, sir.'

'Find him, bring him to me. We are to leave without delay.'

'Yes, sir.' Ekkerlin glanced at the books, hesitated, then began gathering them together.

31

'I will take care of those,' said Standaire.

Ekkerlin hesitated. 'Yes, sir. Thank you, sir.'

Standaire moved to the desk. The books were written in a strange runic language, and the general raised his eyebrows. 'It is a good thing I can make neither head nor tail of your reading material. Were it not so, I might be obliged to report you for reading forbidden texts.' He rested a hand on the books. 'I will secure them in my quarters. No one shall see them.'

'That is greatly appreciated, sir. I will fetch Ballas immediately.' Ekkerlin left the library, crossing the floor in long easy strides.

Gathering the books, Standaire thought again how he was no longer the same man as he had been thirty years ago. Did his treatment of Ekkerlin not prove this? The young Standaire, freshly promoted to sergeant, had been a fierce disciplinarian. A man who stuck rigidly to the rule book. He had court-martialled soldiers for petty offences: gambling, cursing in uniform, even arriving late for training; the troops had despised him. Yet here he was, caring not a jot that one of his Hawks broke the law by reading forbidden texts.

Yes, he had changed. But why?

Age was the answer. Age, and experience. As a young man, he had been full of certainty. There were right and wrong ways of doing things, and that was that. As he got older, he realised it was not so clear-cut. Life was too complex, too chaotic, to be contained by rules, principles, dictums.

One must be pragmatic – that was the only maxim worth a candle, when there was work to be done.

Ekkerlin was an excellent Hawk. Physically tough, absurdly intelligent, cool-witted and courageous, she was an asset Standaire could not afford to lose. So, as far as he was concerned, she could read whatever she liked. He would not notify the

Church. Nor would he try to stop her: if he did, she would be gone in less time than it took for ink to dry upon a page.

Anhaga Ballas ran over Kelledin Moor, sweat streaming over his shirtless body.

He was a big man, six feet eight inches tall, as heavy as a cart laden with masonry stones. His face was a grim slab of flesh, the brows ponderous, the nose thrice-broken. His mouth was perpetually downturned, as if nothing in existence could ever meet with his approval, and his green eyes sparkled with angry insolence. But he was strong. An ox's yoke could rest easily upon his shoulders and, as someone once joked, a quarryman could smash rocks upon his stomach.

And he was *fast*, moving deer-swift across the moors, trying hard to burn off the black mood that had dogged him since sunrise. When his spirits were low, he sought solitude. His dark humours – melancholy, bitterness, rage lacking any discernible source – turned him into bad, dangerous company. Boredom was the spur, he knew. He joined the Hawks because he craved adventure. Yet there were long stretches of time between missions, weeks and months when there was no meaningful way to expend his energy. So he *festered*, growing rotten like an untreated wound. The only solution, albeit imperfect, was to run, run and run, until exhaustion stopped him feeling much of anything.

Picking up his pace, he powered up a steep slope, bracken whipping against his shins. His lungs burned, his leg muscles felt as if they were aflame. His eyes were raw with sweat. His heart thundered.

Good, he thought, darkly.

He crested the slope. Knucker Tarn lay a hundred paces ahead, glittering in the sunlight. Lowering his head, he powered full-tilt to the bank then halted, tugged off his boots, stripped out of his leggings and plunged naked into the water. He swam downwards at a gentle angle until he reached the tarn-bed, twenty feet below the surface. It was gloomy there, and calm, and he sat cross-legged, gripping a clump of waterweeds in each hand to keep from floating up. Closing his eyes, he counted his heartbeats. By the time he reached a hundred and eighteen, a purplish mist was ghosting into his vision and his lungs felt as if they were ripping apart. Letting go of the waterweeds, he swam upward, bursting through the surface and gulping mouthfuls of air.

A rider cantered toward the tarn, leading a second horse by its reins. Grunting, Ballas dived underwater and swam unhurriedly to shore.

'Feeling brighter?' asked Ekkerlin, as Ballas rose close to the bank.

'Piss off.' Ballas wiped water from his face.

'Not a chance. The general wants to see us.'

'A mission?'

'An urgent one. We are to leave straight away; Standaire will explain everything as we ride.'

Climbing out of the tarn, Ballas stumped to his clothes and started to get dressed.

'I hope it is not some bloody spying job, like the disaster at Cralsten Docks. Two weeks peering out of a window, waiting for a dreamers'-weed merchant to appear at some half-derelict warehouse – and he never came. I have never been so bored.'

'We were stationed in a brothel, Anhaga. There was much you could have done to alleviate the tedium.'

'Don't much like whores,' said Ballas, donning his leggings. Sitting, he pulled on his boots. 'They are as joyless as corpses and as cunning as weasels. Can't have fun with someone who'll stab you in the back whilst she is kissing you.'

'If you shun scarlet women, you will lead a very lonely life,' said Ekkerlin. She peered at him. 'Your face . . . I fear it is an obstacle to romance. But then again,' she added, 'it might prove advantageous. If a woman falls for you, you can be sure she is a lady of depth and substance, not some superficial trollop, beguiled by good looks. Of course, it will *help* if she has poor eyesight. And anosmia – the absence of one's sense of smell.' She tapped her nose. 'It can be brought on by a blow to the head. As can concussion, which may lead to impaired judgement – which would also be to your advantage. So, Anhaga, your true love – if she is ever to exist – must be blind, concussed and incapable of smelling a heap of fish guts rotting in the noonday sun.' Ekkerlin laughed. Then grew serious. 'Hop on,' she said, gesturing to the spare horse. 'The general is in a strange mood.'

'His mood is always strange,' scowled Ballas, getting to his feet.

'But never strange in this way. He is . . . distracted.'

Muttering, Ballas strode to the spare horse, patted its side fondly and swung into the saddle.

'Come on,' said Ekkerlin, looping the reins around her hands. 'I'll race you to the Roost. Ready?'

Ballas slipped his feet into the stirrups. 'Aye.'

'On a three count – one, two, ride!' Jabbing her heels, Ekkerlin sped off over the moors. Ballas watched her go, making no effort to follow. He liked Ekkerlin, as much as he liked anyone. But he wished that sometimes, just now and again, she would stop talking quite so much.

CHAPTER THREE

Silver Hoof, the manorial home of Cledrun Mallakos, was three floors high, with mock-battlements running along the roof and fluted pillars flanking the door. Crafted from white stone, the building glowed in the moonlight like a block of ice. At the front, a gravel courtyard abutted on a sward littered with statues of horses, some galloping, others rearing, a few nibbling at the grass. Two dozen guards patrolled back and forth, their tunics emblazoned with silver horseshoes, their hands resting on their swords. Shoulders slumped, the men looked bored, very bored. As well they might. The Hoof lay in the heart of the Clenshire countryside, miles from the nearest town. Ballas suspected it had been a long while since the guards had seen action. They were hired to defend, to fight; yet, in truth, they did little except stroll about, drifting here and there like dandelion spores on a breeze.

Ballas crouched at the railings surrounding the Hoof. Ekkerlin and Standaire knelt close by, garbed entirely in black. Several times, the guards had looked in their direction, then looked away again, seeing nothing.

'Seems Mallakos has got a private army.' Ballas closed his fingers around a railing. Despite the late hour, the metal was warm.

'They will not trouble us,' replied Standaire, quietly. 'They are employed purely to protect the horses in the stables on the far side of the building. They never set foot in Silver Hoof; it is forbidden.'

Ballas scowled. 'What idiot hires men to look after his horses, but not himself?'

'Mallakos is a horse-breeder,' said Ekkerlin, peering at the Hoof. 'The animals are an investment. It is not unusual for greedy men to put money before their own safety.'

'He is rich, is he?'

'Deservedly so, by all accounts. He produces the finest horses in Druine. One of his thoroughbreds is worth as much as a warship.'

Standaire handed Ballas a parchment. It was a map of Silver Hoof's interior, showing every room, corridor and staircase. On the third floor, a square space was labelled *Mallakos's bed-chamber*. Beneath, there was a caricature of a pig's head, grinning, jowls slubbered with food.

'General?' Ballas pointed to the sketch.

'Our informant is the household cook. He says Mallakos is a glutton.'

Ballas looked again at the map, memorising every detail. It took only three heartbeats; as a Hawk, he had been trained to absorb vast amounts of information at a glance. Handing the document to Ekkerlin, he ran through the mission in his mind.

As well as breeding horses, Mallakos collected forbidden texts. Amongst these was a document called *The Loss*, a recent work attributed to Cavielle Shaelus. According to Standaire, first editions were marred by certain typographical errors, rendering them distinct from any subsequent copies; on the Church's bidding, the informant had checked to see if these flaws were present in Mallakos's copy of *The Loss*; they were, and thus it was possible for the Hawks to embark on a crude but effective process by which they would track the text back to its starting point. Simply, they would ask Mallakos who supplied him with his copy, then they would ask *that* person the same question, and so on, until they found the printing press. Then, if Standaire was correct, they would be in close proximity to Helligraine. A rescue operation would follow; the mission would be concluded.

'Let us move,' said the general.

Climbing over the railings, the Hawks sprinted across a patch of open land to a black door set in the rear of Silver Hoof. Steam floated wispily out of a ventilation hole in the stonework. Faintly, Ballas heard the muffled *clack-clack-clack* of something sharp chopping rapidly through something soft.

Standaire tapped on the door. When there was no response, he tapped again, slightly harder. The chopping noises stopped. A pause, then the door cracked open. An eye peered out, as pale blue as streamwater.

'Yes?'

'Cook Warsten?' Standaire whispered.

The blue eye narrowed. 'Who – who are you?'

'The Church has sent us.'

A slow, relieved blink. 'Ah, you are here! Praise the Four. This is excellent.'

The door opened. Thin, grey-fleshed, Warsten had the narrow, joyless face of the permanently resentful. His mouth was as narrow as a steam-slit cut into a piecrust, his hair the colour of whey. He wore a gravy-splashed white apron; in his hand he held a knife, blade flecked with slivers of carrot. He smiled. 'When I informed Father Ransom of my master's misdemeanours, I did not know if anything would come of it. Even when he asked me to check a certain text for imperfections, I was not certain he was taking me seriously. Please, step inside.'

The Hawks entered a large kitchen. A cast iron pan rumbled on a stove, a lump of gammon boiling within. Pheasants hung from a beam amongst sprigs of thyme, marjoram and basil.

Carrots, mushrooms and apples lay heaped upon an oaken table and steam floated everywhere, like vapour rising from a marsh.

'Which one of you is the Scholar of Outrage?' Warsten's gaze shifted from Hawk to Hawk. Scholars of Outrage wore a certain uniform – black leggings, black boots and a black tunic with an even blacker triangle stitched into the breast.

'He's waiting in the lane,' lied Standaire. There was no Scholar of Outrage, except in Warsten's imagination.

'And the other Wardens? You cannot besiege the Hoof with a mere three men.' Glancing at Ekkerlin, he coughed. 'Individuals. Three *individuals*.'

'There will not be a siege. We will arrest your master discreetly. You told Father Ransom the guards never venture into the Hoof.'

'Mallakos forbids it,' nodded Warsten. 'He mistrusts them, says their presence makes him uneasy.' He squinted, uncertainly. 'Are you sure that just the three of you will be sufficient? I expected . . . I have heard that when a collector of forbidden texts is brought to book, it is a loud, riotous occasion. Swords are drawn, blood is shed—'

'Not this time,' said Standaire.

Disappointed, Warsten sighed, swirling the steam in front of his mouth. Then, as he was about to speak, a tiny bell fixed to the wall jangled, jerked by a cord sinking into the stonework.

'That is Mallakos, demanding more food,' he said, drooping. 'From dawn till dusk, dusk till dawn, I await his call, and it is killing me. I cannot recall the last time I had a fair night's sleep. It is true what they say: when a man sins in one fashion, he sins in a dozen others. His fondness for forbidden texts aside, Mallakos's prime vice is gluttony. How the Four must loathe his over-indulgence! And what a challenge it will be for the Forest's demons, when they attempt to rip him apart. There is *so much* of him, you see. They will be hacking and clawing for

39

weeks!' He looked at Standaire. 'He *will* be hanged, won't he? For his crimes?'

'If everything is as you claim,' said the general. 'But we must see the texts.'

'I will show you.' As they left the kitchen, the bell tinkled with greater urgency, threatening to spring free of the wall.

Warsten led the Hawks along several scarlet-carpeted corridors. Then they entered a large, echoing chamber, submerged in darkness. Hurrying back and forth, Warsten lit some lanterns, their light washing over countless bookcases crammed with leather-bound books, gilt and silver lettering winking on their spines.

Ekkerlin gazed around in wonderment.

'Are all these forbidden texts?' she asked, eyes bright.

Warsten chuckled, sourly. 'They are not texts of any sort. Look for yourself, if you wish.'

Opening a bookcase, Ekkerlin drew out a thick tome. By rights, it should have been as heavy as a house brick, but the Hawk handled it as though it were weightless. 'Hollow,' she murmured.

'As are they all,' said Warsten. 'You won't find a single genuine book on those shelves. My lady, you are standing in the heart of a massive lie. My master likes to pretend he is a learned man but, in truth, he cares nothing for knowledge – unless it pertains to horses.' He blew out the taper he had used to light the lanterns. 'Horses, yes – and matters deemed blasphemous by the Church.'

He strode to a bookcase at the far end of the library. Kneeling, he opened the lower door, removed an armful of the hollow books then tugged out the base-board, laying it on the floor.

'This is Mallakos's treasure-trove.' Reaching inside, he pulled out a handful of thin books, each barely more than a pamphlet. 'Reprehensible works, all of them,' he said, spreading them on the desk. 'I feel sullied merely by touching them.'

'You told Father Ransom there were twenty, maybe thirty texts.' Ekkerlin paced over. 'Yet I see only half a dozen.'

'I may have exaggerated,' said Warsten, awkwardly. 'I feared you would not come, if you knew his collection was somewhat meagre.' He raised a finger. 'My motives were good. Mallakos *deserves* to hang; when you meet him, you will sense the evil locked within his monstrous form. You cannot miss it. It darkens every room, sours the air you breathe. I noticed it as soon as I entered his employ. I have led a good, pious life; since childhood, I have prayed thrice daily, read *The Book of the Pilgrims* each evening and attended church on every seventh day. Such immersion in what is holy has granted me an instinct for what is *un*holy: I can spot it a mile off. As soon as I set eyes on Mallakos, I thought, There is a man covered in wickedness, a man who treads the dark path . . . who *skips* along it as merrily as a girl-child gathering flowers in a meadow.'

'Yet you work for him,' muttered Ballas. 'You accept his wages.'

'In the fleshly realm, compromises must be made,' said Warsten, firmly. 'A fellow has to eat, you know. In Paradise, however, I will have no need to drink such a bitter brew. All will be abundance; all will be tranquillity.' The cook's eyes sparkled at the prospect of eternal bliss.

Standaire looked through the texts. Most had complex, pompous titles, Ballas noticed: *Equine Astrology: How the Stars Influence the Development of Horses. The Enlightenment of Sleep: Occult Significances of the Dreaming World. Posthumous Utterances: An Anthology of Words Uttered After Death* . . .

Standaire stopped suddenly, fingers resting on a copy of *The Loss*.

Craning his neck, Warsten said, 'Ah, that is the book with the errors. I assume it is of particular interest?'

41

'You have served us well,' said the general. 'Now, you must return to the kitchen.'

'You intend to arrest Mallakos?'

Standaire nodded.

'May I not observe?'

'No,' replied Standaire.

'But surely, it is permissible. If it weren't for me—'

'Go back to the kitchen,' repeated Standaire, firmly.

Warsten looked hurt. 'But I had assumed—'

'If you want to see your master in distress,' said Ekkerlin, picking up *The Loss*, 'I suggest you keep a close eye on the notice board outside Father Ramson's church. Once Mallakos is sentenced, the date of his execution will be posted there.'

'I admit that I am disappointed,' said Warsten, half to himself. 'But I suppose you know your business. Yes, I will go back to the kitchen. After all, the dogs need feeding.'

'The dogs?' asked Standaire.

Warsten chuckled. 'Oh, that is my nickname for Mallakos's guards. I always cook them a little something during the night. The poor devils are bored to tears most of the time, and a rumbling stomach makes any ordeal a thousand times worse, do you not think?' He laughed. 'I am breaking the rules, of course. Mallakos would go berserk if he discovered I was serving his food to the men. But so what? If the guards hunger, they must eat.' He touched a fist to his chest. 'Believe it or not, a rebellious spark burns within my breast, just as it burned within many of the saints. I am not one to be cowed by petty restrictions.'

The cook smiled, broadly. Ballas knew what he was thinking. In his mind's eye, he saw Warsten telling the guards how he had betrayed Mallakos to the Church. Shoulders drawn back, chest puffed out, the cook would grin and leer, as if sharing a bawdy joke. As the guards congratulated him, he would feign modesty, then suggest they raid the horse-breeder's wine-cellar, so they could celebrate properly. Ballas had encountered men like Warsten often before. Small-minded, petty souls, who could not resist bragging about minor triumphs. Nothing could stop them, neither threats nor the promises of a reward. They could not help themselves. The temptation was too strong.

Therein lay the problem. If Warsten told them about Mallakos's arrest, the guards would want to make sure it was legitimate. They would confront the Hawks, demanding to see a Warrant of Capture – the Church-sanctioned document authorising such arrests; the Hawks did not have one. They might want to speak to the non-existent Scholar of Outrage, too. Why wouldn't they? Mallakos paid their wages. If he was imprisoned – and executed – they would find themselves out of work.

At the very least, Warsten's boastful nature could complicate the mission considerably.

Ballas looked at the Hawks. Standaire nodded, barely perceptibly. Ekkerlin cleared her throat, then said, 'Warsten, it is a fine thing to encounter someone so loyal to the Church. We are in your debt.'

'Oh, I merely wanted to play my part.' Flattered, Warsten stood a little straighter. 'After all, bringing sinners to book is, at heart, a *cosmic* matter, is it not? The Four observe all that we do, and do not do. We are judged for our omissions as much as our deeds. What sort of fellow would I be, if I remained silent? If I had not told Father Ransom about my master's despicable activities?'

'You speak as if you hate your master. Are you not exaggerating his vices?' From Ekkerlin's tone, it was clear she thought he was. Ballas thought so, too. A petty man, Warsten seemed the type who painted everyone black, so his light could shine brighter.

'Exaggerate? Never! Hate? Yes, I suppose I do. But it is –

how can I put it – a *holy hatred*. You already know about two of his sins – forbidden texts and gluttony. But his profession is sinful, too.'

'I see no harm in breeding horses,' frowned Ekkerlin, tucking *The Loss* behind her belt.

'But he *races* them as well,' said Warsten. 'His mounts run at most of the big tracks, where poor, deluded folks place wagers upon them. Gambling is a villainous business. It has been the ruin of many good men – my father included.' A pause, fraught with memories. 'My family had money, once, before he was seduced by the turf. Such a passion can lead in only one direction. Within two years, we were destitute. We lived on the streets, sleeping behind bakeries, grubbing for money in the gutter . . .'

As he spoke, Ballas moved behind the cook.

'I do not blame my father,' Warsten continued. 'He had a weakness. It is men like Mallakos, who fed upon his frailty, that are guilty. There is no wickedness more despicable, than to exploit the vulnerable—'

Ballas punched Warsten across the head. It was a gentle blow, just enough to knock him unconscious. As Warsten toppled sideways, Ballas caught him, lowering him gently to the floor. He removed the cook's apron then, drawing a knife, sliced it into three long strips. With Ekkerlin's assistance, he bound Warsten's hands behind his back then tied his ankles together. The final strip he used as a gag, knotting it tightly across the cook's mouth. Grabbing his shoulders, Ballas dragged Warsten over the polished floorboards and hid him beneath a table in the far corner of the library.

Dousing the lamps, the Hawks then climbed a central staircase to the top floor, and followed a corridor to the bed-chamber that Warsten had marked with the sketch of the pig's head.

Beyond the closed door, someone was unhappy.

'Curse it, Warsten, you dismal streak of rat-piss – where are you? When I give the order, you should come running. You know the rules, you despicable turd.' Then, mumbling, 'Maybe the bell is broken. No; the string is taut. Hm. The indolent cur has probably fallen asleep. This really will not do. I shall deduct a penny or two from his wages.'

Gently, Standaire tried the door handle. It gave a faint click but did not open.

'Warsten? Is that you?' came the voice. 'One moment. I will let you in.'

A bed-frame creaked, relieved of a heavy burden. Footsteps thumped across the floorboards. 'Whatever you've brought me, it had better be worth the wait.'

A key twisted in the lock. The door opened, revealing the fattest man Ballas had ever seen. A purple sleeping robe hung from his shoulders, straining tight against a belly that bulged like a sail catching a strong wind. His face was a dollop of pink flesh, sparkling with sweat; his eyes were large, but his mouth – despite his fondness for food – was a tiny slit, crowded with yellow, stublike teeth. Golden hair lay upon his scalp in limp curls and stubble bristled on his chins, glinting like bronze dust.

Seizing his robe, Ballas clamped a hand over his mouth then shoved him backward into the chamber. He flung him down onto the bed, littered with plates bearing the remnants of numerous meals.

'Make a noise, and I'll rip out your lungs,' hissed Ballas, jabbing a thick finger at Mallakos's face.

The Hawks strode into the chamber. As Ekkerlin shut the door, Standaire paced to the bed. 'Cledrun Mallakos?'

'What? Me? Yes – I mean no.'

'You collect forbidden texts,' said the general.

'Texts – what are you talking about?' Mallakos shook his head.

Ekkerlin held up *The Loss*. Mallakos's face fell, slumping like a glob of molten wax. 'What is that? I've never seen it before—'

Ballas slapped him across the face. 'Do not lie to us.'

'It is the truth! I—'

Ballas slapped him again. Ripples rolled from cheek to cheek and, very quickly, a handprint blossomed on the horse-breeder's pink flesh.

Mallakos's eyes moistened. His lips quivered. Bowing his head, he said, 'You are from the Church, aren't you? I am done for.'

'If we served the Church, Silver Hoof would be aswarm with Wardens, and you would be speaking not to me, but a black-robed Scholar of Outrage. Is that not so?' Standaire spoke as smoothly as an otter gliding through water. He gave Mallakos a moment to digest his words, then said, 'If you answer our questions, we will go, and you shall never hear from us again.'

'Who are you, if you are not Churchmen?' Mallakos looked up, eyes as large as a puppy's.

'That does not matter,' replied Standaire. 'Tell us what we wish to know, and all will be well.'

Mallakos looked from Hawk to Hawk. He had the soft, vulnerable air of a crab stripped of its shell. 'And this question is . . . ?'

'Where did you get *The Loss*?'

Mallakos winced. 'I am sorry, but I cannot tell you. One cannot betray people involved with the Dark Market, for they are a ruthless bunch, and I would pay a terrible price.'

'What do you suppose will happen if you stay silent?' Standaire stared coolly at Mallakos. 'Do you imagine we will shrug our shoulders and go? All you need to do, Mallakos, is utter a few honest words.'

Touching his brow with trembling fingers, Mallakos grew thoughtful.

After a few long, silent moments slipped by, Ekkerlin crouched by the bed. 'Allow me to offer some advice,' she said.

Mallakos looked at her.

'At present, your mind is an ocean full of waves,' said Ekkerlin. 'Each wave is a thought concerning your current predicament, and they are all crashing against one another – so much so, the tiny, fragile boat that constitutes your powers of reason is caught in the middle, storm-tossed and leaking, unable to advance an inch in any direction. Simply, you cannot decide what is for the best. So I will put things in perspective. You fear that if you talk to us, the men you have betrayed will come for you, bent on revenge. Perhaps they will. But Mallakos, if you don't talk, *we* will seek revenge. And we are here *right now*.' She smiled, pleasantly. 'Do you suppose your enemies will send a man quite as ugly as this?' She gestured to Ballas. 'It is not by accident that he is so monstrous. His flesh is an exact mirror of his soul. There is no goodness in this fellow. No mercy. Given the opportunity, he would do terrible things to you.'

'I believe you,' swallowed Mallakos, looking at Ballas.

'Besides, it is likely no one will learn of your betrayal,' continued Ekkerlin. 'We won't tell anyone. What would be the point? We would not gain anything.' She peered closely at Mallakos. 'You do not like whoever sold you *The Loss*, do you?'

'How can you tell?'

'Is he *forcing* you to buy the texts?'

Mallakos shifted, uneasily. 'Me? No one forces Mallakos to do anything! I am rich, powerful and—'

'A victim of blackmail,' interrupted Ekkerlin. 'Do not be ashamed; it is not uncommon. I have met many like you. You have the face of a broken man – a lack of confidence, mixed with frustration. I can spot it a mile off. I have a talent for such things.'

47

It was true, Ballas knew. Ekkerlin had studied how the face betrays emotions. She could read the barely tangible signs indicating whether someone was lying or speaking the truth. Moreover, she could sometimes figure out what the truth was. It was not an exact science, she said. But it worked as often as not. Clearly Mallakos, whose face was almost uncontrollably expressive, was an easy subject.

'We can help you – if you tell us your tormentor's name and where he can be found.' Ekkerlin patted Mallakos's knee. 'You are a rich man. I suspect you have considered hiring an assassin. Am I correct?'

Mallakos nodded, numbly.

'Well, there is no need. Not now. Give us his name, and he will die,' said Ekkerlin. 'He has wronged us, too, but discreetly, keeping his identity hidden. Once we find him, we will ensure he never casts a shadow in this world again. He will find himself in the Forest before he has a chance to fart.'

'Truly?' Temptation sparkled in Mallakos's eyes.

'Truly,' said Ekkerlin.

Mallakos struggled, trying to reach a decision. Then he nodded, solemnly defiant. 'Very well. His name is Marrus Curtlane. You can find him at the Loop.'

'The Loop?' inquired Standaire.

Mallakos frowned, as if the general's ignorance was surprising. 'The racetrack in Sliptere. It is the largest structure of its kind in Druine, a veritable cathedral, a living shrine to all that is glorious about the equine species.' He lifted a hand to his heart. 'I want to be buried there, when my time comes. Just beneath the finishing line, so I can listen to the triumphal drumming of hooves for all eternity.'

Rising, Ballas walked to an oaken trunk, opened it and took out an armful of clothes.

'Get dressed,' he said, dumping the garments on Mallakos's lap.

'What?'

'We are going to Sliptere. You will introduce us to Marrus Curtlane yourself.'

Flummoxed, Mallakos could barely speak. 'But – I have given you his name and—'

'You trade horses. It is in your nature to lie,' said Ekkerlin, straightening. 'What is to say you have not deceived us? We might travel to Sliptere, discover that Marrus Curtlane does not exist – and then what? By the time we return, you will have gone into hiding, or doubled the number of guards patrolling your home.' She shrugged. 'It would make no difference, in the long run. We would still find you. But the inconvenience would be . . . irksome. Put on your clothes.'

'No, please, listen,' said Mallakos. 'I have not misled you. Why would I? The more I consider the matter, the happier I am. In truth, I would pay you – *will* pay you, if you wish – to extinguish Curtlane's flame.' He screwed the clothes into a ball, squeezing it tightly. 'You must have noticed that Silver Hoof contains articles of immense value. The paintings, the tapestries, this goblet,' he waved a hand toward a jewel-encrusted drinking vessel on a bedside table. 'So many things, each worth a small fortune. As you leave, you may take as many as you wish. Whatever you want, it is yours.'

Ekkerlin laid a hand on Mallakos's shoulder. 'Do as you are bidden,' she said.

As Mallakos pulled on his leggings, Ballas grew uneasy. He had a well-honed instinct for danger, and right now, something – he could not say what – was amiss. Disquiet swirling in his guts, he strode to the door and locked it.

Standaire watched him, closely. At that instant, bootsteps sounded in the corridor outside the bed-chamber. Someone grabbed the door handle, twisting it.

'Mr Mallakos?' came a rough, coarse-edged voice. 'There are

intruders loose in Silver Hoof. They tied up Warsten and hid him in the library.'

Mallakos gaped, staring at the Hawks. The door handle shook furiously.

'Damn it, let us inside,' urged the voice. 'Didn't you hear me?'

Whipping out a knife, Standaire touched the blade to Mallakos's throat, the tip dimpling the horse-breeder's salmon-coloured flesh. 'Say only the things I tell you,' whispered the general. 'Inform your guards that you were sleeping. Ask again what happened.'

'Lezluthe, is that you?' called Mallakos, blinking furiously. 'What is going on? I was fast asleep, slumbering like a bear in the cold season, then you start banging on my door. Explain yourself!'

'Two men and a woman,' said the man named Lezluthe, still yanking at the door handle. 'They trussed Warsten up like a chicken and stuck him under a table in the library.'

'The library? What were you doing *there*?' blurted Mallakos. He winced, realising he had spoken without Standaire's permission.

'We were seeking the cook,' explained Lezluthe, swiftly. 'He gives us a little food at this hour each night. When we went to the kitchen, he was not there, but we spotted footprints – very faint, mind you – leading out into the hall . . . Does it truly matter? You are in danger, and we must protect you.'

'Tell them you are perfectly safe,' said Standaire, 'and you are not to be disturbed until they have caught the intruder.'

'Leave me alone,' said Mallakos. 'Find the men and the woman, stick them somewhere secure and I will speak with them on the morrow. In the meantime, do not trouble me again. I need my sleep. Rouse me once more, and I will throttle you like some irksome cockerel, squawking an hour before dawn.'

50

'Mallakos, I urge you to be sensible! Let me post a few guards—'

'Lezluthe, it is not your place to urge me to do *anything*!' Mallakos looked entreatingly at Standaire, unsure what to say next.

'Tell the guards to search the grounds,' said Standaire. 'They must split up into groups of two or three.'

Mallakos did as he was told. Reluctantly, his guards departed, footsteps booming away along the corridor. Mallakos hunched forward, sweat-drops dribbling from his brow.

'Groups of two or three,' he murmured. 'That makes good sense. What chance do my men have against you, if they are banded together in such small numbers? You have done this before, haven't you?'

'Get dressed,' said Standaire, coldly.

Listening at the door, Ballas thought he heard footsteps creeping lightly back along the corridor. Tilting his head, listening, he picked out the muffled hiss of a knife sliding from its sheathe.

'They are still there,' he whispered to Standaire. 'I reckon—'

The door jolted as something thudded against it. With surprising boldness, Mallakos swatted Standaire's knife aside and rolled from the bed. There was a second, louder thud.

Running to the corner of the chamber, Mallakos said, 'My men realise that I am not alone. I will not be able to stop them coming in. But if you surrender, I will ensure they do not kill you—'

A third thud and the door tore out of its frame. Mallakos's guards surged across the threshold, a dozen of them, snarling like pack animals. Ballas knew instantly there were too many to fight. A guard with close-shorn black hair, a goatee beard and a mouthful of cracked teeth ran at him swinging a black-wood cudgel. Deflecting the weapon, Ballas punched his attacker in the face. The man reeled backward, blood bursting from his ruined nose. Two more guards lunged, knives drawn. Spinning, Ballas leapt onto Mallakos's bed, then jumped again, landing on the floor by the window.

He turned. Ekkerlin and Standaire were fighting furiously against a knot of seven or eight guards, but they were already injured, Standaire bleeding from a cut above his eye, Ekkerlin stooping slightly, as if a rib was broken.

More guards poured into the chamber, knives flashing.

Ballas wanted to hurtle over and help his companions, but he knew it would do no good; he might as well dive into a pool of blood-maddened sharks. His thoughts veered sharply. He was a Hawk; he had duties to fulfil. If the mission failed – and it *was* failing – he had to notify Faltriste, so a fresh team of Hawks could be dispatched. And for that, he needed to be alive.

He swept open the curtains. Beyond, a glass door stood open, leading onto a balcony. He started to move through but a strong hand seized his tabard and yanked him backward. Spinning, Ballas swung a bone-splitting right hook into a guard's cheekbone. The man staggered, colliding with two onrushing guards.

Plunging onto the balcony, Ballas climbed onto the balustrade and leapt onto the neighbouring balcony. There, another glass door led into another bed-chamber. Through the darkness inside, he dimly made out a four-poster bed, a writing desk, a wardrobe. Suddenly a sliver of light materialised in the far wall, widening as a door opened. Six or seven guards raced through.

Cursing, Ballas leapt onto the next balcony. Another darkened chamber lay beyond another door. He cursed. He knew exactly what would happen: the door would open, more guards would appear and he would be forced to jump to the next balcony, and so on, again and again, until he had reached the edge of Silver Hoof, and there was nowhere left for him to go.

He looked up, staring at the mock-battlements on the roof-edge. How far above were they? Thirteen feet? Fifteen? Too high to reach, unless he jumped from an elevated surface.

A door opened in the bed-chamber. A flurry of guards rushed through, crow-black against a wash of lamp-light.

Ballas climbed onto the balustrade. Gaze locked on the battlements, he jumped, flinging his hands outward and up. His fingertips scraped stone, and for an instant he thought he had made it, but he fell, dropping onto the balcony. He landed heavily, pain flaring in his ankle.

Reaching the window, the guards jerked the door open and poured through. Ballas swung an uppercut into the first guard's jaw, clashing his teeth together. A second guard swept a knife at Ballas's face, but the Hawk seized his wrist and twisted and pulled, flinging the guard over the balustrade. Then something cracked against the back of his skull. Sparks blossomed in the Hawk's vision, drifting and glittering. Stumbling, Ballas turned as a cudgel swept forward and cracked his eyebrow. Roaring, Ballas grabbed the guard's tunic and, shifting his weight, brought his boot down on the man's knee. The joint broke loose, detaching with a muted *pop*, and the guard fell, yowling. A fourth guard remained, clutching a short-sword. He looked very frightened, very confused. He had entered the bed-chamber with three companions, spurred on by a hunger for glory. Now, he was alone. He licked his lips. His eye whites seemed to phosphoresce like moon-struck sea-foam. He turned suddenly, fleeing the bed-chamber.

Climbing onto the balustrade, Ballas jumped again. This time he found a handhold. Swearing viciously, he hauled himself up. As he scrambled over the battlements, he found himself in a rooftop garden. On all sides, exotic trees and shrubs sprouted from tubs and pots, leaves dripping silver in the moonlight, strange, flesh-slick night-blossoms quivering in the breeze. The air was powerfully fragrant.

Ballas realised he had made a mistake. Climbing onto the roof, he had acted instinctively, eluding the guards by the quickest, safest way. But he had not thought ahead. If he had, he would have gone *downwards*, hanging, swinging and dropping from balcony to balcony until he reached the courtyard. Then he could have sprinted out of the grounds.

He recalled the map supplied by Warsten. The cook had not sketched the garden, but Ballas recalled a swirling line, indicating a spiral staircase, rising from the end of a corridor to the roof. Already, guards would be racing toward that staircase, seeking to rise up and corner him amongst the peculiar, bristling plants, knowing there was nowhere he could escape to.

Looking over the battlements, he wondered if he could get back down.

No, he decided. A guard stood on each balcony, staring upward, a long-bladed sword at the ready.

Somewhere, a trapdoor swung open, smacking against stone. Guards appeared, rising amongst the vegetation like the demons of some small-scale replica of the Eltheryn Forest. Six, seven, eight, nine . . . At least two dozen men appeared, peering through the plants, seeking him like a fox gone to ground.

The breeze strengthened, rustling leaves, creaking twigs. A fat-bodied moth swirled up from a shrub; a few lacewings flittered delicately into the night.

A guard squinted in Ballas's direction. 'There!' he called, pointing.

The other guards turned. Then they were moving, prowling through the plants, slowly, methodically, gazing intently at Ballas. The goatee-wearing guard Ballas had punched in the face barged to the front of the advancing men. His shattered nose was an ugly splatter, dribbling blood over his mouth. His eyebrows were locked in an angry frown.

'Best for you if you surrender,' he shouted. Ballas recognised his voice. He was Lezluthe, the guard who had shouted through the door at Mallakos. Grinning, he held up a crossbow, sleek and lightweight. 'Look what I've got here. Beautiful, isn't she? She cost me a small fortune.'

Ballas said nothing.

'Come now, you *must* be impressed.' Lezluthe's grin steepened into a crescent. 'So far, I haven't tested her on anything living, just gateposts and pumpkins. But now . . . This could be her lucky night.'

As the guards crept closer Ballas broke into a sprint, angling away through the garden, toppling trees, shrubs and saplings, shattering plant pots, trampling blooms. The scent of a hundred shaken blossoms whirled up in his wake, and tiny winged insects bustled chaotically toward the moon. As Ballas ran, the guards fanned out behind him, herding him to the northern edge of the roof. When he halted, Lezluthe was approaching, picking a way through the fallen plants, squinting along the crossbow. Ten paces away, he stopped.

'Our master does not want us to kill you,' he said. 'He wants us to take you alive so you can be questioned.' A sinister emphasis lay on *questioned*. 'But I do not think it is necessary. Your two companions are still alive and in time, they will tell us everything we need to know. If you were to perish, nothing would be lost.'

He adjusted his grip, pursed his lips.

'I am sure Mallakos would understand, if I said you were proving troublesome and we had no choice but to kill you. If I told him you flew into a rage, lashing out like an . . .' he looked Ballas up and down, 'angry gibbon, he would believe it. If I said nothing could have stopped you, except a well-placed arrow – he would believe that, too.' His finger curled around the trigger. 'Come to think of it, you look as though you're on the verge of doing something stupid. What do you say, my boys? Can you see it too?'

'Oh aye,' said a guard. 'There's a look in his eyes.'

'Something's brewing,' said another.

Lezluthe flexed his trigger-finger. 'Then it is settled.'

Ballas stared at the arrow-tip, glinting in the loosing gully. Then he looked at Lezluthe. 'I don't reckon it'll end here,' he said, darkly.

Lezluthe twitched an eyebrow. 'You're going to hunt me down in the afterlife, are you?'

'No,' said Ballas, the breeze stroking the back of his neck. 'We will not have to wait that long.'

Drawing a breath, Ballas jumped backward off the roof and plunged through hollow air.

CHAPTER FOUR

Ballas fell, an involuntary yell erupting from his throat. Overhead, stars whirled and the moon shook, as if cracking free of the firmament. For a heartbeat he feared that he had misjudged his jump, and his life would end, suddenly, on the stableyard cobbles, but he crunched suddenly into something tough but yielding. He continued falling, his body crashing through the thatched roof of an outbuilding, splintering branches and scattering straws. He bounced off a ceiling beam then spun, landing heavily upon a bed.

A pause, followed by a slow creaking of wood. The bed collapsed.

Grunting, Ballas rose onto all fours. Across the room a young man sat upright in a narrow bed, clutching the sheets to his chest. As skinny as a whippet, his sharp-boned face was a mask of baffled terror. He stared stupidly at Ballas, eyes glinting in the light of a bedside lantern.

'What's your name?' Ballas got to his feet.

The young man's jaw worked noiselessly. Striding over, Ballas seized his throat. 'Your name,' he repeated, lowering his face to the young man's.

'F-Felthen,' gulped the youth.

'Trade?'

'S-stableboy for Mr Mallakos.'

'Good. You can be of some use.'

Grabbing the lantern, Ballas hauled Felthen out of bed. Beneath his white nightshirt, the young man's body was painfully thin. Ballas wondered if he was sick, afflicted by some wasting disease. Then he realised it was not so. If Felthen was a stableboy, he probably aspired to become a jockey and as a species, jockeys were puny specimens, favoured for their lightness. The ideal race-rider, it was said, should weigh no more than the whip and stirrups combined.

'Has Mallakos got a favourite horse?' asked Ballas, jostling Felthen out into the stableyard.

'A favourite?' murmured Felthen, confused. 'His best racer is Bayleaf Bright . . .'

'Bring it to me.'

'. . . but Larchfire is the mount he holds most dear. He treats the animal like a sister. The Four knows why. I've never seen such a decrepit nag.'

'Fetch Larchfire. Now.'

Felthen obeyed, slapping barefoot across the cobbles toward the stable buildings. Ballas jogged to a farrier's hut, on the eastern side of the yard. Inside, he found what he was looking for straight away: jugs of oil, sealed with wooden bungs. Grabbing a jug, he went outside, placed it on the cobbles then tugged out the bung. Next, he used a knife to shatter the lantern's glass panels, so the flame flickered raw to the air.

Felthen returned, leading Larchfire. The horse was ancient, head drooping, grey-white fur growing in sparse clumps. If it had ever been a racer, its glory days were long gone. Pathetic, shambling, drag-hoofed, it did not belong on the racetrack but inside a glue-pot.

Putting the lantern on the ground, Ballas picked up the jug, instructed Felthen to keep a tight hold on Larchfire then, carefully, poured oil over the horse. The clear fluid seeped through Larchfire's hair, trickling down its sparse-muscled legs, dripping from its sag-belly. The animal accepted the ill-treatment without so much as a snort.

Footsteps echoed from the courtyard. Moments later, the guards appeared, hurtling around from the front of Silver Hoof. As they approached, a few men faltered, surprised to discover that their prey was still alive. Most likely, they expected to find a corpse, snap-boned and crack-skulled on the outbuilding floor.

'Come no closer,' shouted Ballas, casting the jug aside. Retrieving the lantern, he returned to Larchfire. 'Another step and the horse burns.'

The guards neither stopped nor slowed. They did not know Larchfire was sodden with combustible fluid; they could not see the moonlight glistening on its slick hair, nor smell the strong vapours wafting from the beast. Ballas intended to tell them, to shout a warning, but Felthen ran toward the guards, waving his arms.

'Do as he says! He's covered Larchfire in oil – one spark, and she will go up like a firework!' The stableboy sprinted over to Lezluthe. 'It is the truth, I swear it!'

Lezluthe slowed then stopped. Raising a hand, he halted his men. 'I've had enough of playing tag with this sack of shit,' he said, lifting the crossbow. He squinted, taking aim. 'It's time to end the games.'

'What do you reckon will happen if you kill me?' shouted Ballas, raising the lantern high. 'The lantern will fall, and though I will be dead, so will Mallakos's favourite horse. What then, Lezluthe? I will tell you. Come dawn, you will be looking for a new job.' Catching a wisp of vapour, the lantern-flame surged then shrank.

'I don't give a screaming damn,' said Lezluthe, shrugging. 'I'll find work elsewhere easily enough.' He laughed, sound-lessly. 'It would be a relief, to leave the Hoof. I've never toiled anywhere so dull. Men like me, we need adventure. Aye, that's right. We live for moments such as this, and when they come, we grasp them with both hands.' His expression growing sombre, Lezluthe grew very still, slipping into a Huntsman's Lull – the trancelike state that preceded a killing blow. He moved the bow downwards a fraction. Then he squeezed the trigger—

—and Felthen lunged, knocking the crossbow upwards. The weapon bucked and the arrow rose high, streaking harmlessly over Ballas's head then clattering on the cobbles beyond the farrier's hut.

'You fucking cur!' Lezluthe punched Felthen neatly across the jaw. The stableboy stumbled, fell, then stood again and ran back to Ballas. When he halted, he positioned himself between Lezluthe and the Hawk.

'If you put an arrow in the big man Larchfire will die,' he said. 'I would rather perish than see that happen.'

Lezluthe loaded another arrow. 'Step aside, boy.'

Felthen folded his arms. 'Not a chance.'

Surprised, Ballas said, 'Good lad.'

'Step aside, you lump of badger-shit,' said Lezluthe, lifting the crossbow.

'Stand your ground,' urged Ballas.

'I am frightened,' Felthen whispered over his shoulder.

'Don't be.'

'My life means nothing to Lezluthe.'

'Reckon you're right. But Lezluthe's own life means everything to him, and he knows that if he pulls the trigger, I'll tear out his throat so fast he will not have the chance to piss himself.' He looked to a guard standing close to Lezluthe. 'You there,' he bellowed, pointing.

The guard touched his chest. *Me?*

'Go fetch Mallakos. Bring my companions whilst you are at it.'

60

'Stay where you are,' said Lezluthe to the guard, watching Ballas along the crossbow.

Ballas stared hard at the guard. 'Do as you're told,' he said, dropping his voice a notch. 'Go now.'

The guard hesitated, glanced at Lezluthe, then sprinted from the stableyard.

'Not all of my men are as faint-hearted as Jackrin,' said Lezluthe. 'Felthen, this is your last warning. If you don't get out of the way, you'll get an arrow in your skull. How would you like that, eh?'

'Tell him,' said Ballas, softly.

'What?'

'Tell him how you would like it.'

'I don't think I would like it at all,' Felthen called to Lezluthe. 'It's a damned stupid question to begin with. What did you expect me to say? Do you think I got up this morning and thought, Do you know what I could really do with today? A bit of wood and iron in my brain?' He giggled nervously.

'That settles it, you sarcastic little shit. I'm going to kill you first, then it'll be the big bastard. We'll see what a wise mouth you've got then.'

Lezluthe adjusted his posture, preparing to loose the arrow. A shout rang out.

'Enough! Lezluthe, lower your weapon.' Mallakos appeared, waddling across the stableyard. Eyes boggling, he strode straight to Larchfire. 'Oh, my girl. What has he done to you? You poor creature!' He embraced Larchfire, burying his face in the oil-wet hair of the horse's neck. Then he shot Ballas an angry glance. 'Take that lantern away. If you harm a hair on her mane, I'll rip your guts out. Do you hear?' Then, defiance ebbing, 'Please, back away a few paces. I will deal with Lezluthe.'

As Ballas stepped away, a group of guards appeared, leading Standaire and Ekkerlin. Although both Hawks walked at a steady pace, Ekkerlin remained hunched over, and Standaire limped badly. As they grew close, Ballas saw their faces were bruise-swollen, their hair matted with blood.

'Hurt?' Ballas asked Standaire, as they arrived.

'It is bearable,' replied the general.

Ballas looked at Ekkerlin. 'You?'

'A broken rib or two. Nothing worse.' She grinned, raggedly. 'Promise me you won't kiss them better.'

Mallakos looked up, cheeks gleaming with oil. 'What do you want from me? What must I do to end this?'

'Call Lezluthe over,' said Ballas.

Nodding, Mallakos yelled, 'Lezluthe, we must parley.'

'Aye? Then speak,' called Lezluthe. He lowered the crossbow a fraction.

'What I have to say cannot be yelled across a stableyard. Come to me.' When Lezluthe hesitated, Mallakos shouted, 'You are in my employ and will do as I say.' Straightening, he drew back his shoulders. 'Do you want everyone to learn of your secret passions? I know what you get up to when you are not patrolling Silver Hoof.'

Lezluthe stared uncomprehendingly. Suddenly, his face slackened.

'Yes, it is *that* of which I speak,' said Mallakos.

Lezluthe approached. He looked confused, and worried. Glancing to the guards, he said, 'I don't know what Mister Mallakos is gabbling about. But I reckon I'd better find out. If anyone's been spreading rumours, I'll cut out his tongue and shove it up his arse.'

'What must I say when he gets here?' whispered Mallakos, looking at Ballas.

'Nothing,' replied the big man.

Lezluthe halted five paces away. 'Mallakos, whatever you've heard, it's slander. You mustn't trust gossip. It is—'

Using an underarm throw, Ballas flung the lantern into Lezluthe's face. Lezluthe recoiled, more in surprise than pain and, springing close, Ballas drove a fist into the guard's smashed nose, grinding it into a shapeless nugget of gristle. As Lezluthe fell, Ballas snatched the crossbow from his fingers and, before he could rise, knelt upon his chest.

He jammed the weapon into Lezluthe's mouth.

'It *is* her lucky night, after all,' he muttered, pulling the trigger.

Rising, he rolled Lezluthe over, grabbed a handful of arrows from the quiver across his back and returned.

'Tell your guards to kneel down,' Ballas instructed Mallakos.

'They will not do it. I called Lezluthe over, and now he's dead. I have lost their trust.'

'Horseshit. They know the kind of man Lezluthe was. Reckless, ill-disciplined, glory-seeking – there could not be a peaceful end whilst he lived. Offer to treble their wages, if you must.'

As Mallakos obeyed, Ballas turned to Standaire.

'You fit enough to handle the bow?'

'You have something in mind?' said the general, taking the weapon and arrows.

'Remember when the gymnasium was infested by ants last summer?'

Loading an arrow, Standaire nodded. To Ekkerlin, Ballas said, 'Go fetch some more oil from the hut over there.'

As Ekkerlin departed, the guards sank reluctantly to their knees.

'Not long ago, those men were trying to kill me. Now, I feel sorry for them,' said Ekkerlin, returning with two oil jugs. 'You have inspired me to forgive my enemies. You should become a priest.'

Taking a jug, Ballas strode to the guards, Ekkerlin following.

'Lie down, all of you,' said Ballas.

Some guards settled face-down on the cobbles whilst a few lingered, uncertain. One remained upright, glowering at Ballas. 'What are you playing at, you—'

An arrow sprouted from the side of his head. There was a soft *snick* as Standaire loaded a fresh bolt. The remaining men lay down, muttering, shifting.

Ballas doused the guards in oil, walking amongst them as casually as a gardener watering a vegetable plot. Ekkerlin did the same. The men groaned and cursed, but softly, as if fearing a wrong word would act like a tinder strike. Once the jugs were empty, Ballas and Ekkerlin went back to Standaire.

'Keep an eye on them,' Ballas instructed the general. 'If they move, aim for the cobbles. One spark, and they'll go up like candles.' He grabbed Felthen's arm. 'Come with me.' He led the youth toward the stables. 'I need four horses with good temperaments. The sort that won't panic.'

'Yes, sir.' They ducked into the stables. 'I don't think I'll forget this evening in a hurry,' the stableboy added.

'Nor should you,' said Ballas. 'When we are gone, take Larchfire to the river. Wash every drop of oil from her hair. When you have finished, do it all again, just to be certain. Then set loose all the horses in the stables. Don't want them to starve to death, do we?'

'They won't starve. I'll be here to take care of them.'

'You'll be long gone,' said Ballas. 'Which horses do we need?'

Felthen pointed out the mounts best-suited to Ballas's needs. As he started saddling up a grey mare, the stableboy said, 'Long gone? What do you mean?'

'You cannot stay here,' said Ballas. 'Mallakos is leaving with us, and I don't reckon he'll be coming back. You'd better seek work elsewhere.' He paused, tightening the bridle of a chestnut gelding. 'Before you leave, go to Mallakos's bed-chamber. It's on the top floor. You'll find a jewelled goblet on a bedside table. Take it and sell it. It ought to be worth two or three gold pieces.' He glanced at Felthen. 'Don't go living on the streets, aye?'

'No, sir.'

They led the horses into the stableyard. Ballas instructed Mallakos to choose a mount and get into the saddle.

'I am not sure that I can,' said the horse-breeder, gesturing to his corpulent form. 'It has been several years since I have ridden, and I have acquired a few ounces of—'

'Get up, or I'll throw you onto the bloody thing,' said Ballas. He turned to Felthen. 'Take Larchfire to the river. Do not look back.'

Felthen did not move.

'Do it now. Remember what I said about the goblet.'

'Yes, sir.' Felthen led Larchfire across the stableyard, vanishing into the darkness beyond the farrier's hut.

Ballas took the crossbow from Standaire. Then the Hawks climbed upon the horses.

'We are leaving,' Ballas called to the guards. 'I reckon there is an hour or two until dawn. I want you to stay exactly where you are until the sun comes up. Mallakos will return in a day's time. No doubt, it will be a happy occasion. After all, you will be getting extra wages.' His tone darkened. 'None of you do aught stupid, will you? If you follow us, you'll be joining Lezluthe in the Forest. Imagine it, spending a near-eternity in the company of that dullard.'

The Hawks and Mallakos rode from the stableyard, skirting the oil-sodden guards and rounding the corner to the front of the Hoof.

As the others rode on, Ballas halted. He waited a few moments then, turning his mount, rode back to the stableyard.

As he expected, the guards were getting to their feet. He

understood their intentions, for they would be *his* intentions, if their roles were reversed. Saddle up Mallakos's racehorses, give chase, rescue Mallakos – and obtain a handsome reward from their grateful master.

He glanced at the crossbow. A bolt nestled in the loosing gully.

He lifted the weapon to his eye. Squinted. Pulled the trigger.

The crossbow bucked like a living creature. An arrow flew, striking the oil-greased cobbles near the guards. A tiny spark flared and for a half-instant, there was a blue haze of burning vapour. Then there was nothing except fire. Scrambling to their feet, the guards screamed, thrashing and capering like dancers in some obscure religious ceremony. Glowing embers floated skywards, mingling with the stars. Howls echoed from the walls of Silver Hoof. In the stables, horses screeched in sympathy, banging their hooves against the doors, as if striking a drum-beat to which the men continued to dance, each a black shape spinning and whirling through the unimaginable light.

A guard ran across the stableyard toward Ballas, flames lapping over his outstretched arms, his blackened, half-fleshed skull burning like a torch. Reloading the crossbow, Ballas loosed a bolt into the centre of his forehead. He dropped, and lay motionless. His skin carried on burning, exhaling tufts of smoke.

Grunting, Ballas turned away.

Twenty paces ahead, Mallakos twisted in his saddle. His face slack as an empty wineskin, he stared goggle-eyed at Ballas, his mouth silently forming the words, *No, no, no, you fiend!*

'Ride on, horse-breeder,' said Ballas. 'Ride on, and say nothing.'

CHAPTER FIVE

So, from my long sleep I awake! What compels me to take up my quill, after so many years of silence? What strange force kindles my passionate fires in these, my twilight years? Perhaps it is no mystery. They say a swan sings most sweetly just before its death; maybe this is true of myself.

Whatever; it makes no odds. The urge to write is upon me and I have no choice but to submit.

In my earlier works, I delineated the Pilgrim Church's failings. My books were long, for the failings were numerous, and I acknowledge they were not to everyone's taste. Naturally, the Church denounced my work, and wished to see me hang. But there were others who criticised me too, saying, 'You gripe about the Church, yet offer no solution! You are like a doctor who diagnoses an illness, yet supplies no cure.'

Is this truly a criticism? I would say not. Rather, it is an observation. My focus was purposefully narrow; I had no intent other than to describe what was wrong. And what cure could I provide? None! There are ailments for which the only remedy is so extreme it kills the patient; so it is with the Church and Druine. The Church is too deep-rooted to be removed; wrench it out, and the nation will collapse. Chaos, anarchy, barbarism – that would be our lot if, in a flash, the Church were to vanish.

I know I will attract further criticism for what I am about to say, but my shoulders are broad, my convictions firm.

Our saviours arrived thirty years ago, and we turned them away.

I speak of the Vohorin. They came bent on conquest and we, understandably, resisted, driving them from our shores then, in a campaign of vengeance, crossed the sea and destroyed Vohoria. This venture – described by the Church as the Needful Scourge – ensured that nothing remains of that marvellous land; the people were slaughtered, the buildings razed.

For ourselves, as well as the Vohorin, this was a disaster.

This book will describe what was lost when Vohoria fell, and what we would have gained had we the foresight to welcome the Vohorin into our country and embrace them as our liberators.

It is said that a country – its culture and the psychology of its people – can be judged by its geniuses. Such men are instances in which all that is praiseworthy is manifested in a single being. So I will begin with Jurel Kraike, the sorcerer who spearheaded the Vohorin invasion, and brought to our shores magic unlike any we had encountered.

Ah! Before you protest that his magic was evil, and caused great pain in its victims, remember that the abilities and knowledge used to harm can, under different circumstances, be employed to heal. The blade that pierces the heart may just as easily carve a cancer from the flesh . . .

Extracted from *The Loss* by Cavielle Shaelus

In the fading light, the bell tower was a tall block of solid shadow, jabbing at the star-scattered sky. Leptus Quarvis hurried across the gravel courtyard of Prendle House, a hip-bag bouncing against his thigh. Opening the tower door, he climbed the winding stone steps, his pace slowing. He was in poor physical condition. Had been for a long time. It was his own fault. Years ago, whilst serving as a Scholar of Outrage, he suffered a crisis of faith. Until that time, his piety had been absolute: he believed whole-heartedly in the Four, and every single word in the *Book of Pilgrims* struck him as a self-evident truth. Alas, his piety became a habit, rather than a passion, and like many who believed the same things day after day, he grew bored, and began to question his beliefs. His doubts grew, and one evening he suffered a sickening flash of clarity: the Church's teachings were nonsense. The Four did not exist. There was no afterlife, no Eltheryn Forest. The holy tales intoned from every pulpit in the land were based not in reality, but wishful thinking; at best, they provided comfort in dark times; at worst, they were attempts to control the populace, to jerk it this way and that, like a dog on a leash woven from fear.

This revelation had not been liberating. Quarvis plunged into despair. Worse, he rebelled, ditching his morals for their exact opposites. Gone was the frugal living, the prayers, the obligation to save the souls of the citizenry. A fiery hunger for dissolution arose in their place, one Quarvis embraced with reckless vigour. He drank, gambled and whored; for two years, he pursued his Scholarly duties by day – of all his sins, hypocrisy was the most trivial – and lived like a scoundrel during the night. But it took its toll; as the saying went, *If you shake hands with a demon, expect to lose a finger or two*. Never a robust fellow, Quarvis's health deteriorated. Alcohol robbed him of the desire to eat, and left him suffering from a variety of gastric complaints; the debts arising from his gambling habits filled him with anxiety, and paranoia; and as for the whores – when the girls gave him their bodies, they also gifted him the maladies contained within. He was struck down by an assortment of poxes, most of which were cured, but a few of which still lingered, like the scent of cheap perfume in an abandoned brothel. For two years, he pursued this errant life; a year longer, and it would have killed him. Nonetheless, it had left its mark.

Halfway up the steps, he halted, leaning against the wall. Although he was keen to reach the top, he needed to rest. A minute or two would be long enough.

Last year, he had dismissed a maid from his employ. He overheard her describing him to a new girl, and whilst it was not uncommon for floor-scrubbers to speak harshly of their masters, her words had been unforgivably cutting.

Have you seen him? He is like a chimera, cobbled together from ugly animals. He has the shrivelled face of a monkey, the hunched body of a praying mantis, and is as scrawny and bald as a baby bird that has escaped the egg a month too early! Do you know how old he is? Thirty-five years, if you can believe it! He will look no worse when he is dead, I'd say.

Quarvis might have forgiven her, if her thoughts were not so strongly in accord with his own. He *was* a wretched specimen, an insult to the human form. He could not glance into a mirror without feeling nauseous – and horribly disappointed. Was it fair that he should pay such a high price for his errancy? For a brief spell of self-indulgence? No; it was not.

But it did not matter. At this moment in time, he was one of the most important men in Druine. A history-maker, a crafter-of-the-future.

He carried on up the steps. At the top, there was a small oaken door. He knocked, waited several heartbeats then ducked through.

The belfry had been converted to a sleeping room. Small, sparsely furnished, it was far from homely. There was a narrow bed, a writing desk, and a swirl-patterned rug on the floor. Otherwise it was empty – except for an armchair set by the window overlooking the garden.

Jurel Kraike sat in the armchair, watching nightingales flying through the gathering dusk. Time had not been kind to the Vohorin. Although only in his fiftieth year, his long hair was ice-white, his skin raddled by exposure to intense heat and savage cold. His face was a collision of stark contours and sharp angles, his small dark eyes lit by a fire at once angry and philosophical – as if he was constantly brooding on some displeasing but undeniable fact. Half lame, he relied on a walking branch, crafted from an exotic black wood found only in the Skravian Desert. Not that he had had much use for it since arriving at the house, a month ago. Not once had he ventured outside his tower room. How did he pass the time? Quarvis often wondered. There was nothing to fill the long empty hours. No books to read, no writing materials to use. Only the view from the window which, though appealing, had surely grown tedious by now. And the Vohorin insisted on absolute solitude. This surprised Kraike more than anything else. He had imagined that he and Kraike would have long conversations: together, they would discuss the past and plot out the future. They were co-conspirators, after all. But Kraike preferred silence.

Who was Quarvis to object? He was a lesser man than Kraike. So much so, they practically belonged to different *species*. Quarvis inhabited the world of solid objects, of flesh and bone, of what could be touched, scented, tasted. On the other hand, Kraike – whilst still an occupant of the physical world – was also a sorcerer, and such men perceived reality in a dramatically different way. They saw things concealed from ordinary eyes; they perceived chains of cause and effect that most would dismiss as impossible nonsense. Unless, of course, they were presented with proof. And what greater proof was there, than Kraike's achievements during the Vohorin invasion of Druine? Yes, the invasion failed. But Kraike demonstrated his abilities, and showed the worth of his strange knowledge.

Although he did not possess a ghoulish streak, Quarvis wished he had seen the plague spell at work. A few words uttered by Kraike, and hundreds upon hundreds of Druinese soldiers would burst into flame, the blaze beginning in their internal organs then spreading through their bodies, blackening flesh, charring bone, filling the air with greyish white smoke . . .

'These birds remind me of my homeland,' said Kraike, watching the nightingales. His words caught Quarvis by surprise. Had he misheard? Possibly. Kraike spoke Druinese with a thick Vohorin accent, and sometimes Quarvis struggled to understand.

'The birds?'

'Emperor Grivillus was fond of nightingales,' said Kraike. 'He called them "winged sonnets". He believed he had the soul of a poet. This was one of his many delusions.'

'Was he . . . as bad as some claimed?'

'You shall find out for yourself, if you are willing.' He gestured to the writing desk. A thin book rested upon the polished surface, bound with brown twine. 'And believe it is worth the risk.'

Yes, thought Quarvis. The risk. The book was known simply as *The Chronicle*, and one did not read it, but *use* it. Kraike had warned him that the process posed a danger to both body and mind. So much so, the sorcerer insisted that Quarvis build up his strength beforehand. For three weeks, the former Scholar had eaten bowl after bowl of rich beef broth, imbibed a half-pint of bull's blood each morning, and walked endless circuits around the garden. Peeping from the shadowed windows, the household staff thought he had gone mad, and Quarvis wondered if it was all truly necessary. But it had made a difference. Despite his struggles on the tower stairs, he felt stronger than he had for years. Less frail, at least.

'Nothing valuable is gained without peril,' he said to Kraike.

'Then prepare yourself.'

Taking *The Chronicle*, Quarvis knelt on the rug. Opening his bag, he pulled out a brass bowl and a leather pouch of *lecterscrix*, a narcotic herb. The drug was a rarity in Druine, and had cost Quarvis a small fortune. It looked innocuous enough, as he tipped it into the bowl. A tangle of thin brownish yellow stalks, similar to dried-out grass clippings. Kraike lit a taper from a lantern and, leaning forward, passed it to Quarvis. Quarvis stared at the flame swaying on the tip.

'I ignite the *lecterscrix* then inhale, yes? Whilst I am concentrating on the book?'

Irritation touched Kraike's voice. 'You do *not* concentrate. You let the symbols wash over you, like rainwater.'

'Yes. Of course. And then, I will see the past? I will set eyes on Vohoria, before it fell?'

'You will see Vohoria as it was, forty years ago. It would exist for only another decade; then the Needful Scourge began, and everything was obliterated.'

Quarvis lit the *lecterscrix*. The herb crackled softly, the thin strands glowing red at the edges, and Quarvis feared the whole bowl would burst into flame. It did not do so, but smouldered, exhaling a cloud of green smoke. Immediately, Quarvis gagged. The smoke stank of rotting fish guts. This was unexpected: *lecterscrix* was related to dreamers' weed, a smokeable herb popular throughout Druine, one Quarvis had never used – not even during his debauched phase – but had smelled many times. It had a sweet, crystalline scent, pleasant enough in its way. But this? This was nearly unbearable! Composing himself, he blew out the taper. Then he opened *The Chronicle* at the first page.

There was no writing, no pictures. Instead, a jumble of geometric shapes filled the page, each fitting snugly amongst its neighbours, like the pieces of a mosaic. Some of the shapes he recognised: squares, rectangles, pentagons and hexagons – these were familiar enough. But others were mind-warpingly complex, a confusion of corners and edges, following no discernible mathematical principles. All were sketched in black ink and from what Quarvis had heard, they had been drawn freehand. The overall effect was unsettling. Whether the symbols or the *lecterscrix* was to blame Quarvis could not say, but he grew dizzy, as if he were standing upon a high place and looking down.

He inhaled the *lecterscrix*. The urge to vomit increased, then subsided. His nostrils tingled, his throat tightened. Was this normal? Or was he suffering a bad reaction? He inhaled again. His vision blurred, and when it regained focus, the symbols appeared to be moving, rippling like an ant-swarm. Quarvis was convinced that if he touched the page, the shapes would flow up his arm and envelop him completely, and he would suffocate. Of a sudden, their motion changed, and they whirled as if drawn to the centre of a vortex. With a jolt, Quarvis realised he too was being sucked in – but sucked in where? A feverish panic seized him. Surely this was not the desired effect? Surely this was *not right*?

He cried out. Or thought he did. He could not be certain for a muffled rushing noise, as loud and vigorous as a hurricane, filled his ears. And he could no longer feel his body. He did not know if his jaw had moved, if his vocal chords had vibrated. His physical self had ceased to exist.

Was this it? Was he dying? Had his soul slipped out of his earthly body? Was he hurtling headlong into the Forest?

I am sorry, so sorry, he thought, addressing the Four. *I should have never lost my faith* . . .

He was moving now. At speed. He could not tell if he was rising or falling; he felt as if he were travelling in a direction that lacked any equivalent in the ordinary world. *The Chronicle* had vanished, the symbols were gone. So too the room in the top of the tower. Quarvis raced through a whispering emptiness, a strangely tangible absence, a nothingness so intense that it was an undeniable something . . . and he found himself in a foreign land, forty years ago, long before the Needful Scourge . . .

Winter, and Vohoria is a world of unbroken whiteness.

Standing on the palace roof, Selindak, high secretary to Emperor Grivillus, squints through a telescope and surveys the land.

There can be no doubt: Vohoria is a beautiful place.

A typically fierce frost has settled, sealing everything in a hard glittering white. The countryside gleams; the trees, meadows and fields no longer seem to have sprouted organically from the soil, but appear to have been crafted from porcelain and set down upon the landscape like colossal ornaments. The towns and cities are always white, even in the heat of midsummer: in southern Vohoria, there are quarries from which bone-pale stones are hewn for building materials. But now, their whiteness is intensified a thousandfold; in the cold sunlight, they shine with a near-painful intensity. In the far distance, the Seven Towers – a tribute to the first seven emperors of this noble nation – spear skywards, each an ice-splinter three hundred feet tall. Further off, Selindak sees the capital city of Merrulik, again immaculately white, except for a dark haze of smithy smoke, hanging in the chiming air like a shadow.

Beautiful indeed. Worth fighting for. Dying for.

Revolving the telescope on its tripod, he focuses on Grivillus's private hunting forest, two hundred acres of oaks, sycamores and beeches. He pays close attention to the nearest edge, in particular the foot-worn path winding into the trees. He stares, waiting; but no one emerges.

It does not matter. He is a patient man; he will wait, as a spider waits upon its web.

Selindak is forty-two years old. He is tall, gentle-featured, and slightly stooped – a consequence, Grivillus claims, of his scholastic tendencies.

Spend a lifetime hunched over books, and you may well

nourish the mind, *the emperor once said*. But you will also destroy the body. What is the use of being an intelligent cripple? Why prize a healthy mind over healthy flesh?

Grivillus had exaggerated. But that is his way: the emperor often overstates his emotions, and expresses his own thoughts – as meagre as they are – with excessive force.

Footsteps patter up the stone steps leading to the roof. Selindak turns the telescope, so it points over the countryside once more. An instant later a serving boy appears, red-faced, breathless. 'Forgive me, Secretary Selindak,' he pants, half stumbling. 'It is the emperor – he is unwell.'

'So? He is often unwell. Why trouble me with it?' Selindak's words are harsh, but his tone is gentle.

'That is true,' says the serving boy, pawing sweat from his forehead. 'But he has become . . .' He struggles to find the correct word. 'Unmanageable.'

'How so?'

'The clerks requested he should sign some parchments, and he flew into a rage. He is suffering terribly and, in his pain, he has grown unhinged.'

'Has he taken his medicine?' A subtle emphasis on medicine; the serving boy understood.

'A bottle and a half so far,' he said. 'And it is only two hours past dawn. He is in the throne room. I beg you to speak with him.'

'The colt requires gentling, does he? Very well.'

Leaving the roof, Selindak sets off toward the ground floor. Designed by the architect Nalpurik, the palace is a work of art, encapsulating the Vohorin artistic principles of sparsity and ostentation. Everything is white, of course – the corridors, the floor tiles, the ceilings. Yet there are degrees of whiteness, as any man who has contrasted sea-foam with snow well knows, and it is in a fractionally darker shade that the palace's true beauties are manifest. The walls of every corridor, passageway and stairway are decorated with images of trees. Clustered close together, their branches sprawling, and intertwining, they are not painted on the walls, in the fashion of a mural, but are made of marble and inset in the wall stones. Every step one takes, there they are; no corner of the palace is untouched. The scullery, the privy rooms, the bed-chambers – they are there. The palace is three hundred years old, and the architect Nalpurik was a wise and enlightened man; to him, the trees had a powerful symbolic resonance – one that Selindak recognises too. But Grivillus? And every other soul in the palace? They do not understand; they cannot understand . . .

Selindak enters the corridor leading to the throne room. He can hear Grivillus shouting; the smooth walls and cavernous ceilings can turn the cracking of an ant's knee-joint into a thunderous echo.

'No, no, no!' the emperor yells. 'Can you not see I am ailing? Can you not see this is a poor hour for affairs of state?' A pause. Then, as the echoes fade, 'Why must you pester me? Why must you buzz like flies around my ears? Ah, yes – that is exactly what you are: flies, flies, flies, all of you! And flies must be swatted, if they prove to be a nuisance. You men, all of you, you will hang for this. My guards, seize them and escort them to the dungeons! Tell the rope-master I need three strong nooses dangling from three gallows trees. We will kill them in unison. Three hard snaps of their necks,' he clicks his fingers; it echoes like a whipcrack, 'and my problems will be solved.'

Selindak steps into the throne room. What he sees is profoundly displeasing, although not unexpected. Emperor Grivillus is drunk. His face is fiery red, as if he has been subjected to a blast of air from a furnace. His long black hair falls in greasy scraggles to his shoulders, his clothes are grease-stained and rumpled, and he is barefoot like a savage. His jaw bristles with a five-day beard, his forehead is blemished by scabs, and his drinker's paunch bulges like an inflated pig bladder. He is not the handsome man depicted in paintings. He is large, solid and brutish, more a crude thumbnail sketch than the proud figure rendered in oils. He looks more like a mine-worker than an emperor.

Selindak notices his left eye is bruised. Has someone struck him? A laughable idea. No one would dare. Most likely he has blundered into a doorframe, or tumbled over whilst intoxicated.

Selindak knows why he drinks. Since adolescence, Grivillus has suffered – ignobly, with much self-pity – headaches of rare intensity. Every third day, they strike; Grivillus describes them in a variety of ways. I feel as if my skull is splitting. As if someone is skewering my brains with a red-hot poker. As if giant hands are squeezing my head, crushing it, slowly, so it warps then crumples . . .

The malady is real; for once, Grivillus is not exaggerating. When the ailment strikes, the blood drains from his face; he grimaces involuntarily, his features contorting as if viewed in a defective looking glass; he trembles, vomits and, on occasions, sinks to his knees and clutches his head – as if it could make any difference.

In fact, nothing makes any difference. Vohoria's finest physicians are baffled; the emperor has gulped down potion after potion, and swallowed tablet upon tablet, all to no effect. It seems the affliction will be a constant burden, to be endured until the grave.

He stands in the centre of the throne room, glowering at a trio of clerks. Each of these elderly men, who have served him loyally for many years, holds a wad of parchments against his chest; their gazes are fixed on the guards who are advancing slowly across the room, boot-heels clicking on the tiles.

'Take them,' *Grivillus instructs the guards.* 'I want them to swing before nightfall.'

'My emperor,' *says Selindak from the doorway. His voice is mild, and he smiles faintly, as if nothing is truly amiss.*

Grivillus looks over. 'Ah, Selindak. I trust you will oversee the execution of these . . . these traitors?'

'Traitors, my emperor? But they are merely doing their duty.'

'At an importune time,' *says Grivillus.* 'They are torturing me, Selindak. They might as well be stretching me upon a rack.' *He takes a swig from a bottle of valrux — a colourless spirit, potent enough to stun a horse.*

'Affairs of state can be laborious,' says Selindak, gently. 'And perhaps they ought to have chosen a finer moment. But traitors? They are here, my emperor, because they want Vohoria to thrive. Without your signature upon those documents,' he gestures to the parchments, 'nothing can be done. No hospitals can be built, or taxes raised, or roads repaired; no insurrections can be stifled or—'

'Enough,' says Grivillus.

Unperturbed, Selindak continues, 'And it is not merely your signature they require. It is your wisdom. Where would we be, without your guidance? Your insight?'

'Is that it, Selindak? Do you insult me with flattery?' For a moment, Grivillus's anger seems to rise. His eyes flash; his jaw clenches. He draws back his shoulders, and clenches the hand which does not hold the bottle into a large, knob-knuckled fist. Selindak knows this is a pretence; the emperor is playing a joke. Grivillus's humour is of an unwholesome sort. It invariably arises from the discomfort of others; even in adulthood, he remains the child who laughed whilst incinerating insects beneath a magnifying lens. Selindak plays along, looking abashed. Grivillus's lips quiver; his nostrils twitch. Suddenly, he breaks out in loud, caustic laughter.

'Ah, my secretary — you are so easily gulled!' His eyes moisten with mirth. For a brief spell at least, he has forgotten about his headache. He gulps another mouthful of valrux, then points the bottle at the clerks. 'So, I should spare these gentlemen?'

'Oh yes,' replies Selindak. 'They may have offended you, but their motives were good.'

Grivillus looks at the clerks. Then shrugs. 'Off you go, then. Hurry, hurry,' he makes a shooing gesture, 'or I may change my mind.'

As the clerks depart, scuttling away like cockroaches exposed to sudden light, Selindak takes the parchments from them whilst Grivillus shuffles to the throne and sits, heavily, bracing the valrux bottle between his thighs. 'This is not a good day,' he says, rubbing his head.

'Did you sleep last night?' Selindak inquires, walking toward the throne.

'Not in any nourishing way,' replies Grivillus. 'I drowsed, but never sank into the depths of full slumber. What about you, Selindak? I suppose you slept like a dormouse in winter.'

'I do not share your affliction,' says Selindak. 'If I could take it upon myself, so that you might be released from pain, I would gladly do so.'

'You would regret it,' said Grivillus. 'No one deserves this.' He rubs his head again, takes another, shallower drink of valrux.

Examining the parchments, Selindak says, 'These are important, my emperor. Let us deal with them, and then you may rest.'

Grivillus consents. Unlike the clerks, who tend to labour each point, Selindak proceeds swiftly, dwelling only upon the necessary details. As Grivillus scrawls his signature on the final document, a serving boy — the same who had summoned Selindak from the roof — appears in the doorway.

'Yes, my child?' says Selindak.

'The hunters have returned. They have brought something to entertain the emperor.' The boy's eyes dart nervously to Grivillus. 'They say it will amuse him.'

'Amuse me, eh? Something they found in the forest?'

'It is, my emperor,' replies the serving boy.

'What is it, then? A pheasant that can play the harp? A dancing deer? A pig that recites the poetry of Min-drannek?' Grivillus raises a hand. 'No, do not tell me. I want it to be a surprise.' Grabbing the throne's armrests, he hauls himself onto his feet. He sways, then staggers across the floor, gripping the bottle. 'Life is a war against boredom. Is that not so, Selindak? Go on, boy. Lead the way.'

Outside, in the courtyard, four hunters are waiting. Clad in bear-skins, they are savage-looking men, dirty-faced, beards tangled and *hands filthy. Before them rests a pig-trap, a wooden cage whose door swings shut when the prey ventures within. Inside, a young boy sits cross-legged. He is, perhaps, nine or ten years old, and despite the bitter cold, he is naked. His body is covered in dirt, there are twigs and leaves in his hair, and even though his surroundings are unfamiliar, he is calm, his face blandly vacant, chubby fingers interlaced on his lap.*

Grivillus approaches, kneels. 'What is this, then?'

'We found him in the forest,' *says Lirix, the leading hunter.* 'We cannot say how long he has been in the trap. It is amazing that he has not frozen to death. Look, he is barely even shivering.'

'What is your name, child?' *Grivillus taps on the bars.*

'He has not spoken a word since we came upon him,' *says Lirix.*

'I am sure he will speak now, though. One does not stay silent in the presence of one's emperor.' *Grivillus taps the bars again.* 'Your name, boy. And where you hail from.'

The boy says nothing. Only stares.

'High secretary, would you say the child is a mute? Or merely impertinent?'

Selindak crouches by the cage. Reaching inside, he touches the boy's shoulder. 'His skin is icy. Maybe the cold has shocked him into silence. As for his origins — Lirix, is the wall around the emperor's forest in good condition?'

'As far as I can tell,' *says the hunter. Then, he shrugs.* 'It is old, though. Maybe the stonework has come loose in places, even collapsed.'

'So the boy could have wandered in from outside?'

'It is possible.'

'A stray, separated from its parents, would you say?' *Grivillus looks sideways at Selindak.* 'One who left home and went wandering?'

'The nearest village is twenty miles away,' *says Selindak.* 'If it is so, the child is blessed with considerable stamina. Great fortitude, too, to tread so far in the midst of winter.'

'Those are both Vohorin traits,' *says Grivillus.* 'But it is possible he has been abandoned, is it not? If he is a mute, his parents might have rejected him. There is scant point in nurturing an imbecile.' A dark note enters Grivillus's voice. His amusement, if it ever truly existed, is departing. A tiny muscle twitches at the corner of his eye. His nostrils twitch, his breathing deepens. He flinches as a bolt of pain lances through his skull. Rising, he looks first at the cage, then the hunters.

'Well?' he says.

The hunters stare back, at a loss.

Grivillus swigs from the bottle. 'Do I broil him? Or roast him? Or cut him into pieces and fry him in a pan? You are duty-bound to catch food, my huntsmen. Unless you have deviated from those duties – a crime punishable by death – I can only assume you are offering up this child as a meal. So how should he be cooked?'

Lirix falters. 'My emperor, we did not intend that . . . that you should devour the child.'

Grivillus blinked, widely, in mock confusion. 'No? Then why did you bring him to me?'

'We – we merely thought you would . . . would be interested.'

'As a cat is interested in a ball of wool?'

'No, my emperor. We simply imagined—'

'Did you hear that, Selindak? Our hunters have begun using their imaginations.'

'An unexpected turn of events.' The secretary smiles, not because he finds the emperor amusing, but because he must be placated. The hunters are not wicked men, but they will be punished if Grivillus's dark mood persists. Servants, scullions, doctors and generals have all been executed – after lengthy torture – because Grivillus objected to words spoken entirely without malice. When his head troubles him, he grows irrational. He tries to transform his suffering into the suffering of others.

'The hunters have wandered beyond the bounds of their duties,' he says. 'But I am certain they have also brought good fare for the banqueting table. Is that not so?'

82

'Yes, High Secretary Selindak. Several boars, and a deer. Some of the best specimens we have encountered.'

Grivillus grunts, shrugs – then glowers at the boy. 'The little savage,' he mutters, distastefully.

Kneeling now, hunching low, the child urinates onto the ground. As soon as he has finished, he sits, prises a clod of soil from his knee and mushes it into the urine, turning it into a paste. Then he pulls a twig from his hair, dips it in the paste and, reaching out through the bars, begins writing on the ground, the twig serving as a stylus, the mud-and-piss as ink.

Grivillus laughs. 'He wants to become the court artist.'

The boy works quickly, scrawling on the paving stones, and when the twig is dry, he brings it back into the cage, dips it again and continues.

'The court poet, perhaps.' Selindak moves close. 'He is writing, not sketching.'

Grivillus stares, squinting. 'That is our language, is it not?'

'It is, my emperor.'

'Yet the words make no sense.'

'Not to you or me,' says Selindak, peering at the looping, swirling marks. 'But – yes – an apothecary would understand them. They are part of a chemical formulae – a recipe, if you like, by which an infusion may be prepared.'

'An infusion for what?'

'I cannot say, my emperor.'

The boy scribbles frantically a while longer. Selindak, Grivillus and the hunters watch in silence. When the child lays down the twig, he looks at Grivillus then lifts a hand to his own head, pulls an agonised face and groans.

'He is mocking me,' says Grivillus. 'The hideous little sprite is ridiculing my affliction.'

'Or he is telling you what the formula is for,' murmurs Selindak.

Grivillus does not hear. 'The wretched cur must be drowned, or burned, or buried alive . . .'

'No,' says Selindak, firmly.

Grivillus jolts, surprised. 'My secretary?'

'Before we condemn the child, we must test the formula. Consider your circumstances, my emperor. A child appears in your forest, apparently endowed not only with alchemical understanding, but knowledge of your malady. Who in Vohoria knows of your troubles? It is a secret, is it not?' He strokes his short neat beard. 'We Vohorin believe that the universe operates in a mysterious fashion. Equally, we know that it arranges affairs for our benefit. Is that not so? Are we not the Chosen?' He gestures to the child. 'What is to say he is not a gift? An endowment from the universe itself?'

'You talk like a metaphysician,' mutters Grivillus, sourly.

'They are not without wisdom,' counters Selindak. 'Yes, they may speculate a little wildly at times — but we need not fall prey to the same vice. Indeed, with the formula lying at our feet, we do not need to speculate at all. No; we need only take it to the court apothecary. He will brew it up and deduce its function.' He laughs, softly. 'Though its purpose is clear to me, as it should be to you.'

Grivillus drinks from the valrux bottle. 'Very well. We will do as you suggest. But the child's life depends on the outcome. If the mixture is useless — or worse, a poison — I will assume that he was mocking me. For that, he will pay the highest penalty. If, on the other hand . . .'

In Quarvis's vision, the scene dissolved. For a moment, he saw the geometric shapes, spinning at a furious rate. Then, of a sudden, he was in the throne room once more . . .

Laughing, Grivillus paces back and forth. Now and again, he claps his hands, stamps his foot, shakes his head. Stooping, he takes an empty goblet from the floor and tosses it from hand to hand.

'The child is a miracle,' he says to Selindak. 'Where is he now?'

'In a room in the eastern wing. Awaiting his fate.'

Grivillus laughs again. 'And a glorious fate it shall be. Grant him a bed-chamber in the heart of the palace. Make sure he is given good clothes, and whatever food and drink he requires.' He lobs the goblet high in the air, so it clips the ceiling, and catches it when it falls. 'Has he spoken?'

'No, my emperor.'

'You have no inkling of his name? Where he came from?'

Selindak shakes his head.

'Then we shall keep him.'

'My emperor, he may have parents who are seeking him.'

'Let them seek; they shall not find. He is ours now. As you say, he is a gift from the universe. Think of it, my friend! All the great minds in Vohoria could not provide a remedy. And then, some child with a weak bladder, some mud and a stick appears, besting them all!' He pauses, peering into the goblet. 'Jurel Kraike. We shall call him Jurel Kraike.'

'The Bringer of Harmony?'

Grivillus pats the side of his head. 'I feel as if there is music in here. I cannot think of a more apposite name, can you?'

The scene faded, ebbing into emptiness. The symbols lay motionless on the page, and green smoke wreathed Quarvis, clogging his nostrils, stinging his eyes.

I have seen, he thought. I have seen . . .

His stomach tightened, propelling his evening meal into his throat. Rising, he stumbled across the room, flung open the window and vomited into the garden below. When the spasm passed, he wiped his mouth on his sleeve and turned to Kraike.

'I apologise,' he said, ashamed. 'I did not expect to be so strongly affected.'

'But you *were* affected?' Kraike regarded him with wary scrutiny.

'Oh yes.' Quarvis nodded. 'I witnessed your arrival at Grivillus's palace. You were young, a half-decade from manhood.

85

You wrote an alchemical formula that would cure the emperor's aching skull.' A wave of exultation washed over Quarvis. He fought down a giddy, ecstatic laugh. 'The visions were so vivid! I felt as if I were there. I saw everything; I *felt* everything. I even knew what Selindak was thinking!' He composed himself. He did not want to appear too surprised, for it might imply a certain scepticism toward Kraike's unusual abilities. Returning to the rug, he emptied the smouldering *lecterscrix* out of the window. Then he picked up *The Chronicle*. 'This book is a miracle.' He looked at Kraike. 'How does one create such a thing?'

'The credit is owed to Selindak,' replied Kraike.

Surprised, Quarvis said, 'He too possessed sorcerous gifts?'

'In a small fashion,' said Kraike, turning his face to the window. He breathed deeply, clearing the smoke from his lungs. 'His grasp of the esoteric arts is weak, but effective, within certain boundaries. Beyond composing books like *The Chronicle*, there is little else he can do.'

'You speak of him as if he still lives?'

'He does. He is waiting for us in Vohoria.'

'He must be in his eightieth year!'

'He is too stubborn to die. I learned that much when he was writing *The Chronicle*. The book contains three visions, and each almost killed him.' Kraike looked at Quarvis. 'At the moment of death, the soul leaves the body. This is a phenomenon well known in my culture, as well as yours. Occasionally, the soul departs prematurely, before the body has died. In such instances, it remains trapped in the physical world. You have heard such tales, surely? They are common enough. The grievously ill or injured report that they could see their mortal frames, languishing upon their sick-beds. They could also perceive the room in which they lay, the people gathered around them . . . Before composing a chapter of *The Chronicle*, Selindak cut his wrists. The wounds were deep and life-threatening. So much so, his soul drifted from his body. At the same time, he was inhaling *lecterscrix*; he entered a trance-state and, concentrating on the episode he wanted to depict, engaged in automatic writing. Are you familiar with the term?'

'Of course,' replied Quarvis. 'It is when a scribe writes without conscious thought; he puts down whatever feels *natural* at the time. The Church forbids the practice, believing it makes one susceptible to demonic influence. One may become, the Masters claim, an "amanuensis of the damned".'

A faint smile touched Kraike's lips. 'Your religion is full of crude fears.'

'It is not my religion,' said Quarvis, hurt. 'I abandoned it long ago – except for the truthful elements, such as the existence of the Forest.'

Unperturbed, Kraike continued. 'Selindak composed *The Chronicle* whilst we cowered in the Skravian Desert. To me, his motives were nonsensical. He said it was important that history was accurately recorded, in the greatest possible detail, by its participants. I asked why this was so. He gave no satisfactory answer, claiming only that it was a principle he held dear, and refused to abandon, no matter how dire the circumstances. And how could I doubt his commitment when every time he wrote a chapter, he came close to death? When he opened his wrists, his blood stained the sand deep red; the colour left his face; his heartbeats became tenuous flutters. Our physicians always struggled to revive him; they were convinced he would have perished, were he not endowed with an extraordinarily profound will to live.' He grew reflective for a moment then squinted at Quarvis. 'Do not believe you were exposed to Selindak's thoughts. He transcribed only *some* of what he was thinking. The relevant parts. When he stood on the palace roof, for instance, it seemed he was merely contemplating Vohoria, its countryside, how it was worth dying for. Not so. He was keeping watch for my arrival. Likewise, he knew I had not spent the entire night in the boar trap, but had been put there shortly before the hunters arrived. As for the formula I wrote on the tiles – it was chemically neutral. It had no active properties.'

'How, then, did you cure Grivillus's headaches? Sorcery?'

'I did not heal him. Selindak stopped poisoning his food and drink.'

Quarvis gaped, jaw sagging like a trapdoor.

'Selindak had served Grivillus for ten years,' explained Kraike. 'He knew that one day, someone like myself would need to enter Grivillus's inner circle. Equally, he understood that that someone had to have something to offer, or he would be turned away at the outset. What better than a cure for some malady that blighted the emperor's life? That reduced him to an embittered drunk, and leached away his ambition?'

Quarvis had known none of this. Now, he felt as if he had been accepted into some secret club that welcomed only the privileged few.

'I want to see the second vision,' he said.

'So you shall. But not this evening. You must rest and regain your strength.'

Quarvis wanted to protest. But Kraike was right. His guts bubbled and frothed, and he felt uncomfortably light-headed.

'The morrow, then?' he said, moving to the door.

Kraike did not reply. Once again, he looked out of the window. Night had fallen; no nightingales sang.

Leaving the room, Quarvis trod dizzily down the steep stone steps. Outside the bell tower, he leaned against the wall, inhaling the cool air, trying to get the *lecterscrix* stench out of his nostrils. Despite the lingering nausea, he felt good. Elated.

Moving to the rear of the tower, he crouched by a lavender

bush growing against the stonework. Sweeping it aside, he exposed a trapdoor, which he opened.

Descending a short flight of steps, he fumbled for a lantern, then lit it. Yellow light illuminated a circular chamber some ten paces across. An open-fronted bookcase stood in the centre. Alongside it, a table on which lay a stack of artwork, each depicting a scene of everyday Vohorin life. Rendered in blue paint, against a white background, men and women worked in the fields, fished in rivers, played strange musical instruments. Quarvis treasured these images – but how they paled in comparison to what he had seen in *The Chronicle*! How flat and lifeless they seemed, suddenly. His gaze shifted to the bookcase. Only the topmost shelves were in use; the texts Quarvis collected were hard to come by. Many he had stolen from the Black Archives, the repository of outlawed works beneath the Esklarion Sacros, during his tenure as a Scholar of Outrage. Others, he had purchased on the Dark Market. Thematically, they were split into two groups: some concentrated on Vohoria, its history, culture, religions and philosophies. The rest focused on visionaries, those peculiarly gifted individuals who perceived the spirit realm as clearly as the physical world. Men like Kraike, whose soul travelled every night to the Eltheryn Forest, where he communed with one far greater than himself . . . far greater than any visionary who had existed.

Quarvis took a tiny effigy from the bookcase. An inch and a half long, carved from time-yellowed ivory, it depicted a muscular man in a loincloth, a spear clutched in one hand, an etching tool in the other.

Toros. The Father of Vohoria. The King of Visionaries.

Quarvis stared. Was this a true likeness of Toros? Kraike would know, of course. But Quarvis would not ask. He would find out for himself, soon enough.

For millennia, Toros had dwelled in the Forest. Not as a lost

89

soul, trapped there after death. But as a willing inhabitant, a scholar who ventured into that unspeakable realm to study the magical forces from which it was composed. With every passing moment, Toros learned more and more about the strange tides and currents moving through reality. As his knowledge grew, his powers increased.

It would not be long before he returned to this world. And Quarvis would be there to greet him.

CHAPTER SIX

'This is the Loop, the finest racetrack in Druine,' mumbled Mallakos, gesturing limply to the stadium. 'Here, you shall find the man you are seeking. The man,' he added bitterly, 'who sold me *The Loss*.'

Normally, Mallakos would have been delighted to set eyes on the Loop. It was a colossal structure, the outer wall eighty feet high, decorated with a frieze of galloping horses, their hooves silver, their eyes gemstones glittering in the sunlight. Over the entrance there was a graven stallion, measuring twenty feet from nose to tail with real steam pluming from its nostrils, forced out by a pump hidden inside its cavernous body. It was a glorious sight, and never failed to stir his horse-loving heart.

Until now.

His captors had not treated him badly. On the journey to Sliptere, they ensured he was fed and watered, and not once had they manhandled or mocked him. He had even conversed with the girl, whom he inwardly referred to as the Bookworm, for she had a strangely studious air, and had read the confiscated copy of *The Loss* with some eagerness. Mallakos had asked her if the book was worth the trouble it had caused. She was surprised; had he not read it himself? Mallakos revealed that he had read only one of the forbidden texts in his collection, a work entitled *Equine Astrology: How the Stars Influence the Development of Horses*. He did not explain why he neglected the other works, and the Bookworm had not asked. Instead, she had shrugged and said, '*The Loss* is one of the worst books I have read. An ode to the glories of Vohoria, it claims life in Druine would be infinitely better if we had lost the war. I can only assume the author wrote it as . . . as a joke.'

'It's not worth hanging for, then?'

'You will not hang, Mallakos. We do not serve the Church.'

That much seemed true. Whoever they were, they were not doing the Masters' work. Were it not so, they would have raided Silver Hoof with two dozen armed men, and been accompanied by some cold-eyed, self-righteous Scholar of Outrage. As far as the horse-breeder could tell, they were mercenaries, though they gave no clue who their employers were, or why they were seeking Marrus Curtlane, the bewhiskered savage who sold him *The Loss*.

Mallakos had given all of his captors nicknames. Besides the Bookworm, there was the Blade, the gaunt man, not young, who appeared to be in charge. Then there was the Brute, the lumbering half-beast half-man chimera who had threatened to set Larchfire ablaze. He was terrifying; not only had he incinerated the guards, but he had slept soundly afterwards. No guilt, no remorse. As if he had done nothing worse than roast a few chickens on a spit.

Wading through the crowds, Mallakos led his captors into the Loop.

One thing was certain: he could not return to Silver Hoof. Not with a stableyard full of dead men. No doubt, someone in his serving staff had already reported the incident to the Wardens, which meant that he, Mallakos, was a wanted man. He was not guilty of the murders, of course. But when the Wardens searched the Hoof, gathering evidence, they would have found his stash of forbidden texts. If he was caught, he would be hanged, and the hanging would be preceded by a long spell of torture at the hands of a Scythe, one of the Church's interrogators.

He realised there was only one way he could evade the Church: he had to abandon his current identity and become someone new.

The old Mallakos – horse-breeder, dweller-in-luxury – needed to vanish, replaced by someone wholly unrecognisable. But what would this fresh-minted version of himself consist of? Mallakos could not imagine. He had dedicated himself to horses since he was fourteen years old. He loved everything about them – their smell, their nobility and above all, their natural fondness for him. He did not – could not – view them as mere livestock, as some breeders did. He treated them as friends, even children. How could he live without them? He did not know, but it was necessary. He had to cast off his present existence completely. To avoid being recognised, he would need to avoid the company of other horse-lovers, for he was well known in equine circles. In fact, he needed to go further. Even those who were not acquainted with racing knew of him – or his girth. His tremendous size had earned him a small amount of fame, and if he was to be inconspicuous, he needed to transform himself into a thin man – which meant no more ham and egg suppers, no plates overspilling with roast pheasant, no pies with crusts as thick as kettle lids. Like some primitive hunter-gatherer, he would have to subsist on nuts, berries and roots. The prospect was utterly appalling.

He led the Brute, Bookworm and Blade into the stadium. As he looked at the tiered marble seats, thronged with racegoers, and the oval racetrack of hoof-hardened sand, his heart turned to lead. He would never come here again. It was over, this happy chapter. He felt like a heartsore young man watching his lady walk out of the door, never to return. If it were not for his captors' presence, he would have wept.

93

He took them to the uppermost tier. They sat, Mallakos by the aisle, the Blade alongside him, the Brute and the Bookworm further along.

'Can you see him?' asked the Blade.

Mallakos gazed to the trackside, where Odds Men were taking bets. 'No. But he will come. He cannot resist tossing his money into the wind.'

'He loses, does he?'

'Always. I have never known anyone with such bad luck. By rights, he should have bankrupted himself a thousand times over.'

'You remember what you must do?'

Mallakos scowled. 'I am not an imbecile.'

An official in a red doublet crossed the track, climbed the inner rail and strode to a brass gong, glaring in the noon sunlight. Picking up a cloth-swaddled mallet, he struck it once, sending a loud note wobbling over the stadium. The crowd sank into an excited hush. Emerging from an opening in the arena wall, the jockeys rode to the starting line. As they gathered, Mallakos felt a touch of deep sadness. He observed the eagerness of the animals to run, and wondered where he would ever encounter such enthusiasm again. Certainly not amongst men, who as a species were jaded, and averse to simple enthusiasms. When the officials struck the gong, and the horses broke away, the sunlight gleaming on their curry-combed fur, his sadness deepened, so much so it became physically painful. It was poetry, to watch the horses run, the only sort of poetry Mallakos truly appreciated. It exuded no wisdom, no sophistication, only a vigorous joy in life itself. It made the horse-breeder's heart dance, and the breath sparkle in his lungs. If it was taken from him – which it would be – what would remain? Nothing. He might as well be a clod of soil, or a scarecrow in a field, for all that he would be able to feel of the world . . .

When the race ended, the Blade leaned close. 'Has he arrived?'

Mallakos looked toward the Odds Men. Then grunted.

'There. That is him.' Pointing, he picked out Curtlane. As always, he was dressed entirely in white. And as always, he was slapping the outside rail in frustration. 'Clearly, his luck has not improved.'

'Let us get started, Mallakos,' said the Blade.

Mallakos sighed. 'Very well.'

Rising, he waved a hand back and forth until Curtlane spotted him. Leaving the trackside, the white-clad man loped up the steps. As he grew closer, Mallakos was struck by his ugliness. Somehow, Curtlane's hideously disproportioned face always surprised him; he kept forgetting how cruelly nature had treated him, endowing him with a countenance virtually identical to a bullfrog's. His fat-lipped mouth was preposterously wide; his eyes bulged, and his nose was a grim little stub perforated by two almond-shaped nostrils. He was twenty, perhaps twenty-five years of age, yet the side-whiskers sprouting from his jaw were as wispy as an adolescent's. He probably thought they granted him a rough, tough, masculine air, like the v-shaped scar on his cheek, which he stroked whilst talking to women. In truth, they did nothing of the sort. The whiskers looked like fuzzy mould sprouting from a rotting plum; they were repellent. Garbed in his white shirt and leggings, his fingers bedecked with gold rings, his neck encircled by a fine-linked gold chain, Curtlane had clearly not learned one of life's simple lessons: if you are an ugly man, vanity will do you no favours: fine clothes and jewellery only make your aesthetic shortcomings more strikingly apparent.

Curtlane halted at the bench. 'Ah, Blubberguts! It has been a while.'

'Good day, Curtlane.' Mallakos gestured to the Odds Men. 'I see your fortunes have not improved.'

'Each day my purse grows lighter,' said Curtlane, 'just as your arse gets fatter. How long until your heart judders to a halt, you monstrous lump? It cannot be long now. I would be surprised if you survive the summer, with the heat and all.'

'It is always a pleasure to see you, Curtlane,' sighed Mallakos. 'I cannot imagine why I left it so long since our last meeting.'

Curtlane smiled. Tiny yellow-tipped spots twitched above his upper lip. 'Are these folk with you?' He looked along the bench to Mallakos's captors.

'They are my bodyguards,' said Mallakos.

'They are not your usual crowd. Where is Lezluthe?'

'Unwell. A sore throat, not contagious, but very painful.'

'They look as if they have been in the wars. What happened? Did they get between you and a freshly baked pie?'

'Your jests are tedious,' said Mallakos. 'If you must know, we were attacked by bandits – none of whom fared terribly well.'

Curtlane's gaze alighted on the Brute. 'Now that is an ugly piece of work,' he grinned. 'Where did you find him? A zoo-logical garden?'

'That's the spirit,' said Mallakos. 'Just keep on insulting a man who is twice your size and three times your weight. I am fairly certain he will take it in good part.' He looked at the Brute. The big man's expression was thunder-dark. 'Yes, he is almost definitely laughing on the inside.'

Curtlane rubbed his hands together, rings catching the sunlight. 'Well, fat man – what can I do for you? I doubt you invited me over for a mere chat.'

'I am seeking a text,' said Mallakos, loudly.

'Shut up!' said Curtlane, sharply. He looked around, nervously. 'Not here, you bloated idiot. There are ears everywhere. Outside.'

They left the Loop, Mallakos and Curtlane walking side by side, the Brute, Blade and Bookworm close behind.

'I am hungry,' said Curtlane, as they emerged into the square. 'We should discuss our business over a meal. What do you say?'

'I say that you are a scrounger.' Mallakos glanced at his captors. Their faces were expressionless.

Am I playing my role well enough? he wondered. There was no way to tell.

'As it happens,' he went on, attention returning to Curtlane, 'I, too, have an appetite.'

'Then we shall go to Rendell's Refectory. I crave steak, under-cooked and bloody.'

'Well, I want seafood. We will head to the Inland Harbour.'

Curtlane snorted. 'Fish is the fare of seagulls, not men. We will go to Rendell's.'

Mallakos halted. 'Curtlane, as I am paying, I shall choose the destination. Besides, if you can get me what I want, I will give you money enough for a thousand steaks. I am seeking something quite specific, you see.' He gestured to an alley. 'This is the shortest route to the Harbour. Come if you are interested. Otherwise, I will take my business elsewhere.'

Curtlane stroked his whiskers. 'It is not like you to be so stubborn.'

Mallakos shrugged. 'Times are changing. I am weary of being trampled upon by the likes of you. Now, will you come or not?'

'Lead the way, fat man.'

Crossing the square, they slipped into the alley. The previous year, a fire had torn through the narrow street of shops, ware-houses and mills. In more affluent days, the buildings would have been demolished and rebuilt so trade could resume. Now, though, they stood blackened and abandoned, the roof timbers sagging like the ribs of some charred beast, the stonework soot-darkened, the windows shattered. The air still carried a faint tang of woodsmoke, a scent nearly as comforting as horse-piss-soaked straw. Mallakos sighed. He wished none of this was happening.

Finding the alley deserted, Curtlane said, 'Well, my lump of lard, what is it you want?'

Mallakos glanced again at his captors. The Blade and the Bookworm's expressions were still unreadable. But the Brute was darkly attentive, listening like some outsized tomcat at a mouse hole.

'As I say, I am seeking a text.'

'What is its name?'

'I do not know.'

'Then how can I help you?'

'Let me elaborate. I am seeking a certain *type* of text. A while ago, you sold me a work which rather tickled my fancy, and I would like to read something similar. It was called *The Loss*, if you recall.'

'*The Loss?*' Curtlane frowned, nonplussed.

'You must remember. A very slender thing, maybe ten or fifteen pages long. Printed on coarse paper. It extolled the virtues of Vohoria, before it fell.'

Curtlane raised a dismissive hand. 'Spare me the blather. I sell texts, but I never read them. Why would I? They are a heap of bollocks.'

'But you do remember selling *The Loss*.'

Curtlane thought a moment. 'Aye,' he nodded. 'Now that you mention it—'

A dark shape swept past Mallakos. An instant later, the Brute slammed Curtlane against the wall, a hand locked around his throat.

'Make a sound,' said the big man, 'and I'll snap your neck.'

'Get off me,' croaked Curtlane, squirming. His bulging eyes swivelled, fixing on Mallakos. 'Tell this ape to unhand me!'

'Alas, I cannot,' said Mallakos, stepping back.

'This is outrageous! Malla—'

The Brute punched Curtlane in the belly. 'Stay silent, boy.'

Curtlane slid to the ground, settling on his rump. His face was crimson, his eyes wet. Kneeling, the big man leant close, so their foreheads were touching.

'We are going to talk, you and I,' he said, softly.

'I – I am sorry. I did not mean to insult you. I got carried away—'

The Brute seized Curtlane's jaw. 'Quiet.'

Curtlane swallowed.

'I have one question. Answer truthfully, and I'll let you go.'

Curtlane looked desperately at Mallakos. 'W-what is going on?'

'I do not know,' replied Mallakos. 'But I am certain that now it has started, it cannot be stopped. Far be it from me to offer you advice, but if I were in your shoes . . .' he looked at the text-seller's lower garments '. . . or your piss-stained leggings, I would do as I was told.'

'Where did you get *The Loss*?' asked the Brute. 'Did you print it yourself? Or buy it from someone?'

'I – I cannot remember.'

The Brute grabbed Curtlane's hand and then, adjusting his grip, seized his little finger. 'I was hoping you would say that. See, every time you lie to me, I get to snap one of your fingers. If you run out of fingers, I'll move on to your toes. After that, I will tear off your balls, one after the other.'

'Oh, please,' stammered Curtlane. 'I have—'

'Trouble.' It was the Bookworm who spoke. Laying a hand on the Brute's shoulder, she pointed along the alley.

Three brawny, flat-faced men raced toward them, gripping blackwood cudgels. The Brute cuffed Curtlane across the head. 'Stay where you are,' he said, rising. Sprinting full-tilt at the men he jumped, attaining an incredible height for such a large man. He crunched his knee under the jaw of one attacker whilst simultaneously flattening another with an uppercut. A pace or two behind, the Bookworm caught the third man's wrist and flung him over her shoulder. As he hit the ground, she turned, then stamped on his forehead. He sank into unconsciousness, tongue lolling out of the corner of his mouth. Kneeling, Ballas punched the attacker whose jaw he had broken across the head, hard. He too dropped into the clanging sleep of the pole-axed.

The Brute stumped over to Curtlane.

'Who were they?' he demanded, hauling the text-seller onto his feet.

Curtlane's purple face was turning white. 'I do not know—'

'Horseshit.' The Brute kneed him in the groin, the blow lifting him several inches off the ground. 'The truth, boy.'

'I . . . it is the truth.'

The Blade moved to Mallakos. 'We need somewhere quiet to speak with Curtlane. Somewhere we will not be disturbed.'

Mallakos nodded. 'I know of a place, I think.'

He led them along a succession of streets, venturing deeper amongst the burned-out ruins. He felt as if he were trapped in a bewildering dream. Mallakos was accustomed to a sedate pace of life – of rising at dawn, tending his horses and whiling away the remaining hours eating, drinking and daydreaming. Now, everything was happening too quickly. Whether he liked it or not, he had become his captors' accomplice. He had helped them find Curtlane. He was leading them to a place where the text-seller could be questioned. But that was not what baffled him. Rather, it was how he felt about it. Without warning, something had changed inside him. He had left the Loop feeling beleaguered and broken. But somewhere along the way he had gained . . . gained what? Resolve? Strength?

Truth be told, he felt good. He looked at his captors. In

particular, he focused on the Brute, jostling Curtlane along the alley. Inexplicably, and without justification, he felt as if he were one of them – that he too was an adventurer, a mercenary, someone who did not flinch from a fight or quail at threats. His shoulders drew back involuntarily. His chin lifted.

Halting outside the charred shell of a water-mill, he said, 'We are here.'

The Blade kicked open the door. Beyond, there was a large empty space, ankle-deep in ash. Dust motes glinted in sunlight pouring through a window which, miraculously, had not been shattered in the fire.

The Blade went inside, followed by the Brute and Curtlane. They half-closed the door, leaving Mallakos outside with the Bookworm.

'Whatever you do to him, he has got it coming,' said Mallakos, nodding toward the door. 'What happens now? What do we do next?'

'We?' The Bookworm tilted her head. For the first time, Mallakos noticed she was pretty, despite the bruises. Not a heart-stopper by any means, but endowed with a sturdy, resourceful air that he found appealing. Her eyes radiated intelligence, and she had the wide-yet-shapely shoulders of a lass who was not afraid of hard work. For a silly moment, Mallakos imagined she was his wife. He saw them working side by side, mucking out stables, leading horses around a paddock. She would make an excellent stablegirl, he thought. And certainly, a life amongst horses was more befitting a lady than raiding houses and stamping on heads. 'We do nothing, Mallakos. You are free to go.'

Mallakos blinked. 'Go?'

'We have no further need of you,' said the Bookworm. 'You have taken us to Curtlane; that is all we required.'

'Is this not . . . a little abrupt? I am sure I can be of further service.'

'No, Mallakos. You cannot.' She took a back step toward the door. 'Fare thee well.'

Glancing through the half-open door, Mallakos saw Curtlane kneeling in ash, sobbing. Mallakos did not pity the young man. On the contrary, he realised how much he loathed him. A year ago, Curtlane had approached him with a copy of *Equine Astrology: How the Stars Influence the Development of Horses*, knowing Mallakos would be interested in purchasing it. Oh yes, how the scoundrel had struck at Mallakos's weakest point! Unable to resist, Mallakos bought the book. He believed the transaction was a one-off; he would not see Curtlane again. How wrong he was. The young man returned a couple of weeks later, touting a text entitled: *The Enlightenment of Sleep*. Mallakos tried to turn him away. What do I care about such things? he had said. But Curtlane was persistent. And in his demeanour, Mallakos detected an unspoken threat: buy the text, or the Wardens will hear about *Equine Astrology*. Then where will you be?

Of course, Mallakos realised Curtlane could not inform the Wardens about *Equine Astrology* without implicating himself. No doubt Curtlane knew this too – and knew he also possessed a great advantage over Mallakos: namely, Mallakos was weak-spirited, and fearful of conflict of any sort. In other words, a blackmailer's ideal victim. So Mallakos bought the text, hoping he would be left alone from then on but knowing it would not be so. Text followed text; it became a habit. So much so, Curtlane dispensed with his obliquely threatening behaviour; he would just walk over to Mallakos, utter a few cruel insults, give him a new text, take his money and go.

One of these texts had been *The Loss* – the work that had landed Mallakos in his current predicament and ultimately cost him everything: his home, his stables, his horses, his comfortable life.

'What will happen to him?' Mallakos nodded toward Curtlane.

'That is not your concern.'

'Will he die?'

'Go, Mallakos,' repeated the Bookworm, impatiently.

Mallakos dug a purse out of his pocket. Opening it, he tipped two gold pieces onto his palm. 'Kill him, and these are yours.' He held out his hand.

The Bookworm lifted her eyebrows. 'You jest.'

'Am I laughing? Clutching my sides and rocking back and forth?' He jiggled the coins so they clinked together. 'You need not feel any guilt. More than anyone I have met, Curtlane does not deserve to live.'

'We are not assassins,' said the Bookworm.

'One can be a killer without making it one's trade. Just snuff him out. Please. It need not be a swift, neat job. I would prefer it if it wasn't, in fact. Yes, go at it as cack-handedly as you like. Make a meal of it. I just want him to suffer. And then cease existing.'

The Bookworm closed Mallakos's fingers around the coins. 'Keep them. And leave us alone.' Saying nothing more, she vanished into the water-mill.

Mallakos hesitated, listening. Inside, Curtlane yelped with pain. To his astonishment, the sound did not lift Mallakos's spirits. Opening his hand, he stared at the coins. Then he slipped them in his purse and waddled away.

Ballas held Curtlane's face cheek-deep in the ash. Suffocating, the text-seller thrashed, arms flailing, legs bending and kicking like a swimming frog's. When Ballas hauled him up, ash clung to his spittle- and tear-moistened face.

'You bastards,' spat the text-seller, rising onto all fours. 'You pissing bloody—'

Dragging him upright, Ballas flung him against a wall. 'Who attacked us in the alley?'

'I told you that I do not know—'

'Don't plead ignorance. They were trying to rescue you.'

'It is the truth, damn it!'

Striding over, Ballas raised an open hand. Curtlane cringed, knees sagging. 'For pity's sake, why won't you believe me? I do not have a pissing clue who they—'

Ballas smacked him across the head, the impact loud as a whip strike. Yowling, Curtlane collapsed and rolled into a ball.

'Let us try a different question.' Kneeling, Standaire sat Curtlane upright. 'You sold Mallakos a copy of *The Loss*, yes?'

Curtlane grimaced. 'You know that I did.'

'Where did you obtain it?'

'I cannot remember.'

'Is that the truth?'

'Of course it bloody is!'

Standaire glanced at Ballas, nodded. Once more, Ballas seized Curtlane's head, thrusting his face into the ash. Curtlane struggled, clawing at the floor.

'Stubborn little bastard, is he not?' said Ballas. 'Reckon he'll take a bit of persuading . . .'

The door opened and Ekkerlin entered.

'Mallakos wants us to kill him,' she said, shutting the door. 'He offered us two gold pieces.'

'I'd gladly do it for naught,' said Ballas, Curtlane writhing under his hand.

'He is not proving helpful?'

'Not yet.'

'Grant me a moment with him,' said Ekkerlin, crouching alongside Curtlane.

Ballas let go of the text-seller. Curtlane jerked upright, exhaling a mouthful of ash, then sucking in deep lungfuls of air. This time, he did not curse Ballas. He simply sagged, spitting on the floor, wiping snot-thickened ash from his nostrils.

'Sit up, Curtlane. Let us speak.'

'I do not want to speak,' said Curtlane, breaths hitching.

'But speak you must.' Gently, Ekkerlin manoeuvred him into a sitting position. With her fingertips, she wiped the ash from his face, so it remained only in his side-whiskers and eyelashes. 'Good. Now I can see you.' She smiled, pleasantly. 'What did you say your name was?'

'I did not say. Mallakos told you.' Curtlane winced. 'It is Curtlane.'

'Of course it is. And your first name?'

'Marrus.'

'Spell it for me.'

Curtlane scowled. 'What for?'

'Do as I ask. It is probably best if you do not test my friend's patience too much.' She flapped a hand toward Ballas. 'So far, you have seen only his gentle side. He can be much, much worse. He can make stones scream, when he is in the mood. Now, spell out your name.'

'M-A-R-R-U-S,' said Curtlane, enunciating each letter with faint sarcasm.

'Good. Now, where did you get *The Loss?*' Ekkerlin watched him, closely. In particular, she observed his eyes, noting the direction they moved.

'Like I said, I can't remember.'

Ekkerlin sighed, shoulders drooped. 'You are lying.'

'No I am not.'

'Oh, please.' She gestured to Ballas, who plunged him into the ash once again.

He held him there a long while. Eventually Standaire said, 'He is choking.'

Reluctantly, Ballas dragged him out. Curtlane gasped for

breath, twisted, then vomited on the floor. The Hawks watched dispassionately. Ballas was faintly intrigued by the young man. He sensed he was not the courageous sort. Yet he was behaving with unusual bravery. Most men of his type would have cracked by now.

'Are you going to tell the truth, now?' asked Ekkerlin, wiping the ash from his face once more.

Curtlane stared at her, evenly. 'Who are you? What do you want?'

'You know what we want. If you give it to us, you will be free to leave. It is a simple bargain.'

Curtlane's stare turned into a resentful scowl. Then he sighed, body slackening. 'Very well. Yes, I *do* remember where I got *The Loss*. On Brook Street, there is an apothecary. He keeps a printing press in his cellar. He produces forbidden texts, some of which I sell. The Four only knows why he does it: he is hardly poor. I suppose it must be a matter of principle, some rot about "educating the commonfolk".'

'That is a commendable principle,' said Ekkerlin. 'And if I were to meet this apothecary, I would shake his hand.'

'Then do so, if you like. Leave me alone and cast your shadows over *him*.'

'That is not possible,' said Ekkerlin. 'He does not exist. Or if he does, he did not give you *The Loss*. You see, I have been watching you. When you spelled your name, you looked upwards, to the left. This is the direction your eyes move when you are remembering something. However, when you spoke of the apothecary, you looked upward to the *right*. Hence, you were making something up. Do not feel embarrassed; everyone betrays themselves in this way. It is absolutely unavoidable. Of course, now you know about it, you will fight against it. When I ask the question again, you will force your eyes to move in the direction of remembering. But then, distracted by the effort,

106

you will speak uncertainly, and once again I will know you are lying.' She placed her hands on his shoulders. 'This is your final chance, Curtlane. Deceive us now, and my friend will set to work on your bones. His methods are far less refined than my own, but equally effective.'

Curtlane opened his mouth to speak but Ekkerlin touched his cheek.

'You are going to say that I am – what? Mad? Deluded? Mistaken? But that too will be a lie, one that I will spot. Because you do not believe it yourself.'

Curtlane seemed to fold into himself. Sagging, he stared fixedly at the ash-covered floor. Ballas sensed powerful, contradictory currents swirling through the young man; he wanted to save himself but, equally, he did not want to reveal who had given him *The Loss*. Eventually, he shook his head. 'You are deluded. You are mad.'

'And you, Curtlane, are looking at the ground so I cannot watch your eyes,' said Ekkerlin. 'Ballas, do what you must. Look upon our friend here as an outsized wishbone, waiting to be pulled.'

Leaning, Ballas grabbed Curtlane's wrist—

—and the door crashed open.

Four men surged through. Like those in the street, they carried cudgels, but they were garbed in fine, smart shirts and leggings of black silk. Springing to his feet, Ballas crunched a fist into the nearest attacker's face, shattering his cheekbone. Rising, Ekkerlin slammed the heel of her hand up beneath the jaw of a second, clashing it shut. As the man staggered, she kicked him hard in the groin. Dropping his cudgel, the third attacker unsheathed a knife and ran at Standaire. With an oddly serpentine slowness, the general stood, seized the man's wrist and plunged a forefinger in his eye socket.

At the rear of the water-mill there was movement. Stumbling

through the ash, Curtlane lurched to a glassless window. Casting about a wild-eyed glance, he climbed through and disappeared.

'Bring him back,' said Standaire, cracking the fourth attacker across the cheek.

Ballas ran to the window. Squeezing through, he dropped onto a path running alongside the river, crusted with brown heat-ripened scum. Already Curtlane was thirty yards away, running hard. Every few steps, he glanced over his shoulder. Cursing savagely, Ballas broke into a sprint, gaining ground with every pace. As he grew close, Curtlane fired another backward glance, gave a strangled yowl of panic and jumped into the river. The scum split apart, revealing oil-dark water beneath. Curtlane sank from view, then surfaced a few yards away, cracking upward through the layer of hardened filth and dog-paddling furiously toward the opposite bank. Clambering out, he looked at Ballas and ran.

Ballas followed, leaping as far across the river as he could. He did not make the full distance. Shattering a patch of scum with his boot soles, he plunged into foul, greasy darkness then surged up into sunlight, gulping lungfuls of air. He swam, trying hard not to retch. When he climbed out, flies swarmed around his face and clothing.

Fifty paces away, Curtlane raced like a hare pursued by hunting dogs.

'Help! He's going to kill me! For pity's sake, someone stop him!'

The text-seller swerved into a ginnel. When Ballas rounded the corner, Curtlane was already exhausted, arms flapping, legs getting tangled with one another. Then he tripped, hitting the ground hard.

'No! No! I am sorry! For the Four's sake, show mercy—'

Ballas punched him on the side of his head, knocking him unconscious.

Slinging him over his shoulder, Ballas carried him back toward the mill, crossing the river by a stone bridge a hundred yards downstream. As he went, his sodden, fly-crawled clothes dried out in the sun. A vile faeces-and-rotten-vegetable reek rose around him, and he spat out a mouthful of bile.

He laid Curtlane down outside the water-mill window. Peering through, he discovered the building was empty. Ekkerlin and Standaire were gone. So too their silken-clad attackers.

Something was wrong. Very wrong.

Clambering through the window, he stood still, listening. Nothing. He looked down at the rotting oats on the floor. He could see many footprints where he, the Hawks and the attackers had fought. And there was a second set of prints, small and neat, padding through the sludge to the edge of the room, where they halted. A fifth person had entered the mill. Something caught his eye. Crouching, he found a thin strip of wood, an inch long, the tip stained bright green. A poison dart, like those blown from hollow tubes by jungle dwellers? He spotted a second identical dart a short distance away.

Outside the window, Curtlane groaned. Rising, Ballas stared at the darts, the oats. Then he climbed out through the window onto the path.

CHAPTER SEVEN

Ballas halted the stolen cart outside Blacker's Folly.

The Folly was a hollow spire-shaped structure of black stone. Rising a hundred and thirty feet high, it teetered on the brink of collapse. Fracture lines threaded the brickwork, the window frames were warped, the glass shattered. The conical roof was just timbers, the slates long since fallen away, and birdshit streaked the upper half of the building.

Mallakos had pointed out the Folly when they entered Sliptere, suggesting it would be a good place to question Curtlane.

He said it was erected by Lackloss Blacker, a silk merchant. It was intended to house musicians, painters and sculptors who, despite their talent, could not earn a living from their work. Blacker was to be their patron, feeding and clothing them, and buying whatever materials and tools they needed to pursue their arts. He had a natural empathy for the creatively inclined, believing he too would have pursued an artistic life, had his overbearing father not bullied him into the world of commerce. He believed his gift lay within the 'sphere of habitable beauty' – that was to say, architecture. Thus he designed the Folly himself. Proper architects condemned his plans from the start. It was riddled with flaws, they said. Lacking structural integrity, the Folly would collapse before it was completed and if it did not, it would come crashing down soon after. In this, they were mistaken. Against all odds, the Folly had stood for twenty years. But it never properly fulfilled its intended use. On windy days, it swayed, creaking and shuddering; even when the air was still, timbers groaned, stones scraped and a continual pall of dust hung in the air. The artists dwelled there for only a week; one night a storm struck and, losing their nerve, they fled, never to return – and proved that despite their pretensions to the contrary, they were not willing to die for their art.

Jumping off the cart, Ballas pushed at the door. It was wedged solid. Grunting, he shoulder-charged it open, returned to the cart and whipped back the tarpaulin beneath which Curtlane lay, wrists bound, a gag across his mouth.

Dragging him off, Ballas flung him into the Folly. Inside, he closed the door and looked around.

Once, the ground floor had been a sculptors' workshop. Ballas jostled the text-seller across through a jumble of half-hewn blocks of stone and marble, mallets, chisels and sketch-books, then up some stone steps to the second floor, a music room. An abandoned cello leant against the wall, the varnished wood cracked and crusted with dried mould. A violin lay on the floor, like some strange brown beetle, trampled to splinters, its snapped strings curling like antenna. Another climb, and they reached the top floor, once the haunt of painters. Knocking over a cluster of easels bearing unfinished portraits and land-scapes, Ballas manhandled Curtlane to the far side.

He kicked the text-seller's legs from beneath him. Curtlane landed heavily on his rump, then sagged back against the wall.

'Say nothing,' said Ballas.

Forcing open a rust-jammed window, Ballas looked down. There was a stone ledge below, webbed with fracture lines. Leaning out, he pressed it with his hand. It held firm. He pressed again, placing a little more weight upon it. It would do, he decided.

Kneeling, he tugged down Curtlane's gag. Then he hauled the text-seller to the window.

'Look down,' he said, thrusting the young man's head through the open window.

'You are going to kill me,' said Curtlane, eyeing the drop below. He began to shake beneath Ballas's hands. The sensation pleased the Hawk. He loathed Curtlane the moment he set eyes on him. He inspired a near-primal aversion. Like maggots wriggling in dog shit. Or an outrageously infected wound.

'No. I am going to give you an opportunity to live.'

Grasping his belt with one hand, his collar with the other, he lifted the text-seller out of the window. He lowered him chest-down onto the ledge. His face turned sideways, Curtlane stared over the neighbouring rooftops. He gasped, growing rigid. A feeble trickle of urine seeped from his leggings. 'Please, please, please . . .'

'I do not know you very well,' said Ballas. 'But I have run into folks like you before. You lie, deceive, indulge in a hundred forms of dishonesty. Why? To get what you want. Well, we are going to turn things upside down. You want to live?'

'Of course,' said Curtlane, at a whisper.

'Then you will have to speak truthfully. Reckon you can do it?'

'Y-yes.'

'See, if you don't, I will leave you where you are. Doesn't sound too bad, does it? Except, I will have tied your ankles together. And stuck the gag in your mouth so you cannot shout for help. Now, what do you think will happen? There are two possibilities, as far as I can see. First, you try to get inside. But that means you will have to stand up, and that ledge is pretty narrow. Not to mention weak. Chances are, you will lose your balance and fall. Or the stones will give way under your shifting weight and, aye, you will drop. Either way, you end up on the ground, skull cracked open like an egg. But there is something else that might happen. You might just lie there, paralysed by fear, until the sun sets and the sky darkens. And then you will doze off. But that would be a bad move. You see, men toss and turn when they slumber, and you know those dreams when you are falling? Well, Curtlane, if you try hard enough, dreams really can come true. Do you understand?'

Curtlane made a wheezy yelping noise.

'Let us talk awhile,' said Ballas, leaning on the window-frame.

'Please. Bring me inside.'

'Not yet. I want to know who the men in black silk were. And where you got *The Loss*.' The water-mill attackers' attire was strange. The men had the lustre of professional thugs; so why wear clothes so easily torn and ruined? They looked as if they were dressed for an evening in a sedate drinking club.

'I do not know.'

'You do not know what?'

'The answer to your questions.'

'Which one?'

'Both of them.'

Leaning out, Ballas pushed hard on Curtlane's back. The text-seller squealed, clenching shut his eyes. 'Oh, by the Four's mercy . . .'

'I am getting bored,' said Ballas. 'And when that happens, I do stupid things, things that make no sense. My friend, the girl – she tells me that I am my own worst enemy. When I am in a dark humour – such as now – she insists I go for a long run. She reckons it calms me down a bit. Perhaps I should put in a few miles and come back. What do you think?'

'Do not leave me.'

'Then tell me the truth.'

Curtlane said nothing. Ballas pursed his lips.

'You are protecting someone.'

'No!'

'You fear him more than you fear me – which is strange, given the circumstances. Would you prefer to die than tell me his name?'

'Die? I do not want to die at all.'

'Then tell me.'

Curtlane grew very still. A high breeze stirred his side-whiskers, crusted with riverscum. 'If I do . . .'

'I will bring you inside.'

'And then?'

'You can go on your way.'

'I do not have a choice, do I?'

'Death or life – that is a choice enough for most.'

Curtlane opened his eyes. He stared at the rooftops, then shut them again, disturbed. 'His . . . His name is Sayner Vessen. He is an Odds Man at the Loop.'

'And he controls those men in black silk?'

'No. He sold me *The Loss*. As for those men, I do not know. I cannot guess who they are. Sir, you must believe me. I – I am not a popular man. No one has ever rushed to my defence before, and then it happens twice, in swift succession. It is without precedent. I am confused.' His eyes sprang open, as if he were struck by a revelation. 'Perhaps they were Vessen's men, looking out for me. Both lots. The first linger at the Loop, overseeing everything. Wearing ordinary clothes, they are able to watch me without being noticed. As for those in the silks – they must be accomplices of some sort. But they do not frequent the Loop. I have never set eyes on them before.'

Ballas narrowed his eyes. 'Is this the truth?'

'I am in no position to lie, am I? Please, bring me inside. I think I'm going to be sick.'

114

Reaching down, Ballas dragged the text-seller in through the window. Sitting him against the wall, he said, 'It is heartening, to witness a liar speak the truth. I hear that honesty feels quite good. Rather like shedding a heavy load. My friend Ekkerlin says there is no greater burden than one's conscience, if it is freighted with deceptions.'

Curtlane blinked, nodded. 'You are right, I suppose.' A nervous laugh. 'But I am simply glad to be off the ledge.'

Ballas unfastened the belt around Curtlane's leggings, drew it out of the straps and tugged it tight between both fists. 'Very nice, made of good, strong leather. Cost you much?'

Curtlane was nonplussed. 'Are you robbing me?'

'No. I have many vices, but thievery is not amongst them.' He shoved Curtlane onto the floor. Grabbing his ankles, he folded Curtlane's legs upwards and back, so his heels nudged against his buttocks. Seizing both of the young man's wrists in one hand, he brought those close to Curtlane's feet, and held them there, in the crook of his arm. Next, he took the belt, looped it around the text-seller's wrists and ankles, then drew it tight and buckled it. Curtlane looked strangely like a dead insect, its limbs folded together in death.

'I do not have any of my friend's fancy techniques for spotting lies. If I want to know whether something is true, I have got to take a look for myself. So this is what I will do. I shall speak with your Odds Man and if you are telling the truth, I will come back.'

'Come back?'

Without replying, Ballas tugged the gag back into position. Then he returned Curtlane to the ledge. 'If you are lying, you will never see me again, and you will die up here.' Leaning out, he patted Curtlane's shoulder. Then he pointed to the street below. 'Or down there.'

Withdrawing, he closed the window. Leaning against the

wall, he waited, counting; by the time he reached seven, Curtlane was yelling through the gag.

He continued counting. At twelve, he opened the window.

'What is it? I was halfway to the door.'

Curtlane said something indecipherable. Ballas dragged him inside and removed the gag.

'I – I was mistaken. Got it all wrong. I am so sorry.' Curtlane's face was flushed bright red, yet he smiled, as if despairing of his own absent-mindedness. 'Small wonder that I got so confused. Who could possibly think straight with . . .' his gaze flitted from Ballas to the window, 'with all this going on.'

'What was your mistake, Curtlane?'

'In the past, I purchased texts from Vessen. But not *The Loss*; no, that came from someone else. A priest.'

Ballas peered at him. 'A holy man? Are you confused again, Curtlane?'

'Do not mistake his blue robes for a spotless soul. He is as corrupt as any who has walked the globe. He will spend a thousand eternities in the Forest, when his time comes.' He coughed, savagely. Spittle hung from his lips in shining strands. 'His name is Cellenric. He preaches in a little church on Harp Row, about half a mile from the Loop. He may know about the men in black silk, too. In fact, I am certain that he does. I saw him talking to them once, a while back. I will take you to him.'

'I will make my own way there,' said Ballas.

'No, no. Let me come. I have a knack for talking to men of his kind.'

'Of his kind?'

'Traders of forbidden texts. They have peculiar ways, you see. And—'

Ballas slipped the gag into place. Then he lowered Curtlane onto the ledge.

116

'Our deal still stands,' said the big man. 'Only the details have changed. I will visit Cellenric alone. If he is what you say, I will come back.'

Closing the window, he counted. By the time he reached thirty, Curtlane had not cried out. Satisfied, Ballas left the Folly.

A half-hour later, Ballas sat on a pew at the back of the church on Harp Row. Late-afternoon sunlight streamed through stained-glass windows, dappling the churchgoers with colour. Father Cellenric stood in the pulpit, jaw thrust out, eyes blazing with holy fire. Swept back from his high, strong forehead, his grey hair was sealed in place by a lavish application of grooming oil. He was a small man, maybe five and a half feet in height, yet his mannerisms belonged to a much larger man. He stuck out his chest, clenched his fists and gestured expansively. In a deep, rich voice, at odds with his diminutive stature, he preached about sin. To Ballas, he did not look like a genuine clergyman, but an actor playing a role. His demeanour was a little over-rehearsed; every surge and dip of his voice, every movement of his body and arms, was too obviously designed to impress. Moreover, he looked as if he were enjoying himself a little too much. He seemed to care less about the eternal fate of his parishioners' souls than, simply, putting on a good show.

'Our path is riddled with the flowers of evil,' he said, the words resounding beneath the vaulted ceiling. 'These flowers are called Greed, Dissolution and Unbelief. They belong to the genus named Sin, and their fragrance is Temptation. If we pause on our life's long walk and pick one, as we might a daisy or a bluebell, we take a rash not upon our skin but our very soul. Unlike the prick of a thistle, or the stinging bite of a nettle leaf, it is pleasurable; we feel good, happy perhaps, and therein lies the diabolical trick played by the malign forces teeming

117

within this, the world of flesh: what pleases the senses rots the soul . . .'

Ballas stopped listening. Although he served the Church, he was not a religious man. He could not say he believed, or disbelieved; he simply never gave the matter any thought. He had taken up arms for selfish reasons: military life at once fulfilled certain desires whilst holding particular vices at bay. He craved conflict; for him, violence was not only natural, but necessary: it satisfied some deep, inarticulable and possibly unwholesome yearning locked in the impenetrable caverns of his soul. Yet the violence had to serve a *purpose*. He despised those thunderous, troublemaking oafs often found in taverns, intent upon stirring up discord purely so they could flex their muscles and swing their fists. Indeed, he hated anyone who fought solely for fighting's sake. In his view, such men not only lacked self-discipline, but had no desire to attain it; not so, with Ballas. He considered himself feral by inclination, which was probably true of most men, but he loathed the idea that he was not the master of his own impulses, and was instead carried helplessly along by his whims and urges like a rider trapped on a runaway horse. He had known many who were like that, his father for one, and he rebelled against the weakness of spirit that dominated them, and diminished them, every single day. Could he ever become such a man? Yes, he knew. He suspected he would already be that type of despicable figure, had he not enlisted. He signed up at the age of fourteen, and it had been exactly the right time: he had been on the cusp of manhood, but still malleable, and willing to listen and learn. A year later, six months even, it would have been too late. His descent would have begun, and he would have been as good as lost.

Cellenric continued preaching. Ballas's mind drifted, although occasional phrases slipped into his consciousness. *The weeds of sin must be ripped from the Garden of the Holy . . . The briars of impurity pierce the soul, so we must be wary where we tread . . . Take care what you harvest, for just as a poisonous mushroom may resemble an edible one, so sin can resemble virtue . . .*

Eventually, the sermon ended. At the altar, the churchgoers supped wine from the chalice and accepted Cellenric's blessings. Then they returned to their pews, sang a hymn, and departed. As they left, Cellenric stood in the doorway, bidding them farewell. Ballas remained seated and when the last worshipper was gone, Cellenric looked over.

'My son, why do you linger? Are you unwell?'

Ballas turned to him. 'Not in body, but soul.'

'You have sinned?' Cellenric's eyebrows rose a fraction.

'Deeply, in countless ways.'

'And you wish to unburden yourself? As you can see,' the priest swept an arm across the church, 'there is no confessional booth. But I never cared for them; they have too much of the coffin about them.' He closed the door. 'Tell me what troubles you. I will listen, but not judge. Once, I too was a man of the world, prey to myriad vices. I understand the potency of one's base compulsions.' He started toward the pew. 'You look pained. Have you undergone a flash of clarity? That is, gained a sudden sense of how far you have fallen?'

'I fear it is so,' replied Ballas, softly.

'Then I will sit beside you, and when you speak, hold nothing back. Confession is akin to emptying a chamber-pot: one must pour out every last drop, or the foul smell shall linger.' He smiled, eyes sparkling. 'I am being frivolous, of course. But the Four do not forbid humour, even in one's darkest hours.'

As he neared the pew, Ballas rose swiftly, pacing to the doors and locking them.

'My son?' Cellenric stared, surprised.

119

'I do not want to speak of my sins. I want to speak of *The Loss.*'

Cellenric frowned. 'Forgive me, but I do not understand.'

'Curtlane sent me,' said Ballas, striding over.

'Curtlane? The name rings no bells.'

'He wears white. Sports side-whiskers.' Ballas halted, planting his hands on his hips. 'You gave him forbidden texts to sell.'

Cellenric's face slackened. 'I did *what*? No, no, no. Sir, I am a holy man!' He jabbed his Scarrendestin pendant. 'My opposition to such monstrous publications is unequivocal.' His face turned red. 'Who is this Curtlane fellow? Tell me everything you know, and I shall report him to the Wardens. By the end of the week, he will be dangling from a noose.' He clenched his fists. 'So many good souls have been ruined by false beliefs. When I imagine the Forest, I see not only the souls of the damned, but the souls of the damned *gullible*!'

A sick smile spread across Ballas's lips. 'You are lying, holy man. In the pulpit, you feigned piety quite convincingly. But outrage is far harder to pull off.'

'My outrage is sincere,' breathed Cellenric, heavily. 'You have no inkling how strongly I despise—'

Ballas cuffed him across the head. Cellenric stumbled along the aisle, then whirled, a hand pressed to his temple. 'You savage!'

'What about the men in black silk? Curtlane said you know who they are.'

'Black silk?' Casting his eyes to the church roof, he said, 'In your infinite mercy, please release me from this dream. It is unpleasant, and none of it makes sense.' He lowered his gaze to Ballas. 'I assume the fellows in the silk are scoundrels. When I visit the Wardens, I shall report them as well. I am a merciful soul, but where sin is concerned—'

'Very well,' said Ballas.

120

'Very well?'

Grabbing his robe, Ballas dragged Cellenric to the font. The blue marble water bowl was full to the brim, drowned flies speckling the surface. Ballas plunged Cellenric's face into the water and held it there. The holy man struggled furiously, arms pinwheeling, feet stamping the scarlet-carpeted floorboards. After a ten count, the holy man grew limp. He was playing dead, Ballas knew. No one could drown in such a short time. Of a sudden, bubbles erupted around Cellenric's head, churning the water. Once they subsided, Ballas hauled out the holy man.

Collapsing, Cellenric gulped for air. 'You fiend,' he spluttered. 'You absolute devil!'

'Tell me about *The Loss*.'

'You bloody fool,' spat Cellenric. 'Do you think a man grows omniscient if he nearly drowns? I do not know anything about the text.'

Muttering, Ballas seized him and held him under the water again. As the holy man writhed, he gathered his thoughts. In the Folly, he had reasoned Curtlane was protecting someone. He still believed this. But he doubted the mysterious someone was Cellenric. The holy man was not capable of inspiring fear. When faced with trouble, he blustered, flapped and lied, and lacked any authentic trace of resilience. So why had Curtlane given his name? Was it a decoy? Did the text-seller believe that given some time alone, he *could* find a safe way off the ledge?

No. The holy man knew something. Recognition – and fear – had flashed across his eyes when both *The Loss* and the silk-wearers were mentioned. In some ambiguous way, Curtlane had sent Ballas here. And that, Ballas realised, made a sort of sense. Even on the ledge, Curtlane was afraid of directly incriminating the man he feared. *He* did not want to be the one who gave away the man's name, so he had sent Ballas to Cellenric, knowing the priest would — with a little encouragement — tell him everything he needed to know. That way, Curtlane would not be responsible for the betrayal, and whatever punishment was forthcoming would fall upon Cellenric's shoulders.

The water in the font was pink, blood-tinged. When Ballas pulled out Cellenric, he saw the holy man's nose was broken. Blood sluiced over his face, dripping from his jaw, pattering onto his Scarrendestin pendant.

'You unutterable cur,' said the priest, the words muffled. He struggled loose of Ballas's grasp, swayed then dropped to his knees. Descending onto all fours, he crawled to the altar. Sweeping aside a small curtain fixed to the lintel, he pulled out a bottle of holy wine and uncorked it. 'I will die,' he said. 'Because of you, I will be tossed into an early grave. You are a bane, sir. A pustule ripening on the arsehole of humanity.' He took a deep swallow from the bottle, then wiped a sleeve across his lips. 'There is a particular corner of the Forest reserved for the likes of you. All the theologians write about it. They say it is full of the most awful torments. The demons will—'

'You are going to tell me the truth, are you?'

Another swig, followed by a gasp. 'What choice do I have?' He gazed earnestly at the bottle, cradling it as if it were a newborn. 'Curtlane sent you to me, did he? The ignominious boy. He is always embroiling others in his troubles.' He lifted a finger to probe his ruined nose but thought better of it. 'I play no part in the forbidden text trade. Once, I dabbled, true enough. But this was in the old days, when the profits exceeded the risks. It has been many years since I peddled diabolical books.' He took another swallow from the bottle, draining it. Muttering, he took another from beneath the altar. 'One has to be mad to do it nowadays. And Sensifer Olech is as insane as they come.'

'He is the man I seek?'

'Not if you are sensible.' Cellenric uncorked the bottle. 'A wise man would give him the widest conceivable berth. I remember the days when I did not know of him and, more importantly, he knew nothing of me. He is a businessman. He smuggles narcotics, operates numerous brothels and owns a gambling establishment, Olech's House of Fate. It is a fine place, very luxurious. Crimson drapes, polished tables, a well-stocked bar tended by the prettiest girls in the city. It makes gambling seem the most *sophisticated* of sins.' He took a drink, throat-apple bobbing. 'You spoke of men in black silk. You have locked antlers with them, have you?'

'Not me. My companions.'

'Then I shall forgive your unpleasant behaviour, for clearly you are grieving.'

'They did not die. They disappeared. Kidnapped, I reckon. They were attacked in a water-mill near the Loop. I went outside and when I returned, they were gone. I found poisoned darts on the floor.'

'Poisoned darts? A new tactic, for Olech. Normally he is not so subtle. Why were you attacked?'

Ballas explained a little about Curtlane – that he sold *The Loss*, and he and his companions had been trying to learn where he obtained copies of the text. As he spoke, he watched Cellenric closely. And in a flash, he saw it – a faint, very faint, resemblance between the priest and the text-seller. Cellenric did not possess Curtlane's toadlike eyes and mouth, but his jawbone was of a similar shape, only with Curtlane it had been hidden behind his side-whiskers.

When Ballas finished, the priest said, 'So *two* groups of men attacked. One lot in the alley, the other the water-mill?'

'Aye.'

'Then – it would seem they were defending Curtlane. Trying

123

to get him out of harm's way.' There was a note of disbelief in the holy man's voice, a glimmer of astonishment in his eyes.

'That is what I reckon.'

'And now, Curtlane – he is safe?' He touched the pendant, uncertainly.

'For the time being.'

'Meaning?'

'He will last until dusk. After that, who can say?'

'What have you done to him?'

'You sound concerned, holy man.'

Cellenric laughed nervously. 'I confess that I am not wholly unacquainted with the young man. From time to time, he visits this church, seeking to confess. His conscience troubles him which, in my opinion, is a good sign. It shows he is not beyond redemption. Like a lump of wet clay, his soul can be shaped into a pleasing form.' He shrugged. 'It is my duty to play the potter. I have to save him – from himself and the Forest.' He glanced at the bottle. 'Where can I find him?'

'Do not trouble yourself. I will go to him when my business with Olech is done.'

'When your business with Olech is done, you will be dead.'

'Take me to Olech's home,' said Ballas. 'My chances are my own to take.'

'No, no. You take me to Curtlane first.' Cellenric planted his hands on his hips. His defiance lasted several heartbeats. Sighing, he said, 'There is no point in arguing, is there? Truly, I cannot face any more conflict. Very well. I will do as you ask. But first, I must don discreet attire.'

Grabbing a second wine bottle from under the altar, he shuffled into the vestry. Ballas followed.

'Might I ask a question?' Cellenric pulled the robes up and over his head. Beneath, he wore a linen vest and a pair of baggy

124

breeches. 'Curtlane has betrayed me. Did he reveal my name straight away? Or did it take some, ah, persuasion?'

'A good deal, as it happens.'

Cellenric paused. 'Really?'

'Aye.'

Blinking, he took a grey tabard from a hook. 'I imagined he would drop me in the dungheap at the first whiff of trouble,' he said, thoughtfully. 'Well, that is something.' He caught himself. 'It shows he is not all bad. Perhaps he is treading the road to redemption. As a holy man, this gives me some satisfaction.' He pulled on the tabard. Then he drew on a pair of black leggings and a dark woollen coat, ill-suited for the hot weather.

'Let us go,' he said.

A short time later, Ballas stood on a wide, airy street in a prosperous part of the city. Only several years old, the houses were yet to be tarnished by the elements. Each was two floors high, crafted from cream-coloured stones, topped by dust-brown clay tiles. 'That is Olech's abode,' said Cellenric, pointing. 'There is a magpie perching on— oh, it has flapped away. But you spotted it, yes?'

'Aye.'

'This is a pleasant area, is it not? Quite different from most parts of Sliptere. No rotting vegetables, no stray dogs or beggars. I doubt Olech's neighbours suspect there is a distinctly *un*pleasant character in their midst. But why should they? Olech is no fool; he keeps his professional and domestic lives separate from one another. I only discovered that he dwelled here when I visited a house along the street, to deliver the final rites. In a moment of boredom, I glanced out of the window and saw him, plain as day, unlocking his front door. It gave me quite a chill, to see someone so awful doing something so trivial as twisting a key in a lock – it seems contrary to the laws of nature, somehow.' He took a silver hip flask from his pocket. 'I imagine he can be charming to those who live close by. To them, he will seem a strange, somewhat vain fellow, affable enough. But if they knew about the gambling house, the black-clad thugs he employs to do his dirty work . . . And the Hordelings. Oh yes, we must not forget those pestilential little sprites.'

Ballas squinted. 'The Hordelings?'

'A man is feared for two reasons,' said Cellenric, sipping from the flask. 'First, the revenge he takes upon those who cross him. Second, the probability that he will *discover* the identities of those who wrong him – betrayers, rivals and so forth. The silk-wearers deal with the former, whilst the Hordelings contend with the latter. This city is over-brimming with scum, and the very worst serve as Olech's eyes and ears. Some eighty or ninety youngsters comprise the Hordelings. The youngest is perhaps seven years old, the eldest eighteen or nineteen. They gather information; they eavesdrop, catch rumours and spy upon Olech's enemies.' He scratched his chin. 'I believe Curtlane was a Hordeling once. You see, most of the Hordelings have unhappy backgrounds. Their parents are drunks, or addicted to visionary's root, or are feckless in any of a thousand different ways. To them, Olech is a benign figure. Fatherly, even.' He licked whisky from his lips. 'Fatherly, yes,' he added, quietly. He was silent a moment. Then he looked up at the sky. 'The day is lengthening. I must go to Curtlane. Where shall I find him?'

Ballas thought a moment. If he told the truth, it might complicate matters. Once the priest had rescued Curtlane, his thoughts could turn to revenge – or self-preservation: having wronged Olech by assisting Ballas, he might try to make amends by warning the gambling-house keeper that he was being sought by a large, dangerous, brutish man. Perhaps he would do nothing of the sort. But Ballas could not afford to take the chance. It would be best if he sent the holy man on a wild goose chase. As for Curtlane, balancing on the ledge – he was not Ballas's concern.

'Leave the city and head north,' lied the Hawk. 'On the moors near the city gates, there is a hollow in the ground. It looks like some giant has ripped out a fistful of earth.' Ballas had seen the gouge on the way into Sliptere.

'Yes, I know it,' nodded Cellenric.

'You will find Curtlane with some of my friends. Tell them Trallek sent you.'

'And they will let me take him away?'

'If you utter the password.'

'Which is?'

Ballas thought a moment. 'Clambercrake.'

'After the birds? The *extinct* birds? That nested on cliff-tops yet, lacking any natural sense of balance, kept falling to their deaths?'

'You ought to hurry, holy man,' said Ballas. 'My friends will be watching the sky and sharpening their knives. Once the sun drops, both the world and Curtlane will fall into darkness.'

Taking a step back, Cellenric looked him up and down, as if committing him to memory. 'You are loathsome,' he said, lifting his chin. 'Perhaps I am not the most devout holy man to ever wear the blue, but I have read *The Book of the Pilgrims*, and I know what becomes of men like you. I said it in the church, and I shall say it here: your fate is the Forest, you hideous, cold-hearted bucket of shit.' He turned, paused, then turned back. 'Normally, I would pity anyone who makes an enemy of Sensifer Olech. But not you. No, if Olech is the one who casts you into the Forest, I will count him as a friend for ever. I will buy him fine wine, wash his feet and pray a hundred times each day that he has a long, happy life.' He scowled, his tanned face crumpling. Then he was gone, half striding, half running back the way they had come.

CHAPTER EIGHT

Sensifer Olech peered through the window at the three figures in the cell.

They sat in the gloom, blindfolded, hands tied behind their backs. Two were complete strangers, the first a thin, grey-haired man, the other a young woman who, if her face were not so badly bruised, Olech would have considered taking to his bed.

Both sagged against the wall, shoulders slumped, heads drooping. Even now, they had not fully recovered from the poison darts Olech had blown into their necks at the water-mill. He rarely had the opportunity to use the darts on human prey. It was gratifying to observe how effective they were: within two heartbeats, the man and the girl were sprawled upon the ash-softened floor, sleeping like milk-lulled babies.

The third man was not a stranger, though he had never met him before. There were few in Sliptere City who did not know the name Cledrun Mallakos.

According to his sources, the horse-breeder had been keeping company with Curtlane's abductors, so Olech dispatched his black-clad Peacekeepers to capture him before he left the city. When they brought him to the House of Fate, Olech had scarcely believed his eyes. The rumours about Mallakos's girth were true. He was preposterously, absurdly, *breathtakingly* fat. Olech had had trouble containing his mirth. The horse-breeder bulged like a python that had swallowed prey fifty times too large; his hugeness was almost heroic. It was said that fat men over-ate to assuage their unhappiness, but Olech could not believe this was true for Mallakos: nothing, surely, could make someone *that* miserable.

It was a mystery why anyone would allow themselves to sink into such a condition. Olech was in his sixty-second year, yet looked much younger. At a glance, he would appear to be thirty, thirty-five. He had always taken excellent care of himself. Each day, when he rose, he performed a hundred press-ups, the same number of sit-ups, and various stretches to keep his snake-sleek body taut and limber. He ate carefully, trimming the fat from his meat, sprinkling not so much as a solitary salt-grain upon his potatoes and always, *always*, eating his greens. When the weather was fine, he lounged shirtless on the roof of the House, absorbing the health-giving sunlight. Consequently, his skin was as dark as polished oak. His hair and short-cropped beard were dark, too – the studious application of expensive dyes, imported from the East, ensured every strand was as black as the furthest corners of the night. He looked good. Young, strong, healthy.

He stared at Mallakos. The horse-breeder was weeping, tears trickling from behind his blindfold, sparkling on his cheeks.

Unlike the other two, Mallakos was the ideal prisoner. There had been no need to interrogate him, for he blabbed everything he knew before Olech could ask a single question. He spoke of his abduction from Silver Hoof, the visit to the Loop and their journey to the water-mill. He did not know who his captors were, though he had given them nicknames. The thin man was the Blade, the girl the Bookworm. A third man, a giant he called the Brute, was still at large. And, crucially, he revealed they were interested in *The Loss*, a forbidden text that had caused Olech no end of problems.

Olech turned away from the window. As fascinating as the

prisoners were, they paled in comparison to the contents of the small, low-ceilinged room in which he stood. Somewhat grandly, he called it the Vivarium. On a table by the wall there were three glass tanks, resting side by side. To the untrained eye, they seemed to contain nothing except branches, twigs, leaves and bark chippings. But if the owner of that untrained eye were to put his hand inside one, he would discover his mistake swiftly enough. Alongside the cases were an array of glass jars, scalpels and a single chainmail glove. Donning the glove, Olech flexed his fingers, listening to the links rasp. Then he gestured to the window.

'Bring the girl,' he said to Gruliek, a huge, flat-faced Peacekeeper. The big man was as stupid as a thrice-poleaxed bullock, but obedient.

Gruliek departed, returning a minute later with the Bookworm. He sat her in a high-backed chair bolted to the floor in the centre of the Vivarium, then roughly secured her in place with a series of leather straps.

'Remove the blindfold,' said Olech.

Gruliek did so. The Bookworm blinked, as if waking from a thousand-year slumber. Turning her head, she looked directly at Olech. Small muscles twitched in her face; a certain light glimmered in her eyes. Olech was nonplussed. Then, suddenly, he understood. She was laughing at him, silently.

'Something amuses you, girl?'

The Bookworm looked away. Olech stared, puzzled, then moved to the glass tanks. One contained a species of jungle frog, its bright blue skin slick with venom. This, he had smeared on the tips of the blow-darts. It had served its purpose, but he had no use for it now. No; he would use a far more interesting venom.

He removed the lid of the second tank. Then he picked up a two-pronged skewer, similar to a toasting fork. Carefully, he used it to sweep aside the leaves and, after a few heartbeats, he spotted it – a hothead snake, its brown-green body virtually invisible amongst the twigs and leaves. With supreme caution, Olech lowered the skewer, until its prongs encompassed the creature's body just behind the skull. Thumbing a lever in the skewer-handle, he caused the prongs to contract, seizing the serpent. Instantly, the snake struggled, hissing furiously, tail swiping from side to side, clattering twigs, scattering leaves. Smiling faintly, Olech watched the hothead's brown skull turn bright red, flaring like a hot coal stoked by a strong breeze.

With his gloved hand, Olech seized the snake then lifted it out. Setting the skewer aside, he approached the Bookworm.

'A Keltuskan hothead,' he said, lowering the snake in front of the girl's face. 'Beautiful, is she not? Intriguing, too. Mallakos says you are fond of learning, so allow me to educate you. The hothead's venom is an oddity. It neither kills nor paralyses, unlike most toxins found in nature. Its primary purpose, it seems, is to cause pain. The nature-writer Hailrus believed it reflected a sadistic streak within the creator-god. What other explanation could there be, for a creature that caused suffering for suffering's sake? That itself gained no benefit from the anguish of its victims? Later, though, it was discovered the venom has a secondary property. Namely, the pain is lessened if one speaks truthfully. Quite how this occurs, the natural philosophers are at a loss. They theorise that when one is speaking honestly, the body secretes certain chemicals which have palliative properties. Maybe there is something in this; who, amongst religious souls, has not felt joyous after confessing their sins? Which adulterous man, once the storm has passed, does not experience profound relief that he has told his wife the truth? But the details are not significant. Not for you or I. Or indeed the tribesmen of the Kletuik,

132

who use the venom when appointing a clan-chief. To ensure he does not harbour secret allegiances with rival tribes, they administer the poison and question him; if he is truly loyal, he says nothing to incriminate himself. If he is a traitor, however . . .'

Rising, he carried the hothead to the table. With his free hand, he picked up a glass jar, a thin leather membrane stretched across the top.

'I think you can guess what is coming,' he said, lowering the snake close to the jar, where it hissed, vibrated like a tuning fork then struck, sinking its fangs through the membrane. For a moment of quiet fascination, Olech watched milky droplets of venom patter into the receptacle.

'I have contacts throughout Druine,' he said, setting the jar on the table. 'Men who, like myself, profit from forbidden texts. And they are repeating the same disturbing story, over and over again. Someone has acquired an unhealthy interest in *The Loss*. In particular, they want to know where it is printed. They move from text-seller to text-seller, asking the same question: Where did you get hold of the text? This technique is used by Scholars of Outrage, but these hunters of *The Loss* are not in the employ of the Church. Like yourselves, they have the lustre of mercenaries, and like yourselves, they use the most savage methods. They have tortured and killed many of those engaged in the same business as me. You will understand, I am sure, that I find this troubling. More troubling still, however, is what occurs when the tables are turned. Occasionally, they have fallen prey to those they acted against. They have been chased, cornered and, on several occasions, been a whisker away from capture. But always, they take their own lives.' He nodded, as if confirming this fact to himself. 'They would rather die than reveal why *The Loss* is of such considerable interest. And, of course, who they work for.' He glanced at the Bookworm. Her eyebrows were slightly raised, her expression uncertain. 'Hit a nerve, have I? For certain, I seem to have caught your interest.'

He peeled back the membrane from the jar then, taking a scalpel, he walked to the Bookworm. Kneeling, he set the jar and scalpel on the floor. Then he rolled the Bookworm's tabard sleeve up to the elbow. He probed her skin with his fingertips, pressing it gently, feeling firm-yet-delicate muscles. 'Contrary to the rumours, I am not an unreasonable man.' He looked up into the girl's dark eyes. 'You need not receive the venom, if you confess of your own free will. It really is the most sensible choice.'

The Bookworm's gaze darted to the jar. Olech watched her eyes, closely, seeking fear. And he found it – a thin, uneasy glimmer.

'Speak,' he said. 'For your own sake.'

Blinking, the Bookworm looked at him. 'The Thrisulis,' she said.

Olech frowned. 'What?'

'It is the Thrisulis tribe who use hothead venom. Not the Kletuiks.' She drew a breath, deep and tremulous. 'Torture me, if you must. But remember: there is no torment as severe as being forced to hear an arrogant man speak confidently about things which are simply wrong.'

A vein throbbed in Olech's temple. 'It could have been so much easier for you,' he said, taking the scalpel and carving an incision into the Bookworm's arm. Pulling the sides apart, he poured the venom into the wound.

The venom would not act immediately. Returning the scalpel and jar to the table, Olech washed his hands in a bowl of water, thinking.

Knowledge is power – it was an old phrase, one Olech understood better than most. He had countless enemies, yet he had never suffered an attempt on his life, and he was rarely

134

double-crossed or betrayed. Incredibly for someone of his ill fame, no one spoke badly of him, at least not in public. No rumours were spread, no gossip disseminated. To all intents and purposes, he controlled his adversaries to the same degree he did those who worked for him, and he achieved this through *knowledge*.

Simply, he *understood* his rivals. He knew every detail about their lives – where they dwelled, the taverns they frequented, even what their childhoods had been like. If they hated him, he knew why, and comprehended the exact form their hatred took. If he wished, he could write a biography of each of them; it would be accurate, in-depth and without omissions. Nothing escaped him.

For this, large thanks was owed to the Hordelings. The ragged mob of youngsters, savage, cunning and ruthless, made excellent spies, gathering information like basking sharks scooping up plankton. He had a myriad other sources too: shop-keepers, tavern-masters, corrupt Papal Wardens – anyone, in fact, who kept their eyes and ears open. He knew more about daily occurrences in Sliptere than anyone else. And thus, he could deal with problems before they occurred. Potential assassins were neutralised before they had a chance to grab their knives; likewise, other would-be betrayers suffered retribution before they committed their misdeeds. Olech was master of the destiny of every soul in Sliptere. And, consequently, he governed his own fate to the highest degree. As the owner of a gambling house, he knew better than to leave anything to chance.

When he learned of those who sought *The Loss*, he grew uneasy. *Deeply* uneasy. He feared that one day, they would come for *him*. So he had taken precautions. He had made Curtlane the sole distributor of *The Loss* and, without his knowledge, placed him under constant observation: wherever he went, whatever he did, Olech's underlings were watching. That way, if *The Loss*-seekers came to Sliptere, it would be Curtlane they spoke to. And when that happened, Olech's men would be waiting: they would capture the seekers and finally, Olech would learn why so many people throughout Druine were interested in the text.

That had been the plan. It had not run smoothly, Olech admitted. The men who watched Curtlane at the Loop had failed to capture the seekers; according to Mallakos, the Brute and the Bookworm had dispatched them with alarming ease. Mercifully, a pair of Hordelings were watching along the alley. One informed Olech of what had come to pass, whilst the other followed them to the water-mill then led Olech's Peacekeepers there.

Even then, it had not gone entirely to plan. Two of the seekers had been captured, but the third, the big man, had escaped. As for Curtlane – he was still at large. Perhaps he was already dead. But it did not matter. On balance, the day had been a success. Olech had caught two seekers and whether they liked it or not, they would spill their secrets.

The Bookworm screamed, jerking Olech from his reverie.

Olech turned. The girl was in a dreadful state, skin as white as salt-bleached driftwood, eyes goggling in their sockets, lips skinned back and sweat streaming like molten silver over her bruise-clouded face. Tendons jutted from her neck; a tangle of veins swelled on her forehead.

'Now,' said Olech, kneeling. 'I have some questions for you.'

As soon as Father Cellenric vanished from sight, Ballas strolled to Olech's house, knocked on the front door and waited. When no one answered, he crept down the side of the building, picked the lock securing the rear door and slipped through.

Inside, he wandered from room to room. It could have been the home of any man whose wealth outweighed his good taste.

In the main room, the floor was covered by a jet-black carpet, the walls painted dark red. Bronze statuettes of naked women perched on shelves, tables and ledges, trapped in various erotic postures, several of which would have caused excruciating pain in a living person. There was a bookcase crammed with various volumes, many concerning poisonous snakes and reptiles. Clearly, Olech was fascinated by the creatures. Maybe he saw something of himself in them. Arrogant men often likened themselves to wild beasts; countless times, Ballas had heard some muscle-bound braggart compare himself to a shark, or a lion, or a mountain bear.

According to Cellenric, Olech owned a printing shop. Ballas opened the bookcase.

Working methodically, inspecting one book after another, Ballas sought a work, any work, that had rolled off the serpent-lover's own presses. If this work bore the same typo-graphical flaws as the first edition of *The Loss* – the tailless 'y's and decapitated 'A's – he would know that Olech was the source they were seeking and, therefore, Helligraine was likely to be close by. But he was disappointed. Although he found several books produced by Olech – works on musical theory and a treatise on physical beauty – they were immaculately printed, the lettering perfectly formed.

Upstairs, in the bathing room, a full-length gold-framed mirror was bolted to the wall. Pausing, Ballas inspected his reflection. He looked exactly like what he was: an ugly man engaged in an ugly business. His face was bruised, his left eye bloodshot. Flecks of dried blood clung to his tabard. Wrinkling his nostrils, he turned away.

Olech's bedroom contained a wide bed, covered in silken sheets. Ballas found nothing of interest – except another mirror, fixed to the ceiling above the bed, its purpose both obvious and mystifying. Why would anyone want to watch themselves engaged in the act? No doubt, Ekkerlin could offer a clever explanation – assuming she was still alive.

Although he liked very few people, Ballas found Ekkerlin's company strangely tolerable. True, she mocked him ruthlessly, jesting about his size, foul temper and undeniable lack of physical appeal. Yet he did not take offence. Spoken by anyone else, even good-humouredly, such words would have earned a broken jaw or worse. Not so with Ekkerlin. Although Ballas did not find Ekkerlin's jests amusing, they did not strike the tiniest spark of rage.

And if it were not for Ekkerlin, Ballas would not have become a Hawk.

Whilst the two of them had been serving as ordinary foot soldiers in the Druinese army, she had taught Ballas to read and write, speak Southern Keltuskan, navigate by the stars, decipher a map, and other things that seemed less relevant: to speak politely, even deferentially; to control his anger, and ask questions about matters he was not remotely interested in. In hindsight, Ballas realised she had been preparing him for the Hawks, for the regiment did not allow illiterates to join its ranks, and those who demonstrated a facility for languages were looked upon with favour; also, they favoured fighting men with inquisitive minds and respect for authority. He realised, too, that Ekkerlin was an excellent reader of men's characters. She understood that if he suspected he was being helped in any fashion, Ballas would have turned away, refusing to accept a single lesson. So she educated him subtly, without him knowing it – the same technique employed by trainers of performing dogs, she later revealed. At this, he was too grateful to be offended.

Ballas wandered to the kitchen. He was hungry. In the pantry he found a slab of beef, a pot of mustard and some black bread. He ate greedily, leaning back against the wall, gazing idly at the table set in the centre of the room. Beneath it, there was a plain yellow rug, heel-worn and tatty, out of keeping with the general opulence. Curious, Ballas stamped upon it, lightly, and heard a hollow thud. Interesting. Setting his meal aside, he shifted the table to the far wall then peeled back the rug. Beneath, there was a trapdoor.

Taking a lantern from the living room, Ballas opened the trapdoor and descended into a cellar, where he found an empty bookcase. Three large jars rested upon the uppermost shelf.

One was empty. The other two contained human heads, suspended in a preservative solution.

Raising the lantern, Ballas looked closely.

Despite the solution, the heads were rotting, clods of pale, greasy flesh slithering off their skulls. Their hair floated upwards like waterweeds growing on a riverbed, exposing badly mutilated faces. Their eyes were gouged out, noses pulverised, cheeks and foreheads latticed by knife wounds. Their mouths were stitched shut with black twine, except in the middle, where there was a gap through which their tongues protruded.

Each jar was labelled with a strip of parchment. In a ragged, ungainly hand, the first label read *Gridluk Yearne*. The second, *Sheldrithe Caele*.

There was a label on the empty jar, too. This one said *Sensifer Olech*.

Ballas returned to the kitchen, closed the trapdoor, replaced the rug and lifted the table back into place.

Carrying the mustard, beef and bread into the main room, he sank into an armchair, watching the sky darken, waiting.

Rounding a corner, Cellenric broke into a run.

He tried hard to avoid wallowing in the oh-so-obvious truth: namely, it only took a visit from a stranger to turn one's life upside down.

Although he was a priest, Cellenric did not believe in divine justice. He did not believe in a divine *anything*. The rituals, stories and mythology of the Pilgrim Church were preposterous, but they enabled him to lead a comfortable life. A warm home, good food, limitless wine – all paid for by the Church. If he had to spout pious nonsense twice a day, so be it: it was a fair bargain.

He thought about the old adage, *The wages of sin are death*.

Like so many things the Church said, it was wrong. The wages of sin were not death – indeed, sin made him feel fully alive – but unwanted progeny, if the sin was of a particular sort. Curtlane was his son, sired twenty-three years ago, with a woman he had accidentally – and mistakenly – fallen in love with. Mercifully, she perished during childbirth and, no sooner had Curtlane emerged (even as a baby, he was irksome, his pink face wrinkled with sneering contempt, as if to say, I departed the womb for *this*?) than Cellenric had dropped him off at an orphanage. He hoped he would never set eyes on him again. But, sixteen years later, Curtlane tracked him down. Cellenric could not imagine how he had done so. Nor did it matter. He had acquired, late in a life, a son he neither wanted nor liked. Nor, it turned out, could do anything *with*: Cellenric tried to cure him of his errant ways, to no avail: the boy was bad from head to toe. Remove the wickedness, and nothing of Curtlane would remain except an empty, blank-eyed shell: he was a reprobate through and through.

Eventually, Cellenric washed his hands of him. Or tried to. But the young man returned from time to time, usually to borrow money or, if Cellenric was not in a generous mood, threaten to blackmail him.

Yet he loved his son. He could not say why; it was one of life's mysteries. Poets wrote about the tug of blood, whilst philosophers spoke of the undeniable – occasionally smothering

– bonds of kinship. Whatever the reason, Cellenric feared for the boy. He was held hostage by men who would kill him when the sun set.

Clambercrake, thought Cellenric, over and over, lodging the word in his mind.

The word that could save his son's life . . .

The priest ran full pelt through the city, half drunk, full of panic.

He turned onto a long road. Sensifer Olech's House of Fate lay ahead, a single-floored building of white stone, the doorway mantled by a statue of Mistress Fortune, the presiding spirit of chance-games. A slender young woman, she wore a silken robe, the neck open to reveal a hint of bosom; a pair of dice lay in an outstretched hand, a knowing smile lay on her lips. It was amazing how differently that smile was interpreted. On the way in, it seemed to say, *This will be your lucky day*. On the way out, *Why did you even try? You were doomed from the outset*.

Two Peacekeepers flanked the door, garbed in black silk. As Cellenric approached, they shook their heads.

'Not a chance,' said one, as Cellenric halted.

'What do you mean?' Cellenric looked down at his clothes. His black coat was smart, his boots polished to a black shine.

The Peacekeeper pointed to his broken nose. 'You're bleeding like a bloody fountain. And you're three sheets to the wind.'

Reflexively, Cellenric wiped blood from his nose. Gristle grated; he nearly passed out from the pain. 'I wish to speak with Olech,' he said, gasping.

'To complain? Ha – he will tell you the same thing. No entry for the pissed or blood-drenched. Then he will rip your balls off for wasting his time.'

'Sir, I am not here to gamble. I want to do your master a

141

favour. Once we have spoken, he will be grateful. *Very* grateful. It concerns the, ah, difficulties at the water-mill.'

The Peacekeeper narrowed his eyes. 'You know about that?'

'I do indeed. One of Olech's enemies escaped, did he not?'

'What of it?'

Cellenric smiled; the movement of his lips made his nose ache. 'I have lured the man into a trap.'

'*You?*'

'Do not be astonished. I am not utterly lacking in guile.' He pressed a hand to his chest. 'Go, tell Olech I am here. Say it is Cellenric, the father of Marrus Curtlane. Inform him that I have done the hard work. The rest will be easy.'

Glancing at his companion, the Peacekeeper vanished inside. Stepping back, Cellenric stared at Mistress Fortune, trying to read her smile.

Sagging against the straps, the Bookworm shuddered. Sweat trickled down her face in large greasy globs, and stray strands of hair stuck to her forehead, forming abstract glyphs. Tiny muscles flickered in her cheeks, as intangible as will-o'-the-wisps. She had suffered terribly. But she had not spoken.

If he had been a noble soul, Olech would have admired her resilience. Instead, he was incredulous. Such resistance was not without precedence; he had read of several instances where a victim endured the venom without cracking. But it was unusual, very unusual, and he never expected to witness it for himself.

Crouching, he lifted up the Bookworm's chin.

'You are a rarity,' he breathed. Rising, he kissed her on the forehead. 'An oddity indeed.'

There was a knock at the door.

'You have got a visitor, Mister Olech,' came a muffled voice.

'Send him away. I have other matters to deal with.'

'He insists on speaking with you. He reckons that he . . .

142

Well, the big bastard at the water-mill – the one we did not catch . . . He has lured him into a trap. Beyond that, he won't say aught else.'

CHAPTER NINE

Entering his own home, Olech felt strangely like a burglar, for he was venturing into the unknown. Dusk had fallen. Somewhere in the darkened rooms, the Brute was waiting like a poisonous spider in a woodpile. Mallakos spoke of him in the direst terms, as if he was part man, part beast, part demon of the Forest. But Olech was unperturbed. Mallakos was a coward, and cowards exaggerated. Even if the Brute was everything he claimed, it would not matter: Olech knew how to deal with thugs. For nearly thirty years, he had employed such men, men like the Peacekeepers. By and large, they were stupid, and easily manipulated. He always bent them to his will. And if the Brute resisted? That too was not a concern. What Olech could not bend, he broke.

Lighting a lantern, he climbed the stairs to the bathroom, whistling to himself, as if this was merely an ordinary evening and nothing were amiss.

Placing the lantern on a shelf, he stooped, rinsing his face in a basin of cold water. Straightening, he glanced at the shaving mirror and saw the reflection of someone standing behind him. Or rather, someone's chest, huge, solid, clad in a blood-specked tabard.

Olech's guts quivered. He had expected the intruder to creep up on him. But not so silently. Nor had he expected him to be quite so big. He was, simply, extraordinary.

Olech picked up a towel. Casually, as if nothing was wrong. 'What do you want?' he asked, drying his face.

The Brute seized Olech's throat then slammed him against the wall. Now, Olech could see him clearly. A huge slablike face, cold green eyes, brutally jutting brow, a crumpled snout of a nose – he was the stuff of fever dreams. When he spoke, the sound was like a mineshaft collapsing.

'Where are my companions?' he asked.

Olech lifted a hand to the Brute's wrist. 'You . . . are . . . choking me,' he croaked.

The Brute's grip tightened. 'Where are they?'

'Cannot speak. Barely breathe.' Beneath Olech's suntan, blood was gathering, turning his face bright red. He imagined he looked a little like a hothead.

The Brute stared, then loosened his grip.

Bending over, planting his hands on his knees, Olech sucked in several deep breaths. 'Piss and blood, you could strangle a horse.' Rubbing his neck, he looked up. 'Who are you? Why are you in my house?' He coughed, throat burning. 'Another trick like that, and I'll shout out for the Wardens. They are always patrolling outside. They will be here in a flash . . .' He trailed off. The Brute was sending a dark look that read *Do not toy with me*.

'Very well. I can see you are too bright to be tricked,' said Olech, knowing flattery was an easy way to soothe a stupid's man bad temper. 'Yes, I know where your companions are. At present, they are enjoying the hospitality offered at Sensifer Olech's House of Fate.' He flattened a hand against his chest. 'I am Sensifer Olech and you have my word that your friends are unharmed. Why would it be otherwise? We are kindred spirits, our fates intertwined by the same problem.' He coughed again; he could still feel the Brute's hand around his neck. 'Are you familiar with the phrase, *My enemy's enemy is my friend*?

145

Well, it rings true for you and me – assuming that you have ill-feelings toward the printer of *The Loss*.'

'You know who prints it?'

'We have met,' replied Olech, dabbing his face with the towel. 'And it was not pleasant. Please, let us go downstairs and discuss the matter in comfort. I need a drink to steady my nerves.' He showed his hands to the Brute. They were shaking, badly. He had decided that when he met the Brute, he would feign fear; in its own way, that was also a form of flattery. But he was not pretending. He was genuinely unnerved.

After a moment, the Brute nodded. In the main room, Olech poured a goblet of Mallranian firewater. He took a deep swallow, gasped. 'Would you care to indulge, my friend?' he asked, picking up another goblet.

The Brute shook his head. Olech slumped into an armchair, whilst the Brute perched on the settle.

'Why are you interested in *The Loss*? And the Dogman?' asked Olech, after another sip.

'The Dogman?' asked the Brute.

'The printer of *The Loss*,' said Olech. 'I doubt that is his real name; but some men attract certain monikers, due to their quirks – particularly if their real name is unknown. Set eyes on him, and you would say, *There goes the Dogman*. You would not be able to help yourself; it would be instinctive – and inevitable.' He chuckled. 'Perhaps the fairytale is to blame, the one where the cruel hunt-master is devoured by his own hounds. *He* was referred to as the Dogman as well. Odd how these names persist, is it not? How they spring so readily to mind? Now, sir: a little openness is required, if we are to help one another. No jewels are plucked from a closed casket, as they say. So . . .' He gestured beckoningly. 'Tell me what you know, then I shall do the same. Together, we may solve this problem once and for all.'

146

Something flickered in the Brute's eyes. Olech was unsure if it was a good sign.

'You speak first,' said the Brute.

Olech laughed, despairingly. 'You broke into my home, and you are twice my size. Clearly, you have me at a disadvantage; should you not go first? To put *me* at *my* ease?'

The Brute did not speak. Only stared. Uneasiness bubbled up from Olech's guts. Then something else happened, something unexpected. Olech began to talk.

Olech ran a printing house, producing texts both legal and forbidden. Several months ago, before the heatwave began, he was approached by a man even taller and broader than Ballas. Like some primitive savage, he wore animal furs; around his throat hung an outsized necklace, consisting of animal jawbones strung upon a long rope. He said that he too was a printer of forbidden texts. And he wished to strike a bargain with Olech. He could supply copies of *The Loss* – a text Olech had heard of, though never seen – which Olech could sell on the Dark Market, at an inflated price. In return, Olech was to give him a quarter of all profits and, crucially, swear to print no copies of his own. In the stranger's words, he was to disseminate, not replicate.

Olech accepted the offer. The stranger handed him thirty copies of *The Loss*, tied together in a bundle, then departed. Immediately, Olech broke his half of the bargain; he went to his printing house and began setting the type to produce his own copies of the book. Disobedience, Olech claimed, was part of his nature, as was a refusal to be intimidated. He had barely started when the printing house door opened. Outside, it rained heavily, the night sky slashed by lightning bolts. Standing on the threshold, the stranger stared at him, his huge, shaggy-bearded face solemn. Behind him, something moved in the darkness. Although it was little more than a shape, a *presence*, Olech thought it was a dog . . . a dog as large as a mule. He did not have long to ponder the creature, if that was what it truly was. Without speaking, the stranger placed a sack on the floor then vanished, sweeping out into the night, slamming the door as he went.

The sack contained two things. The first was a human head, bobbing inside a fluid-filled jar. The second was a note, identifying the head as that of Gridluk Yearne, the last text-seller who had broken his contract with the stranger.

Olech had been warned.

Uncharacteristically, Olech was unnerved. For a while, he did not rebel, but remained true to the contract. Every few weeks, he would find a note slipped under the door, and hidden on the roof of the printing house, two dozen copies of *The Loss*, ready for sale. Also, the money he owed the stranger – which he left upon the roof for collection – would be gone. In this anonymous fashion, they conducted business; Olech no longer set eyes on the Dogman, or his accomplices.

After a time, however, he had had enough. He reminded himself that he was Olech, feared throughout Sliptere, and not the sort of man to do another's bidding, or be cowed by threats. Taking a Peacekeeper named Sheldrithe Caele into his confidence, he described the arrangement, and ordered Caele to watch the rooftop hawkishly. When he spotted the Dogman's agent – Olech could not imagine the Dogman himself scrambling up onto the roof – he had to follow him, find where he dwelled and report back. Then, Olech decided, he would take revenge. The Dogman had humiliated him, and he would pay.

Caele did as he was instructed – and never returned. Not in any acceptable form: two days later, Olech found the Peacekeeper's head in a jar on the roof. Alongside it was another jar, empty, bearing a label which read *Sensifer Olech*. There was also another batch of *The Loss*, which confused Olech at first, then gradually made some sort of sense. Combined, the objects seemed to say: You have betrayed me, Sensifer Olech. Do so again, and you will pay. But, for now, you are forgiven and our contract is unchanged.

After that, Olech gave up pursuing the Dogman. He had not only lost his appetite for revenge, but had become preoccupied with something else: throughout Druine, sellers of *The Loss* were falling prey to an unidentified group of men who, as Olech had been, were seeking the text's origins. These sellers were treated badly, often killed. And Olech had no desire to be next.

Olech fell silent. He had not expected to tell the Brute quite so much. He had wanted to reveal just enough to encourage the big man to disclose what *he* knew. Once he started, though, the words floated up from nowhere. Or rather, from a troubled corner of his soul, full of fear, doubt, uncertainty. Until now, he had told no one about the Dogman, except for Sheldrithe Caele – and then, he had said only what was strictly necessary. He had a reputation to maintain. He could not show weakness. He had to be seen only as Olech the Deadly, the Unfearing. But he no longer felt like any of those things. The Dogman made him feel tiny, frightened and worst of all, *old*. He doubted the younger Olech would have been so easily unsettled. Or lain awake at night, sweating in the darkness.

Now, he felt cleansed. And *lighter*. It had solved nothing, of course: the Dogman was still at large. But Olech did not feel quite as bad, which was surely worth something.

He exhaled, slowly. In a way, he was grateful to the Brute for listening – although it was gratitude tempered by an unavoidable truth: he would not have uttered a word if the Brute was going to live long enough to tell anyone else.

'That is my tale, as woeful as it is.' Olech refilled his goblet.

'And it is the truth?'

'If I could make up such a yarn, I'd be earning a fortune as an epic poet.' But it was not the truth. Not entirely. He had omitted one or two details. 'Now, it is your turn.'

'I will speak when you've taken me to my companions,' said the Brute.

'But what about our bargain?'

The Brute did not respond. Sighing, Olech got to his feet. 'I understand. You cannot tell me anything without your companions' permission. You are a team, a unit; you are obliged to act together. Very well. I will take you to them.' He placed his hands upon his hips. 'Before we go, there is something I must show you. It will vanquish any doubts concerning my story.'

'The heads,' said the Brute.

'You have seen them?'

The Brute nodded.

'And here I was, thinking they were well-hidden,' said Olech, ruefully. 'Perhaps I am not as canny as I like to think. Did you notice anything peculiar about them?'

'They had been mutilated,' said the Brute.

'Oh, a blind man could see that! Anything else?'

'Such as?'

'Come,' said Olech, smiling benignly. 'I will show you.'

He led the Brute into the kitchen. Outside the window, the garden lay in darkness. Olech flicked a gesture, unseen by the Brute. Then he stepped back toward the pantry. A heartbeat later, the rear door crashed open. Half a dozen Peacekeepers surged through, launching themselves at the Brute. At the same moment, the front door clattered open and another six or seven silk-wearing thugs plunged in and set upon the Brute, pummelling him as if tenderising a lump of steak.

The Brute fought back, cracking jawbones, splintering ribs. It was a quite a sight, Olech admitted, musing the Brute would have made an excellent Peacekeeper. Alas, fate had different plans. Strolling into the main room, Olech climbed on the armchair and retrieved a blowpipe from atop the bookcase. It was a gorgeous implement, two feet long, emblazoned with the spider-gods of the Melituk tribe. He took a glass phial from his pocket, inside which there was a dart. Carefully, he unstoppered the phial and tipped the dart onto the table. Pincering it between thumb and forefinger, he loaded it into the blowpipe.

He returned to the kitchen. Five Peacekeepers lay on the floor, groaning and bleeding. The rest carried on battering the Brute, whose nose was pulped, lips split and face swollen.

'Back,' called Olech, lifting the blowpipe to his lips.

The Peacekeepers withdrew, leaving the Brute in the centre of the floor. Olech blew, hard. The dart seemed to materialise in the Brute's neck, and the big man did what everyone did, when struck: he plucked the dart from his neck, stared at it, then tossed it aside. He advanced on Olech, growling. But it was already too late. The Brute's legs buckled, he teetered then collapsed, eyes closed, spittle seeping from a mouth-corner.

Olech surveyed the Peacekeepers.

'That,' he said, slapping the blowpipe against his palm, 'is how it ought to be done.'

Ballas woke on a cart-back, wrists tied, blindfolded.

Six years had passed since he had last drunk alcohol. But he still recalled the mornings after, and he felt something similar – nausea, trembling limbs, a savagely aching skull. He moved, stretching his legs, straining against his bonds. He was weak, sluggish. His body did not feel like his own.

The cart moved swiftly, rattling over paving stones. Rolling onto his side, Ballas vomited.

'Sounds like he's awake,' came a voice over the cartwheels.

'That was quick,' said someone else. Raising his voice, he addressed Ballas directly. 'Olech's got a few treats for you. That friend of yours, the bashed-up whore, she's already had a taste. She screamed, aye, screamed like she was losing her virginity – to a bloody *horse*!'

Several men laughed.

'Now, now, Gruliek,' said one. 'Don't you go upsetting him. Best if he saves his tears for later.'

The cart rolled on, jouncing furiously. When it finally halted, and Ballas was dragged off, his legs buckled and he sprawled upon the ground. Jeering, the men hauled him onto his feet. A door opened, and he felt himself jostled along a series of corridors. When they halted once more, a door squealed open and he was shoved over the threshold. He heard several of his captors follow, grab someone and heave them outside.

The door clanked shut. A bolt slid into place.

A familiar voice cut through the blackness. 'Hawk Ballas?'

'General,' murmured Ballas, turning toward the voice.

'Come close.'

Ballas trod carefully through the emptiness until his feet bumped against a pair of legs. 'Kneel,' said Standaire. Obeying, Ballas felt the general's forehead bump against his own. A pair of teeth tightened around the blindfold, then jerked it downwards until it rested crookedly on the bridge of Ballas' broken nose. Ballas hissed in pain, then looked around.

The cell was large but gloomy. Light drifted through a window high up in the wall, illuminating the general, who looked gaunter than ever before. It was an effect Ballas had seen before, once in the dusty side streets of Nenralleth, again in the bandit-prowled woodlands of southern Druine: somehow, adversity *honed* the general, stripping away all that was unnecessary, sharpening him to the barest essence, turning him into an instrument of pure survival. It was at once disturbing and heartening.

'We are not alone,' said Standaire.

Twisting, Ballas spotted Mallakos, slumped against the opposite wall. He wept, softly, tears sparkling on his cheeks.

'Ekkerlin?' Ballas asked Standaire.

'They took her out as you arrived,' replied the general. 'Do you see the window up there in the wall?'

Ballas looked, nodded. The window was too high for him to peer through; presumably, though, the occupant of the neighbouring room could look into the cell.

'Beyond, there is a torture room of sorts,' said Standaire. 'She is in there, now; she has been interrogated once already. She revealed nothing, she says.' He drew a breath. 'She told me that Olech uses a type of snake-venom as a truth serum. It has . . . has affected her. Badly. Her mind is unsound, almost as if she suffered from battleshock. Where have you been, Hawk Ballas?'

Ballas opened his mouth to reply. But suddenly, Ekkerlin cried out in the adjoining room.

'No! Have some mercy! Please, do not . . . you must not . . .'

Ballas shot a look to Standaire. His head tilted back, the general stared emptily at the ceiling. Getting to his feet, Ballas ran his fingertips over the walls, seeking a sharp edge to cut through his bonds. Once his hands were free, he could do something. *Perhaps.*

'Do not bother. The walls are rubbed smooth,' said Standaire.

Ballas grunted, then paced back and forth, trying to force the remaining traces of the dart's poison out of his system. Ekkerlin screamed, startling him. It was a sound unlike any Ballas had heard. It soared beyond the human, even the animal; it was an audible distillation of the purest anguish. Gooseflesh rose on his arms; his hackles stirred. Guts clenching, he turned to the wall with the window, cursing the bricks that separated him from his friend.

Suddenly, Mallakos yelled, 'Be quiet, curse you! Stop skriking! Show some restraint!' He stared fiercely at the wall, the window; eyes goggling, fat face clenched tight, he had plunged into a wild, half-hysterical panic. 'Why must you torture us with your noise, you silly girl! You are not the only one who is suffering.'

Ballas glowered at him. 'You be quiet, fat man,' he said.

Mallakos laughed despairingly. 'I'll make as huge a racket as I please. And never again will I do your bidding. I was your slave once, but no longer. Look where it got me! You have destroyed me, you lumbering oaf. Both of you, all *three* of you – I was happy before you turned up at Silver Hoof. Now . . . He will kill us, you know. Sensifer Olech. He will not set us free. Not when we might run to the Wardens and tell them about this . . . this private prison of his.' His blubbery face tightening, he cried, 'Woman – keep it shut! I do not care about your pain! I have enough of my own!'

Ballas started over. 'My hands are tied, but my feet are free. I could easily kick you to death.'

'Fine! Do it! It would be an act of mercy.'

'Leave him be,' said Standaire, sharply. 'Let him blather, if he wants. He will calm down soon enough.'

Mallakos *did* blather, yelling, sobbing, expelling wordless utterances of fathomless grief. He did not care if it angered the Brute. He was doomed, his life was over, and it was entirely the fault of the big man and his cohorts.

Eventually, he fell silent, exhausted.

He wondered what had brought him to this abysmal pass. Despite his words, it was not wholly the fault of the Brute and his friends. Curtlane should not have blackmailed him, and he, Mallakos, should never have purchased *The Loss*.

Maybe this was too simple. Maybe there was a deeper, meta-physical explanation.

Abruptly, he laughed. Oh yes, there *was* a deeper reason. He was the victim of a cosmic joke, and if he had kept his eyes open, he would have seen it coming a mile off.

At age thirty-three, he had been homeless, penniless, friend-less. He had drifted from village to village, town to town, seeking employment. At night, he slept rough; by day, he foot-slogged onward, hoping that his luck would change. One after-noon, he spotted a young horse standing forlornly in a field. Underfed, alone, it was in a pitiful state; overcome by a feeling of kinship for a fellow sufferer of fate's cruel vagaries, Mallakos climbed the fence into the field and approached the poor beast. He intended to pat it on the flank, scratch its ears, stroke its long sleek neck – in effect, to offer it a tiny crumb of comfort, and to say, I too am alone. We are brothers in despair.

As he approached the horse shied away. Mallakos noticed it limped, badly. After earning its trust, Mallakos inspected the horse's hooves, discovering a stone lodged in the left hind horseshoe. Taking a tiny knife from his pocket, he pried it out and said, 'There we go, my girl. A tiny flicker of darkness has been lifted.'

At that instant, the horse's owner appeared, a sour-tempered, cider-drinking, dog-hearted farmer, who cared nothing for the animal. He and Mallakos struck a bargain. If he toiled as a farmhand, for abominably low wages, Mallakos could take care of the horse, doing with her as he pleased. Mallakos agreed. The farmer was not a lenient master, working Mallakos from dawn till dusk, burdening him with one soul-crushing, back-breaking task after another. Yet Mallakos did not care. He had been struck by an idea.

He had decided to transform the horse, whom he called Larchfire, into a racer.

He knew little about training horses, and Larchfire's early races at the local track were hardly triumphant. Yet he persisted, cultivating Larchfire, working her hard and encouraging her, secretly feeding her the farmer's finest oats, which he kept locked in a shed along the lane. Gradually, Larchfire improved, growing stronger, faster, and gaining an understanding of what was expected when she was on the track. And she began to win. More than that, she started to humiliate the opposition, leaving them stumbling through the clouds of hoof-churned dust she left in her wake. By now, Mallakos was no longer impoverished. Race after race, he wagered as much as he could afford on the girl, and his thoughts turned to entering her in the bigger races in the neighbouring city. Inevitably, there was a downside: inflamed by greed, the farmer reneged on their deal, insisting that Larchfire was – had always been – his animal, and *he* had transformed her into a successful racer. But it did not matter. One night, under cover of darkness, Mallakos led Larchfire from the stables, climbed upon her back and together, they rode away.

The rest was as predictable as a fairytale. Larchfire won bigger, more profitable races, and Mallakos invested his earnings in more horses. These also ran extraordinarily well, bringing in yet more money, which Mallakos once again invested . . .

And so on. Within seven years, the once-homeless Cledrun Mallakos had become one of Druine's wealthiest men.

And now he was locked in a cell, wrists tied, listening to a woman scream as if to split the heavens.

He chuckled, sourly. What had set him on this path to despair? What impulse had flung him into the gnashing jaws of calamity?

A good deed. An act of kindness.

He had prised a stone from a sorrowful horse's hoof and lo, here he was, waiting to die. Yes, a cosmic joke indeed. No doubt, the Four would be pissing themselves, if they existed. So too the gods worshipped in foreign countries. The heavens would be awash with tears of laughter.

Suddenly, he froze. He felt as if he were dropping through empty space. After a moment, he composed himself.

'Gentlemen,' he said, 'if we were to lose our bonds, would we have a chance – a serious chance – of escaping?'

His back to Mallakos, Ballas fumbled against the horse-breeder's chest.

'There. You have it – ah!' Mallakos yelped as Ballas tore the pendant from his neck.

'It is one of those clever sorts with a blade which folds into the handle,' the horse-breeder went on, breathlessly. 'If you—'

With thick, dexterous fingers, Ballas extended the blade. 'It is done,' he said, pacing to Standaire. The two men sat back to back. Ballas sawed at the ropes around the general's wrists.

'I wear it as a lucky charm,' said Mallakos. 'I have never placed much worth in such articles. Now, I wonder if there is something to superstition. Years ago, I used it to pluck a stone—'

'Shut up.' Ballas worked the blade back and forth. The cutting edge was as dull as a barleystalk, but he was making progress. In the neighbouring room, Ekkerlin was silent. Ballas sensed they did not have long until the Peacekeepers brought her back. With a jerk, Standaire broke his bonds, then began untying Ballas's. Once he was free, Ballas returned to Mallakos.

'On your feet,' he said.

Mallakos rose unsteadily, like a bubble rising through dark water. Moving behind, Ballas set to work on his bonds. 'You done much fighting?' he asked.

Mallakos laughed. 'Never. I have always favoured swift feet over strong fists. I am what philosophers call a pacifist.'

'It's an easy habit to break.'

Mallakos nodded, solemnly. 'I do not have a choice, do I?'

'There's always a choice.'

'Not a genuine one, I meant,' said the horse-breeder, swallowing. 'It is life or death, is it not?'

'Yes.'

'Couldn't you and the Blade . . . your friend . . . take on the Peacekeepers yourselves? Killing is your business, is it not?'

'It is. But *you* have got to get stuck in. What is your life worth, if you are not willing to fight for it?'

'About the same as if I refused,' mumbled Mallakos.

Ballas pulled the ropes from the horse-breeder's wrists. 'If you do not play your part, you will not survive. As soon as the Peacekeepers are sorted, I will take your throat in my hands and squeeze until your eyes burst out of their sockets.'

'I wish I could believe you were jesting. But you men are not known for your humour, are you?'

'You men?'

'You are Hawks,' replied Mallakos. 'When you came through the door, that is what the general called you: Hawk Ballas.'

Ballas drew a breath. 'Then we will strike a bargain. Do you want to resume your earlier life at Silver Hoof?'

'Of course.'

'Fight like a bastard, and it shall be so.'

Mallakos trembled. 'Truly? But how – the dead guards in the stableyard . . .'

'We Hawks have the ear of the Masters,' said Ballas. 'If we ask for your sins to be forgiven, it will be done.'

'But my forbidden texts—'

'You have served us well, Mallakos. The Masters will overlook your minor indiscretions.'

Swallowing, Mallakos looked at the door. 'What must I do? How does one . . . how does one fight?'

158

'When the Peacekeepers come, stop being civilised. That is all you must do.'

'Civilised? I do not understand.'

'A civilised man is bred to be mild,' said Ballas, hearing a door open along the corridor. 'To settle his differences in a gentle fashion. That is fine, in ordinary circumstances. But it can also hold you back. When the guards arrive, turn into a savage. Become a primitive, if you like. Bite, gouge, punch, claw – do what you must. Be feral, Mallakos. You ever had a wild horse that refused to be tamed?'

'Never. I have always managed—'

'Piss on that, then,' muttered Ballas, turning to the door. Footsteps sounded outside. Across the cell, Standaire was on his feet. Mallakos had referred to him as the Blade. A nickname. But apt. The general looked as though he could slice sunlight into its constituent colours. Now and again, Ballas feared him, was grateful that they were allies rather than enemies. This was such a time.

'One more thing,' he said to Mallakos.

'Yes?' The horse-breeder's voice quavered.

'When you hit someone, put your full weight behind it; that way, you will send the bastard flying halfway to the moon.'

'Can I have my knife, please?' asked Mallakos.

Ballas held up the knife. The blade was barely more than an inch long. 'This little thing? It won't be any use against what is coming through that door. Not unless you are planning to trim the Peacekeepers' toenails.' He tossed the knife across the cell; the blade pinged brightly against the wall stones.

The footsteps halted. A bolt slid.

Olech watched as the Peacekeepers dragged the Bookworm out of the Vivarium.

He had been surprised when she resisted the first dose of

hothead venom. Now that she had received a second measure without confessing, he was amazed. He wondered if she was a freak of nature, if she had some biological quirk that shielded her from the venom's full effects, that she had hurt, yes, but not enough as she ought. Or maybe the venom was defective – too weak, too diluted.

'. . . big bastard?' came a voice.

Olech blinked. Geliurt hovered in the doorway.

'What?'

'Do you want me to fetch the big bastard?' said Geliurt. 'I'd love to see him get a bit of the venom.'

'It is too soon,' said Olech, distractedly. 'It will be several hours before my hothead has generated enough for another dose.' He cursed himself. He ought to have used the last dose on the Blade. Maybe he would not have fared as well as the Bookworm. Maybe he would have told Olech what he needed to know. But he had wanted to watch the Bookworm suffer a second time. He was not sure why. Maybe because she had corrected him about the Thrisulis tribe. After shooting the dart into the Brute's neck, Olech had gone to the bookcase and consulted *Customs of the Jungle Folk*; she had been right. The Thrisulis used hothead venom when electing a chieftain, not the Kletuik.

Wandering to the window, he peered into the cell.

Something was wrong. The prisoners were on their feet, arms free, blindfolds gone.

'No!' he yelled, but already it was too late. A chink of light seeped through the dark space. The door was opening.

Grabbing the edge, Ballas yanked open the door, startling the two Peacekeepers holding Ekkerlin upright. Ballas powered a straight right into the face of one of them, whilst Standaire struck the other in the throat. Staggering, the Peacekeepers dropped Ekkerlin but Ballas caught her before she hit the ground. Carefully, he laid her down. Before he could rise the first Peacekeeper kneed him in the face, knocking him off his feet. Crimson sparks floating through his vision, Ballas scrambled up, driving his fist into the man's head. The Peacekeeper wobbled and, stepping close, Ballas hit him twice more until he dropped.

A third Peacekeeper grappled with Standaire. Emerging from the cell, Mallakos snatched up a cudgel dropped by a Peacekeeper then, after a pause, struck the general's assailant across the skull. A half-hearted blow, it had no effect. Swearing, Mallakos swung again, channelling every atom of aggression he could muster. The blackwood stick smashed through bone and the Peacekeeper dropped, blood trickling from his ear. Stunned, Mallakos stared at the cudgel as if it were a religious artefact.

'Take Ekkerlin. Sling her over your shoulder, if you must,' Ballas told him.

A fourth Peacekeeper emerged from the room next to the cell. Ballas recognised him from Olech's kitchen; his face was completely flat, pummelled smooth by a life of violence. 'I'm going to cut you,' he said, and Ballas recognised his voice too. It belonged to Gruliek, the Peacekeeper who taunted him on the cart.

Unsheathing a knife, Gruliek slashed at Ballas's face. Catching his wrist, Ballas thundered three lung-emptying blows into his guts. Gruliek sagged, then, cracking his jaws wide open, he lunged at Ballas's throat, intending to bite him like a dog. Ballas slammed the heel of his hand under Gruliek's chin, knocking back his head. Then he twisted Gruliek's wrist, savagely, rupturing the tendons. Yelling, Gruliek dropped the knife and Ballas punched him again and again, driving him backward along the corridor. A powerful left hook sent the

Peacekeeper stumbling into the room by the cell. Following, Ballas hit him once more, in the chest, flinging him backward into a table of glass cases. As he dropped, Gruliek flailed, catching a case seemingly full of twigs and leaves. The case fell, shattering. Gruliek tried to rise, but he was too punch-drunk to coordinate his limbs. He sat still, gazing blankly at Ballas. Then he murmured something and looked down.

Half a dozen bright green snakes crawled out of the case. Hissing, they slithered over his thighs and rested there, pondering their next move.

'Help. Me. Please.' Although he addressed Ballas, Gruliek's gaze was locked on the serpents.

Ballas looked at him, dead-eyed. 'Why?'

'Please—' A snake struck, sinking its fangs into Gruliek's groin. Inspired, several others did the same. Shrieking, Gruliek flailed at the creatures, thrusting his hips to dislodge those whose teeth were embedded in his flesh.

Ballas returned to the corridor, leaving Gruliek. Together, Mallakos and Standaire supported Ekkerlin, who sagged between them, as limp as wet laundry on a line. Her face was pale, lips twitching, eyes uncomprehending. As Ballas strode over, she looked at him. No flicker of recognition crossed her face. No hint she knew who he was.

Ballas had planned to leave the way they had come. But the snakes were slinking out into the corridor, blocking their path.

Moving away, they trod deeper into Olech's House of Fate.

The corridor turned sharply to the right, halting at a rise of stone steps. As Ballas bounded up, a door opened at the top. Three Peacekeepers surged through.

Ballas seized the ankle of one, jerked his leg from under him and, as he fell, stamped on his throat. A split instant later, he slammed a fist in a second Peacekeeper's face whilst Standaire, abandoning Ekkerlin, hurtled up the steps and delivered a blow to the third Peacekeeper's chest. The impact was precise rather than powerful. With a baffled gulping noise, the Peacekeeper clamped a hand against his ribs. Heart spasming, he fell, tumbling down the steps.

Ballas pressed on, passing through the doorway into a small office with a polished mahogany desk and a leather armchair. A portrait of Olech hung on the wall.

Crossing the room, Ballas flung open a second door.

He found himself in the gambling hall. The vast, darkness-edged space was crowded with circular tables where gamblers played dice and card games, their faces sallow in the lantern light. In the centre stood a statue of Mistress Fortune, garbed in her customary white robe, a pair of dice nestling in an outstretched hand. At the opposite wall there was a serving bar, stocked with exotic liquors. Serving girls drifted back and forth, dressed as Mistress Fortune, bearing trays of drinks.

'Where is Olech?' demanded Ballas, seizing a girl by the arm. She was fifteen, maybe sixteen years old. Honey-coloured hair tumbled to her shoulders, and she would have been pretty were it not for a faint bluish tinge to her teeth – a sign she smoked visionary's root.

'Gone,' said the girl. Her gaze was hazy, unfocused. As if she had indulged in the root not long ago. 'He went running out of the doors. He looked . . . *frightened*.'

'Where did he go?'

'How should I know? I'm not his wife.' She giggled at the idea. 'He said something to Welner and went.'

'Welner?'

'His favourite. But then, she does whatever he asks. Her moral compass points southward, as they say. She's game for anything.'

A bell clanged somewhere overhead, its chimes deep and solemn.

'Ah, she's on the roof,' said the serving girl. 'Are you the man who's got Olech running?'

'Reckon so,' muttered Ballas, letting go of the girl's arm.

'Well, now it's your turn to run. That bell summons Olech's Hordelings, as well as every other Peacekeeper in the city. Whoever you are, you are going to be *hunted*.'

They heard the bell, the Hordelings. Those who slept, awoke; those who were awake felt their hearts lurch and blood quicken. The drunk grew sober; those who were rutting abandoned their bedmates, lured by a greater excitement elsewhere.

It had been six months since they last hunted.

They had few pleasures in life. Mired in poverty, they slept on the streets or in half-derelict houses infested by rats, cockroaches and feral cats.

None was beyond his or her nineteenth year. None could read or write, or cared to. They knew only what they needed to survive. Foremost in this was a painful awareness of their place within the natural order. They were scavengers – crows, jackals, vultures, subsisting on whatever they could find. But when the bell tolled, they were preybirds, glorious and deadly, flying from the glove of Sensifer Olech.

And they flew, now, through Sliptere's night-smothered streets. The swiftest raced amongst them, spreading news of those they sought: three men, one a giant, one monstrously fat, the third as thin as a stropped razor's edge; and a woman, afflicted by some undisclosed malady, effectively dead to the world.

They were to be captured, not killed. Their lives belonged to Olech.

Sensifer Olech – the Hordelings adored him. He gave them hope. If they served him well, they would be rewarded. They would be fed, given liquor, even a few coins. Some of the most

164

loyal became Peacekeepers, it was said, whilst others operated his brothels or smuggled narcotics on his behalf. A select few, it was whispered, played a part in Olech's most secret enterprise: selling forbidden texts. They had an excellent life, by all accounts: they dwelled in warm houses, drank fine wine, wore good clothes and never, ever had to grub for coins in the gutter, or steal, or beg.

In desperate circumstances, ignorant folk pledged loyalty to the Four, hoping they would be rewarded in the next world; the Hordelings knelt before Olech, and their rewards, if they came, came in this world, where the greatest joys were those of the flesh.

The Hordelings swarmed through the streets, whistling loudly, so each knew the whereabouts of the others. Gradually, they massed, gathering as if drawn together by some strange magnetic force. The whistling ceased, replaced by shouts, each proclaiming the location of their quarry.

'Sage Street,' called one. Then, as the prey moved on, the cry of 'Lute Street' went up. And so on until, from street to street, until the name 'Sackcloth Row' rang out.

CHAPTER TEN

Stealing a cart from a hostelry near the House, they rode swiftly, rattling through the moonlit streets, cartwheels clattering, the axle creaking as if to snap. Ekkerlin lay on the cart-back, unconscious, sheened in foul-smelling sweat. Mallakos sat alongside her, his flabby face pink with exhilarated terror. On the driving bench, Ballas gripped the reins, urging the horse onwards as fast as he dared. Standaire sat beside him, staring intently ahead.

Once they were a good distance from the House, they would find a physician to treat Ekkerlin. Ballas was unconvinced that any doctor, no matter how skilful, could do a great deal for her. She was dying; he was sure of it. Slowly and inexorably, she was sinking away from the warm light of consciousness and life, and descending toward the abysmal, tideless depths of death. She was too far gone; no clever man of medicine, armed with a legion of draughts, potions and powders, could haul her back up.

Ballas heard footsteps, shuffling and pattering in the side streets, as fast and numerous as a pack of rats fleeing a hungry cat. He looked around wildly, seeing no one in the shadowed gaps between the buildings. Then the whistling started, a flurry of thin shrill notes skirling and looping toward the night sky, each arising from a different set of fingers held bent to a different mouth.

166

A voice cried, 'Sage Street!'

Sage Street – the long narrow road on which the cart moved, lurching and swaying. Tugging the reins, Ballas steered the horse onto another road, the cart tilting dangerously as it rounded the corner. He made a note of the road name: Lute Street.

Somewhere behind, a voice yelled moments later, 'Lute Street! Lute Street!'

Whipping the reins, Ballas drove the cart on at full tilt, then angled onto another road.

'Sackcloth Row! Sackcloth Row!'

Flanked by shops, wallowing in darkness at this late hour, the Row stretched on as far as the eye could see. Heartened, Ballas flicked the reins three times, shouting, 'Go on, girl. Go on, now.' He knew he could not outwit his whistling, running, shouting pursuers. These were the Hordelings, he guessed. And they knew the streets too well. But he could outpace them. A fast horse was easily enough to—

'Slow down!' snapped Standaire, pointing.

Ahead, a barricade of masonry, barrels and stones had been erected, spanning the entire road. Cursing savagely, Ballas yanked hard on the reins, jerking the horse to a whinnying, skittering halt. There was a moment of quietness, in which the air seemed to throb and seethe. Then the Hordelings came, pouring out of the side streets like ants from a shattered nest, a mob of ragged, unwashed youngsters, their prematurely aged faces pinched with fervid glee, their rot-toothed mouths stretched open, their eyes alight with predatory joy. Others materialised on the road itself, leaping gracelessly over the makeshift barricade and running toward the cart in a frantic swarm, screeching and laughing like the demons of the Forest.

No sooner had Ballas glimpsed them than they had arrived, vaulting onto the cart-back, springing onto the driving bench, a tidal swell of filthy, scrawny bodies, stinking of sweat and alcohol. Like an ill-weighted sailing vessel, the cart teetered to one side, then overbalanced, crashing onto the paving stones. Then the true attack began. Howling, shrieking delightedly, the Hordelings fell wolf-like upon the Hawks, biting, punching, kicking, flailing. Ballas lashed out blindly until the sheer oppressive mass of the Hordelings overwhelmed him, crushing him to the ground, threatening to smother him.

He could not say how long the onslaught lasted. Time did not seem to pass amongst the thrashing vortex of limbs, fists, knees and teeth. Curling into a ball, he brunted the blows as well as he could, thinking all the while that this was not a proper – an *intelligible* – way for a Hawk to die, any more than it seemed right that a sickly lion should be devoured by wild ants, a tiny mouthful at a time.

Through the buzzing in his ears, and the snarls and grunts of the Hordelings, he heard someone yell, 'Withdraw!'

The Hordelings continued, blood-frenzied and unreachable.

'I said *withdraw*!' This time, the voice was coarsened by a dangerous, furious edge. One by one, the Hordelings peeled off Ballas, detaching themselves slowly, reluctantly. They did not retreat far, but milled around the cart, loitering, hoping their master would have second thoughts and command them to resume their attack.

'Back away,' came Olech's voice.

As the Hordelings did as instructed, Ballas saw Sensifer Olech dismount from a jet-black mare. Grinning crookedly, planting his hands on his hips, he surveyed the Hawks. Glancing sideways, Ballas did the same. Several yards away, Standaire was propped up on one elbow, head drooping, face swelling with bruises, lips slick with blood. Bleeding heavily from his nose, his coppery hair sticking up in wispy tufts, Mallakos dragged himself into a sitting position and sagged back against the underside of the fallen cart. Ekkerlin lay on the ground, unconscious, her limbs spraddled, her eyes closed.

Olech's grin widened. No shark had ever looked so pleased by the sight of its prey.

'Ropes,' he said loudly. 'You have brought ropes, yes?'

'Aye,' replied a Hordeling, stepping forward. Several lengths of rope were looped around his shoulders.

'Tie them up. Then take them back to the House. These fellows, and that lady, have a long, interesting evening ahead of them.'

As the Hordelings advanced, slipping the ropes off his shoulder, Mallakos raised his hands. 'Wait – no! Wait!' He swung his face to Olech. 'We must speak, you and I. It is a matter of the gravest urgency.'

Olech laughed noiselessly. 'The hour for discussion has long passed, my bloated friend.'

'Trust me, you will be grateful once I have spoken. All is not as it seems – or as you imagine.'

'There will be time enough to parley at the House,' said Olech.

'I am sure there will. But by then, it will be too late.'

'Too late for what?'

The rope-carrying Hordeling approached Mallakos. 'Back off,' snapped Mallakos, jabbing a finger at the youth, who was no more than fifteen years old. 'If that rope so much as brushes my skin, I will not tell your master what he needs to know. And for that, he will not thank you. He shall give you a long and interesting night of your own.'

The Hordeling looked to Olech uncertainly.

'Very well, Mallakos. What do you wish to tell me?'

Mallakos shook his head. 'I will not utter a word with everyone listening. No, not a chance. This is for your ears alone.'

Olech stared thoughtfully at Mallakos. Fat, battered, bruised and in all likelihood concussed, he was not a threatening figure.

'Come over,' said Olech, beckoning. 'Whisper it to me, if you must. But if you are wasting my time—'

'Wasting your time? Sensifer Olech,' said Mallakos, struggling onto his feet. 'I am probably *saving your life.*'

Olech made no effort to disguise his distaste for Mallakos. He was a disgraceful specimen, practically crippled by his ponderous bulk. His body wobbled and as he grew close, Olech could hear his heavy, laborious breathing. He looked as if he could keel over at any instant, clutching his chest; when he halted, Olech could smell his sweat, a revolting garlic-and-onions tang.

'Say your piece,' he said.

'Straight to business, is it? Very well. I trust you know who they are?' Mallakos gestured toward the cart.

'The Bookworm told me nothing.'

'Even though you interrogated her?'

'She held her silence, somehow.'

'And that silence was as good as a confession,' said Mallakos, brightly. 'Really, it ought to have told you everything you needed to know. Who, my friend, are trained to withstand torture?'

Olech shrugged, nonplussed. 'Tell me.'

Mallakos smiled. 'The Hawks.'

Olech stared at the figures scattered around the cart. His blood grew cold. 'Are you certain?'

'They let it slip in the cell,' replied Mallakos. 'They also revealed they are not alone. Others of their kind are in Sliptere and, at this very moment, they will be seeking their missing comrades. Which is very bad news for you, Olech.'

Olech clenched his jaw, thinking. So, it was the Church who sought *The Loss*. And who better to send on such a dangerous errand than the Hawks. Violence, conflict, peril – it was their meat and drink. It all made a horrible kind of sense.

'All is not lost,' said Mallakos, placing a hand on his shoulder. 'I know a little about the Hawks. Unlike most men, they are not interested in revenge. Or settling scores. For them, it matters only that their missions are successful.'

Olech swatted Mallakos's hand away. 'Why should this please me?'

'It means you can negotiate with them. Tell them everything they want to know, and they will move on. As unnatural as it might be, you should play the role of penitent. Say you would have helped them from the outset, if you had known. Apologise, grovel. No one can rise as high in the world as you without an ability to create an illusion.' He coughed, then elaborated. 'First, though, you must dismiss the Hordelings. You did a splendid job of subduing them before, but their passions will spill over soon enough. Look at them. They are like wasps buzzing at a honey-shop window.'

'If they go, I will be undefended,' murmured Olech. Inside his suntanned skull, several thoughts clicked together. 'Which is exactly what you want.'

'Pardon?'

Olech laughed, sardonically. 'Those men and that girl are not Hawks. If they were, they would not find themselves in such perilous circumstances. I too know a little about the regiment, in particular their tendency to plan ahead. They rarely find themselves unmanned by circumstances. Always, they are masters of their destiny. You lied to me, Mallakos.' He laughed again, a little harder. 'What else should I expect from a horse-breeder? Duplicity is not merely your business, but your passion.' He drew back his shoulders. 'You underestimated me. I am not some dung-slubbered halfwit to be tricked by a slug with a viper's tongue.'

Moving close, Mallakos punched Olech in the stomach. At least, that was what it felt like. Glancing down, Olech saw a knife-handle jutting from his guts. Blood-trickles crawled along the blade.

'You were smart enough to spot the one ruse, but not the other,' said Mallakos. 'You poor man, I tricked you twice over.'

Olech considered a reply. But his mind was blank, flooded by the cloudy waters of panic. Even if his wits were sharp, it would have been no use. Blood was bubbling into his mouth, oozing over his lips. Groaning, Sensifer Olech fell to the ground.

The Hordelings stared, stunned, as if they had witnessed some baffling conjuring trick. Some gaped, others scowled, a few murmured.

Drawing a breath, Mallakos raised his arms. 'Ladies and gentlemen,' he called, 'this has been a great day . . .'

During his years of vagrancy, he had rubbed shoulders with folk like the Hordelings. He understood them, knew their fears, greeds and lusts. He knew them better than they knew themselves.

Choosing his words carefully, he denounced Olech.

It was not hard. He did not need to lie. Olech had offered them hope, yet what had he provided, what rewards had he bestowed? Despite their loyalty, the Hordelings were underfed, penniless, inhabitants of the gutter. Which was exactly what Olech wanted. They were useful only because they frequented the shady regions of the city, the cold, dark grots where black business was conducted. Why, then, would he want them to rise up in life? They had helped him, yes – but how had he helped them? What is more, Mallakos said, Olech held the Hordelings in contempt. Why? Because he was rich, and the rich despised the poor – it was a natural law.

As he spoke, the Hordelings grew uncertain. Some were

having their worst suspicions confirmed; for others, Mallakos's words were a horrible revelation. Either way, their hopes were cracking apart like the stonework of Blacker's Folly.

Spreading his arms, Mallakos said, 'Olech is dead; every second, his corpse grows colder. Within a day, it will be rotten; by the end of the week, it will be ashes, drifting from a pyre. But you will live on. You will hunger and, when summer ends, you will shiver. It need not be so. Now is the hour to take what is rightfully yours. In death, Olech will pay what he owes. At present the House of Fate is undefended. The Peacekeepers are gone, scattered like sycamore seeds in a strong wind. What is there is yours. Go, take what you will. In the gambling hall, there is money, much money. And liquor, if you crave sustenance. How many of you have set foot in the House?'

No one replied.

'None? I am not surprised. Olech would rather let an angry grizzly bear across the threshold than your good selves. There is a hidden floor, underground, stuffed with treasures. Yes, you heard correctly. Olech is a rich man, and rich men collect baubles – jewellery, artworks, fine clothes . . . Anything that reminds them of their wealth. And it is all yours, if you choose. Run; take it. Go a-scrumping, if you will.'

The Hordelings stirred, tempted but unconvinced.

'Do you think I am lying? That I, like Olech, would trick you? No, no. You know me, do you not? Surely I am preceded by my reputation? I am Cledrun Mallakos, the finest horse-breeder in Druine and a frequent visitor to the Loop.' A few Hordelings squinted, and nodded. 'You will recall that I petitioned for the kinder treatment of horses during the races. No unnecessary whipping, no over-vigorous heel-jabbing. Why? Because I hate suffering. In horses, men, women and children. It is repugnant in all its forms.' He spoke at length, describing why he hated misery. Not because it was relevant, but because it gave the Hordelings time to think. Already, plots were forming: they were planning to blackmail him for Olech's murder. Or extort money in other ways. Maybe a few were thinking that they could abduct him. But it would not happen. When he next went to the Loop, he would ensure he was well-protected. A dozen bodyguards would suffice.

'You must decide what to do next.' Mallakos planted his foot on Olech's chest – the customary stance of the vanquisher over the vanquished. 'Soon, the Wardens will arrive. If you stay, many of you will be arrested. Go, and you can fill your pockets at the House of Fate. I cannot say you will all grow rich. But you will have money enough for food, wine, maybe a week or two in a good lodging house.'

He waited. Then, to his relief, the Hordelings drifted away. They departed slowly, uncertainly, but that was to be expected. The world had suddenly become a very different place. They felt as if the ground was shifting under their feet, as if the night sky contained constellations hitherto undiscovered. Then one broke into a run, keen to reach the House before the others. And then they were all running, swarming like hornets from a shattered nest. Mallakos watched them go. Light-headed, he looked down at Olech.

Drifting back into consciousness, Olech stared up with damp, fearful eyes.

Ballas watched as Mallakos trotted over.

He felt sick. He ached from toes to scalp. He doubted he had a square inch of flesh unbruised, a bone uncracked. But it was bearable. Preferable, certainly, to the alternative: if the Hordelings had been well-disciplined, he would be dead. Crowding in, jostling one another, none of the savage youngsters had been able to land a clean, forceful blow.

'Finish him off,' said Mallakos, pointing to Olech.

'He lives?'

'The old adage is true: the more evil one is, the greater one's lust for life.' Then, 'I stole the knife from one of the youngsters. *Whilst I was being beaten!* I never imagined that I possessed such presence of mind. That I could plan ahead whilst . . .'

Ignoring the horse-breeder, Ballas got to his feet. He walked over to Olech. Considering there was a knife stuck in his belly, he looked remarkably healthy. His face had not lost a shade of its suntanned hue. His teeth were as white as salt.

'Be rid of him,' said Standaire, walking stiffly over.

'With your permission, I shall interrogate him. When we spoke in his home, he revealed a little about *The Loss*. Some of it was true; some of it, lies. I want to find out which is which.'

'Do what you must. But not here.'

Crouching, Ballas took Olech in his arms and lifted him, as if he were a sleeping child. Olech gasped as the knife shifted. 'What . . . are . . .'

'Shut up. You will have a chance to talk soon enough.'

A potter's workshop stood across the street. Kicking open the door, Ballas carried Olech inside and laid him upon a workbench. Casting about, he saw tools hanging from wall hooks, some sharp-edged. Then he spotted a kiln, hunkering against a wall. Touching the iron door, he discovered it was warm. He opened it a fraction. A gust of hot air blew out. Closing it again, he returned to Olech.

'Want me to pull it out?' asked Ballas, squinting at the knife.

'No! No . . .' Panic lit up Olech's eyes.

'It will only take a second.' He reached out.

'No, damn it, no!' Terror contorted Olech's face.

Ballas shrugged. 'Aye, maybe we should leave it for a physician.'

'A physician? Then you intend to let me live?'

'If you behave yourself.' Straightening, he rolled his shoulders. 'I have seen many knife wounds like that. I'd say you have an hour or so before you start dying. Maybe a little longer. Or shorter. Who can tell?' He shrugged. 'Time is of the essence, either way. Are you going to be helpful? If so, I'll take you to a physician. Aye, I will leave you on his doorstep, bang on the door and walk away. He will feed you a pint of whisky and extract the knife. Then, all will be well. You can go back to the House, and everything will be as it was.'

'W-what do you mean, *helpful*?'

'You lied to me. In your home.'

'No. I spoke the truth.'

'Not all of it.'

'I—'

'Do not deceive me, little man.' Seizing the handle, Ballas yanked out the knife. Olech half-screamed, half-yelped, scrunching shut his eyes. 'Now you have got a half-hour left. I suggest you hurry.' Ballas laid the knife on the bench.

'You b-bastard . . . I will not tell you anything . . .'

Ballas exhaled, slowly. Olech was no fool. He recognised that Ballas was not a merciful man. He knew he would not be delivered to a physician, even if he spoke the truth. And even if he was, there was little that could be done: the wound was deep, his internal organs were damaged, and death was approaching come what may. Olech had decided he would die with dignity which, in these circumstances, meant *defiance*. He would say nothing, except to curse Ballas, and declare he would never, ever tell him what he wanted to know.

It was not a problem; pain could bring even a dying man to his senses.

Grunting, Ballas lifted Olech from the workbench. He carried him to the kiln, opened the door and shoved him inside. Closing the door, he counted to five, then opened it again. He bore

Olech to the bench, laid him out. He had not fared well. His hair and beard were gone, steamed away. Water-fat blisters bulged on his cheeks and his lips were cracked. He trembled like a diseased fox.

'Our contract has changed,' said Ballas. 'Your death is a certainty. But a question remains: what form will it take? More importantly, will it be quick or slow, gentle or excruciating? Will you die with a whisper or a scream?'

Olech said nothing. Ballas grunted. Either the snaky little man was tougher than he had supposed, or he could not accept what was happening to him. Still, it hardly mattered. When a medicine failed to cure a patient, a higher dose was sometimes required.

'Very well,' said Ballas, carrying him back to the kiln. Once more, he locked him inside for a five count. This time, Olech shrieked, the sound muffled by the kiln's brickwork. When Ballas took him out, his shirt and leggings had evaporated and his skin was hot. Red cracks seamed his scalp, fissures oozed across his forehead. His eyeballs were desiccated, his ears wispy tatters.

'I need the truth,' said Ballas, placing him on the bench.

Olech stayed silent.

Defiance? After all that? wondered Ballas.

He doubted it. Prising open his jaws, he peered into Olech's mouth. His tongue was blistered, but largely intact. So why was he refusing to talk? Was he stronger than he had imagined?

'You are a fool,' said Ballas, taking hold of him.

Olech writhed madly. He did not want to go back in the kiln. Then why—? Suddenly, Ballas understood. The problem lay in Olech's throat. Taking a jug, he poured water into Olech's mouth. Olech spluttered, then tried to speak. The words were barely audible, just flutterings in the air.

'Whisper,' said Ballas. 'It will be enough.'

'A village . . . thirty miles east . . . Mist. Lots . . . of mist. There, you . . . you will find the Dogman.'

177

'You knew he was there? Your enemy?'

'I . . . did not dare . . . fight with him . . . He was t-too much . . . even for me.'

'Where in the village can he be found?'

'I . . . do not know. I did not dare . . . pry deeper. I had had enough.'

'Anything else?'

'No . . . except . . .' Olech began crying. 'A . . . quick death . . . you promised . . .'

Nodding, Ballas picked up the knife. Touching it to Olech's throat, he whispered, 'I will see you in the Forest.'

Olech shut his eyes, waiting for the killing stroke. Ballas stared, thinking. Not long ago, this burned, blistered husk had poisoned Ekkerlin. Ballas could still hear her screams, echoing through the interior of his skull. He doubted they would ever fall silent. He doubted, too, that Ekkerlin would live. She had already been taken to death's threshold; by now, she may have passed through the doorway completely.

Gone, for ever.

What a miserable death it would have been.

Agonising. Horrifying. *Unforgivable*.

He lifted the knife from Olech's throat. Then he tapped the blade-tip on his forehead. Lightly.

Olech's eyes cracked open.

'I have changed my mind,' said Ballas.

Olech's char-lipped mouth opened. A muffled meaningless croak emerged. Setting the knife aside, Ballas carried the gambling-house keeper to the kiln.

Ekkerlin sat in a side street, propped against a wall. Her face was as blank and pale as the moon. Her mouth sagged open, her eyes as blank as a stuffed animal's.

Ballas crouched beside her. 'Has she . . .'

178

'She has not stirred. She is locked in a waking sleep,' said Standaire. 'We must take her to a physician. But first . . .' He glanced over his shoulder. Ten yards away, Mallakos paced back and forth, animated by a restless energy. 'We must deal with the horse-breeder.'

'General . . .' said Ballas, gently.

'We have no choice. He knows who we are. He understands our mission.' The general released a long breath. 'I will do what is required. It is my fault, after all. I spoke too loosely in the gambling house.'

'As did I,' countered Ballas. He looked closely at Standaire. The general's skin was grey, his eyes ringed by shadows. He was exhausted, yes – but there was something else, something Ballas could not quite identify. A deeper weariness, maybe. One that could not be cured by a good night's sleep. He caught himself pitying the general. 'I will do it,' he said.

'No, Hawk Ballas. I—'

'What became of Olech?' interrupted Mallakos, striding over. 'Is he—'

'Yes,' said Ballas.

'There is smoke coming from the chimney.' He pointed a chubby finger toward the potter's workshop. 'Did you—'

'Yes.' Suddenly, Ballas rose. 'With your permission, General, I will debrief Mallakos.'

Standaire narrowed his eyes in a way Ballas had seen before. *Are you disobeying me? Is that wise, do you think?* Yet the mysterious something else lingered. The general glanced at the ground then nodded, faintly.

'Debrief me?' said Mallakos.

'Our friendship is over,' replied Ballas. 'You must go on your way.'

'Truly?'

'You have served your purpose,' said Ballas. 'Come, let us

walk awhile. I will explain what you must do next. Regarding Silver Hoof and the dead men in the stableyard.'

'Ah, it seems so long ago,' said Mallakos, thoughtfully. 'Can it really be only a few days? The Masters *will* forgive me, will they not? They will absolve me of my sins—'

'We – and they – are in your debt.'

'Then they will overlook both the corpses *and* the forbidden texts? It was a trifling hoard, but sufficient to send me to the gallows.'

'All will be well,' said Ballas.

Planting his hands on his hips, Mallakos grinned. 'Well, it has been quite an adventure, has it not? Sir, despite everything, I am pleased to make your acquaintance.' Bending, he proffered a hand to Standaire. The general hesitated, then shook it. 'I hope your friend recovers,' said Mallakos. 'I am sure she will. She is remarkably sturdy; if she were a horse, I would be proud to own her. I am sorry if I gave her short shrift when she was suffering. I should have been more sympathetic.' Digging a purse from his pocket, he tipped five gold pieces into his palm. 'Here,' he said, putting them on the ground near Standaire. 'Take her to Doctor Burnlake in the east of the city. He is expensive, but skilful. When my gout flares up, he is the man I go to. There will be some money left over, of course. So treat yourselves. Buy some new clothes, some extra knives – whatever takes your fancy.'

Leaving the alley, Ballas led Mallakos across Sackcloth Row.

'You know, I disliked you at first,' said Mallakos, patting Ballas on the shoulder. 'After all, you doused Larchfire in oil. But that is in the past. And you would not have torched the old girl, would you?'

Ballas looked at him. 'You reckon?'

'You would have rather chopped off your own balls,' said Mallakos. 'I shall tell you how I know. First, you were using

Larchfire as a bargaining tool. As long as she was unharmed, my guards would not have attacked you. If you set her ablaze, however, my men would have had no reason not to rip you apart. Which they would have done. Kill the horse, and you would be signing your own death warrant.'

Ballas grunted. The horse-breeder was perceptive.

'Secondly, most importantly, you are fond of horses. Do not deny it! I have an eye for such things; I can spot the difference between one who treats them merely as transportation, and one who has a genuine admiration for the creatures.' He laughed. 'You are not given easily to happiness, I think. But when you are on horseback, your expression becomes . . . not gentle, but contented. Maybe it is because you see a little of yourself in those noble animals? After all, they prefer silence over chatter, and when they work, they work hard, without making a fuss.'

Ballas grunted, again.

'How old are you?' asked Mallakos, abruptly.

'Twenty-four years,' replied Ballas, unthinkingly.

'You cannot remain a Hawk for ever. It is a young man's game, yes? Oh, the general is an exception, although . . . Well, *you* did most of the dirty work, did you not? Made most of the decisions, too. One could easily be forgiven for thinking that *you* were in charge. Anyhow, when you retire, what will you do? If you are interested, I could offer you an apprentice-ship now.'

'Apprenticeship?'

'I will teach you to breed horses. And, when you are ready, I will give you some breeding stock so you can set up on your own.'

Ballas was perplexed. 'Why?'

Mallakos blinked, as if the answer were obvious. 'I am in your debt. You have saved my life umpteen times over.'

'You would not have been in danger were it not for us.'

'True,' murmured Mallakos. Then, brightly, 'But you sorted out my difficulties with Curtlane. For the last year, he has been like a guillotine blade, hanging over me by a frayed rope. I doubt he will ever trouble me again. No longer will I dread visiting the Loop. Where is the bewhiskered little snot, by the way?'

'That does not matter.'

'Nonetheless, I am grateful. And there is something else. After all this,' he gestured over his shoulder to Sackcloth Row and the gambling house, 'I feel quite different. Sort of . . .' He faltered, then shook his head. 'It makes no odds. Let us talk of practical matters. What must I do?'

'Do?'

'About Silver Hoof. The corpses and texts.'

Ballas led him into a side street, empty except for rats, scratching through rotten fruit heaped against a wall. The Hawk halted but, oblivious, Mallakos walked on a few paces, still talking, until he realised he was alone.

'Ah, so this is it then?' he said, returning. 'Our tearful farewell?'

Ballas did not reply.

Mallakos stared back, puzzled. 'Sir?' he ventured.

Grabbing his shirt, Ballas pushed Mallakos against the wall. At the same time, he whipped out his knife, lifting it toward Mallakos's throat. With unexpected speed, Mallakos grabbed his wrist.

'What? Sir? What are you doing?'

Ballas did not reply. He did not need to. The black sunlight of comprehension broke over Mallakos's face.

'No. This cannot be,' he breathed. 'I did everything you asked. Oh, I know that secrecy is of the utmost importance. You cannot have some fat old blabbermouth strolling hither and thither, telling all and sundry of your mission, but I assure you – I am not he! I will stay tight-lipped. Indeed, I could not speak of our adventure without incriminating myself as a buyer of texts. I would be weaving my own noose!'

Ballas inched the knife closer to Mallakos's throat. 'It will be easier if you do not resist,' said the Hawk, his voice thick. 'It will be a quick death, a gentle death . . .'

'But – but I do not want a death of any sort!'

Ballas grimaced. 'I am sorry, horse-breeder.'

Knees buckling, Mallakos slid toward the ground. Keeping hold of the horse-breeder's shirt, Ballas followed, kneeling, the blade touching his throat.

'Please,' said Mallakos, eyes wet. 'Not now. Not after everything.' Then, 'I will leave Druine! I will emigrate to the east, and you will never hear of me again.'

From nowhere, a cold darkness rose up, enfolding Ballas. He felt suddenly as if he were watching himself from a distance. His body was no longer his own. He stared at his hand, at the thick strong fingers curled around the knife hand, at his huge, bruised, scabbed knuckles jutting stark. He felt no more a living thing than the knife itself.

It always ends like this, he thought. There is never any other way . . .

He met Mallakos's gaze. A single, irrefutable truth shone through the darkness, blazing as clearly as molten steel.

He was a Hawk. He had a job to do.

'Sorry, horse-breeder,' he repeated, applying pressure to the knife.

As Ballas returned to the alley, Standaire looked up.

'It is done?'

Ballas held up a knife, slick with blood. Then he cast the weapon over the rooftops, spinning dark against the starlit sky. Stumping over, he knelt by Ekkerlin.

'Wake up, girl,' he said, lightly slapping the side of her face. 'You cannot sleep whilst there is work to be done.'

'We will find this Doctor Burnlake,' said Standaire. 'Maybe he will prove useful.'

'Make an effort, woman,' said Ballas, peering into Ekkerlin's eyes. He stroked a few strands of hair from her face. 'Never marked you for an idler.'

'Lift her up,' said Standaire. 'The sooner we get her to the physician, the better—'

'He will do nothing,' murmured Ekkerlin, drowsily. Her voice was a thin rustling of air. Her eyes rolled loosely in their sockets. 'Gout is one thing. Snake-venom, quite another. I do not think . . . a few restorative infusions will—' She coughed, savagely. 'Will make a difference. Water, rest. That is what I require.' Raising her head, she looked into Ballas's face. Then grimaced. 'Unless I am already dead. Is this the Forest? Are you a demon? One of the famously ugly ones?'

Ballas grunted. 'Go back to sleep, woman.'

A faint smile touched Ekkerlin's lips. Then her grimace tightened and, clutching her stomach, she vomited blood-tinged bile onto her lap. Suddenly she was shaking, spasming as though gripped by a seizure. Her arms flailed, her jaws clashed. Her head rocked back and forth, cracking against the wall. Grabbing her shoulders, Ballas drew her clear then sat, looping his arm around her shoulders. 'Come on girl,' he murmured. 'Be still, be still, be still . . .'

The fit lasted barely a minute. When it ceased, Ekkerlin shivered, wildly, as if caught in an arctic wind.

'. . . die . . .'

'No, girl,' said Ballas. 'You are not going to die.'

'Die? No. Not die as in, ah, die. Die as in *d-y-e* . . .' She shuddered, spat. 'Olech coloured his beard. Could you not tell? I noticed it in his interrogation room. I cannot recall . . . recall

184

what was harder: refusing to confess, or keeping myself from giggling. A man of his age, with a beard as black as a badger's bollock.' Another lung-stripping cough. 'Is he dead?'

'If he isn't, he will have at least acquired a nice glaze,' said Ballas.

'Did he say anything useful?'

'Aye,' replied Ballas. 'We will be heading to the coast as soon as you're ready. I reckon the sea air will do you good.'

Ravrik Suthe rode through Sliptere upon a grey mare, a handsome creature for which he had not paid a penny: creeping in through the stable door, as stealthy as a cat, he had stolen it from an ostlery adjoining an exceptionally rough, spit-and-sawdust tavern. A bold crime indeed, but Ravrik Suthe was a bold man, capable of conquering his fear just as he had once conquered plates of gammon, pheasant and beef. Of course, this master criminal had aliases: his name might not have been Ravrik Suthe at all. It could just as easily have been Lefris Nathret, or Meriate Shumarfe or Ciruvar Jalvar. It did not matter, for the time being at least. Not until he fled his native Druine for the hot, dust-logged Distant East. No; for the moment, he was who he had always been: Cledrun Mallakos, horse-breeder, frequent visitor to the Loop, possessor of near-limitless wealth.

He had made his choice. He would not – could not – remain in Druine. By now, the Wardens would have discovered the scorched corpses scattered through the stableyard at Silver Hoof; no doubt, they would have found the crime baffling: the usual hows, whys and whos would be rattling through their skulls like trapped bluebottles. They would know only that he, Mallakos, dwelled there; thus, he would be suspected of involvement. They may have found his forbidden texts. So he had to go. And the Distant East was as enticing as anywhere: after all, it was the home of horse-racing. Over there, they bred the finest horses, and their colossal stadiums made the Loop look like a village green. He would set up a stables and go into business. It would be fun, he thought, starting from scratch. Well, not *entirely* from scratch: before he departed, he would visit the various banking establishments where he kept his money, and withdraw as much gold as he could carry. As soon as he arrived beneath the hot Eastern sun, he would find a suitable spot to build a stable and, once it was erected, purchase some breeding stock. Yes, the old Mallakos would continue to exist, reborn in a different country, under a different name.

But first, he had work to do. Blacker's Folly loomed ahead, as rickety in darkness as daylight. Mallakos rode closer, taking his time. He needed to think.

He had fully expected the Brute to kill him. Hawk Ballas – clearly a man endowed with a ruthless disposition. Even now, Mallakos felt the knife-blade pressed against his throat, and the big man's hand, vast enough to crush a pumpkin, pressing hard against his chest. He recalled with a certain shame how he had gibbered and wept, pleading for his life. And he recalled, too, the lightning-bolt of surprise he experienced when the Brute turned away, suddenly, and spun the knife into a rat scuttling close to the wall across the alley.

Oh yes, it had been quite a moment.

'I am showing you mercy,' said the Brute. 'Now, you can do the same – if you wish.'

Dumbfounded, Mallakos said, 'What? How?'

The Brute explained that Curtlane lay bound and gagged on a ledge outside a window on the Folly's uppermost floor.

'Rescue him if you want,' the Brute said. 'Leave him, if you prefer. It is up to you.' Then, he stumped over to the slain rodent and tugged out the knife, glancing at the blade, as if checking it was suitably blood-stained.

A ruse of your own, thought Mallakos, brightly. Very good.

The Brute pointed the knife at him. 'You keep this to yourself,' he said. 'If Standaire learns that I have spared you, he'll cut off my balls and roast them like chestnuts.'

Mallakos raised a finger to his lips. 'He shall hear nothing from me.'

The Hawk stared at him a moment. Then he strode away, as heavy as a shire horse, and vanished into the darkness of Sackloth Row.

Mallakos stopped outside Blacker's Folly. Dismounting, he secured the grey mare to a rusted tying post then opened the front door.

Inside, everything lay in moonlit gloom. A thin dusty pall hung in the air and softly, very softly, the Folly creaked, its ill-assembled stones shifting.

Step after ponderous step, Mallakos climbed to the top floor. He still had not decided what to do. He would take a look at Curtlane then make his mind up – assuming it was not already too late. The bewhiskered oaf could have tumbled from the ledge long ago. How long did the Brute say he had been up there? Since the afternoon. Maybe there was no longer any decision to make.

There were two dozen windows in the large circular space, and Mallakos moved from one to the next, shoving them open and peering out. After five or six such attempts, he found Curtlane. The young man lay upon his chest, his wrists and ankles bound together by a tight-buckled leather belt. The posture must have been agonising. Small wonder he looked unwell. Maybe it was the moonlight, but his skin seemed extraordinarily pale. Crumbs of vomit clung to his lips, and he had soiled himself: a few flies buzzed drowsily around his sullied rump.

Strangely, Mallakos felt no glee. No happy tug of vengeful delight.

Is this what it is like to wield power over a stricken creature? he wondered. Until now, I imagined that I would drop my leggings and piss on the appalling little bastard through the window. Yet I simply do not care. How peculiar. How disappointing.

'Ahoy there, Curtlane,' said Mallakos, quietly.

Curtlane jolted, startled. 'Gmff et nt?' he said, the words muffled by the gag.

'Who is it? Well, who in all the world would you least like to see in a building like the Folly? That is, a crumbling, derelict structure which might collapse under the lightest burden?'

Perplexed, Curtlane lay motionless. Then, 'Mphros?'

'The very same. A lovely evening, is it not? The moon is up, the stars are bright – it is enough to make a fat man dance.' Mallakos broke into a lumbering flat-footed jig, stamping his feet as hard as he could. The entire Folly seemed to shake; dust clouds puffed from the walls. On the ledge, Curtlane trembled, fearing the vibrations would crack apart the stone perch on which he lay. Strangled noises – pleas to stop, Mallakos guessed – escaped the gag, and the horse-breeder obliged, his vast, sweat-slick body juddering to a halt.

'Ooh, I am quite out of breath.' He leant on the window sill. 'Give me a moment, will you?'

Curtlane yammered something; although the stifled noises were unintelligible, Mallakos caught their meaning.

'Do not rush me.' Pulling a handkerchief from his pocket, he mopped his brow. In truth, he was not tired. On the contrary, he fizzed with energy of a kind he had never encountered before – a sort of heightened vitality, as if he were not merely alive, but doubly so. He tossed the handkerchief out of the window; it fluttered dove-pale in the moonlight, then drifted down into the street. Observing its descent, Curtlane whimpered.

'Right. Let us get to business,' said Mallakos, briskly. 'Our mutual friend – the big fellow you insulted at the Loop – has asked me to ask you if you want to come back inside . . .'

'Gnef! Gnef a-oo!'

'. . . so, do you?'

'Gnef! Gnuggy gnef!'

'Sorry, I did not catch that . . .'

'Gnef! Gnef! Gnef!'

'No, I still cannot understand. I tell you what: I will ask again, and you grunt once for yes, twice for no.'

'Gnn,' said Curtlane.

'Wait for it,' said Mallakos, cheerfully. He was having fun, he realised. At some point, he had begun to enjoy himself, and now Curtlane's panic shone in his heart like a pretty flower sprouting from a dunghill. 'Do you want to come in? Once for yes, twice for no.'

Curtlane grunted. Once.

'Really? You are actually happy out there? It is your choice, I suppose. Very well. I will be seeing you, Curtlane. Fare thee well!'

He moved away from the window. A frenzy of cloth-muffled protests erupted from outside. Mallakos returned to the window.

'What? No, no, I am quite certain I said once for no, twice for yes. Nonetheless, we shall try again. This time, we will do it your way: once for yes, twice for no. Do you understand?'

'Gnef,' said Curtlane, eyes bulging. His face turned red. Sweat-drops trickled from beneath his side-whiskers.

'So that is a . . . Is it yes? Or a no? I am not sure which system we are using. For the next bit, when I ask if you want to come in, it is once equals yes, twice equals no. But for *this* part, the preliminary question – is it to be the same? Or the other way around? Goodness, this is confusing. For simplicity's

189

sake, I shall leave the choice to you. Which system would *you* prefer to use when answering the question about, uh, the system we will use, ultimately, to determine whether or not you wish to come back inside – or indeed, remain out there, so high above the ground, with those paving stones so far below, which do not look as if they would provide a soft landing, if you were to tumble. No; there is not much bounce in a stone slab. Anyhow, I digress: which system shall it be? One grunt for yes, two for no? Or two for yes, one for no? When answering *this* question, we shall use one for yes, two for no.'

Curtlane grunted, once; though he was clearly unsure exactly what he was grunting *for*. Again, Mallakos feigned confusion – or half-feigned: he had truly lost track of where they were up to – and the cruel charade continued, until it seemed Curtlane might purposefully roll off the ledge just to bring his misery to an end.

'I can see we are getting nowhere,' said Mallakos. 'I blame myself. I have just climbed two flights of stairs and danced a jig – thus, I have grown a touch light-headed. But what does it matter? I am here, you are there, and I will do what I ought to have done as soon as I arrived. Curtlane, prepare to enter the safety of the Folly!'

Leaning through the window, Mallakos grasped in both hands the belt that held the text-seller's wrists and ankles together. He tugged, gently, appraising Curtlane's weight. He was surprisingly heavy for someone so slender.

Letting go, Mallakos pursed his lips. 'I have no wish to panic you, but this may be trickier than I supposed. Truth is, I have not lifted anything heavier than a plate of suckling pig in many a long year. You know, I am starting to think that you are right: I *have* let myself go somewhat. Nonetheless, I will make the best of what I have got. I shall tug and heave until you are inside – unless my heart gives out partway through! What

I am saying, Curtlane, is it will not be a smooth ride. So brace yourself. Now, are you ready?'

Curtlane made a noise simultaneously indicating he was ready, and would never, ever be ready.

'Excellent. Here we go.' Leaning out again, Mallakos seized the belt as he had before – and *pulled*, straining like a thin heifer giving birth to a gigantic foal. Although he could not see it, he knew his face had gone a deep shade of purple; his cheeks and forehead felt as if they were on fire. His eyes swelled from his sockets, his nostrils flared and his jaw locked tight. Groaning with effort, he hauled Curtlane up level with the window. Now came the tricky part: dragging him over the frame. Groans toughening into roars, Mallakos heaved—

—then felt the belt slither free of Curtlane's wrists and ankles. The young man fell but, lurching forward, Mallakos grasped his shirt collar with one hand, his side-whiskers with the other, and yanked him through the window. Stumbling backward, stars swimming in his vision, Mallakos clattered through some easels then fell on his rump.

Curtlane lay on his side, sobbing. Mysteriously, his arms and legs remained behind his back, as if the belt were still in place. Clambering to his feet, Mallakos waddled over, knelt and unfastened the gag.

'Cramp! I've got pissing cramp!' yelled Curtlane. 'Ah, shit, shit, shit!'

'Is that it? Not a word of thanks?'

'I am in agony, you fat f—'

'—unny thing about cramp,' said Mallakos. 'All you want to do is keep still and wait for it to pass. But my physician says one must fight against it.'

Mallakos seized one of Curtlane's arms and manipulated it back and forth at the shoulder, as though operating a water pump. Curtlane yowled, thrashing to be set free.

'Now, now,' said Mallakos, moving on to the other arm. 'You have been marvellously courageous so far. Do not spoil things by squawking like a mouse-frightened woman.'

'Piss off! Just *piss off*!' Wriggling loose, Curtlane half-crawled, half-dragged himself away over the dust-covered floorboards. Following, Mallakos set to work on Curtlane's right leg.

'Hold still,' he urged the text-seller. 'Better by far if we—'

'Damn it!' Curtlane surged to his feet, screamed in pain then fell. 'Stay back,' he warned, raising a fist. 'Any closer and I will . . .'

Will what? wondered Mallakos. He stared keenly at the young man. To his surprise, he saw genuine fear in his eyes. It could have been left over from his time on the ledge, and the less-than-ceremonious fashion Mallakos had brought him inside. But he did not think so. The young man was clearly petrified of something existing in the present moment; and that something was Mallakos himself. Glancing down, he noticed that blood covered his right hand. Olech's, of course. He flexed his fingers, then touched his face, discovering bruises. The Hordelings' handiwork, from when the cart toppled and the vile earwigs swarmed over the Hawks and himself. Incredibly, Mallakos had stayed calm throughout the ordeal. Oh, he had yelled, cursed and lashed out. But that was only natural. What he had not done was degenerate into a gibbering, weeping wreck.

Unlike Curtlane, on the ledge.

He took a sudden step toward the young man. Curtlane recoiled, budging himself up against the wall.

'Stay back,' he repeated. This time, Mallakos recognised the true nature of the words: they were not a warning at all but a plea. He wondered, vaguely, whether Curtlane would ever cease to be himself. Would *he* be transformed by adversity, at some future point, into someone better, brighter, stronger? Would the massive forces of some ordeal turn the turd into a diamond? Who could say. He was still young. There was always hope.

'Would you like me to leave?' Mallakos asked.

'Yes, I would. Sod off back to your pies and truffles, you flabby bastard.'

Mallakos smiled pleasantly. He felt no animosity toward the young man. Not now. His days of striking fear were over; he was a toothless dog, a de-clawed cat. A spider trapped beneath an upturned cup.

'Well then,' said Mallakos. 'I shall do as you bid.' He dug his purse out of his pocket, opened it, then tossed two copper coins to Curtlane. As they landed on his lap, Curtlane winced, as if they were scorpions.

'What are these for?'

'New clothes,' said Mallakos. 'Consider it a farewell gift.'

He gestured to Curtlane's shit-stained leggings.

'Some advice,' he said, half turning away. 'If one loses control of one's bowels at the first whiff of trouble, one might consider dressing in a colour other than white.'

'Aw, piss off you—'

Mallakos stopped listening. Already, he was pissing off, crossing the easel-crowded floor and heading down the steps.

Outside, he untied the mare and clambered into the saddle. Leaving the city by the northern gates, he rode over the silent moon-washed moors. His thoughts drifted eastwards. Horse-breeding aside, how would he live, once he was out there? He had a few ideas. He would commission the construction of a grand house in the airy, white-bricked style favoured in hot countries. Perhaps – or perhaps not – he would call it Dusty Hoof. It would have a large garden, a pond of golden carp and, naturally, a massive and luxurious stable block. He would eat the local foods, reputed to be healthier by far than the fatty, gristly fare found in the average Druinese kitchen. Obviously, he would face certain difficulties: he would need to learn the language and customs of his new homeland. And with his white skin, he would stand out like a scrap of linen on a black silken bed sheet. But so what? He quite fancied being an intriguing novelty.

His mind wandered; he rode on. Soon, his reverie was broken by a voice coming from a deep gouge sunken in the rich moorland earth.

'Clambercrake! Clambercrake!'

Mallakos looked over. A man in a long woollen coat flapped toward him. His grey hair was tangled, his nose broken. In his right hand, a silver hip flask caught the moonlight.

'Clambercrake! Where is my son? Do you have him?'

Heeling the mount into a trot, Mallakos left the man behind. This was not the night for tending to a stranger's woes — particularly if the stranger was drunk, blood-stained and raving about extinct birds. No; it was a night for moving onward, and planning, and simply being alive.

CHAPTER ELEVEN

The Vohorin were not a religious people. A few practised a gentle form of pantheism, but most were agnostic, happy to accept that existence is full of irresolvable mysteries. Of course, in the early days, they forged their own myths and legends, and none is more interesting than that of Toros, the posthumous founder of Vohoria.

In ancient times, Toros was a shaman and tribal leader, revered for his kindness, wisdom and strange abilities, who dwelled in the land that would eventually become Druine. One evening, when the moon shone full and bright, he ate some magical berries and sank into a trance. Leaving his body, his soul entered the Eltheryn Forest – The Realm of Breathing Trees, as it was then known – and remained there, so Toros might study this realm where all is composed not of physical matter, but magic in its rawest form. His purpose was simple: he would learn what he could and, at some later date, return to the mortal world, and use his discoveries to help mankind. Understanding this would take a long time, and his body would not survive, so he etched into the walls of an underground cave a lengthy spell, known as the Origin, which would enable a talented sorcerer to bring him home from the Forest.

Soon after he entered the Forest, he did indeed perish, in body but not soul. In accordance with his instructions, his tribespeople devoured his corpse and bore his bones eastwards, across a strip of land – now lost beneath the sea – into an uninhabited territory in the east. They named their new home Vohoria, and so, a nation was born. It can be said with certainty that every Vohorin who fought, and fell, in the invasion of Druine was a descendant of these settlers. And these settlers themselves belonged to the same stock as we Druinese, for they shared a common land, and were separated from one another only by tribal allegiances. Indeed, there were no physiological differences between the Vohorin and the Druinese. Our skins were the same hue, and we were of equivalent stature . . .

But how our cultures differed! Whilst all but a few Vohorin had forgotten the Toros myth, we still clung – and cling – to the fairytale nonsense spouted by the Pilgrim Church! In essence, they are the same tale; in fact, I would go further, and say the story of the Pilgrims is a bastardised version of the Toros myth. Consider this: in both, a mystical figure or figures enter the Forest for the sake of humanity. But there is a conspicuous difference: Toros intended to help the living, whilst the Four offer assistance only to the dead – and not all the dead, mind you. Their favours are reserved only for the faithful. What manner of philanthropy is that? One utterly in keeping with the Church's presiding principle of 'Do as we say – or suffer the consequences!'

Millennia before Vohoria fell, the Vohorin abandoned their belief in Toros. They had no need of it; the existential tenets enshrined in the tale were well-established in the hearts of the people. Simply, embrace life, and do not fear death. Thus, Vohoria was a wondrous land. Whilst Druine sank, and sinks yet deeper, into decay, Vohoria boasted magnificent architecture, great art and philosophy, and a populace that was truly free.

And we would be free too, if we had accepted our invaders

as liberators. Instead, we cling to the Church like an idiot-child suckling at the teat of its long-dead mother, not realising that what he believes is nourishment is truly a poison.

Extracted from *The Loss* by Cavielle Shaelus

Kneeling on the rug, Quarvis lit the *lecterscrix*. It had been a difficult day for the former Scholar of Outrage. The previous evening, he had used *The Chronicle* for the first time. It had been an exhilarating experience and afterwards, although nauseous and dizzy, he had not felt too bad. But this had been merely the calm before the storm. And what a storm it was! All night he lay in bed, sweating, shivering and vomiting green-tinted bile. Several times, to his shame, he had wondered whether the visions contained in *The Chronicle* were worth it. When dawn came, and hard sunlight speared through the curtains of his sleeping room, he had squirmed like a lobster in a pot of boiling water. His regrets intensified, and he was perversely tempted to abandon the entire enterprise – to leave the house, and Kraike, and forget he had ever heard of Toros. He could start a new life elsewhere, and embrace an existence free of pain and drama . . .

By the afternoon, his spirits revived, and he contemplated his earlier thoughts with complete objectivity. He had done what he always did, when he suffered: unable to cope with the discomfort, he had imagined himself as *someone else* far removed from his current circumstances. He had done the same when he suffered his crisis of faith: no longer able to believe in the Four, and the Church, he had refashioned himself as a distinctly *un*holy man – a drinker, gambler and user of whores. He loathed this cowardly, deluded impulse, this cringing sourness embedded in his character. As the *lecterscrix* began to smoulder, he vowed he would not submit to cowardice again, no matter how ill he felt during the night.

As the green smoke rose, stinking like a sunstruck harbour at low-tide; he opened *The Chronicle* at the second page. Like the first, it was crammed with geometric symbols. He glanced at Kraike, watching from the armchair. Then he inhaled the foul-smelling smoke, drawing it deep into his lungs.

On the page, the shapes rippled . . .

Ten years have passed.

Jurel Kraike has matured into a slender young man, his face so smooth-skinned and sharp-featured it might have been fashioned by the same craftsman who sculpted the nightingales atop the courtyard wall. He is in the courtyard now, garbed in a thick fur-and-leather coat; it is autumn, and Vohoria is sealed in glittering frost. Three iron cages stand before him, each containing a prisoner dragged from the palace dungeons. These men, pale and emaciated, as naked as the day they were born, shiver violently in the cold. Scrubbed clean by servants, they do not even have the usual layer of prison-filth to keep them warm. But they sense this is the least of their worries. They watch Kraike, warily, as he strolls around the cages, a predator circling its prey.

From a second-floor window, Selindak and Grivillus are also watching. Time has treated Grivillus kindly. No longer a frequent drinker of valrux, nor blighted by the headaches created by the poison Selindak mixed into his food, he is strong, healthy and occasionally playful. He spends the mornings hunting, the afternoons dealing with affairs of state. In some respects, he might be considered a good emperor.

'Perhaps you should tell me what our friend is up to,' he says, gazing contentedly into the courtyard. 'You must know; you and he are always talking together.'

'I am sworn to secrecy,' replies Selindak. 'Kraike insists that I explain nothing, so the impact of the demonstration will not be lessened.'

Below, Kraike reaches into a cage and seizes a prisoner's arm. The prisoner recoils, as if Kraike's touch is scalding hot. Kraike's lips move,

198

whisperingly; he lets the man go. Then he leaves the courtyard and enters the palace. When he arrives in the chamber, he is unsteady on his feet, and sweating so badly that when he removes his coat, the cotton clothes beneath cling to his thin body like an extra layer of skin. He flops onto a couch, then lies down, exhausted. Grivillus approaches, baffled, but Selindak lightly places a hand on his forearm.

'Forgive me, my emperor,' *he says,* 'but Kraike must be permitted to rest. He has expended a great deal of energy.'

'What? He merely grabbed a prisoner and spoke a few words—'

'Those words took indescribable effort,' *says Selindak.* 'Trust me. I know what sights await you, and you will not be disappointed.'

'How long must I wait?'

'One hour. Perhaps you would like to do the honours?' *He gestures to an hourglass resting on the window sill.*

'Do them yourself,' *says Grivillus. Although his mood is generally calm nowadays, there are still occasional flashes of temper. The old Grivillus has been tamed, to a degree, but a residue of his old self remains, lingering like bloodstains on the cuffs of a murderer's sleeve.*

As Grivillus departs, Selindak turns the hourglass. The sands flow; settling into a chair, he watches Kraike, already immersed in a restless sleep.

When the sands run low, Selindak summons a servant, intending to send him to fetch Grivillus. But it is not necessary. Before the servant can depart, Grivillus returns of his own accord. A good sign, thinks Selindak. Despite his irritability, the emperor is interested.

'Well?' *he says, moving to the window.* 'I see nothing except that which I saw before – three ragged men, frightened and shivering. At least they have stopped shitting themselves.'

'It will not be long now,' *says Selindak, glancing at the hourglass.* 'Only a few minutes more.' *Gently, he taps Kraike's shoulder. Kraike opens his eyes, then sits up, mumbling. For a moment he is disorientated. Then he joins Grivillus at the window.*

After a time, he taps the glass. 'There. It is starting.'

Selindak hurries over. In the courtyard, the prisoner whose arm Kraike seized is acting strangely. His face is full of horrified wonder, his eyes widening, his lips working noiselessly. From sitting cross-legged, he gets to his feet, then backs up against the side of the cage. Suddenly, his abdominal muscles tense, jamming hard against the hair-fine skin covering his stomach; his mouth stretches open, and he releases a scream as desperate as that of any trapped animal. He collapses against the cage, then slides to the ground. An instant later he is on his feet again, patting furiously at his own body, as if swatting at a legion of invisible insects. Then the patting ends, and the prisoner wipes his hands over his legs, torso and arms, as if brushing something away; his movements are as frantic and clumsy as someone gripped by a seizure. Spittle hangs from his lips, snot pours from his nose, and his cries startle the crows from the tree-tops in the nearby forest.

'Entertaining though it is,' murmurs Grivillus, 'this is hardly impressive. Some poison has clearly been used — cleverly applied, I suppose, when Kraike grabbed the man's arm.'

'There is no poison,' says Selindak, softly.

'Then . . .' Grivillus trails off. A red blemish has appeared on the prisoner's stomach, roughly circular, the size of a dinner plate. It spreads and broadens, flowing up the man's chest to his shoulders, and down to his hips, loins and legs. Thin tendrils of smoke trickle from the inflamed areas, and the man flings himself back against the cage, yowling hoarsely, tufts of smoke floating from his mouth. Covering his face with his hands, he rubs frantically; when his hands are lowered, his eyeballs are gone, the empty sockets charred black. His hair shrivels from his scalp and his scalp steams and blisters; he drops onto his side, writhing; every inch of skin glares red; then it blackens, growing crisp, like a cut of pork left hanging over a cook fire.

'He — burns?' says Grivillus, stupidly quizzical. 'But there are no flames . . .'

'Oh, they are there,' said Selindak. 'But they cannot be seen in the

bright sunlight of this frosty morning. Look, the other men are succumbing.'

It is true: the remaining prisoners are patting and stroking and shrieking in an identical manner to the first. When the spasms cease, all three men are nothing but skeletons wrapped in stiff black meat, jaws hanging open, limbs folded to their chest.

A thin pall of smoke hangs over the courtyard. Gradually, the crows return to the trees; in the sudden silence, their cawing is very loud.

Grivillus stares, absorbing what he has seen. He turns to Kraike. 'What have you done?' he asks, not in a tone of rebuke, but wonderment.

And now comes the hard part, thinks Selindak. It is one thing to cause men to burst aflame buy violating the commonly held laws of nature; quite another to explain it to a man whose intellect is not as sharp as a razor, but as dull as a cushion.

But Kraike manages admirably, speaking in terms simple enough for a child to understand. During his long hours of study, for which Grivillus occasionally mocked him, he has gained an insight into the magical arts, and Grivillus has witnessed the culmination of his labours: a plague spell, capable of spreading swiftly from man to man, which destroys its victims by kindling a fierce heat in their innards. Notice, he says, that I cast the spell only upon the first prisoner. It was he who spread it to his fellows, by the mere fact of his close proximity.

Grivillus is delighted; he declares that the spell will enable Vohoria to conquer the globe. Who could fight back against such an inexorable and mysterious weapon? But Kraike says the spell is too dangerous to be unleashed indiscriminately, for it can slay Vohorin just as easily as the enemies of Vohoria. However, in Druine there is a source of power, the Origin, which will allow him to refine the spell to such a degree its effects can be contained, and only its chosen targets destroyed. We need only use the spell to conquer Druine, he says. Once *the Origin has been used, and the spell refined, the true conquests can begin . . .*

Quarvis surfaced, briefly, then was plunged back into the whirling shapes.

Six months have passed.

A swarm of Vohorin warships float at anchor, resting as still as stones on the night-darkened waters off the south-eastern coast of Druine. They arrived at dawn, gliding through the curling mist, each a black shadow, creaking softly. Once they had ventured as close to the coast as they dared, the Vohorin battalions disembarked, some ten thousand men splashing through the shallows onto the beach. As they scrambled up the sand dunes, their white armour gleaming in the grey, drizzle-streaked light, they resembled a horde of crabs, venturing inland to overwhelm some stricken creature.

The Tide Watchers, the Druinese defenders of the coast, were caught off-guard. Because of the mist, they had not seen the ships until it was too late. By the time they had taken up arms the Vohorin were upon them, hacking, slashing, cleaving; swords sang, battleaxes crunched, arrows murmured.

It was a beautiful sight, Selindak had thought, watching from the emperor's ship, a telescope raised to his eye. There was no shade of red as vivid as that of Druinese blood splashed upon white Vohorin armour. No music that pleased the heart like a Vohorin battle cry and no painting that stirred the soul like the sight of so many Vohorin slaying so many Druinese. Of course, the Druinese were not the Vohorins' natural enemy. Far from it: they were the same race, the same bloodline.

As he watched the battle, Selindak thought, *Those men are possibly killing their own distant relatives.*

Now, Selindak sits on a small stool in the hold of the emperor's warship. The low-ceilinged, candle-lit space has been converted into a *torture chamber. In the centre of the floor, there are two long benches. A Druinese prisoner of war lies on each of them, restrained by thick leather straps. The walls glitter with the apparatus of interrogation: hanging from tiny pegs there are scalpels, the blades of varying lengths and shapes, some hooked, some curved like a boar's tusk, others perfectly straight, their sharpened edges glinting. Implements as crude as carpentry tools rest on a table. Gristle-crunchers, bone-splitters, hammers, mallets, spikes, pliers and copper tubes slender enough to slip down a man's throat, so boiling water can be poured directly into his stomach. On a shelf there are jars of poisons. Some cause indescribable pain; others, hallucinations so alarmingly vivid reality itself seems like a vague dream. In the months preceding the invasion, Kraike studied the art of torture. In a specially prepared dungeon, he practised on prisoners drawn from the same jail as the three men on whom he demonstrated the plague spell. His companion in all things, Selindak attended these sessions, observing that Kraike did not take pleasure in causing distress. But nor was he harrowed by it. Simply, he was neutral, as coldly analytical as a mathematician solving a complex equation. And this was disturbing: Kraike had a gift for treating living, suffering creatures purely as a means to an end. For a time, Selindak had been troubled. Then he realised that Kraike's dispassionate approach was the correct one: the ends were worthy of the means, no matter how monstrous they were.*

The first Druinese prisoner has already experienced Kraike's gift for torture. His naked flesh, moon-pale, gleams with blood. His eyeballs are missing, his jaw crushed; his legs have been flayed and the skin pulled over his feet, where it trails to the ground like a pair of half-removed leggings. His stomach has been sliced open, his intestines heaped upon his chest; incredibly, this did not kill him: as Kraike once explained, a good interrogator keeps his subjects alive for as long as possible. So he suffered further agonies, his fingers crushed, his shoulders wrenched from their sockets. Eventually, he expired, the violated mechanism of his body shuddering to a stop.

During the torture, in fluent Druinese, Kraike questioned the prisoner. But he learned nothing of true significance. Nor did he want to: the interrogation was not intended to acquire information but terrify the second, as-yet-unharmed prisoner on the neighbouring bench.

It worked marvellously well. This prisoner mewled, wept, sobbed and cursed as he heard his countryman's cries. He strained against the straps securing him to the bench; he trembled savagely. Now, he seems to have sunk into a type of terrified stasis. He lies there, barely moving, gaze fixed on the ceiling. When Kraike approaches, scalpel in hand, the prisoner tenses; when Kraike presses his fingertips against his belly, the prisoner groans.

'No, no, please . . .'

Kraike's lips move; he whispers a few soft words in a language neither Vohorin nor Druinese. Then he withdraws his fingers. As if he has had a better idea, he returns the scalpel to a wall peg. Then he returns to the prisoner. Leaning close, hands braced on the bench edge, he says, 'I am weary. But once I have slept, I shall return. I suggest you contemplate your circumstances. When the sun rises, you must decide.'

'D-decide what?'

Ignoring him, Kraike leaves the hold. Rising from the stool, Selindak follows, crossing the blood-splashed floor planks and climbing the steps through a trapdoor onto the deck.

The sky is clear, the stars and moon bright. Except for the gentle creaking of the ships, there is silence. Selindak follows Kraike along the deck to the prow. Grivillus is waiting; wordlessly, the emperor turns an hourglass resting on the bulwark.

They wait.

After a time, there is movement back along the deck. The trapdoor leading to the hold cracks open, there is a pause then the second prisoner climbs through. He runs to the ship's side and flings himself over into the sea.

Selindak feels a pang of relief. He was uncertain if the simplest part of the ruse would work: when Kraike leant close to the prisoner, telling him he must decide, he had loosened the buckle on the strap around the frightened man's wrist. With one hand free, the prisoner had been able to undo the other straps and make his escape. They had taken the idea from an old Vohorin conjuring trick; it was so laughably crude, and so strongly associated with vulgar entertainment, it seemed implausible that it should have a place in warfare.

The prisoner swims ashore, reaching the beach a safe distance from the Vohorin camp. Then he is away, scrambling through the dunes, vanishing onto the grassland beyond.

Bending, Selindak picks up a telescope from the deck and raises it to his eye. He can see the prisoner, sprinting the dark mile to the Druinese camp.

'He will have such a tale to tell,' Selindak murmurs.

Again, they wait. Then, just before the final sand grains fall, a scream rings out from the enemy camp. A small blot of fire pierces the darkness, visible even without the telescope. It sways back and forth, lurching and twisting, then drops to the ground like a tiny comet. Its light fades. Surprised, appalled shouts drift from the camp.

Once more, they wait.

Casting the plague spell is a perilous business, Selindak knows. For the first half-hour, it lies dormant in the victim's body; it cannot be spread. After that, however, it is fantastically contagious. By now, every man in the Druinese camp ought to be infected, the malady speeding from one to the next as swiftly as a flying arrow. If the prisoner had not escaped the hold by the twenty-fifth minute – Kraike can read an hourglass with near-unnatural precision – he would have been killed where he lay and his corpse dumped overboard. If he had blundered too close to the Vohorin soldiers on the beach, he would have been pierced by fifty blazing crossbow quarrels.

Selindak watches the Druinese encampment. There is a sudden blossoming of orange-yellow light so bright it casts a haze into the night sky. Thousands of men scream, their yells blending into a single, almost orchestral cacophony. The grasslands are a single fireball, surging, billowing; tiny sparks scatter through the darkness . . .

Striding over, Grivillus snatches the telescope from Selindak. Lifts it, looks.

His expression is that of a child seeing snow falling for the first time.

And the look of wonderment is there the following morning, as the emperor, Selindak and Kraike wander through the Druinese encampment. On all sides the black-fleshed dead lie on the grass, glistening under a cool layer of dew – several thousand husks, clench-jawed and eyeless, as brittle as month-old fly carcasses snagged on a spider web.

Grivillus's emotions are simplistic: he is delighted by the plague spell's potency, and feels in a vague way that Druine has already fallen. Kraike is subtler: he feels only a type of bloodless satisfaction: the spell works, all is as it should be.

For his part, Selindak is curious. What was it like for those who died? Those poor doomed men, plunged into a bewildering cauldron of fire? Fire erupting from themselves?

Crows pick at the corpses. Flies swirl and dip.

'The Origin will grant you powers greater than this?' It is Grivillus who speaks. His voice is soft.

'Yes, my emperor,' replies Kraike.

'Very good.' Grivillus nudges a charred corpse with his boot. 'Very good indeed. I trust that we are to continue in the same fashion? Kidnap an enemy soldier, infect him, then permit him to escape to his fellows?'

'Yes,' says Kraike.

'There is beauty in something so simple,' the emperor muses. He wipes ash from his boot onto the wet grass. He sniffs, glances at the sky. 'Let us march on, and play our clever trick again and again, until our work is done.'

*   *   *

The shapes grew still; surfacing, Quarvis found himself back in the room. Rising, he carried the bowl of *lecterscrix* to the window.

'You lied to the emperor,' he said, tipping the embers into the garden. 'About the Origin's purpose, I mean. I assume Grivillus would not have approved of your desire to resurrect Toros?'

'Neither approved nor understood,' murmured Kraike. 'Toros – at the time – was largely forgotten. Grivillus knew nothing of the visionary and if I had told him, he would not have believed me. A nonsense story, he would have said. A vulgar myth. If he *had* believed, however, the invasion would have never gone ahead, and Selindak and I would have been executed.'

'For what crime?'

'Treason,' replied Kraike. 'Dissent. Rebellion – the exact charge would not matter. Grivillus would have considered Toros to be a rival, therefore an enemy; thus Selindak and I would be deemed conspirators. You must remember, the emperor inherited his title when he was fifteen years old. He had grown to consider Vohoria to be his property, his plaything. He would have tolerated no rival. So we deceived him. Our plan was to conquer Druine, find the Origin and use it; then we would slip away, back to Vohoria, where Toros's bones are hidden. The resurrection would occur and Grivillus . . . for him, all would be lost.'

Something occurred to Quarvis. 'You said Toros had largely been forgotten *at the time*.'

Kraike looked at him, waited a moment, then nodded. 'After the Scourge, when we fled into the desert, there was a renewal of faith.'

'Toros is worshipped again?'

'By some,' said Kraike.

Quarvis tingled with delight; he had not expected this. 'You must tell me more,' he said, moving from the window.

'On the morrow, perhaps,' said Kraike. 'Once you have used *The Chronicle* for the final time, we will speak further. It will be, I think, an enlightening evening.'

CHAPTER TWELVE

The Hawks walked across open moorland. Overhead, the sky was ferociously blue, the sun blazing as if to incinerate the globe. Dark flies skirled out of the long grasses, heat-dazed, lethargic; stonechats snicked drowsily in the distance, and the air shimmered, as if seen through wet glass. By Ballas's reckoning, this was the hottest day of the year so far.

Yet, two hundred yards away, there was mist.

In the potters' workshop, Olech had mentioned mist. Ballas found it strange that he should speak of such a small detail, whilst on his deathbed. Now he understood. Lying on low ground, at the bottom of a steep slope, the village was smothered in sea-fret so abnormally thick a man could drown in it. The white vapours covered it like a gently rippling linen shroud, thinning occasionally to give a hint of some solid structure – a cottage roof, a bell tower – then thickening again, returning to its natural, and strangely *un*natural state.

Gulls cawed over the unseen ocean. Ballas licked his lips, tasting salt.

'Whitelock,' said Ekkerlin, thoughtfully.

Ballas grunted. 'What?'

'As the village does not appear on any map, we may call it whatever we like. I propose Whitelock, after the village in the old folk tale, that was overrun by moon-pale phantoms,' explained Ekkerlin. 'I imagine that if such a place existed, it would look something like this. And our Whitelock is a lost village, just like the one in the story.'

'A lost village?' Ballas looked closely at Ekkerlin. It had taken her two days to recover from the hothead venom. She had lain in a narrow bed in a room above a tavern, sweating, groaning and shivering; she had vomited copiously, and when she slept, she always awoke suddenly, roused by some nightmare that had her trembling like a sycamore leaf. It had not been easy; she resembled nothing so much as a drunk surfacing from a month-long binge. Now, she was back to normal, more or less. Certainly, she had lost a little weight, and she was fractionally less talkative than before. But an ordeal of the kind she had suffered was bound to take its toll. Sometimes, Ballas thought he could still hear her screaming through the walls of the cell.

'An abandoned settlement,' said Ekkerlin. 'Sometimes, the inhabitants move away because the things they rely upon to sustain them have gone. The sea no longer yields fish; the soil has grown barren; the specific reasons vary, of course. Other times, though, they are wiped out by plague, and the entire place sinks into silence.' Drawing a breath, she squinted into the mist. 'I suspect Whitelock was forsaken for a different reason. Simply, the mist appeared, and the villagers faced a choice: stay and grow mad, or leave and stay sane. No one could dwell there for long without losing their wits. As a species, we require daylight and, just as importantly, we must be able to see the horizon. Without either, we grow unstable, disorientated. The world stops making sense.'

They walked on, halting when the mist grew so thick they could barely see one another.

'We shall go in separately,' said Standaire, whispering. 'Look around; see what you can discover. Return to this spot in a half-hour.'

*   *   *

210

As soon as he entered the mist, Ballas grew uneasy.

Often, a Hawk's survival depended on the clarity of his senses; danger frequently presented itself in subtle ways – sounds captured at the very edge of hearing, an incongruity glimpsed in the corner of the eye, a faint scent floating somewhere it ought not to be found – yet the mist obliterated everything except itself.

Ballas's vision shrank to a few feet in any direction, and what he did see was always dark, ambiguous, the vaguest hint of something solid. Every external noise was muffled, deadened by the sea-fret yet, at the same time, every internal sound – Ballas's breathing, his beating heart – was absurdly loud, so much so they could have frightened the birds from the rooftops, had there been any. Pressing on, he slowly gained an impression of the village. Most of the buildings were half-derelict cottages, the roof-thatch tumbling loose in soggy clumps, the sills, eaves and doors rotting. Underfoot, the ground was wet mud, putting forth thin grey weeds which drooped listlessly, leaves and stems sagging under their own weight.

Despite the slow-tumbling motion of the mist, the air seemed still – a breath trapped in the throat of some gigantic animal. Once, Ekkerlin had spoken of foreign religions who believed the afterlife was not a realm of torment but boredom; the landscapes were bleached of colour, no plants grew nor flowers bloomed, and time was locked in a single unending moment. These were hells worth fearing, decided Ballas. They were enough to drive a sceptic to prayer.

Halting at a cottage, he peered through a front window, seeing a plain room, furnished with two simple chairs and a table. The floorboards were bare, the walls blotched with dark mould, the ceiling-corners strung with cobwebs. No one had dwelled there for a long time, it seemed. Muttering, Ballas moved along to the next cottage; again, the building was untenanted. He did this over and over until, on his fifth attempt, he found himself gazing into a room showing signs of habitation. For certain, it was no palace: as with the earlier cottages, mould crawled over the walls and the furnishings were monastically spare. But a heap of blankets rested on the floor, along with a sweat-browned pillow, and a plate rested on a table, laden with a half-eaten meal that looked reasonably fresh.

Not wishing to be seen by the occupant, if he was present, Ballas drew back from the window. At the same instant, footsteps scuffed along the lane, the noise mist-choked and dull. Swiftly, Ballas ducked into the gap between the cottage and its neighbour and waited. As the footsteps drew close, their owner coughed, a hoarse, soggy bark, arising from lungs that might themselves have been corrupted by the black mould. Tensing, Ballas drew his knife, but the footsteps halted, abruptly, and the cottage door opened then closed. Another cough came from within, then there was silence.

Sheathing the knife, Ballas moved on.

For a while, he wandered, musing that Ekkerlin had been completely correct: a fellow could easily lose his wits in the skyless, horizonless village, where the greyish white light seemed to emerge not from the sun, but from the mist itself, like the pale luminescence of decaying shellfish in a darkened cellar. Although he recognised it was juvenile, Ballas could not shake off the feeling that the mist was in some inarticulable sense *alive*, that it was a formless, engulfing entity of the kind found in fever dreams which, by inexplicable means, had gained a presence in the real world.

Who would willingly dwell in Whitelock? he wondered – but it was not a difficult question to answer: it was a good home for anyone who craved secrecy, who wished to conduct their business away from prying eyes. But this could not be the only reason. A text-trader could be discreet, even in a busy city. As far as Ballas could see, there was no advantage to imprisoning Helligraine here, when he could easily be locked up in an attic, or a cellar, for an indefinite period. No. There had to be another reason why Whitelock had been chosen — and whatever it was, it was important, for no one would reside in this Four-forsaken, sanity-scouring nowhere land unless it was necessary.

Contemplating this, Ballas walked on until he encountered another cottage, the windows boarded over, the door hanging an inch or two ajar. Warily, he peered through — and grunted with surprise, his eyebrows lifting, then falling and locking in a frown. He stood motionless, listening for footsteps in the mist; hearing none, he stepped into the cottage.

The cottage had been converted into an armoury. Swords, knives and morning stars rested in several oaken racks, all polished to a shine, their blades whetted sharp enough to slice through granite. Battleaxes were propped against the walls whilst thickets of bows, long and short, bristled in the corners alongside tables laden with red-fletched arrows. There was enough weaponry to arm a small militia and when Ballas chose a short-sword at random, sliding it out of the rack and swinging it from side to side, testing its heft, he found it was a killing tool of excellent quality. Any soldier would be pleased to possess such a weapon; returning it to the rack, he picked up a battle-axe, discovered that it too was of the highest order. Setting it back against the wall, he wondered what purpose the armoury served. Were the weapons intended to defend Whitelock's occupants against intruders? Against Wardens and the like? If this were so, why were they stashed away, where they could do no good, rather than residing in the occupants' hands, ready for use at a moment's notice? Maybe these were not the only weapons in Whitelock; maybe the occupants *were* armed, and this horde was surplus to requirements? But there was a chance the weapons had been collected for aggression rather than self-defence. Aggression against whom? Olech? Were the Whitelockians planning to attack Sliptere, marching into the city like the invaders of some foreign land, and slay the gambling-house owner and his Peacekeepers? It was a pleasing idea, but deeply improbable. If the Whitelockians *did* crave a secret existence, they would not embark on any such ventures, guaranteed to catch the Church's attention.

Brooding on this riddle, Ballas left the armoury and wandered, and without realising it, he drifted in the direction of the sea, halting abruptly when he heard the crunching roll and tumble of waves crashing onto a shale-strewn beach. He looked around, then paced to a large bulky structure, crouching darkly in the mist. A boatshed, he realised. Inching warily to the glass, he looked inside, his gaze alighting on a printing press in the centre of the room. A long table-like structure, similar in appearance to a wine-press, it was a relatively new invention. These devices excited Ekkerlin enormously; she believed they would revolutionise the transmission of knowledge. Handwritten parchments were expensive and few citizens could afford books, thus folk were generally ignorant, and relied solely on priests and Church-sanctioned schools for their understanding of the world. This would change, Ekkerlin believed. Although expensive to purchase, printing presses could produce documents cheaply, and quickly – operating one of the ingenious contraptions, a man could match the day's labours of a dozen quill-wielding copyists in mere minutes. They were excellent news for folk like Ekkerlin, who wanted every man, woman and child to cram their heads with interesting, stimulating material; likewise, they were a great asset for the makers of forbidden texts. Only the Church and its scribes opposed them, decrying them as their fiercest adversary in the ever-raging war against sinful thought.

Around the boatshed, tables were set against the wall, laden with parchments stitched together by red thread, whilst a stack of wooden crates loomed in a corner. Moving to the front of the building, Ballas tested the door and, finding it unlocked, stepped inside. He experienced a brief flash of disorientation: the boatshed felt *strange* in a way he could not put his finger on. After a few moments of mild confusion, he understood: with the doors closed and windows sealed, the interior was completely empty of mist, and he felt as if he had slipped into a world within a world or, in a peculiar fashion, risen from a pool of cloudy white water into grey daylight. Already, tatters of mist floated over the threshold, creeping like some sluggish vaporous mould. Shutting the door, Ballas moved to the table heaped with red-stitched books. Straight away, he saw they were forbidden texts: their titles alone screamed their profane, heretical nature.

Jumping at Shadows – Why Men Fear the Non-Existent Menaces of Gods, Demons and Eldritch Entities of Every Complexion.

Pig and Troughs – An Inquiry into the Ceaseless Greed and Avarice of the Blessed Masters.

Let the Forest Be Thy Guide – A Proposal for Adopting in this World the Morality of the Demons Who Frequent the Next.

Opening *Let the Forest* at a random page, Ballas read:

. . . and our ethics are those of low creatures – the earthworm, grub and insect, whose lives are short, unhappy and bereft of value. A demon of the Forest exists in an infinitely more nourishing state. It does not cower in fear, but recognises it is the master of its own destiny, and the destinies of others . . .

Ballas stopped reading; he had seen everything he required: the text bore the same typographical imperfections as Mallakos's

copy of *The Loss*, the capital A lacking its top, the lower case
y missing its curling tail. If the theory was right, and slave-
scribes were imprisoned close to the presses that printed their
work, the implications were clear: Helligraine was somewhere
in the village. The Hawks had only to rescue him, and that
was it: the mission was over, except for a ride to Prendle House,
the home of Leptus Quarvis.

Ballas moved to the door – then froze.

He heard voices in the mist, approaching the boatshed.
Cursing, he sought a hiding place. There was only one possibility. Striding over, he slipped behind the stack of crates and
crouched, sinking as low as he could, his bruised muscles and
battered bones aching. Breathing heavily, heart thumping, he
waited.

The door opened, revealing two figures, one short and plump,
the other as tall and thin as a garden rake. As they entered
their features gained clarity in the clear air. The plump one
wore an eye patch cut from sackcloth, and beads of moisture
trickled over his bald, liver-spotted scalp. The other sported a
thin grey moustache, drooping over a slender mouth quirked
in a permanent smile. He was the first to speak.

'What does it matter to *you*, Skrulien? You never bothered
to learn your letters. You could not read any of this stuff,' he
flapped a hand toward the book-covered tables, 'if your life
depended on it. You're as ignorant as a month-old pig turd.'
He spoke good-naturedly, and one-eyed Skrulien did not seem
offended.

'All I am saying,' said Skrulien, shutting the door, 'is that
we spend all our time printing horseshit. Sometimes, it makes
me feel no better than some holy blowhard, spouting nonsense
to a churchful of imbeciles.'

'You're saying we're akin to priests?'

'More or less,' said Skrulien. 'The way I see it, them who

read our books are not too different from the dullards who fill up the pews during a religious service. Both will gobble up any old dross, won't they? They're like baby sparrows in their nests, beaks cracked fully open, waiting to be fed.' The moustached man frowned, perplexed, and Skrulien elaborated, 'They eat their mother bird's vomit. Have you never seen it?'

'I was raised in a city,' replied the moustached man, moving to the printing press. He squinted at a tray of iron letters, running his fingertips over them, checking they were in order. 'I had better ways to entertain myself than watching birds fly, fish swim and donkeys mate. Fetch the ink, will you?'

Skrulien took a wooden flask from the end of the table. Tugging out the stopper, he emptied it into a deep rectangular dish, the dark fluid glooping, tiny splashes spattering the floorboards.

'Maybe it is all horseshit,' said the moustached man, tapping the lettering, 'but it is a horseshit made of gold, aye? We won't topple the Church if we're armed with pitchforks and homemade spears.'

'We've got weapons enough,' said Skrulien. 'Or haven't you noticed?'

The moustached man's shoulders slumped, as if this was old ground he was tired of treading. Nonetheless, the smile lingered, hovering like a dragonfly over a millpond. 'We are not the only ones fighting this war,' he said. 'You *know* that, Skrulien. We're merely a single unit in the greater army. Some of the weapons are ours, aye, but the others are destined for our compatriots' hands. When the time comes, we'll send them to those who need them, and then . . .' The smile twitched, curling fractionally upwards at the edges. 'Then the Scarlet Twilight will settle upon Druine, and the streets will foam with the blood of holy men, and our bellies shall slosh with sacred wine, plundered, imbibed and grown merry upon.' He uttered this

217

with a grandiose flourish, as if he *was* a pulpit-bound priest intoning some pious truth. Chuckling, he tapped Skrulien's wrist. 'It will not be long now,' he said, gently. 'Not long at all, according to the Dogman. As we speak, he will be parleying with Cal'Briden, arranging the final details, setting the date, the hour . . .'

Behind the crates, Ballas jolted, recognising the name Cal'Briden. It took a moment or two to place it precisely, to fully grasp its significance, but the details swam sluggishly into his consciousness and he recalled that Cal'Briden, a fantastically wealthy former silk- and spice-merchant, had been quietly sowing seeds of dissent against the Masters for several years. An enigmatic figure, no one knew where his enmity arose from some private grudge, or he had a philosophical antipathy toward the Church. Nor was it known where it would take him – whether he was happy to remain an angry voice, grizzling and snarling in the wilderness, or whether he would incite an actual revolution. Now, it seemed this mystery was solved.

Sceptically, Skrulien said, 'You reckon so?'

Dipping a thick-bristled paintbrush into the ink tray, then sweeping it back and forth over the lettering, the moustached man said, 'You do not?'

Skrulien huffed, rolling his shoulders. 'Ha! "Any day now, it will not be long, brace yourselves my boys, for the storm is soon to break" – the Dogman makes such promises over and over, yet we never budge an inch outside this damned village. We buy weapons, honing the blades and buffing the steel until they gleam as bright as bloody stars – but do we ever get to use them? Nah. We just skulk about this place, bored out of our skulls, and then, when we grow disillusioned, the outsized bastard dares to question our dedication! You've heard him, haven't you, when one of us asks when, exactly, the Scarlet

Twilight will fall. He blows up like a bloody volcano.' Skrulien clenched his fists. A scowl tightened his face. 'Are you ever tempted to up and leave?' he asked, suddenly. 'To say "To the Forest with it all" and go?'

'Never,' said the moustached man, dipping the brush in the ink tray again.

'Then you have the patience of saint.'

'Or the good sense of a fox,' said the moustached man, applying ink to the lettering. Even though he pursed his lips in concentration, the smile remained. 'When it is in danger, a fox goes to ground. It is the only way of avoiding the hunts-man's dogs. What I am saying,' he lay down the brush, 'is that, like the fox, we must remain inconspicuous. What do you think would happen if you were to leave? Do you think the Dogman would let you go on your way? Or would he let fly those bloody dogs of his?'

'There are ways of avoiding hunting dogs,' said Skrulien, uncertainly. 'If you had a head start, and bathed in a tarn, even a muddy pool, the bastards would not be able to find your scent—'

'Such tricks might work with Druinese dogs, I suppose. But the Dogman's foreign beasts? Would you want to take the chance?'

'Enough,' said Skrulien, uneasily. 'You know that I do not like to *think* about the creatures, let alone talk of them. When is the Dogman getting back?'

'This evening, or the morrow's morn,' said the moustached man, casting about for something. He sighed, then grew concil-iatory. 'My friend, I genuinely believe the Twilight is not far away. The Dogman is no fool. He knows there will come a time when our restlessness will grow too strong and, dogs or not, we will desert him. Then where would he be? Without us, his men-at-arms, he is no use to Cal'Briden. If we went, the merchant would cast him aside like a bolt of rotten silk. What use is a general without his soldiers? Whether he likes to admit it or not, the Dogman needs us.'

Skrulien fingered his eye patch then nodded, heartened by his friend's words. 'I've never looked at it that way before.'

'You never look at anything that way,' commented the moustached man. 'With clarity, logic and reason, I mean. Like the Dogman's dogs, you consist of base impulses, nothing more. Now, bring me some parchments.' He patted the machine. 'We have got work to do. If we do not get this batch printed by the time the Dogman returns, he'll throw a tantrum.'

'He's like a big bloody baby, isn't he?' grinned Skrulien. 'What are we rolling out this time, anyway?' Turning away, he stumped toward the crates behind which Ballas was hiding. The Hawk knew that in a heartbeat or two, he would be discovered and, if he was honest, he was glad. Certainly, it would complicate the mission, but his knees, thighs and back were aching abominably, and he wanted nothing more than to rise and stretch his muscles.

'Some tripe about summoning demons to make yourself immortal,' said the moustached man, squinting at the lettering. 'According to this, they can make you impervious to every physical threat encountered in the mortal world.'

Skrulien took a crate from the top of the stack, clutched it against his chest then stepped back, gaze alighting on Ballas.

'Reckon you better get summoning,' said the Hawk, drawing back his fist.

Ekkerlin watched Standaire and Ballas vanish into the mist. She did not follow, but lingered, thinking.

She had suffered horribly in the gambling house. The hothead venom was a peculiarly savage form of truth serum, attacking both body and mind at once. She felt as if a thousand red-hot needles had pierced her body, sizzling through flesh, muscle and bone. And she had suffered ghastly hallucinations, of three varieties – a monstrous triptych.

First, she was in Soriterath, standing before the Penance Oak. Here, the severed heads of convicted magic-workers were nailed to the branches, and they sang to her, their jaws swinging jerkily up and down as if tugged by wires, their eyes rolling in delight. Their song was abrasively discordant, obeying neither the laws of harmony nor melody, and hypnotically repetitive; of the song's words, she recalled nothing. Not that it mattered. She doubted they would make sense. After all, the entire scene was absurd. How could the heads sing, without lungs to push air through their vocal chords? How could their mouths and eyes move, when their brains were as dead as clay? Nonetheless, the scene was horrifying, partly due to a secondary effect of the venom: it had cranked up Ekkerlin's emotions to an unbearable pitch. If she had encountered the singing heads in real life, she would have mastered her fear. She might even have been calm enough to study them, to work out exactly how they functioned. Not so in the hallucination. She had been overwhelmed, like an arachnophobe upon spotting a spider. Every sliver of cool-headedness, restraint and rationality had fled, driven out by pure fear.

The second phase was equally distressing. She was trapped in the Eltheryn Forest. Demons attacked from all sides, tearing flesh from her bones, ripping her tongue from her mouth, her eyes from their sockets. When she ran, she tripped over her own entrails; when she screamed, nothing emerged save an outrageously huge blood-bubble, swelling from her lips like a glossy scarlet balloon. According to myth, the Forest languished in eternal night. Yet here the sun shone, and a clear blue sky stretched over the tree-tops. Strange, yes – but not unusually so for a hallucination.

The final vision was the standard material of nightmares. She raced along endless white corridors, fleeing a presence – or presences – she could neither see nor hear. Now and again she glanced back and maybe – *maybe* – she glimpsed her pursuer but if she had, she could not remember the form it had taken.

Throughout, Olech's voice had whispered questions in her ear.

Why are you seeking the origin of The Loss*? Who sent you? Who pays your wages?*

She knew that her ordeal would end if she answered. Yet she resisted. Twice, she suffered the venom; twice, she stayed silent.

Why? Where had she found the strength? Was it pure stubbornness? Loyalty to the Hawks? An understanding of the mission's importance? Or something as crude as her dislike for Olech? She did not know. She employed various tactics to overcome the venom. She had tried – vainly – to take her mind elsewhere, to ponder philosophical problems. She had repeated to herself that the torment would pass, if she were patient. She even attempted to take an interest in the hallucinations, to treat them as objects of curiosity. Nothing worked.

But she had endured. Precisely how was a mystery.

Drawing a breath, she entered the mist. A grassy slope led down into the village. She walked slowly amongst the cottages, the mist enfolding her like a sheet of gauze.

She could remember nothing about the hours after the gambling house. The escape, the trouble on Sackcloth Row – all were a blank. She regained consciousness in a boxy room above a tavern, where Standaire and Ballas supervised her recovery. Ballas recounted Olech's demise, imagining it would lift her spirits; it had not. She did not bear grudges, no matter how badly she had been wronged. What was the point in rejoicing over Olech's death, when he was significant only as far as he related to the mission? Beyond that, he meant nothing to her. But then, she suspected the gambling-house owner was – had been – inclined to feuds, battles and petty vengeances. What if he had lied to Ballas in the workshop? What if his spirit had not been broken by the knife wound, and repeated roastings in the kiln, and he had decided his last act should be one of defiance? What if he had lied about Whitelock? Certainly, the village seemed uninhabited . . .

Suddenly, a vile stench touched her nostrils. Sweat, fur and something else. Corruption, she realised. A raw wound left untreated. It seemed to emerge from a dark, low building to her right. A stable, adjoining a tavern. Approaching, she cracked open the upper half of the door and peered inside.

Through mist-laced gloom, she saw what appeared to be a heap of old furs, slung in the corner to rot. As her eyes adjusted, she realised she was mistaken. It was a dog, as large as a young horse, sleeping with its huge shaggy head resting between its forepaws, saliva dripping from the gigantic fangs jutting from its lower jaw, its flanks stretching and shrinking with every breath that half rasped, half whistled from its cavernous chest. Its eyes were closed, its muscles slack, but its tail, as thick as a mooring rope, twitched, and occasionally swept from side to side. The creature was not only very big but very old. Its fur grew in scraggly clumps, and there were bald patches of pale mottled skin, as unwholesome as the flesh of a poisonous toad-stool. The dog's slumber was deeper than ordinary sleep; it spoke of exhaustion, of the inescapable weight of an excessively long life. Ekkerlin stared, mesmerised, until the dog snuffled, and its slitted eyes cracked open. Withdrawing, she shut the door silently.

A dog of such size was impossible, she thought, then realised her error. Such beasts were rare, but they *did* exist. A century ago, a dog-breeder in the Distant East had created hunting hounds of such improbable size he was accused of sorcery. She doubted magic had played any part, and the animals were engendered by nothing more sinister than careful interbreeding. The man – his name was Crava, she recalled – was beheaded, his remains burned on a pyre along with those of his dogs.

Something occurred to Ekkerlin. Olech had referred to *The Loss*'s supplier as the Dogman; when talking to Ballas, he'd said he had glimpsed a dog similar to the one in the stable. Chances were it was the same animal and, as those who were fond of dogs preferred to keep them close by, it was possible the Dogman himself dwelled in the tavern next door.

Moving to the tavern, Ekkerlin looked through a window. She saw a common room, stripped of tables, settles and chairs, empty except for a green divan, a stack of parchments and an ornamental vase in the Eastern style, from which protruded a rolled-up scroll. Warily, she tested the door handle: unlocked. Opening the door as quietly as she could, she stuck her head inside, listening. She heard nothing. She sniffed, noticing the air was stale, indicating the building had not been occupied for days, even weeks. Crossing the threshold, she closed the door then went straight to the parchments. Handwritten, the script cramped yet flowing, the uppermost page was entitled, *A Treatise of Predatory Virtue: How the Church Enforces Goodness by Means of Shame and Guilt – by Cavielle Shaelus.*

'Blood and sand,' whispered Ekkerlin. The document had been written recently: the title was new enough to be unfamiliar to Ekkerlin, who had read all Shaelus's older works, and the ink lay dark and fresh upon the page. She leafed through the rest of the stack, encountering page after page of the neat, tiny handwriting. Several other titles flashed across her vision. *The Metastasis of Belief*; *The Obscene and Needless Hardship Endured by Penitents*; *Incense and Sceptres: Warfare and the Church* . . .

And finally, *The Loss.*

Ekkerlin straightened. Was Helligraine here, in the tavern? Silently, she crept up the stairs to the second floor, where she found three rooms, all empty. Returning to the common room, she went to the door, preparing to leave, satisfied she had found at least a small sign that Helligraine was – or had been – in the village. Then she remembered the scroll sticking out of the vase. Kneeling, she took the vase in her hands, removed the scroll and unfurled it. It was a letter, written in Frivilis, one of the many languages found in the Distant East.

My esteemed friend,

I am so glad you and I have come to an agreement. I cannot say I find our bargain entirely pleasing, for I am a rich man, and like all rich men, I am accustomed to getting my way. But I have only myself to blame. Never again will I underestimate the abilities of a Druinese when it comes to the game of buying and selling!

I accept your offer. For ten thousand gold pieces, I will purchase your tame scribe. In my country, Cavielle Shaelus is well known and highly regarded, admired for both his scholarship and his relentless tweaking of the Church's nose. I will gain much credit amongst my rivals for obtaining the gentleman as a pet. They may boast of their golden mansions, extensive harems and gilded seafaring vessels, but they will fall silent when I parade the inestimable Shaelus before them!

My intermediaries will meet you in Harvedrake on the twenty-third of Julver. You will escort them to your village, where they will take possession of the scholar and pay what you are owed – assuming the scholar is in a serviceable condition. By your own account, he is very old, and although you have not mentioned it, I fear there is a danger he may not survive the sea journey to my country. You will understand, therefore, the need for an inspection to be performed to ensure Shaelus is ship-shape, so to speak. You say you have treated him well, as far as possible, given his circumstances. I dearly hope so. If he is in an unacceptable state, you may keep him, just as I shall keep my money.

Re'anthe Nemthe.

The twenty-third of Julver was a week away. Therefore, Helligraine was still likely to be in the village.

Suddenly, Ekkerlin heard shouting. She rolled up the scroll hastily and slipped it in the vase. Dark shapes rushed past the window. She opened the front door a fraction and peered out, just in time to see three men vanishing into the mist. Footsteps rang out through the village. Doors opened and closed, the echoes travelling strangely through the mist.

Somewhere, a cry rose up. 'There's an intruder! The bastard killed Skrulien!'

Standaire walked through the mist, senses alert, footsteps silent. Since Olech's revelations, he had grown uneasy. Throughout Druine, others were seeking Helligraine. Who were they? Olech had assumed it was the Church. In the lodging room, whilst Ekkerlin recovered from the venom, the general and Ballas had discussed the matter. A simple soul, Ballas offered the simplest explanation. If Shaelus was worth abducting once, he was worth abducting *twice*. First, he had been snatched from Grimlarren Moor. Now that his texts were proving popular, it was unsurprising others would want to put him to work for themselves. Thieves steal from thieves. Why shouldn't text-makers do the same?

Standaire doubted it was so clear-cut. But he could not say why. And what other explanation was there? Faltriste had not dispatched any other Hawks to find Helligraine. Would he have hired mercenaries to do the task? Definitely not. Often ill-disciplined and corrupt, they could not be trusted with either Helligraine's safety or his secret — that he had been Cavielle Shaelus in his former life.

Standaire pressed onward through the mist.

The damp air made his joints ache — a sure sign of his gathering age. It was no surprise. Lately, his physical deterioration had grown increasingly obvious, no more so than during the escape from the gambling house. Fighting the Peacekeepers, he noticed that he relied more on experience than strength and speed. As a cadet, new to military life, he had been told it would eventually be the case, if he served into later life. It is a sad day, a senior officer had explained, when a fellow wins a scrap not because he is tough, fast and healthy, but because he has a good memory for the fights that have gone before. To rely on one's mind rather than one's fists — it is the beginning of the end.

At the time, the officer's words made no sense. A victory was a victory, by whatever means; nothing else mattered. Except it *did* matter. A great deal. Experience took up the slack, so to speak, but it could go only so far. Unless it was backed up by *some* strength, *some* speed, it was useless. And the day when Standaire's physical competence dropped below the mark was approaching. He could feel it, not only in his body, but in other, insidious ways. The constant mental tiredness, the perverse boredom he felt, even in the midst of crises, the vague sense of futility more befitting an adolescent than a man of his many years. They suggested, stridently and unshakeably, that the candle was burning low, the flame drowning in wax, and if his mind refused to acknowledge it, his spirit certainly did. The clouds were gathering; the crows sang. Increasingly, one question imposed itself again and again, as unceasing as a mantra:

How much longer? How much longer?

227

Grimacing, Standaire leaned against a cottage wall. This was not the hour for gloomy introspection, if such an hour existed. He had work to do, obligations to fulfil. How much longer? It did not matter. Not yet; not now.

He moved on, peering through windows. The nature of the search irritated him. Although he proceeded methodically through the village, he felt as if too much was being left to chance. It would be easy to miss Helligraine, if he were out of easy view. Equally, it would be impossible to spot him if he were lodged in an upstairs room. As Standaire tried to imagine where he would hide a Blessed Master, if he were the kidnapper, he spotted a bulky shape through the mist. With its distinctive silhouette – a spire rising skywards, a long low section to the rear – it was unmistakably a chapel.

'Surely not,' the general murmured.

But why not? What better place than a holy building? What greater amusement for the kidnapper, than to imprison a Master in a church? What more delicious irony could there be? What better joke, to appeal to the uncultivated mind of a criminal?

As he approached, Standaire saw that although many slates were missing from the spire, the roof itself was in good condition. Moving alongside the worship hall, he looked in through a window. First of all, he noticed the ecclesiastical furnishings were gone, the pews ripped out, the altar removed. Then he spotted the desk – a dining table, in fact – with a lantern glowing on the corner. Last, he saw the old man, hunched over a parchment, writing, his quill darting back and forth as swiftly as a dragonfly over a millpond. His white hair had grown to collar-length, and a tangled beard sprouted from his jaw. His features were aquiline, dignified, stately. He wore the rough garb of a peasant, a field-worker. Yet Standaire recognised him. He had seen him several times before, in the great hall at the Sacros.

Helligraine.

The Master stopped writing. Frowning, he slowly turned his face toward the window—

—and Standaire jerked away before he could be seen.

His chest grew tight, and he could barely breathe. A dry chuckle rose in his throat.

Are you bored now? he asked himself. Does everything seem futile?

He released a long breath; the mist swirled in front of his mouth. He gathered his thoughts. What came next was clear enough. He would meet the other two Hawks on the moors, as they had arranged. Then they would return to the chapel and set the Master free. Next, there would be a ride to Prendle House, the home of Leptus Quarvis. And that would be it: the mission would be over.

Something stirred at the edge of Standaire's vision. He turned. Helligraine stared through the window, his eyes luminously blue.

General? mouthed Helligraine, squinting.

Standaire nodded. *Yes, your holiness.*

You have come for me?

Yes. We have come for you.

Gasping, Helligraine looked skywards, to the heavens. *Thank you*. He clasped his hands, as if in prayer. *Thank you . . .*

That instant shouts rang across the village. Standaire jolted, startled. Beaming, Helligraine tapped the window.

Your Hawks?

Pointing to the desk, Standaire made a *be seated* gesture.

Helligraine frowned, confused. Standaire understood. Why should I return to the desk, Helligraine was wondering, when I will be rescued in a matter of moments?

Now, many footsteps were echoing through Whitelock. They seemed to be coming from every direction at once – an acoustic trick played by the mist, the general hoped.

229

Take your seat, Standaire instructed Helligraine. The holy man's cheerful expression collapsed into dismay.

Something wrong? Then, realising this was no time for questions, the Master did as he was bade, shuffling to the desk and sitting.

Several sets of footsteps bounded toward the chapel. Standaire hurried to the rear of the building. He waited, listening.

'Well?' said a man, curtly.

'The old bastard is still inside,' said a second.

'That's something at least,' said a third. 'The Dogman would burst a bollock if aught happened to the scribe.'

'Do you reckon it's true? That Skrulien's dead?'

'I fucking hope so. I hated the one-eyed bastard. He thought he was so smart . . . Who do you think did it? Not one of us, surely. Probably some—'

A strong forearm looped around Standaire's throat. 'Get back here, boys. I reckon I've got him, whoever he is!' A knife-tip touched Standaire's eyeball. 'Make a move, and I'll blind you, you snot-rag.'

Three figures appeared. Rough, ragged men, their faces pale and hair matted with salt.

'Well then,' said the nearest. 'What shall we do with—' Arching backward, he dropped to the ground. The man beside him turned then reeled back as a blade swept out of the mist and opened his throat. Thrusting his arm up behind his captor's forearm, Standaire yanked forward, breaking the man's grip. Spinning, he jabbed three rigid fingers into his throat. The man staggered. Standaire unsheathed his knife and jammed it hilt-deep into the man's ribcage. As the man fell, Standaire turned. The third attacking villager lay on the ground, clutching his stomach. Kneeling, Ekkerlin wrenched out her knife and slashed his throat.

'He is here,' she said. 'I found a letter that—'

Standaire gestured to the chapel. 'In there.'

'Shaelus?'

'Helligraine,' corrected the general.

CHAPTER THIRTEEN

For many years, Ekkerlin had been an admirer of Shaelus's writings. No: admirer was too feeble a word. She *adored* his work; his mind was at once expansive and acute, he possessed a turn of phrase to shame the greatest poets, and he had taken considerable risks in the pursuit of knowledge. His earliest books – particularly the account of his journey to the Dalzerte Gardens – had filled her with a compulsive need to learn, to understand the world around her, and the theoretical worlds that lay beyond. Ostensibly, this passion might appear at odds with her service to the Four. The Church forbade various strains of learning, did it not? But the Church was a man-made institution, clumsily attempting to keep the populace in order. Of course it tried to shackle the minds of ordinary folk. And of course it claimed that there was no need to pursue such knowledge to begin with, for the Church was divinely endowed with an absolute comprehension of all that existed in this world, and everything that constituted the next. The idea was laughable. So laughable, it was easy to ignore. Like Shaelus, Ekkerlin believed that true enlightenment, if it was to arise at all, would come from a process called 'syncretism', in which the learning found in various religions, cultures and traditions was carefully combined. Even if this approach failed, there was one undeniable consequence: it made life more interesting. The shackles were cast off, the blinkers removed, the ears cleansed of echoing sermons; every day, the mind tingled with the prospect of a new excitement.

She shared something else with Shaelus: restlessness, an adventurous urge, a desire to *see* and *do*.

A life consisting solely of thoughts and ideas was not enough; it had to exist alongside experiences. The image of a learned man as a dry, cobwebby ghost, rarely venturing beyond his library, was inaccurate more often than not. True scholars not only savoured knowledge, but sought it out for themselves; they travelled, took risks, trod perilous paths; they drank from the fountainhead, not the stream. This was why she had joined the army. What better way was there to see the world? To encounter the joys and horrors of life in all its myriad forms? She had signed up not only to fight, but to learn. And now, by some peculiar quirk of destiny, she was here, staring through a window at the scholar she admired beyond all others, the man whose example she had followed.

Strangely, she was disappointed, as if she was contemplating a painting which, although impressive from a distance, consisted only of crude and clumsy brushstrokes when viewed close to. What was Shaelus, but an old man, hunched at his desk, nervously turning a quill between his fingers? She did not know what she had expected. But this was not it. He resembled a vagrant, a ditch-dweller. Or a soak, supping away his life in the corner of a tavern. Nothing hinted that a powerful, idiosyncratic intellect buzzed and crackled in that white-haired head. But then, maybe the intellect was gone, dried out by long service to the Church . . .

Shaelus turned his face to the window. To Ekkerlin.

And she saw it – a hungry, questing glitter in his eyes. His aged, dishevelled appearance dropped away, and she beheld a man full of intelligence, determination and clarity. Setting down the quill, he got to his feet. As he walked to the window, he limped slightly, but even that was impressive: it seemed to say, I have been through much, and will gladly go through much again.

Standaire returned from the front of the chapel. She had told him about the letter in the tavern. He knew that if the document was correct, the Master could be whisked away to the East within days, or taken now as Whitelock was under attack. The general agreed that they had to act.

'The door is sealed,' said Standaire. 'You have brought lock-picks, Ekkerlin?'

'Yes,' replied the Hawk, delving into her pocket.

As Ekkerlin produced the small devices, Helligraine shook his head. Standaire watched as the holy man mimed inserting a key into a lock, and trying – but failing – to twist it. Then, indicating the imaginary lock, Helligraine gestured open-handedly, scowling, as if he had been offered a plate of rotting food. His meaning was clear: the lock was faulty, and could not be picked.

Useless, mouthed Helligraine. Then, tapping lightly on the windowpane, Might I suggest . . .

'I do not believe we have a choice,' said Ekkerlin.

Standaire nodded, unhappily. *Step back*, he told Helligraine, unsheathing a knife.

Raising a finger, Helligraine scuttled from view. He returned with a thick woollen coat, which he laid on the floor beneath the window, to deaden the noise of falling glass. Then he backed away several paces and waited.

Standaire pressed the knife-tip against a lower corner of the window. He struck the handle with the side of his fist. Nothing happened. He struck again, and the window shattered. Carefully, he broke the remaining fragments from the frame. Then he held out a hand to Helligraine.

'Your holiness,' he said, beckoning the Master outside.

'Alas, General, it is not so simple,' he said. 'I fear that you have failed to observe something important. It is a completely understandable oversight, of course, but – well, when one encounters an old friend, who one has not seen for a long while, and whose health is giving one concern – it is natural to focus upon *him*, rather than his surroundings. And I daresay the desk got in the way. My own body too, from time to time. But look.' He gestured downward. A black chain snaked across the floor stones, one end secured to a manacle around his ankle, the other attached to an iron loop sunken into a heavy slab. Standaire grimaced; had not noticed it. Now that he saw it, though, he could barely see anything else.

'Misdirection,' said Helligraine. 'A friend for the stage-conjuror, but an enemy to the Hawk, it appears.' He cocked his head, listening to the shouts racing through the village. 'I expect that ghastly racket distracted you, too.'

'And *you* did not think to mention this, your holiness?' said Ekkerlin, surprised.

'Why would I?' replied Helligraine blithely. 'You are Hawks. Such obstacles are your meat and drink.'

Climbing through the window, Ekkerlin knelt, inspecting the manacle. It was a crude circle of steel, held shut by an unwieldy lock. She swore.

'Hawk Ekkerlin?' said Standaire, clambering inside.

She rapped her knuckles against the manacle. 'It is too crude to be picked. I could try, but it would be useless.' She looked up at Helligraine. 'When a key is used upon the lock, does it open smoothly?'

'Far from it,' said Helligraine. 'Like the door, it is always something of a struggle, a wrestling match if you will. But surely, if it is old, it ought to be easily sprung? From what I understand, the more sophisticated the lock, the harder it is to open. That is the natural tendency of all things, is it not?

235

The more complex and finely balanced something becomes, the more difficult it is to be compromised.'

'That is true of codes and glyphs,' remarked Ekkerlin, rising. 'But not locks. Often, simpler is better.'

'Then what must we do?'

Ignoring the question, Ekkerlin trailed the chain, seeking weak links. Finding none, she examined the iron loop, probing the mortar where it sank into the floor stone. She shook her head.

'No joy?' inquired Helligraine, gently.

'No, your holiness. General, what . . .' She fell silent. There was no need to speak. The general was asking himself the same question. *What must we do? What* can *be done?*

Striding over, it was Helligraine who spoke. 'I believe we must employ decisive methods,' he said, turning the chair so it was adjacent to the desk. Sitting, he reached into the space beneath and pulled out a dirty glass bottle. When he uncorked it, a strong astringent smell floated out. 'Mellavian godspit,' he said, tossing the cork aside. 'A potent spirit, believed to possess restorative properties. Every evening, my captor, the Dogman, gave me a small cupful. He said it would keep me in good health. Maybe it would have done, or maybe it would only have kept me compliant, but I never drank it. Rather, I decanted each measure into this vessel, saving it for the hour of my escape. If what I planned can be termed an escape. Rather, it would be merely the trading of one torment for another . . .' He swished the liquid around the bottle. 'Godspit is enormously potent. There is enough here to end my life. I confess there were long, dark hours when I was tempted . . . when the Forest seemed preferable . . .' He shook the memory away. 'Now, though, it shall serve a different purpose.'

His gaze flitted sharply between the Hawks.

'One of you must find a different purpose for your sword, too: you must turn it into a physician's tool.'

Ekkerlin glanced at Standaire.

'Your holiness?' said the general, approaching the desk.

Lifting the bottle, Helligraine swallowed a mouthful. A shudder tore through his body. 'Mercy, it is worse than I recalled. Has either of you served as a battlefield surgeon?' Bending over, he tapped his foot. 'If the manacle cannot be removed, she must go, I fear. A clean strike from a sharpened blade should suffice. The godspit will serve as an antiseptic . . . once it has served as anaesthetic.' He took another swallow, grimaced then gasped. 'Get on with it, will you?'

Ekkerlin felt panic rising. 'There must be another way.'

Helligraine laughed; already, he was a touch tipsy. 'A wise Keltuskan once wrote, *Must, must, must — a word oft-spoken by the desperate, but rarely uttered by the rational . . .*'

'Krenef Nilgen,' said Ekkerlin, recognising the quote.

Helligraine's eyebrows lifted. 'Very good, my girl. You are familiar with his works?'

'Yes.'

'And you are not, I hope, the worst type of reader? That is, one who consumes without digesting? Who devours wisdom, yet learns nothing?' Another sip of godspit. Another laugh. 'Drink a little, if it will soothe your nerves — and steady your hand. For you have been a surgeon, have you not? I saw you flinch when I mentioned it.'

Closing her eyes, Ekkerlin drew her sword. 'He is right, General. There is no other way.' When Standaire did not respond, she opened her eyes again. The general stared fixedly at Helligraine, his lean face sombre.

'Is this truly what you desire?' he asked Helligraine.

'Desire? No. But I am willing to endure it.' He swung his gaze to Ekkerlin. 'Be on with it, my girl. If I sup much more of this stuff, you will have to carry me out of this village . . .' He hesitated, catching himself. 'You will probably have to do so, come what may. But you take my point.'

'You must lie down, your holiness,' said Ekkerlin, the words seeming to come from a great distance away. Her hands were shaking. The sword felt preposterously heavy.

Rising from the chair, Helligraine did as he was told. He lay on the floor stones, staring at the rafter-crossed ceiling. He looked like a graven figure craved into a coffin lid. In his right hand, he held the godspit bottle. With his left, he drummed his fingertips on the floor, impatiently. Raising the Master's leg, Ekkerlin rested his foot on the chair. Then she drew her sword. She was suddenly aware that she was sweating heavily. Her skin quivered and twitched, as if trying to crawl off her bones. A sour metallic taste flooded her mouth. She did not know if the venom was to blame. Or whether the procedure itself was unnerving her. As Helligraine deduced, she had served as a battlefield surgeon. She had amputated many limbs, and performed procedures that were infinitely more intricate and perilous. Yet she felt herself unravelling, a thread at a time. Drawing a breath, she looked at Helligraine—

—but the old man raised his head, suddenly.

'Your holiness?' Ekkerlin heard a quiet desperation in her voice. For a moment, it seemed the Master had worked out a different solution. One that did not involve steel and bloodshed, sundered bone and severed tendons.

He stared fixedly at his foot, perched on the chair. Then he smiled, drunkenly. 'Just making sure you've got the right limb up there,' he said, chuckling. Then, lowering his head to the floor stones, 'Continue.'

Ekkerlin touched the sword to Helligraine's ankle. 'Your holiness, are you certain?'

'It is the only way.'

Slowly, Ekkerlin raised the sword above her head.

* * *

It had ended badly for plump, one-eyed Skrulien. As he hefted the crate, Ballas slammed a raw-knuckled fist into his face. As he fell, eye patch askew, Ballas drew a knife, plunging it into the soft, yielding skin of his temple. The moustached man, with his ever-flickering smile, sprinted from the boathouse. Ballas followed, but as soon as the man vanished out the door, he was gone, swallowed by the mist.

Gone, yes – and shouting at the top of his lungs.

Intruder! There is an intruder! He's killed Skrulien . . .

Driven by instinct, Ballas ran, hurtling through Whitelock, heading for the moors. As he went, he realised this natural, unthinking reflex was the same one that had driven him onto the rooftop garden of Silver Hoof. Contained within the moment, it seemed sensible. Yet ultimately, it was the worst thing he could do. He might escape with his skin whole, but the villagers would follow, and he would lead them to Standaire and Ekkerlin, who were likely to be running too.

He halted, breathing heavily. Running footsteps sounded in the mist. Fighting the impulse to hide, he stood in the centre of the lane, waiting.

The footsteps grew closer. Two dark figures appeared.

And still he waited . . . and when the men came, he did not move, but allowed them to collide with him. The first fell, spinning to the ground.

'Watch where you're going, you clumsy fucker!' he shouted, sprawling.

The second man stared at Ballas. There was a fleeting spasm of recognition – the recognition that comes with seeing something unfamiliar, something heard about but never witnessed. He started to open his mouth but Ballas dropped him with a thunderous right hook. Then he ran, cutting back through the village toward the beach. In his wake, the first man shouted, 'He is here! He is here! He's going toward the sea!'

239

Ballas sprinted, passing the boatshed then stumbling down a steep slope onto a beach littered with shale. The mist was thicker here, blowing off the iron-grey sea in thick, rolling swathes. He paused, formulating a plan. He had to return to the moors at some point; he could not remain in the village for ever. It was wisest to track northwards for a few miles, he decided, then angle to the east, returning to the moors a good distance away from the meeting point described by Standaire.

He broke into a brisk jog, conserving his energy. Gradually, he heard the shale scuffing and rattling, disturbed by the boots of running men. He paused again, listening. As far as he could tell, through the sound-warping mist, the footfalls originated from somewhere behind. He tilted his head; behind, yes – and from the sides. He ran again but already, dark figures were emerging, spilling onto the beach like black vapours released from an alchemist's flask.

'Here,' shouted someone. 'To me! To me!'

Picking up his pace, Ballas pounded over the shale but the figures moved quickly, swarming around him, penning him in. He stumbled to a halt. The men stood five or six paces away, their faces half clear in the mist. They regarded him warily, but with hunger. They stood there, not speaking, uncertain what to do next.

Ballas spat onto the beach. 'Move aside,' he growled.

Incredibly, the crowd started to part. For a moment, Ballas believed that his words had done the trick. Clearly, the villagers feared him. Or each man, individually, feared that *they* would be the one to face reprisals, if they did not obey. Thus, they separated in unison . . .

Ballas was mistaken. They were not stepping aside to allow him through.

Rather, they were letting someone else stride through. Two men, peeling through the mist, one leading a large creature on a leash. Four-legged, large and solid. At first, Ballas thought it was a pony. As the mist receded, he discovered he was wrong.

It was a dog, a hound, bigger than any he had encountered. *Much* bigger. For certain, it had seen better days. Old, its fur growing sparsely, its fangs yellow and crooked, it looked as if it was a year or two from death. Yet it exuded power. Even its infirmities – a pronounced limp, a drooping, low-sunken head – added to its appearance of heavy solidity, of vast energies trapped within its bulk. One eye was white, the other grey and vigilant. Lifting its head a fraction, it sniffed the air.

The men halted ten paces away.

'What do you think?' said the one holding an iron chain attached to the hound's collar. 'Shall we give Old Jess a run?'

'Nah. The Dogman wouldn't approve. She's his dog and she runs only when he says.'

The other man gazed at his fingers, curled around the chain. 'But the Dogman's not here . . .'

'He will be back by nightfall. If he finds out—'

'Aye, Linke,' said someone in the crowd. 'We've got the intruder. That'll be enough. Maybe on the morrow, we'll be back here, and Jess shall have her day.'

Raising its head, the hound sniffed the air. A low rumbling growl shook its throat. It sniffed again; a black-mottled pink tongue swiped over its fangs. Then it strained lightly on the leash, as if to say, *Yes, I must.*

'She's got his scent,' said the chain-holder, Linke. 'Would be cruel to hold her back, wouldn't you say?'

'It's not your decision,' came another voice from the gathered men.

'I'm holding the leash. Of course it's my decision.'

'That's not what I meant. '

'Go Jess,' said Linke, dropping the chain. 'He's all yours. Entertain us, if you will.'

The hound did not move. It stood still, sniffing, reading the salt, sweat and seawater scents on the air. Then its gaze dropped to Ballas. Lowering its heavy head, it charged.

Ballas reached for a knife.

Ekkerlin held the sword above her head, poised to strike.

Focusing on Helligraine, she saw in her mind's eye the gristle, bone and sinew, swaddled in ripe red flesh. A single strike, and it would be over. A hard well-aimed blow, and they would be free to leave Whitelock.

Yet she could not move. She stood, arms aching with the sword's weight, muscles flickering, sweat streaming over her face.

'Hawk Ekkerlin,' came Standaire's thin, dry voice. 'Do what you must.'

Ekkerlin licked salt-rich sweat from her lips. Still she could not move.

'If you will not do it, I will,' said Standaire, tersely. She saw him at the periphery of her vision, a brooding figure, seized with impatience.

'Follow your orders, Hawk,' slurred Helligraine. His eyes were locked on the sword. The Four only knew what the sight of the weapon was doing to him. Did he view it as an ally, part of the force that would liberate him from Whitelock? Or an adversary, on the brink of causing indescribable pain? Or did he see it for what it was: just a strip of forged steel, sharp along both edges?

'Ekkerlin,' said Standaire, pacing over. 'Give me the sword.'

Seizing her wrist, he gently lowered her arms. Then he took the sword in his hands.

'I am sorry, General,' she murmured.

'Silence.' Standaire positioned himself by Helligraine's ankle. Then he lifted the sword. 'Ready, your holiness?'

'I have been ready a good while,' said the Master, shutting his eyes.

Suddenly, a scraping noise echoed across the chapel. A key sliding into a keyhole and grinding, raggedly, inside an ill-made lock. Ekkerlin whirled, staring. Standaire lowered the sword and blinking, Helligraine sat upright.

'Hide yourselves,' he said, getting clumsily to his feet. Turning the chair, he sat down at the desk, picked up his quill, dropped it then picked it up again. Standaire and Ekkerlin each hid behind a wide stone pillar. The key grated in the lock, and whoever was on the other side swore savagely, banging the door with the heel of his hand.

'Bastard thing, bloody bastard thing,' came a voice. 'Bloody prick-wrenching, bollock-twisting thing . . .' The key grated, then the door jolted. The handle turned and the door opened, revealing three men. Entering, they paused, looking around.

'You're still here, scribe? That is good,' said one of them, jaw covered by a thick red beard.

'Where else would I be?' replied Helligraine, mildly.

The red-bearded man's gaze alighted on the broken window. Tendrils of mist snaked around the frame, clutching and grasping, like diaphanous fingers. 'Someone has broken in.'

'Nonsense,' replied Helligraine. 'Rather, a writing utensil broke out. An inkpot, hurled by me in frustration.'

'Are you drunk, scribe?'

'Of course. The Dogman left me a little godspit, for all the good it has done me. Sir, I am in pain. Hence I hurled the inkpot – there is, I understand, certain analgesic properties attendant on violence. I drank the godspit hoping it would numb the discomfort . . .' Bending, he rubbed his ankle. 'My manacle is eating through my flesh. Every third day, the Dogman brings a jar of ointment to treat this recurring wound. Yet he has not visited.'

'He is away.'

'Yes, I am aware of that. As he entrusted you with my well-being, I assume he gave you the ointment. Yet you have been lax in your duties. Do you have it with you?'

'I have no time for this, scribe,' said Red-beard, half-snarling. 'As long as you are in your place—'

'But you will bring it later?'

Red-beard shrugged. 'Perhaps I will.'

'Perhaps is not good enough.' Helligraine rose, suddenly. 'You have the key, for the manacle?'

'Yes. But I have not the time—'

Standaire was the first to move. Springing from behind the pillar, he hacked the sword into Red-beard's neck, half-decapitating him. Simultaneously, Ekkerlin sprinted to another man, jamming a knife through his ribcage. Unsheathing a dagger, Standaire dispatched the third man. As Ekkerlin closed the chapel door, Standaire rummaged an iron key from Red-beard's pocket. Hurrying over, the general unlocked the Master's manacle.

Helligraine got unsteadily to his feet. Swaying, he leaned on the desk.

'Can you walk?' asked Ekkerlin, moving alongside.

'I am too drunk to walk,' said Helligraine, blinking widely. 'But no man is ever too drunk to dance. Come, my girl, let us jig our way out of the village.'

The dog sprang at Ballas, striking him high on the chest. Falling backward, the Hawk felt the knife slip from his fingers, heard it clatter on the shale. Planting its forepaws on his shoulders, the dog lowered its vast, dripping jaws toward his face. Its breath reeked of decay, of internal organs rotting whilst they lived. Yelling, Ballas gripped the shaggy fur around its throat and pushed, forcing back its head. Growling furiously, the dog strained to lower its head again, blood-tinged spittle dripping from its teeth, splashing greasily onto Ballas's cheeks. Already, the muscles in Ballas's arms burned. The beast was far heavier than he had expected, and he felt its bulk compressing his ribcage, flattening it by imperceptible degrees.

Their uncertainty gone, the villagers formed a circle, cheering on the dog. Through their yells, Ballas heard the murmuring shush-shush of seawater crumbling on the beach. Somewhere, a seagull cawed.

'Come on, Jess,' someone cried. 'Take off the fucker's face!'

The dog began thrashing like a shark on the deck of a fishing boat, snapping and writhing, each movement squeezing a little more air from Ballas's lungs. If it wished, the dog could stop fighting and simply lie there, suffocating him like a boa constrictor. Ballas did not have much time. His arms were trembling with weakness; soon, they would give way completely and the dog would be upon him, its ugly fangs grinding through his skull, crushing it as if it were a wren's egg.

Letting go of its throat, Ballas jammed his left hand under the beast's jaw then did the same with his right. Someone in the crowd laughed.

'The big bastard's got spirit,' he said. 'For all the difference it will make.'

Maybe it would not make any difference. Maybe he would die here, on this beach, in a desolate village choked by sea-fret. In a way, this possibility did not trouble him. All men died, eventually, and the circumstances were rarely more than a foot-note. On countless battlefields, he had heard the terminal utterances of wounded comrades, and whilst they complained about the pain, and the bald fact that they were dying – always too soon, always for a cause that seemed abruptly absurd – they never mourned the location, or who had wielded the blade. Ultimately, such details were irrelevant.

Opening the fingers of his right hand, he groped upwards, fingers following the dog's muzzle until they reached something soft. Locking his forefinger straight, he plunged into the soft warm jelly of the dog's good eye, the eye untouched by the milky haze of blindness. Yowling, the dog flung back its head and Ballas, hooking a leg over its back, rolled it down onto its flank. Bracing a hand on its throat, Ballas straddled it, whipped a knife from his belt and plunged the blade into the creature's ear, driving the steel several inches deep, so it tore through the grey slush of its aged brain-tissue.

Its yowls growing shrill, the dog spasmed wildly. Wrenching out the dagger, Ballas got woodenly to his feet. He realised that he was exhausted. A warm pain flowed through his chest, indicating a broken rib. He sucked in a few deep breaths.

The villagers stared. They were silent now, each bearing a hazy, fearful, distant look, one Ballas had seen before. It was the look of someone who had just realised they had supped a poison. Who knew that although they were safe for the time being, their skies ahead would be dark, agonising.

Sheathing the dagger, Ballas drew back his shoulders.

'Which one of you is next?' he growled, looking from man to man.

No one stirred, standing as motionless as the trees of a petrified forest.

'Well?' roared Ballas. 'No takers?' He turned to the man who had brought the dog, Ol' Jess. 'What about you? No? Then step aside.'

Ballas strode through the villagers. Once he was out of sight, enfolded by the mist, he broke into a sprint, tearing northwards over the shale.

Ballas returned to the moorland cave where they had hidden their horses before entering Whitelock. The horses were gone – a good sign, perhaps. If Helligraine had been rescued, he might have been given the third mount to ride. But ride where? Ballas surveyed the cave, focusing on the rocks scattered over the ground. One bore a white cross scratched onto its upper face. Kneeling, he turned it over. On the underside, there was a single word, scraped there by a sharp edge.

Redberry

Ballas knew the name. Redberry was a town twenty miles to the north-east. It looked like he had a long walk ahead of him.

The walk swiftly turned to a run. It was ridiculous: he had escaped Whitelock barely an hour ago, yet the familiar restlessness had returned. But then, why would it not? The mission was as good as over and as far as Ballas could tell, his future consisted of nothing except weeks, maybe months, of idleness at the Roost.

When he arrived at Redberry, several hours later, night was falling. He walked the streets until he spotted a small cross sketched in dirt on the white painted door of a tavern. Inside, he asked the tavern-master where his friends might be found. Then he climbed the stairs to the second floor.

The lodging room was small and damp-smelling. The Hawks were there, sitting on the bare floorboards. An old man perched on the edge of a narrow bed. As Ballas entered, he looked over. A filthy white beard bristled on his jaw. His hair was long and greasy. He wore the rough garb of a manual worker – practical rather than elegant attire.

'You are alive,' said Ekkerlin, rising.

'Reckon so,' muttered Ballas, shutting the door.

'This is the one you have spoken of?' said the old man. 'Anhaga Ballast?'

'*Ballas*,' corrected Ekkerlin, playfully. 'Though "ballast" is

a far better name. Our friend is big, heavy and in most circumstances, worthless. Yet he keeps our ship on an even keel.
Anhaga, this is Blessed Master Helligraine.'

Ballas started to kneel.

'No, no,' said Helligraine. 'We will have none of that here.
I owe you my life. And my sanity. If I had spent another hour
in that ghastly village, I would have lost my wits.' He eyed
Ballas's claw-torn clothes. 'You encountered trouble?'

'A handful of villagers,' said Ballas, rising. 'And a dog as
big as a horse and as old as time.'

'Jess,' said Helligraine, thoughtfully. 'You and she . . .
clashed?'

'Aye.'

'And you triumphed? That is, Jess . . .'

'Dead.'

Helligraine gasped, rolling his eyes skywards. 'The Dogman
will not take this well.'

Ballas shrugged. 'Depends on how he looks at it. On the
one hand, he's lost a dog. On the other, if he's good with a
skinning knife, he's gained a rug.' He looked at Standaire.
'Permission to get some food, sir.'

Ballas went down to the common room, bought a bowl of
stew and ate slowly, his mind wandering. When he returned
to the lodging room, the candles had been extinguished and
everyone was sleeping, Standaire and Ekkerlin lying on rough
blankets on the floor, Helligraine stretched out on the bed –
Ballas settled on some spare blankets, shut his eyes and sank
into a deep slumber.

He woke a short while later.

Helligraine was writhing on the bed, seized by a nightmare.
'Too late . . . too late . . .' he shouted, over and over. Opening
his eyes, Standaire rose on one elbow, staring. Rubbing her
face, Ekkerlin, who was nearest to the Master's bed, made an

I'll deal with this gesture, then gently shook Helligraine's shoulder.

'Your holiness, wake up. You're dreaming,' she whispered, forcefully.

Helligraine's eyes flicked open. He looked around, confused. 'Hm?'

'You were dreaming. And talking in your sleep.'

'Was I?' Helligraine sat up against his pillows. 'What was I saying? I hope it was something profound.'

Ekkerlin told him, and he shook his head.

'That stands to reason,' he said, picking crumbs of sleep from his eyes. 'I dreamt I was on Grimlarren Moor, the site of my abduction. It all happened so quickly, you see. One moment we were riding along – myself, my aide and twenty Papal Guards. And then, before we knew it, we were surrounded by the Dogman's men. Oh yes, they came suddenly, springing from behind trees and boulders, and surging out of a nearby gully like hornets from a shattered nest. As soon as they appeared, it was too late. They were armed with bows, swords and axes. And my goodness, how they could use them! But you have encountered those dreadful savages in the village you called Whitelock.'

'With respect, the ones we met did not strike me as especially competent.'

Helligraine chuckled. 'That is true,' he said, eyes twinkling in a sliver of moonlight that pierced the curtains. 'But the Dogman was present on the Moor. He controlled everything; I suppose one might say that the villagers responded to his commands just as his dogs obey his whistles and shouts. But without his guidance, they are useless, mere strays, purposeless, self-indulgent, controlled by their base impulses.' His expression darkened. 'The Dogman is a fearsome soul. Big, strong, clad head to toe in animal skins. He wears this ridiculous

249

adornment around his neck, a long rope strung with the jawbones of various animals. Why must tough men insist on being *seen* as tough? Even when it serves no purpose? But he knows his business. After all, the abduction was a success. Within a week, I was chained up in the chapel, writing forbidden texts . . .' He leaned back into the pillows, as if struck by a sudden fatigue. 'It was appalling – nay, revolting – to be reunited with that scoundrel, that bane I thought I had left behind.'

'Bane, your holiness?'

'Cavielle Shaelus,' said Helligraine, quietly. 'I thought he was gone for good. Banished, cast out, reduced to a nothingness. But he was still there. Inside me.' He bumped a scrawny fist against his chest. 'To write the texts demanded by the Dogman, I had to become Shaelus once more. At first, I resisted. When I wrote, I *pretended* that I was he; I impersonated him, nothing more. But it was enough to stir him from his slumber, the slumber I had mistaken for death. He arose within me like some vile spirit. And yes, I became him once more – at least when I was holding a quill. As soon as my day's labours ended, it was as if some frightful miasma had lifted and I could see what I had turned into, if only temporarily. I cannot describe the shame, Ekkerlin. To be Shaelus once more – twelve months ago, I would not have thought it possible. But now . . .'

'But surely you acted under duress? Surely the Dogman drove you to it, with threats?'

'Oh, that is true enough. He promised a variety of torments, if I did not do what he wanted. For a savage, he is remarkably inventive.'

'Then you should feel no guilt. You did only what was required to survive.'

'No, girl. You do not understand.' An agonised vehemence crept into Helligraine's voice. He gripped the bedsheets, tightly; he closed his eyes. 'The Dogman forced me to work. But he did not make me *enjoy* it. And enjoy it I did. Do you hear? It was exhilarating to be Shaelus again. Liberating. I cast off my piety, my obedience to the Four, and I felt free. But freedom comes at a price: one is alone, and thus undefended against forces much larger than oneself.' Opening his eyes, he peered at Ekkerlin intently. 'I speak of spiritual terrors. When one embraces the Four, one obtains their protection in the next world. But if you do not, you will find yourself at the mercy of all the Forest has to offer. And amongst everything the Forest offers, mercy is nowhere to be found. You will suffer for eternity. *I* may suffer for eternity, given my crimes. I sinned, not so much in writing the texts, but in taking pleasure in the process. I do not know how I shall redeem myself, how I will become the man I was before Whitelock.' He squinted. 'You seem confused. No; disappointed.' A frown. Then, 'I think I know why. You are a literate girl; in the chapel, you showed familiarity with the writings of Krenef Nilgen. Perhaps you are familiar with Shaelus's works too? And cannot bear to hear him denounced by the one who knows him best? You may speak freely. I shall not excommunicate you if you admit to reading forbidden texts. How could I, given all that I have done?'

'It is true,' said Ekkerlin. 'I am fond of your – his – work. And it pains me that you should speak of him as if he lacked merit. He had a fine mind, a bold spirit—'

'What use is a fine mind, if it is put to destructive purposes? What value a bold spirit, if it carries one in entirely the wrong direction? He loathed the Church; yet the Church benefits us all, if we let it. Indeed, it is our only hope for a posthumous existence free of anguish.'

'It is not his anti-clerical writings I admire,' said Ekkerlin, carefully. 'But his exploration, his histories of lost civilisations.'

'They too were anti-clerical, in purpose if not form. They

were intended to show that although the Church claims absolute knowledge, it is not so: there are other ways a people may live happily, and obtain grace in the afterlife – if the afterlife exists, which Shaelus doubted.'

Ekkerlin hesitated. 'Shaelus's books – were they the truth?'

'Spiritually? No.'

'But in terms of what you did, what you saw?'

'Me?' A note of disapproval.

'Shaelus,' corrected Ekkerlin.

'Yes, they were true. Shaelus's detractors claimed his works were overblown fantasies, grandiose fictions designed to gain fame, admiration and money. They were mistaken. Shaelus never wrote a false word, or exaggerated the tiniest detail. On the contrary, he was tempted to play down his adventures. He recognised that if no one believed his stories, his stance against the Church would not be taken seriously either.'

'So, when Shaelus walked the Desolate Gardens of Dalzerte, days before they were destroyed by the Salandier barbarians—'

'It was exactly as he described.'

Ekkerlin was surprised. She had assumed his adventures in the Desolate Gardens were exaggerated. They struck her as a touch *too* extraordinary. Playing cat and mouse with a barbarian horde, evading capture on numerous occasions, then spending a tranquil evening walking the overgrown paths . . . She was glad it was true. It was the first of Shaelus's books she had read. And it had kindled in her a hunger for adventure; without it, she may never have joined the military.

'And the boat journey through the Whirling Waters to Ralparrak? And the plundering of the Bear Tomb—'

'Shaelus never lied,' interrupted Helligraine, sharply. 'Although it would have been better if he had, for his truths were more sinful than any deception.' Sighing, he patted Ekkerlin's shoulder. 'Forgive me if my tone is harsh. I understand your curiosity, misguided though it is. But I would prefer not to speak of the past. Of *him*. Let us look to the future instead. The general says I cannot return to the Sacros.'

'Not yet,' said Ekkerlin. 'We are to stay at the home of Leptus Quarvis until Blessed Master Faltriste has exposed whoever is responsible for your abduction.'

'Ah, Faltriste. He is a good man, but . . .' Helligraine stared at his hands, fingers interlaced upon the blankets. 'I fear he is ill-suited to the task. He lacks steel; he is too kind-hearted and easily deceived. I will pray for him.' He looked across the room to Ballas. 'It seems our chatter is keeping our friend from sleeping. I apologise, sir. We will be silent from now on.'

'My thanks, your holiness,' said Ballas. He closed his eyes, heard the bed creak as Helligraine settled himself, and dropped into a heavy sleep.

CHAPTER FOURTEEN

Sitting in the village hall, Cramlecke wondered if this would prove to be the worst night of his life.

In his twenty-nine years, he had suffered many bad nights. Most folk would not believe it was so. A thief, murderer and – just the once – rapist, they would assume he was rarely troubled by fear. That he seldom considered consequences. In this, they were mistaken.

The Dogman had returned an hour ago. Cramlecke did not know who broke the news that Ol' Jess was dead. Maybe he had discovered it for himself, wandering to the stables to pay the monstrous dog a visit, and finding it empty. But he did know, that was certain: his bellows of grief and rage tolled over the village like a bell struck by an angry god. The ocean had fallen silent; the stars had withered, the moon grown a paler shade of white. Cramlecke was glad he had not *seen* the giant's outburst. Like most in the village, he had been locked inside his home, cowering.

But no longer. Word spread that the Dogman had called an assembly and so it was that every villager had gathered in the hall, where they sat cross-legged on the bare floorboards, like prisoners awaiting execution. Cramlecke felt sick. His bowels pulsed like a tide-teased sea anemone, his hands trembled and he had chewed his bottom lip until it was soft and bloody. It was no consolation that everyone else felt the same, that the air crackled with collective fear. Nor was it helpful that Ol' Jess's death lay squarely at the feet of two men, Linke and Wessil. They would all suffer because of those two imbeciles. Why, in the Four's name, had they set the dog on the stranger? What were they thinking? They knew she was too old and sick to fight, that she puked up her meals and shat herself without shame. Had they expected to win the Dogman's approval by giving the dog a run? Or were they merely trying to entertain themselves? To introduce a little drama to the tedium of village life? If so, they had succeeded. Blood and sand, they had succeeded.

That was not the only thing that had gone wrong. The scholar had vanished from the chapel. Long ago, the old man had been quite famous, having earned the Church's enmity by writing forbidden texts. Forced by the Dogman to ply his trade once more – he had retired, apparently – he was earning much money for the Scarlet Twilight. Sold on the Dark Market, his books enabled them to purchase weapons and meet other expenses which, according to the Dogman, were required to overthrow the Pilgrim Church. What these expenses were, the Dogman never said. But the Twilight was a huge operation, spanning the length and breadth of Druine, and such ventures did not come cheap.

Even now, in the midst of fear, Cramlecke was excited by the Scarlet Twilight. In essence, it was a revolution, though a bloodier – and swifter – one than had ever gone before. Under the control of Cal'Briden, a Church-hating former merchant, hundreds of small militia units lay hidden throughout the country. When the call came, they would rise up and overthrow the Church, toppling the ancient institution *in a single night*. How? Oh, that was the good part. Some folk, weaklings mainly, claimed that violence solved nothing. How wrong they were! Armed to the teeth, the Twilight Men – of which Cramlecke was one – would march into every town and city, slaughtering Churchmen and torching holy buildings until, come dawn, nothing of the Church would remain except smouldering rubble and crow-pecked corpses. The scheme was crude, yes. But it would be effective. What was the Church, but a legion of robed idiots, spouting holy nonsense? What, therefore, would be left if those prattling imbeciles were dead? Nothing; nothing at all.

After the Twilight passed, Cal'Briden would take power. By all accounts, he was a just man, fond of the commonfolk. Aided by those he called his generals – men like the Dogman, who had led each unit to war – he would fashion a new Druine, one built upon fairness, free thought and tolerance. Admittedly, there would be a touch more bloodshed after the Twilight, for some poor, deluded folk, clinging to the Church's teachings, would make things unnecessarily difficult. Nonetheless, they would be dealt with easily enough. And then, once the nation was fully restored to its senses, a bright future would beckon. Cal'Briden was intelligent; he knew how to manage farmland so no one starved and, of a compassionate nature, he had promised to construct hospitals, orphanages and other establishments to help the needy. *Only when the incense-fragranced hands of the Church have been pried from our throats,* he once said, *can the good people of Druine inhale the sweet vapours of life.*

Cramlecke shuddered, as fear reasserted itself. Gazing around, he noted his fellow Twilight Men looked considerably unheroic. As well they might. The mere *thought* of an angry, grief-sore Dogman could buckle the stoutest warrior's armour. Few had seen him since he learned of Ol' Jess's death. Those who had painted a peculiar picture: the shaggy-bearded, fur-clad giant on his knees, clawing the ground and weeping, eyes red, dribbles of snot hanging from his nose. Anguish did not shrink him, they said. It *enlarged* him, trebling his size, increasing his intensity fourfold. He had been both pitiful and terrifying. And somewhere, out in the village, he was heading toward the hall.

Seated next to Cramlecke, a man named Rublen chuckled.

'Something amuses you?' demanded Cramlecke, bitterly. It seemed unfair that someone should not be sharing his fear.

'It's funny to see so many folk shitting themselves,' said Rublen, looking around the hall. 'Don't you think?'

'No, I don't.'

'Shitting themselves *needlessly*, I should have said. There: is it funny now?'

'Ol' Jess is dead. The scholar has vanished. And you think we shouldn't be afeared?'

'Nothing is going to happen,' said Rublen, picking a bit of fluff from his leggings. 'Do you know what the Dogman will do? He'll come stumping in, roaring and raging, and rattling the jawbones on that stupid necklace of his. He'll make threats, blustering and farting – and then? Nothing. You see, there is naught else he can do. The Twilight is almost upon us, Cramlecke. And that means he needs us. We are his army; without us, he will have no one to lead. And without anyone to lead, he is no use to Cal'Briden. The merchant will drop him like a hot potato, and he will no longer be a general in the Twilight. That's the last thing he wants.' He scratched his chest. 'He cannot afford a mutiny. Not now, not so close to our night of action.'

'I suppose you're right,' murmured Cramlecke. 'But I still feel . . .' He trailed off as the door swung open, revealing a swathe of mist-curdled darkness.

'Here we go,' said Rublen, rubbing his hands together. 'Brace yourself, old friend. This is going to be quite a performance.'

Clenching his fists, Cramlecke tried to remain calm. He told himself that Rublen was right; the Dogman would not push them too far. Oh, he would make sure everyone suffered. He would scare seventy-three shades of shit out of them and when he was done, their ears would be ringing, hearts pounding and bodies trembling like storm-shaken aspen leaves – but that would be all. There would be no beatings, no deaths. Whatever was coming would be bad, yes, but bearable.

For a long time the doorway remained empty, and Cramlecke wondered whether the Dogman was there at all. Perhaps a breeze had blown open the door, and the giant was elsewhere in the village, brooding, mourning . . . Then he smelled the wet-stone-and-bracken aroma of pipesmoke. Squinting, he saw curls of bluish vapour floating through the mist. The Dogman was there all right. So why hadn't he come through?

Suddenly, two dark spherical objects flew through the doorway, spinning through the air close to the ceiling then dropping. One landed, skidding and bouncing over the floor-boards whilst the second, incredibly, fell into Cramlecke's lap, coming to rest in the gap between his thighs, lodging itself there like an egg in a bird's nest.

Cramlecke looked down. Linke's face stared back up, eyeless, noseless, earless, his jaw hanging open.

Cramlecke surged to his feet, dislodging Linke's head. Casting about, he looked to the others for – for what? Sympathy? Help? No. He wanted to know they shared his horror. That they too were alarmed, that they hovered on the cusp of panic. But no one was paying attention. As one, they stared at the doorway, still empty except for mist, darkness and a thin, winnowing ribbon of pipesmoke.

They waited. And waited.

Then there came a noise like the ending of the world. It was the sound of mountains collapsing, of the earth fracturing and rivers bursting to steam, of the sun cracking loose and hurtling to earth, charring the air through which it travelled.

'This village,' roared the Dogman, 'is *dead*.'

The giant said nothing more. And he did not appear in the doorway either. He was still there, of course – the pipesmoke continued drifting, floating in thick clouds now, as if the giant were breathing heavily. His half-absence was disturbing; it wound Cramlecke's nerves tighter and tighter. In his guts, pressure was building; he wanted to defecate. A similar tension tingled in his eyes, for he was close to tears. His lungs did not seem to be working properly, and it was a miracle his legs had not given way. He realised he *wanted* the Dogman to appear. It did not matter how loudly he shouted, how savagely he shook his fists or who he singled out for ill-treatment; anything would be better than waiting.

Punch us, kick us, do whatever you like, thought Cramlecke, wretchedly, just get it over with.

The Dogman did not set foot in the hall. Instead, out in the night, he whistled – three loud sharp blasts. Cramlecke's bowels opened. Groaning, he looked accusingly at Rublen, who was slack-faced, a hand covering his mouth.

'You said nothing would happen,' said Cramlecke, weakly.

Rublen did not hear. Nor did Cramlecke, truth be told. As his mouth moved, his ears picked up a different noise. Claws, clattering over stone, heading through the night toward the hall. All around, the villagers were getting to their feet.

Stand if you must, thought Cramlecke. It will make no difference.

He did not see the dogs arrive; too many Twilight Men blocked his view of the doorway and, even if this were not so, he had closed his eyes. But he heard them, those animals, the offspring of Ol' Jess, yelping and barking, obscenely happy, murderously jubilant. Even this was too much. As the first men began screaming, Cramlecke's legs gave way. Dropping to the ground, he curled into a ball. That too would make no difference. But it was all he could think to do.

CHAPTER FIFTEEN

I did not witness the destruction of Vohoria. In one sense, this is a mercy, for I doubt my sanity would have remained intact, had I seen that fine civilisation torn apart by barbarous hands. Yet, as a historian, I bemoan my absence from that bleak event for it is my duty to record what others are in no position to see and, if it is possible, make them understand.

I have spoken to Druinese soldiers who partook in the Needful Scourge. As one might expect, their feelings vary. Some are haunted, not by the destruction wrought upon a noble culture, but the individual acts they committed: one does not, after all, easily forget the slaughter of innocents. Others claim they were fulfilling their obligations to the Church, and suffer no guilt; still others take a quiet pride in their efficiency, and dedication to duty. Of course, there are vainglorious idiots, who mistook their rampage for heroism; every conflict attracts such imbeciles, who love bloodshed almost as much as they love themselves.

Nonetheless, there is some consistency in their accounts. They speak of narrow streets foaming with blood, of frightened men, women and children taking their own lives rather than losing them to their tormentors; they describe sadism on an unprecedented scale, and the strange, compulsive urgency with which they surged through the country, feeling as if they were taking part in a race as much as a war. They spoke of the heavy exhaustion experienced at the end of each day, when their muscles were worn out with cutting, hacking and chopping, and the grim camaraderie of fighting men waging battle in a foreign land.

Not once, however, did any of these veterans claim to have feared for his life. And this casts a black light upon the whole venture, does it not? The Scourge was not a war, but a cull, an attempt – successful, alas – to obliterate a people.

To those who protest that after invading Druine, the Vohorin deserved what they received, I say this: Druine itself, under the malign leadership of the Church, has seized countless lands, and done so without any significant reversal of fortune. By your own logic, Druine deserves a taste of its own repugnant medicine. Maybe, one day, this will come to pass, and the Church will discover what it is like to feel a heavy boot upon one's neck. But if ever such a day arrives, it is a long way off, and I shall not live to see it.

Extracted from *The Loss* by Cavielle Shaelus

'You are sweating,' observed Jurel Kraike as Quarvis entered the room.

'Oh, it is nothing,' replied Quarvis, shutting the door. 'The steps are steep and I am tired.'

'Is that all?' Kraike watched intently from the armchair, a wizened, white-haired spider in the centre of a web. Behind him, a golden dusk filled the window. Nightingales swept back and forth, singing their sweetly mournful song.

'All?'

'This evening, you will use *The Chronicle* for the final time. Are you frightened of what you might see?'

'Frightened? No. Uneasy, perhaps.' Crossing the room, he took *The Chronicle* from the writing desk. Kneeling on the rug, he took the brass bowl from his bag and opened the *lecterscrix* pouch. As he filled the bowl he felt Kraike's gaze upon him.

'I confess to a certain . . .'

'Yes?'

'Dread.' He looked at Kraike. To his surprise, Kraike nodded, understanding.

'Selindak nearly died composing the final vision. It was not the blood-loss that brought him to the edge, he said, but the emotional strain. If it affected him, it will affect you too. If you believe it will prove too much . . .'

'No. If I do not see, I shall not understand.'

Kraike lit a taper from a lantern. 'You can never understand, Quarvis. Nor can I.'

Frowning, Quarvis accepted the taper. 'I am confused. If you were present, yet cannot—'

'Light the *lecterscrix*. Inhale. Learn.'

Kraike did as he was told.

It is the fourth night of the invasion. The Vohorin forces are forty miles inland and, in essence, nothing has changed. By day, the soldiers fight, employing the traditional methods; by night, Kraike infuses a prisoner of war with the plague spell, then allows him to escape back to his countrymen. An hour or so later, the plague takes effect, and the enemy burns, incinerated from within. Then, the following day, the Vohorin march deeper into Druine, and the process is repeated. It has become a routine, this slaughter and immolation; in a way, it is as dull and predictable as the work-day of an office clerk. Only the scenery changes: on the first day, the prisoners were infected in the hold of a warship; now, they take the blood-taint in a tent, pitched a hundred yards apart from the main Vohorin encampment.

On this, the final evening of the invasion, all is as it always is. Two prisoners are strapped to benches; braziers burn, spilling gritty smoke, and racks of torture-tools glint in candlelight. Selindak perches on a stool, watching Kraike work, listening to winged beetles colliding against the tent walls, each impact a tiny whipcrack. Flayed, blinded, his internal organs heaped upon his chest, the first prisoner breathes his last, shuddering into the irreversible stillness of death.

The second prisoner seems not to notice. Since his arrival, he has prayed constantly, begging the Four to grant him the fortitude required to endure such ordeals. His piety is so intense, he appeared oblivious to his companion's suffering. Of course, it cannot be so. He will have heard the man's screams, his entreaties, and a hundred other things: the slow cracking of his fingerbones as the pliers twisted, the hiss of a red-hot spoon scooping his eyeballs from their sockets, the sullen squelch of his vital organs as they were lifted, one by one, from his abdomen. He knows what is coming, and no matter how earnestly he petitions the Four, he will be afraid. Horribly, desperately afraid.

Clutching a blood-wet scalpel, Kraike looms over the prisoner. He is skinny, this man, his ribs jutting like those of a stray dog. He is young, too: his soldier's beard is wispy, his jaw covered in pimples, his eyes bright and fresh, as if prolonged use is yet to tarnish their lustre. Kraike seeks signs that he is frightened, and finds them: he has chewed through his bottom lip, dried piss stains his legs and his heart beats rapidly, flexing the skin above his ribs.

Kraike flattens a hand against the prisoner's abdomen. As he does so, he moves his other hand, the one gripping the scalpel, to the leather strap securing his right wrist to the bench. With the dexterity of a pickpocket, he loosens the buckle then brings back his hand, so the scalpel touches the prisoner's belly. The movement is fluid, swift, and completely undetectable; distracted by the empty hand against his stomach, the prisoner feels nothing.

Kraike murmurs the spell-words, half to himself. Then, in Druinese, he utters the same words as every preceding night.

'You will stay here until morning,' he says, withdrawing the scalpel.

'Once I have slept, we will speak. Contemplate your circumstances. When the sun rises, you must decide.'

Moving away, he reaches behind his back to untie the strings of his leather apron. Suddenly the man is moving, tearing free of the loosened strap, grabbing Kraike's arm and yanking him back, so the sorcerer falls, sprawling atop the prisoner. Faster than an eye-blink, the prisoner snatches the scalpel from Kraike's grasp and plunges it toward Kraike's throat. Rising from his stool, Selindak lunges, knocking the prisoner's hand aside. Still moving, the blade slithers wide of Kraike's throat, sinking into the apex of his collarbone, and the prisoner grinds it hilt-deep, yelling and snarling.

'Go home,' shouts the prisoner, as Kraike falls to the ground. 'We know what you are doing. We do not know how you do it, or which dark entities you call upon for your power. But you cannot trick us any longer. We know, we know, we know — and we outnumber you two hundred to one. You cannot burn us all, you dog!'

Guards plunge into the tent. Unsheathing a sword, one hacks the prisoner's head from his neck, whilst the others rush to Kraike. The sorcerer lies perfectly still, blood welling around the knife-blade then trickling over skin that grows paler by the heartbeat . . .

Like a drowning man, Quarvis surfaced from the vision, gulping for air. Then he plunged again, sucked in by the shapes whirl-pooling on the page . . .

The Vohorin flee Druine. They take seriously the prisoner's claim that the spell is no longer a secret; even if they did not, they could not fight on, for Kraike's knife wound has become infected, and the sorcerer is feverish, incapable, hovering on the threshold of death. They have suffered the ultimate reversal: their dreams of conquering Druine have turned into a desire to simply survive. Furthermore, they know the Druinese are plotting revenge: their armies are massing, their own warships setting sail, their hearts burning with a hunger for vengeance.

Those who understand Druinese history know that the Church is never content to repel its enemies, or subdue them: it must obliterate them, always, on every occasion . . .

Jurel Kraike sleeps on a narrow bed in the hold of a warship, which has been converted to an infirmary. Outside a small window, the blue sea rolls, glittering in sunlight. Selindak has not left Kraike's side throughout the voyage. Although his health is improving, the sorcerer remains very sick. His skin is as white as the nightingales in the palace courtyard, his breaths are the murmuring hiss of water travelling through a rusted pipe and his sweat, ever-flowing and abundant, stinks like a freshly opened tomb. He will live, no doubt. But to what end? He will survive only to witness the destruction of Vohoria. If Selindak were to climb up-deck and raise a lens-tube to his eye, he would espy Druinese warships on the horizon, their black sails blazoned with the red triangles which, he understands, represent Scarrendestin, the holy mountain.

Of a sudden, the door opens. Emperor Grivillus stumbles through, clutching a bottle of valrux. He looks as he did all those years ago, when he was wracked by skull-aches. His hair is greasy and unkempt, his clothes stained, his eyes bloodshot and lips pale. Slamming the door, he lurches over to Kraike.

'Wake up,' he says.

'Let him sleep,' says Selindak. 'It will aid his recovery.'

Nostrils quivering, Grivillus empties the bottle over Kraike's face. The sorcerer splutters, but it is merely a reflex: he does not waken, only groans and twitches.

'He is pretending,' says Grivillus. 'He is as awake as you or I, Selindak. I expect the pair of you were conversing until you heard my footsteps approaching. Then, this yellow-hearted coward feigned slumber, believing I would not hold him to account if he was taking his rest.'

'My Emperor, his repose is genuine. I—'

'Wake up!' Bending, Grivillus yells the words into Kraike's face. 'Damn it all, you worm-ridden cur – rouse yourself!' Then, clenching a fist, he punches Kraike's knife wound, swaddled in bandages. Once, twice, three times in swift succession. Groaning, Kraike opens his eyes.

'Ah, he returns,' snarled Grivillus. 'What have you got to say for yourself?'

Kraike has not spoken since the attack. He does not speak now, only stares up at the emperor.

'Well? Spit it out. You promised that within weeks, we would have conquered Druine. You, with your precious spell – triumph was a foregone conclusion, you said—'

'My emperor, he made no such promises. He said there would be risks,' says Selindak.

'Silence,' spits Grivillus. 'I want to hear what he has to say, this man who has shattered Vohoria.'

'He cannot speak,' says Selindak, calmly. 'Permit me to answer on his behalf. As I said, we knew our quest would not be without peril. And that is the vital word – we. You approved of this venture; without your consent, it would never have happened. If memory serves, you were as keen as anyone to set sail—'

Grivillus smacks Selindak open-handedly across the face, knocking him from his stool onto the floor.

'Maybe he did speak cautiously,' breathes Grivillus, 'but he dangled his pretty little spell before our eyes, enticing us, enticing me. When tempted by such power, who would have chosen to stay at home? What sane man would have turned away from conquest? When a whore lifts her skirts, the stoutest soul is tempted. And that is all Kraike is, to my mind. A pestilential whore, who fills you with desire yet leaves you with nothing except shame . . . shame and ruination . . .'

Grivillus lifts the bottle to his lips, finds it empty, then lowers it again. 'Or maybe he is something worse. Maybe,' he licks his lips, 'he is a traitor. For certain, any turncoat would be proud to match his accomplishments. Oh yes, he would congratulate himself most heartily as he watched his enemy's homeland go up in flames.'

266

'You are drunk,' says Selindak, getting to his feet. 'You have not uttered a word of sense since you came here. I suggest you go on deck, vomit the valrux from your system and inhale the sea air until your head is clear.'

Grivillus turned. 'Vohoria has not yet fallen,' he spat. 'Whilst it still exists, I remain emperor – your emperor, Selindak. I hold the power of life and death over you, and everyone on this vessel. Do not forget it; know your place, old man.' The emperor strikes Selindak again, with a closed fist this time. The high secretary spins, crashing into a medicine cabinet. The glass-panelled door shatters; jars spill out, smashing on the floorboards. Grivillus stares at the broken glass and for an instant, his gaze is dreamily malevolent, before hardening with resolve. 'The very existence of this betrayer is an insult,' he says, regarding Kraike coldly. 'I will not let him see the outcome of his handiwork. I will not give him the satisfaction of watching Vohoria fall.' Reaching up, he smashes the bottle on a ceiling beam then stands motionless, glass splinters falling around him like oddly shaped hail. 'It is over, Kraike,' he says, holding the bottle-stub over the sorcerer's throat—

—and then he arches his back, a thin gasp escaping his lips. As he falls, Selindak steps aside, letting the scalpel-handle slither free of his grasp. The blade is jammed into Grivillus's lower back, wedged between two vertebrae, and when he tries to rise, the emperor finds his legs are useless. He stares at them, disbelieving. Then he looks up at Selindak.

'You will pay,' he breathes, groping for the scalpel.

'No, my emperor,' says Selindak, picking up the bottle-stub. 'I do not believe that I shall . . .'

The vision faded; Quarvis waited, expecting another phase of the time-lost drama to begin. But there was nothing. The symbols lay motionless on the page, as inert as pebbles on a streambed.

'Disappointed, Quarvis?' asked Kraike.

Stirring himself, Quarvis rose and carried the bowl to the window. 'No. I learned a great deal.'

'But you did not see what you feared,' said Kraike. 'The fall of Vohoria, the citizens slaughtered in the streets, the great buildings vanishing in flame.'

'It is a strange omission.' Quarvis emptied the embers into the garden. 'Such catastrophes are the meat and drink of conventional histories.'

'How could it be included in *The Chronicle*, when Selindak did not observe it? By the time the Druinese arrived, we were halfway to the desert. I was still feverish, unaware of anything except the hallucinations that capered through my mind, and Selindak – he did not look back. An odd lapse for a historian, perhaps. But nothing was lost. One act of barbarism looks much like another.'

'I expected to see the desert,' said Quarvis, taking *The Chronicle* from the rug and placing it on the desk.

'There was little *to* see. Thousands upon thousands of Vohorin, seared by the sun during the day, freezing to death by night. Hunger, sickness, desolation – they too are the same wherever they are encountered.'

'Thousands upon thousands? The Church boasted that it had *annihilated* the Vohorin people.'

'A lie,' said Kraike. 'If they had followed us into the desert, perhaps it would have been so. But the Druinese soldiers had no appetite for the endless sands; they were not equipped for such a journey. I suspect they believed we would not last long, either. To the untrained eye, the desert is a vast, harsh emptiness, yielding neither food nor water. But some amongst us knew how to survive. We *endured*, Quarvis. And we rediscovered our faith.'

'The Erethin were amongst those who fled into the desert,'

continued Kraike, naming the priestly order which had kept faith in Toros when everyone else had cast him aside. 'They preached; the people listened. Vohoria's collapse was punishment for forsaking Toros; only faith in the Visionary-amongst-the-Trees could restore our shattered nation.'

'And they believed?' Hearing the hope in his own voice, Quarvis detected a hint of zealotry. In a more subdued tone, he added, 'The faith grew strong?'

'Eventually,' replied Kraike. 'The Erethin did not merely preach, but ensured Toros was central to our lives. Prayers were uttered before every conceivable activity: hunting, cooking, fetching water, copulating . . .'

'Children were born in the desert?'

'They were the most faithful of all,' said Kraike. 'They knew no different.'

Quarvis tapped his fingertips on *The Chronicle*. 'All was not lost. And so much was gained.'

'Vohoria is not the land it once was. When the converts ventured back into what remained of the towns and cities, they brought their faith with them. Now, it is a holy land, governed by the Erethin.' His gaze hardened. 'What did you *truly* fear about the final vision?'

'I – I did not want to see Vohoria fall.'

'Yet you seemed disappointed when you were denied exactly that.'

'I remarked that the omission was strange, nothing more.' Quarvis grew cold. There *was* something more, something he had hoped the sorcerer would not suspect.

'Do not deceive me,' said Kraike. 'Your guilt is written upon your face.'

Quarvis swallowed, nodded. 'The Church claimed your invasion was repelled by the Four's intervention. They gave no details, except to say a glorious miracle occurred, and your armies had no choice but to retreat. I feared they might be telling the truth.' He raised a hand. 'I knew it was not so. I can see through the Church's lies easily enough. Nonetheless, I . . . I was uncertain. I am sorry; I have always been prone to doubts. It is a failing of mine.'

'Do not speak too harshly of yourself,' said Kraike. 'It is better to be a man who requires evidence, than one who believes every appealing fantasy that comes his way. Your doubts are gone, I trust?'

'Yes. The Four played no part, only an assassin.'

A smile. 'And you will not torment yourself by interpreting the assassin's actions as miraculous? You will not wonder if the Four entered his heart, granting him extraordinary courage?'

Quarvis chuckled. 'I shall leave such convoluted – and dishonest – interpretations to the Masters.'

'Very wise,' said Kraike. As Quarvis moved to leave, the sorcerer said, 'Do you intend to accompany me to Vohoria, when the time comes?'

'If it is permitted.' Quarvis was astonished that his voice remained level. He wanted to see Vohoria more than anything else – except the resurrection of Toros. For a moment, he feared that Kraike would say it was *not* permissible. That his talents were required elsewhere, perhaps.

'Good,' said Kraike. 'You will be a welcome addition to the Erethin.'

CHAPTER SIXTEEN

Waking shortly before dawn, Ballas left the tavern and wandered the wide, clean-swept streets of Redberry.

The mission was over, more or less. And Ballas's black mood had materialised, closing around him like a dark rendering of the Whitelockian mist. Soon, he would be back at the Roost, submerged in a world of tedium. Long hours would pass, filled by an unsatisfying nothingness. No drama, no excitement, just seemingly endless boredom.

He crossed a market square. All around him, local citizens were setting up their stalls, preparing for the day's trade. Their lives did not amount to much, thought Ballas. But they laughed and joked, enjoying the fresh warmth of the new-risen sun, and seemed happy enough. He envied them. They were content with their lots, satisfied with their humdrum existences. Once, he had craved such a life: he envisioned himself with a wife, some children, working dawn to dusk in quiet joy, raising cattle, growing wheat . . . Idyllic, perhaps, but he knew it would prove unendurable: the boredom would kill him.

And that was the problem, he thought as he left the market. A part of him was continually dissatisfied, no matter the circumstances. He could be basking in riches, wanting for nothing, entertained by a legion of dark-eyed, half-clad women and his heart would still be as numb as a lump of clay. Only when he was embroiled in blood, thunder and disruption did he feel good. No, good was too strong a word. Rather, he felt *alive*. And that too was a problem, for these moments were far from pleasant: they were crammed with the terror, dismay and half-panic of a hunted animal cowering in undergrowth.

On a long street, he caught himself peering through the window of a vintner's shop. There, bottles of whisky, wine and brandy nestled on a bed of straw, gleaming in the early light. His palms itched; his mouth felt dry. He had brought a little money, enough for a half-bottle of something strong, something that would take the edge off his low mood.

'Ah, up with the larks, are you?' The shopkeeper stepped out of the doorway, rubbing his hands. Fond of his own wares, he had a liquor-swollen nose, as red and bulging as a strawberry, and scarlet veins spindled through his cheeks. 'You seeking aught in particular? Why not step inside – there's bound to be something to tickle your fancy. I've got oceans of everything.' He beckoned through the doorway.

Staying put, Ballas stared at the window display, wondering which spirit he would like best. It would have to be something Standaire would not detect upon his breath; technically, the mission was not over, and Hawks were forbidden from indulging whilst on duty. One of the colourless liquors, like Keltuskan firewater. Potent, soothing but *discreet*. To be safe, he would return to the market and eat something covered in spices. A garlic-roasted chicken, maybe. Or peppered steak.

'You got Halvike Clear?' he asked the shopkeeper.

'As many bottles as there are stars in the sky,' replied the man, disappearing inside.

Ballas walked to the doors, then paused, his attention caught by a deep voice rumbling from some distance along the street.

'An old man, dressed like a vagrant,' said the voice, booming softly like thunder rolling through a distant valley. 'White hair and a white beard, both as grubby as a whore's bedlinen. Mind you, he's got a regal sort of face. And there's intelligence in his eyes. He will not be alone.'

Ignoring the shopkeeper, Ballas strode to the end of the road. Peering around the edge of a building, he realised he had walked further than he expected. He was near the city gates. A group of Wardens were conversing with a very tall, very broad man. Garbed in furs, with a jawbone necklace hanging around his throat, Ballas recognised him, not by sight, but by description.

This was the man Olech had spoken of.

This was the Dogman.

Warden Commander Raisle had changed over the years. His hair had grown grey-white, his face had gained a cragginess which, in the proper circumstances, lent him an imposing air, and his eyesight was slowly failing. But the change he noticed more than any other was his ever-increasing impatience. Once, long ago, he had earned the nickname 'the Stone' because of his stolid, unemotional demeanour. No longer. Behind his back, his fellow Wardens referred to him as 'the Kettle'. Once his heat is rising, they said, he flips his lid and billows steam.

Right now, his lid was flipping.

He ought to have found the visitor amusing. Garbed in animal skins, with a string of animal jawbones hanging around his neck – at a glance, he spotted the mandibles of a badger, fox, deer and what might have been a shark – he looked like a savage that, by some miracle, had found himself transplanted into the modern age. His hair was long, straw-yellow, as bushy as a hayrick, and a beard of equal thickness and disarray sprouted on his jaw. Yet he was well-spoken, enunciating his words carefully, in the deep, rich voice of a stage-actor. Maybe *that* was what he was: a thespian who had lost his troupe, and was seeking them in Redberry. But that was of no odds. For several minutes he had badgered Raisle, asking the same questions over and over again.

'An old man,' he said, 'dressed like a vagrant. White hair and a white beard, both as grubby as a whore's bedlinen. Mind you, he's got a regal sort of face. And there's intelligence in his eyes. He will not be alone.'

'I do not care whether he is travelling with a legion of singing monkeys,' snapped Raisle. 'It is not my job to reunite you with your missing friend.'

'What harm would it do?' The stranger pouted – an odd expression for such a large man. For some reason, it bolstered Raisle's suspicion he might be an actor. As a breed, they had slightly overactive faces. Always, they were gurning, smirking or employing any number of exaggerated tics and grimaces. And to think – they considered such facial gymnastics to be an art form!

'For the last time,' said Raisle, fighting to keep his voice level, 'you are free to seek out your companion for yourself. But I cannot assist you.'

The stranger puffed on his pipe. That too was something that irritated Raisle. He had no objection to the habit itself; he enjoyed a bowlful as much as the next man. But the stranger had a particular way of smoking that was uniquely annoying. He sucked on the pipestem slowly, *reverently*, as if engaged in some sort of sacrament.

'"Cannot",' said the stranger, thoughtfully. 'Are you playing a little loose with the definition, Commander?'

'Loose?'

'Do you actually mean *cannot*? Or is it *will not*? If it is the latter, you are guilty of dishonesty – and, as a Warden of high rank, you ought to be ashamed.'

Raisle's face grew hot. 'How dare you tell me what I should be ashamed of! Very well. I meant *will not*, as I have explained a hundred times already. Now, seek out your friends, if you must, or leave my town. I shall not tolerate any misbehaviour from your sort.'

The stranger sucked on his pipe, paused, then took the implement from his mouth. Slowly, he banged out the ashes onto his palm, then scattered them on the ground. He refilled the bowl from a leather pouch, ignited a taper from a torch burning by the gates, then relit the pipe. 'What makes you think you have a choice, regarding what you will – and will not – tolerate?' he said, blowing a thick miasma of smoke into the air.

'These stripes say I have a choice,' snapped Raisle, jabbing a finger to the three red bars on his tunic shoulder.

'They do, do they? No,' smiled the stranger, shaking his head. 'Clearly, you are confusing authority with power. Of the former, you have much. Of the latter, you are barren.' Taking the pipe from his mouth, he fingered the tobacco, thoughtfully, as if finding meaning in the smouldering strands. 'I will grant you one chance to reconsider. You have been manning these gates since nightfall yesterday evening. Do not deny it; you are squinting like an undenned badger, plunged suddenly into sunlight. You will have seen my friend enter Redberry. As he is unfamiliar with the town, he will have asked where he could find lodgings and you would have told him.' He smiled. 'You gate-keepers take backhanders from tavern-owners, do you not? In exchange for a few coins, you put business their way.'

Raisle's anger flared. Admittedly, the accusation was true – but that was not the point. The stranger had no business accusing him of dodgy dealings. 'Enough,' he barked. 'Get out of my town. If you don't go of your own free will, you will be escorted through the gates.' He placed a sinister emphasis on *escorted*, insinuating his departure would be less than gentle. Understanding, a couple of guards approached the stranger.

'Stay back,' said the stranger, raising a hand. Then, he lifted that same hand to his mouth, bent his fingers and whistled, releasing three sharp, piercing blasts.

Alongside the gates there was a watchtower, overlooking the moorland beyond Redberry. The Warden manning this vantage point began yelling. 'Close the gates! Close the gates, damn you!' The Warden's name was Servus, and he was as unflappable a character as Raisle had ever encountered. Yet his voice was panic-cracked, as shrill as a startled piglet's. He pointed stupidly at the grasslands, eyes agog. 'For pity's sake, close them!'

The stranger was smiling. 'You had your chance,' he said.

Six colossal hounds loped through the gate. Gathering around the stranger, they yapped and gribbled, manifesting the strangely painful over-excitement unique to the canine species. At first, Raisle could not believe his eyes. The dogs were *huger* than huge, each the size of a young horse. Their fur was steel-grey, their jaws warped by a preponderance of large, spittle-greased fangs. He stared, astonished. He could have been no more startled – or incredulous – if the Four themselves had strolled into Redberry.

The stranger tapped his own shoulder, mimicking Raisle when, moments ago, he had pointed to the markings of his rank. 'Your stripes give you authority,' he said. 'But they do not grant you any *power*. Powerful is the man,' intoned the stranger, 'surrounded by dangerous friends.' He knuckled the dogs' heads, slapped their flanks and tickled their chins, clearly enjoying their company. 'What do you say, my girls? Shall we show this buffoon what the embroidery on his tunic is worth? Stripes indeed!' With appalling slowness, he lifted his fingers to his mouth again and whistled, four times. Peeling away from their master, the hounds set upon the Wardens around the gates. Despite their size they moved swiftly, leaping upon the men and ripping out their throats with their colossal jaws.

A few Wardens turned and ran, but the dogs pursued them, leaping high upon their backs and clamping their jaws around their helm-encased heads, fangs buckling the steel.

Raisle stared at the stranger. His anger had evaporated, supplanted by fear. He too turned and ran, even though he knew it was useless. When he felt a pair of strong paws strike his upper back, he was not surprised. And it was with a strange sense of relief, and gratitude that his fear was coming to an end, that he heard the steel of his helm crumpling.

'A fur-clad giant, bedecked with jawbones,' said Helligraine, ashen-faced. Sitting on his bed, he hurriedly tugged on his boots. 'That is the Dogman. And his dogs are here? Sweet mercy, we are doomed. We should have ridden through the night, not pausing until we reached the home of Leptus Quarvis.'

Standaire opened the lodging-room door. 'We will escape them, your holiness. Our horses are close by.'

'They can run swifter than any mount,' said Helligraine, rising. Then, cupping a hand to his ear, 'Can you hear it? They are frolicking.'

Breathing heavily from his breakneck run to the tavern, Ballas listened. Barking, muffled by the window-glass. And something else, something disturbing. Screams, cutting through the early morning air.

'Dogman has a contract with his dogs,' said Helligraine. 'In exchange for their loyalty, he grants them certain rewards. Now and again, he permits them to play. Those cries you hear arise not from fear, but pain. Is it not so?'

Ballas could not tell for certain but he suspected the Master was right.

'He is quite mad,' Helligraine went on. 'Always, he has teetered on the crumbling edge of sanity. Now, the ground has given way, and he is tumbling into the black abyss of lunacy.

The letter from the Easterner is at the root of this. He stood to make a lot of money from selling me; now the bargain lies in ruins. He is here, I wager, to seize me come what may, deliver me to the Easterner, take his money and disappear. This is all my doing.'

'Come, your holiness,' said Ekkerlin. 'We must go.'

They hurried down to the common room. A trio of drinkers sat at their tables, sipping their drinks slowly, listening to the barks and screams drifting in from outside.

As Standaire headed for the door, Ballas caught his arm.

'A poor idea,' he said, tilting his head to the window.

Outside, a hound loped along the street, sniffing the air. Standaire froze, absorbing the size of the creature. Then he slid the door bolts, quietly.

'What's happening out there?' asked a red-faced drinker as he got to his feet. 'It sounds like the Forest has ruptured and the town is full of demons.'

'It is worse than that,' muttered Ballas, striding behind the serving bar.

'Aiy!' snapped the tavern-keeper. 'You cannot come back here. If you want something, I'll bring it over. Go on, take a seat.'

Ignoring him, Ballas ducked into a back room. A door stood in the far wall, obstructed by barrels and crates full of bottles. Casting them aside, Ballas tried the door. It was locked. Returning to the serving bar, he held out a hand to the tavern-keeper.

'Key,' said the Hawk.

The tavern-master scowled, nostrils quivering. 'You must be jesting. You walk in here—'

'Give me the key,' repeated Ballas.

'Not a chance. This is my establishment. And besides, no one makes demands of *me*, not here, not anywhere.'

Ballas spotted an iron key resting on a shelf behind the bar. As he reached for it, the tavern-master grabbed his wrist. 'You be leaving that just where it is,' he said – then dropped as Ballas headbutted him.

As he fell, the tavern-keeper caught hold of the shelf, tearing it from the wall. Bottles fell, exploding into shards. Stooping, Ballas grabbed the key. As he did so, the front door jolted, struck by something solid. Hurrying into the back room, Ballas jammed the key into the lock. He gave it a twist, but it did not budge. Cursing, he tried again. No success.

Ekkerlin appeared, jostling him aside. 'Let me try – before you snap it.' She worked the key, twisting it gently one way then the other. When it clicked, she pulled open the door. At the same instant the front door crashed open. The drinkers cried out; Ballas heard chairs falling, then a throaty, furious snarling.

Ekkerlin, Standaire and Helligraine rushed into the street. Snatching the key from the lock, Ballas followed. As he turned to shut the door, a drinker stumbled into the back room, his clothes blood-soaked, a flap of claw-torn flesh lolling from his cheek. As he lurched toward the door, Ballas held out a hand, intending to pull him through, but the dog was there, suddenly, lunging into the back room. Cursing, Ballas slammed the door and locked it.

They went to the stables across the street to retrieve their horses. As they grew close, Ballas realised it was a pointless errand. Fear-maddened, the horses whinnied and bucked, banging their hooves on the door and walls.

He swore, bitterly. Obvious questions surfaced in his mind. What now? Where do we go?

'Anhaga,' said Ekkerlin quietly.

A second dog stood at the end of the street. Its head tilted back, it sniffed the air, seeking a scent.

'Their eyesight is poor,' murmured Helligraine. 'But their sense of smell is astonishing. Like sharks, they can detect their prey from miles away.'

Ballas turned away from the dog. Two hundred yards away, there was a three-floored building with gleaming brass window frames and a bronze-lettered sign hanging over the door. *Laindek's Exquisitorium*. On either side of the door was an oil painting, shielded from the elements by glass: the first depicted a pie resting in a lake of gravy, steam floating from a slit in the crust, the second a broiled salmon on a bed of parsley.

It was their only escape route. Racing over, Ballas yanked the doors open. The Hawks and Helligraine plunged through. Ballas slammed shut the door then slid the bolts, one near the top of the door, the other near the bottom. He turned to face an eating hall cluttered with circular tables. Twenty or so men were breaking their fasts, digging into greasy heaps of bacon, eggs and fried liver. Despite the dog, Ballas felt his appetite perk up. His guts rumbled.

A blue-liveried waiter approached. In one hand, he held a clay teapot by the handle. In the other, three beakers, all balanced on his palm and outstretched fingers. 'No, no, sir. You cannot lock the door. Our diners will not—'

'If you open this door,' warned Ballas, 'your diners will be *dined upon*.' The door shuddered as the dog flung its weight against it. The bolts strained; a nail popped loose, clattering onto the floor. The teapot and beakers dropped from the waiter's hands. Hot tea lapped against Ballas's boots. A few diners rose, staring at the door. Others froze, spoonfuls of dripping meat hovering beneath their lips. Another thud; the door shook. The waiter stepped back, eyes widening.

'By the Four's mercy, what—'

'Stay away from the windows. All of you.' Ballas barred the

door, sliding the wooden beam into its iron fittings. A delaying tactic, no more.

Sprinting across the hall, Ballas opened the door into the kitchen. A huge oven expelled thick waves of heat. The air shimmered with vaporous grease. A tubby man wrapped in a gravy-splattered apron fried black pudding slices in a pan, shoving them back and forth with a spatula. 'Vallingen,' he said without looking up. 'Tell those fussy idiots out there that if they claim this batch is underdone, I will be roasting their kidneys for the midday meals. Ungrateful pigs. They would not know fine cooking if it—' He glanced over. Realising Ballas was not who he thought he was, he pointed the spatula at the Hawk. 'Get out. Whoever you are, you have no business in my kitchen.'

Swatting the spatula aside, Ballas strode to the far wall. There was a door, flimsy-looking and bolted shut. Next to it, a small square window.

As Ballas peered out, a dog appeared. He momentarily thought it was the same one that had been battering the front door. But it was slightly bigger, and a long scar parted the shaggy fur on its right flank. Ballas stepped back before the dog spotted him.

'I said get out!' The cook grabbed Ballas's shoulder.

'Stay away from the window. There are dogs outside. Large ones.' Ballas pushed the man aside.

The cook was incredulous. 'Dogs? Ha! You stray into my place of work – then give me orders? Why should I not look out of the window? *My* window?' Hands on hips, he stumped belligerently to the window. A heartbeat later the glass shattered, the dog's head bursting in through a flurry of shards. The window measured barely three handspans up and across, and the beast travelled only eight or nine inches through until its bulky shoulders jammed against the frame. But it was far enough. Its jaws clamped hard on the cook's head, one set of fangs piercing the top of his skull, the other crunching upward beneath his chin. Bones crackled; gristle popped. The dog pulled back from the window. The cook collapsed, his face no longer a face at all, but a grotesque red blossom of raw meat. His skin was gone; so too his jawbone.

Ballas nearly pitied him.

'Up,' he said, returning to the hall. He paced toward a staircase. 'There is no other way.'

They climbed. The first floor was a dining hall, identical to the one below. As they hurried to another staircase, the Exquisitorium's front doors crashed open, the bolts springing from the wood, the bar snapping. Men shouted; chairs clattered onto the floor. Then: barking, loud enough to fracture stone. Suddenly, the entire building was full of screams, some shrill and pure, like a high note played on a flute, others disintegrating into ragged raspy yowls as they strained into the upper registers. All echoed up the staircase with such clarity it seemed the stricken men were there, on the first floor, as invisible but tortured presences.

'What do we do?' It was Helligraine who spoke. Despite his white hair and age-creased face, it was easy to forget he was an old man, burdened by an old man's frailties. Exertion pinkened his cheeks. Sweat trickled down his face. He breathed heavily and shallowly, as if the air was polluted by noxious vapours. A frantic light danced in his normally placid eyes. He was frightened. Ballas suspected he also felt strangely cheated: to have escaped the Dogman, only to be recaptured a day later? An agonising twist of fate. So severe, perhaps, it was enough to make him wish he had not been rescued at all.

Another staircase rose to the next floor. Here, there was nothing except an expanse of bare floorboards, a few chairs and a ladder leaning against the wall beneath a trapdoor in the ceiling. Sprinting over, footsteps thudding, Ballas climbed the ladder and swung open the trapdoor. Early sunlight washed over him. Somewhere, birds sang. He hauled himself onto the Exquisitorium's flat roof.

Wheezing, Helligraine followed him up the ladder. As he neared the top, Ballas proffered a helping hand. Helligraine swatted it away, almost playfully.

'Forgive my wretchedness a moment ago.' He clambered up. 'The dogs momentarily unmanned me.'

Once Ekkerlin and Standaire were through, Ballas hauled up the ladder and shut the trapdoor. Not an instant too soon. The instant the trapdoor was down it bounced up a few inches, propelled by the blood-washed snout of one of the dogs leaping up from below. The trapdoor lay twelve or so feet above the floor; there was no chance the dog could get through. Nonetheless, Ballas stepped on the trapdoor, holding it down with his considerable weight. The wood jolted beneath his feet as the dog jumped again. Ballas's hackles twitched. He looked around.

The marketplace lay in the distance. Tattered blood-sodden figures sprawled amongst upended stalls. Some lay motionless, as lifeless as the meat-vendors' plucked chickens and scrubbed pigs; others crawled, writhed and spasmed, their vital juices gathering in vivid pools. Others, unharmed but shocked, drifted to and fro, heads in their hands, sleepwalking through the carnage. A breeze lifted, carrying the sounds of weeping and groaning to the rooftop. Ballas shuddered. He had not heard this combination of noises since childhood. His mind drifted for a moment, rolling back to the green valley that was once his home. He began sinking into a reverie, but Helligraine moved beside him.

'We are safe up here, yes?' The Master's composure had returned.

'Reckon so,' said Ballas, distantly.

'So what do we do?'

'Wait.' Ballas shrugged. 'The Wardens will sort out the dogs.'

'Do you think so?'

'I saw some carrying shortbows. If they have any sense, they'll smear poison on the arrowtips.'

'Wardens – with good sense? Despite your impious demeanour, I think you must believe in miracles.' Chuckling, Helligraine patted Ballas's shoulder.

Ballas did not share the holy man's good humour. His instinct for trouble quivered, like an insect's antennae. Something had changed. Something subtle, something barely noticeable. The dog had jumped only twice at the trapdoor; finding the barrier unyielding on both attempts, it had given up trying to break through. This was understandable. Any dog would behave in the same way. But these dogs were unusually intelligent, according to Helligraine. Faced with an obstacle, they would not abandon their assigned task. They would think, as far as they could, and find a solution. Ballas knelt. Listened. Hoped to hear signs that the dog who pursued them was somewhere below, waiting. Claws scratching on floorboards, an occasional frustrated snarl, heavy breaths rumbling from a colossal chest – anything would do.

There was nothing. Only silence.

Ballas looked beyond the rooftop. A second building of equal height stood next to the Exquisitorium. A flight of stone steps rose from an opening onto the rooftop. What was the neighbouring building used for? Nothing, Ballas recalled. It stood empty – except for a team of workmen, toiling within. Tilting his head, he listened. Through the wallstones, he heard cries of fear and pain. His gaze flitted to the gap between the Exquisitorium and its neighbour. How far? Ten, fifteen feet? Close enough for a dog to jump.

He looked to the other side of the Exquisitorium. There was

a third building ten paces away. With an adequate run up, a Hawk could leap the distance. But Helligraine? In his adventurous younger days, perhaps. Not now. Despite his elevated spirits, the Master still breathed laboriously. Oceans of sweat poured down his face. His eyes were faintly heavy-lidded and he stooped slightly. Exhaustion was setting in. Terror had driven him this far. Now, he was rapidly becoming a spent force. Abandoning the trapdoor, Ballas grabbed the ladder and laid it across the gap between the Exquisitorium and the third building, forming a makeshift bridge. As he did so, Helligraine whispered, 'What? Are the Four mocking us?'

Ballas turned. A dog bounded up the steps onto the roof of the disused building, followed by a second.

'Get Helligraine over,' Ballas snapped at Ekkerlin. 'I will hold the dogs at bay.'

Ekkerlin did not argue. Taking his elbow, she led Helligraine to the ladder.

The dogs gathered at the roof-edge. Trembling with pent-up energy and scenting the air, their half-blind eyes lifted to the sky. Ballas moved to the edge of the Exquisitorium roof. Faced them. Waited. If they jumped – when – he would drop low and punch upwards. A well-aimed chest strike *might* be enough to flip them backward into empty air. If he was lucky. If they did not both jump at the same time. But if they did come over together? He would flip one and do whatever he could with the other.

It was odd, he mused, with the chilly breathlessness he often experienced before violence. He hated the prolonged periods of boredom in between missions. But when the missions came, he did not enjoy the danger. He felt sick, frightened, horribly mortal. It seemed that he could not cope with either state: in their own ways, tranquillity and drama were equally unbearable. He looked at the dogs. Either of the creatures could be the death of him. He observed their heavy, implacable muscles, the red-stained fur around their mouths, the fangs that had already done so much damage and were sharp enough to do so much more. Intelligent as they were, he doubted they possessed an imagination. And without imaginations, they had no notion of death. Thus, they could act fearlessly. Excitement floated off their huge bodies like waves of heat from a brazier. It was as pure and sweet as springwater, uncorrupted by apprehensiveness. Doubt. Caution. He envied them; they had the advantage.

Standaire stepped beside him.

'Are they over?' Ballas asked. He did not dare look away from the dogs.

'Halfway. Helligraine has gone first, Ekkerlin following close behind.'

Silence. The dogs caught their sought-after scent. They padded to the roof-edge. How badly impaired was their vision? Could they see the drop between the buildings? Could they sense it in some other way? Instinctively, he patted the knives sheathed on his belt. He grimaced. The weapons would be useless against these creatures. If he had the time and opportunity, coupled with considerable good fortune, he might drive a blade through an eye socket into the brain. Or slash open a belly so the guts poured out. But it was not likely. The dogs moved too quickly. Any movement was registered a fatally long time after it happened. It was like trying to pick out the individual wingbeats of a hummingbird.

'They are over,' said Standaire.

'I suggest you follow them, sir. If the dogs jump once you're over, knock the ladder away. Then leave. Helligraine is our priority.'

Wordlessly, Standaire moved away. He was gone a five count before the first dog leapt. Ballas realised immediately he had underestimated the creatures. With the shortest of run ups, the dog sailed over the gap—

—and over Ballas's head.

Paws scuffed as the dog alighted on the rooftop. Ballas whirled. The dog bounded toward Standaire, who had just knelt to cross the ladder on all fours.

'General!' Ballas dived full-length, seizing the dog's hind paw. The coarse fur scratched against his palm. He felt iron-hard bone and steel-tough tendon. The dog scrabbled forward, dragging the Hawk several feet. Standaire glanced back. Twisting, he drew a knife and swept it at the dog's throat. The dog jerked back, dodging the blade by inches. Then it twisted, its paw breaking free from Ballas's grip. Scrambling to his feet, Ballas kicked it beneath the jaw. Miraculously, the blow struck home, knocking back the creature's head. Attacking from behind, Standaire slammed the blade into the dog's spine, then, straining, wrenched out the weapon. Blood welled from the wound, trickling through the grey fur like lava through a forest of dead trees. Yowling, the dog spun and lunged again at the general. Grabbing the thick fur around its rump, Ballas dragged it several paces away from his superior. Abandoning the ladder, Standaire took five long paces from the roof-edge, ran, then jumped. As he flew over the gap, the dog tore free and followed, springing like a horse over a gate. Swiping out a hand, Ballas caught its trailing paw, gripping it for a fraction of an instant before it jerked free.

It was enough to diminish the dog's momentum. As Standaire landed on the opposite rooftop, the dog launched itself over the gap, soared a distance then sank abruptly from view, plummeting to the street below. There was a muffled smack as it impacted on the paving stones. Overbalancing, Ballas stumbled, caught himself. Standaire stood alongside Ekkerlin and Helligraine.

'Come now, Hawk Ballas,' he ordered.

Ballas glanced over his shoulder. On the rooftop, the remaining dog was readying itself to jump, scuttering back and forth.

'No, General. If I go, it will follow.' It was the truth. The first dog fell because Ballas had hindered its flight. If he had not done so, it would easily have made it over. 'Get yourselves away.'

'Anhaga!' It was Ekkerlin who called out. 'Do as you're told. Together, we will stand a better chance if the dog *does* follow.'

'Shut up.' Ballas did not look at Ekkerlin. '*You* do as you are told – and piss off.' As soon as he spoke the dog jumped. Ballas ran, hoping to meet it as it landed. He was too slow. As soon as its paws touched the roof it leapt again, its wide-open jaws hurtling toward the Hawk's face. Anticipating the move, Ballas dived, rolling sideways. He stood. He reached for a knife. Before he could draw the weapon, the dog rushed at him. He dived and rolled again. The dog spun, then stood, flanks expanding and contracting with every breath. Watching him. Sizing him up. Calculating its next move. Ballas's heart turned to lead. Whatever the next move was, it was likely to prove fatal. Fighting these dogs was different from fighting Ol' Jess; these were young, fit and healthy.

The Hawk was exhausted. His body felt absurdly heavy, his clothes as weighty as armour. He looked into the dog's eye. The dog no longer seemed an animal. It was a mechanism, a soulless contraption specifically designed to rend flesh. It existed solely to bring death. It was no different from an axe-blade. A hangman's noose. A phial of poison. Ballas felt his nerves cracking apart. His composure shattering. His stomach writhed. His eyes stung. A part of him wanted to kneel and offer his throat to the dog. Do it. Get it over with. But a stronger part of him wanted to live. In some red-lit corner of his mind, something fractionally less than an idea flared.

An instinctive notion of what he should do. Something that would not – could not – have occurred to him if his mind were clear.

Turning, he ran to the roof-edge. Slowed at the last moment. Stepped off.

Falling, he twisted. Grabbed the edge. Hung there, fingers straining, knuckles jutting. A shadow fell upon him. He looked up.

The dog gazed down, blood-fouled saliva dripping languidly from its fangs.

Ballas heaved himself up several inches. He thrust up his right hand, seizing the fur covering the dog's throat and the flesh beneath. Roaring with effort, he pulled, simultaneously hauling himself up and dragging the dog off the roof. The creature fell, tumbling past the Hawk like a lump of broken masonry. Struggling, Ballas wrenched himself onto the rooftop. He lay face-down for a moment.

When he lifted his head, he discovered he was not alone.

CHAPTER SEVENTEEN

The Dogman ought to have been a laughable figure, decked out in furs, the jawbone necklace hanging around his throat, the pipe clamped between his teeth.

But Ballas felt no urge to mock him. The Hawk was uneasy. Worse, a touch fearful. He wondered if the Dogman's size was the cause. Ballas rarely encountered men of a height equivalent to his own. And the Dogman was taller, much taller. Broader too. Sweeping his gaze up and down, Ballas thought, *There is naught I can do. There is no way in. He is too solid, too large. Wherever I hit, however hard, he will not fall, he will not break . . .*

A faint smile hung on the Dogman's lips. He seemed pleased with Ballas's disquiet. Removing the pipe from his mouth, he tapped the hot ashes onto his palm, held them up a moment then blew them away.

'You are a dead man,' he said, tucking the pipe in his pocket. 'In a world swarming with possible errors, you have made the biggest mistake of all. You did not do so knowingly. No, you acted in ignorance. This is true of every man who crosses me. If they had the tiniest inkling of the storm that would break over them, of the fiery rains that would fall, they would think twice.' He stroked his beard. 'Do you believe this will end well for you?'

Ballas did not reply. He knew what was coming. Violence followed a pattern, starting with harsh words, insults and threats, which served not only to intimidate but grant each combatant a chance to size up his adversary. Then the combatants would square up against one another and, when the tension rose to a certain pitch, the first punch would be thrown. After that, both fighters turned into Forest demons, feral and ruthless. Any pretence of grace, elegance and fairness evaporated. Men did not fight like the heroes of epic poetry. They became flailing, spitting, snarling distillations of the survival impulse.

Ballas often followed the pattern. On this occasion, however, the idea appalled him. He did not want to size up the Dogman, for the more he regarded the giant, the greater his unease became. And there was no point in attempting to intimidate him; the Dogman knew he had the advantage. Yet Ballas paused, observing something akin to madness in his eyes. It was not pure lunacy, the kind afflicting the chattering inmates of an asylum. No, it was mediated by self-control. Knowing it lurked within him, the Dogman treated it as a source of energy, as something to be utilised, like the tension in a drawn bowstring.

Ballas licked his lips. Hesitated. Then, leaping to his feet, he charged, intending to knock the Dogman to the floor. If he succeeded, he could unsheathe a knife and slash the man's throat; it would be over in a dragonfly's heartbeat. Anticipating the move, the Dogman danced aside and Ballas hurtled past. Halting, the Hawk spun – and the Dogman punched him squarely in the face. The impact was astonishing; Ballas reeled, purple sparks flaring in his vision. Grinning tightly, the Dogman advanced, flurrying blows into his head and chest, a bewildering hailstorm of concussive shocks. Ballas raised his arms in defence. But the onslaught had already stopped.

Pacing backward, the Dogman said, 'I admire your ambition. A little sapling like you, facing up to an oak. Very commendable.' He was barely out of breath. 'Would you like to try again?'

Ballas decided he would. But it would not be a fair fight. He reached for the dagger at his hip. His fingertips fumbled against the sheathe. Empty, he realised. He must have dropped the weapon. He reached to another sheathe; that too contained no blade. Blinking, he looked past the Dogman. All four of his knives lay twenty yards away, glinting in the sunlight.

'I was a pickpocket in my youth,' said the Dogman. 'I learned that like a stage-conjuror, one must employ the art of mis-direction.' He threw a few air-punches. 'Not the subtlest way of diverting one's attention, I grant you. But effective.'

Spitting on the ground, Ballas took stock. His lips were burst, his nose crushed and left eye was swelling shut. His ribs ached, as if broken, and his guts throbbed. He glanced at the trapdoor. He could jump through, if he wished. But to what end? The dog was waiting below. No, he realised, not one. But four, swarming in the gloom, rattling their claws, huffing and yelping. He looked to the neighbouring building, wondering if he could leap across as the dead hound had done. He suspected he could – but only if he was granted a long run up. He looked to the other rooftop. Helligraine and the others had disappeared, and the ladder – even if there had been some way he could have scrambled along it swiftly enough to elude the Dogman – was missing. He was trapped, he realised.

The Dogman prowled toward Ballas. Without hesitating, Ballas rushed at him, catching him off-guard with a succession of bone-splitting punches. Only a few found their target; the Dogman bobbed and weaved, as nimble as a champion pugilist, and replied with blows of his own, catching Ballas on the cheek and forehead with appalling ease. A whining, buzzing noise arose in Ballas's ears, as if locusts swarmed inside his skull. Every impact plunged him momentarily into darkness.

This is too much, he thought, stumbling away to the other side of the roof. He stood then, punch-drunk, fell to his knees.

As he did so, the Dogman scooped up his knives and tossed them off the roof. 'Best if you are not tempted, yes?' he said. 'Now, how are you feeling? Are you fit to continue? I am not a physician, but you look a little shaken up. Surprised too, if I am not mistaken. But that is to be expected. I daresay this is a novel experience for you, getting trounced in a fair fight.' Chuckling, he rubbed his hands together. 'You are getting everything you deserve. You and your companions have caused me a great deal of trouble. Worse, you have nearly– *nearly* – lost me a huge amount of money. I intended to sell Shaelus to an Eastern merchant next week. Yet, when I returned to my village yesterday, I discovered the old bastard is missing. Thus, I have been forced to go on a hunting expedition. Still, there are worse things that can befall a man. After all, I have enjoyed myself thus far. It is nice to see my dogs get some exercise.'

'What about the revolution?' said Ballas, seeking to delay the Dogman from any further attack.

'Revolution?' frowned the Dogman.

'The Scarlet Twilight.'

'Who told you about that? One of the villagers, I assume. Ah, those poor mistaken fools!' He laughed uproariously. 'The Twilight is a vulgar ruse. I needed some men to keep an eye on Shaelus, and to assist me in other ventures. For one month, I trawled the taverns of Northern Druine, seeking outlaws of every complexion, men who loathed the Church and would gladly do my bidding, if it would lead to that institution being flung into the privy pit of history. Once they had been, ah, *recruited*, I took them to the village and yes, they gulped down my lies like pigs at a trough. To a man, they believed they would be heroes. It is amazing how easily stupid men are gulled. Prey upon their fancies, and they are yours.'

'I saw the armoury.' By degrees, Ballas's head was clearing, his balance returning, the purple sparks fading from his eyes.

'It is the little details that make a deception,' shrugged the Dogman. 'Give an idiot a bit of steel and tell him he is a warrior – well, he will believe it, won't he? It makes no difference if he is as yellow as piss-stain on a condemned man's leggings. He thinks, Yes, I *am* the stuff of legend, and soon everyone shall know it.' He pulled the pipe from his pocket, looked at it, then returned it to his pocket, as if remembering suddenly where he was.

'You took a risk,' said Ballas.

'So what?'

'A *stupid* risk,' said Ballas. 'If those men *were* idiots, and they hated the Church, what was to say they would not avenge themselves on the Master whilst your back was turned?'

'The Master? What are you speaking of? The old man is barely even the master of his own bladder.'

Ballas's head cleared a touch more. 'His name is Helligraine.'

'There is only one Helligraine I know of, and he . . .' Confusion touched the Dogman's eyes. Then realisation dawned.

The Dogman stared. For several long moments he did nothing else, was *capable* of nothing else. Ballas sensed his mind spinning like a pinwheel firework, spraying sparks in every direction. His thick brows creased, uncreased, then creased again. His nostrils twitched. Instinctively, he reached into his pocket for his pipe, then caught himself, realising this was a poor time for languid contemplation.

'I did not know,' he said eventually.

'Horseshit. You abducted Helligraine from Grimlarren Moor. You *must* have known he and Shaelus were one and the same.'

'True, I *did* abduct Helligraine – but not from Grimlarren.' The Dogman laughed, coarsely. 'Helligraine has been missing for how long? A full year?'

'More or less.'

'He has been in my possession for a mere four months,' said

294

the Dogman, fingering the jawbones. 'Not that I knew it. No, to me he was Cavielle Shaelus, the scholar, the adventurer, the wolfsbane in the Church's holy wine . . . When we are reunited, I will congratulate him. Not once did he give the faintest clue that he was truly a man of the scarlet. As you implied, it might have cost him his life, if he had done so. My villagers would have submitted to their base passions; their hatred for the Church would have brimmed over, and neither I nor my dogs could have stopped them from ripping him apart. All things considered, he had a powerful incentive to keep his true nature hidden. And yet . . .'

The Dogman looked skywards, thinking. Ballas was tempted to charge him, whilst he hung in this distracted state. But he did not move. In the dazed, punch-drunk recesses of his mind, certain thoughts were forming, disturbing and unwholesome. He wanted the Dogman to continue speaking.

'Yet he did not seem to consider himself a Master. As far as I could tell, he thought of himself as Shaelus, and no one else.'

'What are you speaking of?'

'The circumstances in which I found him,' said the Dogman. Then, 'This changes everything. Shaelus, a Blessed Master — without knowing it, I acquired *two* assets instead of one. I shall be able to charge my friend in the East twice the money for the old man! He is rich, though; he will pay up.' He shook his head, wonderingly. 'Life is so strange,' he murmured.

'What were Helligraine's circumstances?' asked Ballas.

'Why should it concern you? Soon, you will be dead.'

Ballas did not reply. He did not need to: it was obvious that the Dogman wanted to tell his story, whatever it was. It was always the way with men like him: vain, boastful and self-regarding, they enjoyed nothing more than recounting their exploits, no matter how trivial or stupid.

'Do you believe in destiny? I do,' said the Dogman. 'Chance

encounters, random accidents, strange coincidences – they conspire to set a man on a certain path.

'In early spring, whilst travelling to conduct some business in Fallongrail, I was caught in a rainstorm. I took refuge in Heronsgate Town, a miserable nowhere-place, which I would have never visited, were it not for the downpour. As I sat in the common room, drying myself by the fire, a fellow settled close by. He warmed his hands at the fire, even though he was already warm enough: his face had a rosy pink glow, and perspiration glistened on his forehead. Straight away, I marked him for a scoundrel: we rogues can spot one another, you know. I expect he recognised that I too had no reverence for the rule of law. We fell into idle conversation. Observing his clothes were dirty, and there was dust in his hair, I asked if he had been travelling and, like myself, had come to Heronsgate to avoid the rain. He told me he had been labouring on an archaeological site, far out on Brellerin Fell. The work was strenuous, the pay derisory and, having had enough of being treated like a slave, he had fled, taking with him a wooden casket containing the other men's wages.

'He laughed as he told me this; I laughed too, not because I found the theft amusing, but because I wanted to put him at his ease. I suspected he had something more to tell me, and I wanted him to speak freely, without caution.

'And so he did.

'He claimed the dig was overseen by an elderly man who, on several occasions, had been referred to by others as "Cavielle Shaelus".

'He asked if knew the name; I said I did. We spoke a little about Shaelus's reputation, and the high prices his writings bring on the Dark Market. My new friend had an idea, one guaranteed to earn him a small fortune. But he needed help. Let us team up and kidnap Shaelus together, he said. Then we can force him to write forbidden texts – new ones, of course – which we can sell on the Market.

'I was sceptical. Could the legendary Shaelus be unearthing relics on Brellerin Fell? My friend promised he would prove it.

'Shaelus, he said, did not dwell at the dig site itself. Averse to the clangour of pick axes on stone – the archaeologists were hacking through rock, trying to gain entry to an underground cave – and the rough banter of the workers, he dwelled in a large tent a half-mile away. My friend said Shaelus was a creature of habit, living each day in an identical fashion to the last. He visited the site three times each day: at dawn, noon and dusk.

'We went to Brellerin Fell, arriving when the sun was at its zenith. We peered into the tent and, as my friend predicted, the man who might or might not have been Shaelus was not present. His belongings were there, though, in particular a thick bundle of forbidden texts, written by others than himself, and a stack of his own writings, the ink dark and fresh. I read a few paragraphs of the latter, and recognised the peculiar beauty of his prose. Thus, I was in no doubt: the elusive Shaelus was close by, and ripe for the taking.

'My friend and I retraced our steps a good distance, then hid behind some boulders. We would be safe here, he promised. He was half right. *I* would be safe; he, sadly, would not. Before he could so much as squeak in protest, I slit his throat. I have never been inclined to share my treasures with anyone. Besides, how could I trust him? He had betrayed Shaelus. What was to say he would not betray me?

'When night fell, and all was quiet, I returned to the tent. Shaelus was sleeping. I woke him, force-fed him a sedative draft and once he was unconscious, carried him over my shoulder, found a horse and rode away.' He shrugged, as if it had been as simple as tying his bootlaces.

'Two weeks later, Shaelus was imprisoned in Whitelock, and those clownish villagers were acting as his guardian. There. That is all there is to it. Except – I must give you my thanks. Helligraine is Shaelus, Shaelus is Helligraine – I would never have guessed, were it not for you. My Eastern friend will pay double for the old man! You can go to your grave knowing your last deed was a generous one. How many men can say that?'

The Dogman advanced, slowly, a glacier sliding over ancient moorland. Ballas got to his feet. Now the talking had stopped, he was dizzy again. And horribly weak. His body felt like a lump of chopped meat, glistening on a butcher's block. The buzzing in his ears was very loud.

There was no way out, he realised as the Dogman drew closer. The final sand grains were trickling through the hourglass. He had known it would end this way, or some way similar. A Hawk always felt the presence of a Black Day, heard the Eternal Craftsman chipping an inscription into his gravestone. But this feeling had *always* been with Ballas, long before he joined the regiment. Since childhood, it had followed him, and he heard it in the cawing of crows and the mumblings of slow, lazy, endless rivers. He hoped that when the hour came, he would accept it dispassionately. That his blood would not stir, his heart not quicken. But he was disappointed. The sky was gorgeously blue and the sun, punishingly hot throughout summer, seemed warm and benevolent. He did not want to leave it behind. Simply, he did not want to *go*. Dully, he watched the Dogman traipsing closer.

Abruptly, he recalled a dream he had experienced frequently since childhood. Although the setting varied, the essence was always the same. He was fighting some unbeatable foe in a high place, a place close to the sky. The conflict lasted a long while until he realised he could not triumph without sacrificing himself. In these dreams, he bull-charged his adversary, seizing him in a bear-hug and launching them both off the high place, and they fell, spinning, to the ground. Always, Ballas woke before the terminal impact.

He did not believe that dreams were premonitions. But he knew they could offer guidance, in a distorted fashion.

Dropping his shoulders, he ran at the Dogman. As they collided, Ballas clenched his arms around the Dogman's body and ran on, his face buried in the giant's furs, the stink of dog-sweat and pipesmoke filling his nostrils. The Dogman stumbled backward, growling, and Ballas believed he had him, that at any moment he would feel the rooftop sag away, replaced by empty air. Of a sudden, the Dogman twisted, breaking loose. Overbalancing, Ballas sprawled flat. Rolling, he started to rise but the Dogman kicked him in the head, hard, then flung him onto his back and sat upon him, straddling his chest.

'Here it ends,' he said, drawing back a fist.

He punched Ballas in the face, again and again, the onslaught rocking the Hawk's head from side to side, rattling his brain inside his skull like dice in a gambler's cup. He felt oddly as if he were drowning, drowning in skin and knuckles, and he felt, too, as if he were drifting away, as if he were riding a tiny boat over a dark ocean, heading for a black, limitless horizon. Blood bubbled into his throat. He could not breathe. He could barely think. He was dissolving, sinking into nothingness.

Abruptly the blows stopped. Ballas opened his eyes. Squinting, the Dogman leaned close.

'You are not dead, I see,' he said, breathlessly. Then, 'If I was an honourable soul, I would spare you, saying you had earned a little mercy. Alas, I am a pragmatist, and I know well that it is folly to—'

Reaching up, Ballas seized the back of the Dogman's neck with his left hand. With the right, he grabbed the shark's jawbone strung to the necklace. Roaring, he jammed the razor-sharp teeth into the Dogman's throat. And *pushed*.

The Dogman's eyes widened. His mouth sagged open . . .

And Ballas submitted to darkness.

He woke, trapped beneath something heavy.

Confused, he thought he was back in Blacker's Folly and the ill-made edifice had collapsed, trapping him under its stones. He opened his eyes, slowly, painfully. Dimly, he saw an outrageous shock of yellow hair. Then he caught the stench of sweat-fouled furs. Grunting, he rolled the Dogman's body from atop his own. He lay motionless, the sun warm against his face.

Someone was shouting. Grimacing, he sat up.

A Warden stood on the roof of a neighbouring building, pointing a crossbow. Ballas rose, swayed, then fell. He crawled to the trapdoor, opened it. Four dogs lingered below, oblivious to their owner's death. He turned to the Warden to demand that the bow and arrows be thrown over. The man had disappeared.

He crawled to the Dogman's corpse. Hands shaking, he stripped it out of its furs then, sitting, he removed his own garb. With effort, he donned the furs, then removed the jawbone necklace from the Dogman's neck, noticing the shark teeth had sunk halfway into the giant's throat. Although inevitable, the Dogman's death had not been quick.

That was good, decided Ballas, looping the adornment around his neck.

He got to his feet. He drew the Dogman's pipe from his pocket, stuffed it with tobacco. In a different pocket, he found a flint and steel and soon, the pipe was burning, the tobacco exhaling clouds of smoke. He puffed and sucked, so the vapours billowed thickly around him; he had never used a pipe before, and it was not a pleasant experience.

Drawing up the furs' hood, Ballas opened the trapdoor.

He lowered himself into the room. The Dogman's surviving dogs swirled around him, taking his scent, greeting him with yelps and yaps. Clenching the pipe between his teeth, Ballas walked through the Exquisitorium, descending the staircases to the ground floor. The front door sagged open, hanging crookedly from its hinges.

Outside, two dozen Wardens waited in a half-circle, crossbows poised. They looked terrified, weapons rattling in their grasp.

Ballas stood in the doorway. Behind him, the dogs gathered.

'The dog's keeper is dead,' he said. 'You'll find his corpse on the roof.'

'Who are *you*, then?' asked a Warden, whispering loudly.

'Don't reckon it matters. But I'll tell you what *is* important. As soon as I step aside, you'll be face to face with the dogs. Best make your arrows count.'

Knocking back the hood, he stepped into the street and walked away.

A Warden cried out, startled. Then Ballas heard two dozen arrows, rattling out of their bows, thunking into the dogs. The animals growled, yelped and whined, but Ballas barely heard them. The buzzing in his ears was loud again. He was exhausted and he wanted to sleep.

Ballas caught up with the others five miles north of Redberry. They were riding fresh horses, either stolen or purchased back in the town, and Ballas himself was attired in a new tabard and leggings, bought hastily at a tailor's shop.

Ekkerlin laughed when she saw him. 'What has happened? The bruises and blood I can understand – but as for the rest?' She gestured to his clothes. 'Have you experienced a sudden growth spurt?' Ballas looked down. His garb, the largest articles he could find in the hosier's, were several sizes too small, his leggings rising halfway up his shins, his tabard sleeves terminating midway between his elbows and wrists.

'Be quiet,' grunted Ballas.

Helligraine did not share Ekkerlin's good humour. Instead, he was fretful. 'The Dogman,' he said, wringing his hands. 'Is the dreadful giant – is he gone?'

'He is dead,' replied Ballas, sullenly.

'Was his demise quick?'

'Quick enough.'

Nodding, Helligraine asked, 'And the means by which he was dispatched?'

'He was bitten by a shark,' said Ballas.

'Thirty miles inland?' frowned the Master.

'Some folk are born unlucky, I reckon.'

'Shark or not,' said Helligraine, brightening, 'I am in your debt, Hawk Ballas. You are a credit to the regiment. Once I have returned to the Sacros, I will ensure you are honoured. How far is it to Quarvis's abode? Will we be there by night-fall?'

'It is a two-day ride,' said Ballas.

'So long? Ah, well – let us keep an easy pace. It is a miracle you can sit up in a saddle at all, given your injuries.'

Heeling their mounts, they set off toward the north-west. After a time, Ballas gestured discreetly to Standaire, and the two men slowed their pace, lagging out of the Master's earshot.

For a short time, Ballas did not speak.

'Well?' said Standaire.

'He is a liar.' Ballas glowered at Helligraine, twenty paces ahead.

'The Master?'

'He has deceived us.' He recounted the Dogman's confession on the rooftop: that he had not ambushed the holy man on Grimlarren Fell, but kidnapped him from an archaeological site in the north; that, knowing him only as Shaelus, the Dogman had had no inkling he was a Blessed Master.

When he finished, Ballas looked at his bruised, swollen knuckles.

'The rogue element within the Sacros — I reckon we know who it is, General.'

For two days they rode to Prendle House, the dwelling place of Leptus Quarvis. The journey was uneventful — no fights, no chases, and certainly no dogs . . .

. . . except for a small, wiry stray — a ratter, thought Ballas — sniffing by the side of a moorland road at noon on the first day. He took pity on the lone, dishevelled creature. Halting, he dismounted then took a piece of dried beef from his saddlebag. When he approached, the dog backed away nervously, its dark eyes never leaving the morsel gripped between Ballas's thumb and forefinger.

'You don't trust me, do you?' said Ballas.

He trod closer, smiling benignly. The dog scuttered further back. Grunting, Ballas placed the beef on the ground and returned to his horse.

'I do not blame you,' he told the dog as he remounted. He looked over his shoulder toward Helligraine, riding with the other Hawks a hundred paces behind. 'Go on, take the food, boy,' he said to the dog. 'It won't kill you. But if that old sod throws you anything, be on your guard. Aye, give it a good sniff before you swallow it down. If anyone can't be trusted, it is him, not me. I reckon he'd toss you a lump of poison and say it was sugar.'

It was true. Helligraine had deceived both the Hawks and the world at large. To begin with, he had staged his abduction from Grimlarren Moor — an action resulting in the slaughter of twenty Papal Guards. Then he had lied to the Hawks, claiming the Dogman had taken him from Grimlarren, and he had been imprisoned in Whitelock ever since. He had not mentioned the archaeological dig on Brellerin Fell – which, it seemed, was the very reason he had fled the Church. Ballas was curious: why was the dig so important? Why would an aged man abandon a comfortable life to go grubbing about in the soil?

This was one mystery; there were others.

Olech had revealed that the Hawks were not alone in seeking the source of *The Loss*. Who were these other people? Had *they* intended to rescue Helligraine? If so, who did they believe he was? Helligraine, the absent Master? Or Shaelus, the errant scholar? Or both: was Helligraine's former life not quite the well-kept secret the Church believed?

The questions swarmed like gnats, and the answers could not be found by logical means: there was too much Ballas did not know to make any sound deductions: it was like trying to solve a puzzle with half of the pieces missing.

On the evening of the second day, as they rode along a dirt track leading to Prendle House, Ballas asked himself a question that he could answer with a reasonable amount of confidence.

What did *he* think about Helligraine? Not as a Master. Or a supposedly reformed writer of forbidden texts. But as a man.

He realised that he liked him. He recalled their first meeting, in the lodging room at Redberry, soon after the adventure in Whitelock. When they were introduced, Ballas had started to kneel in deference to the holy man's high rank, but Helligraine had stopped him.

No, no. We will have none of that here. I owe you my life . . .

There had been no trace of imperiousness. Throughout the journey, too, he had not behaved like a man of status; he had not complained about the poor food and inferior lodgings they encountered, except in jest. Nor had he demanded special treatment of any sort. He had acted, in fact, as if he and the Hawks were of equal standing. And Ballas had warmed to him.

Despite his lies.

And that was the thing. It was easy to forget Helligraine's deceptive nature – at least when he was close by.

The previous day, Ballas had warned the stray to be wary of the Master. Talking to the dog in such a way, Ballas had been amusing himself; but the sentiment was sincere. Helligraine was not to be trusted. Yet, a half-hour later, when they had stopped by a stream to rest, Ballas had found himself liking the Master once more. He half-forgot about his deceptions; if he had been a sensitive soul, he might even have felt a tiny pang of guilt for speaking badly of him to the dog.

Helligraine was a trickster of a rare kind. He did not win trust by what he said. Or how he said it. He did not even say things people believed because they *wanted* them to be true. No; he was both subtler and bolder. Something in his bearing, some strange indefinable quality, caused folk to set aside their doubts and forget that they had cause to disbelieve every word he said. Bluntly, he made people forget who they were dealing with.

A high boundary wall encircled Prendle House. Through a wrought-iron gate, Ballas saw a well-tended garden, a bell tower and the house itself, two floors high, built from dull brown stones. Tugging on a rope, Standaire rang the summoning bell.

'I expect you are looking forward to a comfortable bed,' Helligraine said to Ballas. 'Somewhere soft to rest your bruised flesh and battered bones, yes?'

'A bed makes no difference once you are asleep,' replied Ballas, guardedly.

'True, but surely a plump goosedown mattress aids the *journey* into slumber?'

'Maybe,' said Ballas. 'But Hawks don't need much rest. And when we sleep . . . we sleep with one eye open.'

PART TWO

PROLOGUE

. . . and here is there, in the Forest.

The tall, broad oaks are not the wholesome trees of the corporeal world, but warped monstrosities, their boles twisted, their branches snaking sinuously to form — so it seems — unreadable sigils. Their bark glistens darkly with a gelatinous fluid, reminding Kraike of the effluvium covering a newborn baby, and they breathe, these trees, ever so slightly, their trunks flexing with every in and out breath, their thick roots pulsing.

The oaks grow closely together but there is space for other vegetation to thrive. There are thornbushes, their barbs long and curved; clumps of wet grass, infested by dark beetles with overlong antennae; and a variety of fungi, some bulbous, others slender and tapering, all dripping with a sweat-like liquid, erupt from the dark earth. Overhead, the oak branches intertwine, but there are gaps through which a red moon shines, full and fat, a perfect blood-drop on the floor of a surgeon's room.

In the Forest, there are no stars. Nor clouds. No rain falls; no wind blows. Time does not pass here. Everything is locked in a single unending moment.

Thirty paces ahead stands Toros. The barest essence of a man, he consists only of what is needed for survival. His slender body is locked solid with muscles so sleek, stark and sinuous they do not seem to be muscles at all, but smooth lumps of gristle. Blood-fat veins ensnare his chest, arms and legs; he is naked, except for a loincloth and,

309

hanging around his neck, an amulet crafted from a piece of black bark, torn from one of the oaks and threaded upon a string of braided grass stalks. His entire body is hairless; although white as milk, his skin bears a faint bluish tinge, a subtle phosphorescence of the kind observed in certain deep-water fish; his heavy-browed, heavy-jawed face is neither cruel nor kind, but purposeful — the countenance of someone concerned purely with practical matters. And his eyes — they are not eyes in any meaningful sense, but glistening black orbs, with neither whites nor irises; yet they are expressive in a way Kraike cannot understand. Kraike knows that if he were to venture close, he would see swirls of colour glossing their surface, an iridescence like oil upon water.

But he does not — cannot — venture close. In the Forest, he is no longer a man, but a soul, lacking matter, density, weight — a tangible nothingness. Nonetheless his body — no, his being *— feels heavy.*

He stands, stares, hoping that for once Toros will not notice him . . .

No; it is too late. Toros stirs, his gaze alighting on Kraike. At first, the shaman does nothing. Only watches. Then he tips back his head and roars at the sky.

Although the cry is delivered full-heartedly, Toros's mouth stretching wide open to expose teeth sharpened to fierce little points, the noise is muffled, as if travelling through water. Even so, it is the most appalling sound Kraike has ever heard. Terrified, he too cries out, involuntarily — a pathetic non-sound, too feeble to stir the air.

Why has Toros roared? Because he is angry, and wants Kraike to understand how deep that anger runs. More than that, he wants to attract the Forest's demons. He wants them to come through the dark trees, prowling like wild animals lured by the scent of some injured creature.

And come they do, three of them, emerging from the moon-splashed redness between the oaks.

It is believed there are an infinite number of infinitely varied demons in the Forest. Kraike is unsure if this is true. He has seen the same types of demon, again and again. Perhaps some are more common than others; maybe certain regions of the Forest are frequented by certain types. Whatever the explanation, these demons are well known to him.

The first is Curlew, a bird as big as a man, walking with a man's upright posture, its dark-feathered wings folded cape-like around its body, its black-taloned feet digging into the ground, its beak a monstrous curving barb as long as a sword, sharp enough to pierce steel. The second is Hateful Embrace, a man whose bones erupt in sharpened stubs through his flesh. And the third—

How Kraike hates the third. The Spirit of Innocence is a boy-child, its body swaddled in puppy fat, its face warped by a gleeful grin so obscenely outsized that the demon's stub nose is pushed up between its eyes, and the eyes themselves are scrunched shut by the pressure of its up-surging cheeks. It brandishes two long knives, the blades shining star-bright; skipping and hopping, he clanks the weapons together, striking up music only he finds pleasurable.

The three demons advance on Toros. Spotting the amulet, they halt, abruptly; somehow, the symbol keeps them at bay. They hesitate, uncertain. Then they turn to Kraike.

Kraike knows what will follow. He has endured it thousands of times before.

He knows, too, there is no point in fleeing. In fact, the most sensible option is to accept what is coming, and wait.

But this is also the impossible thing. He can no more stand there, resigned and unresisting, than he can sprout wings and fly away.

The demons approach, slowly, as if sizing him up. Curlew's feathers glimmer in the blood-hued moonlight; its long beak casts a longer shadow. Embrace moves cautiously, whilst Innocence skips, hopping from foot to foot, full of eagerness and impatience.

Then they are running, hurtling toward Kraike, Innocence leading the way, followed by Curlew then Embrace.

Spinning on his heel, Kraike breaks into a sprint. Almost immediately, he trips over a clump of vegetation, sprawling face-down on the Forest's strangely warm soil. Scrambling up, he sets off again, tearing between the trees, low-hanging twigs scraping his forehead, thorn-riddled undergrowth clawing at his shins.

Where is he running to? Where, in the Forest, can he find sanctuary?

There is only one refuge in this nightmarish land: Paradise.

And Kraike knows he will not find it. Nor does he hope to. Even if he knew its location, he would not reach it before the demons caught him.

And catch him they will: glancing back, he sees they are gaining ground.

'Leave me be!' he shouts, noiselessly. 'I do not deserve this!'

He runs on and, hazarding another backward glance, sees that Curlew has vanished, and only Embrace and Innocence remain. He knows what this means. Behind the two remaining demons, snapped branches and broken twigs fall lazily to the ground, floating down as gently as dandelion spores. He glances up, peering through the Forest roof at the patches of sky visible through the branches.

A shadow sweeps overhead, momentarily occluding the moon.

Ahead, more twigs and branches fall. Curlew descends, wings beating, alighting gracefully on the ground.

Kraike stumbles to a halt. Curlew is twenty paces ahead, blocking his way onward. Innocence and Embrace are forty paces behind, getting nearer with every passing moment.

He turns, intending to run away to his left. That way, he will avoid the demons – but for how long?

Not long at all.

He has taken two or three steps when the air ripples and Curlew glides toward him, twisting and spinning through the trees, its perfectly black, perfectly circular eyes fixed upon him. Kraike raises a defensive hand—

—and Curlew's long evil beak skewers his palm as easily as a darning needle piercing silk and, travelling on, plunges into his upper

312

chest, just below the collarbone. Screeching, Kraike falls backward, the beak slithering out from the wound. He starts to rise but Curlew plants a foot on his upper arm, the knife-sharp talons sinking into his bicep. Then Embrace is there, kneeling, seizing Kraike's other arm between hands of sharpened bone-spikes; the spikes sink deep, and Embrace starts ripping off dripping lumps of flesh; then it grips Kraike's arm again, and rips again, pulling off more flesh; it will do this over and over, Kraike knows, until his arm is naught but bones.

Prancing over, Innocence sits on Kraike's abdomen. Its hideous, grin-corrupted face practically glows with feverish excitement; it is hard to imagine a happier child. It thrusts a knife two inches deep into the hollow in the centre of Kraike's ribcage. Then it wrenches the blade from side to side, cracking the bony structure open; for such a small creature, its strength is extraordinary.

Laying the knife on the ground, Innocence inserts its fingers into the newly made gap and prizes open Kraike's ribcage, exposing the heart and lungs within. Innocence claps its hands, delighted. Then, dipping its head, it begins to eat, snuffling and wallowing like a pig at a trough.

The pain is astonishing.

Kraike screams, and screaming looks sideways, past Embrace, to Toros.

Toros stands five paces away, watching, his face empty of emotion. 'Why me?' yells Kraike. 'Why did you choose me?'

Kraike jerked awake in the little room at the top of the bell tower. He lay on the floor by the bed and for a heart-ripping moment he believed he was still in the Forest and the walls were trees, the ceiling a dark tracery of branches.

Gathering himself, he got stiffly to his feet, sweat-soaked, shaking, his throat as dry as the Skravian Desert sands. He poured a cup of water and drank it, slowly.

For Kraike, the Forest had not always been a place of crunching fear and savage torments. Once, he had enjoyed his nightly visits; more, he had yearned for them, for they had nourished him, and filled him with a sense of purpose.

In the old days, Toros had not been his tormentor; he had not summoned demons, watching coldly as they tore him apart. Far from it: he had been Kraike's mentor in the magical arts.

His guidance took an unusual form.

In the Forest, certain rules prevailed. Such a rule was that one soul could not communicate with another. Two souls, both speaking the same language, would find each other's words inexplicably unintelligible; likewise, if they attempted to convey meaning through sign language, the gestures – no matter how simple, or self-evident their meanings were – would prove baffling. Metaphysicians believed this rule was an essential to the suffering caused by the Forest: if souls could converse, they could offer one another comfort and, perhaps, form alliances capable of fighting off the demons. In the Forest, it seemed, a condemned soul had to be alone, bewildered and helpless.

Thus, Toros could not teach Kraike in the usual fashion. He could not give lessons, like a schoolmaster addressing a classroom. He could not endow Kraike with facts, principles or methods of analysis.

What he could do, however, was infinitely stranger – and much more useful.

Standing close, he would gently place his hands on Kraike's shoulders and stare purposefully into his eyes. Faint, barely detectable vibrations passed from Toros into Kraike's immaterial form, each a mere whisper, a tremor as soft as an ant's heartbeat. It was during such communions that Kraike noticed the iridescence in Toros's eyes, the various colours swimming brightly over the depthless blackness; and it was at these moments he was overwhelmed by a powerful sense of pride, for Toros had chosen him as his – his what? Apprentice? Understudy?

When the sessions ended, Kraike would awaken and, although he had not learned anything new, he existed in a fractionally different way. Toros changed his instincts, his reflexes, not in an animal sense, but an intellectual and perceptive sense. After each communion, Kraike saw the world with heightened clarity; he noticed the hitherto hidden connections between things and, importantly for a prospective sorcerer, the normally undetectable web of cause and effect which encompassed everything that existed, and could exist. Not only that, he understood how this web and those connections could be manipulated, how they could be exploited with extraordinary results – such as the plague spell.

Of course, Kraike's transformation was gradual, occurring in tiny increments, beginning when he was a baby mewling in the crib . . .

. . . and ending, abruptly, with the failed invasion of Druine.

Somehow, Toros knew Kraike's attempt to locate the Origin, the spell cut into stone that would bring the shaman back to life, had ended in catastrophe. And it enraged him. The communions ceased; the demon-attacks began. It was obvious that Toros could gain nothing useful by watching Kraike suffer – nothing, at least, that would help him escape the Forest and return to the physical world. But, although he was a disembodied soul, existing in an immaterial world consisting of magical energies, Toros possessed the same desires as any living man who believed he had been badly let down. He wanted to exact revenge. He wanted his own disaster to become Kraike's disaster, too. Toros, the wise shaman, endowed with astonishing abilities – he was no better than a foul-tempered husband who thrashed his wife for overcooking his evening meal.

So Kraike once thought. Now, he realised it was untrue.

Selindak, and others, had told Kraike that he was privileged

315

to have been chosen by Toros to receive his nightly communions. Toros, they said, was capable of forming such a bond with
only one person at any time; it began when that person was
born, and ended only upon his death. During this period, Toros
could be visited by no other soul, no other individual capable
of wandering the Forest.

And this, Kraike believed, was the real reason Toros allowed
the demons to eviscerate him, night after wretched night. The
shaman wanted to push him over the edge, to shove him into
a chasm of despair so deep, so relentlessly awful, Kraike would
commit self-murder. Then Toros could choose someone new to
take his place.

Ostensibly, this plan made no sense. Why would Kraike take
his own life, knowing he would find himself in the Forest as
a result? Why would he plunge himself into the very torment
he sought to avoid? Why, when he would be not only a visitor
to the Forest, but a resident, continually assailed by demons?

Toros understood that Kraike, in his desperation, would fall
prey to the absurdest notions. He would believe it was best to
get the torments over with, and have his soul cleansed, so that
the Four – or any of the similar deities found in various religions – would take him to Paradise. He would become a believer,
a believer in whatever brought him comfort and hope.

Toros was no fool; Kraike had indeed felt these inclinations.

Once, out in the desert, he had even attempted the deed . . .

But that was a long time ago; things were different now.

The Origin had been located, and excavated.

Soon, Kraike was certain, he would redeem himself in Toros's
eyes, and the nocturnal torments would end.

CHAPTER ONE

The Lost Gardens of Dalzerte – who can say what wonders are to be found in that time-forsaken place, that sole-surviving testament to the existence of the Dalzertians? Who can say where the Gardens themselves are to be found, if they are to be found anywhere at all?

Learned men have expended much ink – an ocean's worth – on speculations, theories and studies. Good for them, I say: a fellow needs a hobby, after all. But I say, too, You fools! How can you discuss a place you have never visited? Plundered from one another's writings, your knowledge is second, third, fourth, fifth-hand, at best, and no more credible than the fairytale about the lizard and the singing egg.

But I, Cavielle Shaelus, have found the Gardens, and walked their tangled paths . . .

Extracted from *A Glimpse of the Lost Gardens of Dalzerte*
by Cavielle Shaelus

Prendle House was a mansion, two floors high, crafted from brown stones. Beyond the wrought-iron gates in the boundary wall there was a gravel courtyard, a sprawling garden and a bell tower, rising from a neatly cropped lawn.

Dusk had fallen. Overhead, nightingales swirled, singing to the encroaching night.

Standaire rang a bell by the gate. Squinting, Ballas saw a face appear at a first-floor window; it withdrew hastily and moments later, a little man clad in black scuttled out of the front doors. He was a peculiar specimen, short in stature, so skinny his leggings gathered in baggy rumples around his knees. He was hunched, his scalp hairless except for a few wisps, his face as pale as soap. As he neared the gates, he picked up his pace, then slowed down, then sped up again, as if gripped by a mixture of excitement and uncertainty.

'Is it . . . can it be . . .' Halting at the gates, he stared at Helligraine, his little eyes blinking furiously. 'Is it you?'

'That depends on who you are expecting,' replied Helligraine, perching upon the chestnut gelding he had ridden since leaving Redberry. 'If you were expecting a manifestation of the Four, you will be disappointed. But you are waiting for Helligraine, once of the Church, soon to be of the Church again . . .' He stroked his thick beard. 'Do you have any grooming shears, Leptus Quarvis?'

'Your holiness,' gasped Quarvis. 'Oh, my goodness . . . You are safe and – and you are here!'

'Open the gates, my friend,' smiled Helligraine. 'We have come a long way. I trust your larder is well stocked? And there are soft cushions on your chairs? I for one am blighted by the most insufferable saddlesores.'

Fumbling a key from his pocket, Quarvis unlocked the gate. As he tugged it open, trotting backward in tiny steps, he turned his face to an outbuilding at the far end of the garden.

'Girls!' he shouted. 'You are needed! Come here immediately! Chop chop!' A door opened in the outbuilding. Three young women emerged, dressed in housemaids' greys and whites. Quarvis's attention returned to Helligraine.

'Oh, your holiness, I feared the worst!' Dropping to one knee, he bowed his head. 'But then, who did not! When your corpse – *a* corpse, clothed in scarlet – was found, every pious soul in Druine groaned in despair. But it was not you! And now you are here, at my humble home, with your skin whole!'

Dismounting, Helligraine touched Quarvis's shoulder. 'On your feet,' he said. 'It is not proper that a fellow should kneel before his guest. By rights, *I* should be kneeling before *you*. I have dangerous enemies; by accepting me into your home, you are taking a considerable risk . . . Unless the sour business in the Sacros has been resolved?'

'Not yet, alas,' said Quarvis, rising. The housemaids arrived. 'Stable the horses then prepare an evening meal. And we will need rooms for each of my guests – on the western side, I think, so they are not woken too early by the sun.'

As the serving girls led the horses away to the stables, Quarvis took the Hawks and Helligraine into the house. They followed a corridor into a lounge, furnished with well-upholstered settles, a divan and several deep armchairs. Despite the opulence, there were signs of piety. Holy trinkets rested on shelves, alongside a copy of *The Book of the Pilgrims*, and a huge, gloriously vivid tapestry of Scarrendestin hung on the wall. Quarvis might have retired from being a Scholar of Outrage, but his faith still seemed strong.

'So,' said Quarvis, eyeing the Hawks. 'These are your liberators, I assume?'

'Indeed they are,' said Helligraine. 'Allow me to introduce General Standaire, commander of the Hawks. You may be familiar with his name.'

'Oh yes! And such a name it is! Everywhere it is spoken, it glitters, as if gilded – unless one is an enemy of the Church: then, it shines like steel.' Quarvis shook Standaire's hand; the general gave a slight nod of acknowledgement.

Quarvis turned to Ekkerlin. 'And you, my dear?'

'Hawk Ekkerlin,' replied Ekkerlin. When she shook Quarvis's hand, the former Scholar winced.

'My goodness. A very firm grip you have there.' Disengaging himself, Quarvis wriggled his fingers and laughed, as if enjoying a good joke. Then he turned to Ballas. 'And you, sir, who blocks out the light? Who could scale Scarrendestin in three long strides?'

'Ah, he is Anhaga Ballas,' said Helligraine. 'A fine friend and fearsome enemy. Stay on his good side, if you can. And remember, it takes a lot of food to sustain a fellow of his size.'

Quarvis and Ballas shook; the Scholar's hand was soft and damp, like an unshelled oyster.

'Please, be seated,' said Quarvis, gesturing.

The Hawks sat on a settle; Helligraine sank into an armchair.

'As the girls are elsewhere,' said Quarvis, 'I shall fetch the refreshments myself. What do you crave?'

Helligraine asked for red wine; the Hawks requested water. Quarvis bustled away, returning with a pitcher of water and a bottle of ruby-dark wine. Taking five goblets from the cabinet, he poured the drinks.

'Marvellous,' said Helligraine, sipping the wine. 'So much better than Mellavian godspit.'

'Godspit?' frowned Quarvis. 'Why would you sup that frightful stuff? A droplet could melt through iron.'

'It is a long tale,' said Helligraine. 'No doubt we will speak of it soon enough. But first, what news from the Sacros?'

'I have not heard from Faltriste in nigh on a week,' said Quarvis. 'But our communications were never very frequent. You must understand that he was afraid of being discovered; thus, he wrote to me only when it was strictly necessary.' He raised his goblet. 'To your enduring good health, your holiness.'

'And that of my saviours,' added Helligraine, nodding to the Hawks.

'Your saviours.' After drinking the toast, Quarvis settled into an armchair. Suddenly he grew solemn, his good cheer fading like a gaudy painting left in the sunlight. 'Your holiness, *where have you been?*' Then, catching himself, 'If you do not wish to speak of it—'

'No, no,' said Helligraine dismissively. 'You ought to know.'

He recounted the story the Hawks knew was a lie. He said that he had been snatched off Grimlarren Moor not because he was a Master, but Cavielle Shaelus; he had been taken to a mist-seized village and forced to write forbidden texts by the hound-adoring Dogman.

As Helligraine spoke, Ballas gazed steadfastly into his goblet. He did not so much as glance at Ekkerlin or Standaire; in such looks, secrets were betrayed. He noted, however, that as he told his tale, the Master was utterly convincing. Every inflection in his voice, every cadence, belonged to a troubled man reliving his misfortunes. Even now, Ballas wanted to believe him, and felt strangely guilty for not doing so; Helligraine's tone made his disbelief feel like a moral crime.

How can you doubt me? Can you not hear my pain?

To conclude, Helligraine described the effect of the ordeal on his soul.

'It was dreadful, Quarvis. I feared my faith would collapse.'

'But it did not. It brunted the storm and stood firm.'

'I contemplated self-murder . . .'

'And you resisted.'

'Even so . . .'

Silence fell, and lingered. Abruptly, to break the low humour, Quarvis said, 'And these fine gentlemen – and lady . . . I trust they lived up to their reputations? As Hawks, I mean.' A light gathered in Quarvis's eyes, one which Ballas recognised: it was the hungry glow of someone keen to hear a story. He had seen it a hundred times before. Weak men, barely strong enough to crush a wasp, adored tales of heroism. In some inexplicable way, it made *them* feel heroic, too. Already Quarvis was drawing back his shoulders and sticking out his flat chest as far as it would go. He gripped his goblet tightly, as if he might crumple it. His lips glistened.

'You must tell me everything,' he said to Standaire. 'Leave nothing out.'

The general's face remained impassive. But Ballas sensed his discomfort. As did Ekkerlin.

'I will tell the tale, if I may,' she said. 'The general is a man of action. He does not dwell on past glories.'

'*Past* glories? But these glories are merely days old! Nonetheless, I take your point. Speak on.'

Ekkerlin recounted the mission from Silver Hoof to the present. Quarvis listened raptly; when the tale ended, he sagged in his armchair, exhausted.

'Unimaginable,' he said, shaking his head. 'And it affirms one's faith, does it not? Clearly, the Four played their part in your triumph. How else could you have survived?'

'Now, Quarvis,' said Helligraine, gently. 'Let us give credit only where it is due. I did not detect the Four's intervention. The Hawks succeeded on their own merits. If the Four *had* stepped in, well, my friends would have had a much easier time of it.' He sipped his wine. 'Ballas knows this better than most. You will have noticed how badly bruised his face is; it has healed considerably since he fought the Dogman. He was in a dreadful state after that brawl, on a rooftop in Redberry.' Another sip. 'You must tell Quarvis what happened. This fellow, the Dogman,' he looked to Quarvis, 'was twice the size of Anhaga. Made him look like a pygmy.'

'Truly?' Astonished, Quarvis leaned forward, teetering on the edge of his chair. An inch further and he would have fallen. 'Spare no details, Hawk Ballas. I am intrigued.'

Reluctantly, Ballas spoke. 'Me and the Dogman fought. I took a beating and when he sat on my chest, ready to deliver the killing blow, I grabbed the shark's jawbone he wore around his neck and stuck it in his throat.' A shrug. 'I passed out. When I woke, he was dead.'

Denied a long, lurid story, Quarvis blinked, disappointed.

'One thing you must understand about Anhaga,' said Helligraine, 'is that he is not much of a speaker. I have pressed him for a full account several times and always, he tells the tale in two or three sentences.' He smiled playfully. 'I think he imagines that men like you and I – that is, holy men — cannot withstand profanity.'

'Profanity?' queried Quarvis.

'I suspect strong words were exchanged before the fight,' said Helligraine. 'Is this not what normally happens? The tongue lashes before the fists fly?' He wagged a knowing finger at Ballas. 'There *was* some to-ing and fro-ing, I am sure.'

'A few hard words were spoken, aye.'

'Such as? I am intrigued.'

'None worth mentioning. Our minds were set on murder. We weren't trying to impress each other with our wit.'

'Well, the Dogman is dead,' nodded Helligraine. 'That is all that matters.'

A short time later they were taken to a feasting hall. Outside the windows, night had fallen. The housemaids brought fried steak and boiled potatoes, dripping with peppercorn gravy. The Hawks ate silently whilst Quarvis told Helligraine about the various comings and goings in the Church. Once the meal was over, the maids showed the Hawks to their rooms on the western side of the house. Each room contained a wide bed, a washbasin in a wooden stand and a reading chair against the wall.

Alone, Ballas sat on the bed, unlacing his boots.

There was a knock at the door.

'Are you clothed, Anhaga?' It was Ekkerlin.

'Come in, if you must,' said Ballas.

Ekkerlin entered, followed by Standaire.

'What do you make of Quarvis?' asked Ekkerlin, closing the door.

'He is an irritating little turd,' said Ballas, removing a boot. Beneath, the woollen sock was stiff with dried sweat. 'Hopping about like a flea, jabbering like a chimp . . .' He peeled off the sock. His feet were dust-grimed, the toenails cracked. 'He acts as if Helligraine pisses wine and shits butterflies. I wanted to slap him.'

'*Acts*,' said Ekkerlin. 'Believe it or not, you used exactly the right word.'

Heaving off his other boot, Ballas glanced up. 'Aye?'

'It was all a performance,' said Ekkerlin. 'Some men are not natural liars; they blush, stammer, trip themselves up – you can spot them a mile off. The problem is, they are too self-conscious; they cannot deceive whilst they are being themselves. So, for these folk, the best thing is to pretend to be someone else entirely. They adopt false, often outlandish mannerisms, hoping their eccentric behaviour will conceal their falsehoods.'

The other sock came off; Ballas tossed it into the corner. 'So Quarvis is not an obsequious buffoon?'

'I doubt Faltriste would trust him, if he were.' Ekkerlin looked to Standaire. 'General, are you required to inform Faltriste that Helligraine is safe?'

'That duty falls to Quarvis,' replied Standaire.

'I suspected as much.' Moving to the window, Ekkerlin drew the curtains. 'We have all been wondering whether Faltriste is in league with Helligraine, yes? Whether there is not one rogue element in the Church, but two?'

She looked over. Ballas grunted; Standaire nodded.

'Now we are here, at the house, it seems likely Faltriste *is* involved,' she said. 'Since we left Redberry, Helligraine has had several chances to slip away, if he so wished. The night we stopped in Splintercliff, for instance he could have run off then, and I doubt we would have found him again in such a large city. But no, he stayed with us, which means he came here *willingly*. He did not try to return to the archaeological dig. Or anywhere else. So, we can assume that he *wants* to be here. And, as this location was chosen by Faltriste, we must assume that he trusts Faltriste – and why would he do so, except that Faltriste is also part of whatever furtive scheme he is involved in?'

'What about Quarvis? Do you reckon he is involved?' asked Ballas.

Ekkerlin frowned. 'Of course he is.'

'Because he put on an act? Maybe he was just trying to ingratiate himself with Helligraine. I have seen it often before: when they are keeping company with the powerful, some folk abandon their dignity and creep and crawl to make a good impression. What is to say Quarvis was not doing the same?'

'If Quarvis was genuinely trying to earn Helligraine's admiration, would he have debased himself so badly? It was impossible to regard the version of Quarvis that we saw with anything but contempt. Honestly, you understand so little about human nature.' She patted Ballas's shoulder. 'But you avoided Helligraine's trap, I grant you that much.'

'Trap?'

'When he asked about the fight.'

'I would have been a bloody fool if I mentioned what the Dogman told me,' muttered Ballas. '"Oh, Helligraine – just before I killed him, the big bastard let slip that he did not snatch you from Grimlarren Moor, but an archaeological dig on Brellerin Fell. Naturally, I thought naught of it. Why would I? It is but a trivial detail, of no significance whatsoever . . . "'

'Helligraine was not interested in *what* you were saying,'

said Ekkerlin. 'Rather, he was watching your face closely, seeking signs that you were leaving something out. Perhaps he would have found them, too, if you had not cunningly allowed the Dogman to pound your face into a bruise-swollen pulp. As it was, your features betrayed nothing of import. The Master might as well have tried to gauge your mood by contemplating your arse. General, what is our next move?'

'Our next move, in a game where the rules are hidden?' said Standaire. 'There is nothing we can do, except keep our eyes and ears open.'

CHAPTER TWO

Alone in the lounge, Helligraine allowed his mind to drift. By rights, his thoughts should have ventured toward the future – the Origin, the resurrection of Toros, and the new world that would blossom upon the shaman's return. Yet it was not so; he found himself gliding backward, into the past. This was perfectly natural, he knew – he had read countless biographies of great men who had grown reflective during the lulls preceding their finest accomplishments – and he felt no urge to resist. Instead, like a wood-and-paper kite torn from its owner's grasp, he let the winds of memory blow him wherever they pleased . . . and he was carried back to a time before false names, scarlet robes and endless hours labouring in the Sacros' Black Archives . . .

There is no beauty in this desert, thinks Cavielle Shaelus, stumbling over the sand. No poetry . . .

How long has he been trekking through the Skravian Desert? He cannot say. Weeks, months, years – it is all the same. Somewhere during the journey, he wandered off course and now he is lost, a desiccated stick-thin figure lurching through a wilderness of dunes.

He has not eaten in days. This morning, he drank the last few droplets from his water canteen. His lips are cracked, tongue swollen, and skin peels from his face in translucent tatters. His eyes are burned raw, his throat a simmering corridor of flame. He no longer sweats, shits or pisses. He is dried out to the core; a stray flame, and he would ignite like kindling.

By day, when the sun is savage, he yearns for the ice-cold nights. At night, as freezing winds groan over the contoured sand, he yearns for the searing day.

At all times, day or night, he yearns for death.

Why does he not lie down and die? Vultures are circling, after all: they know it will not be long. But his body is no longer under his control; it plods on automatically, the muscles working and limbs moving of their own accord. He is trapped in an unstoppable gyre of motion. Whether he likes it or not, he will walk until he drops . . .

And he does drop.

One noon, the mechanism jams; his legs buckle and, making no effort to catch himself, he pitches face-first on the sand. He turns his head, so the coarse grains are against his cheek. He closes his eyes. He does not feel at peace. Nor is he troubled.

This is what it is, he thinks, sliding into oblivion.

He is woken by water splashing onto his face. His eyes open. A circle of faces, shielded from the sun by white linen, peer down at him. He tries to rise, but a gentle hand holds him down. He tries to speak but his tongue is too dry and swollen. Strong arms slip beneath his body, and he is carried into a leather tent.

He is laid out on a groundsheet and immediately falls unconscious. When he wakes, night has fallen. Someone has covered him in thick blankets. Outside the tent, the wind moans, as if lamenting his survival. Inside, a stranger sleeps alongside him. A woman, in her twentieth year or thereabouts. Her skin has been frazzled dark by the sun. Her hair is black, curling out from beneath a fur-lined hat. As he stares, her eyes open, and the irises are the cool green of tropical waters . . .

He stays in the tent for two days. Wordlessly, the woman brings him water and food, a type of stew that sticks to the roof of his mouth and is difficult to swallow. He says nothing to the woman, nor feels any curiosity about who she is, or why she and her companions have rescued him. He is too dazed to ask questions. He cannot form coherent thoughts. He feels like a barely sentient scrim of dust, a cognizant heap of ashes.

He spends a lot of time asleep.

He wakes to shouting. His eyes snap open. It is night time; he hears the wind, and feels the cold. Outside the tent, there is a great disturbance. He sits up, for the first time in days. He opens the tent flap and looks out.

There is a campfire, spitting sparks into the night sky. Armed with spears, his rescuers – five men and the woman – are rushing frantically back and forth. One of the men is injured, slumped on the sand, blood spilling black from his lower leg. In the darkness beyond the fire, something hisses, then growls, then hisses again. Shaelus has never heard such a noise before; it makes his spine quiver.

Suddenly, a dark shape rushes into the firelight. It is the size of a sheepdog, although its legs are much shorter. Its back is covered by a curved shell, from which a weasel-shaped head protrudes. Two dark eyes nestle above a snub nose, and its mouth is an explosion of crooked fangs. It surges at one of the men, a spray of sand rising in its wake. Panicking, the man strikes it with the pointed end of the spear; repelled, the creature races toward another man, who hurls his spear at it; the weapon bounces harmlessly off its shell, and the creature hurtles on, until its intended victim escapes by leaping over the fire. Thwarted, the creature chooses a new target – the green-eyed woman who, Shaelus notices, is unarmed.

Without thinking, Shaelus rushes out of the tent, dives full length and, hooking his fingers under its shell, rolls the creature onto its back. For a moment he lies with his face inches away from the creature's spittle-glistening fangs. An instant later, a spear sinks into the beast's leathery underside. Hissing ferociously, squirming like a man in a fevered sleep, it grows still.

Hurrying over, the woman kneels beside Shaelus. Relieved, but filled with nervous energy, she says the Vohorin words for 'thank you' over and over.

'Enough now,' says Shaelus, sitting up. 'You saved my life, and one good turn deserves another.'

These are the first words Shaelus has spoken in days; the woman is astonished.

'You are Vohorin?' she asks.

'I am seeking Rirriel Klaine,' he replies, avoiding the question. He does not dare admit he is Druinese; he cannot say how the others will react if they find out he is bound by nationality to those who destroyed their country.

'Then we shall take you to him,' says the green-eyed woman. 'My name is Crenfriste; my companions and I are hunters. We have come from the settlement, seeking rare game.'

'Your settlement – is it close by?'

'A day's walk,' says Crenfriste. 'That is all.'

Settlement is too small a word to describe the home of the Vohorin exiles. It is a city, of sorts, acres upon acres of tents stitched from tanned leather, sprawling endlessly over the sand. A river flows close by, tinged green by waterweeds; berry-bearing trees stand upon the banks, casting wavering shadows on the water. Crenfriste explains that only eight thousand Vohorin escaped the Scourge but the population is now close to twenty thousand; Vohoria is rising, she says, one birth at a time.

Rirriel Klaine is a recluse. He dwells with his uncle in a tent set apart from the settlement. According to Crenfriste, he has few dealings with the exiles at large. He rarely leaves his tent; he is, she says, a living nothingness. When she asks why Shaelus wishes to speak with him, Shaelus avoids the question. He does not tell her that he is carrying a letter from a certain man in Druine, one who wears the black robes of a Scholar of Outrage.

330

Crenfriste disappears into Klaine's tent. When she emerges a short time later, she holds open the tent flap, beckoning him inside.

'Who are you? What do you want?' says Klaine immediately.

Klaine is of indeterminate age. His long black hair tending to grey, his face creased and body gaunt, he could be forty years or a hundred. He looks haggard, as though he has not slept for many years, or carries an unbearable burden upon his shoulders. Nonetheless, his eyes are lively, but cold. Next to him, cross-legged on his mat, is a man Shaelus takes to be his uncle. He is old, of that there is no doubt. Lean, bald-headed, his wispy beard is as white as moonlight. He watches Shaelus attentively.

'I have a message to deliver.' *Shaelus hands Klaine a folded parchment, sealed with a blob of red wax. He has been tempted to open it on many occasions. Always, he restrained himself.*

Klaine breaks the seal with a yellowing thumbnail. He reads the document; his expression does not alter.

'Leave,' *he instructs Shaelus, passing the letter to his uncle.* 'Return tomorrow, at dawn.'

'A short meeting after such a long journey,' *says Crenfriste as he emerges from the tent.*

'I have travelled further for less,' *replies Shaelus, truthfully.*

They walk to the river. Sitting on the bank, Shaelus listens as Crenfriste describes life in the settlement. Then, as she discusses the despair most felt at being forced to abandon Vohoria, she stops mid-sentence. 'You are Druinese, are you not?'

Shaelus swallows. 'If I were to say yes . . . would it matter?'

'Did you fight during the Scourge?'

Shaelus shakes his head. 'I have never been loyal to the Pilgrim Church.'

'Then I can bear you no grudge. And your people are not entirely to blame. Our downfall was the arrogance of our leaders.' *She releases a long breath.* 'What is your business with Klaine and Maritus?'

'Maritus?'

331

'His uncle.'

'*I am delivering a message, that is all,*' replies Shaelus.

'*From Druine?*'

'*I would rather not say.*'

Crenfriste nods, understanding. '*Did Klaine treat you courteously?*'

'*I have had colder greetings,*' said Shaelus. '*But warmer, too.*'

The next morning, Klaine gives Shaelus a sealed letter. He is to deliver it to Faltriste. Accompanied by a group of hunters – although, disappointingly, Crenfriste is not amongst them – he is escorted through the desert until the ruins of Vohoria are visible on the horizon.

Saying his farewells, he begins the long journey back to Druine.

'The Hawks are sleeping,' said Quarvis, entering the lounge.

Helligraine stirred, drifting into the present. 'You are certain?'

'Their doors are closed. There is silence.'

'Silence means nothing,' said Helligraine, rising from the armchair. 'The big man, Anhaga – have you noticed how quietly he walks? He could creep up on a deer without it noticing.' He looked at Quarvis. He had encountered the former Scholar several times before. Always, it had been the same: with his hunched, withered body, he provoked in Shaelus a type of primal aversion. Even if he had not been repulsive to the eye, he would have remained disgusting: although he was intellectually, as well as physically inferior, he was always inordinately pleased with himself. He subverted nature's primary principle: that only the strong, in mind and body, should survive.

'You should have poisoned them,' said Helligraine, as they moved to the lounge door.

'I mistrust narcotics,' said Quarvis. 'They are unreliable – except for *lecterscrix*. Oh yes, *lecterscrix* is quite a substance. I have used *The Chronicle*.'

'It was enlightening?' Helligraine was not interested.

'Oh yes. You have not used it, have you?' A frown.

They went into the hallway.

'I have not had the opportunity,' said Helligraine, voice dropping to a whisper. 'Nor do I have the inclination. I know what happened.'

'You know that Selindak murdered Emperor Grivillus?'

'Yes.'

'That is good,' said Quarvis, thoughtfully. 'Although – and I am sure you will agree – *knowing* something is different to *understanding* it. Unless you witnessed Grivillus's last moments, you cannot comprehend how badly everything hung in the balance. Kraike lay unconscious in the creaking hold of a warship; Grivillus thundered in, crazed by bitterness, maddened by *valrux*. The emperor blamed Kraike for the invasion's failure, even accusing him of treachery – a ridiculous notion! When anger obliterated the last shred of his sanity, Grivillus smashed a bottle and touched the jagged end to Kraike's throat. To see the glinting edge against Kraike's flesh, knowing that one hard thrust would end not only a man's life, but cast into the abyss a glorious future for everyone on the globe . . . It was terrifying! Mercifully, Selindak dispatched the emperor, plunging a scalpel into his back, so he dropped to the floor, paralysed like a fly when a spider's venom takes effect. Then he seized the broken bottle, did Selindak, and . . . Well, I am certain you can imagine what followed.' He looked earnestly at Helligraine. 'Imagine if Selindak had not acted so boldly? If he had hesitated, even a fraction of a heartbeat? How different everything would be.' Then, quietly, 'How appallingly, atrociously different . . .' Laughing suddenly, he drew back his sleeve, baring his forearm. 'Look. I've caught gooseflesh just thinking about it!'

They halted at the front doors. Quarvis pulled a key from his pocket. 'Emperors always seem to perish at the hands of those closest to them,' he said, silently twisting the key in the

333

lock. He opened the door. Moonlight glowed on the white gravel of the courtyard. 'Small wonder they are so paranoid.'

They crossed the courtyard to the garden. As they approached the bell tower, Helligraine glanced uneasily at the first-floor windows of the house.

'I lodged the Hawks on the other side of the building,' said Quarvis, in a tone of quiet pride. 'Even if they are awake, they will see nothing.'

In the bell tower they climbed the steps, Quarvis wheezing slightly. Helligraine felt a pang of mean-spirited satisfaction: the former Scholar was half his age, yet he was struggling. For his part, Helligraine experienced nothing worse than a gentle aching of the knees. Purposefully he picked up his pace. He wanted Quarvis's struggles to worsen. He wanted – yes – the decrepit little man to know he was inferior.

By the time he reached the top Quarvis was sweating. He knocked three times on a door, then bowed his knobbled little head to the wood, listening. Catching some unheard signal, he opened the door.

They went through.

The room was lit by a single candle, positioned on the floor so its glow was not visible through the window. Kraike sat in an armchair, slumped like a bundle of twigs heaped in a wheelbarrow. He was crooked and gaunt, his hair white as sea-foam. His pale, sleek face stared through the gloom. Helligraine gazed at him. He had met Kraike only once before, in the desert, when he called himself Rirriel Klaine, and dwelled in a small tent with Selindak, once high secretary to Grivillus, then posing as a semi-recluse called Maritus.

The sorcerer had aged terribly; he looked like a diseased tree, awaiting the woodsman's axe.

Foreboding touched Helligraine. Has he lost his wits? Is he mired in dotage? Is he . . . is he *capable*?

Suddenly, Kraike rose. Grabbing a walking branch, he limped to Helligraine and embraced him. 'Shaelus,' he said. 'The stout unbreakable sinew, the wire that binds the bones. The inward force that has held everything together.' Breaking the embrace, he stepped back. He smiled, stiffly, but not without warmth. 'It is good to see you. If I had known who you were when we met on the sands, if I had guessed at your abilities, and how you would serve us . . . I would have treated you with greater respect.' He returned to the armchair and sat. With a crooked hand, he gestured to the bed; Helligraine perched on the edge.

'I feared you were lost,' said Kraike.

'I was, for a time.' Briefly, Helligraine recounted his abduction from the archaeological site and his incarceration in Whitelock. Already, it seemed as unreal as a fever dream.

As he spoke he glanced at Quarvis. Would *he* have recovered so quickly? Would *he* have been able to set aside the hardship and frustration with such speed? No. The little man would have been destroyed by the experience.

'Did you lose hope?' asked Kraike when Helligraine finished.

Helligraine shrugged. 'I took each day as it came, and occupied myself with the texts I wrote. Did Quarvis show you *The Loss?*'

'It is a touching, if overblown eulogy,' remarked Kraike, dryly. 'I assume it was composed for a purpose greater than satisfying your captor?'

'Oh yes. I made sure it contained details that only Faltriste would recognise as true,' said Helligraine. 'Nothing substantial, just a certain phrase here and there. Also, I adopted my old, distinctive style – that alone was proof that I was alive. As for the text itself – its very existence allowed the Hawks to find me.'

Kraike nodded. 'You have missed much during your absence. Quarvis tells me the Origin has been uncovered.'

'Is this so?' Helligraine looked sharply at Quarvis; he had

been snatched from the dig during its earliest stages; he had not laid eyes on the Origin.

Quarvis beamed, his eyes bright. 'Oh yes,' he said, fingers fluttering like pale limp anemones. 'It is a marvel. A vast cave, the walls inscribed with the Universal Script. What a remarkable achievement! It is said that Toros created it in a single night; the strength required to etch so many symbols, with such precision, into solid rock . . .' He shook his head. 'It would defy belief, if it were not true.' The fingers grew still; he planted his hands on his hips. 'The excavation was finished three months ago. Were it not for your disappearance, Jurel Kraike would have used it by now. Is that not so?' He looked at Kraike, seeking confirmation.

'What happens, happens,' said Kraike, unconcerned. 'We sail the vessel, but do not control the ocean.'

'Quite so,' said Quarvis. Then, to Helligraine, 'I assume you still have the *optos*?'

Helligraine bridled. 'In other words, you are asking if I have lost it?'

'Surely you can understand my concern? Without it we may not proceed, and after everything that has befallen you . . .'

Quarvis's concern *was* understandable, supposed Helligraine. The *optos* was a tiny desiccated berry, no bigger than the red fruit of a holly bush, with powerful narcotic properties. When he created the Origin, Toros ate handfuls upon handfuls; loosening the tight cords of rationality, they enabled the user to perceive the world in metaphysical terms, heightening his visionary abilities. In this sense, it was similar to *lecterscrix*, only far more potent. The shrubs that produced it were extinct, and Helligraine possessed what was possibly the last surviving specimen; without it, Kraike could not use the Origin.

'It is safe,' said Helligraine. 'I buried it in the ground near the Origin.'

'In the hope it would grow? And the species could thrive once more?' A joke, from Quarvis. He chuckled, happily, then grew serious. 'Will it not have rotted in the soil? The weather is fine at present, but months ago there were storms and—'

'It is wrapped in leather and sealed in a casket.'

'Good,' nodded Quarvis, satisfied. 'One cannot take chances.'

'That is true,' said Helligraine. 'So, let us discuss *your* responsibilities. I trust you have a plan for removing the Hawks? We cannot simply leave them behind when we travel to the Origin. I am still in their care, so to speak; they would follow us. Moreover, I do not believe they trust me.'

'Surely you have not let slip about—'

'I said they do not trust me,' interrupted Helligraine. 'I did not say they know anything. So, what is your plan? Poison would have been the obvious solution. But as you have no faith in the proven toxic properties of certain substances . . . substances that cannot be detected by taste or smell, and always yield a fatal result . . .'

'On the morrow, I will ride to the Origin; when I return, I shall be accompanied by those men most suited to murder.'

'You must also notify Faltriste of my safe return,' said Helligraine.

'I am one step ahead of you,' replied Quarvis. 'When I went to fetch the wine, I took time to dispatch a messenger bird. Faltriste will receive word this evening.' He wiped a hand over his slickly glistening scalp. 'At last, everything is proceeding as it should. These are great days, are they not? Great days indeed.'

CHAPTER THREE

Daylight seeped through the curtains, falling across Ballas's eyes. He awoke, grunting. Sometimes, a long night's sleep refreshed him. Other times, such as this, it had the opposite effect: he felt as if he had been bludgeoned.

Rising, he padded to the washstand and rinsed his face with tepid water from the bowl. Outside the window, birds sang, obnoxiously loud, unspeakably cheerful. Donning a tabard and leggings, he padded barefoot down the staircase and went through to the feasting hall.

Helligraine, Ekkerlin and Standaire sat at the long table, breaking their fasts. The general was in a bad humour. His stony face, sleek and chiselled, bore no clear trace of emotion but Ballas recognised the tiny tell-tale signs: a fractional tightening of the lips, a subtle tension in his shoulders and a faraway glint in his eyes, as though his dark irises reflected something bright and splintered in the distance.

'Ah, Anhaga! You have risen,' said Helligraine, looking up from a bowl of porridge. 'I trust you slept well?'

'Well enough,' murmured Ballas, settling next to Ekkerlin.

'Today is a good day,' said Helligraine, in tones of quiet excitement. 'As you will observe, Quarvis is absent: he is on the open road, galloping to the Sacros. He intends to meet with Blessed Master Faltriste, and return as swiftly as he can – bearing fair tidings, one hopes. He estimates he will be gone five days, maybe six, certainly no more than seven.' He stroked the white linen shirt he had been given by Quarvis on his arrival at the house. 'As comfortable as this borrowed attire might be, I yearn for the scarlet robes of my position.' He chuckled. 'And yet, how often I cursed them! Not in the spirit of blasphemy, you understand. Far from it. But a Master is a mammal, after all, and prone to mammalian discomfort. The robes are as hot as the heart of the sun, and as heavy as a cloak of lead. And as for the Scarrendestin pendants – wrought from gold, they weigh as much, I'd say, as the holy mountain itself. They made my neck ache.' He scooped up another spoonful of porridge. 'But these are paltry complaints. Many folk suffer infinitely worse than I. They say a happy man counts his blessings, whilst a wise man gives thanks for the absence of minor discomforts.' He popped the porridge into his mouth.

Ballas ate his meal silently, then went into the garden.

He sat on a marble bench, the gathering sunlight warm against his skin. A few moments later, Ekkerlin emerged from the house and sat beside him.

She peered at him. 'Well, did it work?'

'Did what work?'

'There was a pitcher of milk on the dining table,' she said. 'I assumed you were trying to curdle it with your face. Sweet grief, Anhaga – you look as if it is raining piss and you've left home without a hood.'

'Aye? And what of Standaire? He was less than cheerful.'

'His anger is justifiable. Quarvis left an hour before dawn. He did not consult the general, or even give him a hint that he intended to leave. He just went, before he could be stopped. Not that the general could have stopped him. Faltriste's instructions were clear: once we arrived here, the whole matter was to be turned over to Quarvis. He is in charge. But his stealthy departure seems suspicious, wouldn't you say?'

Ballas shrugged.

'Yesterday, I observed that he is not a natural liar,' continued Ekkerlin. 'Maybe *that* is why he left so early. Any later, he would have encountered Standaire and been required to offer an explanation. The lie itself would be simple enough. But delivering it? He is an appalling actor, is Quarvis. And he knows it. I suspect he feared he would give himself away . . .' She nudged Ballas. 'You are not listening.'

'No,' said Ballas. His gaze was fixed on a black beetle, climbing up a grass blade. At the top it halted, shell glinting; it lingered, then started down the other side. Ballas grimaced. The restlessness he experienced in Redberry before the dogs arrived, had reappeared. It weighed heavily upon his spirits; soon, he knew, it would ripen into something dark, something destructive. Without anything to focus on, he grew . . . feral, he supposed. That was the word Ekkerlin had once used. By a strange coincidence, she had likened him to a wild dog: during the hunt, he was savage, yes, but disciplined. Once the chase was over, however, he grew erratic.

He stood. 'I am going for a run.'

'You cannot,' said Ekkerlin. 'Standaire has forbidden us from leaving the grounds. Besides, you ought to rest.'

She was right. Physically, he had not fully recovered from his fight with the Dogman. His body was bruised, his muscles ached, and his cracked ribs had not yet healed. But resting – that was easier said than done. He eyed the garden. Roughly rectangular, it measured a half mile along each side. One circuit would equal two miles . . . But no; he hated running in circles: it lacked even the illusion of purpose.

'Be easy,' said Ekkerlin, quietly. Ballas looked at her. She knew; she sensed he was unravelling.

Ballas scowled. 'There is naught to do here.'

'Quarvis has a small library—'

'That is fine for you. But me?' His scowl deepened. 'Piss on it,' he muttered, rising. 'Piss on the whole damned thing.'

The day passed slowly, every minute dragging like a flensing beneath the skin. Ballas simmered, a cauldron of black bile. At midday and dusk, he ate his meals in the feasting hall, devouring the offerings savagely, his teeth grinding through the steaks as if ripping them straight from the carcass.

It was childish, he knew. Here he was, a Hawk, sulking like an adolescent. But knowing this made no difference: the feelings were so thick and heavy, and rose with such stubborn force, he could not tamp them down.

When night fell, he asked a housemaid if Quarvis possessed any sleeping draughts, strong enough to knock him out until morning; it would be best, he decided, to hibernate through this burning winter of the soul. But the housemaid said no, Quarvis did not; nonetheless, she doubted that her master would mind if Ballas took a bottle of wine from the cellar. Not the good stuff, mind you, she added. Only the vintages resting on the uppermost levels of the rack. Or the whisky, arranged on a table in the corner.

Useless, thought Ballas, retiring empty-handed to his room.

He lay down on his bed, the mattress at once too hard and too soft. He glowered at the ceiling through the darkness. Eventually, he slept—

—and woke, abruptly.

How long had he slumbered? He cracked open the curtains. Not long, it seemed – the moon hung in the same part of the sky as before he lay down.

Slumping onto his pillow, he waited for sleep to return. It did not. Nor would it, he realised. When he woke naturally, of his own accord, there was at least a chance he might doze off again. But when he had been woken *by* something – it

341

did not take much: a creaking branch, a bird scuffling in the gutter — there was absolutely no possibility of returning to the world of dreams. He was awake, and there was nothing he could do.

Except . . .

An idea sprouted. At first it was a cringing, timorous thing, so weak it seemed merely the *idea* of an idea; but it strengthened, rapidly.

Sitting up, Ballas swung his legs around and planted his feet flat on the floor.

Would it hurt to take a bottle from Quarvis's cellar, as the housemaid had suggested? He need not drink until it was empty. A few mouthfuls would be enough to make him drowsy. A few mouthfuls, yes — just so he could get back to sleep?

Standaire would not approve. But the general would not find out, if Ballas was careful. He would bring the bottle to his room — uncorking it downstairs, so the *pop* would not disturb the upper floor — and when the morning came, he would dispose of it discreetly: give it to a housemaid, perhaps, or simply toss it over the boundary wall into the fields.

What harm would it do? None, as far as Ballas could see. And the benefits were obvious: he would sleep, wake up refreshed and maybe — *maybe* — the foul mood that had dogged him would have disappeared.

He stood — then hesitated.

Yes, he thought. This is always how it used to begin. Not with a need but an excuse.

Before joining the army, Ballas had lived rough in various cities, keeping company with criminals, derelicts and down-and-outs. Although he was only twelve years old, he had shared their sour wine and cheap cider, discovering that his thirst was far stronger than his fellow drinkers': when they sipped, he swigged; when they sought a gentle numbing of the senses, he pitched himself headlong into liquid oblivion. And he could always find a good reason to do so, a justification that convinced no one, even himself.

I am downcast . . .

I need to forget how I got here, and why . . .

I need to steady my nerves before I go out stealing . . .

He could not count the times he had awoken in some unfamiliar place, battered, bruised and bloodied, with no idea how he had got there, or what he had done to earn his wounds, or what wounds he might have inflicted on others.

Each time, it had begun with a small sip; each time, it had ended with injury, desolation and despair.

Horseshit, thought Ballas, stepping onto the landing. I am no longer a child, as wild as a moorland cat. I am a soldier, a Hawk; I possess self-discipline. I am not that *boy* any longer.

He trod silently down to the ground floor.

The cellar lay beyond a door under the staircase. Slipping through, Ballas felt a faint stirring of apprehension. Did he truly need wine to sleep? Could he not simply suffer a restless night instead?

His thoughts swerved in a different direction.

Silver Hoof, Sliptere, Whitelock and Redberry – each place had yielded a separate ordeal. Did he not deserve a reward? Some recompense for his suffering? The Dogman had nearly killed him, for pity's sake! Should he begrudge himself a splash of wine after all he had been through?

The cellar lay in absolute darkness and Ballas had brought neither a lamp nor a flint and steel. It did not matter. Groping blindly, he shuffled through the lightless space until his fingertips encountered something smooth – and glassy.

The bottom of a wine bottle, hovering at chest height.

He groped a little more, locating dozens upon dozens of bottles, nestling in a honeycomb-shaped rack. He ran his fingers

343

over them, anticipation stirring in his gut. He grew breathless. Carefully, he drew out a bottle, weighed it in his palm.

This will be enough, he thought, turning away.

He took a step toward the door. Halted. Turned back.

Another one, perhaps? he wondered. When he lived on the streets, some eight years ago, he had not been half the size he was now. He had been tall, and broad-shouldered, true, but his body had lacked bulk. Back then, it had taken two bottles to get him tipsy. Performing a rough, haphazard calculation, he decided that nowadays, *four* bottles would be required for the necessary sedative effect.

Padding to the rack, he extracted another bottle—

—and froze, hearing a barely audible creak of door hinges somewhere above.

Motionless, he waited, listening.

Another creak, as the door swung the other way, then footsteps treading along the corridor leading from the banqueting hall to the hallway. A pause, then a key twisting in the front door. The door opening, closing.

Returning the bottles to the rack, Ballas climbed the cellar steps into the hallway then went through into the lounge. Moonlight flowed through the window, gleaming on the gold-threaded Scarrendestin tapestry; the holy oddments on the mantelpiece cast small, insignificant shadows.

Warily, he looked through the window. A lone figure walked across the white-gravelled courtyard, a plate of food in one hand, a stoppered jug in the other.

Ballas recognised the swept-back hair and shaggy beard immediately.

Helligraine.

Leaving the courtyard, Helligraine trod the short distance over the garden to the bell tower. At the door, he carefully placed the plate and jug on the grass, dug a key from his pocket and unlocked the door. Holding the door open with his rump, he bent to pick up the food and drink then disappeared inside.

Sitting in a chair near the window, Ballas watched and waited.

After half an hour, a tiny window opened high in the tower. Helligraine appeared, emptying of a bowl of glowing embers into the garden. He sucked in a few breaths of night air, then sagged over the sill, as limp as a washrag, his shoulders shaking as if he was vomiting. He stayed that way a short while. Then, straightening, he turned; gesturing shakily, he appeared to speak to someone within the room. The conversation did not last long: a moment later, he vanished from sight.

He remained in the tower another half hour. When he reappeared, he locked the tower and set off toward the house, veering slightly from side to side as though intoxicated, dabbing at his nose and eyes with a handkerchief.

Leaving the lounge, Ballas hurried up the staircase to his room. He was already in bed when he heard the front door open and close. He listened to the stairboards creaking as Helligraine climbed to the upper floor; when the holy man passed Ballas's room on the way to his room, he heard his breaths, wet and raspy, like those of someone stricken by a winter chill.

Very quietly, Helligraine's door clicked shut.

Ballas lay in the moonlit gloom. He remained restless, but this was a different kind of restlessness – a type of buzzing, itching excitement.

Ballas had a sense of purpose now. He knew what he would do on the morrow, when the sun rose and birds sang.

Shutting his sleeping-room door, Helligraine went to the washbowl on the windowsill and rinsed his face. The evening had been a disaster; he had never felt so unwell.

He had attempted to use *The Chronicle*.

Following Kraike's instructions precisely, he had knelt on the carpet, lit the *lecterscrix* and gazed passively at the sigils covering the first page. Very little had happened. Yes, the sigils had quivered, like fresh-hatched larvae. But beyond that? Nothing. No visions had presented themselves; the past had not sprung into the present. The sigils had grown still and, desperately, he had inhaled more of the foul-smelling smoke, dragging it into his lungs as deeply as he could; still nothing. Another inhalation and then—

—he had passed out.

When he woke, Kraike was kneeling over him, shaking his shoulder. How weak he had felt. How pathetic, how puny.

Quarvis had managed it. So why hadn't he?

He dried his face with a towel, rubbing a touch harder than was necessary, the coarse fibres abrading his skin like a hairshirt. He peered into a small mirror hooked above the bowl. His eyes were faintly bloodshot. His nose, the nostrils reddened by the *lecterscrix* smoke, would not stop running.

Quarvis must not hear of this – these were his first words on awakening.

Kraike had nodded, understanding.

Not a word, Helligraine emphasised.

He disliked Quarvis more than anyone he had met. There was something uniquely ignominious about men like him: mediocre souls, convinced of their own worth. In normal circumstances they were – just about – tolerable; Helligraine could brush them off like insects. He would give them a hard look, a faint sneer, and they would flee, their lesson well learned. But he could not send Quarvis away. He was part of the plan; he would not be going anywhere. Not until Kraike had used the Origin, at least. After that, however, he would serve no purpose. He was – always had been – a thing of convenience, performing the simple chores which would have been a waste of Helligraine and Faltriste's time. He had paid the Origin's excavators – those who demanded payment; not all did – and ensured they were fed and watered, and furnished with the proper equipment. He had arranged for messages to be delivered to various people, when it was necessary. And lately, he had played housemaid to Kraike.

Yes, housemaid – an apt enough term. For what had Quarvis been all along, but a servant? An errand boy?

Could he not see this for himself?

Probably not, thought Helligraine. Men like Quarvis were not famed for their self-awareness. They did not see themselves as others saw them. They were gnats who thought they were eagles, minnows imagining they were sharks . . .

And yet Quarvis had successfully used *The Chronicle*. He had seen Vohoria, as it was during Grivillus's reign. He had witnessed the early successes of the invasion, and its ultimate failure. He had seen the murder of Grivillus himself. Had seen the events Kraike had lived through.

And he, Helligraine, had been denied.

Sitting on the edge of his bed, he wiped his nose. His hand-kerchief was dripping wet. Cursing, he tossed it across the room.

Why Quarvis, he wondered, and not me?

The answer was obvious, he decided. He and the former Scholar were temperamentally different. By nature, Helligraine was sceptical; he required proof, evidence; he could not believe something simply because he wanted to. Inevitably, this raised certain barriers in the mind, barriers which had to be broken, if belief was to occur. But Quarvis? That slop-witted sprite had no barriers. His bald little head was empty of all critical facul-ties; he was a splatter of wet mud, waiting to take the imprint of a bootsole. He never asked why, or how; he never tried to understand the plausible, or raised a dismissive hand against

347

the absurd. He *accepted* things too readily and surely, this had enabled him to use *The Chronicle*? He was not intelligent enough to understand how strange the book was, how its effects ran contrary to nature's laws. He was not bright enough to fight against it, as Helligraine had done. Small wonder he had experienced the visions.

But Quarvis would not see it that way.

No; his success with *The Chronicle* would strike him as – yet another – proof of his worthiness.

How your song will change, thought Helligraine, lying down. How abruptly it will crash into a minor key; how suddenly it will turn from harmony to discord.

CHAPTER FOUR

Of the Dalzertians, little is known, except they lived, and died, several thousand years ago. We would know nothing of their existence at all, were it not for the folk traditions of other tribes who, even now, speak of them with a mixture of wonder and opprobrium.

So what can we say about the Dalzertians, with any degree of confidence?

They were no more technologically accomplished than their contemporaries; they did not erect structures that seem impossible by current standards, nor did they master hydraulics, or invent devices to view the night sky, or any of the extraordinary things attributed to other vanished cultures. For this, there is a possible explanation: beyond manipulating the physical world just enough to ensure their survival – they farmed, dug wells and so forth – they were concerned primarily with their spiritual lives. They were amongst the first to gain an awareness of the Eltheryn Forest; they had shamans, visionaries and alleged magic-workers of every description. And they were aesthetes too, perhaps believing – or falling prey to – the notion that beauty and truth are not only intertwined but, at heart, one and the same . . .

Extracted from *A Glimpse of the Lost Gardens of Dalzerte*
by Cavielle Shaelus

Dawn light infiltrated Ekkerlin's sleeping room. Looming over the bed, Ballas prodded the Hawk's shoulder once, hard.

Mumbling, Ekkerlin twitched, then opened her eyes. 'Anhaga?'

'Get up. You are needed,' said Ballas.

Rubbing her eyes, Ekkerlin sat up. 'What is happening?'

Ballas told her what he had seen the previous night: Helligraine creeping into the tower with food and drink, vomiting out of a window and talking to someone inside the room beyond. He also recounted his swaying, stumble-footed return to the house afterwards.

'You think there is someone in the bell tower?' Ekkerlin climbed out of bed. She had slept in her day clothes. As was commonly said at the Roost, 'When trouble calls during the night, one should need only to reach for one's sword, and not one's leggings.'

'I reckon so,' said Ballas.

'Quarvis claimed that the house is unoccupied except for us and the housemaids.' Ekkerlin pulled on her boots.

'Aye,' said Ballas, cheerfully.

'You sound pleased that – perhaps – Quarvis has lied to us.'

'It adds a bit of spice,' said Ballas, truthfully. He felt a thousand times better than the previous day. 'As soon as we have eaten, I'll take a look inside the tower. I need you to keep Helligraine distracted.'

'It should not be difficult,' said Ekkerlin, lacing up her boots. 'Have you spoken of this to the general?'

'Briefly. He approves.'

'Very well then. Let us go.'

In the feasting hall, Helligraine sat at the far end of the table. His eye-whites were bloodshot, his nostrils red and raw. A handkerchief bulged behind the hem of his sleeve, ready to be plucked out if the need arose. Grey sags hung under his eyes. Seeing the Hawks, he raised a melodramatic hand.

'Ah, my friends – keep your distance! I appear to have contracted an ague,' he said. 'It came on as I lay in bed. I hope I did not disturb your sleep: every time I sneezed, it resonated like a blast from a bombard; when I blew my nose, I swear the foxes in the fields must have gone to ground, fearing they had heard the huntsman's horn.'

'Your holiness,' said Ekkerlin, taking her seat. 'You look like—'

'Death warmed up? Or cooled down by several degrees? Do not fret, my girl. It is a half crumb of nothingness; it will not kill me. At my age,' he placed a hand against his chest, 'one is susceptible to unhealthy surprises. My bedsheets were changed yesterday; I wonder if the housemaids washed them in a soap disagreeable to my constitution. Who can say? Maybe I ought to avoid the garden, just to be safe. It is not impossible that some flowering plant has . . .'

Trailing off, he pulled the handkerchief from his sleeve and sneezed into it.

'Forgive me,' he said, wiping his nose. Tears trickled from his eyes. 'I hope my small explosions will not affect your appetite.'

They did not. The housemaids brought plates of scrambled egg and trout, boiled and thinly sliced, dusted with black pepper. Ballas ate quickly. As he neared the end of his meal, he nudged Ekkerlin's foot beneath the table.

She said, 'Your holiness, might I posit an adventurous appraisal of your malady?'

'Of course. No; wait. Let me guess.' Helligraine squinted at her with his pinkened eyes, as if she was a landmark on a far-off hilltop. 'You are going to suggest . . .' He fell silent as another sneeze brewed, his mouth opening and nostrils trembling. When it failed to materialise, he went on, 'Cardingale's theory of the mind-imbalanced body, yes?'

'Yes,' confirmed Ekkerlin.

'Well then,' said Helligraine. 'What would your first question be, if you were a physician working in accord with the theory?'

'I would ask if you have ailed this past year.'

'And I would say no, not once. Of course, my *spirits* were heavy whilst I was in Whitelock, and in Redberry, when the dogs came, I experienced agitation of unusual severity. But physically, I have barely suffered. So . . .'

'So it is possible, according to Cardingale, that now all is well, and you have returned to favourable circumstances, your body has transformed your psychical suffering into a tangible ailment.'

'That is what Cardingale wrote,' agreed Helligraine. 'But what of Shilkaine's discussion of the same matter? Would he not say that I caught this affliction, whatever it is, whilst I was in Whitelock but some hidden part of my mind, recognising my situation was poor enough without being made worse, compelled my body to, ah, *defer* the sickness until now, when I am better equipped to cope?'

'That was Shilkaine's belief,' said Ekkerlin, 'but Delfraisin pointed out an obvious inconsistency when he observed . . .'

Rising, Ballas quietly took his leave; with any luck, Ekkerlin and Helligraine would be discussing impenetrable medical theories for some time to come.

Outside, he crossed the sunlit garden to the tower. He tried the little door at the base, but it was locked; this was no surprise. Moving to the spot beneath the window and crouching to unlace his boots, he noticed the embers Helligraine had emptied from the bowl the previous evening. At a glance, they resembled the dusty black flecks of scorched pipe tobacco. But a few strands of unburned vegetation lingered, and they were unlike any tobacco he had seen. If anything, they resembled dreamer's-weed, a commonly used recreational narcotic – which would, perhaps, explain Helligraine's vomiting fit the night before, and his sickly condition this morning: whilst many enjoyed the drug without ill effects, others reacted badly.

Removing his boots, Ballas looked up at the window, eighty feet overhead. Then he eyed the stonework beneath, following it down to the ground. The interlocking stones were craggy and poorly fitting, riddled with finger- and toe-holds.

Ballas started to climb.

Although a big man, he was agile – agile, Ekkerlin had once said, in the improbable fashion of an orang-utan, all bulk and muscle and a strange, dexterous lightness. Maybe so; but six feet up, Ballas's feet and fingers slipped, and he tumbled heavily onto the grass. Cursing, he got to his feet and tried again. At the Roost, when overtaken by restlessness, he not only ran flat out until his heart ached and lungs strained; he climbed the small crags scattered through the further reaches of Kelledin Moor. This was a tiny act of disobedience; Standaire forbade any unnecessary activities that could injure the Hawks, rendering them unfit for service. But when his dark moods descended, Ballas did not – could not – give a weasel's hiss about anything except annihilating those moods. He did what he had to do; and now, at least, it was serving a purpose.

Halfway up the wall, he was struck by a thought so forceful it nearly dislodged him a second time.

What if he had drunk the wine in Quarvis's cellar? He would not have stopped at two bottles, or even three. As likely as not, the housemaids would have found him in the morning, unconscious on the cellar floor. And then what? A swift dismissal from the Hawks, if Standaire were to hear of it. And after that . . .

Pushing the thoughts aside, Ballas continued climbing, acknowledging that in a peculiar way he was indebted to Helligraine for inadvertently pulling him back from the brink.

You've done some good, old man, he thought, albeit by accident.

He reached the window. Halted. So high up, he was transformed. Sensing the huge immovable solidity of the ground beneath, feeling the close-yet-distant proximity of the sky above, he recognised he was, in the great scheme of things, neither more nor less significant than a dust-mote, a floating spore, a wisp of smoke. But even such minuscule things had a presence, and were observable; he had to be careful. He did not want to be seen by whoever was in the tower, if there was anyone there at all.

Raising a hand, he gripped the sill.

Could the room be empty? Possibly. Aye, Helligraine had spoken to someone, but did that someone exist? Could the Master have been hallucinating, after using the narcotics? Could the room be nothing more sinister than a den for indulging in dubious substances?

Grasping the sill with his other hand, Ballas heaved himself up to the window. Warily, he looked through.

The room itself was unextraordinary. A bed, a small writing table and a rug blazoned with a swirling design. Then Ballas spotted an armchair so close to the window he almost missed it . . . and almost missed the old – no: ancient – man who sat there, his hair as dully white as bone chippings, his face sharp-featured and weather-coarsened, his chin sprouting a sparse beard the same lustreless hue as his hair. Ballas stared, no longer feeling the unshifting weight of the world below and the limitless reaches of the sky above. He was aware only of the shrivelled, time-broken marionette mere inches from his face, separated only by a thin sheet of glass. Mercifully, the figure

354

was looking in the opposite direction, into the depths of the room; but his obliviousness would not last.

Did not last.

The figure's head tilted minutely, like a dog catching a faint scent. His shoulders tightened as he prepared to turn in the chair.

Ballas lowered himself from the window, sharply. His toes slipped free of the stonework and he hung from the sill by his fingertips. Grunting, he tilted back his head and looked up, expecting to see the old man's bony face and narrow shoulders at the window, his gaze resting accusingly on the interloper who had scaled the tower.

But he did not appear. If he *had* detected a presence, he had dismissed it, as what – a bird flying past and casting a shadow?

Straining, Ballas climbed down the tower. Five feet from the bottom, he heard Ekkerlin's voice echoing through the house's opened doors.

'Your holiness, you said you would avoid the garden, in case the flowers were making you sick.'

In the cheerful, guileless voice of an accomplished liar, Helligraine replied, 'A man is wise to fear certain things. Knives, swords, poisons and the noose – but flowers? No, my girl, I have had a change of heart. One must not tremble in the face of nature's sweetest adornments. I will not cower before clematis, or balk at rosebushes! Nor will I dread the rhododendron.'

Ballas darted behind the tower, out of sight, emerging when Helligraine and Ekkerlin were halfway down the garden, walking side by side, chatting and pointing at flowers.

Ballas found Standaire at the table in the feasting hall, finishing his breakfast. He told the general about the mysterious figure in the tower.

'Thank you, Hawk Ballas,' he said, his face yielding no trace of emotion. 'Now go. I must brood awhile.'

CHAPTER FIVE

'Your move, general,' said Ballas.

The words seemed to come from far away. Standaire's attention remained fixed on the burnt-orange dusk outside the lounge window. Were it not for his current circumstances, he would have found the house a fine place to rest, an excellent spot for a retired general to live out his retirement. He recalled the gentle dread he had felt, not long ago, about leaving the military, and his confusion at how a man was supposed to spend his time once his life's work was done. Now, he craved such unending respite; this mission, riddled with deceit, had worn him out.

'General, it is your move,' repeated Ballas.

Yes, thought Standaire, his gaze returning to the chessboard. *It is*.

They were halfway through a game. The pieces lay scattered across the black and white squares, and for a moment Standaire could not remember which pieces could perform which moves; the carved nuggets of ivory and onyx might as well have been pebbles on a stream bed. He could not even recall which colour he was playing. Not that it mattered: he did not care for chess. It was a game, therefore a distraction. A wealth of mental effort lay behind each move – but for what? They had no significance beyond the confines of the board. A fraction of an inch past the edge, and the whole endeavour became meaningless.

'No more,' he said, toppling his king. 'Where is Ekkerlin? Helligraine?'

'The library, talking about the Four knows what.'

Standaire looked out of the window at the bell tower. 'You are certain you saw someone?'

'Aye.'

'Then I shall look.' He stood; he had waited long enough. All day he had tried to strike upon the wisest course of action; he had considered his duties to the Church, and Faltriste, and even the deceiver Helligraine. To no avail. It was impossible to decide what was for the best, or what could be done without betraying at least one of the interested parties. People spoke of being caught in webs of intrigue, and though the phrase was well worn, it was accurate. Standaire felt as if he was imprisoned in a net of strands, coming from all directions, stopping him from taking a step forward, or back, or to either side.

But no longer.

Rising, he left the lounge, and the house, and strode across the garden to the tower.

The door was locked; he shoulder-charged it open.

Entering the tower, he bounded up the winding stone staircase. A mixture of exhilaration and relief swirled through him.

At last, he was doing something; finally, the prevarication had ended.

A thought struck him: whoever resided in the tower room would have heard the door collapsing inward. Was he preparing himself for the approaching intruder? Reaching for weapons, priming himself to attack?

Ballas claimed the man was old, a jumble of loose bones slouching in an armchair, as slack as a corpse.

Even so, thought Standaire. *Even so . . .*

At the top of the staircase stood a small black door. Standaire grasped the ring-handle and twisted, expecting it to be locked.

But the mechanism moved, well-oiled and frictionless. Standaire pushed the door open, braced for whatever might come.

What came was infirmity. Ballas was right: the mysterious occupant was as old as time. Sitting in the armchair, his gaze was blank, his facial muscles as limp as wet laundry. Spittle trickled from the corner of his mouth, tracking down to his jaw, glistening in the final dashes of dusk sunlight. His long-fingered hands rested loosely on his lap, and his shoulders drooped, weighed down by the burden of his many years. With his dull white hair and dull white beard, he looked *tarnished*, spent, spoiled, a relic. More, he looked imbecilic, like one of those poor aged souls whose wits died long before their bodies did. He did not react to Standaire's sudden arrival. No muscles twitched; no light, however faint, flickered in his dark eyes. It was as if the general was not there.

Standaire stared, at a loss. A strange guilty awkwardness moved through him, flowing up from the soles of his feet.

What now? he wondered. Do I simply leave?

No, he decided. Not yet.

There was no need to hurry. Oblivious to everything, the man in the chair did not care if he came or went. For all it mattered to that broken figure, as nerveless and insensate as a scarecrow, the general could have danced a jig upon the floor-boards.

And Standaire still had questions that required answers.

Why had Helligraine visited the tower the previous night? Why had he smoked some unidentified narcotic, the remnants of which he had emptied into the garden? How come the housemaids knew nothing about the tower's occupant? Why was Quarvis keeping his presence a secret?

Standaire had breached the tower seeking certainty. Instead, he had discovered only more mysteries, more doubts and ambi-guities.

Remaining in the doorway, he cast about. The room was nothing special; simply furnished, it could have been an upmarket lodging room. The plasterboard ceiling, he noticed, was stained by a residue of greenish smoke, presumably from the narcotics. Maybe Ekkerlin could tell precisely which variety of combustible herb had created it; her knowledge of such matters – *all* matters, in fact – ran deep. Standaire lowered his gaze. The old man had not stirred; in his mouth corner, tiny spit-bubbles winked, stirred by his slow, shallow breaths.

He is pitiful, thought Standaire. Yet I cannot pity him.

It was true: he was disturbed rather than moved by such sights. Compassionate people uttered truisms such as, *The poor dear, ruined by his old age. He does not deserve this. To live a good life, and be punished in such a fashion* . . .

The general's response was more pragmatic, almost accusing. *You left your suicide too late. You lived until you were too weak to wield the blade or pour the poison. Do you regret it? Do you wish you had annihilated yourself whilst you had the strength, if not the desire?*

Something caught his eye: a book, several pages thick, resting on a writing desk.

Glancing at the man, he left the doorway. Walked over. Picked up the book. The pages were scuffed, blunt-edged; it had seen better days. Opening it, he was confronted by a page filled with geometric shapes. The next page was the same, and the one after that. Was this the old man's handiwork? A relic from his younger days? Perhaps he had been an architect, and used the book to practise the precise drawing skills necessary for his trade. Or maybe it marked the beginning of his mental decline: it was easy to imagine him, his wits sliding into nothingness, sketching the shapes over and over, filling page after page, driven by a sense of purpose no one – not even himself – could understand.

It happened suddenly, and Standaire had no time to react. The old man surged up from the armchair, casting off his dotage like a cloak. A knife glittered in his hand, and the old man swept it upward, into Standaire's stomach. Gasping, the general staggered back into the doorway. Seizing a walking branch propped against the armchair, the man limped briskly over, and Standaire realised he was not old at all, this gaunt white-haired figure, only diminished by what – adversity? Suffering? Hardship? The man raised the branch, then swung it at Standaire's skull. Standaire lurched back reflexively, and the branch struck the door frame, the force wrenching the makeshift weapon from the man's hands. Taking another step back, Standaire felt the world fall away from beneath him, and he too was falling, tumbling down the winding staircase, limbs flailing, the knife jolting against the steps.

Close to the bottom he stopped, his head on the lowermost step, his legs trailing up the staircase. Rolling onto his side, he scrambled to his feet. There was, he noticed, a lot of blood sluicing from the knife wound, soaking his tabard and leggings, glistening on his boots, gathering in a puddle on the floor stones. Above, the walking branch clicked slowly, methodically, on the steps; the man was descending, as patiently and ruthlessly as a spider approaching an insect snagged upon its web.

Lurching through the door into the garden, Standaire yelled Ballas's name. Perhaps the Hawk would hear him; perhaps not. Standaire took a few steps over the grass toward the courtyard, his body as heavy as a sack of lead. The sky was growing dark. Was it the sudden rush of gloom that often followed the death of dusk, and the arrival of night? Or did it emerge from within? Was he passing out?

Another few steps and he looked back at the tower. The doorway was empty.

But only for a moment. The man appeared; he did not

venture across the threshold, only watched, as if pondering whether it was worth crossing the blood-splashed lawn to end the general's life. Standaire was not easily intimidated, but there was an unsettling dispassionate gleam in the man's eyes, one that spoke of appraisal, calculation.

'Ballas!' shouted Standaire again, his voice appallingly weak.

His legs gave way, and as he fell, he twisted, to avoid trapping the blade between his body and the ground. Lying on his side, he saw the man had made his decision: Standaire's life was *not* worth the walk across the lawn. No; there was something else he had to do. Coolly, he angled away from the tower to the gates at the far side of the courtyard, delving a key from his pocket as he went. He unlocked the gates, then drew them open, exposing the countryside beyond, the fields and trees sunken in the new settled darkness. A quick glance at Standaire, and he was gone, limping into the environs beyond the boundary wall.

Standaire lay still. His blood was warm, but his body felt cold.

Come on, he urged himself. *Do not submit.*

He lifted himself onto all fours. Ballas appeared in the doorway to the house. Stared.

'Ekkerlin!' shouted Ballas into the building. Then he was running, as fast as a boulder tumbling down a mountainside. He knelt by the general.

'The old man?' he asked.

Standaire did not reply; he did not need to. Ballas looked around, scanning the garden, the open gates. Now, for the first time, waves of pain radiated from the knife wound. Clenching his teeth, Standaire lowered his head.

Hurtling across the courtyard, Ekkerlin crouched beside Standaire. Her gaze flashed from the wound, to the blood, to the general's face, growing paler with every heartbeat.

'We must get him inside,' she told Ballas.

Ballas stared into the darkness surrounding the house. Minutes ago, he had been playing chess against Standaire. Now, the general had taken a wound which, unless the laws of nature were suspended, would prove fatal. A knife, buried handle-deep in the guts – it meant only one thing.

He rolled the general onto his back. Then, slipping his hands beneath his knees and back, he lifted him as if he were a sleeping child. As he carried him to the house, Ballas spotted Helligraine in the doorway.

'Sweet mercy!' cried the holy man. 'What has happened?'

'Be silent,' muttered Ballas, approaching.

'The general – no! I do not understand. And the gates, they are open . . .'

Helligraine lingered in the doorway, wringing his hands. He seemed utterly at a loss; his confusion appeared genuine.

But it would, wouldn't it? thought Ballas, getting close.

Helligraine, the liar, the unceasing deceiver – he could convince the sun it was a raincloud. Ballas experienced an upsurge of rage. He was certain that, if he had not been carrying the general, he would have killed Helligraine on the spot – a single skull-cracking blow would have been sufficient.

'Move,' he growled at Helligraine, who had not stirred from the doorway.

'Yes, oh, I am so sorry.' Helligraine backed into the hallway so Ballas could pass.

'Take him to the feasting hall,' said Ekkerlin, following.

Ballas took several steps then halted, turning to Helligraine.

'Come with us,' said Ballas, quietly.

Helligraine frowned, as if the Hawk's words made no sense.

'Help us treat the general,' said Ballas. 'We need your assistance, and we shall have it, whether it is given willingly or not.'

'Ekkerlin is a trained surgeon,' said Helligraine, uncertainly. 'Is that not so? In Whitelock, when it seemed I must lose my foot—'

'Come with us,' repeated Ballas, a dark edge seeping into his voice.

'I do not see what use I will be. It has been many years since I played a part in any medical endeavour, and my hands are not as steady as they once were, and . . .' He trailed off, suddenly, and Ballas knew the Master had spotted his ruse. He did not want Helligraine's help; far from it: he wanted to keep an eye on the holy man.

'Come with us,' said Ballas a third time. 'Or I will break your fucking legs.'

Reluctantly, Helligraine obeyed.

In the feasting hall, Ekkerlin cleared the chairs from around the dining table. Ballas laid Standaire on the wooden surface. The general was still conscious, but fading, like a candle flame shrinking to the wick. His face was grey, his gaze unfocused. Sweat sparkled on his forehead and his breathing was shallow.

'You are right,' said Helligraine, approaching the table. 'I must help; I should do what I can.'

'You've already done enough,' said Ballas. He pointed to the far wall. 'Sit there.'

'But if I can be of some use—'

'You'll do as you are told.' Seizing his upper arm, Ballas jostled Helligraine to the far wall. Thrusting him to the ground, he bent, his face inches from the holy man's. 'I have had enough of your—'

'At ease, Anhaga.' It was Ekkerlin who spoke, peering at the general's wound. Already, blood was dripping from the edge of the table, spattering on the floor stones. 'We need medical supplies.'

'Where are they kept?' asked Ballas, straightening.

'I do not know. Ask the housemaids – and hurry.'

Glancing at Helligraine, Ballas strode out of the hall into the adjoining kitchen. It was empty; at this late hour, the housemaids were abed. A small door in the far wall took him along a narrow corridor toward the housemaid's quarters. A second door blocked his way; flinging it open, he loomed into the candlelit space beyond.

Three housemaids sat on narrow beds, chatting. As one, they turned astonished faces to the door; as one, they screamed. As well they might. Covered in blood, hands glistening red, his wide, heavy face garishly smeared, Ballas thought he must have resembled a demon of the Forest.

'Medicines,' he snapped. 'Where?'

The girls continued screaming. Stepping inside, he yanked a maid onto her feet. 'Needles, threads, bandages – *where?*'

'The kitchen . . . a cupboard . . .'

'Show me.'

In the kitchen, the maid opened a cupboard. Inside, a few odds and ends lay on a wooden tray: a roll of lint, a single needle, a spool of thread, a handful of dust-covered jars.

'This is it?' demanded Ballas.

'When our master sickens, he visits the physician in town,' apologised the girl. She looked Ballas up and down. 'What has happened?'

'It's none of your business,' said Ballas, grabbing the tray. 'Return to your lodgings.' He rushed back to the feasting hall. Ekkerlin was leaning over the general, a hand pressed upon his forehead.

'Still with us?' asked Ballas, putting the tray on the table.

'By a whisper,' breathed Ekkerlin.

Turning, Ballas saw that Helligraine had risen to his feet. 'I told you to sit.'

'You did,' breathed Helligraine. 'And I have chosen to disobey.

364

The general has saved my life. And I shall repay the debt, if I am able.'

'Able? Maybe you are. But willing? That is another matter.'

'Anhaga?' said Helligraine, taken aback. 'Of course I am willing—'

'You say it is so,' retorted Ballas. 'But your words are worthless. One in every twenty is true, perhaps. As for the rest . . .' He carried a chair to the wall, then shoved Helligraine into it. 'I am weary of your lies.'

'Lies? I am a servant of the Church! It is neither my nature nor desire to dissemble.'

'Aye? Then tell me about your friend in the tower. He is the one who stabbed the general.'

'My friend? I—'

'I saw you, last night,' said Ballas, seizing a scarlet curtain, drawn back from the night-darkened window. 'You went into the tower, spoke with someone, threw up out of the window. This morning I climbed the tower and I saw him. An old man, as thin as a twig.' He tore the curtain from its rail, then laid it flat on the floor. Drawing a knife, he sliced off a long strip, two inches wide. 'Then this evening, the general paid him a visit. And now . . . now, here we are. Who is he?'

The colour drained from Helligraine's face. 'Why did you not ask? I would have told you all you needed to know.'

'Do you reckon we would have trusted you?'

'Why do you keep speaking as if I am a liar? I do not understand.'

'And still it goes on.' Ballas drew Helligraine's arms behind the chair-back, then tied his wrists with the strip of curtain. 'Then again, perhaps, you truly do not understand. So I'll explain. Before I killed him, the Dogman told me a few interesting things.'

'Such as?'

'He did not abduct you from Grimlarren Moor. No, he took you from an archaeological dig on Brellerin Fell, and you'd been in Whitelock for only four months when we found you.'

'And you believed him?' Helligraine laughed. 'It is – was – the Dogman's nature to cause trouble. Think about it: you were about to take his life. So what does he do? What shall be his final gesture? He decided to die in the manner that he lived: amongst discord. He uttered a few words designed to cause chaos. It would serve no great purpose, of course – except to grant him a little satisfaction before darkness fell, and he found himself in the Forest.'

'You are wrong,' said Ballas, tying Helligraine's ankles to the chair legs with the remaining length of fabric. 'He told me long before he knew he would perish. I said something that caught him off guard. Maybe the Dogman is normally a liar. But even liars tell the truth, when they believe there will be no consequences. What harm would it do, to reveal everything to me, when I would be dead within moments? Besides, Helligraine – I do not trust you. You are too smooth, too *likeable*. Your every gesture is designed to earn affection. Ekkerlin has seen through you, too,' he added. 'As I told Quarvis about Redberry, you were watching me the same way Ekkerlin watches folk to see if they are telling the truth. You and she know the same techniques, and she saw you, trying to read my expression, my mannerisms . . .' He stepped back. 'Who is the man in the tower?'

'The Dogman lied,' persisted Helligraine. 'Lied for the sake of lying. Even if you were about to die, it'd make no difference. The Dogman would be unable to help himself; deceit was a compulsion he could not govern.'

Ballas picked up the knife. 'Answer my question, or I'll cut the truth out of you.'

'Anhaga,' snapped Ekkerlin from the table. 'Cool yourself and come over. You are needed.'

366

'I am going outside,' said Ballas, tapping the knife against Helligraine's cheek. 'I am going to find the man in the tower, and I will make him talk.'

Turning, he went to the table. Standaire fluttered in and out of consciousness, floating between the worlds of light and dark.

'You are stronger than me,' said Ekkerlin. She pointed to the knife jutting from Standaire's belly. 'Before you go, pull this out.'

'Hold still, General. It shall be over in a moment.' One instant, Ekkerlin's voice echoed strangely, as if rising from an immeasurably deep chasm. The next, it boomed loudly in Standaire's ears, as forceful as a wave crashing against a cliff face.

Hold still, she had said. It shall be over in a moment.

But how long would that moment last? wondered Standaire. In itself, not long – time it took for a sand grain to fall through an hourglass, perhaps. And yet, this tiny fraction of time might constitute the rest of his life. A knife leaving the body was every bit as murderous as when it entered.

Leaning over the table, Ballas gripped the knife. Standaire closed his eyes, not out of fear, but resignation.

What will come, will come, he thought.

Truth be told, he already felt as if he were dead. As if he were – yes – a ghost. The feasting hall was only tangible now and again; the table seemed to solidify, then liquefy against his back, growing hard then soft, hard then soft, as if the physical world was in a state of flux, and he was the only constant.

Absurd, he thought, dimly.

Faces swam behind his closed eyes. He saw fellow soldiers from years ago, some returning home battle-weary but unbroken, others interred in shallow graves, many more abandoned where they fell. He saw battlefields bogged with blood and skies bustling black with crows. He saw endless journeys on warships rattling with swords and shields, and sails bulging in the wind, storm-black and stitched with the red emblem of Scarrendestin. He saw the Sacros, and its ever-changing procession of Masters, and the Penance Oak, baubled with human heads. He saw his hands, his fingers curled around a succession of sword handles, growing older, the smooth skin of youth coarsening, the tendons tightening, the veins rising. He saw his father, whose rigid demeanour he had adopted as his own, and his mother, whose loving selflessness he had never been able to comprehend. He thought he saw his wife, but could not be certain; he had not set eyes on her in nearly two decades. A pang of regret: he had neglected her, badly, and their daughter; they had gone, and he could not blame them.

This is what I have been, he thought. This is what my life has amounted to.

But surely, it was all *anyone*'s life amounted to. Time flowed, and men and women were borne along on the current, scarcely aware of how fast the waters ran, or that they would ride this river only once. Yet there were those who knew, or seemed to know, and revelled in the mere fact of being alive. They felt the breakneck pace of the water, yes, but took time to admire the scenery as it raced past, to watch clouds forming and dissolving in the sky, to listen to breezes whispering in the trees and to allow themselves to be gilded by sunrises and sunsets . . . Standaire had encountered many such men, when he was a recruitment officer for the army. Dreamy-eyed youths, with slumped shoulders and weak handshakes – they seldom lasted longer than a week at the training camps. Standaire had condemned their indolence, their lack of motivation. Where is your fight, your fire? he had asked. Now, he wondered if they were, in some unknowing way, *wise*. Did they instinctively understand that effort changed nothing? Did they feel the river flowing and, knowing they would be carried along until their dying day, decide to accept things as they were, and enjoy whatever came their way? Did they choose to *appreciate* the world, rather than change it?

Standaire had done the opposite, and achieved nothing. A lifetime of strain, peril and commitment, and here he was, lumped on a table, slipping away one ruby-red droplet at a time.

His essence was already gone, he knew. He was no longer thinking like Standaire; his thoughts were those of a stranger. He wondered if this stranger had always been there, waiting for a chance to speak. He wondered, too, what his life would have amounted to if the stranger's voice had been stronger, and he, Standaire, had heard it, now and again, and listened . . .

A sudden wrenching tug in his belly, so strong he felt as if he was being lifted off the table . . .

And blackness poured into his vision.

The moon was not bright enough; beyond the boundary wall, the countryside lay in darkness and shadow. Ahead, a hedge-row-flanked lane trailed toward the horizon. On either side, fields, empty except for a few oaks, and the occasional hawthorn bush.

Following the outer face of the wall, Ballas sprinted a circuit around the grounds, his gaze fixed on the gloom-swathed landscape, hoping to spot something – *anything* – hinting at the old man's presence. A silhouette, a shifting shadow, he did not care. But his hopes were low. He was not relying on skill, on his years of training and experience, but luck. And so far, good fortune had been conspicuously absent from the mission. From the outset, everything had gone wrong. If Ballas was superstitious, he would fear the whole enterprise was cursed.

Returning to the gates, breathless not only from exertion but anger, he strode into the courtyard.

Through a candlelit window in the feasting hall, he saw Ekkerlin's silhouette, stooping over the table, tending Standaire's wound. He looked through the garden, with its crooked rose-bushes, and flowerbeds, and fruit trees. Then he ran, covering the large garden in less than a minute, inspecting every shadow, every tuck of darkness, even peering up into the thin fruit trees, in case the old man was hiding in the branches.

He was flailing, he realised. Clutching at straws.

Piss on it, he thought, returning to the courtyard.

He looked around, rage thickening in his blood.

'Where are you, you ugly old cunt? Show yourself!'

As expected, there was no reply. Then Ballas looked at the tower.

Surely not? he wondered.

Running through the doorway, he bounded up the steps to the room at the top. He did not expect to find the old man, slouching in the chair. He did not expect to be the beneficiary of any good fortune whatsoever.

Yet this was not so.

The man was not there. But when he glanced out of the window, the moon slid out from behind the clouds, and Ballas spotted other men, riding over the fields from the west. A dozen or so, a half mile away, heading toward the house. Despite the darkness and distance, Ballas recognised their lead rider: Leptus Quarvis, his hunched, crumpled body bouncing in the saddle. Suddenly, another figure appeared, on foot a short distance away.

The old man, waving a walking branch above his head.

The riders halted. Dismounting, Quarvis spoke with the old man, raising a hand to his forehead in what might have been dismay. Then he shouted something to the riders, and they were off again, their easy trot abandoned for a full-blooded gallop.

The wound was cleansed and stitched; a bandage encircled the general's stomach: already, bloodstains soaked through the white lint, something Ekkerlin chose to interpret as a good sign: only the living bleed.

She wiped her fingers on a clean piece of lint. Only the living bleed, she thought again. Then winced. Since when did I take comfort in truisms? And hollow ones at that?

Since now, she decided. What remained but hope, no matter how irrational? She would pray, if she believed it would do any good.

'He is Quarvis's uncle,' said Helligraine from the chair. Ekkerlin started; the holy man had been silent whilst she worked on the wound. 'The man in the tower, he is Quarvis's blood kin.'

Ekkerlin turned. 'Is that so, Helligraine?' She heard it, then, a certain emphasis in her voice when she spoke his name. As if to say, You *are* Helligraine, aren't you? Certainly, you are no longer Cavielle Shaelus, the writer I revered, the adventurer, the historian, the essayist who railed against the Church's worst excesses. That man *is* dead, as you claimed that night in Redberry. You are someone else now, someone deserving only of contempt – or worse.

'He is tired, sick, and requires care,' said Helligraine. 'I promised Quarvis that whilst he was absent, I would do what was necessary.'

'When we arrived, Standaire asked who else dwelled at the house. Quarvis mentioned the housemaids, but no one else. Certainly no uncle in the tower.'

'Wild horses would not have dragged the truth out of him,' said Helligraine. 'His uncle, you see, is an embarrassment. Since leaving the Church, Quarvis has developed certain beliefs not entirely in accord with scripture. He has become – to a degree – a proxilist. He believes that congenital illnesses are divine punishment for the sins of one's distant forebears. His uncle, like others in his family, suffers from bralaxia, a disease not unlike syphilis.'

'I know what it is,' said Ekkerlin tersely.

'Of course you do,' nodded Helligraine, apologetically. 'But the truth is this: Quarvis fears that he too carries the malady. Perhaps he does. You have seen how stunted, how pathetically withered he is. This might be the earliest manifestations of the disease – a disease which, like any other passed from generation to generation, is considered by proxilists to be an irrefutable indicator of, shall we say, *spiritual degeneracy*. In short, Quarvis believes he is tainted, and can be purified by neither penitence nor prayer; he fears his tenure in the Forest will be a long one . . . I pity him. But I admire him too. For all their absurd theories, proxilists are compelled to nurse their stricken relatives, no matter how inconvenient – or unpleasant – it might be. Quarvis's uncle is nearing the end of his life. His mind is gone, more or less, and he is in constant pain. To alleviate his suffering, he inhales the fumes of burning visionary's root every evening; it transports his tormented, reeling mind to happier places, and enables him to sleep. However, he cannot be trusted to use the substance without supervision. Unattended, he would absorb too high a dose, and slay himself; or he would set himself ablaze in his attempts to ignite it. Ballas *did* see me vomiting through the tower window – but only because the smoke filled the small room and I, unaccustomed to narcotics of any description, reacted badly. As for the general – Quarvis's uncle is not usually aggressive. I can only assume that, startled by our friend's sudden arrival, he lashed out in panic. As I said, the poor soul is somewhat unhinged. Even it were not so . . . Well, who would not be alarmed by the sound of doors being kicked in? Who would not believe he was in danger, and ready himself to act accordingly?' He grimaced. 'If only you had asked, I would have taken you up and showed him to you myself. Perhaps I would have introduced you as friends—'

The feasting hall door crashed open.

'Riders,' said Ballas, entering. 'A dozen or so, led by Quarvis.'

'Praise the Four,' said Helligraine. 'Clearly, Quarvis has returned with an escort to take me to the Sacros.'

'Horseshit,' said Ballas. 'Quarvis has not been gone two days. He could not have ridden to the Sacros and back in that time.'

Helligraine gave a little shrug. 'When you arrived, he sent a messenger bird to Faltriste. Obviously, the Master dispatched riders here immediately and, by chance, Quarvis encountered them on the road, turned around, and came back with them.'

'Horseshit again,' snapped Ballas. 'They were riding through the fields, from the west. Soriterath lies in the north.'

'Riders may be forced to take a detour for any number of reasons,' said Helligraine, calmly. 'Listen, Anhaga. Untie me. I understand your confusion and, yes, your foul humour. I too would rage if something wicked befell one I hold in high regard.' His gaze flitted to Standaire. 'But it will not look good if the Church's men find me tied up like a common criminal. Release me, and I will not speak of the matter. Ekkerlin,' he looked at her, 'your wits are cooler than Anhaga's. Surely you can see I am talking sense?'

Ekkerlin could see no such thing. She knew only that she could not trust Helligraine – and that the riders were getting closer. She heard hooves drumming on the fields, accompanied by the clink and clatter of harnesses.

'We must take the general upstairs,' she said to Ballas.

Ballas stared uncomprehendingly.

'Trust me,' urged Ekkerlin.

Slipping his arms beneath Standaire's legs and back, Ballas lifted him from the table and carried him as he had before, high against his chest, as though he was a sleeping infant.

Leaving Helligraine behind, Ballas and Ekkerlin went into the hallway. Sprinting to the door, Ekkerlin looked into the courtyard, just as the riders poured through the gates. Twelve men, as Ballas had claimed, and she noticed they were not armed, at least with conventional weapons: an assortment of pick-axes, mallets and hammers hung from their mounts, as if – her mind sparked; connections flared – they had ridden out from a mine, or a quarry . . . or an archaeological dig.

She turned. Ballas was halfway up the staircase.

'Remember Kalbaste?' she said, naming a mission from years ago.

Ballas grunted. 'The whisky bottles are on a table in the corner,' he said. Nodding, Ekkerlin raced to the cellar.

CHAPTER SIX

Never one for futile struggles, Helligraine did not strain against the strips of curtain cloth binding him to the chair, but simply sat there, waiting for his rescuers to arrive. To an onlooker, his placidity would seem remarkable. *Such calm, in the face of such ill treatment*, they would say. *He must have mastered one of those exotic philosophies, whose adherents do not allow any ordeal, no matter how serious, to upset their inner calm.*

Nothing could be further from the truth.

Helligraine felt sick, and it was a thousand times worse than a few lungfuls of *lecterscrix*.

A question burned in his mind: was Kraike alive or dead?

When he returned to the feasting hall, fresh from hunting the sorcerer, Ballas had given no indication either way. If he were not a Hawk, Helligraine would have interpreted his silence as a sign of failure. But Hawks were unlike ordinary killers. They did not bask in their triumphs; they did not boast, or brag, or even mention their successes unless it was strictly necessary.

And that was the troubling thing: with Standaire grievously wounded on the table, and a horde of riders approaching, it had not mattered – at that moment – whether Kraike remained in this world or not. The Hawks had other considerations, other priorities; why speak of something which would neither help nor hinder them, when urgency was of the highest import?

Figures sprinted past the windows. Then, a flurry of footsteps as three riders emerged from the kitchen, clutching makeshift weapons. Two pick-axes and a heavy-headed mallet – crude, but effective, thought Helligraine. He doubted that even Ballas could survive a pick-axe embedded in his chest.

He knew the men; they had excavated the Origin. They knew him too, though it took them a moment to recognise him through the long hair and shaggy beard he had grown in Whitelock.

Rushing over, they began untying his wrists and ankles.

'Where is Quarvis?' asked Helligraine, speaking fluently in the Vohorin tongue, the native language of his rescuers. Over a year ago, these men had smuggled themselves into Druine to work on the Origin. Helligraine suspected a few had also tried – and failed – to find him after his disappearance.

'Keeping his distance,' remarked one, with a note of disapproval. 'Him, and this fellow who waved us down as we got close to this place.'

'Describe him,' said Helligraine.

'Old, by the looks of him. Lame, too – he carries a walking branch.'

'And he is unhurt?'

'As far as I could tell.'

Screams sounded somewhere beyond the house. High-pitched, full of helplessness, they were not the cries of the Hawks. Helligraine looked queryingly at his rescuers.

'Quarvis wants the housemaids dead,' said one. 'He insists that we take no chances. "Who knows what those bitches have seen or heard," he said.'

'I doubt that is the reason,' muttered Helligraine, in Druinese. Quarvis had disliked the housemaids in the way characteristic of any physically repellent man, long past his prime, when confronted by youth and beauty. Without meaning to, the girls

376

had tormented him and now their petty, spineless master had done the petty, spineless thing: he had taken his revenge. Not personally, of course. *That* would have required too much guts. But the job was done and for Quarvis, that would be enough.

Freed from the chair, Helligraine stood, rubbing his wrists; Ballas had tied the knots so tightly he had lost the circulation to his hands. Helligraine glanced at his fingers; they were tinged purplish-blue. In other circumstances, he would have cursed Ballas and, even though he was not a vindictive man, wished some awful punishment upon him. But not now. Why bear ill feelings toward someone who would be dead within minutes?

'The Hawks are on the upper floor,' said Helligraine.

'Quarvis says there are three of them.'

'One, the general, is badly wounded, probably unconscious. He will give you no problems. But the other two . . . Make quick work of them. Do whatever you must.' He hesitated, then placed a hand on the nearest rider's shoulder. 'You are willing to die for our cause, are you not?'

'A thousand times over,' said the rider.

Once will be enough, thought Helligraine. 'Then throw caution to the wind, and fall upon your prey like wolves.'

Leaving the house through the kitchen, Helligraine strode through the garden to the courtyard. Climbing into the saddle of one of the horses, he glanced through the front doors. A dozen men, broad and brawny, honed by long months shattering stones, gathered at the staircase, preparing to climb to the upper floor. Strangely, Helligraine did not rejoice at the know- ledge the Hawks would soon be dead. He could take or leave Ballas, of course: thundering brutes like him were ten a penny. But Ekkerlin was a different matter. It was a shame that such a lively, all-absorbing mind such as hers should be shut down before it had a chance to truly flourish. She would, he thought, have made a fine writer of forbidden texts.

Heeling the horse, he rode through the gates into the countryside. Quarvis and Kraike waited a hundred paces away, both on horseback.

'Are you hurt?' Helligraine asked Kraike.

'No. Only impatient,' said the sorcerer.

'Then let us ride,' said Helligraine. 'We have a good distance to travel, and I see no reason to delay.'

Ballas carried Standaire to the top of the staircase then, turning left, bore him into a sleeping room at the far end of the landing.

Although there was a bed, he laid Standaire on the floor carefully, as if he were a priceless, breakable object. Several moments later Ekkerlin appeared, clutching an armful of whisky bottles.

'How did you know?' she asked, putting the bottles on the floor.

'About the whisky? It does not matter.'

Bootsteps scuffed in the hallway, then boomed upon the stairs.

Wordlessly, Ballas bounded along the landing, halting at the top of the staircase. Below, halfway up the scarlet-carpeted step, there were eight or nine riders. Seeing Ballas, they halted. They were not frightened, he knew. Only curious. They wanted to get the measure of the man they were about to kill. To size him up, pinpoint his weaknesses. Is he physically dangerous? Yes. Is he armed? No, except for a blood-wet knife tucked behind his belt. Could he kill us all, if he wished? If we attacked him one by one, yes. But as a group, a horde? Not a chance. We would overwhelm him.

None of the men moved. The first to attack, they knew, would receive the worst treatment. Perhaps the knife would be

378

used. Maybe, given their prey's high vantage point, he would be kicked in the teeth before he got close enough to do any damage. Inwardly, each rider asked himself the question: Who will be first? And as always in such circumstances, it was followed by the same thoughts: Not me. No; the duty belongs to someone else.

And then, Why is no one else taking the first step? Why is everyone just standing here, doing nothing?

It was a temporary pause, Ballas knew. Sooner or later, the riders would come to their senses.

Drawing back his shoulders, he planted his hands on his hips.

How long did he have?

Out of the corner of his eye, he saw Ekkerlin kneeling on the sleeping-room floor, her back to him, hunched over the bottles. Next to her, a bedsheet lay in a heap; alongside it, strips of white cloth, raggedly cut.

He looked at the riders. Sensed their restlessness. Their hesitancy was dissolving; the dam wall was fracturing; soon the flood would come.

'Well?' said Ballas, his voice echoing down the staircase. 'What do you want?'

The riders at the back of the group looked at one another, whilst those at the front stared fixedly at the Hawk.

'Come on, boys,' said Ballas. 'Speak up.'

A few riders whispered amongst themselves. Ballas could not be sure, but it seemed they spoke in a foreign language.

'You there.' Ballas pointed at one of the whisperers. 'Don't keep it to yourself. Tell me what you said.'

The whisperer shouted something in his unintelligible tongue. The riders laughed, loudly, coarsely.

'If you are going to insult me,' said Ballas, 'use a language I can understand. Aye? Let's have it again, in Druinese this time. I do not know where you hail from, but when you talk, you sound like a pig snuffling snout-deep through shit.'

A sidelong glance. Ekkerlin was on her feet, retrieving something from a small table in the corner. A flint and steel.

'Where do you come from?' Ballas asked the riders. 'It isn't Shamfira. Or Boran-Klette. Nor is it Keltuska: although it's a barbarous place, the people aren't entirely without good manners. You lot, though – you stand sniggering like schoolboys watching donkeys screwing. So go on, tell me.'

Click – a flint and steel being struck.

A rider carrying a pick-axe pushed through the group. 'I speak Druinese,' he said, the words drowning in his unplaceable accent. 'I say you are boastful for a man who soon will die.'

Click click click.

Come on, woman, thought Ballas. Hurry it up.

Ballas sneered at the rider. 'What was that? I am wearing nice boots for a prostitute?' Grimacing, he shook his head. 'Try again. You aren't making any sense.'

'That is not what I say,' said the rider, irritated. 'I say we kill you.'

'You want to kiss me?' He pursed his lips. '*Kiss* me, yes? An unusual threat. But horrifying nonetheless.'

Click click. Scrape. Click.

'You mock me, you gibbon. No more!' The rider sprinted up the steps, holding the pick-axe above his head. Jumping down several steps, Ballas caught the makeshift weapon by the handle, then powered a straight left into the rider's face. As the rider fell, Ballas yanked the pick-axe from his grasp.

Click click. Then, 'Anhaga.'

Ballas looked along the landing. Five whisky bottles lay at Ekkerlin's feet, a strip of burning cloth jammed into each of their necks; a sixth rested in Ekkerlin's hand, ready to be thrown. Nodding, Ballas returned his attention to the staircase.

The pick-axe wielder got to his feet. 'You . . . you damned cunt!'

'Ah,' said Ballas, 'that I *do* understand.' He spun the pick-axe at the rider, the curved blade hammering into his chest. The man toppled back, and before he had even hit the ground, the other riders were trampling him as they charged up the staircase, weapons in hand. Something moved in the edge of Ballas's vision.

A bottle, thrown by Ekkerlin.

Ballas caught it, then flung it down on the top of the staircase. The glass shattered, spilling whisky, which ignited, flinging up a waist-high barrier of flames. The nearest riders were caught in the fiery surge. Two tumbled backward, away from the blaze, whilst a third lurched through. Ballas punched him in the face, once, hard enough to split his skull from pate to jawbone. Ekkerlin tossed a second bottle; stepping back from the flames, Ballas caught it, then lobbed it over the heads of the riders. It seemed to fly through the air with a sluggish languor, as if moving through water; when it fell, it exploded at the base of the staircase, and another low barrier of fire sprang up, trapping the riders. A third bottle arrived, which Ballas smashed onto the floorboards at the side of the staircase; now, if a rider were to leap over the bannister, he would land in a trembling puddle of fire. Ballas shattered the fourth and fifth bottles on the ceiling, so the whisky tumbled like a blazing rain onto the riders. The sixth bottle he smashed on the landing itself.

The entire process took only a half-dozen heartbeats. Already, the staircase was thick with smoke. Through the grey-black pall, Ballas saw riders, fire-wreathed and yowling, sprinting out of the hallway into the courtyard. Others, less fleet-footed or level-headed, writhed on the staircase, flesh blistering, hands clawing at the blackened, smouldering carpet.

He ran into the sleeping room at the end of the landing.

381

Already, Ekkerlin was climbing out of the window, as sleek and supple as a rat slithering into a drainpipe. An instant later, and she was gone.

Bending, Ballas picked up Standaire and went to the window. Ten feet below, Ekkerlin stood upon the flat roof of the house-maids' quarters.

'Ready?' called Ballas. Ekkerlin nodded. Gripping his wrists, Ballas lowered Standaire feet-first out of the window. Reaching up, Ekkerlin seized the general's ankles. Bending through, Ballas lowered Standaire as far as he could, then let go. Clumsily, Ekkerlin caught him; overbalancing, she fell back onto the roof, the general's limp body sprawling on top of her.

Scrambling up, Ekkerlin dragged Standaire several yards across the rooftop. With considerable effort, Ballas squeezed through the window, his broad shoulders jamming against the frame; for a moment he was wedged, like a cork in a bottle; then, breaking free, he fell head-first onto the roof, twisting at the last instant, landing hard upon his shoulder.

Winded, he got to his feet.

'Hurt?' asked Ekkerlin.

'Does it matter?' Lowering himself off the roof, he dropped several feet into the garden. Ekkerlin followed, landing lightly on the lawn.

'Weapon?' asked Ballas.

'None,' replied Ekkerlin. 'Does it matter?'

'Reckon not,' said Ballas.

At the far end of the garden, five — no, six — riders were visible, clothes smouldering, tufts of smoke drifting wispily through the pale moonlight. To Ballas's surprise, they did not retreat, despite their injuries. Instead, they jogged toward the Hawks, some still clutching their pick-axes and mallets, others empty-handed.

'They are dedicated, I'll give them that,' murmured Ekkerlin.

'Some foreigners have more guts than good sense,' said Ballas, pulling the knife from behind his belt.

'Foreigners?'

'Later,' said Ballas, running to meet the nearest riders.

Some men, it was said, fought as if their lives depended on it. Others – the truly dangerous ones – plunged into combat as if their souls were at stake. Some riders were merely singed, their skin reddened; others were badly burned, their faces and hands blistered, their flesh blackened and cracked. Yet all fought ferociously, as if their fire-wrought wounds were of no import. Charging at Ballas, the nearest rider swung a pick-axe, aiming the blade at some indeterminate point in the Hawk's torso. Ballas leaned back, the weapon cleaving empty air, then lunged, grabbing the haft and headbutting the rider hard enough to knock him from his feet. He slammed the axe-blade into the man's forehead, then wrenched it out, bones crackling. To his right, two riders advanced on Ekkerlin. Charging over, Ballas jammed his knife into one rider's lower back. As he did so, Ekkerlin punched the second rider in the throat, then ripped the heavy-headed mallet he carried from his grasp. He sprawled on the grass, his skull sagging inward like a rotting pumpkin.

Three riders remained. The first Ballas dispatched with the pick-axe, aiming high, the blade ripping a chunk out of his throat. Ekkerlin knocked the jawbone clean off the second man's face then shattered his skull, as she had the first. The final man was unarmed, and casting the axe aside, Ballas thundered several lung-emptying blows into his stomach, caught him as he fell then snapped his neck.

He stepped back. The garden seemed to reel and shake with the aftershocks of conflict. Smoke rolled across the sky, blocking out the sun. The air heaved and Ballas, feeling something tap lightly against his elbows, spun around, his fist drawn back.

Ekkerlin raised empty hands. 'At ease, Anhaga.'

Ballas lowered his fist.

'We had better move the general,' she said. As she spoke, there was a creaking of timbers, a groan, and the house's roof collapsed, spraying a swarm of red sparks, disgorging a rolling cloud of smoke.

They sprinted to the housemaids' quarters before the smoke sloughed over it. Ballas climbed onto the roof and carefully lowered Standaire down to Ekkerlin. Together, they carried the general to the far side of the garden. They lay him down beside a rosebed. The unwholesome grey hue of his face had worsened; he looked as if he was a brine-soaked corpse washed up on a beach. Pressing her fingertips beneath the general's jaw, Ekkerlin said, 'There is a pulse.'

'Strong?'

'Strong enough for now.'

With nothing else to do, Ballas sat cross-legged on the grass, watching Prendle House decline into scorched timbers and ash.

Chapter Seven

Their demise was peculiar in form, if not essence. Many cultures have suffered implosions – destructive collapses of law, civility and established customs – leading to their end, but few fell apart in such an extraordinary manner as the Dalzertians. They did not disintegrate gently, but savagely, extinguishing their light by means of that most frightful deviation from natural law: cannibalism.

The accepted theory is this: the crops had failed, the stored food was exhausted, and the Dalzertians had little choice but to dine upon one another – to make a meal of their mothers, a feast of their fathers, and so on. When this period of deprivation passed, those who survived were so appalled by their deeds, they left the region, and travelled elsewhere to start anew. Such a process would take months, most likely years; and here, this theory is at odds with the folk tales.

Tribes dwelling close by claim the Dalzertians destroyed themselves overnight. Their ravenous anthropophaginian orgy lasted between sunset and dawn, and would have gone on longer, were it not for a 'flash flood of bright water' that swept through the region, cleansing the settlement of its inhabitants, both alive and dead.

What are we to make of this? What could inspire such a

singular night of barbarity, in which one man dined upon another, as if he was of no more value than a pig?

Extracted from *A Glimpse of the Lost Gardens of Dalzerte*
by Cavielle Shaelus

Dawn broke over Brellerin Fell, sunlight sparkling on the dew-spangled grass. On all sides, limestone boulders glowered darkly. Small black insects hovered in the air, and tiny pale moths fluttered from the bracken as the horses' hooves tramped through, crushing leaves and stalks.

Sitting in the saddle, Helligraine was practically concussed by fatigue. They had ridden through the night, maintaining a brisk pace, and although the first few hours had been delightfully thrilling, he had soon grown weary.

This is how it is for men of my age, he reasoned. Every frenzy of vigour, every flash of excitement, is followed by a rapid collapse. We burn out quickly, too quickly.

Quarvis suffered in an identical fashion. Perhaps it was worse for him: he had only just returned from the same journey before embarking again, nourished by neither sleep nor rest. As they rode, the former Scholar had flopped and swayed in the saddle, inching involuntarily toward sleep; several times, he had come close to falling off his mount. On each occasion, Helligraine had been seized by hope:

Yes, tumble off and snap your neck, you inglorious gobbet of snot, he had thought. You are no use to us any longer. And would not a pathetic, farcical death be apt for one such as you – a pathetic, farcical little man?

But he had not fallen, always catching himself at the last moment, and they had ridden on through the endless depths of the night.

Only Kraike seemed untroubled by fatigue. A skilled horseman, he rode with a type of sinewy grace, anticipating every jolt and jounce so perfectly he barely shifted in the saddle, and it appeared his mount was much less running than gliding over the lumpy ground. He kept his gaze locked on the horizon, his expression barely altering.

Helligraine suspected a part of him was already at the Origin, swallowing the *optos* berry, preparing to acquire knowledge that had lain hidden for millennia. If he felt nervous, even overawed by the task, it did not show. He was calm, as calm as a chess player who knew he would checkmate his opponent with his next move, come what may.

When the excavators' tents came into view, Helligraine's underslept eyes mistook them for a flock of brown, leathery birds roosting on the grass. He blinked, then realised his error. Of a sudden, his weariness vanished; his youthful zeal returned, and he heeled his mount into a brisk canter.

'Why such haste?' called Quarvis from behind. Then, 'Oh, of course – you have not seen, have you? You disappeared before the work was complete.'

The tents were pitched at the edge of a deep gully. Drawing up, Helligraine dismounted. Only six excavators were present, clad in leggings and vests, their skin browned by the sun; the rest had gone to Prendle House to eliminate the Hawks. Immediately, each man got to his feet; several reached for their knives.

'It is I, Cavielle Shaelus,' said Helligraine, in the Vohorin language. 'Look beyond the beard, and you will recognise me clearly enough.' The excavators did as they were bidden, then nodded and moved aside.

Hardly a warm welcome, thought Helligraine. But what had he expected? Handshakes and dancing? They disliked him, always had. Before his abduction, he had worked them ruthlessly hard;

when they thought he was not listening, they called him *acaratix* – the Vohorin word for 'slave-driver'. Most likely, they also called him worse, much worse; despite his obvious allegiance to Vohoria, he was of Druinese birth, and such taints were not easily ignored. *His* countrymen had destroyed their homeland; *his* countrymen had driven their parents and grandparents into the burning desolation of the desert. When they gazed upon Helligraine, they did not see the scholar who sought not only to restore Vohoria, but lift it to the pinnacle of nations: they saw the oppressor, the annihilator, the butcher of women and children, bathed in the red glow of the Scarrendestin symbol stitched into the black sails of invading warships. Yes, to them he was the embodiment of an ordeal – and they should have known better. Why? Because he, every bit as much as Kraike, was – would be – responsible for returning Toros, the founder of their nation, their long-forgotten, now-remembered demigod, back into the world. Each excavator was an Erethin, a priest dedicated to Toros; each would perish a thousand times over in his name. Their loyalty was beyond question; thus, they had been entrusted to unearth the Origin. Admittedly, when it seemed the task was too great for a mere eighteen men, Helligraine had hired a few non-Vohorin to break the stones – and it was one of those men, he was certain, who had betrayed him to the Dogman.

He picked his way down the gully wall.

Ahead, there was a cave entrance, burrowing into the dark stones beneath the moors. When he had first arrived, the opening was jammed solid with boulders. It had taken the excavators a full month to break the stones with their pick-axes, mallets and chisels. Once the opening was clear, their labours continued; against expectations, the cave itself was crammed with yet more boulders, stacked and wedged from the floor to the ceiling. Progress had been painfully slow; they felt as if they were tunnelling to the centre of the globe.

Helligraine halted at the cave entrance. Inside, all was darkness.

'I need a lantern,' he told an excavator.

A lantern was brought. Helligraine still did not venture inside. He was seized by a sudden, breathless nervousness. His heart pounded, his blood grew as hot as lava. It was absurd; he felt like an adolescent on the verge of losing his virginity. His guts sloshed, his hands shook. His mouth went as dry as the desert sands.

Control yourself, he thought.

It was easier said than done. Locating the Origin was his life's work. At least, the only work he had done that meant anything. Yes, he had written countless texts; true, he had scandalised the Church, and in doing so, become a household name. But compared to this, it was all so much fluff. After all, many people – rebellious poets and pamphleteers, for instance – had gained a similar degree of fame. How many, though, could claim to have *directly* changed the course of history? How many could say they were not merely passengers on the ship, but the helmsman, guiding the vessel into new and glorious waters?

Rousing himself, Helligraine ducked into the cave. He wanted to spend some time alone with the Origin. A minute or two, at least.

He walked carefully, boots slithering over loose stones, the lantern casting warped shadows over the walls. He had dreamed that he would be the first person to set eyes on the Origin, once the cave was cleared. The Dogman had denied him this honour, this thrill, and whilst he felt a faint trace of bitterness, he knew it did not matter. Nor, he realised, did it matter that finding the Origin was his life's work. No; not at all. Toros's return to the mortal realm – that was the only significant thing. Everything else was merely a footnote, easily – and justifiably – forgotten.

In this cave, Toros had died. And dying, accomplished something astonishing.

And *this*, Helligraine realised, was the source of his nervousness.

To him, the cave was a sacred place. Just as Scarrendestin, the holy mountain, was sacred to those faithful to the Church. Naturally, there were differences: the story of the Pilgrims was a beguiling myth, nothing more, whilst Toros's story was pure, irrefutable fact. Yet the emotions Helligraine felt – a lightness of spirit, a quivering of mild awe – were undoubtedly the same as those experienced by a believer. He had suspected he would feel *something*. But nothing quite so intense. With every footstep it grew stronger, until he felt as if something rarefied, something indescribably sweet, was pouring into him, whilst something inside himself – love, perhaps, not only for Toros but existence itself – was rushing out of him, filtering through his pores and spreading through the cave.

Ridiculous, he thought. You are overly tired and, consequently, prey to absurd sentimentality. This cave is merely a place where something happened. It has no special properties, save those existing in your imagination.

Serving as a Master, he had seen believers swooning over relics. A tatter of cloth, purporting to be a fragment of a Pilgrim's shirt. A tooth, fallen from a Pilgrim's jaw during a bout of fasting. Even a scab, in a glass case, supposedly peeled from a Pilgrim's wound – how he had ridiculed the faithful's devotion to these petty articles.

Do you think those artefacts are genuine? he had thought. And if they were, what difference would it make? In themselves, they are merely objects. Yes, they were – so you imagine – once owned by certain people, whom you hold dear. But so what? Are they really worth such convulsions? Such eye-rolling? Such imbecilic cooing?

Yet he was not immune, it seemed.

He raised the lantern. And he saw.

Superficially, it was exactly as Quarvis claimed. Written in the hard-angled, ruthlessly geometrical Universal Script, the Origin was etched into the black stone walls, each sigil no larger than a hazelnut. Yet the finesse of its execution was breathtaking; it bordered on the unnatural. The straight lines were *perfectly* straight, compensating for every crease in the stone; the angles were as precise as any diagram in a trigonometrist's textbook. It was believed Toros had used only primitive tools, for nothing else was available: the most persuasive theory was that he had employed a sliver of diamond, sharpened by natural forces – or possibly magic – as a scribe. What else could make such neat incisions in solid stone, in an age before steel? But surely, even with a diamond keener than any blade, it would have taken unimaginable effort to create even a single sigil. A great deal of time, too. How long, for a modern craftsman to fashion just one of those dazzlingly precise markings? An hour? Two? Toros had completed the Origin in a single night . . .

A single night, thought Helligraine, to inscribe a singularly remarkable spell. A spell that would, millennia after its composition, resurrect its creator; a spell that would restore flesh to Toros' ancient bones, would generate a beating heart, a murmuring brain, and a billion billion nerve-endings poised to apprehend the corporeal world . . . a spell that would draw Toros's soul into its once-abandoned, now-remade shell, and reanimate it, so that the eyes saw and the ears listened and the tongue moved, stirred by knowledge of immeasurable depth.

Stepping back, the circle of lantern light widening like a blossom opening to the sun, Helligraine discovered the Origin was *massive*.

The cave measured forty paces end to end; from floor to ceiling it was eight, maybe nine feet high. And the inscriptions covered every square inch, except for its lowest and highest points, where it would have been impossible even for Toros to work effectively.

Involuntarily, Helligraine took another step back, as if struck by an ocean wave. His legs grew weak; he nearly dropped the lantern. A thin, near-hysterical laugh emerged from his throat.

'Sweet mercy,' he breathed, shaking his head.

A single night – all this, in a single night . . .

Suddenly, nausea rolled through him. In his vision, the sigils quivered and writhed, as they had upon the pages of *The Chronicle*, that night in the bell tower. No doubt, the cause was the same: the human mind recoiled from such a profusion of regular shapes, and the body responded sympathetically: the gorge stirred, the throat tightened, an icy sweat broke upon the skin. Alarmed, Helligraine shut his eyes. Then, warily, opened them again, just a fraction, so the Origin hovered in his sight as a harmless blur, a semi-distinct smudge.

How . . . How?

But he knew the answer. He had contemplated the process by which Toros created the Origin every day for the past fifteen years. By ingesting an *optos* berry, which heightened his visionary powers, Toros was able to split his soul into two parts. The largest, dominant part travelled to the Forest, where, using his unparalleled instincts and intellect, Toros was able to acquire the knowledge required for the spell contained in the Origin; as it did so, the lesser part of his soul, still inhabiting his physical body, etched the spell into the cave walls. Then, the physical body perished – perhaps from exertion – and the smaller part of Toros's soul joined the greater in the Forest.

How simple it seems, thought Helligraine, when one cannot truly comprehend even the basic details of the process.

'Marvellous, is it not?' Quarvis's voice broke the silence – tore it apart, like the obscene cawing of some ugly bird. His contemplative mood shattering, Helligraine turned. The former Scholar approached, his small feet scuffing over the loose stones, a wide grin twisting his appalling little face. With a crooked-fingered hand, he gestured to the Origin. 'Defies belief, yes?' He shook his head, wonderingly. 'When I first saw it, I nearly collapsed with . . . What is the word? Awe, I suppose. Yes, yes,' he nodded, eagerly. 'I was, quite literally, awe-struck.' Clenching a fist, he gave the air a timid punch. 'Awe-*struck*,' he repeated.

At the far end of the cave, Kraike appeared. Accompanied by an excavator, he inspected the inscription. Helligraine watched him closely, seeking signs of what – delight? Exultation? Wariness? Kraike's face remained stonily impassive. For him, the Origin was not something to be admired, like a work of art. Nor could it inspire wonder: as a sorcerer he – unlike Helligraine – could not perceive it as a splendid mystery. No; he had at least *some* inkling of how it functioned. And that was at the heart of it: for Kraike, it was something to be used.

Kraike stared a while. 'Fetch the *optos*,' he instructed Helligraine.

'So soon? Do you not wish to rest first? We have ridden far—'

'Fetch the berry,' said Kraike. 'I wish to begin straight away.'

Leaving the cave, Helligraine rode half a mile to the tent where he had dwelled before his abduction. He was half surprised to find that it was still there, pegged firmly to the ground; inside, he discovered that nothing had changed. The crudely fashioned writing desk, pallet bed, and heaps of parchments were exactly as he had left them.

Drawing a knife, he slashed the groundsheet, then tore the incision wide open, exposing the soil beneath.

With his bare hands, he dug, like a dog salvaging some buried treat. Five or six inches down, his fingertips encountered something solid. Scraping away the remaining soil, he drew it out – a steel casket the size of a jewellery box. He flipped the clasp then lifted the lid. Inside, there was a dried-up berry, brown and shrivelled. Snapping shut the lid, and sealing the clasp, he left the tent and rode back to the Origin.

The excavators had been busy inside the cave. Two dozen lanterns burned, some arranged in a semi-circle against the wall, others hanging from tall wooden frames; combined, their light illuminated every square inch of the inscription. The effect was hallucinatory; the sigils seemed to quiver and tremble twice as violently as before and, carrying the casket to Kraike, Helligraine kept his gaze lowered, unwilling to suffer another bout of nausea.

Opening the lid, he held out the casket to Kraike. Kraike took the berry between his thumb and forefinger; Quarvis bustled close, squinting.

'So that is it?' said Quarvis. 'The last *optos* in existence?'

'Leave,' said Kraike, suddenly.

'If you like, I can stay and, ah, supervise,' said Quarvis. 'Perhaps it would be safer if I—'

'Do as you are bidden,' said Kraike, sharply. His face tightened; in the lantern light, his eyes flashed. He looked like a viper poised to strike. But beneath the anger, Helligraine detected something else: fear.

Of what? Using the Origin? Perhaps. Goodness knew what the process would entail. It could prove to be psychically, even physically, painful. Enough, perhaps, to push Kraike to the edge of insanity.

Maybe his fear was a simpler sort – a fear of failure.

So much rested on the sorcerer's narrow shoulders. Had any man ever borne such a responsibility?

'Come,' Helligraine said. 'Let us do as we are told.' He hesitated, tempted to wish Kraike good luck. But luck had no part to play.

They left the cave. Outside the sun was very bright; dawn had departed, a new day had blossomed.

Alone, Kraike gazed at the inscription.

He had imagined it would be much smaller – the same size as a page from *The Chronicle*, maybe. When he set eyes on it, he had felt his resolve crumbling, his determination dissolving.

No, no, this is too much . . .

He had sent the others away, fearing they would spot his unease. He insisted on using the Origin straight away for the same reason a man pulls a deep splinter from his flesh the instant it gets lodged there: postponing certain tasks made them infinitely harder. And it did not matter that Helligraine's concerns were well founded, that he *was* tired, and *did* need to rest. No; this was the moment for action, and he would do what had to be done, weariness be damned . . .

Be damned – a phrase so casually used, yet so poorly understood.

Every time he slept, Kraike tasted damnation. He knew exactly what awaited a lost soul in the afterlife; he had seen the breathing trees, the demons, the blood-red moon. He feared it, as any man would; and it was the reason he was here, in an underground cave, a withered berry resting in his palm, a vast tract written in the Universal Script writhing in his vision.

He was not loyal to Toros. How could he be? Ever since the invasion failed, the visionary had tormented him. His nightly trips to the Forest had evolved from a gentle communion, in which Toros taught him the magical arts, to a punishment.

And this punishment served a purpose: it was a goad, a snapping whip, designed to keep him working on his allocated task.

Your torments will end, Toros seemed to say, each time the demons assailed Kraike, *once I am free of this place*.

In the desert, unable to travel to Druine, the essential *optos* berry lost without a trace, Kraike had plunged into despair – a despair unmitigated by hope. *How* could he do what Toros demanded? It was impossible! In the Forest, he had tried to explain this to the visionary, to no avail; either he did not understand, or care, or continued to believe the punishments served a purpose. Sometimes, Kraike wondered if Toros *enjoyed* watching him being torn apart by the many-formed abominations, if he treated it as an entertainment.

Soon, though, the torments might end. If he used the Origin successfully, and every other part of the plan flowed smoothly, Toros could be in the world of flesh within a month . . .

And then?

Then a torment of a different kind would infest Kraike's mind. Kraike was mortal; one day, he would perish, and find himself trapped in the Forest, not as a visitor, but an inhabitant. He would join the legion of lost souls incarcerated in that infinitely vast, infinitely awful prison of trees and demons. Unlike most – *any*, perhaps – he understood what this entailed, and the mere prospect of it was sickening. So much so, even if Toros returned, he would be unable to experience a single moment of happiness, or contentment: his remaining years would be spent in trembling anticipation of his ultimate fate.

Unless, in his gratitude, Toros granted him a reprieve.

No, not a reprieve, for that suggested only a delay, and Kraike yearned for something permanent.

When he died, he wanted to go elsewhere. Paradise, perhaps; it hardly mattered, as long as it was not the Forest. He had already served his time in that realm. It would be unfair, if he was forced to go back.

He put the berry in his mouth. Chewed. A taste of dust flooded his mouth. He gazed at the Origin. And waited.

Dawn sunlight flooded the room at the top of the bell tower.

Ekkerlin hunted for clues like a scavenger seeking carrion: she did not care what she found, as long as she found *something*.

She was disappointed. Except for a smear of green smoke residue on the ceiling, there was nothing.

She left the tower. Across the courtyard, the fire-wrecked, smoke-blackened remnants of the house smouldered. She went into the stable building, empty but for Standaire, sitting against the wall, sipping at a cup of water.

He had survived. The knife blade had not pierced any vital organs — a stroke of good luck of the type referred to as a 'seamstress's blessing': the odds of it occurring were the same as threading a needle by throwing both the needle and the thread at one another, and having them collide in mid-air. He had suffered a night of fevers, sweats and pain. And it showed. His flesh was grey, his eyes shadowed, his breathing the raspy murmur of a shallow stream moving over stones.

He had not spoken since waking, an hour earlier.

Now, he looked at Ekkerlin.

'How long have you served as a Hawk?'

The question caught Ekkerlin off guard. 'Three years,' she replied.

'Then you are well acquainted with our rules — and principles.'

'General?' Ekkerlin frowned, nonplussed.

'If a Hawk is injured, he must be abandoned, if it benefits the mission. You should have left me behind and pursued our assailants.'

'We could not do so, General.'

'Why not?'

'You are not merely a Hawk. You are our general, and all orders must come from you. We could not act without your permission.'

Standaire's eyes darkened. 'What of the principle saying you should use your wits? Your initiative? What has been gained by saving me, when you could have pursued Helligraine?'

'With respect,' said Ekkerlin, perturbed, 'our mission was to bring Helligraine to the house, and wait for further instructions. That mission is over; if there is to be a new one . . .' She shrugged. 'Its nature has not been determined.'

Standaire laughed, bitterly. 'Ekkerlin, I never expected this of *you*.'

'Expected what?'

'Hiding your mistakes behind technicalities. You *know* you should have followed Helligraine.'

'Untrue,' said Ekkerlin. 'We did not know what was for the best. If we followed Helligraine, what would we find? More men, determined to kill us? In numbers which neither I nor Ballas could overwhelm? What then, General? With you, me and Anhaga dead, no one would know about Helligraine's crimes. Would it be wiser, then, to notify the Masters of everything that has occurred? I doubt Ballas and I would even be granted an audience. If we were, would the Masters believe us? If we told them that Helligraine is alive, and engaged in some sort of . . . of *conspiracy*, would they say, "This sounds reasonable. We must investigate?"' She shook her head. 'They would laugh at us. Then send us to the gallows for treason.'

'Words, Ekkerlin. Just words.' Wincing, Standaire got to his feet. 'Where is Hawk Ballas?'

'Burying the housemaids,' said Ekkerlin.

'Tell him we are to leave immediately.'

Ekkerlin did not ask for where. Disturbed by the general's strange mood, she left the stables. At the far end of the garden, Ballas tamped down the green turf with a shovel. He had laboured on the grave plots since dawn. Ekkerlin doubted this respectful gesture arose from a soft heart: since when did the big man care about treating the dead with dignity? Most likely, he was bored, and sought to occupy his idle hands.

'Anhaga,' she called, waving. 'We are on the move.'

Jabbing the shovel into the ground so it stood upright like a grave-marker, he stumped over, wiping sweat from his face. As he grew close, Ekkerlin saw his expression was strange. Distracted, melancholic. Perhaps he *did* have a soft heart. Or maybe this was simply a morning when strange moods prevailed.

'Where to?' asked Ballas, reaching the courtyard.

'Wherever the general says.'

CHAPTER EIGHT

Noon, and the heat gathering in the gully was unbearable.

Climbing onto open moorland, Helligraine spotted Quarvis sitting alone, hunched over something in the grass, his small face intent. Approaching, Helligraine saw that the mysterious something was an animal skin, scraped clean of fur, decorated with clumsily executed primitive artwork: hunters spearing boars, bears and deer; men with symbolically huge phalluses, women with vaginas large enough to drive a cart through; exotic, long-extinct ferns and fruit bushes.

'What is that? Where did you get it?' asked Helligraine.

'Hm? Oh, this.' His reverie broken, Quarvis looked up, squinting against the sunlight. 'The Erethin found it in the cave.' He patted the skin with his fingertips. 'I was wondering if it might be Toros's handiwork.'

'Unlikely,' said Helligraine, sitting. 'Do you think he would amuse himself with third-rate daubings?'

'Surely a visionary cannot be, ah, *visioning* every hour of every day? Surely he needs distractions and, dare I say it, hobbies like the rest of us? Besides, this daubing, as you call it, is immaculately preserved. Would this not indicate that magic was at work? Some marvellous preservative force?'

Helligraine stared at Quarvis. The little man was monstrously stupid. He suffered from a malady common amongst the excessively faithful: he saw everything as a sign that his idol not only existed, but existed in glorified fashion: every object they had touched, every trace they left on the world, was an indication of their glory, their miraculous nature.

'The cave was more or less air-tight,' said Helligraine. 'It would be magical, Quarvis, if the skin *had* deteriorated.'

Quarvis chuckled. 'Oh, you joyless sceptic – I was joking. You are not the only one with knowledge of ancient artefacts. But this, I maintain, was Toros's handiwork. Look.'

He turned the skin over. On the other side, there was a series of similar diagrams, rendered in ochre. Each showed half a dozen circles, connected to one another by sometimes straight, sometimes curving lines. Evidently, the artist was dissatisfied with his work, for each diagram had been crossed out with wide, angry smears of the same ochre that had been used to create it. It was easy to imagine the artist completing a diagram then, frustrated by its inadequacy, striking it out.

'Do you know what these are?' asked Quarvis.

Helligraine did; they were neither novel nor astonishing. 'Maps, showing the hypothetical connections between dimensions. Some believe there are other worlds, joined by ethereal pathways. There is our world, the Forest, and many more.' He flapped a dismissive hand over the diagrams. 'It is nonsense at worst, wild speculation at best.'

'Toros did not think so,' said Quarvis. 'Assuming this *is* his handiwork.'

'You understand nothing, and see less,' muttered Helligraine, sourly. 'Toros *entertained* the idea, perhaps. Then he dismissed it. Did you fail to notice that the diagrams have been obliterated? Even the most gifted men wander down dead ends, from time to time. By nature, they experiment with ideas and actions; occasionally, experiments fail – and those failures are as important as the successes.'

401

Helligraine's voice had grown strident; Quarvis raised his eyebrows.

'Your tongue is sharp enough to gut a pig carcass,' said Quarvis. 'I imagined that when this moment came you would be in a better humour. Instead, you are griping like a vinegary old maid.'

'You take too much for granted,' said Helligraine, rising. 'You sit there, looking as if our success is assured. But I ask you, have you no sense, no inkling, of the risks Kraike is taking? You have seen the Origin. Have you not, for even half a second, wondered if it might prove *too much*? That it might destroy the sorcerer? Kraike's task is without precedent. Toros wrote the spell; but maybe he . . . he overestimated the ability of another to read it. Absorb it.'

'Kraike is not some child leaping into fast-flowing water, oblivious of the current's strength,' said Quarvis, mildly. 'He knows what he is doing; he will not be swept away.'

'He has been in the cave since dawn. Now it is noon. We have waited too long.'

Helligraine picked his way down into the gully. He felt sick; he knew better than to trust his moods: whether one was in a fearful humour, or a jubilant one, it made no difference to the outcome. But he could not stifle the pre-emptive despair that crawled over him like some noxious mould. It had arisen the instant he left the cave and, with every slow-passing moment, intensified, until he was certain the entire venture would end in failure. Were other men, at vital points in history, besieged by such doubt? Probably not. Great warriors, empire-expanding tyrants and the like believed their success was preordained; triumph was their destiny, their gilded fate. How could Helligraine entertain the same illusions, when he had spent a lifetime writing about failure? He had wandered the ruins of once-glorious civilisations, civilisations that must have seemed as if they would last for ever. He had seen the toppled, ivy-wreathed statues of leaders whose names were now forgotten. He immersed himself in books whose authors had sunk beyond obscurity, and whose theories – once persuasive – now seemed quaintly preposterous. Yes, he understood it quite clearly: ambition concluded in decay, and in time all dreams died a death.

Reaching the gully floor, he strode to the cave.

'Give me a lantern,' he instructed an excavator.

The excavator, as lean and keen-eyed as a racing dog, frowned. 'You cannot enter the cave. Kraike has forbidden it.'

'I will deal with his objections, if they arise. Now do as you are told.' When the excavator did not move, Helligraine nodded, sharply. 'Very well. Lantern or not, I shall go in. The sun is high and bright; the cave will not be completely dark.' He took a step forward. Moving close, the excavator laid a strong hand upon his shoulder, restraining him.

'It is forbidden,' the excavator repeated. 'Kraike must not be disturbed, his concentration broken.'

Swiping out, Helligraine knocked the man's hand away. 'Yes? What if his work is done, but he is lying in the gloom, stricken by the after-effects of the endeavour? What if he will perish without our help? A sorcerer is but flesh and blood; his gifts reside in the mind, not the body. They are prone to sicknesses and convulsions as much as the rest of us.' He turned to enter the cave. Again, the excavator restrained him, seizing his upper arm.

'What would you know about it, *acaratix*?'

'What would I know?' Incredulous, Helligraine tried to break free. This time, the excavator's grip held firm. Helligraine felt the gristle-and-whipcord strength of the man's labour-honed fingers. 'I located the Origin. I travelled to the Skravian Desert to tell Kraike all was not lost. I am the mortar binding this endeavour together. Without me—'

'I asked what you knew. Not what you had done.'

Helligraine scowled, confused by the distinction.

A slick smile touched the excavator's lips. 'You are not Erethin. You cannot comprehend the processes Kraike is engaged in. His world, his thoughts and instincts, are as strange to you as a bird's to a fish.'

'And because you are Erethin you have some insight I am lacking?' He laughed, scornfully. 'You have read none of the texts I wrote, have you? If you had, you would know that I place no worth in titles, plaudits or declarations of rank. A man is but a man, regardless of what he calls himself.'

Now, it was the excavator who seemed confused. His smile faded, but did not diminish; rather, it grew subtler. 'Do you think we Erethin are chosen at random? That we draw lots or roll dice?'

'I expect the process is more convoluted,' said Helligraine. 'But it will amount to the same thing. A holy man, of whatever complexion, requires no skills, save an ability to *appear* holy.'

'Has Kraike spoken of *The Chronicle*? It is a document which—'

'I know what it is. I have held it in my hands.'

'Did you use it, *acaratix*?'

'Does it matter?'

'Clearly, you did not. But maybe Kraike spoke of its origins – who created it, and why?'

'We have not discussed it, no. And I do not see its relevance to our current situation.' He looked into the cave. He wanted to rush into the darkness, as much to escape the excavator as assist Kraike.

'Selindak created *The Chronicle* in the desert, some time after your visit,' said the excavator. 'He believed it was time to renew our faith in Toros. He understood that religion would prove essential to rebuilding our culture. For this, he required priests – priests unlike those found in *your* culture. That is, priests who had an authentic kinship with the figure they revered.' He blinked; the smile twitched. 'Priests who, like Toros, were blessed with visionary talent. *The Chronicle* is not merely a work of history; it is a test. Only those with innate visionary abilities can use it, can see the scenes it depicts. An aspirant would inhale the smoke of burning *lecterscrix* then, once the trance had passed – if it occurred at all – answer questions regarding what he saw. Naturally, these questions pertained not to the incidents themselves, for these swiftly became common knowledge. Rather, Selindak would ask about certain details, insignificant in themselves: the colour of our late emperor's belt during one scene, for instance. Or the scars marking the body of a particular prisoner on whom the plague spell was tested. And so on. For each aspirant, there was a different set of questions.' He gestured to the other excavators, listening intently along the gully floor. They seemed amused. And satisfied, as if they had waited a long time for this moment. 'Was I right to assume you have not used *The Chronicle*?'

Helligraine did not reply.

'But you tried, yes? Of course you did. From your reddened eyes and nostrils, it is clear you inhaled *lecterscrix* not long ago.'

'Unhand me.' Helligraine tried to squirm loose from the excavator's grip. 'I will not be goaded by the likes—'

'Likes of me? Of *us*?' He looked to his fellow excavators. 'It is as we suspected, my boys. We, the slaves, are superior to our master. But we hid it well, did we not? We feigned respect; we acted obediently. We accepted his insults, and worked until we dropped, when he asked it of us. We bit back our rage, day after day, and not once did we break his head with our mallets.' He laughed; the others laughed. He let go of Helligraine's shoulder. 'Go, *acaratix*. Sit down and—'

He fell silent, his gaze drifting to the cave. Over the blood drumming in his ears, Helligraine heard stones sliding, accompanied by the slow *click-clack-click* of a walking branch. In the darkness, something stirred. Then Kraike appeared, stumbling into the sunlight, as pale as salt-bleached driftwood, blood trickling from his nose and mouth, his eye-whites flaring red as lava. Sweat soaked his hair, his clothes were plastered to his body, and he trembled wildly, barely able to keep hold of the branch. Suddenly, he pitched forward. Swooping in, the excavator caught him, laying him gently on the ground.

'Sweet mercy,' said Helligraine, kneeling. He laid a hand on Kraike's forehead; his flesh sizzled. 'Feverish. We must—'

A flurry of spasms shook Kraike's slender body. The sorcerer's eyes rolled, the irises vanishing then reappearing; his hands clenched and unclenched, his fingers hooking like claws around some invisible prey; veins bulged on his forehead, his breath came in deep, stuttering, wheezing gasps. His boot-heels pounded the ground, and from head to toe, he vibrated like a lute string plucked by heavy hands.

Pushing Helligraine aside, two excavators crouched by the sorcerer, restraining him gently but firmly.

This is the form my failure shall take, thought Helligraine, staring. This is when the earth shakes, the sky falls, and I become the cracked, fallen statue of a forgotten emperor . . .

The seizure passed. Kraike lay still, eyes closed, body slack. Suddenly, his eyes snapped open. With a screeching yowl, he lashed out at the excavators, pawing madly with slack-fingered hands; then he shrank back, curling into a ball. An excavator laid a hand on his shoulder; the sorcerer recoiled.

'You are safe,' said an excavator, softly, in Vohorin.

'All is well,' said another. 'Be calm.'

Kraike relaxed, the tension dissipating slowly, like dew evaporating from a sun-struck lawn. Stretching out, he lay on his back. He stared at the sky, at the tract of never-ending blueness, then closed his eyes.

'It is done,' he said hoarsely. '*It is done.*'

A half hour later, Helligraine rode to his tent. Inside, he spread a blanket over the groundsheet and lay down. Back at the gully, Kraike was sleeping; he decided he might as well do the same.

So, the excavators possessed visionary powers – twelve men endowed with the same gifts as Kraike, albeit in an uncultivated form: he had expected it to be rarer, that peculiar talent.

And Quarvis, that weedy know-nothing hobgoblin – he was Erethin, too! It seemed perverse. But, Helligraine reasoned, there was neither rhyme nor reason as to whom the universe granted its finest gifts. How many poets, painters and sculptors seemed undeserving of their genius? How many were so defective in character, intelligence and temperament that their abilities were not only incongruous, but appeared to be the punchline of an unfathomable cosmic joke?

Naturally, the Erethin believed they were special. Even now, Helligraine heard their sly, arrogant laughter.

It is as we suspected, my boys. We, the slaves, are superior to our master.

Believe it if you wish, thought Helligraine, sourly.

If he had had his wits about him, he would have retorted with a quote from the philosopher Lerrinthe: *It is not a man who is superior; it is his achievements.*

Then, a few words of his own:

And what have you achieved? Broken stones, that is all. Hardly warrants a hagiography, does it?

And finally, the inevitable.

Were it not for me, the Origin would not have been found, and Toros would remain trapped in the Forest for the rest of time.

407

He shut his eyes.

Odd, he thought, how petty rivalries persist in the midst of the greatest triumphs. Today, though only a few know it, the future has been changed in a more drastic, more fundamental way than ever before, yet still there are squabbles born of status and vanity.

And the Erethin, he wondered. How strong were their powers?

Not strong enough to shatter stone, he thought, fading into sleep. No, they still needed to wield mallets like common quarrymen.

He dozed in the restless, in-and-out-of-consciousness manner of someone too fatigued to stay awake but too excited to sleep. When he awoke, it was to the sound of hooves, thumping dully over the moors.

Sitting up, he opened the tent flap and crawled out.

Slouching in the saddle, swaying as if only half-conscious, a lone rider cantered toward the gully. Rushing to him, the excavators helped him from the saddle. As soon as his boots touched the ground, he collapsed. Joined by Quarvis, scrambling out of the gully like a hairless rat emerging from a sewer pipe, they knelt around the man, heads lowered, as if listening to words softly – painfully – spoken.

Climbing onto his own mount, Helligraine rode over.

As he grew close, Quarvis left the group and walked to meet him.

'Ah,' said Quarvis. 'What a quandary of emotions you shall soon find yourself in.'

Helligraine halted. Despite his chirping, faintly mocking tone, Quarvis wore a solemn expression.

'I mean,' he went on, 'you passed a death sentence on the Hawks, a group of people you admired, possibly even liked. One way or another, your feelings were bound to be mixed, like sour wine and stale water . . .' He pointed. 'That man, he is the only Erethin to survive the attack on my former home. Goodness knows how he managed to ride this far; there was a blaze, his flesh is blackened like toasted bread, and he has not slept for two days . . . Although he sleeps now. Deeply, eternally, if you catch my meaning. He spat out his last words and croaked.'

Helligraine's guts turned cold. 'And those words concern the Hawks?'

'The lummox and the girl are alive,' said Quarvis. 'As for the general, well, that is uncertain.'

CHAPTER NINE

But, friendly reader, you will have questions which must be answered, if you are to take my account seriously.

Where is Dalzerte? How did I find it, when so many had tried and failed?

Dalzerte lies – or lay – in the Prinsalline Tropics, approximately three hundred miles south of Delgrallis, four hundred east of Quenterren, two hundred west of F'qrain. It is gone, now; soon after my departure, the Salandier Hordes swept in and, driven by holy fervour, laid waste to the Gardens. I was fortunate to arrive mere days before those primitive zealots, and more fortunate still to leave before they appeared and began their rampage.

But my greatest fortune was to find the Gardens at all. I had not been seeking them; rather, I was merely passing through on my way to F'qrain, in the hope of acquiring certain relics. I confess that, travelling alone and lacking a guide, I had grown lost, due in large part to the extraordinarily foul weather – a mixture of hail fierce enough to pierce the skin, and winds that seemed to blow from every direction at once. Disorientated, I blundered into an area seldom trodden, and those few who did venture so far afield did not see what I saw, for the weather that I had been roundly cursing for days had swept away the ground beneath which the Gardens lay, leaving them exposed, as they had not been for millennia.

Granted, this seems improbably fortuitous, and even if I were to take an oath that it was true, you would be forgiven for remaining sceptical. But bizarre coincidences occur all the time. Stand on any street corner, and you will overhear so-and-so saying such-and-such happened, and surely divine intervention was at work, for what else could explain something so unlikely coming to pass? We need only listen to tales of gamblers who, on the verge of losing everything, were rescued by an incredibly rare roll of the die, or lost children who, many years later, find themselves sharing a jug of ale with a stranger who, it transpires, is their father.

Extracted from *A Glimpse of the Lost Gardens of Dalzerte*
by Cavielle Shaelus

They arrived too late; they knew that they would.

Before leaving the house, they suspected the horse-tracks pounded into the moorland grass would lead them to Brellerin Fell: the makeshift weapons used by the attackers were the type of tools, Ekkerlin observed, that might be used at an archaeological dig, if rocks needed to be smashed and soil ripped up, and she suspected that Helligraine had unfinished business at the site. In this, they were right; but, with the general injured, they were forced to keep a slow pace: when they reached the Fell, after a day and a half of riding, there was no sign of Helligraine, Quarvis or the old man from the bell tower. All that remained were a few unoccupied tents, some discarded tools and heaps of shattered stone stacked along the floor of a gully some twenty feet deep.

Dismounting, they climbed down into the gully. A cave sank into the gully wall.

'Is this it, do you think?' asked Ekkerlin, peering into the cave.

Ballas shrugged. 'Whatever Helligraine was seeking, it will not be there now. The old bastard will have taken it away. What do you reckon it was? A book?' But Ekkerlin was not listening. It was noon, the sun hung directly above the gully, its light feebly penetrating the cave. Squinting, Ekkerlin peered silently at something inside. Something that momentarily wiped her face clean of all expression. She looked like a village fool, baffled by a jigsaw puzzle.

'See if you can find a lantern,' she told Ballas.

Ballas did as he was told, locating a lantern near the abandoned tools. A little oil sloshed in the bottom. Climbing the gully wall to the horses, Ballas retrieved a flint and steel from a saddlebag then returned. Ekkerlin had already ventured inside; Standaire lingered by the entrance, a hand pressed against his stomach.

Ballas had seen Standaire in pain before. Yet the general had never seemed quite so *diminished* as he did now. The wound seemed not only to have damaged his body, but his spirit. As always, he was quiet, speaking only when necessary. Yet his customary inexpressiveness had dissolved. His hard, lean face twitched, scowled and grimaced, as tides of discomfort washed through him. He clenched his fists and, just occasionally, sighed, as if receiving unhappy news. More, he was distracted. His thoughts were elsewhere; he did not seem entirely present. He seemed less a man than an apparition.

'You coming in, General?' Ballas asked, lighting the lantern.

Standaire blinked, nodded.

They entered the cave. Standing close to the opposite wall, Ekkerlin gestured impatiently.

'The lantern,' she breathed. 'Be quick, Anhaga.'

Striding over, Ballas raised the lantern high – and nearly stumbled. The wall was covered in tight, angular symbols, each crammed against the other, rising almost from the floor to the ceiling. He stared, then swore.

'They are moving – the symbols . . .'

'It is an illusion,' said Ekkerlin. She pressed a finger to one of the markings: although the symbol continued to writhe and wriggle, like a maggot on a fisherman's hook, Ekkerlin's finger remained perfectly still. Nothing pushed at it, or vibrated beneath it. Suddenly, she turned away from the wall.

'It is making me nauseous,' she said, looking at the ground.

Ballas allowed his gaze to linger. Then he too looked away.

'These sigils comprise the Universal Script,' she said. 'Metaphysicians believe it is the language of the creator-god – or gods, if one holds with the Eastern beliefs.'

'Aye? What does it say?'

Ekkerlin frowned. 'How would I know? I am not a god.'

'No, but your head is stuffed with archaic nonsense. Can you not translate it?'

'Nobody can,' said Ekkerlin. 'It is a language one does not read, but *feel*. It is said that visionaries, if they ingest certain narcotics, enter a trance state in which the Script *flows through* them, and in this way they absorb its knowledge. This knowledge, it does not exist in their conscious mind, but their *underminds* – the part of the mind which controls the bodily functions we do not think about, such as breathing, the beating of our hearts and, in your case, farting.' A fleeting smile. Then, 'One of the narcotics is said to be similar to visionary's root – the substance Helligraine claimed the old man used to alleviate his illness. The same substance which might have left the green stains on the ceiling in the bell tower.'

'The old man had a book written in this language,' said Standaire, softly. 'I saw it – briefly.'

Ekkerlin grew thoughtful. 'Then it is not unreasonable to assume the man, whoever he is, is a visionary. And he came here to absorb all *this*.'

'But you've got no idea what it means,' said Ballas.

413

'It is not some graffito scrawled on a piss-house wall,' said Ekkerlin. 'It is said the Script is the fundamental condition of existence; the universe, and everything in it, is this language made tangible. Some maintain that a gifted visionary can peer at a natural object – a blade of grass, a beetle, bird or gadfly – and see the Script glowing within it; the more complex the entity, the more complex the Script. It is the recipe from which all creation is made.'

'We are miles from a stableyard,' said Ballas, 'yet I can still smell horseshit.'

'Do not be so dismissive,' replied Ekkerlin. 'Whoever cut these symbols into the stone took the Script seriously. As did Helligraine. Do you imagine that he, of all people, would pursue a fool's errand? That he would risk his life for some absurd fancy?'

Before Ballas could reply, stones clattered on the far side of the cave. Turning, he raised the lantern. Three men charged toward the Hawks, brandishing pick-axes.

Setting down the lantern, Ballas charged at the nearest man. A few yards away, he jumped, high, jamming his boot down hard on the axe-blade as he descended, forcing it to the ground. Landing, then spinning, he punched his assailant on the back of his head. Dazed, the man stumbled forward. Moving close, Ballas hooked an arm around his throat and jerked, snapping his neck. The two remaining men raced toward Ekkerlin. For an instant, it seemed Standaire was nowhere to be seen. Then Ballas glimpsed his silhouette in the cave mouth, his hand lashing forward with a stiff flick of the wrist. An unseen knife spun through the darkness, slamming into one man's temple. The other attacker swung his pick-axe downwards at Ekkerlin. Diving sideways, Ekkerlin dodged the blade by barely an inch. Rising, she grabbed the pick-axe handle, and fought to disarm her assailant.

414

Snatching up the first man's pick, Ballas sprinted over.

'Preserve him!' shouted Standaire, the words slurred with pain.

Dropping low, Ballas swung the pick-axe, the blade sinking through the soft flesh behind the attacker's knee, then yanked it free. Tendons tore; screaming, he dropped.

Grabbing the lantern, Ballas ran through the cave, seeking more attackers. Finding none, he returned.

'You know what you must do,' said Standaire, still a dark, slender shadow in the cave mouth. He lingered a moment, then was gone.

Ballas and Ekkerlin carried the attacker out of the cave, onto the moors.

In the gully, Standaire knelt by a shallow spring, bordered by purple flowers. He bent forward, intending to rinse his face. Pain flared in his stomach. He stood, swaying slightly. Then he sat on a boulder, staring abstractedly at the cave entrance.

I ought to court-martial myself, he thought.

If such a thing were possible, he would have accused himself of cowardice. When the attackers emerged from the darkness, he had fled the cave, plunging out into the safety of the gully. He had moved without meaning to; some yellow-hearted reflex animated his limbs, and he had much less run away than been carried off by a body acting of its own volition.

But it was a poor excuse. How many deserters *contrived* to escape the battlefield? Not many, the general knew. Most were overwhelmed by their circumstances and, involuntarily dropping all notions of honour, dignity and valour, became timid animals, fleeing from a predator's scent.

Only when he was outside did his courage return. Moving to the cave mouth, he had thrown his knife at an attacker – but that too was an action tainted by cowardice. He had not cared whether it struck home: he had simply wanted Ballas and Ekkerlin to *believe* that his disappearance had been part of a plan, one born of cool wits and experience. He wanted them to think, He is too injured to fight in an ordinary fashion, so he must employ unconventional tactics.

That the knife found its target was a stroke of pure good luck. Standaire had thrown without aiming; it had been a gesture . . . No, a *deception*, as shameful as any perpetrated by Helligraine.

He lowered his gaze to the spring. The flowers trembled in a mild breeze.

He had not expected to survive the knife wound he received in the bell tower. Nor had he wanted to, if he was honest. Lying on the table in the feasting hall, he had been ready to die, willing to draw death over himself like a dark blanket. His existence could no longer be justified; he was a spent force, a force that even in its prime, flashing and crackling with purpose and passion, had accomplished nothing of enduring worth.

Somewhere across the moors, the attacker cried out; Ballas shouted at him, his words muffled by the oppressively hot air.

Again, Standaire's gaze wandered to the cave.

Is this not proof that I am finished? he wondered. Here I sit, a dead man unexpectedly still living, enmeshed in a conspiracy both puzzling and grave, and yet I feel nothing.

Nothing except disappointment.

The old man in the bell tower — if only he had thrust the knife a half-inch higher or lower, to the left or the right.

Another cry of pain. Standaire sat, waited.

A hundred and thirty years earlier, a physician named Emircke Summer was arrested by the Church, tried in a Papal Court and hanged. His crimes were twofold. First, he had performed a series of experiments on living subjects in order to determine how pain travelled through the human body. Second, he produced a forbidden text detailing his discoveries, which were as revolutionary as they were unpleasant. He created several charts in which various tortures were ranked according to effectiveness, efficiency and subtlety. The latter category was particularly innovative: he found that certain 'violations of the mortal frame' could, if applied simultaneously, yield unendurable levels of pain.

For the best results, and the quickest, he wrote, *it is necessary to aggravate two or more regions of the body at once; the discomforts arising from each shall interlace, and various effects will be produced. Primary amongst these is a feeling of unbearable imprisonment in the subject; his various agonies form the bars of a cell through which he is desperate to escape . . . and to do so, he will confess any truth, no matter how dearly or for how long he has held it a secret.*

Summer's text was incredibly rare. Only a few copies were produced and, written in a language of the physician's own invention, it was accessible only to those with a knack for code-breaking. Ekkerlin had deciphered the text several years ago. Believing it might prove useful, she had circulated it amongst the Hawks, with Standaire's blessing; now, it was an essential component of the regiment's advanced interrogation procedures.

It worked marvellously well. Although the attacker resisted at first – his resilience startled Ekkerlin – he eventually confessed all that he knew, gasping out the words in the harsh language of the Vohorin.

Now, he lay dead amongst a heap of boulders. Ekkerlin and Ballas returned to the gully.

'It is done,' she told Standaire.

The general stared blankly at a small spring fringed by purple flowers.

'Sir?'

Standaire looked up. 'What have you learned?'

Ekkerlin told him. The inscription on the cave wall was the Origin, a source of immense magical power; the old man in the tower, who had used it the previous day, was Jurel Kraike, former ally of Emperor Grivillus, long believed dead. His intention was to resurrect Toros, the mystic who, according to myth, founded Vohoria millennia ago. As for Vohoria itself – many of its inhabitants had survived the Scourge, and returned to its towns and cities. The country, once broken, now reviving, was Kraike's destination; Shaelus, Kraike and Quarvis were travelling with the surviving excavators. And the excavators – they were no ordinary labourers, adept at nothing except breaking rocks. They were Erethin, priests of the Torosian faith. In a burst of defiance, the attacker had said, *We control Vohoria, just as one day we will control the globe* . . .

It seemed almost insignificant, now, but the attacker revealed that it was the Erethin who had attempted to track down Shaelus. *We failed to find him, time and time again, he had said, with bitter amusement. But you delivered him to us. We are very, very grateful.*

The attacker also revealed less esoteric information. Malluvis, an Erethin, had been assigned to return to Soriterath, and meet a contact named Dexler in The Grinning Dog, a tavern near the Sacros. But Malluvis was amongst those slain in the cave.

Standaire listened without speaking. When Ekkerlin finished he asked, 'If our ranks were reversed, what would you decide?'

'Decide, General?'

'Our next move. What would it be?'

Ekkerlin glanced uneasily at Ballas. Standaire had not responded to the revelations in the way she had expected. He seemed uninterested, unconcerned. Maybe it was understandable. His wound was painful; he was visibly tired.

'I would pursue Helligraine and the others,' she said. 'I'd try to catch up with them before they set sail for Vohoria.'

'And then?'

'Kraike I would kill,' said Ekkerlin. 'He is too dangerous to be allowed to live. As for Helligraine and Quarvis – I would take them alive, if I could.'

'Then that is what you must do.' Standaire's gaze alighted on Ekkerlin, but she sensed that he did not see her. Not properly. 'You and Ballas should leave immediately. You have to cover a lot of ground.'

'And you, General?'

'I will ride to the Sacros and break the oath I made to Faltriste. I will inform the Masters of all that has come to pass.'

He gestured to the horses.

'Go, both of you.'

And they went, without farewells.

For a while, Standaire lingered in the gully, gazing at the spring. Then he rose, climbed the steep walls and walked to his horse.

Murmuring with pain, he swung into the saddle. He looked around; already, Ballas and Ekkerlin were small dark specks, shrinking into the horizon.

He did not have to return to Soriterath, he knew. If he wished, he could go elsewhere, and live out his remaining years in some remote corner of the country, an obscure, solitary figure, minding his own business until time succeeded where Jurel Kraike's knife had failed, and he soughed into the grave as unnoticed as a mouse slipping into a wheatfield.

But he heeled his mount and rode.

Somewhere in the past forty years, he had ceased to be a man, becoming instead a mechanism, or maybe a worker ant, fulfilling its purpose because it lacked the wit or instinct to do anything else.

*   *   *

419

After three days' riding, Ballas and Ekkerlin arrived at Bluecurl Harbour. Night had fallen. Roped to the quayside, a dozen boats bobbed on the shifting water — fishing vessels, large enough to hold five or six men, creaking with every dip and swell of the tide.

In a small hut, a solitary candle burned, then lapsed into darkness. The door opened. A little man emerged, whistling tunelessly.

'You the harbour master?' asked Ekkerlin, approaching.

'Aye,' said the man, locking the door. 'And I am done for the evening. Return on the morrow, and we'll speak then. I've got a jar of whisky at home, begging to be drunk, and I'll be—' Glancing over, he fell silent. Suddenly, he laughed, cawing like a gull. 'A-ha-ha! It is *you two*, is it? This puts me in a bit of a bind.' He looked Ballas up and down. 'Well, the matter is settled. The bind is unbound. Money is about as much use to a dead man as feathers to a crab. Odd that he did not mention *how* big you were . . .'

'He?' inquired Ekkerlin, although she already knew the answer.

'An old fellow, eyes bright as a cat's. A very persuasive manner, he had. Not threatening, just . . .' He gestured airily with the hand that held the key. 'He was the sort who could easily win a fellow over. Most fellows, anyway. But not me. I've learned that the calmest waters have an undertow; trust them too much and you'll be gargling brine before you know it.' Slipping the key into his pocket, he planted his hands on his hips. 'He wanted me to pay a few of the rough boys to kill you. Gave me a bag of silvers and said, "If they ask about me, play dumb; pretend you haven't seen me or my companions. If they don't believe you, make sure they get their throats cut. Ditch their bodies in the sea, chop them up to bait the lobster-pots. I don't care."' He chuckled. 'He didn't put it as plainly

420

as that, mind you. He had a poncy way of speaking that made me feel like I was drowning in flowers.'

Ekkerlin smiled. 'But you refused his offer?'

'Of course not!' said the harbour master, grinning. 'I took his money, aye, without any intention of doing what he asked. I'm not one for doing other people's dirty work.' He sniffed. 'The arrogant old shit, thinking folk can be so easily bought. He was asking to be conned.'

'Where is he now?'

'On the water,' said the harbour master. 'He and his mates sailed off at first light yesterday. I doubt they'll be coming back. They'd had their boat moored here for a month or so, and it just sat there, untouched. It caused some resentment, I can tell you. The lads reckon the harbour should be used only by fishermen, and these characters, by sticking the boat there and doing naught with it, were taking up a valuable mooring spot. There was a bit of a set-to when your, ah, friends arrived. I thought it might turn nasty, particularly when this little chap, all hunched and hairless like a prawn, started yelling that the lads should know their places . . . But the old one smoothed things over. Like I said, he was very persuasive.'

Ekkerlin nodded. 'Who else sailed with him?'

'Apart from the prawn? Three younger men, and another with a walking branch, his face as wrinkled as a cormorant's anus.'

'My thanks,' said Ekkerlin. 'Go to your whisky, and have a restful evening.'

'What now?' asked Ballas, as the harbour master departed.

'We steal a boat,' said Ekkerlin. 'And we sail.'

CHAPTER TEN

So, there it was: unsought but found, the Lost Gardens of Dalzerte.

I will not bore you with descriptions of my surprise and delight; you could no more appreciate my feelings than you could taste the flavours of a good meal I might recount.

I beheld it, first, from a high vantage, atop a hill of sand and mud. Did I recognise it straight away? A part of me certainly did for the eventual realisation of what I saw was preceded, for several moments, by a gathering and tremulous excitement. It was one of those occasions, I suppose, when the conscious mind lags behind one's instincts; as soon as my mind caught up, however, I broke into a headlong sprint, and was most likely whooping and prancing like a madman. I cannot clearly remember; the next thing I knew, I was in the Garden itself, standing where none had stood for thousands of years.

Extracted from *A Glimpse of the Lost Gardens of Dalzerte*
by Cavielle Shaelus

Sea travel contained many perils. Whirlpools, storms, sea beasts both mythic and real – these were the stuff of epic poems and song. But the greatest danger, and the one least avoidable, was rarely mentioned: boredom.

In his younger days, Helligraine had spent much time at

sea. Back then, he whiled away the time writing texts. On this voyage, lacking writing materials – and, if he was honest, any desire to write – Helligraine was bored to an extraordinary degree. It seemed the journey would never end, and he would spend the rest of time in that little boat, crawling over the blue-green ocean.

Predictably, Quarvis did not share his suffering. As he had used *The Chronicle*, the Erethin considered him one of their own. These three men, muscled from hard labour, treated the puny runt as an equal, teaching him seacraft, tutoring him in the Vohorin language. Oh yes, Quarvis was having the time of his life, and his happiness only compounded Helligraine's misery.

Then there was Kraike.

The sorcerer stayed silent for nearly the entire voyage. Although he had recovered from the eye-rolling, body-wrenching spasm that followed his use of the Origin, he was a changed man. He spent long hours lost in thought, and his ever-vigilant gaze was a thousand times more attentive: he watched the bright shoals of fish, and the whales and dolphins cruising by the boat, with unsettling intensity. On one occasion, he treated Helligraine to that same unnerving stare.

'What is it?' Helligraine had quipped. 'Have I sprouted a tail?'

'I perceive the world so differently,' said Kraike, his gaze breaking. 'I understand life at its most fundamental level.' He pointed to a basking shark in the distance. 'That creature . . . When I gaze upon it, I do not merely see the beast in its entirety. Nor do I see the organs of which it is composed – the skin, heart, lungs and so forth. I see the tiniest elements that constitute its physical being. I do not simply perceive the tapestry, but the threads, and the wisps from which the threads themselves are made. And beyond the wisps, I see the atoms, the minuscule dots from which everything is built. With this knowledge, I can reshape life. I can alter the forms of living things; and I can restore Toros from his bones. Before, I was a destroyer; now, I am a creator.'

'And the soul?' Helligraine had asked.

'The soul is not physical,' said Kraike. 'I can claim no special insight . . . But Toros? He has spent millennia in the Forest, where all is magic, where all is constructed from the same mysterious substance as the soul — perhaps he will know what I do not.'

The conversation ended; Kraike resumed his contemplative silence.

The suffocating boredom returned. When Helligraine heard seagulls screeching, and spotted their white forms against the blue sky, he experienced relief so strong it exhausted him as much as it invigorated him.

The harbour was no larger than the one at Bluecurl, and proved the point that where there was poverty, there was also uniformity.

As the boat bumped against the dock wall, Helligraine gazed at the small, ugly buildings crouching close by, cobbled together from stones salvaged after the Scourge, and thought, *I could be anywhere*.

It was true. If he had not kept a constant eye on the sun as they sailed, he might have believed the boat had discreetly turned around and carried them back to Druine.

The docks were purely functional. Fishing boats tilted at anchor; barrels of salted cod and herring, and branch-woven crab- and lobster-pots stood on the quayside. And that was it; there was nothing more. No statues, no taverns, no street musicians earning a few coins by playing traditional Vohorin songs and, if he was not mistaken, no brothels where exponents of the oldest profession could prey upon those with healthy impulses and sickly morals.

Depressing, thought Helligraine, as the Erethin disembarked.

No girls, no games, no liquor, songs or grandeur . . . The Vohorin spirit has been truly expunged.

As Helligraine moved to leave the boat, Quarvis caught his arm. 'The others and I have been thinking—' he began.

'The others, Quarvis?' interrupted Helligraine, tugging himself free.

'The other Erethin and I, we have reached a decision. Whilst we are ashore, you and I must not parley with the locals. If we were to open our mouths, you see, we would surely give ourselves away.'

Helligraine frowned, nonplussed. Then, 'You are referring to our ability to speak the Vohorin language?'

'As I have discovered during our voyage, it is a complex language, full of pitfalls and snares. So we must tread warily. There is a secretive aspect to—'

'Quarvis,' snapped Helligraine. '*You* might struggle, but I do not. I can speak Vohorin as fluently as anyone born on this island.'

'Technically, that is true,' agreed Quarvis. 'Now that I've made my own attempts, I admire all the more your grasp of this most convoluted tongue. You are a natural. And yet, you are not natural – a natural Vohorin, I mean. Your words are exemplary, but your accent . . .' He gestured to the Erethin, waiting on the quayside. 'They tell me it is, ah, *conspicuous*. They say that you sound like a foreigner.' He chuckled. 'As perverse as it may seem, they claim I sound more like a born-and-bred Vohorin than you – albeit one who has suffered a grievous blow to the head. But yes, to return to my point – we must be discreet. There is, as I was saying, a secretive aspect to our time here. The Vohorin mistrust outsiders in general, and the Druinese in particular. Can you imagine what would happen if they discovered we belong by blood, if not inclination, to their oppressors?'

'We are serving Toros,' said Helligraine, darkly. 'Surely we would receive a warm welcome.'

'If you consider a branding iron up the arse *warm*,' said Quarvis. 'Look around. Have we been greeted by fanfares? Are there sedan chairs waiting to carry us on our way, along roads strewn with rose petals? No; only a few Vohorin know of our plans. Although most are loyal to Toros, there are rebellious elements who have not seen the light. Thus, we must be careful.'

'He speaks the truth,' said an Erethin, stepping onto the boat. His name was Lujaek. He was the copper-haired fellow who had shown Helligraine such disrespect at the Origin, calling him *acaratix*. Not once had he spoken to Helligraine during the journey. Not once had he even looked in his direction. Helligraine had wondered if his attitude would improve once they set ashore. Maybe then, he thought, he would stop brooding on how hard he had been forced to work, and consider instead what had been accomplished. Clearly, it was not so. Lujaek was an ingrate, Helligraine decided. The type of man who, if drowning after a shipwreck, would rebuke his rescuers for taking so long to arrive he had ended up cold and wet.

'Vohoria is not the land you remember,' said Lujaek. 'You must accept my knowledge, and submit to my guidance.'

Of course it is not the land I remember, thought Helligraine, stepping ashore. When last I visited, the populace was skulking in the desert, the streets were empty, the buildings ruins . . .

But how, he wondered, had Vohoria changed? It appeared Quarvis, with his talk of 'rebellious elements', had a vague understanding – gleaned, no doubt, from his discussions with the other Erethin. But what did he, Helligraine, know?

Nothing, he realised.

He was wholly ignorant of Vohoria's current state. In a way, this was understandable: he had spent the past several decades concentrating on finding the Origin; few thoughts unconnected with the task at hand had entered his mind. Occasionally, yes, he had wondered how the desert-dwellers were faring. But so what? To wonder about something was quite different from considering it with any degree of intensity. He had assumed . . . What had he assumed? Simply, the Vohorin would return to Vohoria, and continue living with the same dog-eared harmony as upon the sands. Their values would not alter, for their plight remained the same: they were a noble people suffering the after-effects of a monstrous invasion. What difference would it make, if they dwelled between walls of stone rather than animal hide?

Rebellious elements – the phrase buzzed in Helligraine's ears. Clearly, his assumptions had been wrong. And there had been nothing to contradict them. Vohoria was separated from Druine by a wide ocean and following the Scourge, there had been no communications between the two nations. As far as Druine was concerned, Vohoria was a dead land, its people extinct; and if anyone thought otherwise, they did so secretly, and made no tangible efforts to discover whether their suspicions were accurate, for the Church had forbidden its citizens from sailing to the home of its former enemy. As for the Church itself – during all his years as a scholar, and his brief period as a Master, Helligraine had not heard Vohoria mentioned once. It was as if the place no longer existed.

A shameful thought struck him: why had he not questioned the Erethin as they excavated the Origin? Surely they would have given him answers, even though they disliked him?

He had not even thought to ask. Perhaps he had been too preoccupied with the Origin itself. Perhaps he had not thought it important: after all, the entire globe, immeasurably vast, would be transfigured upon Toros's return. What importance did Vohoria – a relatively small island, home to very few people – have in the great scheme of things? What value *could* it – or anywhere – have when, soon enough, it might be transformed beyond recognition?

Nonetheless, he winced. Such a lack of curiosity was unforgivable for a scholar such as himself.

Leaving the docks, they entered a patch of grassland. Ahead, a road sloped up toward a hill a quarter mile away. A crowd had gathered on the summit; as far as Helligraine could see – like everything else, his eyes had grown weaker over the years – they were staring at some sort of structure, a statue or standing stone, striking black against the glaring sun. As they walked closer, Helligraine grew uneasy. Something about the sight disturbed him. He considered asking Lujaek, but decided against it. He did not want to give the Erethin the satisfaction of knowing he had him at a disadvantage. So he bided his time, saying nothing. On the hill top, everything became clear.

The focus of the crowd's attention was a man of middling years, strapped upright to a wooden board rising from the ground. He was naked, his flesh bruised, as if he had been beaten. A leather strap encircled his waist, another crossed his chest, whilst a third secured his throat. He looked like a patient planted upon some strange vertical operating table. In his eyes, there was the peculiar terror found in sick men who recognised that surgery was inevitable, and wanted only to get it over with. The board, Helligraine noticed, was crusted with old blood; whatever was about to happen had happened before. The grass beneath the board was similarly stained; so too the straps.

'What is this?' murmured Helligraine.

Moving through the crowd, a broad, heavyset man positioned himself beside the board. Clad entirely in brown, sporting a thick beard of the same colour, he resembled some gigantic bear – one which, with his drowsy, heavy-lidded eyes, had just woken from its winter sleep.

The crowd's quiet chatter sank into silence; the Bear's gaze drifted from man, to woman, to child.

It was then Helligraine noticed his belt. The black band was overlaid with leaves elegantly cut from green cloth, and the upper edge of each leaf was tinted red, as if touched by the light of a blood-coloured moon.

Helligraine looked to Quarvis. *A priest?* he mouthed.

An Erethin, corrected Quarvis, bobbing his head.

Lifting his chin, the Bear began, 'Toros cast himself into the Forest. Why? So he could study the mysterious forces of the universe. To what ends? To improve the lot of humankind. He was born into a primitive age. He saw with absolute clarity the horrors of disease and starvation. And he knew they were not inevitable. Man might have lived scarcely better than beasts, but he recognised that beasts they were not. He knew that they could break the shackles of their existence. That they could climb out of the squalid mire of hunger and infirmity.

'But it would be no easy task. Knowledge would be required – knowledge as deep as the ocean, as exalted as the sun burning in the heavens.

'Knowledge that cannot be acquired in this world.

'So he journeyed to the Forest. And there he remains, learning, until he is ready to return.

'Need I speak of his suffering? Are any of you ignorant of the Forest? Of the demons that shred the flesh? And how that flesh heals, so it might be shredded again? And how that the flesh is not flesh at all, but the soul itself – and thus, all pain is magnified a millionfold?

'All Toros asks is that we ease his pain. How do we do so? Through prayer. Must I explain the effect of prayers upon our saviour?

'Perhaps I should, for this creature,' he gestured to the man strapped to the board, 'would appear to be oblivious. Our

429

prayers act upon Toros's demon-ravaged soul like a cool poultice on burned flesh. They subdue his torment; they serve as an anaesthetic. Our words, uttered on bended knees, diminish his agonies, and assure him that he has not been forgotten. They remind him that he is loved by those he serves.

'How little effort it takes to pray! A trip to the temple, a few words softly uttered – that is all! Yet it is too much for this man. Yesterday morn, I noticed he was absent from morning prayers. Afterwards, concerned for his wellbeing, I visited his home. He claimed to have slept through the bells that summon us to the temple. "Such things happen," I said, and forgave him.

'When he was not at noon prayers, I found him in his cowfields. "Did you not hear the bells?" I asked. "No," he said. "I am deaf in one ear, and when they sounded, I must have been turned the wrong way." Again, I forgave him: a man must not be punished for his bodily shortcomings.

'But I sensed deception. At dusk, I did not myself ring the bell, but had an acolyte perform the task, whilst I watched his farmhouse from afar. What did I see? This scoundrel, this obnoxious specimen,' he glared at the man, 'standing in his doorway, grimacing, as if disgusted by the bells, and sickened by everything they represented. Then he vanished inside and locked the door.

'Why would he behave so abhorrently?

'Because, my faithful friends, he is allied to forces opposed to Toros, forces which thrive upon his suffering . . .

'I speak, of course, of the Forest's demons. One must believe – for logic allows no alternatives – that he is communing with Toros's tormentors, and these entities, despicable in ways we cannot comprehend, have instructed him to prove his loyalty to them. Thus, his actions were not merely those of an unbeliever: he did not attend the temple, as some do, and simply *pretend* to pray. No; he had to make a stand! To actively rebel! Thus, his absence was a gesture, a way of saying to his foul cohorts, "Look! I will defy the will of Toros's emissaries in this world, and they shall know it!"'

'This is untrue,' croaked the prisoner, his voice a parched rasp. 'Why would I defy Toros? Why would I throw my lot in with his enemies? Enemies who exist purely to harm people like me? What sense does it make—'

The priest punched him across the face. Hard. Bones crunched; the man's jaw sagged open, broken.

'Do you expect us to tolerate such prattle? To listen whilst you spout demonic words?' The priest drew a knife, the blade long and curved. 'The hour has come for you to be embraced by the demons you hold so dear.' Raising the blade, he carved a deep incision beneath the right side of the man's ribcage. Reaching through the opened flesh, he rummaged, as if rooting out a blockage in a sewer pipe. Blood flowed over his wrist, soaking his sleeve; eyes narrowing, he seized something. Then, grunting, he dragged out the man's liver, glistening in the sunlight. He held it aloft, so all could see. Then he jammed it into the man's mouth, forcing it as deep as it would go. The man spasmed against his straps, vibrating like a plucked lute string, his eyes rolling like a frightened horse's. His ribcage expanded and contracted as he fought to breathe around the liver. Then he sagged, head drooping.

The liver slid a few inches from his mouth, creeping like some bloated slug, and it seemed for a moment it would fall to the grass. But, catching upon something, it stopped, and hung there, fly-speckled and dripping.

Turning, the Bear continued addressing the crowd.

Legs weak, heart pounding, Helligraine stumbled away to a rock and sat down. He felt sick. Not at the evisceration itself – he had seen worse in foreign countries, where crude, savage

431

customs were practised – but that had been performed in Toros's name.

It was absurd. He had read countless texts that attempted to piece together details of Toros's life. All were in agreement: as far as was known, Toros *had* entered the Forest to gain knowledge to improve the lives of ordinary folk. But only part of this venture was concerned with remedying the physical ills the Bear spoke of. Toros believed that once people ceased to suffer, they would be free to think, to dedicate their minds to higher matters: in essence, his return would be the start of an unending era of enlightenment. But the Bear had acted contrary to Toros's ultimate wishes: he had punished and *silenced* a man for no reason other than expressing disbelief. He had ignored the irrefutable principle that enlightenment could exist where dissenters are plunged into darkness. By slaughtering the man, the priest had turned his face away from the values essential to the progression of knowledge: argument, conflict, debate. He had killed him for the mere act of standing for something other than his own beliefs.

Assuming he was guilty. Helligraine suspected the charges were false. Worse, he believed the Bear had invented them purely to reinforce his authority. And to say that a failure to attend prayers indicated allegiance with demons – what a leap of logic that was!

As for the value of prayers – this, too, was horseshit. Not once had he seen Lujaek and the other Erethin praying. Not on the boat, nor at the Origin.

I should have expected this, thought Helligraine. Holy men are the same the world over. Full of righteous savagery – or savagery they insist is righteous.

The crowd drifted away, some walking down to the docks, others heading for a village half a mile away. Lujaek chatted with the Bear; Quarvis stood close by, attentive, eager to be involved. As for Kraike — he gazed wonderingly at the dead man.

Rising, Helligraine strode to the priest.

'What was that?' he demanded. 'Do you suppose Toros would be proud?' In his anger, he spoke in Druinese. To his surprise, the Bear answered him in the same.

'Ah, you must be Cavielle Shaelus.' He smiled condescendingly, as if Helligraine was some nuisance to be tolerated for the greater good.

In Vohorin, Lujaek said, 'Shaelus, this is Valenke. You would have encountered him sooner, if fate had not intervened. He was to work on the Origin but, as he rode to the docks to sail for Druine, he fell from his horse and broke his arm.' He looked at Valenke. 'At the time, you considered it an appalling misfortune. In hindsight, I would say it was a blessing. We called Shaelus "the slave-driver". Not because he worked us hard, but because he was cruel and aloof. He was worse than any demon.'

'You object to the sinner's treatment?' Valenke asked Helligraine. 'You, a man of Druine, where heads are nailed to trees?'

'I have railed against the Pilgrim Church for my entire life,' breathed Helligraine. 'And this,' he indicated the prisoner, 'is worse than anything the Church has dreamed up. Would you like me to tell you why? The Church preaches "virtuous ignorance"; it believes that piety requires a type of foolishness, a refusal to think and learn, lest the mind be corrupted by wayward thoughts. But Toros insists on enlightenment. When he returns, he will spread understanding amongst the masses. But you, you hypocrite! You silence those who—'

'Are you questioning scripture, Cavielle Shaelus?' interrupted Valenke, leaning close.

'What scripture? There is no scripture. Toros left no writings behind.'

433

'True. But throughout the ages, he has dictated instructions to certain Erethin. Whether it pleases you or not, *this*,' he pointed to the prisoner, the liver gleaming between his lips, 'is utterly in accord with his wishes.'

Helligraine thrust out an empty hand. 'Show me.'

Valenke tilted his head, puzzled.

'Give me a copy of your scriptures,' demanded Helligraine. 'I want to see for myself.'

'I am a Low Erethin,' said Valenke, mildly. 'Only the High Erethin have copies; they inform us of Toros's will.'

'Then they have lied to you.'

'Enough,' said Lujaek, sharply. 'Shaelus, you must tame that tongue of yours. You were urged to say nothing once we left the boat. Now you are not only speaking, but spouting blasphemies. Abstain, or I shall cut out your tongue.' Then, to Valenke, 'We require horses.'

'Arrangements have been made.' Valenke dug a wooden token from his pocket. 'The next village is a mile or so away. You will be given lodgings and horses.' He clapped Lujaek on the shoulder again. 'It is good to see you, my friend.'

'And you, Valenke.'

They set off along the road, walking slowly. They had gone twenty paces when Helligraine halted, suddenly.

'Wait,' he told Lujaek. Turning, he strode back to Valenke. 'I have something to ask of you,' he said.

Valenke's eyes narrowed. 'My forgiveness?'

Ignoring the jibe, Helligraine said, 'There is a danger that we have been followed by those less than sympathetic to our cause. You must watch out for them. One is a woman, dark-haired, robustly built. There is a thin man, barely wider than a bamboo cane, getting on in years, though he may not accompany them. With any luck, he is dead. And the third . . .'

'Yes?'

434

'He is a big man,' replied Helligraine. 'Twice the size of you. Imagine an ox fused with a gorilla, and cursed with the face of a boar.'

'You want me to kill them?' Valenke's hand moved to his knife, resting in its sheathe.

Helligraine chuckled, sourly. 'I would like to see you try,' he said. 'But no, you are not to lay a finger on them. If you spot them, send a warning, so we might be prepared.' In a quiet corner of his mind, a sneering voice piped up, *Prepared how, exactly?* 'Give no clue that you are watching for them. The girl is exceptionally perceptive: keep your cards close to your chest.'

'Mind your language,' said Valenke. 'Such turns of phrase are blasphemous. Toros has forbidden gambling: in Vohoria, no dice are rolled, nor card games played. Watch your step,' he patted the wooden board, 'or you will be next.'

As Helligraine turned away, the Bear's laughter was loud in his ears.

Night was approaching when they reached the village – and a storm, the onyx-black clouds rolling across the sky with preternatural speed.

The village was little more than a shanty town. Before the Scourge, the humblest peasants dwelled in stone-built houses, but here, everything was clumsily constructed from unpainted, mould-speckled wood.

I could be anywhere, thought Helligraine again, as they walked to their lodgings. This could easily be some squalid district in Soriterath, home to folk as poor and greedy as rats.

They entered a two-storey boarding house. Lujaek produced the token given to him by the barbarous Valenke, and the house-master accepted it with a nod.

'We've got five strong horses in the stables,' he said. 'Though

I suspect you will not be riding out this evening.' As he spoke, a thunderclap shook the building. The walls trembled; the rafters creaked. A second thunderclap rang out, and Helligraine glanced upward, half expecting the ceiling to come crashing down.

Their rooms were on the upper floor. The Erethin and Kraike were to share one room, whilst Helligraine and Quarvis took the other.

Helligraine's room was furnished with two narrow beds, covered with flea-riddled blankets. Exhausted from the sea crossing, Quarvis lay down immediately, his knees drawn up to his chest, head bent forward and hands clasped; he resembled a child resting in its mother's womb.

Helligraine lay down. After an hour or so he rose, unable to sleep. Opening the shutters, he watched the storm break. Rain pounded the open ground outside the lodging house, transforming the sun-hardened soil into a bubbling mudslick. Lightning fell, casting the dilapidated village in silver; thunder tolled, shaking the marrow in Helligraine's bones. He contemplated Valenke. His earlier sentiments resurfaced: *holy men are the same the world over* . . .

'For pity's sake,' came Quarvis's voice. 'You are letting the wind in! We've got a long journey on the morrow. I must sleep. Close the shutters, Helligraine. Close them tight, and go to bed.'

'We will strike a bargain,' said Helligraine. 'I will close the shutters, and you will call me by my proper name from now on. I am Shaelus, not Helligraine; I am not – never was – a holy man. That name is the symptom of sickness I willingly suffered; I will not answer to it any longer.'

'Whatever you wish,' said Quarvis. 'Just close the shutters.'

Shaelus closed the shutters, lay down and slept.

CHAPTER ELEVEN

They left the village at first light, riding along the dirt road which, soaked by the storm, had become a strip of glooping black mud. The storm itself was long gone; the sky was clear, the sun shone brightly, and the grasslands had a fresh, rinsed-out look, the boulders gleaming, the wildflower blossoms glowing.

Shaelus was in a low humour. He was preoccupied by Valenke's words the previous day. The bearlike Erethin had spoken of scriptures dictated by Toros. What was to be made of that? A part of Shaelus feared it might be true. But a stronger part of him was convinced it was not. By nature, holy men were liars, and one of their favourite deceptions was to claim they possessed a text that justified their authority. The truth was, even if Toros had not composed any such work, the Erethin would claim that he had. Such fabrications were an essential component of any theocracy.

Theocracy – that was what Vohoria had become. Just like Druine, and countless other ignorance-benighted lands.

It will pass, Shaelus told himself. Once Toros returns, there will be enlightenment. And brutes like Valenke will learn the error of their ways.

Around early afternoon, they entered the remains of a large town, seemingly untouched since the Scourge. The white stone buildings stood scorched and empty; human bones lay amongst the overgrown vegetation, blotched with green mould; skulls gazed from nettlebeds, vertebrae lay scattered like dice. The town was unnaturally still, as if holding its breath. Shaelus was intrigued. The village they left that morning was a ramshackle place, ill-built and leaking. Would it not make sense for the Vohorin to reinhabit somewhere like this?

He drew up alongside Lujaek.

'A question,' he asked. He was loath to speak with the Erethin. But his curiosity was too great.

'Speak on, slave-driver,' said Lujaek.

'This town is empty, yes?'

'Apart from rats, birds and stray dogs.'

'Why does no one dwell here? The buildings seem sturdy enough. With a bit of work—'

'We have forbidden it,' said Lujaek, sighing impatiently.

'We?'

'The Erethin. We control where the people live. Our country is underpopulated; to ensure our numbers rise, we compel people to dwell together in certain towns and cities. You cannot find a mate if you live in isolation.'

'And couldn't they reside here? It seems a waste. A serviceable town, neglected—'

'You are not a practical man, are you?' Lujaek glanced over, green eyes coldly glittering.

'Meaning?'

'You are obsessed with metaphysics,' said Lujaek. 'Yet the realities of the physical world elude you. We Erethin must keep a watchful eye on our fellow Vohorin. We are the law-makers, and law-keepers; without us, all would be chaos. Thus, we make sure the commonfolk live in places we can observe with little effort. This town is remote; the roads are bad. How are we to supervise them? To ensure they do not stray?'

'What if someone decides to dwell here?'

'It rarely happens.'

'But when it does?'

'Such behaviour is deemed sinful. You have seen what happens to sinners.'

They continued riding. Gradually, grey clouds crawled into the sky. Rain began to fall, the paving stones darkening, a cold wind gusting along the empty streets. Another storm? No, just the tail end of the previous night's downpour. Nonetheless, shelter was required. Lujaek halted outside a two-floored building.

'Wait here,' he said, dismounting. 'I will make sure it is safe.'

'Safe?' asked Quarvis, hunching against the raindrops.

'There is a forest over the way.' Lujaek pointed beyond the town. 'It is not unusual for wild animals to make places such as this their homes.' He disappeared through the doorway, returning moments later. 'Come inside.'

Tying their mounts to lumps of tumbled masonry, they went in. The building had been a stonemason's workshop. Chisels, hammers and a variety of other tools lay scattered across the floor. A flight of wooden steps led to an upper floor.

Shaelus sat in the corner. As he settled, Quarvis crouched beside him.

'You must not let it trouble you,' said the little man.

'Do you think I am so tender-hearted I would grieve for an abandoned town?' Shaelus chuckled humourlessly. 'I have travelled the globe, and seen far worse than this.'

'No, no.' Quarvis shook his head. 'I am speaking of something, ah, *deeper*.'

'Namely?'

A tiny shrug. 'That I am an Erethin, and you are not.'

'You are not an Erethin,' said Shaelus. 'Where are your robes? Where is your belt with the blood-tinged leaves?'

'Maybe I have not been formally invested,' said Quarvis. 'But I have an Erethin's talent.'

439

'Why should I care? I am not susceptible to envy.'

'That is good,' nodded Quarvis. 'Very healthy, too. Jealousy rots a man from the inside out. But I was thinking that if our roles were reversed . . . Well, I would feel a little like an outcast. You are the only one here who lacks magical ability.'

'And what exactly are your abilities? What can you do that I cannot?'

'I can use *The Chronicle*,' said Quarvis.

'So? In itself, it serves no great purpose.'

'But it is a start, is it not? A sign that I am capable of great things? Lujaek says that when Toros returns, he will act as our tutor; he will teach us to use our talents. He will *cultivate* them, as if they were seedlings. But that is by the by. Shaelus, I wanted to make sure there is no animosity between you and me. And, yes, I would not want you to think that I look down on you. After all, you have made a massive contribution. Were it not for your cleverness in finding the Origin, Toros would remain trapped in the Forest. In your own fashion, you are – dare I say it – a hero.' Quarvis smiled; it reminded Shaelus of the incision cut into the sinner's abdomen.

'Let us not speak of this,' said Shaelus.

'Why not? We are friends, you and I. Should we not discuss such matters?'

We are not friends, thought Shaelus. And you know it. You are goading me, you malignant sprite. Your tone is one of concern, yet inside, you are smirking like a poor man hearing of a rich man's death. You vulgar homunculus! Do you think I cannot see what you are doing?

Suddenly, Lujaek strode to the doorway. Peering out into the rain, he cursed.

'What is it?' asked Shaelus, rising.

'*Virulin*,' said Lujaek, reaching for a knife.

Shaelus did not recognise the word. 'What—'

440

'Bandits,' hissed Lujaek. 'Eight or nine of them. Granted the chance, they will kill us. Dogs like these – they find freedom in chaos. Believing Vohoria is doomed, they act as they please.'

Through the glassless window, Shaelus saw them – eight men, dressed in rain-slicked leathers, eyeing the horses. Each sported a tangled beard; their faces were clouded with the grime of travel.

Stroking Shaelus's horse, one said, 'Fine beasts, aye? You could smash rocks on their backs! So sturdy, so strong. Far better than our nags, eh?'

'Then we shall have them,' said another.

'In good time,' said the first. 'First, we'll speak with their owners. The riders of such animals cannot be without money. Perhaps they will show us some charity.' Turning, he looked through the doorway. 'There they are, watching us. I expect their hearts are full of pity and compassion. "Those poor souls," they'll be thinking, "out there in the rain – is there any way we can help them?" He drew a knife; the other *virulin* did the same. Slowly, they prowled toward the building.

'Upstairs.' It was Kraike who spoke, his voice firm and low. He pointed at a blonde-haired Erethin. 'Are you prepared to do your duty toward Toros?'

'My duty?' The Erethin's name was Wivus, recalled Shaelus. He was the only excavator Shaelus did not dislike. Soft-spoken, he kept his head down and worked hard.

'Come.' Kraike led him upstairs. The rest followed.

The roof long since tumbled down, the upper room was open to the sky.

'Lujaek, keep the *virulin* from ascending the steps.'

'I will do what I can.' Positioning himself at the top of the stairs, Lujaek unsheathed a knife. Footsteps sounded below. Then, a laughing voice.

'Ah, looks like we aren't getting a warm welcome.'

'Stay back,' said Lujaek. 'Or I'll cut the throats of every one of you.'

'Bold words,' came the voice – that of the *virulin* who had petted Shaelus's horse. 'I take it that you've noticed there are eight of us, and six of you. Of those six, three are too old or withered to fight. What chance do you think you have? Safer by far if you do as we ask.'

'Maybe we cannot kill you all,' said Lujaek. 'But the first up these steps is certain to die. Which of you wants to make the sacrifice? Who will lay down his life for a few horses?'

'Horses and your money,' said the *virulin*.

'Our purses are empty,' said Lujaek. 'Take the horses, if you must. They are all we have . . .'

As Lujaek and the *virulin* spoke, Kraike ushered Wivus to the wall.

'There will be pain,' said the sorcerer. 'But when it passes, there will be glory unlike any you have known. And a freedom so exquisite you will want to weep.'

'I – I do not understand,' said Wivus, uneasy.

'You do not need to,' said Kraike, laying his hands on the Erethin's shoulder.

For a moment nothing happened. Then Wivus cried out, his soft features distorting with pain. A blue haze formed around his body, glowing as softly as a will-o'-the-wisp. His skull swelled, inflating like a balloon, until it was nearly spherical; his skin darkened and, for an instant, Shaelus wondered if he was burning at the touch of an unseen flame, like the victims of the plague spell. But this was different. The darkness arose not from charred flesh, but black feathers, pushing out through his face, bristling and gleaming slickly in the blue light. Bones crunched; a long curved beak sprouted from where his nose had been; his eyes turned into perfect circles, the whites dimming to grey, the irises glooming jet-black. A ripping sound, and

442

his chest swelled, tearing open his tabard; beneath, his body was covered by the same dark feathers that encased his head. The blue light intensified, and Shaelus clenched shut his eyes. When he opened them, the Erethin's arms were replaced by wings, folded around his body like a cape. His legs had thinned, the feet transformed into talons.

A curlew, thought Shaelus, stunned. He has become a curlew as big as a man . . .

No, he realised. Not a curlew. *The* Curlew, one of the Prime Tormentors, a demon found in most regions of the Forest.

'Step aside,' Kraike ordered Lujaek as the blue light faded.

Doing as he was bidden, Lujaek looked at the Curlew. And swore, softly.

'Your courage deserted you, has it?' the *virulin* called up the stairs. 'Well, it's too late. If you'd done as we asked straight away, we might've spared you. But now . . . The *virulin* appeared on the steps. His gaze alighted on the Curlew. His sneer-twisted mouth flattened out; his lips quivered. Slowly, the Curlew turned its head, its beak pointing at the *virulin*. Stumbling a step back, the *virulin* fell down the stairs.

'Get out of here! Run!' he shouted as he hit the bottom.

The Curlew did not follow. Instead, it hopped atop the wall, watching the ground outside the building. Below, the *virulin* sprinted to their horses, a hundred paces away. Cocking its head, the Curlew observed its quarry a little longer. Then, spreading its wings, it leapt from the wall and swooped.

Hearing wingbeats, every *virulin* looked up as one. Gliding low, Curlew plunged its beak through the skull of the nearest man. As he fell, Curlew snapped back its head, drawing its beak free, landing gracefully on its feet. Pacing over, it plunged its beak into the forehead of another *virulin*. Again, another backward jerk of the head and it was loose. The remaining *virulin* ran, vanishing amongst the buildings. The Curlew stood in the rain, its beak dripping red. Then, taking a run up, it launched into a low glide. It too disappeared from sight; only a series of distant screams indicated it had found its prey.

Weak, shaking, Kraike looked at Shaelus. 'Is it not as I claimed?' He grabbed his walking branch, propped against the wall. 'I am no longer a destroyer. I am a *creator*.'

CHAPTER TWELVE

If I were not an educated man, the Gardens would have been
unlikely to kindle strong feelings of any sort; some things are
rendered extraordinary only by our knowledge of them. An
ignorant observer would have seen a vast tract of land, silted
with sand and mud, littered with small blocky stones, not
dissimilar to milestones, threaded by numerous intercoiling
paths. At best, our uninitiated visitor would imagine it to be
the remains of an ancient, oddly designed pleasure garden, of
the kind enjoyed by rich men across the globe.

I, of course, knew better, and set to exploring this long-lost
place, this site where a small civilisation rose and bloodily fell.

Extracted from *A Glimpse of the Lost Gardens of Dalzerte*
by Cavielle Shaelus

'Anhaga!' exclaimed Ekkerlin. 'You have been blessed!'

Gripping the tiller, Ballas scowled. 'What are you talking
about?'

'Brinus, the heathen god of sailors destined for shore, has
bestowed upon you the wet ribbon of benediction.' Laughing,
she pointed at his chest. 'See for yourself.'

Ballas looked. A streak of green-white birdshit clung to his
tabard. Glancing up, he spotted a lone seagull, gliding overhead.

'Land ahoy,' said Ekkerlin, wryly.

Dusk was falling when they reached the coast. Not wishing to draw attention to themselves by mooring at the docks, they put to on a sheltered beach a mile away. Climbing a cliff face, they emerged onto flat ground. The landscape was not dissimilar to Druine's, Ballas noted, all sweeping, hill-contoured grassland, studded with limestone boulders. The similarity was hardly surprising. Millennia ago, the two countries had been part of the same landmass, albeit joined by a long, narrow causeway, which Toros's original followers crossed before settling in Vohoria.

A trifle unsteady on his feet — after so long at sea, the ground seemed to surge and tilt in memory of the waves they had left behind — Ballas followed Ekkerlin toward the docks.

'Reckon we'll need a map?' he asked.

'I shouldn't think so. Everything is locked away in here.' Ekkerlin tapped her head. 'Years ago, I was fascinated by Vohoria. Shaelus's writings caught my interest, and I learned everything I could about the place — its language, customs, beliefs and, of course, geography.'

Helligraine's image materialised in Ballas's mind's eye. He wondered what would be most satisfying — killing the old man, or delivering him to the Sacros to be interrogated, tortured and executed. He did not think he had ever loathed someone so *intimately*. He and the Hawks had risked their lives countless times for his sake, and all the while, he was deceiving them. He had turned them into unwitting servants of a potentially dangerous enemy. He had made fools of them all.

He wondered if it was worse for Ekkerlin. She had idolised Shaelus; he had been the prime mover in her intellectual development, had stoked her natural fires of curiosity. She probably believed she was in his debt, in some oblique way. And yet, he had betrayed her too. Surely she was stung? Surely, in a strange way, it was a worse torment than Olech's venom?

At the docks, they found a fishing boat matching the description given by the harbour master in Bluecurl. They stared, as if the crude, double-sailed vessel might give a clue as to Jurel Kraike's location. Then Ballas noticed a young fisherman, watching from twenty paces away. Realising he had been seen, the man focused on the nets he was untangling. Then he glanced over again, warily.

'Give me a moment,' said Ekkerlin, striding over.

For a brief spell, she conversed with the young man, speaking in the Vohorin tongue. Their exchange was good-humoured, and when Ekkerlin returned, she tapped Ballas on the forearm and led him away from the docks.

'Reckon I'm going to be a barrowload of good here,' said Ballas. 'I can't understand a word of Vohorin. To my ears, it sounds like a sack of rivets tumbling down a staircase.'

'It is a harsh tongue,' agreed Ekkerlin. 'But do not fret: if you stick to the story I told the fisherman, you won't need to say a thing.' She patted him on the shoulder. 'You are my brother – and a mute. Ah, if only it were true! Not the brother part; that would be a nightmare. But if you were unable to speak, how much quieter my life would be! I wouldn't have to listen to your grumbling and grousing, your sour prattle and sulky moping. Then again, you've taught me some interesting profanities over the years. So perhaps I am in your debt . . . in a grubby sort of way.' She cleared her throat. 'The fisherman wondered why we were interested in the boat, particularly as it was of a Druinese design. I told him I wanted to purchase it. Who were its owners? Did he know them? He told me they were strangers. They arrived yesterday, six of them: two old men, three young, one a fellow who resembled a malnourished baby bird.'

Leaving the docks, they set off along a dirt road. Ahead, a hill rose into the fading light. As they drew close, the air began

447

to stink of sun-rotted meat – an odour that not only clogged Ballas's nostrils, but reached down his throat like an invisible hand, intent on turning his stomach inside out.

Upon the hill they found the mouldering corpse of a man, naked, strapped to a wooden board. Blood crusted the lower half of his torso. A long, deep incision puckered the flesh under his ribcage. A large, dark object protruded from his mouth, like a monstrously bloated tongue. Squinting, Ballas saw it was an internal organ.

'What do you reckon? His heart?' he asked Ekkerlin.

'I do not think so.' Her gaze alighted on a noticeboard. Reading aloud, she translated as she went:

This man, Levus N'kalen, was a sinner of the worst order. After failing to attend prayers, it became clear he was in league with the demons, whose company he shall now keep for all eternity. In accordance with the principles of the Doctrines, his liver was cut from his body and placed inside his mouth, for such is the punishment for those who oppose Toros, our servant and master.

'Interesting,' said Ekkerlin. 'In some cultures, the liver is associated with knowledge. As demon-worship is considered a crime of the mind – to contact demons, one must possess certain types of knowledge – it is not uncommon for the liver to be central to such punishments. Indeed, putting the liver in the victim's mouth – to silence him, symbolically, and prevent him spreading his knowledge – is a practice found in various cultures. But not Vohoria. This is new, Anhaga.'

Ballas grunted. 'Does it matter?'

'Probably not. It is interesting, nothing more – you great incurious lump.'

They walked on, not knowing where the road would lead.

As dusk turned to night, the moon brightening and stars shining, they reached a tiny village of shoddy wooden buildings.

'Behold the glory of Vohoria,' muttered Ballas.

Ekkerlin did not reply. She wore an expression Ballas had seen often before: her eyes were glassy, yet strangely focused; she tapped fingertips against her bottom lip, again and again; she appeared lost in a world of her own. But this was far from the truth. She was thinking deeply about something. Suddenly, a gentle tension swept through her features.

'Horses,' she said. 'The fisherman said Kraike and the others *walked* from the docks. But they will not remain on foot for long. Shaelus would not cope; nor Kraike, with his bad leg.' She nodded to a long, low building. Straw lay on the ground outside the closed door. 'Let us speak with the stablehand, if we can.'

Approaching, they knocked on the door. A man's voice rose from within. They entered.

The stable was lit by a single lantern, hanging from a nail. The fragrance of horse sweat purged Ballas's senses of the rotting-meat stench of the sinner. Four horses shifted in the gloom, two white, one brown, the other grey. One snorted, another scraped a hoof.

Slouching on a stool, the stablehand was in his fourth decade, a potbelly straining against a dung-streaked white vest. He had the slovenly look of someone compelled to do the same tedious job, day after day. On seeing Ekkerlin, his eyes brightened. He sat up straight, drew back his shoulders. Then, noticing Ballas, he recoiled a touch, as if he had been caught trespassing.

Ekkerlin laughed, said something in Vohorin. She talked with the stablehand, whose body language was easily deciphered even if his spoken language was not. Waggling his bushy eyebrows roguishly, he made a series of lame jokes, his face glowing with pride. There was a presumptuously intimate aspect to his bearing, as if he had known Ekkerlin a long while, and his hands hovered restlessly, as if they might reach out and touch the Hawk at any moment. Ekkerlin humoured him, but Ballas heard the hollowness within her laughter. She was tolerating him as best she could. As the conversation ended, the stablehand leaned close. The good humour dropped from his face. Growing serious, he hiked a thumb toward the lodging house.

Ekkerlin nodded, thoughtfully.

'Ballas,' she said, turning. She said nothing more. But Ballas understood. Stepping over, he punched the stablehand across the head. The man flew from his stool, as if flung by a gale. He lay amongst the straw, unconscious.

'He propositioned me,' said Ekkerlin as they saddled up two horses.

'What did he offer?'

'In exchange for wandering my, ah, "unexplored territories", he promised a steak pie.'

'And you refused?'

'He promised a pie, but said nothing about gravy.'

Ballas grinned. 'Good girl,' he said. 'I am glad you didn't sell yourself short.'

They led the horses outdoors.

'Kraike and the others passed this way,' said Ekkerlin. 'They spent last night at the lodging house, then set off to Calvaste Town. The stablehand overheard them talking as they left. They will be boarding with a High Erethin named Harvus.'

Mounting their horses, they rode.

CHAPTER THIRTEEN

Riding through the gathering dusk, Shaelus wondered if the others had been disturbed by the Curlew as much as he had. In his mind's eye, he saw the transformation over and over, replaying endlessly: the grotesquely swollen head, the flourishing feathers, the beak sprouting like a knife. And then the smooth swooping flight, the graceful glides and savage kills . . . He wondered if the Erethin, Wivus, had enjoyed it. More, he wondered if anything remained of Wivus *to* enjoy it.

He did not think so. By the time he launched himself from the wall, the Erethin was no longer human. He had become the Curlew; his instincts were those of the demon. His body had changed, but so had his mind.

Afterwards, Shaelus had asked Kraike what would become of Wivus. Would he eventually revert to human form? Or would he be the Curlew for evermore?

Kraike did not know. He had never cast such a spell before; its consequences were a mystery.

As they left the town, they had found the remaining *virulin* scattered over the dirt road, dead, skewered by the Curlew's beak. The Curlew itself was nowhere to be seen. Kraike theorised that he had fled into nearby woodland.

He is a Forest demon, he had said. It is likely he will be drawn to an approximation of his natural habitat.

It was then that, for the first time, Shaelus regarded Kraike with trepidation. Fear, even. It was unsettling for a man to possess such powers, powers without precedent, that had been depicted only in fairytales and myth.

And Quarvis – that simpering dolt, who practically worshipped Kraike, was also unnerved. In the middle of the afternoon, Shaelus overheard a conversation between the little man and Lujaek. He missed the start, but it was obvious he had expressed his disquiet, and Lujaek was trying to mollify him.

'I too was disturbed,' said Lujaek. 'But the feeling will not last. It sprang from novelty, from seeing strange powers boldly used. More than that, it seemed to defy a principle we are all born with, and cling fast to throughout our lives: namely, that once something has a certain form, it should maintain that form for ever. I can speak only for myself, but when I saw the transformation, it was akin to seeing a badly broken arm, with the bone protruding through the skin: one recoils, not just in sympathy, but because the proper form has been corrupted. Yes, I was mildly perturbed that Kraike transformed our friend into a *demon*. Did we not witness the execution of a man who consorted with the vile denizens of the Forest? But then, I grew pragmatic. What better killing tool is there, than a demon? What possible device could have annihilated our attackers so effectively?' He drew a breath. 'My friend, I was unsettled purely because what I saw was *unusual*. Or out of place, so to speak. Nothing more. Was it not so with you?'

Quarvis grew thoughtful. 'I cannot say. When I try examining my own feelings, they become lost behind a fog . . .'

'Were that fog to lift,' said Lujaek, 'you would agree with me. And remember, Kraike's powers can be used to heal as well as harm. The same talent that created the Curlew can cure disease, blindness, and defects of every description. What will the resurrection of Toros be, but a healing act? From his bones, his entire body will be grown anew.'

If Quarvis was soothed, Shaelus was not. His thoughts had turned to Toros. He could not shake off the idea that Toros *had* dictated a set of scriptures, which did not justify but *demanded* the type of cruelty shown by Valenke. It was a slim possibility, yes, but if it were true . . .

How much do I really know about Toros? he wondered. Yes, he had read a number of biographies. But they were speculative at best. What else could they be, when the visionary had been dead over two thousand years? Evidence of Toros's true nature was sparse yet, in Shaelus's imagination, the shaman was a tangible, well-defined figure – not physically, but psycholog-ically. He shared – *seemed* to share – many of Shaelus's own qualities: courage, determination and, in particular, a restless, all-consuming hunger for knowledge. Where had Shaelus obtained this picture of Toros? Whilst the biographies *had* suggested these traits, Shaelus had not accepted them at face value; when it came to subjective judgements, he trusted his own instincts more than anyone else's. From where, then, had this version – *his* version – of Toros sprung?

Where else, but from within himself? Sceptics maintained that gods were invented by men, in their own image, and not the other way around; and the more pious a fellow was, the stronger the resemblance he perceived between himself and his notion of the god he worshipped. Toros was not a god, true; but he was every bit as enigmatic as any divine entity, and Shaelus wondered if he had, to some extent, modelled Toros upon himself. Had he, in a fit of unconscious egotism, imagined Toros as a primitive replica of himself – as if to say that Shaelus the scholar and Toros the shaman were cut from the same cloth? That they could have been brothers, were they not born millennia apart?

Is that why I admire him so much? he thought. When I marvel at Toros, am I effectively marvelling at myself? Am I no better than a vain youth, beguiled by his own reflection?

Grimacing, he pushed the idea from his mind. But his ease was short-lived. Another troubling question cropped up.

How much do I really know about Kraike?

About as much as he knew about Toros, he realised. He only spoke to the sorcerer about practical matters. Ordinary discourse – gossip, idle chatter, joke-telling – was alien to them. Consequently, Shaelus found it impossible to regard Kraike as a living, breathing man, endowed with traits and tendencies, possessing a healthy range of emotions. He looked upon him as a device for bringing about certain events, a mechanism by which Toros could be reborn. Nothing more.

A strange pang of loneliness touched Shaelus.

None of these men mean anything to me, he thought, looking at the others. Nothing at all.

Dusk sank into night and they arrived at Calvaste Town. Leading them to a white, comfortable-looking house, Lujaek dismounted and knocked thrice on the black-painted door. After a long pause and a scuffling of feet, a woman of middling years answered. Her face was haggard, her dark hair threaded with grey. Shaelus guessed she was a housekeeper, or a maid: her hands were scoured red, as if they had spent a long time in the hot soapy water of a washtub.

'Yes?'

'High Erethin Harvus is expecting us,' said Lujaek.

The woman frowned. 'He has mentioned no guests.'

'He did not know the day of our arrival. But he will be pleased to see us,' promised Lujaek. The woman closed the door. As they waited, Shaelus gazed at the moon. It was almost full, and gleamed like a polished silver coin. The same light that spilled on the village also fell upon the woodland near the abandoned town, reflecting – perhaps – upon the cruel dark eyes of the Curlew. Was it still out there, the new-hatched demon? Or had it perished? Was that its fate – a short period of savage good health, followed by death? He tried not to think about it.

Along the building there was a candlelit window. The bulky silhouette of a man hunched at a desk, writing. The house-keeper's silhouette appeared; the man leaned back in his chair, nodded, then continued writing, his quill moving with greater speed than before.

'Please, come in,' said the housekeeper, opening the door. 'It is as you said. High Erethin Harvus is happy to receive you.'

She took them along a hallway into a small lounge, furnished with several divans and a low table.

'My master will not be long,' she said, lighting candles. 'He is composing a sermon for the morrow. He is very conscientious; no poet has ever taken such trouble over his words. He always says, "The better the sermon, the stronger the prayers." I swear, he feels Toros's pain as if it was his own—'

'Ah, my guests,' came a loud, throaty voice. Harvus entered, a short, stocky man, with shoulders as wide as a bull's. He was not old, maybe forty years, but his face was florid, his blond hair thinning. A sizeable paunch strained against his robes and he moved with an odd light-footed waddle, as if wary of step-ping too heavily on the floor. *Gout?* wondered Shaelus. Probably. Even a country on its knees had its share of over-indulgers.

'Do you require feeding?' asked Harvus.

'We have not eaten since noon,' said Lujaek.

'Then you shall eat now.' Harvus turned to the housekeeper. 'There is cold meat in the larder, yes? Good. Boil some potatoes, and the carrots that were brought to temple as a gift.' Sweat sparkled on his face. 'It is humble fare, I am afraid. But nour-ishing. Please, be seated.'

Shaelus sat alongside Quarvis on one settle, the Erethin on another. Kraike sank into an armchair.

'I wondered when you would turn up,' said Harvus, slouching into a chair. 'A month ago, I received a message from High Erethin Laiven at the Varristen. He said I should expect you, and treat you to the highest hospitality. Who am I to refuse instructions from one of Toros's greatest servants?' He interlaced his fingers across his paunch. 'I confess, he explained very little to me. Nothing at all, to be truthful. He did not say who you are, or why you are here. Could you enlighten me?' He cleared his throat. 'I assume it is holy business? And you are all Erethin?' He looked amongst the group. His gaze alighted on Shaelus. 'Ah, you radiate piety like no other. I assume from your white hair and silver beard that you found your faith in the desert? Perhaps you were amongst the first to be called.'

'I am not an Erethin,' said Shaelus, then caught himself. He had not intended to speak; Lujaek had forbidden it. But he was tired, and for a heartbeat, he lost focus.

Harvus's yellow brows sank low. 'Not an Erethin,' he murmured, a dangerous edge in his voice. 'Nor a Vohorin, if I am not mistaken. Your accent is strange. Where do you hail from?'

Shaelus froze, uncertain. It was Lujaek who came to his rescue.

'He is Druinese,' he said, plainly.

Harvus's brows dropped even lower. His red face grew several shades redder. 'He . . . he is one of the enemy?'

'Far from it,' said Lujaek, mildly. 'If there was an order in the universe, he would have been born on these shores, not across the water. He has no love for his homeland. I'd say he despises it as much as any of us.'

'And I would say that is impossible. His people—'

'They are not my people,' interjected Shaelus, feigning offence. 'I have naught but hatred for Druine. I would happily watch every stinking acre burn to the ground. My nationality is a tragic accident of birth, nothing more.'

'Can he be trusted?' Harvus looked squarely at Lujaek. 'The Druinese are notorious liars – even worse, I'd say, than demons: for demons cannot conceal their true nature, whilst a Druinese man, using clever words and smiles . . . They keep their malignancy well-hidden, the Druinese; they are like poisonous worms lurking within wholesome apples, or the toxic redness in middle of undercooked pork—'

'High Erethin Harvus,' said Lujaek, firmly. 'If you object to his presence, you must take the matter up with Laiven. Tell him his judgement is faulty; inform him that he has erred. Then—'

'Enough, please.' Harvus raised a hand. 'Forgive me. You have been here only minutes, and I have already proved myself a dreadful host.' He looked at Shaelus. 'I beg your forgiveness, too. You must understand how easy it is for one such as me to bear a grudge against one such as you – even if it is unjustified. In my defence, I say that I am not normally so hot headed. Before you arrived, I was writing a sermon dealing with the Scourge. As you can imagine, it put me in a resentful humour.' He nodded. Then, 'I ought to be pleased, I suppose.'

'Pleased?' asked Shaelus.

'That a Druinese has seen the light. You have embraced our beliefs, yes?'

Shaelus said that he had.

'Are there many like you? Converts, that is?'

'Not yet,' replied Shaelus. 'But I am sure the faith will spread.'

Harvus grinned, baring yellow teeth. 'Of course it will! It is inevitable. As I wrote in my sermons, our faith sustained us during our exile. What does that indicate? Why, it is the one true path! That it is *metaphysically* correct was never in doubt: *The Chronicle* alone proves that true magic works within the Torosian faith. Alas, that is seldom enough to convince unbelievers. They require proof that it is practically useful; that it will benefit them, in the mortal world. Well, to them I would say, "It enabled us to survive unimaginable deprivations! We endured the desert! What more evidence do you need?"'

A while later, the housekeeper took them into a small dining room. They ate a meal of cold ham, beef, pickles, potatoes and carrots – the finest food Shaelus had tasted since leaving Prendle House – then were shown to their sleeping rooms. Mercifully, they were each granted a room apiece, and Shaelus would not have to share with Quarvis, who snuffled and muttered in his sleep.

Lying in bed, Shaelus expected to doze off immediately. But something nagged at him – a feeling that there was something he needed to *do*.

Something he had wanted to do for a while, in fact.

He remained there for nearly an hour, thinking.

Suddenly, he sat upright.

'Of course,' he murmured. 'Weariness has turned me into an imbecile.'

Climbing out of bed, he opened his sleeping-room door. Outside, the landing lay in darkness. Moving to a washstand in the corner of the room, he lit a candle, working the flint and steel as quietly as he could. When flame glowed, trembling on the wick, he followed the landing to the staircase and went down.

He padded barefoot through the building until he found the room at the far end, through whose window he had seen the silhouetted form of Harvus, labouring at his desk. Inside, he found a study, the walls lined with bookshelves. Although heaped with parchments, the desk itself was of highly polished mahogany, its surface reflecting the candle flame as clearly as a mirror. He drew a handful of parchments from the shelf. Searching through them, he discovered they were Harvus's sermons, written in a bold, splodgy hand. Returning them to the shelf, he peered into the bookcase. The volumes inside were uniformly slender. Unlike Druinese texts, their titles were not imprinted on their covers, so Shaelus leafed through them as swiftly as he could, glancing at the title pages, then replacing them. Again, he did not find what he was seeking.

Sweat trickled down the back of his neck. His hands shook.

What do I expect to gain from this? he wondered. Nothing of any practical use, that is for certain. Then what?

The answer appalled him.

Peace of mind. That, ultimately, is what I am looking for.

He grimaced. Since when had he, Cavielle Shaelus, craved psychological comfort? His entire life had consisted of stress, peril, uproar. He had taken it effortlessly in his stride. But now . . .

He rifled through the parchments on the desk. Harvus's newly finished sermon lay on the top: entitled *Scourge and Renewal*, it began, *We were cast into the sands, and out of the sands we came, harrowed but fortified. The sun beat us into a stouter substance, like a steel blade beneath the swordsmith's mallet* . . .

Pompous arse, thought Shaelus. Then grew still.

He had found it – the *Doctrines of Toros, as Revealed to the Twelve Visionaries*.

Nervously, he glanced at the study door. Closed. Cocking his head, he listened intently. Nothing – no creaking floorboards, no shuffling footsteps.

The *Doctrines* was a hundred pages long. He would not have time to read it all. Nor would his nerves withstand the strain: already, a powerful, sickening unease coursed through his body. If Lujaek were to discover he was reading a text reserved only for High Erethin . . . And Quarvis – what if that repugnant hobgoblin caught him in the act? He would tell Lujaek, no doubt, running to him like a schoolboy reporting a classmate for some paltry misdemeanour.

Drawing a breath, he leafed through the *Doctrines*.

Predictably, it began with a brisk retelling of Toros's life. His shamanism, his magical abilities, his leadership of the Briach tribe. Then it progressed to the creation of the Origin and his entry into the Forest.

Impatient, Shaelus flicked through to the halfway point.

For Toros made the highest sacrifice, a sacrifice greater even than death. For the sake of knowledge, he put himself at the mercy of demons, who tore at the very essence of his soul. His suffering, for us mere creatures of flesh, is unimaginable, for the soul feels pain a thousand times more keenly than our mortal bodies . . .

He looked further down.

Such is the nature of the Forest, that the tormented soul cannot find refuge in insanity, for the wits remain stubbornly clear, and every aspect of the ordeal is fully comprehended . . . This was the design of the creator-god, who formed the afterlife as he did our world of stone and air, water and fire . . .

Then:

Those with faith in Toros will endure mockery, isolation and persecution, for the righteous path is strewn with thorns and sharp-edged flints, yet this is the path we must tread, with unshod feet, and we must take heart, for Toros will return when the hour is ripe, and the unbelievers will believe, whether they wish to or not, and if they beg forgiveness, only Toros, in his endless wisdom will decide if it should be granted or withheld . . .

'How often have I read such rot before?' murmured Shaelus. 'How many holy books contain such trite sentiments? How many ill-spirited scribes, claiming enlightenment, have penned such turgid dross? This book – it stinks like a dungheap! And there is more than a whiff of plagiarism . . .'

Skipping a dozen more pages, he read:

The man who kills must be punished, if the act was not committed in self-defence. To balance the crime, and restore order to the universe, the killer must die and, as wanton murder is essentially an animal act, he must meet his doom in a similar fashion: he is to be slain by beasts, be them bears, boars or lions, spiders, snakes or insects.

The adulterer shall be castrated; he will not perish, but be condemned to a life lacking in desire. If, by mischance, his desires persist, they will remain unfulfilled, and he will endure yearnings for which there can be no resolution.

The mind is a precious gift; for the sake of thought, intelligence and perception, Toros cast himself into the Forest. So it is that the man who clouds his mind with drink or narcotics shall be beaten with wooden sticks, and whipped across the back, until he is half-mad with pain. Only then will he appreciate the value of a sound mind . . .

Disgusting, thought Shaelus. This cannot be right. These cannot be Toros's principles.

It went on.

Music is a distraction, luring our energies away from the pressing concerns of existence. The punishment for those who indulge in this reprehensible pastime must vary according to the nature of their crime. The players of wind instruments will have their lips removed so they can blow no more, and those whose implements of sin were stringed will have their fingers broken, and twisted, so severely they cannot heal, and never again will they strum or pluck.

The painter is guilty of falsehood. Their pictures represent the truth yet, as they engage only one of the senses – that of sight – they are inaccurate, and therefore deceptive. Thus, he must be robbed of his own senses, as far as is possible. He will be blinded with hot iron, so he cannot see. His tongue shall be seared, so he cannot taste. Needles shall pierce the delicate mechanisms of his ears, so he cannot hear. The inside of his nostrils will be cauterised, his ability to smell extinguished. Only his sense of touch shall remain – and what will he feel, except the salty warmth of tears upon his cheeks? In this manner, he will discover the error of his ways . . .

'You dog!' boomed a voice.

Shaelus whirled. Harvus stood in the doorway, clutching a lantern.

'I was right,' breathed the Erethin, lips quivering. 'You Druinese cannot be trusted. Perhaps you have tricked Laiven into believing you are an ally. Maybe you have convinced Lujaek you are loyal to Toros. But I knew from the outset you were a deceiver.'

Shaelus held out his hands. 'You do not understand,' he said.

'What is there to understand? The *Doctrines* are not for your eyes. Yet here you are, creeping about like a burglar—'

'I needed to know—'

'No, you did not,' said Harvus. 'If you had questions, you could have asked me. I would have revealed whatever I thought suitable.' His eyes narrowed. 'But that would not be good enough, would it? You do not trust me. You believe that I would have lied.' He smiled, malignantly. 'That indicates a guilty conscience, does it not? A liar believes everyone else is a liar, too.'

'I—' Shaelus did not complete the sentence. Striding over, Harvus punched him in the stomach. Flailing backward, Shaelus crashed into the bookcase, shattering the glass panel. He sank to the floor, stomach throbbing, barely able to breathe.

Harvus loomed over him. 'On your feet,' he growled. 'I want to strike you again.'

Shaelus did not move. Around his legs, glass shards winked in the candlelight.

Stooping, Harvus grabbed Shaelus's tabard.

'I said get up!' Surprisingly strong, Harvus dragged Shaelus onto his feet, then drew back his fist to launch another blow. Suddenly, there was a dull crack. Harvus arched backward, rising onto his tiptoes, one hand clutching at the base of his spine. He stood like that for a moment, then dropped, groaning.

Kraike stood behind, gripping his walking branch like a staff, his austere face seized by rage, his dark eyes flashing.

'Dare you manhandle one of my party? Dare you ill-treat my companion?' He whacked the staff into Harvus's shins. Yowling, the High Erethin curled into a ball.

'Are you hurt?' Kraike glanced at Shaelus.

'The breath is knocked out of my lungs,' panted Shaelus. 'But otherwise . . .'

Limping to the desk, Kraike drew out a thick-cushioned chair. 'Be seated,' he said. 'Rest.'

'What—' Lujaek appeared in the doorway, clad only in leggings.

Kraike jabbed Harvus with the branch. 'Take him away. Put him in his room, or the cellar – anywhere you wish, as long as I do not see him before we leave.'

Pacing over, Lujaek hauled Harvus onto his feet.

'He – he was reading the *Doctrines*!' protested Harvus, jabbing a finger at Shaelus.

'What of it?' asked Kraike.

'It is forbidden!'

'Forbidden by who? You?'

'No, but there are rules . . . they must be followed . . .'

Lujaek manhandled Harvus to the door.

'You cannot do this!' shouted Harvus. 'I will not be imprisoned in my own home!'

'Be rid of him, Lujaek. Tell him to count his blessings. If he does not anger me again, I shall not report him to Laiven, and his life will be spared.'

Lujaek jostled Harvus through the door, then disappeared. Harvus's protests echoed through the house, then fell silent.

Closing the door, Quarvis sat cross-legged on the floor in front of Shaelus. In the candlelight, the sorcerer's features lost their abrasive edge. He looked worried. 'Your breathing – it is steady now?'

'Improving,' nodded Shaelus.

'What of your heart?'

'My heart?'

'You are no longer the man I encountered in the desert,' said Kraike, almost fondly. 'Your hair is grey, your body thin. Time has taken its toll, as it does to all of us. The mechanism falters; the resilience is lost.'

'Painful truths,' agreed Shaelus. 'But my heart, though pounding, is sturdy enough.' A faint smile. 'I shan't keel over, if that is what you fear.'

Growing thoughtful, Kraike laid the branch lengthwise across his lap, drumming upon it with his fingertips. 'I should have guessed you would creep into Harvus's study,' he sighed. 'Valenke told you that the *Doctrines* were not for your eyes. And then we come here, where a copy is just waiting to be read.' He chuckled. The sound caught Shaelus by surprise. He had never heard Kraike laugh before. 'What should we have expected? Tell Cavielle Shaelus there is a book he must not touch, and what will he do? Did you read much before Harvus arrived?'

'Enough to become confused,' said Shaelus. 'And relieved. The book is not authentic. It contains principles that are stolen from other faiths. Its authors were bandits, literary *virulin*, if you like.'

'Stolen? I do not think so. By all accounts, its authors were honest men. As for the similarities with foreign texts – they are to be expected. Every faith has its own visionaries. Inevitably, they discover the same truths, independently of each other. So it is with our visionaries. They did not steal; they simply found things out for themselves.'

'You believe the *Doctrines* are genuine?'

'There can be no doubt.' He peered at Shaelus. 'You seem unhappy.'

'This book is barbaric.' Shaelus laid a hand on the *Doctrines*. 'Every page is full of hatred and oppression. I cannot – it does not seem – I . . .'

'Yes?'

'I cannot serve Toros, if this is what he stands for.' He watched Kraike closely, expecting a reaction. The sorcerer's thoughtful expression did not waver.

'I know very little about the Pilgrim Church,' he said. 'But is it not claimed that one day, the Four will return to this world? And there will be harmony?'

'That is what the faithful believe.'

'And until that time, the world will remain essentially imperfect? There will be no stability, no earthly Paradise? And the best one can hope for is to stifle discord as far as possible? The Torosian faith adheres to the same principle. We believe the globe will remain chaotic until Toros returns. Before the Scourge, Torosians practised their faith in secret; few in number, truly

465

committed to their cause, they encountered neither dissent, disobedience nor enmity. However, this has changed; now that they govern Vohoria, they have discovered exactly how unruly, how venomously *deluded* the populace can be. Thus, they must do whatever is required to maintain order. Man is a barbarous creature, driven by unwholesome urges. Egotism, vanity, a willingness to bear grudges – these affect nations just as they affect households. Most people are impervious to reason; most refuse to do as they are told, even if it is in their best interests. If the beast is to be tamed, the whip must be wielded. If the *Doctrines* seems harsh, it is because it *has* to be. Gentle methods simply will not work.' He looked keenly at Shaelus. 'You have not spotted the implication, have you?'

No, Shaelus had not. The confrontation with Harvus had left him flustered. His mind whirled and swam like a river in spate. And his stomach hurt.

'The *Doctrines* pertain only to the period *before* Toros returns,' said Kraike. 'Once he is here, the text will serve no purpose. Indeed, its cruelty – as you consider it – will be deemed antithetical to his philosophy. The globe, from its northern to southern poles, will be harmonious. Every individual will perceive himself to be a vital thread in a gorgeous tapestry.' He nodded. 'There will be *enlightenment*.'

'So you say,' murmured Shaelus. 'But what form will this enlightenment take? How will it spread?' His tone was not sceptical. Only curious.

'Truthfully, I do not know,' replied Kraike. 'Toros's methods are a secret only he knows. But there are theories, concocted by wiser heads than mine. Selindak, for one. Once, I questioned him, just as you are questioning me.' A soft laugh. 'Selindak asked me who I believed shaped the world more than anyone else. He was speaking not of individual men, but a class of people.'

'I would say holy men,' said Shaelus. 'They govern both practical and metaphysical affairs. On one hand, they set taxes and send us out to war. On the other, they reshape our spirits, as far as they can.'

'That is the answer I gave. It is wrong. The truth is subtle. So subtle, it is rarely noticed. Our lives are governed by those who manipulate physical matter. In particular, those who *discover* how matter can be manipulated. Look around you! A thousand years ago, this room would have been inconceivable. Parchment, candles, glass – can you imagine the world without them? What of bronze, iron, steel? Or clay? Ceramics? What of the alchemists, whose discoveries are so important? We may not sing about these men, but we feel their hand in everything we do.'

Frowning, Shaelus asked, 'So you are suggesting Toros will transform matter for our sakes?'

'Selindak believes so. But he believes, too, that is not Toros's ultimate purpose. Listen. Human woes arise because we compete for resources. This impulse, this *need*, lies behind wars, be they between tribes or countries. What, then, if Toros ensured that no one would starve? Or go thirsty? And medicines – *effective* medicines – were available to all who needed them? Selindak believes that Toros will not coddle us, like a mother tending to a helpless child. Instead, he will teach us how to look after ourselves. He will educate us, so we may manipulate the world, so it yields everything we need. He will teach us how to farm, not in the laborious, plough-dragging, seed-sowing fashion currently employed, but in subtler, more efficient ways. He will grant us the knowledge to concoct medicines for every ill. He will explain how we can extend our lives, if we choose to do so.'

Kraike raised a finger.

'At a glance, it will seem he is offering a *physical* utopia.

Yet there is much more to it. He believes – according to Selindak – that one's capacity for spiritual contemplation is reduced by bodily need. Who can ponder the divine, when their stomach is growling? Who can muse about the heavens, when they have a boil that needs lancing? Or a relative who is gravely ill? Who, when our imperfect machines of flesh give us trouble, can ponder anything except their pain?'

'There are Eastern mystics who treat suffering as a pathway to spiritual freedom,' said Shaelus, doubtfully.

'Why would they think such a thing? I shall tell you: they are trying to make the best of a poor situation. In those regions of the globe, everyone goes hungry. There is no comfort, no respite from all that harrows the flesh. Thus, these mystics – understandably, I suppose – have transformed their suffering into a virtue. But they are deluded. And even if they were not . . . Do you think the common man thinks as they do? That they see the holy in a weeping sore? Or are elevated by a raw-nerved growth?'

He shook his head.

'Toros will not give us Paradise,' he said. 'Instead, he will grant us lives in which we may ponder Paradise, and dream, and appreciate the myriad works of the creator-god. The people will be enlightened, yes. Thus, they will avoid damnation. No more souls will be punished in the Forest.' He smiled, his eyes glittering. 'The demons will stand idle. The Hateful Embrace's spikes will bear not a drop of blood, Innocence will smirk no longer, and the Curlew . . . It will have no prey to swoop upon.'

He got to his feet.

'Take the *Doctrines* to your room, if you wish. I doubt that Harvus will object a second time.' Turning, Kraike departed.

Shaelus looked at the *Doctrines*, resting on the desk. He was tempted to learn more. But he decided against it. Kraike's words had lifted his spirits; his doubts, though faintly lingering, were largely assuaged. He did not want anything to spoil his mood, to diminish the ease he felt.

Rising, he blew out the candle and went to bed.

Chapter Fourteen

Initially, I explored randomly, like a dog in a field of flowers. Soon, though, I resolved to adopt an orderly approach. And what better way to view the Gardens, to experience them in a fashion not wholly dissimilar to the Dalzertians, than to follow the paths?

Once, the path-stones had been black, onyx-like perhaps, but the sands had scoured them to a brownish hue. Nonetheless, they were quite visible, and easy to follow – though not, I might add, easy to fathom. They conformed to no recognisable pattern, seeming to sprawl, loop and meander without rhyme or reason, one moment striking boldly forth, the next curving back, as if gripped by doubt. In short, it was a remarkable confusion, as tangled as those trails left overnight by slugs and snails; yet there was, I believe, some order, even if I was unable to delineate it.

Extracted from *A Glimpse of the Lost Gardens of Dalzerte*
by Cavielle Shaelus

It was early afternoon. Riding past a deserted town, the whitestone ruins rising like a mouth of broken teeth, Ekkerlin spotted bodies on the road ahead. A tremor swept through her. Could the corpses belong to Kraike and his company? Had the Hawks' work been done for them?

It was not so. The four bodies belonged to strangers – roughlooking men, bearing swords and knives. Looking down from her horse, Ekkerlin noticed something unusual. Tugging lightly on the reins, she halted her mount.

'Hold on, Ballas,' she said. 'Grant me one moment.'

Swinging from the saddle, she examined the corpses. Each had been killed in an identical fashion: some sharp implement – a spear perhaps – had penetrated their skulls, two through the forehead, the remaining two through the back. Whatever the weapon was, it had been employed with considerable force: it was not easy to drive an object through bone. The bodies were starting to rot; she guessed they had lain there a day or two.

'Ekkerlin,' said Ballas, gesturing further along the road.

Ekkerlin looked. A couple of hundred yards ahead, away to the right, an old man crouched at the edge of some woodland. He hacked at something large and dark on the ground. A bear, realised Ekkerlin, squinting. A big one, too.

Remounting, she and Ballas rode over. Immersed in his labours, the old man did not notice them until they were a few paces away. Shirtless, his bare chest and arms were covered with blood, and a few red flecks soiled the spray of white hair billowing from his scalp. He was cutting at the bear with a short-bladed knife, trying to carve it up, presumably for the cookpot. He was making little progress. A swathe of fur had been peeled back, but the knife had trouble breaching the thick-muscled meat beneath.

He looked up, sharply. 'A man has to eat,' he said in Vohorin.

'It is only right the hunter should enjoy the spoils,' said Ekkerlin.

She looked at the bear. A hole gaped at the midpoint between its eyes, identical to those she had seen in the corpses. She noticed a couple more perforations, one below its right ear, the other buried in the bristling fur around its throat.

'But you are not a hunter,' she said to the old man. 'You are a scavenger.'

'There is no disgrace in that,' he replied. 'Better that I eat this beast than the maggots.' He struggled with the knife, veins jutting on his arms and shoulders.

'My brother will help you with that,' said Ekkerlin. Then, in Druinese, 'Anhaga, lend this fellow a hand.'

Dismounting, Ballas knelt by the bear. Taking the knife, he set to work, sawing the blade through the rich red meat.

'What language did you just speak?' the old man asked Ekkerlin.

'Keltuskan,' Ekkerlin lied. Knowing how much the Vohorin despised the Druinese, she thought it wisest to disguise her origins.

Pursing his lips, the man nodded. 'I thought so. Do you hail from that land?'

'We both do,' said Ekkerlin. 'Myself and my brother.'

'Are we trading with your country once again?'

'In a small fashion,' said Ekkerlin.

'Good,' said the old man. 'Vohoria is too isolated.'

'Those men, that bear,' Ekkerlin gestured to the corpses, 'were killed by the same person. Their wounds are the same – a neat little hole.'

The old man shrugged. 'It looks that way. I don't care. I just want to eat.' He watched as Ballas pulled a clod of dripping meat from the carcass. 'He is making swift work of it.'

Lumping the meat on the grass, Ballas raised his head, suddenly. He stared straight into the trees. His eyes narrowed. He got slowly to his feet. A tension seized his massive shoulders and his nostrils twitched like a dog's. His fingers flexed around the knife handle.

His body language was familiar; Ekkerlin had seen it countless times before. He had spotted something in woodland. A threat.

'What is it, Anhaga?'

'I do not know,' murmured the big man.

'Another bear?'

'No. It is the wrong shape. Nowhere near bulky enough. But it is large.' His squint deepened. 'It is a good distance away, and the trees are too dense. I cannot see it clearly. But I am certain it is watching me. Watching *us*.' He grunted. 'If I don't go to it, it will come for us. This will not take long.'

He took a step toward the trees. Springing to his feet, the old man grasped his arm.

'No! Stay where you are!'

Ballas looked at him, nonplussed.

'You are safe out here,' said the old man, flustered. 'It never leaves the woods. Just kneel back down and keep on harvesting the steaks.' Licking his lips, he nodded. 'Yes, do that. Stay here, and keep cutting.'

Ballas turned to Ekkerlin.

'He says you aren't to enter the woods,' explained Ekkerlin. 'He wants you to continue working on the bear. I suggest you do as he says.'

Kneeling, Ballas resumed his labours, slower now, his gaze never straying from the trees.

'It?' said Ekkerlin to the old man.

The old man frowned, shrugged.

'What else am I supposed to call a wild beast, hm?' A defensive edge to his voice. As if he was covering up for a mistake – one which infuriated him. 'Your friend has seen another bear, nothing more. Perhaps it's this one's mate. Who can say?'

'It is not a bear,' said Ekkerlin. 'My friend has seen – and killed – many grizzlies. Enough to fill a thousand cookpots. And he says it is not a bear.'

'He is wrong,' said the old man, turning away.

'No,' said Ekkerlin, with cool gentleness. 'You are lying.'

473

She placed a hand on his shoulder. He flinched. 'A man may lie for many reasons. Self-interest, shame, the sheer pleasure of deception. Most often, though, fear is the cause. What is in the woods?'

'It will not harm us. Not unless we go inside. People have passed by on this road, and none fell foul of it.'

'I believe you. But tell me what it is.'

The old man turned to face her. His lean, poverty-wizened face had grown several shades paler. 'A bird,' he said. 'As tall as you are. Its legs are those of a man, but its torso is feathered, the chest bulging, and it has wings. And despite its size, it flies as well as any proper bird. Its beak is this long.' Parting his hands, he measured out ten or twelve inches. 'Sleek and curved. And what a fine weapon it makes! Jab, jab, jab – as fast as a striking cobra.'

Shuddering, he rubbed his arms.

'I live in the town back there,' he said. 'Until yesterday, five of us dwelled amongst the broken stones. We have no desire to live where the Erethin tell us. No, we crave an independent life. But after the bird-man appeared, my companions lost their nerve and fled to the coast. Can't say I blame them. I, however, am set in my ways and I stayed. Perhaps it would not have been so bad if we had not seen the creature come into being . . .' He chuckled, a touch hysterically. 'It did not hatch from an egg, if that is what you are thinking. It was a man, to start with. A young fellow, travelling with a group. They were attacked by *virulin* – bandits, yes? – and one of his party laid his hands upon him, and spoke, and a light the colour of an early summer dawn glowed around him. Slowly, he turned into the creature, then brought down the *virulin*. None survived. There are more bodies in the town, if you want to see.'

Ekkerlin smiled, softly. 'That is not necessary. Can you describe the young man's fellow travellers?'

474

The answer did not surprise her.

'The one who changed him was lame in the leg, with a face sour enough to make a lizard sweat. There was an old man, sprightly enough, and another fellow who seemed sickly and feeble – if he was a puppy, I would have drowned him. There were two more, younger and stronger. Once the bird-man had done its work, they rode away.'

'In which direction?'

The old man pointed up the road. 'As they departed, I ventured as close to them as I dared, weaving between the buildings, scuttling as stealthily as a rat. I was curious, I suppose, despite my fear. As I drew near, I overheard one of them – the weedy little man – ask how long it would take to reach Calvaste Town. I think he wanted to get indoors as soon as he could. And slide the bolt. And cower under the bedcovers.'

The old man sighed, trembling, as if alleviated of a great burden. He said nothing more, only watched Ballas stacking up lump after lump of meat. All counted, he cut out half a dozen sizeable steaks.

Ballas and Ekkerlin remounted. As they rode off, the old man did not wave or say farewell. He simply picked up the meat, clutched it against his chest and scampered toward the ruined town.

They rode in silence. Eventually, Ekkerlin said, 'What do you know about necromancy?'

'I gather it is every married man's most dreaded nightmare,' said Ballas. 'Imagine it. Your mother-in-law dies. You experience a great sense of relief. Then the next thing you know, some bastard with a grimoire brings her back.'

As he made the quip, Ekkerlin realised Ballas was uneasy. Whatever he had seen, it unnerved him. When the big man joked, it was usually to conceal some other emotion, usually fear. Yes, the bird-man hybrid – even though he had seen only

475

a vague hint of it – had tugged at his nerves. That was why he had wanted to stride into the woodland and confront it. Ballas preferred to face his fears, no matter how severe.

'There is a theory – a persuasive one – that necromancy is essentially a form of healing,' said Ekkerlin. 'When someone dies, they start to rot almost immediately. It is not always obvious, for the decay starts deep within the body, where it can be neither seen nor smelled. If a corpse is to be restored to life, this decay must be reversed.'

Ballas shrugged. 'What of it?'

'To cause the reversal,' said Ekkerlin, 'the necromancer must be able to manipulate matter. To repair it, to change it. *Regrow* it, if you will. This is what Kraike intends to do to Toros's bones. But it seems he can use that skill for other purposes. He can transfigure the living, turning them into something different from their natural state.'

'As with the bird-man,' said Ballas.

'Yes. And the bird-man proves that the Origin was a success. Whatever hopes we had that Shaelus was pursuing a fool's errand are now gone.'

'You had such hopes?' asked Ballas.

Ekkerlin shrugged. 'I know enough about the subject to be sceptical,' she said. 'And also enough to be cautious. We took a gamble coming here. But it has paid off – so far.'

CHAPTER FIFTEEN

It took Standaire seven days to reach Soriterath.

The journey had been difficult. The first two days, the pain of the knife wound had forced him to ride slowly. On the third day, he grew weak and nauseous, feverish. In Cardliste Town he found a physician's surgery. It was late evening and the small building lay in darkness.

Dismounting, he trod to the front door on trembling legs and knocked. A light blossomed in an upstairs window. A silhouetted face appeared, then withdrew. Moments later, the door opened. The physician was very young, no older than twenty-two.

'I trust this is an emergency?' he said.

'An infected wound . . .' Standaire leaned heavily against the door jamb. 'You must help me. I have no money to pay you. But I am a servant of the Church, and you will be rewarded in good time.'

'A servant of the Church? I have been practising only eighteen months; do you have any idea how often I have heard that said, in an effort to get free treatment?' He lifted his chin. 'I shall tell you: never. The Church and men of my profession are natural enemies. They believe one should suffer one's ills with pious valour; we believe it is better not to suffer at all. Either you are telling the truth, or you've concocted the worst lie imaginable.' He laid a hand on Standaire's shoulder. 'Either way, I pity you. Come in, before you collapse.'

Standaire spent three days at the surgery. In an upstairs room he sweated, groaned and shuddered through a fever. On the morning of the fourth day he departed, thanking the physician and promising the money he was owed would soon be sent to him. The physician did not want him to go. 'It is too soon,' he said. 'You are not fully recovered.'

Ignoring his advice graciously but firmly, Standaire went on his way.

Of course, the physician was correct. Although the fever had passed, and the wound's gross inflammation had ebbed – at its height, the infected flesh burned like a branding iron – Standaire was terribly weak, and constantly tired. The remainder of the journey passed in a drowsy, sagging haze.

And now, as he rode through the city gates into Soriterath, he felt no better. He could not recall ever feeling so feeble. But he had work to do.

Since leaving the Origin, he had changed his plans. Originally, he had intended to march into the Sacros and inform the Masters of all that had come to pass – including Faltriste's involvement. He realised now, however, that this would be foolish. Faltriste would deny everything, and probably accuse Standaire himself of some sort of betrayal. If he *was* going to accuse Faltriste – he would have to, sooner or later – he needed evidence.

And to get evidence, he needed money.

It was late evening; a crescent moon glowed palely against the star-spattered sky. At this hour there was only one type of place where money could be reliably obtained.

Riding westwards, Standaire entered a prosperous district where the buildings were new, not yet tarnished by time, and the wide streets were illuminated by a succession of lanterns mounted on steel poles. Ostensibly, it appeared a tranquil, civilised place – the type of area where the city's most dignified and wealthy residents dwelled. And so it was: yet such places always had a seedier side. Entailing a certain amount of power, wealth intensified the animal instincts of men; and wealth, with its connotations of respectability, allowed those instincts to be concealed by those who submitted to them.

The sign on the street corner read *Tulip Road*. Here, brothels crowded side by side, huddling like thieves exchanging stolen goods. These were not the downmarket establishments common throughout Druine. Catering for the affluent, they employed only the cleanest, prettiest girls – and charged accordingly.

Standaire tied his horse outside a three-floored brothel. Over the door, shielded by a sheet of glass, there was an oil painting of a white wax candle surmounted by a scarlet-glowing flame. Slipping into an alley, Standaire waited.

Soon, he heard footsteps. A short, portly man strode along the road, his footsteps brisk and furtive. It was a warm night, yet he wore a long woollen coat, the collar turned up, and a wide-brimmed hat pulled so low over his eyes it was a miracle he could see where he was going.

Stepping out of the darkness, Standaire grabbed his coat and hauled him into the alley.

'Stay silent,' he said, thrusting the man against the wall. He pulled the hat from his head and tossed it on the ground. Then he stared at the man's face. Closely.

'I know you,' he said, frowning. A lie. He had never seen the man before in his life.

'No, no, you cannot,' said the man. 'I mean, I do not know you. So how can you know me?'

'I *recognise* you,' elaborated Standaire. He took a chance. 'I assume your wife does not know you are here?'

'Listen,' said the man. 'At a glance, I'd say you are a man of the world. You must surely know how tedious . . . how unbearably *drab* a woman can become after many years of marriage.' He forced a companionable smile. 'A woman's desires

479

wither long before her husband's. Oh yes, her lust wilts as swiftly as cress planted in dry soil, while a fellow's ardour – it is as unkillable as a briar bush! Thus, I am faced with a choice between disloyalties. Do I take a mistress, to whom I may develop genuinely fond feelings? Or do I – ha! – smell the flowers on Tulip Road? The ladies here are very fine but, given their trade, romance is out of the question. Yes, I am betraying my wife by coming here. But it is a smaller betrayal than the alternative. I am unfaithful with my loins but not my heart.' He nodded, as if he had made an irrefutable point.

'Would your wife accept your reasoning?'

'Oh, I doubt it,' said the man. 'She is not a temperate woman. Nowadays, her only passion is anger – searing, self-righteous anger.'

'Then I will not tell her,' said Standaire. 'As long as you give me your purse. And the rings upon your fingers.'

'You are blackmailing me?'

'You have placed a moral burden on my shoulders,' said Standaire. 'I *ought* to tell your wife; I *want* to tell her, for she should know what sort of man she is married to. But if I stay silent – well, I will be uncomfortable. And for that, I require compensation.' He placed a hand against the side of the man's face. A lazily threatening gesture. 'Do you understand?'

A quarter hour later, Standaire rode to a messenger house, a mile and a half from the Esklarion Sacros. Inside, he strode to the serving counter, behind which stood a fat man, his copper goatee glinting in the light of a half-dozen lanterns.

'Two sheets of parchment,' said Standaire.

Goatee gave him what he asked for. Moving to a low writing shelf jutting from the wall, Standaire dipped a quill in an inkpot and on the first parchment wrote:

Origin used successfully. Kraike and others heading to Vohoria. Hawks dead.

He folded the letter, sealing the edges with candlewax.

On the second parchment he wrote a longer letter. This, he sealed in the same manner. On its outer face he wrote an address:

The Grey Building
Kelledin Moor

Tucking the first letter behind his belt, he carried the second to the counter.

'This must be sent immediately,' he told Goatee.

'Kelledin Moor? I did not know there was aught there.' He shrugged. 'We will dispatch it at first light. It should arrive in four or five days' time.'

'That is too long,' said Standaire.

Another shrug. 'What can I do? I employ only so many riders.'

'It will be worth your while.'

He hesitated. 'Aye? What's the worth of this worth?'

Standaire placed the stolen purse on the counter. Opening it, Goatee peered inside. It contained half a dozen silver coins, and Standaire virtually saw their reflections flashing brightly in his eyes.

'Are you serious?' Goatee asked.

'They are yours if you send the message straight away.'

Turning to a doorway leading to a back room, the man called, 'Luspus! Come here – now!'

A boy scampered out.

'Find Greville,' said Goatee. 'He got back nigh on an hour ago. He'll have either gone home or slipped into the Broken Hoof. Tell him it is urgent – and profitable.'

481

The boy vanished, returning a short time later with a pock-marked man wearing an aggrieved expression. The mingled scents of pipesmoke and warm ale wafted from his clothes.

'Damn it all,' he said to Goatee. 'I'd barely taken my first sup when this whelp appeared and began chewing at my ankles.'

Goatee explained everything, then handed Greville a silver coin, which calmed him as swiftly as a tranquillising infusion. He peered at the address on the letter, then complained that Kelledin Moor was very big, and he was unfamiliar with the area. Taking a third parchment, Standaire wrote down directions, pointing out the various landmarks he should use to orientate himself.

'The grey building is a barracks,' he said. 'You may not receive a warm welcome. If so, say, "The red river overspills its banks."'

'What's that supposed to mean?'

'It doesn't matter. Just say it, making sure you utter those exact words. Repeat them to me.'

'The red river overspills its banks.'

'Now, take a long hard look at me so, if asked, you can describe my appearance in perfect detail.'

A touch perplexed, Greville obeyed.

'Now ride,' said Standaire. 'If you keep a good pace, you will be there by dawn.'

Leaving the messenger house, Standaire paused, leaning back against the wall. So far, he had done nothing more than rob a man and write two letters. Yet he was exhausted. His body was heavy, as if his clothes were weighted with lead ingots, and tremors rippled through his hands and shoulders. He wanted to sleep. He believed he could slumber soundly for a whole day and night, if he had the chance. But this was not the hour for rest.

He rode to a district of derelict buildings. After a little searching, he found what he was looking for: an abandoned edifice whose floor consisted not of solid stone but wooden boards.

Kneeling, he pried up several boards. Beneath, there was a dark space, empty except for cobwebs and rat droppings, deep enough to hold a full-grown man, if he was lying down.

Good, thought Standaire, slipping the boards back into position.

Leaving, he rode onto a long street of shops, deserted at this late hour. Finding a rope-maker's, he broke down the door, grabbed several coils of rope, climbed onto his horse and returned to the derelict building.

He placed the ropes on the floor next to the loosened boards. Then he departed.

An hour later he entered The Grinning Dog, the tavern named by the Erethin Ekkerlin had tortured at the Origin.

It was a spit-and-sawdust hostelry, the type populated during daylight hours by those determined to drink away their hangovers and, during the night, those keen to plunge head-first into rowdy, booze-sodden oblivion.

Purchasing a jug of water, Standaire sat at a corner table. He drank, the water warm and stale-tasting. He cast about, seeking anyone who looked as if he was waiting. And *sober*. He doubted Faltriste would entrust something so important to anyone lacking enough self-discipline to stay clear-headed. Most of the tavern-goers were soused. Some sang, others told jokes too loudly, and most had the loose-eyed, slack-muscled faces of the intoxicated. After a time he spotted a thin fellow, sharp-jawed, his face almost perfectly v-shaped, resting on a settle against the opposite wall. With a jolt, Standaire realised the man was staring at him.

Dexler? mouthed Standaire.

The man's eyes narrowed a fraction. Rising, Standaire crossed the floor, halting at the man's table.

'Are you Dexler?' he asked.

'Who I am is not important,' he said. There was a caginess in his voice that suggested yes, he *was* Dexler. But, hearing his name coming from a stranger's mouth, he did not want to admit to it. Not yet. Not until he was certain.

'I have come from Brellerin Fell,' said Standaire, plainly.

A slight tremor in the man's left eyelid. 'Is that so?'

'I have something for your . . . employer.'

The man flicked a gesture at the stool on the opposite side of the table. Sitting, Standaire plucked the letter from his belt.

'I do not know you,' Dexler said.

Standaire nodded. 'You were expecting Malluvis.'

Dexler did not speak.

'He could not come. He is dead.' He held out the letter. 'This explains everything.'

Dexler took the letter, turned it over in his fingers. Standaire wondered if he would open it. If he did, it would prove that he was *deeply* involved in Faltriste's plot, and privy to the Master's secrets. If he did not, it would be clear he was merely a dogsbody, a hired hand.

Dexler tapped his fingers against the letter. 'What is your name?'

'Bracklen,' said Standaire.

'Well, Bracklen, you cannot leave Soriterath. Not until my employer, as you call him, has seen this letter.'

'In that case, you must help me.'

'Help you how?'

'It is no great thing,' said Standaire. 'This is my first visit to Soriterath. If I am to remain here, I will need lodgings. But I do not know where to look.'

484

'That is hardly my problem,' said Dexler.

'True,' said Standaire. 'But if I cannot find somewhere warm to sleep, I will leave. Do you suppose your employer would be pleased?'

'There are decent boarding houses to be found on Callender Street.'

'I said that I am new here. I do not know where Callender Street is. You might as well have offered me a hammock on the moon.'

As if overcome by weariness, Dexler rubbed his eyes. 'So, what do you want?'

'Take me to Callender Street, if you think it is suitable. I will need money, too.'

Rising, Dexler gave a noiseless laugh. 'Anything else?'

'That will be all.'

They left the tavern. As they walked, Standaire watched Dexler closely, seeking vulnerabilities. In his enfeebled condition, he knew he could not best the man in a fair fight. He would have to take him by surprise – a sharp blow to the throat, perhaps. Or – if he could manage it – a concussive strike to the head. Then he would load the man onto his horse, and bear him to the derelict building with the loose floorboards. He would tie him up with the stolen ropes, gag him, then conceal him in the darkened space beneath the boards, amongst the cobwebs and rat droppings. And then?

Then he would go to the Sacros.

No, he decided. Not this evening. It is too late. The Masters will be abed, and they will not receive my visit with good grace. I want them to be in a good humour when we meet. Otherwise, they may not treat my claims seriously. And their heads must be clear, too. They must be capable of weighing up my words, considering them carefully, and deciding that yes, I am speaking the truth.

'Do I fascinate you?' said Dexler unexpectedly.

'What?' asked Standaire.

'You are watching me very closely.'

'I observed that you have a military bearing,' said Standaire. It was true. Even after a short period of service, soldiers acquired a particular posture that stayed with them their entire lives. They stood a little more upright than most, their eyes were vigilant, and their movements were languidly precise: they neither hurried nor faltered. 'You were in the army?'

'For five years,' said Dexler. 'And yes, it has been said many times that I have a military bearing. As do you . . . General.' He turned his face to Standaire. The vigilant eyes betrayed a knowing smugness. It was the look of a card player the moment before he reveals a winning hand.

Standaire considered denying he was a general, or a military man of any sort. But he did not get the chance. No sooner had Dexler spoken than a hard object cracked against Standaire's head and he sank into darkness.

He woke in a long corridor of black stone, the walls and ceiling curved. A sewer, he realised. There was no smell of excrement. Only the heavy, musty odour of stagnation. A *disused* sewer, then.

His wrists and ankles were tied. A cloth gag was fastened across his mouth. His skull ached. Fractured, perhaps. Or at least cracked open.

Dexler stood close by, accompanied by a slightly larger man who, despite a sizeable ale-gut, also had a military demeanour.

'You awaken,' said Dexler, playfully. 'That is good. I suppose I ought to explain. Yes, why not? It will do no harm. I know who you are, General, not because I served under your command – I am way too young for that – but because I was there, near the war memorial, when you spoke to Faltriste all those weeks

486

ago. The Master is a cautious man. He knows better than to wander the streets alone at night. I was secreted in an alleyway; once, you looked straight at me, and I feared you had spotted me. But no, the shadows were deep and dark, and you saw nothing.

'I expect there are things you would like to say to Faltriste. Equally, he will have many questions for you. This letter, I assume, is a fabrication?' He patted the document, tucked behind his belt. 'I cannot second-guess him, but I think he will pay you a visit tomorrow evening. In the meantime, Heron here,' a gesture to the other man, 'will keep an eye on you. I advise you to make no effort to escape. If Heron so much as *thinks* you are trying to slip out of your bonds, he will break your knees.' He turned to Heron. 'It will be a long evening. Let us hope it does not become too eventful.' He walked away, shrinking into the shadows.

Standaire watched him go. Oddly, he did not sink into despair. He did what he knew was the most sensible thing, under the circumstances: lying on his side, he closed his eyes and slept.

CHAPTER SIXTEEN

At various junctures along the paths, I would encounter one of the small stone blocks I spoke of earlier. Engraved onto each – sandworn yet distinct – was a picture of a single flower, such as a tropical orchid. These images, I believe, denoted the design which the Gardens were intended to follow. It is my theory – and I can see no alternative – that these markers described which plants were to grow where, rather like the guideposts one sees in large vineyards, where a great variety of grapes are grown.

Many of the flowers were of an unfamiliar type; plants, like animals, suffer extinctions, and many of the most intriguing specimens are sadly consigned to the compost heap of history, when it would be nicer by far if they continued to grace our fields, plates and ornamental pots. But a few were recognisable, and endure to this day: carvilex, fangloste, burgencrade and habis, to name a few. The botanists amongst you may notice a commonality to those names: their corresponding plants are all psychotropic, which is to say, they yield peculiar effects when ingested, be it imbibed in an infusion, eaten, or set alight and the vapours inhaled. Could it be, I wondered, that the Gardens were essentially a living herbarium, in which plants capable of inducing 'mystical' states of mind were cultivated?

Extracted from *A Glimpse of the Lost Gardens of Dalzerte*
by Cavielle Shaelus

An eight-foot-high boundary wall encircled the Varristen, the Vohorin equivalent of the Sacros. The building itself was striking: an upright cylinder of white marble, some hundred feet tall, inset with small circular windows and surmounted by one of the most striking statues Shaelus had ever seen: a replica of a Forest oak, fashioned from black-painted steel, bedecked with leaves of some stiff green material which, attached by hinges, fluttered in the breeze.

It was a taste of the old Vohoria, thought Shaelus, passing through the gates. Were it not for the oak upon the roof, the Varristen could have stood in Grivillus's time, or any period in the last five hundred years. The sight of it heartened Shaelus. It proved that Vohorin craftsmen had not lost their talents, or forgotten their old methods. It proved, too, that despite the austerity extolled by the *Doctrines*, the Vohorin taste for grandeur still existed.

The interior was not disappointing. A High Erethin showed the travellers to their chambers, leading them along endless corridors of cream-tinted marble. It was here that Vohoria was governed, the Erethin explained. In the Varristen's countless rooms, Erethin performed bureaucratic as well as spiritual duties, preparing the nation for Toros's return. It was the heart of Vohoria, he said, the mind and the soul.

In his chamber on the top floor, Shaelus went to the window.

Glavven City sprawled before him. Again, he thought, *A hint of the old Vohoria!*

Except for the oaks. Statues identical to the one on the roof sprouted on virtually every street, dark and jagged against white stone buildings. Initially, their omnipresence struck him as overbearing. Then he reminded himself that for all his flaws, Harvus was correct: the Torosian faith had enabled the exiles to endure the desert and, on returning, build their lives anew. The statues were designed not only to reinforce that faith, but remind the citizens of the travails they had left behind. And, from such reminders, strength could be drawn.

Weary from travel, Shaelus sat in a chair by the window and dozed. He was awoken by a knocking on the door.

'Enter,' he said, in Druinese. Wincing, he repeated the command in Vohorin; for a moment, he had believed he was in the Sacros.

The door opened. An Erethin entered, bearing a clean pair of leggings, a vest and a cotton tabard. 'For the temple,' he said, laying them on the bed. 'Prayers begin in a quarter hour. You will be summoned when it is time to go.'

'Prayers?' said Shaelus.

'In the *vasriux*,' said the Erethin, using the Vohorin word for 'cathedral'. With a short bow, he departed, closing the door.

As Shaelus dressed, his heart grew heavy. Loyal to Toros or not, he did not want to attend a sermon. Like holy men, they were the same the world over: Harvus's notes had proved as much. Always, the same things were said, albeit in different ways. *Follow the true path. Do not allow your faith to waver. Sinners will suffer, and we must rejoice at their pain.*

But what else could a sermon consist of? And what else did they *need* to consist of? For the congregation, simple sentiments were always enough. They were not interested in metaphysical complexities, or the philosophy of religion. They wanted to treat their deities not as supernatural beings, whose very existence was a glitch in the fabric of reality, but as friends, companions – as, in essence, ordinary people endowed with a few extraordinary properties. In order to understand the divine, they reduced it to its basest level: gods, who fashioned the world out of nothing, who created the seas, the sun and moon, and everything that walked, crawled and flew – what were they, but men? Artists, perhaps, who used the universe as their canvas, but men nonetheless.

490

The Erethin returned and escorted him to the main gates. Quarvis was waiting; Kraike and Lujaek were nowhere to be seen.

Leaving the Varristen, the Erethin led them through the streets.

As they passed an oak statue, Shaelus noticed something interesting. In his chamber, he had observed how darkly they stood out against the white buildings. Now, he saw that they possessed a secondary darkness – that of their shadows, falling against the pale stonework. These shadows were more treelike than the statues themselves and as the sun moved, they would move too, their branches twisting and sprawling, their boles bending and elongating – as if, like the Forest's trees, they had an unnatural air of sentience.

Inventive, thought Shaelus. *What does Druine have of equivalent ingenuity?*

The temple was a low, circular building, constructed from the ubiquitous white stone, set in a small garden. Shaelus and Quarvis followed the worshippers through the main doors.

And as he entered, Shaelus gasped.

The interior was onyx-black. The change in light was so sudden, he was momentarily blinded. He feared that he had been struck by some sudden malady – a stroke, a blood clot on the brain. Light trickled through several window-slits high in the wall, too feeble to properly illuminate the worship space, but what Shaelus could see made him shudder. Oak statues – a dozen at least – rose from the ground, their branches groping over the prayer benches, their wide boles blocking the most obvious routes forward and back. This was what the Forest would be like, Shaelus decided, if it atrophied. A woodland of motionless stone.

He glanced at Quarvis.

'Isn't it wonderful?' whispered the little man, beaming.

Shaelus raised a finger to his lips. Quarvis winced, realising he had spoken in Druinese. He coughed into his fist, as if to suggest his utterance had been a cough too, albeit one sounding strangely like a language.

You minuscule fool, thought Shaelus. Wonderful? It is supposed to represent damnation! Would you grin and skip if you were in the true Forest?

Yet it *was* wonderful, in an unsettling way. Although he cared nothing for the symbolism, Shaelus admired the artistry. As he sat on a bench, the door closed. Several Erethin, perching on gantries, drew curtains across the window-slits. Pure darkness fell; a wooden panel slid open in the ceiling. Beyond, there was a circular window of red glass; noon sunlight poured through it, bathing the temple in light the colour of fresh blood. The trees spilled shadows; everything glowed.

Such symbolism, thought Shaelus. *Such ingenuity . . .*

It was as if the worshippers had been transported to the Forest. For an instant, the effect was absolutely convincing: if one were to wake up in the temple, one would believe that one had died and gone to the afterlife.

Gradually, the effect's potency faded. At the front of the temple, a High Erethin stood on a bier and spoke; the sermon began.

As Shaelus expected, it was nothing extraordinary. The Erethin spoke of sin, redemption, and the hope offered by Toros. Shaelus began to feel uneasy. He could not say exactly why. Perhaps the sermon was to blame; maybe it was the tree-and-bloodlight effect. Most likely, it was a combination of the two. But he was overtaken by an intense claustrophobia. His legs trembled. Sweat broke on his skin. He felt appallingly weak. He gritted his teeth, fighting against the sensations.

They will pass, he told himself.

But they did no such thing. On the contrary, they intensified, and Shaelus grew nauseous. Getting to his feet, he struggled away from the prayer bench and lurched to the rear of the temple. He grasped the door handle; a large hand seized his wrist.

'No,' whispered an Erethin. 'You may not leave during a service.'

'I am unwell,' said Shaelus, jerking free.

'Your departure will be considered an act of blasphemy,' said the Erethin, reaching for his wrist again.

'Blasphemy be damned,' hissed Shaelus, yanking the door open. Bright noon sunlight spilled across the threshold. Stumbling across the garden, he sat on a small stone bench, head bowed, heart racing. Slowly, his breathing grew steady. The sweating ceased. His terror faded.

Curse it all, he wondered. What happened there?

As he sat, he looked along the street. He felt, dreamily, as if he was in old Vohoria. The illusion swiftly faded. Certain things were missing, things which had given Vohoria its old flavour. No musicians played in the streets; the air was not filled with the airy chords and faintly dissonant melodies that had once formed a counterpart to birdsong.

The players of wind instruments will have their lips removed . . . those whose implements of sin are string will have their fingers broken . . .

The artists were gone. Shaelus had fond memories of happy amateurs, sitting on benches with pads resting on their laps, fine-bristled brushes in their hands, painting the world as it passed by.

The painter is guilty of falsehood . . . he must be robbed of his senses as far as possible . . .

The drinking shops were gone. With a few exceptions — Emperor Grivillus, notably — the Vohorin had not been excessive drinkers. Instead, they gathered at sundown, tippling gently, gossiping cheerfully, as the light dimmed and the day's weariness set in.

The man who clouds his mind with drink . . . shall be beaten with wooden sticks, and whipped across the back, until he is half-mad with pain . . .

'This is only temporary,' he told himself. 'Once Toros returns, the *Doctrines* will no longer apply. These sanctions will be lifted, the prohibitions abolished . . .'

A group of grey-clad men strode past the temple, bearing swords. Each wore on his chest the emblem of an oak, just as Papal Wardens sported a Scarrendestin triangle. These were the *traumerin*, the Vohorin lawmen. Unlike their Druinese counterparts, their purview was not only legal, but spiritual. They were ever-vigilant for sinful acts; if the Erethin were beetles, the *traumerin* were their twitching antennae. As they passed, they glanced at Shaelus. He wondered what they saw: an old man, unable to find a space in the temple? Or one who had forsaken worship, because he'd felt as if he was suffocating? Either way, they did not disturb him.

The service ended. The doors opened and the worshippers filed out.

Shaelus stayed on the bench, head bowed. Out of his eye-corner he saw a brown robe draw close, encircled by the leaves-and-bloodlight belt on an Erethin.

'I ailed,' he said, without looking up. 'Would you rather I had stayed in my seat, and puked? Would that not also be considered blasphemy?'

'The first time we met,' came a woman's voice, 'you were sick. Sun-struck, dehydrated, raving.'

Shaelus looked up. A woman of middling years gazed down, smiling faintly. Her face was haggard, as though her life had been hard. But there was a simmering vitality in her eyes, as though the hardship had passed, and been replaced by comfort. Her black hair was laced with grey. Shaelus blinked. He had seen that face before . . .

'Crenfriste?' he asked, rising. He could scarcely believe it.

'Cavielle Shaelus,' she said, placing a hand on his shoulder. 'What brings you to Vohoria?'

Shaelus was unable to speak. Crenfriste, he thought, after so long . . .

'Oh, I think I dropped my purse here on my last visit,' he said, stupidly flippant. 'It contained the keys to my front door. I haven't been able set foot in my home for the past, oh, fifteen years . . . I fear my pot plants may have perished.'

'Have you found them?'

'Not yet,' said Shaelus. 'But one lives in hope.' He coughed. 'I am here with Rirriel Klaine,' he said, using the false name Kraike employed in the desert.

'Another message for him? I have not seen him since we left the desert.'

'Not a message,' said Shaelus, evasively. 'More a shared venture.'

Crenfriste nodded, seeming to sense that Shaelus was unwilling to discuss it further. 'I saw you in the temple. When you fled, I feared I would be unable to find you again.'

'Oh, that – I was overwhelmed by the occasion,' said Shaelus. Again, evasiveness: it seemed his every utterance was cloaked in secrecy.

'You can cross a desert, yet be laid low by a sermon?'

'I am old, if you have not noticed. My desert-crossing days are over.'

'How long will you remain in Glavven?'

'I leave on the morrow,' replied Shaelus, regretfully.

'Do you have comfortable lodgings until then?'

'Oh yes,' said Shaelus. 'I am residing in the Varristen.'

'Ah, the Varristen has been my home for nearly a decade. I am a High Erethin, now.'

'So I noticed.' Shaelus eyed the belt. 'Were you one of the first?'

She nodded. 'I used *The Chronicle* in the desert. Will your evening be filled with idleness or purpose?'

'No purpose, other than to rest,' said Shaelus. 'I have travelled far these past weeks. I find journeys less agreeable than I used to.'

'Will you be too weary to converse with an old friend?'

Shaelus grinned. 'Of course not!'

'Very well. We shall meet at my chamber. It is numbered fifty-seven, on the second floor. Let us talk of times gone by.'

'Yes, let us do so. Sun-induced delirium is one of my favourite topics.'

'And fights with the *clatterix*,' added Crenfriste, referring to the dark, hard-shelled creature Shaelus had killed that night, a seeming eternity ago.

Shaelus watched Crenfriste walk away. The last traces of claustrophobia were gone. He smiled. Was there any ill that could not be remedied by unexpectedly meeting an old friend?

'What game are you playing?' Quarvis's hissing voice punctured Shaelus's good feelings. 'Running from the sermon like that. I have never been—'

Shaelus raised a finger to his lips. 'If you must speak,' he said, 'speak in Vohorin.' Quarvis stared, flushing. He opened his mouth, then shut it.

'No?' said Shaelus, in Vohorin. 'Good.'

As Shaelus stood, a *traumerin* paced across the garden.

'Cavielle Shaelus?' he asked, drawing up.

Shaelus squinted, warily. 'Yes? If this concerns the upset in the temple . . .'

'The temple? No,' the *traumerin* frowned. 'It concerns High Erethin Harvus.'

Shaelus tensed. Had the gout-riddled, red-faced windbag reported him for reading the *Doctrines*? It would not matter if

496

he had, he supposed. Lujaek would smooth things over. But even so . . .

'He has sent a message,' said the *traumerin*. 'Before you left Calvaste, you claimed you were fearful of being pursued.' He glanced at a piece of paper. 'A big man, a woman—'

'Yes, yes?' Shaelus's heart stopped beating.

'Yesterday, they visited Harvus's home. The High Erethin was absent, mercifully, but they interrogated his housekeeper.'

'And they know where I am?'

'I fear it is so,' replied the *traumerin*. 'Do not worry; you will be well protected. I shall escort you back to the Varristen. As we go, you must describe your pursuers in as much detail as you can. If they enter the city, we shall arrest them.' He smiled, reassuringly. 'You have nothing to fear, sir. Nothing at all.'

'I want to kill him,' said Ballas, watching Shaelus set off along the street. He stood in an alleyway with Ekkerlin, a hundred paces from the temple. They had been in the city barely a half hour when they heard the bell ringing. Ekkerlin assumed, correctly, it was a call to prayer. Following the chimes, they had hastened to the holy building. Now, Shaelus and Quarvis, escorted by several grey-clad men, set off along the street. Discreetly, the Hawks followed.

'Restrain yourself,' murmured Ekkerlin. 'He is not the true threat.'

She was right. They had hoped to find Kraike at the temple. If they had, their mission would be over by now: they would have rushed at the sorcerer, killing him where he stood. Then – if it were possible – they would have fled the city.

Ballas had doubted it would be so easy. This was not a mission where things ran smoothly.

They followed Shaelus to a tall cylindrical building, gleaming frost-white in the sunlight, a colossal black oak mounted on the roof. The edifice was surrounded by a high perimeter wall; as Shaelus disappeared through the gate, Ballas said, 'So, what do you think? Is this where Toros will be resurrected?'

'From the oak, I'd say this is a holy building. So perhaps, yes, Toros will be reborn here.' A little shrug. 'Truth be told, I do not know.'

'Truth be told,' said Ballas, 'it doesn't matter. We know what we've got to do.'

'We have to find a way in, locate Kraike and kill him.'

'Nice and simple, aye?'

'In principle, if not performance,' said Ekkerlin. 'To begin with, we must steal a pair of *traumerin* uniforms.' She glanced at him. 'The law-keepers, dressed in grey. I overheard someone mention their names.' A nod. 'Once we are inside, we split up, and do what we must.'

Something occurred to Ballas. 'Steal uniforms, you say? Look at me! Do you reckon we'll be able to find one to fit? Can you remember how you laughed after Redberry, when I had to buy the first set of clothes I could find?'

'I don't believe I shall ever forget,' said Ekkerlin, smiling. 'Your leggings stopped halfway up your shins and your sleeves barely reached your elbows. You looked like a jester. But do not worry. Your abnormal anatomy is not an insurmountable obstacle. We will try to enter the building with the tree at night, when the light is poor, we'll stretch out the leggings, and you can wear your sleeves rolled up. Failing that, I'll find you a pig's bladder on a stick, teach you a few jokes and we'll say you've been hired to give Toros a little post-resurrection good cheer. After millennia in the Forest, he'll need it, yes? Far better to wake to dirty jokes than prayers, joylessly intoned.' Her smiled faded. Her eyes grew dull. 'I do not think we will survive this,' she said. 'It will be one thing to enter the building, another to leave with our skins whole.'

'Reckon you're right,' said Ballas. 'Promise me one thing.'

'Name it.'

'If you survive, and I do not, make sure I am buried in well-fitting clothes,' he said. 'I'd hate for some archaeologist, a future Shaelus, to dig me up and say, "Ah, a clown! He brought laughter into the world!"'

'No one will ever, *ever* say that about you,' said Ekkerlin.

Night fell on the Varristen.

Shaelus walked the corridor to the door marked fifty-seven. Clearing his throat, he knocked, lightly. A pause, then Crenfriste answered.

'Ah, you came!' Stepping aside, she let him into her chamber, identical to Shaelus's. A pair of candles burned, filling the room with a weak but warm glow. 'Would you like something to drink?' She raised a finger. 'If you request wine, or *valrux*, I will be forced to report you for impious behaviour.'

Shaelus chuckled. 'It is good to see that you treat your duties so seriously,' he said, settling in a chair. The curtains were drawn back from a circular window; outside, the moon shone, illuminating the city streets. The oak statues cast sinister shadows against the white stones. The effect had entirely lost its power, Shaelus discovered. Such was the way with novelties, he knew. They beguiled one moment, then grew tedious the next.

'I have apple juice, or water,' said Crenfriste, moving to a table.

'Apple juice,' said Shaelus. 'Unless it is a trap, and I shall have my liver cut out for choosing it.' He spoke jocularly, yet there was an unintended edge to his words. He had found it difficult to stop thinking about the sinner.

'No trap,' promised Crenfriste, filling a cup from a clay jug. 'You have seen a Mortification Board, then?'

'Yes, on a hilltop near the docks on the western coast,' replied Shaelus.

'Did it disturb you?' asked Crenfriste, proffering the cup.

'I have seen worse,' said Shaelus, accepting the drink. 'I confess, it surprised me. I had not imagined Vohoria would . . .'

'Yes?'

'Embrace punishments so readily,' he said. 'After the desert, I thought there would be greater leniency. Suffering softens the heart, so they say.'

Crenfriste sat opposite Shaelus. 'Or hardens it, depending on who you listen to. But the *Doctrines* are very clear, regarding the treatment of sinners.'

'Indeed they are,' said Shaelus.

Crenfriste raised her eyebrows. 'You have read them? I did not realise you are an Erethin.'

'I – ah, well: a copy fell into my hands. Being a curious soul, I looked.'

'And?'

'The rules are strict,' said Shaelus. 'But necessarily so. Only discipline can hold chaos at bay. Though . . .'

'Yes?'

'I miss the music. And the painting. It seems a shame that this dimension of Vohorin life should be forbidden. But the prohibitions are only temporary.'

'That is what you have been told?'

'By Rirriel Klaine. But, Crenfriste – surely we should talk of lighter matters? As I said this afternoon, I am weary, and if we discuss stuffy subjects, I may doze off.'

'Of course,' said Crenfriste. 'When one is an Erethin, dwelling in the Varristen, one can forget how to make small talk. Idle chatter is one thing I miss about the desert. Out there, there was time enough to talk and daydream.'

'And now, you are encumbered by duties?'

'I serve Toros. Is there a better way to spend one's life? And, like many Erethin, I prefer to be busy than idle. It fends off a certain melancholia.'

'A melancholia?'

'The sort that accompanies pride,' said Crenfriste. 'My children, two boys, are also Erethin. When they became of age, they were sent to study at the *cultrallus* – a school for those destined to wear the belt of holy office.' She tapped the bloodlit leaves around her waist.

'They have no choice in the matter?' asked Shaelus, perturbed. In Druine, a young man could enter a seminary only if he wanted to.

'None,' replied Crenfriste. 'Not that it makes a difference. They would have gone, even if I had forbidden it. I shall never forget their delight when they used *The Chronicle*, and saw old Vohoria – despite the grisly nature of the visions. They are eight and ten years old, now. I have seen neither of them in eighteen months.'

'So, an Erethin's talents are hereditary?'

'It is said that we are Toros's descendants; we have his blood in our veins – and thus, we share his talents, albeit to a lesser extent,' said Crenfriste. 'Both my husband and I were Erethin.'

The word caught Shaelus's ear. '*Were?*'

'He died in the desert,' said Crenfriste, lifting the cup to her lips.

'I am sorry,' said Shaelus, quietly.

'You knew him, in a fashion. He was in the hunting party that saved you.'

Shaelus nodded. Truth be told, he could recall none of the men from the group. Only the green-eyed woman, whose life he had saved in return for saving his own.

For a time, they spoke of lighter matters. Their conversation paused when a candle guttered, fizzing into darkness. Rising,

501

Crenfriste twisted the waxen stub out of its holder and replaced it with a fresh candle. She ignited a taper from the room's still-lit candle, but did not touch it to the wick of the new one. Instead, she stood still, head bowed. 'Shaelus,' she said. The serious tone in her voice seemed to darken the room by several shades. Shaelus grew suddenly uneasy.

'Yes?' he ventured, warily.

'I know why you are here.'

A tightness in Shaelus's throat. 'Of course you do. I told you. I am here to conduct business with Rirriel Klaine.'

'There is no Rirriel Klaine. Only Jurel Kraike.' She turned to him. In the poor light, shadow gathered beneath her eyes. Every minute lived, every breath taken, suddenly showed on her face. The vitality vanished; she looked harrowed, as if she had borne a heavy burden for a long time. 'In the desert, many of us knew Klaine's true identity. We said nothing. Deprived of power, he seemed harmless enough. We knew, too, that his uncle was in fact Selindak.'

'Ah,' said Shaelus.

'I know why you are here,' she said. 'I know that soon, Toros will be resurrected. And then,' she touched the taper to the candle, 'there will be enlightenment.' She gazed heavily at him. 'It will be a glorious moment, will it not?'

Shaelus nodded. 'Of course.'

'But you have your doubts.'

'Me?' Shaelus flattened a hand against his chest. 'No. None at all. Would I have travelled all this way, if it were so?'

'You expected one thing and found another,' she said, blowing out the taper. A trickle of smoke floated to the ceiling. 'What *did* you expect? The old Vohoria, immaculately restored? Or a new Vohoria, where the people were free?'

She sat in her chair.

'I watched you in the temple,' she said. 'You *panicked*, Shaelus.

Even in the red light, I saw the blood drain from your face. You were trembling so badly the bench vibrated. Your skin radiated heat, and you were sweating . . . I was seated behind you, a little to one side. I saw it all. You looked as if you realised you had made a terrible mistake.'

'I realised no such thing,' replied Shaelus, truthfully.

'Not consciously, perhaps,' said Crenfriste. 'But there are two levels to the mind. The upper level thinks, whilst knowing it thinks. The lower level is more discreet. It works away, unnoticed, doing the hard, instinctive work. Occasionally, it understands something important, and tries to tell the upper mind. But if the upper mind will not listen, the lower mind lights a distress beacon, so to speak. In some instances, this beacon takes the form of a persistent, seemingly sourceless unease. In other cases, the body rebels. One falls ill. Or suffers a bad turn . . .'

Shaelus felt routed. A phrase blossomed in his mind:
The trickster has tricked himself.

'It is not so,' he said, hoarsely. He sipped the apple juice.

'No?'

'No.' He shook his head, firmly.

'Then let us assume you suffer from small doubts. That is natural, is it not? Second thoughts strike at the start of any grand scheme.'

The apple juice felt sticky against Shaelus's lips. Wiping a sleeve across his mouth, he put the cup on the floor. 'As you say, it is natural.'

'Then speak of them.'

'And you will put my mind at rest?'

'I will answer honestly,' said Shaelus. 'If you answer *me* honestly.'

They had spent the afternoon on the rooftop of a shop, laying low, waiting for day to dissolve into night.

Their plan was simple, yet perilous. Once darkness fell, they would ambush some *traumerin*, kill them and steal their uniforms. The killings had to be bloodless, for fear of staining the garments that would serve as their disguises.

This would be the easy part – and the only part the Hawks were sure would run smoothly. Every other element of the plan was shrouded in uncertainty.

They would go to the oak-topped holy building, and enter through the gates – assuming the *traumerin* standing guard would permit it. If they did not . . . That depended on how many of them there were. A manageable number – say, five or six – and the Hawks would kill them, steal the key to the gate and let themselves through. If the guards were too numerous, the plan would hit a dead end. Nothing could be done, except leave quietly and think of something new.

If they got into the holy building, they would split up. Then they would face a choice. If the building seemed flammable, the wooden beams and rafters exposed, the walls hung with tapestries and floor carpeted, they would start two fires at different parts of the building. Retreating into the courtyard, they would wait for Kraike to escape the building – if he was not burned alive – and, in the smoke and firelit chaos, slay him. If the building was not likely to catch alight, they would methodically search each floor until one of them located the sorcerer and destroyed him.

Now, the sky was dark. A warm breeze rolled over the rooftop.

'I reckon it's time,' said Ballas. There was a leaden quality to his voice – the heaviness of a gravestone toppling onto gravel.

We will not survive this, Ekkerlin had said.

She was right, Ballas knew. All day, he had felt like a condemned man making the infinitely long, yet not long enough, walk to the gallows. Every minuscule darkening of the sky was

504

a voice whispering, *Soon, soon, soon*. Despite the sun's heat, he was cold much of the day. And he was colder now.

'You are right,' said Ekkerlin, woodenly. 'Let's get it over with, yes?'

They climbed down from the rooftop. Hearing footsteps, they hid in the dense shadows of an alley and waited. Ballas counted three pairs of boots approaching at a steady, measured pace.

'No blood,' Ekkerlin reminded him.

'I'll do my best,' whispered Ballas.

The law-keepers walked past the alley. Three men, carrying pikestaffs.

The Hawks stepped out. Approached from behind.

Something – Ballas did not know what – alerted the law-keepers to their presence. One of the men turned sharply. Comprehension flashed in his eyes; he yelled something in Vohorin. Cursing, Ekkerlin sprang forward, unsheathing her knife, jamming it into the man's throat.

No blood . . . ? thought Ballas.

Clearly, the plan had changed. Leaping in, Ballas drew his own knife, stabbing a *traumerin* through the eyeball, driving the blade into his brain. As he did so, Ekkerlin punched the remaining law-keeper across the head, several times, until he dropped to the ground, eyes rolled back, the whites gleaming brightly in a splash of moonlight. Ballas stamped on the man's neck. Vertebrae popped.

Ballas looked uncomprehendingly at Ekkerlin.

'He said, "It is them!"' explained Ekkerlin, breathlessly. 'Anhaga, they recognised us. We are being hunted.'

No sooner had she spoken than there came the drumming beat of many footsteps, pounding along the road. A cry went up.

Turning, Ballas and Ekkerlin ran.

* * *

'How do you know about the resurrection?' asked Shaelus. 'It is a secret; even High Erethin have been kept in ignorance.'

Crenfriste nodded. 'If I were to answer you, you would not understand. Not yet. So let us speak of your doubts. I should imagine the *Doctrines* is foremost amongst them.'

'That was the case, until I spoke to Kraike,' said Shaelus. 'Because of certain similarities, I wondered if their ideas were stolen from other religions. Kraike assured me it was not so: all mystics draw upon the same truths, so yield the same revelations.'

'That is correct,' said Crenfriste. 'And Kraike would know. After all, he wrote the *Doctrines*.'

Shaelus frowned. 'I thought the Twelve Visionaries were responsible.'

'No, just Kraike. He wrote it in the desert. I saw him do it.'

Crenfriste's words struck Shaelus like an icy blast. 'Kraike has not mentioned this,' he said, numbly. 'In fact, he indicated the opposite was true.'

'He lied,' said Crenfriste, plainly. 'Let me explain.

'It happened four years after you visited the desert. Dalvrek – my husband – and I had gone hunting at night. Returning to the camp, we spotted a figure sitting alone by the river, rocking back and forth and weeping. It was Kraike; realising something was wrong, we ventured over. As we grew close, we saw he held a knife against his wrist, poised to make a fatal cut. As I was gravid with my first son, Dalvrek urged me to keep my distance. I did more than that: I knelt behind a *grivelin* bush, where Kraike could not see me, yet I could hear every word he spoke. Dalvrek went to Kraike, and disarmed him. Then, breaking into tears, Kraike confessed the reason for his despair. Ah, the things he said! At this time, the Torosian faith was well established. We knew about Toros, his promises; a

506

few of us had used *The Chronicle.* Kraike explained that all was not as it seemed. Every night, he said, his soul travelled to the Forest. It had done so every evening since infancy; in the old days, Toros was a benign figure, teaching him the magical arts. But since the failed invasion of Druine, he had become Kraike's tormentor. He would watch as the demons tore Kraike apart. It was agony, he said. The soul is infinitely more sensitive than human flesh; the mildest abrasion is indescribably painful. But the gnashing teeth and ripping claws of the demons . . . Speaking of this matter, Kraike sobbed, piteously.'

She sipped her apple juice.

'We Erethin preach about the soul's susceptibility to pain. We tell the worshippers to imagine what it is like for Toros, suffering demonic assaults in perpetuity. We say that prayers will help him. But it is not so. Oh yes, these prayers help his earthly followers maintain order: if a person is obliged to visit a temple several times each day, he has fewer opportunities to be disobedient, and he knows full well that every Erethin watches his congregation closely, trying to pick out those whose faith is imperfect. But as for Toros himself, the prayers do not – *cannot* – assist him, for he is not suffering. According to Kraike, he possesses an amulet that keeps the demons at bay. Before the invasion, he stood close to Kraike, so the demons would not harm him, either. But no longer.

'While my husband took Kraike to his tent, I wandered to the riverbank where Kraike had been sitting. There, I found a clay bowl full of burned *lecterscrix*. More *lecterscrix*, scorched to ash, lay scattered by the water. Heap after heap of it. Clearly, Kraike had inhaled a vast amount of the stuff – enough to have killed most people.'

'But not him,' said Shaelus.

'So it would seem,' said Crenfriste. 'I believe he had intended to kill himself with the narcotic. But when he failed, he decided to adopt a more traditional approach: he intended to cut his wrists.'

'But wait. This makes no sense,' said Shaelus. 'If Kraike perished, he would be cast into the Forest. The demons he sought to avoid would be waiting.'

'But Toros would not,' said Crenfriste. 'The Forest is infinitely big, a realm without boundaries, and a damned soul always walks alone. Solitude – no, loneliness – is a vital aspect of the torment. No succour can be granted by the company of others, even if they too are suffering. The lost must face their punishment in isolation.'

'Kraike wanted to die so he could be free of *Toros?*'

'So he told my husband, as they walked away. The demons were dreadful; but Toros himself – even though he never raised a hand to Kraike – was far worse. He has a certain *presence*, Kraike said. As if he belongs neither in the mortal world nor the Forest. As if . . .'

'Yes?'

'As if he belongs *nowhere*.' She drew a deep breath. 'Once my husband and Kraike were gone, I returned to my tent and fell asleep. When morning came, my husband had not returned. I sought him out in the camp, to no avail. So I visited the tent shared by Selindak and Kraike. Both men were present; I asked if they had seen Dalvrek. Selindak said they had not. He was lying, of course; he would have been there when Dalvrek brought Kraike back. I nearly – *nearly* – said as much. But I held my tongue.'

'Why?' asked Shaelus, plainly.

'Selindak had initiated the resurgence in the Torosian faith,' explained Crenfriste. 'And doing so, he had grown ruthless. Or at least, his ruthlessness had grown more evident. He did not tolerate dissent. In his own way, he was a tyrant. If I had spoken out, he would have killed me – and my unborn child. And I knew that he had brought death to my husband as well. Dalvrek had heard Kraike's confession, much of which contradicted everything Selindak taught the other exiles. Toros was not suffering; nor was he benign. A week later, Dalvrek's body was found in a far-off part of the sands. I have no doubt he was murdered. But insects had devoured much of his body, and thus, the fatal wounds were lost.

'I grieved, as one would expect. To conceal what I knew, I even sought solace from Selindak. I asked all the stupid, desperate questions common amongst the grief-stricken: Why did this happen? Is this part of a plan?'

Closing her eyes, she squeezed the bridge of her nose between her fingertips. Evidently, the memory still upset her.

'But let us not be distracted,' she said. 'As I said, Kraike was also in Selindak's tent when I visited the day after Dalvrek vanished. He was still under the influence of *lecterscrix*; it would take days for the amount he had taken to leave his system. He was sitting upright on a cushion, a wooden board resting on his lap, and a parchment spread on the board. He was writing, Shaelus. Writing at great speed, the quill scraping and rasping on the page. He was in a trance state. Beside him there was a stack of parchments, all covered with his handwriting. I only glanced at him, but I knew what I was seeing: the residual *lecterscrix* had opened up a pathway and he was communicating with Toros. Or Toros was communicating with *him*.

'Three days later, the *Doctrines* appeared. Selindak announced that he had sent a team of Vohorin to a reputedly sacred place in the north of Vohoria, where they communed with Toros, and they had returned with the document. He considered it a great triumph. No mention was made of Kraike's involvement.'

'Then the text *is* authentic,' said Shaelus. 'Only the authorship is spurious. Perhaps . . . perhaps Selindak can be forgiven the deception. You said that he was responsible for the renewal of faith. If the exiles knew his companion, Kraike – Rirriel Klaine – had composed the *Doctrines*, it might seem that the religion existed primarily for *his* benefit, not the Vohorin as a whole.'

'Perhaps,' said Crenfriste. Shaelus heard her scepticism as clearly as a note struck on a wine glass. She looked at him, coolly expectant.

He cleared his throat. 'Kraike told me the *Doctrines* are not important. As soon as Toros returns, they will serve no purpose. His new-found knowledge will transfigure *everything*. The old rules will no longer apply. Mankind will become harmonious; there will be no need to punish sinners, for instance, for no one will sin. Enlightened, they will choose what is good, and neglect all that is evil.'

Closing her eyes, Crenfriste laughed without making a sound.

Like a lamb entering the world during a midwinter freeze, the Hawks' plan had died almost as soon as it was born.

They sprinted through the darkness-swathed city, hurtling along streets haunted by artificial oaks, moonshadows falling crookedly on the white stone walls.

There was a principle observed by the regiment, one which left a bitter taste in the mouth of every Hawk. Although the populace treated the Hawks as if they were near-mythical warriors, driven by pride and honour, the opposite was true: they were pragmatists. They knew they were not the heroes of epic poems, or war songs crooned in taverns by bards eager to make easy money; they did not embrace gestures of 'glorious futility', where fighting men, knowing all was lost, strove to *die a good death* – whatever that meant. No; unless their deaths served a purpose, they were obliged to survive, and to *escape*.

Standaire had impressed upon them a simple fact: a Hawk was a resource. If he could not fulfil his function at one particular moment, he had to preserve himself for a later time, when he might be of use. No needless risks were to be taken, no vainglorious stand-offs either engineered or accepted.

A Hawk was useful only if he was alive.

Ballas and Ekkerlin raced through the city, heading toward the city gates. A dozen *traumerin* followed, a hundred yards behind, shouting, drawing attention to their location.

Once they were outside the city, Ballas was certain they would be safe. Although there were no hiding places out there, on the grasslands, he knew that he and Ekkerlin would out-run them easily enough.

And then?

He would not worry about that now.

The gates came into view, flanked by flickering torches, guarded by *traumerin*. Ekkerlin cursed. A moment later, Ballas saw why: the gates were sealed, locked shut by a heavy wooden bar.

'The wall,' breathed Ekkerlin. 'We have to find a way over. Or through. Its structure may not be sound; perhaps parts of it have fallen.'

Ballas heard the pessimism in her voice.

Clutching at straws, he thought. We are drowning, aren't we?

They ran on. There was nothing else they could do.

'What amuses you?' asked Shaelus.

But he knew. A sick feeling unravelled in his stomach. He felt disorientated, like a chess player upon witnessing his opponent playing a move that altered the entire complexion of the board. He lifted the cup to his lips. Empty, except for the dregs.

'The *Doctrines* were written for the future as much as the present,' said Crenfriste, rising. Taking the jug of apple juice,

511

she refilled Shaelus's cup. As she did so, Shaelus became aware his hands were shaking. 'Think about it. We Erethin are encouraged to breed with one another. Why? To fortify the Erethin bloodline. This suggests that the Erethin will be important once Toros has returned.'

Shaelus nodded.

Crenfriste placed the jug on the writing desk. 'You said that you read the list of prohibitions in the *Doctrines*.'

'They appalled me,' said Shaelus. 'The punishments are awful.'

'The Torosian faith bans anything it considers distracting,' she said. 'Anything that lures the mind away from the divine.'

'The divine being Toros,' commented Shaelus.

'If a mind is empty, it will be filled by faith – that is the guiding principle. The prohibitions exist for two reasons. First, to maintain order amongst the commonfolk. And second – more importantly, I think – to prevent those latent Erethin, whose talents have not yet been discovered, from being seduced away from their true calling. It is said the spiritual impulse is fundamentally the same as the impulse toward art, music, poetry. Thus, an Erethin might easily dedicate himself to playing the *zaelier* when really, he ought to be serving Toros.'

Shaelus winced. 'But – but what use will the Erethin be? Toros has promised enlightenment. And enlightenment resides in the mind; it is what one knows, rather than what one does. What does it matter if an Erethin does not exploit his gifts? Enlightenment will still have occurred; the world will still be altered.'

Crenfriste did not speak. She did not need to. Shaelus suspected that his face betrayed the revelation unfurling within him.

'We have been deceived,' he said.

'I believe so,' she said. 'Deceived outright. And by omission.' She swirled the juice inside her cup. 'There is much even I, a

512

High Erethin, do not know. I have considered my ignorance for a long, long time. And I believe . . . I believe that, although I cannot discern the secrets themselves, I can at least perceive their outline.'

The city wall was well constructed. There were no portions where it had fallen to rubble. Nor was it climbable: the stones were too smooth, too snugly interlocking; it might as well have been constructed from ice.

Their secondary plan – finding a building close to the wall, climbing upon its roof, leaping onto the wall and risking the thirty-foot drop to the ground beyond – was also unlikely: no such buildings stood sufficiently close to the wall.

So they pressed on, hurtling through the moon-splashed dark, outpacing one group of law-keepers only to be sighted and pursued by another.

It could not go on for ever, Ballas knew. Eventually, they would tire. And if they managed to find a secure hiding place – so what? How long could they remain concealed?

There was another danger.

When the sun rose, the bells of every temple, large and small, would ring, summoning the city's inhabitants to prayer. It was likely the Erethin would speak of the intruders in their midst, the hateful Druinese dogs that had trespassed into their fair city.

Our enemies are amongst us. Find them, kill them! Do unto them as they did unto us during the Scourge!

Suddenly, something hard and metallic clanged against Ballas's forehead. He stumbled, bright pinpricks of light jangling in his vision. Glancing back, he saw a *traumerin* emerging from an alley, gripping a pikestaff in both hands. Through sheer good fortune, or incompetence on the *traumerin*'s part, Ballas had been struck with the flat of the blade; if he

513

had encountered the cutting edge, he would have been trepanned.

Six or seven law-keepers surged from the alley. Up ahead, a larger group appeared, a dozen or so, stampeding along the road.

There was no escape. Nowhere to run to.

Unless . . .

'Get on the rooftops,' said Ballas, pointing to a graven oak thirty yards away.

Ekkerlin ran to the stone tree. Grabbing the lower branches, she hauled herself up, climbing to the top then jumping onto the roof of a building.

Ballas tried to do the same. He ran to the tree, seized the branches and began to climb. Five feet off the ground, he felt strong arms close around his lower legs, yanking him downward. He looked. A *traumerin*. He tried to keep climbing, but fell, dropping to the ground.

Casting the swords and pikes aside, the *traumerin* drew their clubs and waded in, pounding at him until he lost consciousness.

'What do you believe the Varristen is?' asked Crenfriste.

'It is the centre of the Torosian faith,' said Shaelus. 'It is the beating heart; here, decisions are made . . .' He trailed off. Crenfriste was shaking her head, slowly.

'To all appearances, you are right,' she said. 'But if it was truly the case, wouldn't Selindak be here?'

'I assumed he was,' replied Shaelus. 'I expected to be reunited with him at some point.'

'He dwells in the north,' said Crenfriste. 'He issues every edict, gives every command. In the Varristen, we merely enforce his will.'

'Where in the north, exactly?'

514

A mirthless laugh. 'I do not know. No one in the Varristen does. We receive his missives and do as he bids.' She tilted her head toward Shaelus. 'I expect you will find out before long. What is your ultimate destination? Where are you riding *to*?'

'I have not been told. Naturally, I have asked. But then, maybe it is wisest to keep it a secret. I understand there are some who oppose the Torosian faith. If they were to learn where we are going, they might . . . I know not . . . ambush us, I suppose . . .'

There was a knock on the door.

'Enter,' said Crenfriste, loudly.

The door opened. A clerk stepped through. Surprisingly, he did not address Crenfriste. Rather, he turned his face to Shaelus.

'Sir, I bring good news. We have apprehended one of your pursuers. The big man.'

'Is he alive?' Shaelus did not feel delighted. Or relieved. He accepted the news numbly, as if it was no longer of any import.

'Yes, sir. He is incarcerated in the city prison.'

'And the other one, the girl?'

'She remains at large. But I am confident she will be found before long.'

'My thanks,' said Shaelus, quietly.

His message delivered, the clerk departed.

Crenfriste watched him closely. 'You do not seem cheered by the news,' she remarked.

'It is what it is,' replied Shaelus.

'Disingenuous,' said Crenfriste. 'Half the *traumerin* are seeking your pursuers. Clearly, they pose a significant threat. Yet you seem unconcerned that one has been arrested. I think I know why.' She leaned closer. 'Your mind is occupied with graver matters. You are trying to make sense of everything I have told you. I will make it simple for you, my friend. Every step of the way, you have been deceived. Kraike has lied about the

Doctrines. He has lied about his relationship with Toros. And – well, let us see if he has spun you another yarn. Why is he letting you travel with him?'

The question caught Shaelus off guard. 'Why? I—'

'Are you going to witness Toros's resurrection?'

'I believe so,' said Shaelus.

'I believe so too,' replied Crenfriste. 'But why? What purpose will you serve?'

'No *actual* purpose,' said Shaelus. 'But it was I who located the Origin, who have made Toros's return possible. I suspect that . . .'

'Yes?'

'I expect that Kraike is grateful. And thinks it is right that I should be rewarded for my efforts. There is a certain loyalty between us, I think.'

'The decision will not have been Kraike's,' said Crenfriste. 'Selindak will have made the choice.'

'So? His reasons will be the same.'

'Do you think so? There is something you must know about Selindak. Something I discovered in the desert.' She took a drink of apple juice. 'He *loathes* those who are not Erethin. He refers to them as cockroaches, scum, the product of an inferior bloodline; he said that non-Erethin are as intelligent as cattle, but less useful, for they produce no milk and their flesh is not good to eat. These were not isolated outbursts. Day after day, he repeated these slanders.' She gazed into her cup. 'How many of your group are non-Erethin?'

'I am the only one,' replied Shaelus.

'Yet you ride with them.'

'As I say, gratitude, loyalty—'

'Selindak does not feel such things toward non-Erethin,' said Crenfriste, firmly. 'He regards you as tools to be used, a means to an end. He loves you no more than a physician loves the

516

needle he uses to lance boils. And for you, Shaelus, this has troubling implications. When you found the Origin, you had not served your purpose; you had served only *one* of your purposes. Selindak expects something else from you. Something *more*.'

Shaelus's throat grew dry. He drank a little more apple juice. It did not help.

'Such as?'

'Crenfriste shrugged. 'I do not know. But you have a choice. You can carry on with your quest, ignorant of where it will lead, but trusting all will be well, even though you have been deceived so often before. Or . . .' She did not need to finish the sentence.

'Why are you betraying your faith this way?' Shaelus stood. The room felt suddenly oppressive; he needed to go.

'It is not my faith I am betraying,' said Crenfriste, getting to her feet. 'It is my *talent*. I did not ask to be born with Toros's blood in my veins; I did not choose to become an Erethin. It was an accident of birth, nothing more. I am like a poet who abandons his work, because it revolts him; a musician who lays down his instrument, because his compositions make him sick. And yes, I am frightened, Cavielle Shaelus.'

Walking to Shaelus, she pressed her hand flat against his chest. Shaelus felt his heartbeats echoing against her palm, each rapid strike a mallet crashing onto an anvil.

'As are you, I think,' said Crenfriste.

Pulling away, Shaelus opened the door. 'I must go. I need to think. I will see you on the morrow.'

He returned to his sleeping room. Inside, the curtains were closed and all was darkness. Without bothering to light a lamp, he sat on the edge of his bed, sagging forward, head bowed, forearms resting on his thighs.

He tried to think clearly. But it was impossible: he had

learned too much too quickly. And every scrap of knowledge caused a physical response: he groaned, shuddered and cursed, sweat dripping from his forehead.

It was pathetic, he thought. A mind as powerful as his, suddenly useless when he needed it the most.

What, then, do my instincts tell me? he wondered. What does my under-mind say?

He forced himself to stop thinking. He concentrated on *how he felt* — as if he were not a thinking creature, but an animal.

Animals — they knew without knowing that they knew. They appraised the world in a way utterly removed from the intellect. Their wisdom was reflexive, and inarticulable.

It was also reliable.

Three quarters of an hour later, he knocked on Crenfriste's door.

'Enter,' came the Erethin's voice.

He entered. Crenfriste sat at the writing desk, though no parchments were spread before her. Perhaps she too had been thinking.

Shaelus knew what he had to say.

I refuse to do Selindak's bidding. But it is possible, is it not, I will be forced to do so? That I will be coerced, no matter how strongly I object? As long as I am alive, that is a possibility. So I require a poison, a deadly infusion. Bring it to me, and I will drink it.

He opened his mouth. The words would not come.

He was no longer frightened. He was *terrified*, balanced on the knife-edge of panic.

He did not fear Kraike, Selindak or even Toros.

No. He had seen the Curlew — or a facsimile. And for the first time in his life, he feared the Forest.

Is this how believers feel all the time? he wondered. Are they haunted constantly by thoughts of a harrowing afterlife?

As a Master, he had reviled those who sought salvation through prayer and piety.

You act as if you are virtuous, yet you are merely self-serving. Day after day, you say you love the Four, but it is a lie. You are merely making certain noises, and particular gestures, in the hope you will be guided through the Forest to Paradise. What are you, but flatterers, flattering for a purpose?

Now, he understood them. And sympathised.

'When I leave on the morrow,' he said to Crenfriste, 'I will plunge a knife into Kraike's back. I require a poison to smear on the blade, to ensure he does not survive.'

'You imagine that will prove possible?' Crenfriste shook her head. 'When you leave tomorrow, you will be accompanied by a bodyguard of Erethin, all sworn to protect Kraike. You won't be able to get close enough to spit at him.'

'Surely there will be moments when I can strike? Perhaps not straight away but—'

'Unlikely,' said Crenfriste.

'Then what can I do?'

'I do not know,' said Crenfriste. 'But let us think.'

CHAPTER SEVENTEEN

I walked each of the paths; even now, I can feel the stones
beneath my unshod feet. I would have gladly spent many weeks
there, meditating on the uses to which the Gardens were put
by the Dalzertians. But it was not to be. The Salandier Hordes
came, and obliterated the Gardens, so not a single pathstone
remained in its place, or flower-glyphed block left unbroken.
No sooner had Dalzerte risen than it fell again, destroyed by
the barbarous hands of men filled with incoherent passion.

Extracted from *A Glimpse of the Lost Gardens of Dalzerte*
by Cavielle Shaelus

Crenfriste was right: Kraike was getting bodyguards.

Looking out of his sleeping-room window, Shaelus watched
ten well-armed Erethin gathering in the courtyard. Each man
wore a sword at one hip, a dagger at the other. Stablehands
brought strong, well-groomed horses, snuffling and stamping
in the cool dawn light; the Erethin inspected the animals,
ensuring everything was in order. The sight made Shaelus think
of a small militia, preparing for a battle they were confident
they would win. Quarvis stood amongst them, chin lifted,
hands on hips, puffed up with pride; and then there was Kraike,
already on horseback, a wizened stick of a man, his white hair
gleaming.

Shaelus touched his fingertips to the window.

If I were a young man with steady hands, he thought, I could end this right now. I would need only a shortbow and a poison-tipped arrow.

He imagined himself opening the window, raising the bow, drawing back the string – and *thunk*, an arrow erupted from Kraike's head, toppling him from his horse – and somewhere in the Forest, Toros yowled, knowing he would never be free . . .

He no longer held Kraike in awe. Or even high regard. He no longer considered him an extraordinary man, singled out by fate for a high calling. Simply, he saw an ordinary man who happened to possess extraordinary powers. He was no different from a tavern brawler, who had picked up a few exotic fighting moves from overseas. A singer who knew the best songs. A fiddle player capable of performing faster runs than his rivals. His talent was undeniably unusual, yes. But so what? He was still a man, nothing more.

A man – and a coward.

According to Crenfriste, Kraike served Toros to spare himself from nightly ordeals in the Forest. For this reason, and no other, he was willing to bring Toros back to life, and risk changing the world in potentially dangerous ways.

Could there be a starker example of selfishness? Selfishness, driven by cringing, ignominious fear?

'Am I any different?' murmured Shaelus. 'Last night, I should have asked Crenfriste for poison. But fear stayed my tongue.'

There was a knock on the door.

'Come through,' said Shaelus.

An Erethin entered. 'Sir, it is time to depart. Your companions are waiting.'

'Of course. I will be down shortly,' said Shaelus.

'They are restless, sir. It—'

'I said I will be down in a moment,' snapped Shaelus. Startled by the old man's venom, the Erethin withdrew. But he did not close the door: another visitor was waiting: Crenfriste.

But he did not close the door: another visitor was waiting: Crenfriste.

Entering, she shut the door then proffered a folded parchment.

'It is done,' she said.

'He trusted you?'

'Eventually,' she said.

'The letter I wrote to him . . . I chose my words so carefully,' said Shaelus. 'I do not believe that I have ever laboured so hard on a few small paragraphs. It is not in my nature to apologise; and he had no cause to trust me. And yet, my words convinced him?' His gaze darted to the parchment. 'He agreed, yes?'

'He did,' said Crenfriste, handing over the document. 'Although he did not care for the letter; it was the jar of acid that won him over.'

Unfolding the parchment, Shaelus was confronted by the largest, clumsiest handwriting he had ever seen. 'Anhaga Ballas writes as if he is punching the words into existence,' he said. He read the note aloud, but quietly, translating it from Druinese to Vohorin as he went: it described where Ekkerlin was most likely to be hiding, and what she would be planning, if anything; Crenfriste listened, nodding.

'Do you think you can help?' asked Shaelus, when he finished.

'Yes,' nodded Crenfriste. 'But now, I must go. I have to make preparations.'

'You have the other letter? You have not lost it?' He heard an unfamiliar earnestness in his voice.

'Of course, Cavielle. Do not fret.'

'Then I too must go,' said Shaelus. 'I have kept Toros's prime servant waiting long enough. They are growing restless, apparently.' Impulsively, he embraced Crenfriste — a chaste, fatherly gesture. 'I have long wanted to change the world,' he said. 'Now, I want only for it to stay the same. What is it they say about old dogs learning new tricks?'

Crenfriste withdrew. 'Travel safely, Cavielle Shaelus.'

Moving to the door, Shaelus grinned. 'Safely? Never!'

He sensed the Erethin's resentment when he entered the court-yard. How dare he keep them waiting!

If only they knew how little I cared, he thought, as he was led to his horse. *To the Forest with the lot of them!*

Quarvis bustled over. 'At last,' he breathed. 'Why the delay, Shaelus?' His words carried a judgemental edge. His small hands moved to his hips, his twisted little chin lifted a few inches. He was truly in a belligerent mood. He stared accusingly at Shaelus like an emperor surveying an exceptionally unwhole-some subject.

Abruptly, Shaelus understood why. A leaves-and-bloodlight belt encircled Quarvis's waist.

'You are a true Erethin now?' he asked.

'I was invested last night,' replied Quarvis. 'It is customary for the ceremony to be conducted in the temple but, given our circumstances, there was no time to make proper arrangements. So I took my oath in one of the Varristen's grand halls.' He chuckled, spittle glinting on his teeth. 'How many can say they've held superior positions in not one but *two* religions? First I was a Scholar. Now — well, you can see.' He stroked the belt as if it were a warm animal.

'Which gives you the greatest pride?'

'Pride is irrelevant,' said Quarvis. 'Truth is all that matters. In the Pilgrim Church, I chased after illusions. Now, as a Torosian, I tread not only the righteous path, but the path that actually leads somewhere. You know, it occurs to me that—'

523

'I must get to my horse,' said Shaelus, walking on.

Once he was in the saddle, Shaelus focused on Kraike.

You are a liar, he thought. A trickster – as am I. At first, I did not know. Well, let us see which of us plays the game better than the other.

The gates opened; they rode.

Ekkerlin peered over the edge of the flat roof, watching the prison where Ballas was incarcerated. She had been there since dawn, observing the comings and goings, trying to devise a way of setting the Hawk free. But she was at a loss. Only a small portion of the building was visible, a white stone cube measuring twelve feet square; the rest lay underground. She had no idea of the layout, or how heavily it was guarded. Simply, she knew too little to do anything.

She closed her eyes. She was hungry, tired and thirsty – any one of which would have dulled her wits but, combined, made her feel as if her mind was composed of nothing except dust, vapours and soap-bubbles; her thoughts floated, drifted and slithered; she could not concentrate on anything for very long.

She rolled onto her back. It was nearly midday. The sun shone with unrepentant savagery; the sky was a glaring, caustic blue.

How long could she stay here? She did not dare leave the rooftop. The *traumerin* still patrolled the streets, though their fervour had diminished since the previous night. They moved slowly, methodically, like oxen pulling a plough. If they spotted her, though, that would change: within an instant, the oxen would turn into wolves.

Of a sudden, there was a bouncing, knocking sound close by, followed by a rolling, skittering noise. Ekkerlin sat up. A stone had appeared on the rooftop, wrapped in a parchment tied with string. Frowning, she retrieved it, cut the string and opened out the parchment.

Ekkerlin, it began.

She recognised the handwriting; she'd seen it on countless parchments, spread over a writing desk, in a derelict chapel in Whitelock. She glanced at the signature to make sure: *CS*.

'Sweet grief,' she murmured, then read the letter in its entirety.

Ekkerlin,

You are not oblivious to the ways of scholars. You understand our faults better than most. Moreover, you understand how an idea, if it is sufficiently beguiling, can render an intelligent man as stupid as a maggot who, believing it is an emperor gorging on a feast of strangely spiced meats, is devouring naught but dog shit.

It transpires that I am not immune to this failure. When I pursued the Origin, my vision narrowed: I grew obsessed. I believed I was feasting, when in truth I was battening on excrement. Now, I see this: I understand that the thing I chased after, that I desired with every atom of my being, was not only worthless, but dangerous.

I cannot claim credit for this revelation. The lady who has delivered this letter is the one who opened my eyes, and exposed my foolishness. I urge you to forgive me – and, above all else, trust her. Her name is Crenfriste. She wears the belt of an Erethin, but she has no love of Toros. She will do what she can to set Ballas free.

CS.

Warily, Ekkerlin crawled to the other side of the roof. A dark-haired woman, with startling green eyes, stared up.

'Anhaga Ballas needs your help,' she said, in Vohorin. 'You

525

can understand me, yes? Shaelus said you are fluent in my language.'

Ekkerlin did not speak. She was too stunned to think clearly.

'Come down,' said Crenfriste. 'What do you have to lose? You cannot leave this city without my assistance.'

Ekkerlin hesitated, then did as she was bidden.

Ballas considered the jar of acid, hidden behind his back.

It would take no effort to unstopper the vessel, dissolve the chains and break free. He knew it was unlikely he would escape – ten armed guards stood beyond his cell door – but at least he would die fighting. More precisely, at least he would avoid a public execution. To be delivered to the noose or execution-er's blade, helpless, humbled and above all *acquiescent* . . . It was unthinkable.

Be patient, he told himself.

The cell was very warm. Beyond the windowless space, noon must have arrived. He drowsed a little, then heard footsteps in the corridor.

The lock grated. The door creaked open.

A young woman in a clean brown robe stepped through. Her hair was cut close to her scalp, and she was badly hunched, as if her spine was bent. Around her waist was a leaves-and-blood-light belt; under her arm, she carried a case fashioned from black wood. Turning to a guard, she said something in Vohorin. Her voice was appallingly raspy, a coarse wind blowing over desert sands. The guard nodded; the woman raised a crooked finger to an ear, and made a plugging motion. The guard laughed, uttered a short reply. Then he departed, closing the door.

The woman approached, shuffling across the cell. Suddenly, she straightened.

'Good afternoon, Anhaga,' she said. 'I am here to interrogate you.'

Ballas had recognised her the moment she had entered the cell. But then, the disguise wasn't meant to fool him. 'Ekkerlin,' he said, quietly. 'Your hair, your posture, your voice – did you model your disguise on Quarvis?'

'Not on purpose,' replied Ekkerlin. Crouching, she put the black case on the floor. 'I just made the obvious changes.'

'I can understand the hair and bent back,' said Ballas. 'But the rasp?'

'If the guards cannot hear me,' she said, 'they cannot detect my faulty accent. Where is the acid?'

Twisting, Ballas retrieved the vessel.

'Crenfriste – the lady who visited you – stole it from a torture chamber in Varristen, the holy building. From what she says, the building is much like the Sacros.' She unlatched the case. 'And I am playing the role of Scythe.' Lifting the lid, she revealed four long-bladed knives. 'Your plan left a little to be desired,' she said. 'The one you wrote on the note to Shaelus: *Get Ekkerlin in and together, we will get out.* I admire its optimism, true. But its practicality? And level of detail?' She frowned. 'Why did you trust Crenfriste?'

'Instinct,' shrugged Ballas. 'Besides, if she was tricking me, what did it matter? I had naught to lose.'

'You gave instructions where she might find me,' said Ekkerlin mildly. 'You were risking my life.'

Ballas grunted. 'Again, what did it matter? You were already as good as dead – and you know it.' He tilted his head to the door. 'Do you reckon we've got a chance?'

'You do know there are nearly a dozen men out there, bored to tears, desperate for excitement?'

'We've faced worse odds,' said Ballas, unstoppering the jar of acid.

'Yes? When?'

Ballas thought a moment. 'Recently? Mallakos's stableyard.

And that street in Sliptere, with the Hordelings swarming over us like spider crabs.' He slid the jar to Ekkerlin.

'Mallakos's men were fools, the Hordelings children,' she said. 'But I take your point.' She picked up the jar. Sniffed it, then withdrew, eyes watering. 'Goodness. It *is* strong. It is as if they have bottled your sweat after one of your runs. Hold still,' she said, leaning over Ballas's shackles. 'I'll try not to splash any on your groin.' She poured, carefully, tipped the colourless fluid on Ballas's chains, as close to the shackle-pieces as she dared. The iron bubbled, fizzed, then trickled into a silver slurry.

'Right,' said Ekkerlin, backing away. 'Your turn.'

Ballas strained against his shackles. Despite the acid, the chains were still strong. As he heaved, his face turned purple, and tendons stuck out on his neck.

'Make a little noise,' said Ekkerlin. 'The guards are expecting it. You are being tortured, remember?'

Ballas roared, his voice filling the cell from floor to ceiling. Ekkerlin flinched, glancing at the door. The shouting helped, Ballas found. He felt the chains weakening, their integrity diminishing. His wrists broke free. Sitting, he braced his feet against the wall and pushed, working against his leg-chains.

'Come on, Anhaga,' said Ekkerlin.

Ballas doubled his efforts, his roars turning to bellows; the chains snapped, suddenly, and he propelled himself backward across the cell floor. His face felt hot; his eyes were itchy — burst blood vessels, he assumed — and blood trickled from his nose. He got to his feet, swaying dizzily.

'Give me a moment,' he said, leaning against the wall. Through the closed door, he heard the guards' laughter. He listened, allowing the noise to seep into his system as if it was a drug designed to cause violent rage. Within a few moments, he was not just ready to leave, but eager.

'Let's get this over with,' he said. Ekkerlin handed him a

pair of knives from the case. 'We'll sweep through the bastards like a flash flood, aye?'

'Whatever is needed, we shall do.'

Ballas yanked open the door. Three guards stood outside; Ballas slashed their throats before they could react. As he did so, Ekkerlin swept past, stabbing a fourth guard in the chest. Angling past, Ballas stormed along the corridor. Two more guards fumbled for their swords. Leaping, Ballas slammed his bootsole in the chest of one, knocking him back, whilst jamming his weapon into the neck of the other. Landing, he stamped on the fallen guard's throat and pulled his sword from its sheathe. Ekkerlin brushed past, dodging into a side room where several guards were getting to their feet. By the time Ballas entered, three men lay dead.

In the corridor, footsteps sounded.

Returning, Ballas saw a lone guard fleeing to the door, his appetite for a fight gone. Ballas chased and, as the guard reached for the door handle, he dived, grabbing the man's ankles and yanking him back.

The guard shouted something in Vohorin. His tone was one of pleading, but Ballas shrugged.

'If you want to get anywhere with me,' he said, 'you'll have to speak in Druinese.' He sank a knife into the man's belly.

Silence filled the prison.

'Reckon we're done,' called Ballas, panting.

Glass shattered in the side room. There came a smell of smoke, undercut with burning flesh. Frowning, he paced over. Ekkerlin emerged as he got close.

'Crenfriste advised us to burn the place down,' she said. 'If the Vohorin think we are dead, they won't follow us. This is all,' a gesture took in the slain men, 'a horrible accident.'

They returned to the corridor. Through the closed door, they heard cartwheels rattling close, then stopping.

Warily, Ekkerlin opened the door. 'Come,' she said, beckoning to Ballas.

A cart waited outside, Crenfriste on the driving bench. Shutting the door, the Hawks clambered onto the back and hid beneath a tarpaulin. A pause, then the cart moved forward.

'You are safe now,' came Crenfriste's voice over the dull clopping of hooves on sun-baked earth.

Flinching against the sunlight, Ekkerlin rolled back the tarpaulin and sat up. They were outside the city, trundling through grassland. Glancing at the sky, Ballas grunted, then closed his eyes. Instantly, he sank into a fathoms-deep sleep. The big man could slumber anywhere, Ekkerlin knew. He had slept through sea-storms and hurricanes; once, in the Keltuskan jungle, he climbed a *yurik* tree to escape a lion and, cradled by the high branches, drowsed as comfortably as a milk-lulled child.

Ekkerlin climbed onto the driving bench alongside Crenfriste.

Although she had many questions, she did not speak straight away. She gazed at the grasslands, unappealing in themselves, yet suddenly endowed with a type of vivid glory. The sky, whose blueness had grown monotonous, seemed gorgeously deep and vast. Even the horse pulling the cart, a thoroughly average example of its species, kindled feelings of appreciation.

She was alive, all was not lost, and her entire being resonated with gratitude.

'I am in your debt,' she told Crenfriste.

'You can repay me by listening,' replied the woman. 'Shaelus says you have an extraordinary mind, almost equal to his own.'

'Have you read any of his writings?'

'None.'

'Then you will not understand how greatly he is exaggerating.

There has never been anyone like him. His mind is unique.'
Ekkerlin was uncertain how she felt about Shaelus. He had
been her idol, then her betrayer and now, it seemed, her saviour.
Objectively, though, she could not escape a particular truth:
intellectually, he inhabited a universe all of his own.

'Do not overestimate him,' said Crenfriste. 'He is old, now.
Last night, we talked until dawn. He admitted his powers are
waning. He is growing forgetful, his analytical sharpness is diminishing. He is painfully aware that his arrogance is no longer
justified.' Glancing over, she smiled. 'He said the young Shaelus
would not have played a part in Kraike's scheme. Partly because
he instinctively refused to be any man's servant. But mainly he
would find it boring, to concentrate on a single subject for a
long time. And *that* is at the root of his problem, he said. In
his younger days, he could absorb unimaginable amounts of
information very quickly, without effort; it was a reflex. Whatever
came his way, he gobbled it up and digested it, as naturally as
a crow in a field of corpses. Shortly before he was approached
to join Kraike's scheme, he had noticed this gift was waning.
And that, he claimed, was part of the reason he agreed to locate
the Origin. It was an endeavour requiring only a narrow field
of knowledge; a specialist, which is what he became, has to
know and understand only a few things, albeit deeply. Thus,
he would not need to retain his vast sprawl of knowledge any
longer, as it served no purpose. When he started to forget, it
would not matter; he would probably not even notice.'

'How bad has it become?' asked Ekkerlin, stunned.

'Objectively, it is impossible to say; one can neither weigh
nor measure memories. But Shaelus is no longer the man
I remember from the desert. Back then, he believed he was
invincible. Now, he recognises – possibly obsesses over – his
own vulnerability. He is frightened and disgusted by what his
fear has made him do.'

'He is . . .' Ekkerlin hunted for the right word. 'Repentant?'

Crenfriste laughed – a dry crackling noise, like autumn leaves burning on a bonfire. And, like a bonfire, it radiated warmth. 'He has grown forgetful, not been lobotomised! The spark is still there. This morning, he was determined, resolute and, yes, *impressive*, in a dog-eared fashion. Proud, too – as if he had resurrected *himself*.'

'Is that truly the case? Or did *you* play necromancer?'

'I could have done nothing without his consent,' said Crenfriste. 'Last night, when we talked, it was obvious from the start he was caught in a crisis. His bearing was that of one seeking reassurance yet knowing deep down that it will not come. You will be wondering what we spoke of. Well, I shall tell you. Keep your ears open, Ekkerlin, and forget nothing.'

Although Crenfriste spoke for a long time, the account of her conversation with Shaelus seemed to take only a moment. Ekkerlin listened, mesmerised, as revelation followed revelation. She learned that Kraike wrote the *Doctrines* after a suicide attempt; that Selindak loathed those who were not Erethin; that Kraike was not Toros's willing servant, but his slave, tormented by dream-visits to the Forest; she discovered that Shaelus had witnessed the transformation of an Erethin into the Curlew, one of the more common demons; that the Erethin were descendants of Toros; and that it was likely that Shaelus, even though he had located the Origin, was still of use to Kraike – although how, she could not say.

'Shaelus is worried,' concluded Crenfriste. 'He does not know what is expected of him, but hopes it will remain a mystery – which it will, if you kill Kraike.' She sighed, a thin fluttering of air. 'But that is no simple task. Ten Erethin are acting as his bodyguards. It will be a miracle if you get within striking distance.'

'We have our methods,' said Ekkerlin, quietly. Her voice sounded oddly distant; her head buzzed with all she had learned. 'What about you, Crenfriste? What will you do? Simply wait to see how everything transpires?'

'What choice do I have?' She halted the cart, then climbed down. 'You have many miles to travel; you must take the cart.'

'And you?'

'I will return to the Varristen,' said Crenfriste, 'and carry on with my duties. Oh – there is something I forgot to mention. Two miles along the road, you'll find a field of *gliswen*, a wild-flower with gorgeous purple petals. Burn it. Shaelus wants a sign to show that you are following him.' Delving into a pocket, she handed Crenfriste a magnifying lens. 'He also says that you must keep your eyes open as you travel, for he will attempt to communicate with you.'

'My thanks,' said Ekkerlin. 'I will awaken Anhaga, so he can say farewell.'

'Let him sleep,' replied Crenfriste. 'I fear you will both need as much rest as you can get. Now go. You have work to do.'

After a quarter hour, they found the *gliswen* field. Ballas still slept; jumping from the cart, Ekkerlin knelt amongst the flowers and, using the lens to focus the sunlight, set them ablaze. Although the blossoms were moist, the woody stalks burned eagerly. Soon, the entire field was alight, spilling thick crimson smoke into the sky. Ekkerlin watched for a moment, then climbed onto the cart and rode.

CHAPTER EIGHTEEN

Standaire woke to the sound of footsteps, the steady hard-heeled *clack-clack* of boots upon stone.

Cracking open his eyes, he groaned softly. His hands were bound behind his back, his wrists tied at his ankles, and hard, angry cramps turned his back and shoulder muscles into agate-hard blocks. His mouth was burningly dry and his eyes were raw. His head throbbed, skull bones pulsing like some strange undersea creature.

He got his bearings. He was in a disused sewer beneath Soriterath. Directly opposite, a glass-panelled lantern glowed, illuminating two men. The first was called Dexler; Standaire had encountered him in The Grinning Dog tavern. The second, Heron, had attacked him from behind as they walked through the streets, coshing him unconscious.

How long had he been in the sewer? Impossible to say. In this rounded corridor of stone, far removed from the upper world, the standard measures of passing time were absent: there was no sun, inching across the heavens. No birds singing. Night did not fall.

Hearing the bootsteps, Dexler and his companion got to their feet. They stood straight-backed, shoulders squared. The thought struck Standaire again: military men.

The footsteps grew closer. A second lantern floated through the darkness, silhouetting a slender, bald-headed man, walking stiffly but purposefully. Closer still, and Standaire recognised him: Blessed Master Faltriste.

Of course, he thought. Who else would it be?

Twenty paces away, Faltriste became fully visible. His liver-spotted scalp, greased with sweat, gleamed in the lantern light. His dishevelled preybird face was at once calm and caustic – as if he was stoically enduring some foul taste in his mouth. He carried a leather bag. His small, vigilant eyes alighted on Standaire.

'Ah, the useful fool,' he said, halting. 'Yes, the useful fool – who has grown wise, and is therefore useful no longer.' He set his lantern on the floor. 'Depart,' he instructed Dexler and his companion. 'But do not wander too far. You will be needed before the night is out.'

The two men strolled away along the sewer.

'You are resilient, General. I'll grant you that much. By rights, you should be dead.' He gestured to Standaire's tabard. With his arms wrenched behind his back, his knife wound had ripped its stitches and dried blood darkened the fabric. 'A fresh wound, I see. Would you care to tell me about it?'

Standaire did not speak. Nor would he, no matter how hard – or violently – Faltriste coerced him. During an interrogation, one word inevitably led to another, and it made no difference whether that word was an insult, a lie or a profanity: the first crack had materialised in the dam wall, the aversion to speech had been lifted, and the probability of confessing was increased a hundredfold. Better by far to stay locked in silence. To treat the tongue as if it was a lump of wood, inert, useless. Ekkerlin had employed the tactic when Olech interrogated her. Standaire would employ it too. He stared evenly at Faltriste, keeping his face completely inexpressive.

Pouting slightly, Faltriste nodded. 'It would be best – for us both – if we conversed not as adversaries, but gentlemen.

When I called you a fool, I did not truly mean it. Occasionally, I tend toward the dramatic flourish. It is a trait shared by many Masters. Our profession is not merely spiritual, but ceremonial. We dress in outlandish attire, give sermons from the pulpit, and perform various rituals designed to induce in our audiences feelings of awe and grandeur. We are really no different from actors parading on stage, and thus, we fall prey to an actor's affectations. But this is what it is to be human, yes, General? We are all actors, in our own way. Only when we forget that we are playing a role do problems arise.'

Opening the bag, Faltriste drew out several sheets of parchment. He selected one, held it aloft.

'Your military records, General.' He squinted. 'You have served the Church for nearly forty years. Started out as a common footsoldier, then rose swiftly through the ranks. Became a general, then founded the Hawks.' He nodded. 'Not terribly interesting. But later on, when it discusses your activities as a Hawk – well, my ears pricked up, so to speak. The common-folk hold your regiment in high regard. *Absurdly* high, I'd say. Ask a milliner or a tanner or a stableboy, and they'll speak as if you are all men of myth. You are cunning, dangerous, *invincible*; you fight as no men have ever fought before, and you beat odds that would give the most compulsive gambler pause for thought. You are legends, General.

'Why should this be? It cannot be down to the regiment's prowess alone. I suspect that a certain wish-fulfilment is to blame. Ordinary men like to believe that *they* could have been Hawks, if their lives had turned out differently. Thus, by admiring you, they to an extent admire themselves. As for the women – well, what does a woman want, but a strong, violent man who can protect her?

'But there is another component to your fame – an absence, rather than a presence. You see, your failures are never spoken of. That is true, is it not? I am not holding you responsible, General, but it is the way of the world: when someone or something is revered, it is natural to talk only of the triumphs, and hold one's peace about their calamities, their disasters.

'And your career has not been bereft of such things, has it?'

He consulted the document.

'There was the fiasco in Northern Kalmuriss. According to this,' he tapped the parchment, 'you sent twenty-two of your finest men into an ambush. It says here that you were not forewarned about the dangers, or the impending attack. In fact, there was no reasonable way you could have known you were sending those brave – or foolhardy – souls to their deaths.' He lowered the parchment. 'But you and I know that is not true, don't we? There had been many such ambushes in the region. You ought to have at least been on your guard, and not dispatched the Hawks during the hours of darkness. It was, I understand, a cloudy night, too. Not a single beam of moonlight fell to earth. What an advantage that gave the attackers! You might as well have blindfolded your Hawks. Or hooded their eyes, I suppose.' A faint smile. 'All were butchered – after several hours of torture. A dreadful waste of life.'

His gaze returned to the document.

'Then there was Gallvallen Hall. Four Hawks infiltrated the inner circle of a narcotics smuggler, only to be betrayed by one of their number. I believe he was bribed by the smuggler? How easily his loyalty to the regiment evaporated, once he was offered a few gold coins. Again, one may lay the blame on your doorstep. You judged the betrayer as fit enough to be not only a Hawk, but to engage in covert work. How wrong you were!'

Faltriste smiled knowingly at Standaire. As if to say, I am striking a tiny hammer upon your nerve-ends, am I not?

Standaire admitted that he was. Neither the Kalmuriss nor Gallvallen incidents were truly his fault. It was the nature of a Hawk's work that unexpected circumstances arose. Life was not predictable; it was impossible to foresee every eventuality. Nonetheless . . .

'And then there is my favourite,' said Faltriste, brightly. He spoke like a schoolteacher stirring up excitement in a class of bored infants. His tone was deliberate, Standaire knew. He was trying to provoke a reaction, to make him so angry that he could not refrain from speaking. It was of no odds what he said. Whether he called the Master a filthy name, or promised that his plans – whatever they were – were doomed to failure . . . The dam wall would crack; his tongue would be loosened.

'Can you guess what it is? To my mind, it reveals a good deal about your character,' continued Faltriste. 'I am talking about Fardlen's Leap, during the riots three – no, four – summers ago. You sent three Hawks to assassinate the primary troublemakers, the ringleaders of the disturbances. They were captured, and subjected to prolonged torture; day after day, they were mutilated, their fingers and toes sliced off, their eyeballs removed, their teeth wrenched out. Their tormentors made sure you knew about it, for they placed the body parts at prominent spots around the city. And what did you do? Launch a rescue operation? That would have been the decent action. Send in a large number of Hawks to spring their colleagues from their confinement, and bring their suffering to a close.'

Faltriste blinked, slowly.

'But you did not do so. Not a finger was lifted, a knife whetted for combat. Simply, you allowed your men to suffer, then die.'

The risks of a rescue were too great, thought Standaire. Nothing was as simple as you think.

'I do not doubt you can justify your inactivity,' Faltriste continued, as if reading Standaire's mind. 'You could tell me

538

that the situation was complex, fraught with hidden perils. You could tell me, too, that a Hawk knows better than to expect to be rescued: if you fall into the enemy's hands, you are on your own. Is that not an unwritten principle? I believe so. But what a tawdry principle it is! To my mind, it can arise only from one source. You would say it is pragmatism, a balancing of risk against gains. I, however, am certain it arises from a disregard for the wellbeing of others. And this, Standaire, is a moral crime of which you have been guilty, again and again, throughout your career.

'The disasters I have spoken of – and many others – all have one thing in common: namely, when you made your tactical decisions, your monstrous errors, you were always far from harm's way. You were not an active participant in the dangerous elements of each mission. You were safely ensconced in the Roost, sending your men back and forth like chess pieces; or, if you were present, you kept a cautious distance, presumably to avoid being drawn into the chaos. From a self-preservation perspective, this is eminently sensible. But from a humane viewpoint . . .'

Closing his eyes, Faltriste shook his head.

'I took no pleasure in reading these reports,' he said. 'I believed that you were a good man. And even though we are now on opposite sides of the fence, so to speak, I remain disappointed.'

His eyes snapped open.

'General Standaire – the coward, the leech. The man who treats others' lives as playthings. Or rather, counters in a game of chance. Is that not the case? You take risks only when *your* life is not at stake. You do not hesitate to put others in peril, to plunge them into situations from which they are unlikely to emerge alive. But when it comes to jeopardising *your* skin, you are as timid as a church mouse. Is that not so?'

If it was true, thought Standaire, bitterly, I would not have hunted for Helligraine.

And yet, Faltriste's words gnawed at some part lodged deeply within him. He recalled the pitiful despondency he had felt at the Origin – and the way he had retreated from the cave when the attackers rushed out of the darkness.

Perhaps Faltriste is right, he thought. Maybe I was not always what I am now . . . what I have become. Maybe it crept up on me, by invisible degrees.

His face grew hot. His headache grew stronger. He felt rage – not at Faltriste, but himself. He had never, *ever* demanded the Hawks do anything he was not willing to do. At least, not on purpose. But what if he had done so without realising it? What if he had undergone some subtle change of character? Had acquired a certain callousness which he had *mistaken* for pragmatism? Callousness, yes, combined with cowardice? A cowardice that he was only now beginning to recognise?

'And there is my proof,' said Faltriste. 'I deliver unto you all these unpleasant truths, yet your face remains as it always is: not a true face, of flesh, muscle and bone, but a lump of graven stone. No spark of humanity. No hint of emotion. Not a tightening of the lips, an unhappy glimmer in the eyes. Just – *nothing*. I wonder . . .'

He tapped the document against his palm.

'I said that we Masters are actors. And this is true. But some of us inhabit our roles to such an extent that it is impossible to say where the role ends and the man begins. The two merge; a unity is born. When prayers are uttered, every word is sincere; when a genuflection is performed, there is a true belief that a mere swiping of the hand,' he sketched a triangle in the air, 'has some genuine metaphysical potency. To what extent, Standaire, does your exterior tally with your interior? Are you as dispassionate as you appear? I can understand that a military man of rank needs to appear detached, if he is to carry an air of authority. But is this . . . this *figurine* really you? It is so difficult to tell for sure.'

Turning, he shouted along the corridor.

'Dexler, Heron – come here. You are needed.'

As the two men returned, Faltriste pulled a wooden flask from the bag. He tugged out the stopper, sniffed then shuddered.

'Feed this to him,' he said, passing the receptacle to Dexler. 'Make sure he drinks it to the last drop. If he resists, clamping shut his lips like a reluctant child at dinner time, smash his teeth and jam the bottle into his mouth.'

Taking the receptacle, Dexler approached.

Instinctively, Standaire wanted to do exactly what Faltriste said he might: keep his mouth tightly closed, and tilt his head away from the flask. But he did not do so. One way or another, he would be forced to drink whatever was in the flask and if he struggled, he would gain nothing except a mouth of broken teeth. Dexler slipped the flask into his mouth then, seizing his hair, yanked his head back.

Standaire drank. He did not know what he expected. Some truth serum, perhaps. Instead, he found himself swallowing whisky diluted with water.

Why? he wondered.

It made no sense. But it did have an almost instantaneous effect. His face grew warm, his eyes seemed to grow mildly weightless, floating lightly in his sockets. A gentle numbness poured into his limbs; his body did not feel entirely his own. He was not a drinker; nearly a year had passed since he had last imbibed. He disliked the lessening of self-control caused by liquor. Even a small amount frayed the edges of his restraint.

That is it, isn't it? Some interrogators illicit confessions by

541

causing pain. But you, Faltriste, are inducing comfort instead. You want me to relax, become too casual . . .

'Very good,' Faltriste told his accomplices. 'You may go now. But, as before, stay close at hand.'

Dexler and Heron vanished along the sewer. Faltriste took a second document from the bag. 'It says here you have a wife and daughter. Is this true?'

Standaire did not say a word.

'It *is* true,' said Faltriste. 'Daylight is seldom mistaken.' He blinked, as if surprised. 'Oh, but of course! You will not be familiar with Daylight. The Pilgrim Church is an institution of many secrets. Daylight is . . . How shall I phrase this? The espionage equivalent of the Hawks. Except – naturally – they do not share your fame. For them, obscurity is the order of the day. Hence, not even you have been told of their existence. Only we Masters are aware of their activities. Whilst it is true that you and your Hawks act as spies from time to time, you are entrusted only with tasks the members of Daylight would find insultingly easy. They really are quite astonishing. Unlike you, they are not fighting men. On the contrary, they tend to be meek, unimposing specimens – the sort of people who never earn a second glance, and couldn't frighten shit out of a sheep. But that is one of their great virtues: no one suspects them of anything, for they do not seem capable of anything. They took their name from a line in the naturalist Brassal's book concerning foxes: *Behind the soft fur and bright, benign eyes, their minds are as fast as lightning, as methodical as waterclocks and keen as knives whetted by a thousand strokes; and though it hunts through night's heavy dark, the all-comprehending fox dwells in perpetual daylight . . .*

'If there is a mystery, Daylight will solve it. The unit gathers information as effortlessly as an orchard-keeper collecting apples. Even I,' he pressed a hand against his chest, 'am impressed. But I digress.

'Daylight wrote this report for me. It is very enlightening. It pertains to your family — if such a term might be applied to the woman and girl you so heartlessly neglected. Are you curious to hear how they are keeping nowadays? It has been nearly two decades since you last saw them. Surely, you have questions? Well. Your wife is in good health, it seems. She has not taken another husband, but has not lacked for lovers. Your daughter — well, this is excellent news. She has been wedded for four years, to a scrivener. And you are a grand-father, General. A little boy. His name is Jarle, if you are interested. Have you never been tempted to track them down? Without wishing to appear cruel, you are no longer a young man. Usually, when a fellow reaches your stage in life, he seeks reconciliations . . .'

Again, Standaire maintained his silence. But it was not easy. A strong part of him wanted to strike the Master. To drive his fist into his gaunt, aged face, and smash his skull to dust.

'If you were to meet them, what would you say? What explanation would you offer for your desertion?' A glance at the document. 'It says here that your wife *left* you which, technically, means that she is the deserter. Have you taken heart from that fact? *She is the one who ran, not me* . . . But you did not pursue her. You did not try to make amends. You simply let her go — and your child, of course. It is a terrible thing, I understand, to simply allow a child to drift out of one's life. It violates every natural law. Do you ever gaze upon yourself, and wonder who you truly are? And, importantly, what you will leave behind? When a man passes away, what remains of him? His money, if he is wealthy. His reputation, if he is well known. But these are transient things; they do not last. No; the best a man can hope for is to leave a child behind, who is his own not only in terms of blood, but *outlook*. That is to say, he shares his father's bearing, his approaches — his *virtues*. What did the philosopher Hrakis call children? *Flesh-echoes.* An ugly phrase, but apt.'

Faltriste no longer reminded Standaire of a time-battered preybird. He had become a wolf, youthful, vital, coolly sizing up its quarry.

The alcohol was taking effect. The general's anger rose, seething like lava inside a volcano. But he remained in control; he would not erupt. He would not speak. The whisky was potent, but not enough to set him gabbling.

'What did you think of Leptus Quarvis?' asked Faltriste. 'I know precisely what he thought of *you*. A day or so after your arrival, he sent me a letter in which he called you a – forgive the language – *a cold, purely functional turd . . . a creature without a heart, whose mind possesses such a narrow focus – that of performing his duties – everything human is excluded from his being.* He went on to say you have the dead eyes of a whore going through the motions with a paying bedmate. Admittedly, there are worse ordeals than being maligned by Quarvis. One can swat away his insults like gnats. Even so, you and I both know he is not without insight. One of his virtues is the ability to change his mind, and revise his opinions.'

A pause. Faltriste stepped a little closer.

'Two days ago, I received a second letter from our withered friend. He said he had revised his opinion of *you*. I have the letter here.'

He bent to retrieve the document, but stopped, straightened and planted his hands on his hips, a satisfied smile on his lips.

'Daylight was correct,' he murmured, half to himself. He gestured to the flask standing upright on the floor. 'No doubt you thought I force-fed you alcohol to loosen your tongue. Untrue. I force-fed you to loosen your *face*. When one is soused, one can maintain a degree of control over one's actions and words – as long as one's indulgence is not too severe. However, even a small amount of liquor diminishes the control one has over one's countenance. When he is in good cheer, a drunkard grins excessively, so he looks like some painted mummer portraying the Spirit of Joy; when disgruntled, he scowls so aggressively his brows clench and form furrows deeper than those found in a farmer's field. When a lady takes his fancy, he leers like a gargoyle, without realising it; when he is enraged, his visage transforms into the snarling, teeth-bared mask of an ape. These are all extreme responses; there are subtler ones too. Surprise and confusion, for instance.

'General, I did not come here expecting a full account of all that came to pass. I came to have a single question answered: is Leptus Quarvis alive?

'And you just answered it. If he was dead, your alcohol-unfettered countenance would have betrayed confusion when I revealed I had received a letter from him two days ago. As your expression did not shift, I can deduce this did not strike you as strange. Therefore, Quarvis is still alive. And my plan – of which you were a part, albeit unwillingly – continues as it should. If there had been any terrible catastrophe, and he survived, Quarvis would have reported it to me in person. He would have clambered upon his horse and bounced all the way to the Sacros.'

He drew open his coat – the same calf-length black garment he had worn when they met at the war memorial, weeks ago. He drew a knife from the sheathe affixed to his night-black belt.

'Do you ever consider your legacy, General? Do you ever wonder how you will be remembered? Oh – make no mistake: you will not be forgotten. Whether you realise it or not, you are playing a vital part in history. Not Druinese history, alas. Not the dust-and-cobwebs history of the Church, either – for that institution's history is almost over.'

He knelt before Standaire.

'All good things come to an end, General. All tools must be discarded when their usefulness is over. Cast out the rusted ploughshare! Be rid of the leaking bucket!'

He touched the knife to Standaire's throat.

'No last words, General?'

A strong part of Standaire was tempted to utter some searing last statement – to promise Faltriste that his plans would crumble to ash, sooner or latter. That he was deluded. But no – at the moment, the only dignity he could find lay in silence.

'Very well, General.' Tension crept into Faltriste's arms. His breathing sped up. His gaze became peculiarly focused. 'Farewell – and my thanks. The Erethin are in your debt.'

A cry echoed along the sewer. Then the muffled thud of something soft and heavy dropping onto stone. Faltriste blinked, tilting his head.

'Dexler? Heron?' he called, keeping the knife against Standaire's throat.

Another cry, brief and muted, cut short before it had a chance to ring out. Then footsteps, proceeding at speed.

Two men emerged from the darkness. Standaire recognised them: Halger and Frense, two Hawks who, until recently, had been lodged at the Roost.

The words of the first letter Standaire sent from the messenger house flashed through his mind.

Halger and Frense –

Proceed to Soriterath immediately. Keep vigil at the Sacros tunnel that emerges close to the war memorial. Follow anyone who emerges.

This is a matter of the gravest import. Tell no one.

GSt.

*   *   *

546

'What—?' Faltriste jerked to his feet.

Standaire gazed up at Faltriste. Now would be a good time to speak, he decided. 'The fool *has* grown a little too wise, has he not?'

Turning, Faltriste ran down the sewer, away from the approaching men. It was almost comical – an old man, his body long-sunken into dereliction, capering like a spider with a missing leg into the darkness beyond the lantern light.

'Retrieve him,' Standaire instructed the Hawks as they drew close.

'It won't be much of a chase,' said Frense, pacing briskly after the Master.

Kneeling, Halger picked up Faltriste's dropped knife. 'Are you injured, sir?' he asked, sawing the blade through Standaire's bonds.

'Just a little drunk,' replied Standaire.

Halger frowned.

'Faltriste is employing an eccentric interrogation technique,' said Standaire. 'He prefers hospitality over hot irons and sharpened steel.'

Frense returned, gripping Faltriste's coat collar. The Master's pale face had flared a bright angry red. His mouth worked noiselessly, mechanically.

'You shall all hang for this!' he yelled, voice echoing.

'The other Masters will decide who wears the noose,' said Standaire, rising.

'Oh, that is your plan, is it? To haul me before my brethren?' Faltriste laughed, his eyes flashing; he reminded Standaire of a sanatorium inmate, jabbering at imaginary enemies. 'You will not be believed. I am a Master! And you . . . you are merely a jumped-up soldier. I will say you suffer from battleshock. That, traumatised by your military work, your wits have fled.'

'It will take only a few riders sent to the Origin to prove my story.'

'You have seen the— No. No! I will deny all knowledge.'

Standaire smiled for the first time in a long while. 'If that is so, Blessed Master Faltriste, you have nothing to worry about.'

CHAPTER NINETEEN

They spent a day and a half on the road, taking turns to drive the cart whilst the other slept. Naturally, Ballas slumbered as if drugged, plunging into sleep's abyss as soon as he lay down. Ekkerlin had no such luck. Each time she tried to doze, Crenfriste's revelations buzzed inside her head like bluebottles in a jar. The High Erethin had explained matters as clearly as possible, and Ekkerlin had had no trouble understanding. But therein lay the problem: whilst the *facts* were clear, their implications were ambiguous.

First, there was Toros himself. What sort of man was he? Was sort of man would he be, if he returned? Ekkerlin had read numerous texts about the visionary's life but, written millennia after Toros's death, all were wildly speculative. He was an unknown quantity and, as far as Ekkerlin could tell, his motives were a mystery. True, the Erethin spoke of enlightenment, but this idea did not ring true: how many men of history had gone to the same lengths as Toros for the sake of others? Altruism was a powerful force, but it had limits. To spend millennia in the Forest, with or without a demon-repelling amulet, for purely benevolent reasons – it was unthinkable.

Was he motivated, then, by ordinary ambitions? Did he seek power? Glory? Again, these seemed unlikely, and for the same reason: would anyone, sane or mad, crave these exalted things fiercely enough to commit themselves to the Forest for thousands of years?

There was another possibility: immortality. But surely Toros understood that the notion of everlasting life was a sham? That the body, be it through accident or natural processes, would eventually perish? Even if this were not so, what appeal would immortality have for Toros? Surely, regardless of his powers, he would fall prey to boredom? The quiet despair of knowing that his existence would never end?

These thoughts swarmed through Ekkerlin's mind. For certain, though, they did not plague Ballas.

Midway through the second day, the massed hoofprints of Kraike and his companions veered off the road. The Hawks followed, cutting through grassland, then halted at a river, sparkling in the sunlight. There they found a sycamore tree, its bole rubbed smooth, as if a rope had been looped around it. The damp soil of the riverbank was flattened, suggesting a riverboat had been moored there.

The river flowed swiftly, faster than Ballas and Ekkerlin upon their cart.

Ballas scowled; Ekkerlin cursed. She had expected killing Kraike to be difficult. She had not anticipated catching up with him would also be a problem.

What if we arrive too late? she wondered. What if it is not the sorcerer we must kill, but Toros himself?

They followed the river, meandering through the grasslands. After a day and a half, they found a black-painted barge, tied to a willow tree. The vessel was deserted. Rooting inside, the Hawks discovered nothing of interest. But, as they were about to depart, Ekkerlin spotted a cross carved into a deckboard. Alongside, there were two letters, cut by a sharp blade.

Leaving the barge, they spotted a trail of footprints through the grass stalks, heading westwards. After several hours, they crested a low hill, curve-backed like a whale, topped by a few scraggly oaks.

Beyond, the ground sank away—

—and there was an oak forest, sweeping toward the horizon.

'*Bral-kavis*,' said Ekkerlin, softly. 'Roughly translated, it means *Brawlsnare – which in turn means "place of hunting and trapping"*. It is an ancient forest, a wildwood, much like Shardenblack in Druine.'

Riding down, they halted at the forest's edge.

Jumping from the driving bench, Ekkerlin walked amongst the trees. The temperature dropped, the sun blotted out by the branches overhead. She inhaled the scents of the forest: ferns, mosses, damp stones and moist soil. A dead silence oozed from the trees, broken only by birds clattering amongst the twigs.

Something caught her eye. Another cross, this time carved into oak. Vaguely misshapen, it had clearly been executed in haste. But it was enough. A marker, a tiny statement left by Cavielle Shaelus, saying, *I have passed this way.*

Of course he had. Next to the oak, a strip of boot-flattened soil cut between the trees. Kneeling, Ekkerlin inspected the broken grass stalks. Sap seeped from every fracture; the tracks were relatively fresh. A day old, perhaps. Maybe a little longer.

She went outside the forest. After the claustrophobic gloom, the sun seemed very bright, the grasslands extraordinarily vast. She told Ballas what she had seen. Together, they unhitched the cart, freed the horse to wander, and entered Brawlsnare.

As dusk fell, seeping into the forest like golden dust, they reached an area where the grass was flattened in great swathes, and the ashy remnants of a cookfire lay inside a circle of grey stones. Presumably, this was where Kraike and his companions had rested for a night – but which night? How far ahead were they?

Casting about, Ekkerlin spotted another cross carved into a tree bole. Next to it was an arrow, pointing downward. Brushing aside the long grass around the tree, she found a small square of folded parchment.

Opening it carefully – it was damp and liable to tear – she was confronted by Shaelus's handwriting. As she read, she heard Shaelus's voice – strong, focused and, even now, playful.

So it begins! We are the mice, you the cats!

You cannot imagine my relief when I saw the smoke from the burning flower-fields. I could barely contain my delight. My fellow travellers were utterly oblivious to the meaning of the red fumes pouring into the sky. They assumed – fools! – it was merely the sort of wildfire common during hot weather. But for me, it was akin to a rope tossed from a ship to a drowning man.

I cannot say what use these missives will be to you, my Hawks. For me, they serve a solid purpose. I have discovered that my mind is not what it was. When I was young, I could juggle a thousand competing thoughts at once, and analyse them, without the aid of a pen and parchment. No longer, alas. Maybe I have spent too long relying on writing materials (in the Dark Archives, trying to deduce the location of the Origin, I made copious notes, though took care to burn them at the end of every day) and lost the knack of thinking purely in my head. Maybe I am simply suffering from the withering effects of age.

Either way, the cause is not important. I am what I have become – namely, a man who cannot think unless he has a quill between his fingers.

In writing these letters, I am primarily setting my own thoughts in order. As Crenfriste will have mentioned, it seems I am destined to serve a purpose beyond finding the Origin. As to this purpose, Kraike has told me nothing, which suggests it is something I would neither approve of nor enter into voluntarily.

We are accompanied by a guard of ten Erethin. All are young men, well armed, although I cannot say whether they are competent in the fighting arts. For certain, they are taking great care of Kraike. Unlike the rest of us, the sorcerer does not walk, but is carried upon a litter. He spends most of the time sleeping, like a cat on a sunlit windowsill; I suspect he is conserving his energy for when it is needed.

We left this camp on the third day of this month. I suspect that you are several days behind in your pursuit, for we made excellent time when we travelled on the river.

I will write again as soon as I can.

Your faithful, and uneasy, servant,

CS.

Ekkerlin passed the letter to Ballas.

'He isn't one for brevity, is he?' said the big man when he finished reading.

'As he said, he is setting his thoughts in order,' replied Ekkerlin. She looked at Ballas. *He* would never suffer from Shaelus's fear that his mind was losing its sharp edge; he would never struggle to arrange his ideas in some clear, fathomable fashion. His worldview was crunchingly simple. And she suspected that he liked it that way. 'According to the date, we are a day and a half behind Kraike. A lot of ground to cover.'

'Then we'd better get moving.'

They walked into the night. As the moon rose over the trees, spilling silver light through the leaves, Ballas realised that

Ekkerlin was exhausted. She moved sluggishly, her feet scuffing over the twig-littered ground. Her gaze was glassy and unfocused.

She had been finding it hard to sleep, Ballas knew. He had asked her why. She'd told him it was always the way when she was pondering an intellectual matter.

It dominates me, she had said. I obsess over it. The philosopher Melrek said that at the heart of every person, there is a paradox, an internal contradiction. Mine is this: I adore mysteries and puzzles, yet I can find no peace until I have solved them. They drive me mad.

As the night deepened, the sky above the trees sinking into a rich blackness, Ballas made a decision.

'You need to rest,' he said.

'I shall be fine,' she replied, after a long hesitation – as if she had not understood him straight away. 'Let us keep moving.'

'No,' said Ballas. 'You're no use to anyone if you are half-asleep. The way you are plodding on, I reckon Leptus Quarvis could probably beat you in a footrace.'

'Very gracious of you to say so, Anhaga.'

'Rest,' repeated Ballas. 'I'll grant you a couple of hours.'

They did not seek out a suitable place to stop. Amongst the dense oaks, and the ground riddled with thornbushes, there was nowhere to bed down, except the path itself.

Ekkerlin lay down, pillowing her head on her hands – an oddly girlish posture. She fidgeted, then tumbled into a doze.

Ballas sat on a mossy boulder, thinking.

The forest was blissfully silent. The world of strife, uproar and disruption seemed a long way away. True, Ballas needed those things – the thrill of violence, conflict, narrow escapes. But he did not *like* them. Much of the time, he hated them. Yet he needed them, too. He supposed this was the paradox locked within his own heart.

In the moonlight, he grinned.

Once, he had asked Ekkerlin to make sense of these feelings. He had expected the Hawk to give a philosophical answer. Instead, she compared him to a *grisuse* spider.

After mating, she had said, *the male acts as a bodyguard to the newly impregnated female. Do you know what he does so he can better fulfil his function? So he can move with greater speed, and agility?*

Ballas said that he did not.

He bites off his own penis, Ekkerlin had said. *Biologists believe he does not make a rational choice to do so. Rather, he is compelled by an irresistible instinct. Even for a spider, I expect it is unpleasant to chew off your manhood. Yet he does so and, essentially, you do the same. You are a slave to your instincts, yearnings and compulsions. You may not like what they force you to do, but you acquiesce. Your behaviour is natural — and unavoidable . . .*

Now, Ballas brooded on her words. She was right, of course. But one day, he would be unable to act on his nature — at least legally. In five years, maybe ten, he would no longer be strong or quick enough to be a Hawk. Then what? He had no idea. He could not imagine a different life for himself. Some folks, he knew, could plot out their futures to the tiniest degree. Not him. However hard he tried, he could not look ahead; his thoughts crashed into a solid wall of dark stone, which he could neither penetrate, skirt around or climb over.

He had not mentioned this to Ekkerlin. Nonetheless, he knew what she would say. *You cannot contemplate the future because you do not believe you have a future. You live each day as if it was your last — not in a happy-go-lucky fashion, but like someone stumbling through mist, convinced every step takes him closer to a cliff-edge.*

He gazed at Ekkerlin, sleeping soundly.

And what about you?

She had plans — of that, he was certain. He sensed she would not remain a Hawk much longer. What would she turn her hand to? Something connected to the life of the mind. She would become a philosopher, perhaps. Or a poet – albeit one who compared warriors to spiders who bit off their own child-makers. When she read Shaelus's letter, her eyes had brightened. Her expression had grown simultaneously excited and serene. As if to say, *This is it; this is where I belong. This is my world, the world of concepts, and conversations with intelligent souls.*

Suddenly, Ballas's hackles twitched. He felt as if he was being watched. A woodland animal on a nocturnal prowl? He did not think so.

Warily, without moving his head, he lifted his gaze from Ekkerlin to the gloom-soaked woodland beyond.

A lone figure stood between the trees. It was tall and slender, masculine. For a few long heartbeats, Ballas stared, noticing that the man – like all things half-bathed in moonlight – had an eerie quality, as if he were neither of this world nor the next.

Slowly, the man drew something from his shoulder – a shortbow. Reaching behind, he pulled an arrow from a quiver. But he did not nock it. He simply watched Ballas, as if sizing up prey.

Ballas's gaze darted away to the side.

Standing level with the man, twenty paces away, was another figure – shorter, stockier, also armed with a shortbow. He too gazed at Ballas.

Ballas nudged Ekkerlin with the toe of his boot – a gentle tap, nothing more. Wrenched out of her first decent sleep in days, Ekkerlin opened her eyes. She did not speak, or sit up. She barely stirred at all. As a Hawk, she knew an abrupt – but discreet – awakening augured ill. She looked at Ballas. The big man hunched forward casually, as if merely adjusting his posture. He extended the first two fingers of his right hand.

Two strangers.

Curling his index finger and thumb, he formed an *o* shape.

Watching us.

Ekkerlin licked her lips; her saliva glistened in the moon-light.

Armed? she mouthed.

Ballas bent the first two fingers of his right hand, as if crooking them to draw back a bowstring. As he did so, he looked up again.

The first stranger was nocking the arrow. Out of his eye-corner, Ballas saw the second doing the same. Ballas's breathing gathered pace, his heart's slow drumming accelerating into a heavy *thump-thump-thump*. A metallic taste seeped in his mouth. Sweat trickled down the back of his neck.

The first stranger raised his bow, taking aim. His sighting eye folded into a squint. Tension crept into his shoulders.

Ballas timed his dive perfectly, flinging himself sideways off the boulder. He felt the arrow stir the air where, an instant ago, his head had been. Landing heavily on the ground, he scrambled up and charged through the long grasses and clawing thornbushes toward the man. His companion loosed his arrow, but the shaft *clopped* into a nearby tree bole.

Ten paces away, Ballas saw the stranger was garbed in browns and greens, his face darkened by a layer of dirt. He had the look of a hunter. Or a poacher.

The stranger turned to flee. Swiping out a massive hand, Ballas seized the collar of his tabard and yanked him back. The man scrabbled for a knife sheathed at his hip; Ballas caught his wrist with one hand, punched him squarely in the face with the other. The man's head jerked back, nose exploding in a shower of blood and snot. Grunting, Ballas kneed him in the groin, so powerfully the man rose several inches off the ground. Unsheathing his own knife, Ballas cut his throat.

He turned. Ekkerlin and the second man circled each other, knives in hand. Muttering, Ballas picked up the first man's bow, then pulled a white-fletched arrow from the quiver. Briskly, he nocked the arrow and took aim. He released; the arrow tore through the moon-tinted gloom, slamming into the side of the second man's head, the impact flinging him into a thornbush.

'Any more?' whispered Ekkerlin as Ballas strode over.

'None that I saw.' Standing stock-still, the Hawks listened for sounds of either retreat or advance. Swishing grasses, snapping twigs, the murmuring *shush* of weapons being unsheathed. There was nothing, except for the restless silence of the forest.

Bending, Ekkerlin dragged the corpse out of the thornbush into the open. His face was that of a man of middling years. His eyes had rolled back in their sockets, so only the underside of his irises were visible. His mouth sagged open; a black beetle, an inhabitant of the thornbush, tramped along his lips, before losing its footing and tumbling into the tooth-lined cavern beyond.

Ekkerlin lifted his tabard.

'Erethin,' she said, pointing to the leaves-and-bloodlight belt around his waist.

'One of Kraike's companions, you reckon?'

Spitting on her fingers, she wiped dirt from the man's face. 'No, I do not think so. His skin is too pale.'

Ballas looked at her, queryingly.

'He has not spent much time in the sun,' explained Ekkerlin. 'And this summer has been relentless, has it not? Everything is scorched.' She rubbed a little more dirt away, revealing skin as white as stonemason's plaster. 'He has dwelled in shade for a long time. This forest is his home, perhaps.' She squinted at the arrow jabbing from his head. The fletching, Ballas noticed, was not *completely* white. Rather, the feathers were decorated with a black circle fringed with triangles, their pointed ends sticking outwards. Ekkerlin noticed it too. Leaning close, stroking the feathers, she grew lost in thought. Ballas could practically hear her mind working, ideas sliding and interlocking like the pieces of a bewildering puzzle.

'Give me the bow,' she said, holding out her hand.

'It's a good weapon,' said Ballas, doing as he was told.

A good weapon, yes. And it gave him hope. If the circumstances were right, he could use it to kill Kraike. Until now, he imagined the assassination would be intimate – a whites-of-the-eyes, breath-on-the-neck killing. Armed only with knives, it had seemed likely either he or Ekkerlin would have to plunge a blade into the scrawny sorcerer. And to do *that*, they would have to find a way through his bodyguard of Erethin. Even if the killing itself was successful, it was unlikely they would escape with their lives: outraged, vengeful, the Erethin would rip them apart. Probably. But now, it was possible to kill Kraike from a distance. Ballas saw it in his mind's eye: a solitary arrow, cutting through the gaps between the trees, then crunching into the sorcerer's skull. That would be all it took. A flying arrow, well-aimed, and Toros's millennia-long scheme would come to an end. And then, he and Ekkerlin could flee the forest, running like apple-thieves startled by an orchard-keeper. A crude escape, no doubt. But it would work well enough. Sometimes, life boiled down to the simplest things.

Ekkerlin turned the bow over between her hands, squinting. 'Well, this is interesting,' she said. She pointed to an engraving just above the leather-wrapped handle. At first, Ballas could not see it. Wiping sweat from his eyes, he looked closely and saw the same circle-and-triangles symbol as the one on the fletching.

He hazarded a guess. 'The sun?' he said.

'Very good, Anhaga,' said Ekkerlin. 'We will make a semiotician out of you yet. Of course, you are only half right. The *circle* is the sun, but the little triangles are teeth.'

'Like those of a shark?' He recalled the colossal whites that had prowled around the boat as they sailed to Vohoria. They had seen one slaughter a seal; it had glided toward the doomed creature then, at the last moment, crashed upward through the surface, its jaws stretched open, its throat horribly pink and endlessly deep, its teeth a palisade of splintering, crushing cutting tools. Then the seal was gone. All that remained was a scrim of brine-diluted blood, spreading on the surface.

'Not a shark,' replied Ekkerlin. 'A *harbinger* fish. They inhabited the rivers and deeper streams of the hot countries. Alas, they are extinct now. But back then, they were revered.' She glanced at him. 'Primitive tribes often adopted certain animal species as their "spiritual mascots". And within each tribe, certain animals were said to represent certain professions. Usually, they were quite obvious: weavers were symbolised by spiders, wise men by owls . . . But *this* symbol,' she prodded the teeth-and-sun, 'is a little more complex. The countries where the harbinger fish were found were not merely hot, but burningly, blisteringly, *murderously* hot. We are going back several millennia now,' she added. 'Maybe more. But the sun was considered to be an enemy – an angry god, intent on either incinerating his creations in disgust, or punishing them for their innate sinfulness. Whilst a few tribes tried to placate this fiery deity by sacrifices and prayer, others rebelled. They stood firm against this cruel god and, in a gesture of defiance, included it into the panoply of symbols they used. As everyone knows, if you stare at the sun, you are blinded; thus, one is forced to keep one's eyes lowered – a universal gesture of subservience and fear. The primitives seemed to recognise this and decided that if they could not gaze at the sun without bad consequences, they could at least look at *representations* of it with complete impunity. So the sun symbols became emblems of their defiance. This meaning changed over time, evolving, as meanings are wont to do. In the end, these simple circles represented courage.'

'And the teeth?'

'They marked out the hunter's trade,' said Ekkerlin. 'They stood for the harbinger fish's ability to stalk, kill and devour prey. So this symbol,' again, she stroked the fletching, 'indicates that this fellow,' a gesture to the corpse, 'is – *was* – a hunter and, as he does not fear the sun, one of great courage.' She looked at Ballas. She wore the same bright-eyed expression as when she had read Shaelus's letter. She was in her element, an otter gliding through river water, a golden eagle coasting over mountaintops. She seemed almost *unnaturally* alive. Vaguely, Ballas envied her. When had *he* ever felt such high feelings? Just once, of late – when he stood in Quarvis's darkened wine cellar, his fingertips touching the bottles nestling in the rack.

Ekkerlin looked through the trees to where she and the hunter had fought. Rising, she swished through the long grass then knelt. She picked up a bag, held shut by a wooden toggle. Opening it, she peered inside and drew out a pheasant. 'Freshly killed,' she said. Delving into the bag, she took out a smaller bag and looked inside. 'It's full of snares,' she said. 'I'd say that these men were not in this forest to protect Kraike, but to gather food. Which means there is a settlement somewhere.'

'Somewhere close, aye?' Ballas secretly hoped so. A brisk walk through the night – a run even, if Ekkerlin could manage it – a loosed arrow, a breakneck gallop from the forest, and all this could be over.

'Who can say?' said Ekkerlin. 'There may well be store-lock throughout the forest, little grots and nooks where the huntsmen's catch can be stored and kept fresh until it is time to go home. A river, maybe.'

There was no point staying where they were; Ekkerlin would not sleep again that night. Taking the bows and arrows from the corpses, they set off through the forest, moving at a steady, mile-swallowing plod.

*　　*　　*

561

As dawn broke over the tree tops, Ekkerlin suddenly said, 'Yes!'

'Yes?'

'It was a struggle, but I managed it.' She turned to Ballas. Her face bore the glow of a child delighted by an unexpected gift. 'There were seven tribes who used the sun-and-teeth symbol. The Rimlusians, Slavrinas, Dalzertians, Elpireans, Gralfarrens, Crastoneans and the Irriunians.'

'Aye? What of it?'

Ekkerlin shrugged. 'I do not know. I have been trying to remember, that is all.'

Ballas grunted, then nodded. Useless or not, Ekkerlin's deduction seemed to have diminished her weariness. That was good; it was something.

CHAPTER TWENTY

Standaire sat at a long oaken table in the Seventh Hall, a vast wood-panelled chamber on the top floor of the Sacros.

All twenty-seven Masters were in attendance. Almost all were old men, white-haired, faces creased and jowly, a touch bleary and confused by a sleep rudely interrupted. All were clad in heavy scarlet robes, their gold Scarrendestin pendants glimmering in the candlelight.

Rymise was foremost amongst the Masters. He had served the Church longer than any of his colleagues. He was in his ninetieth year. His pale skin was nearly translucent, his white hair thinner than spidersilk. Dandruff speckled the shoulders of his robe, white against the scarlet, and his eyes watered constantly. His breathing was irregular, as if his lungs were bellows worked by someone unable to find a rhythm, and he looked as if he might fall asleep at any moment.

'General Standaire,' he said. 'This is most . . .' a long pause as he sought the right word, 'unexpected. To be torn from one's bed before the larks sing — it is without precedent. Equally unprecedented is your treatment of Faltriste. I understand . . . the Guards inform me . . . that you brought him to the Sacros with a coat draped over his head, concealing his features, and declared at the gates that he is a traitor, and Druine is to go to war. That is why we were, ah, *hoisted* from our pillows, blankets and comfortable dreams. This is an emergency, our aides told us. Conflict approaches, they said. And yet it is not so. What we find is that a decorated military commander has, what, *kidnapped* a Master? Arrested him?' He turned to Faltriste. 'What term would you use?'

'Term? I . . . I do not know.' Faltriste blinked, hazily, as if he too had been woken from a gentle sleep. 'Forgive me, my brethren. I too am tired and, as you can imagine, somewhat stunned. The earthquake has passed, but the aftershocks are still felt.'

'Do you require a cup of wine?' asked Rymise. 'To soothe the blood?'

'A little time is all I need,' said Faltriste. 'I am sure that once Standaire has given his side of this sorry story, I shall be well enough to give mine – if that is what you wish, Master Rymise.'

'A sensible plan,' said Rymise, steepling his fingers. 'General, we are all intrigued. I hope your explanation satisfies our curiosity – although I cannot conceive how it may justify your actions. To *manhandle* one of the Four's anointed servants . . . to—' Wincing, he raised a hand. 'No; I must not forejudge. Speak, and I will listen with an open mind.'

Every Master looked at Standaire. For a moment, the chamber seemed to spin, the wood panels blurring, the lantern flames whirling.

'It is a long tale,' said Standaire, his voice strangely small. He cleared his throat. 'It will take some time.'

'Then begin,' said Rymise, impatiently. 'You are reputed to be a man of few words. I suggest that you prove it.'

Standaire did as he was told, starting at the secret meeting with Faltriste near the war memorial. As he spoke, wading through the tale, he grew uneasy. To his own ears, it sounded absurd, and he felt waves of incredulity rolling out from the Masters too; it was not the magical element they objected to – as clergymen,

564

they treated the supernatural as if it was concrete fact. Rather, it was the notion that they had been betrayed by two of their scarlet-clad fellows which stretched their belief to breaking point. By degrees, Standaire sensed he was losing them; the truth pushed them too far. He felt like a child lying to a parent, weaving an increasingly implausible tale; when he finished, he looked up, and found the Masters staring as if some bizarre insect had fluttered into the hall and alighted on the table.

A heavy silence settled – the type of silence that descends on a battlefield when the final blow has been struck.

At last, Rymise said, 'That is your story, General?'

'It is,' replied Standaire.

Nodding, Rymise exhaled a tremulous breath. 'Very well. Blessed Master Faltriste, are you able to give your account? Have you recovered from your ill treatment?'

'Recovered? I doubt that I will ever be the same again. My brethren,' he looked around the table, 'this evening I have learned much about tragedy. I have discovered, too, the high price of loyalty. As you will know, the general has served the Church well over the years. About that, there is no dispute. But the man sitting before you is no longer the general. The man I knew – we *all* knew – was courageous, steadfast and dedicated. But this poor soul, he is merely what remains of that great man. He is suffering from battleshock. You are familiar with the term, I trust?'

A few Masters nodded. Most remained motionless.

Faltriste sighed; it was as if he was exhaling his very soul. 'Battleshock is a malady that our physicians have recognised only recently. Its precise mechanisms are unknown, but the affliction is essentially this: if a fellow, such as a soldier, witnesses or partakes in violent, bloody actions, he can, over time, grow a little mad. We have all experienced this in a small form, in our daily lives. We receive news, say, that knocks us off kilter.

565

If a loved one dies unexpectedly, we feel unmoored, do we not? The world strikes us as strange and alien. Naturally, we recover; we get our bearings, and carry on as before. But in extreme cases, it is not so: the madness lingers, and the sufferer descends into delusions and paranoia. His thoughts are habitually irrational, his sense of reason deserts him; his mind is akin to a spinning-wheel firework that slips its nail, tumbles to the ground and whirls crazily in the grass, spitting sparks in every direction. In here,' he tapped his head, 'there is naught but chaos. It is sad, very sad.'

'To be clear,' said Rymise, 'you are suggesting the general has lost his wits?'

'I believe so,' replied Faltriste, nodding gravely. 'I should say that battleshock rarely occurs instantaneously. Often it takes months, even years. It is a process of erosion, decay and gradual decline. The sufferer does not *fall* into madness, as if it were a hole; he *goes* mad, as if he is walking a long, unhappy path.'

'With respect,' said Rymise, mildly, 'the general does not strike me as mad. His tale is . . . *elaborate*, shall we say. But his demeanour is not that of a lunatic.'

'The afflicted do not always rave, jabber and chew their wrists,' said Faltriste. 'And you did not see him earlier this evening.'

'Yes, the business in the sewer,' said Rymise. 'I assume you deny Standaire's account?'

'Just as I would deny a heresy,' replied Faltriste. 'I shall tell you exactly what occurred. First, though, I should say that I cannot counter the general's claims about this cave he calls the Origin, or the continuing survival of Jurel Kraike, or the nonsense about this Toros character. How does one refute a story that comes out of nowhere? That falls from the sky without warning? There was no meeting at the war memorial. Nor do I believe that Helligraine lives. This part of the tale is a bolt from the blue. My involvement with the general begins this evening.

'Two Papal Guards, Dexler and Heron – loyal men, who often guard my door at night – were drinking in The Grinning Dog, a tavern popular amongst our sworn protectors. There they spotted the general, seated alone in a corner. Wishing to provide good company, they introduced themselves as former military men and, with the general's blessing, joined him at his table. They hoped to parley with this man they admired, to banter and crack the rough jokes favoured by fighting men. Alas, they became aware that all was not well. The general was not only drunk – surely you can smell the whisky on his breath? – but rambling incoherently, as he has, in a calmer fashion, rambled to us just now. He spoke of conspiracies, long-dead visionaries, sorcerers and Vohoria.

'Dexler and Heron realised his wits were addled by something worse than liquor. They decided to seek help. Gently, they removed the general from the tavern, intending to take him to a physician. Outside, however, the general grew violent – and a violent Hawk is something to be feared. They subdued him, forcibly; at a loss what to do next, they hid him in the sewers, tying him up as if he was a wild beast. As the general struggled against his bonds, they were hit by another fear: what if he had harmed someone during the evening? What if, in his madness, he had killed? The bond between military men is strong. They did not wish to see the general punished for crimes committed whilst insane.

'So, they returned to the Sacros and knocked on my door. They explained what had come to pass and I, long an admirer of the general, went to the sewers. I attempted to placate him, not without success; I suspected that battleshock comes and goes in waves, and I encountered him when the tide was out.

'But the mad can be cunning, too. What I did not know,

or even suspect, was that he had sent a letter to the Roost, demanding assistance. So it was that two other Hawks appeared in the sewer, slayed Dexler and Heron, and abducted me.' He raised a hand. 'I insist those men are not punished. Unaware that the general was unwell, they acted in good faith. Where are they now?'

'In a cell,' replied Rymise.

'Release them,' said Faltriste. 'Or treat them well, whilst they are there. They do not deserve what has befallen them. If required, I will personally grant them a dispensation.' He rubbed his face. 'And that is it, my brethren. There is nothing more that I can tell you.'

Rymise grew thoughtful. 'I have a question, if I may.'

'Of course,' said Faltriste. 'Speak on.'

'Did you leave the Sacros through the tunnels, as the general claimed? He said his Hawks were posted at the exits, awaiting your emergence.'

Faltriste nodded, gravely. 'I did use the tunnels,' he said. 'As for the general's prediction that I should do so . . . It is a remarkable coincidence. Or perhaps not: when a fellow is paranoid, he assumes his persecutors live by the laws of secrecy, and conduct their business in the shadows. It is natural for the general, who knows of the tunnels, to assume that I would use them rather than walk out through the gates, where all could see.'

'Why *did* you avoid the gates?'

'It was for the general's sake,' replied Faltriste, smoothly. 'I did not want anyone to discover where I was going, for I wanted no one to know of the low ebb to which our friend has fallen. You must remember that I, like you, had been woken abruptly from deep sleep. Under such conditions, one rarely thinks clearly. Secrecy was at the forefront of my mind. *No one must know of the general's straits* – this phrase circulated in my head, endlessly.

568

Consequently, I became a touch obsessed. Maybe using the tunnels was a little extreme, but at the time, it made sense.'

Rymise nodded, satisfied. 'And this is your account in its entirety?'

'It is,' said Faltriste.

'Is there anything you wish to add?'

'Only that which I am certain we have all observed,' said Faltriste, sadly. 'When a good man suffers cataclysmic misfortune, we ask, "What has the poor soul done to deserve *this*?" The answer is always, *Nothing*. This is not true in Standaire's case. He brought his fate upon himself. How? By serving the Church. On the battlefield, and during missions as a Hawk, he has seen sights that no man should rightly see. He has waded through blood, heard the screams of the dying, and gazed clear-eyed into the darkness of the human soul. For the sake of the divine, he has fought the unholy; for the sake of goodness, he has struck hard against evil. His sickness has arisen in a way no sickness should: it has grown, like some poisonous fruit, from the rich soil of virtue. The general is a good man; he is, I daresay, the best of men. Thus, I am loath to see him punished. Yes, little of the old general remains. But what are we to do with what is left? Instinctively, I do not want him to be punished, even though his crimes are grave. Would the Four say that the afflicted must be condemned for their afflictions? No, they would not.

'I suggest that, for his own sake, the general is incarcerated, and a physician with knowledge of battleshock is sent to his aid. Maybe he can recover, with the proper treatment. If he cannot, at least we can say we did what we could.'

He looked round the table.

'Is this not the wisest course of action?'

The Masters murmured their agreement.

'Let us not decide hastily,' said Rymise. 'Outside, it is still dark, and resolutions are best reached when the sun is up, and the world is light. I propose that we follow the first part of Faltriste's plan: namely, the general is imprisoned.' He looked directly at Standaire. 'Do not consider this an act of judgement,' he said. 'It is a temporary measure, until we determine how best to proceed. Guards,' he gestured to a pair of liveried guardsmen, 'escort the general to the nineteenth cell. See that he is given food and water, if he should need it.' A sly light flickered in the Master's eyes. 'If the Sacros alchemist is awake, instruct him to brew an infusion that will lessen the effects of alcohol.'

The guards moved uncertainly toward Standaire. Without resisting, he stood and allowed himself to be taken away.

'A tragic turn of events,' said Rymise as Faltriste rose from his chair.

'Indeed,' replied Faltriste. 'To gaze upon the general and feel pity, as if he were a stray dog, shivering in a gutter . . . This is a sorrowful day for the Church.'

'The documents Standaire brought from the sewer—'

'His military record? And Daylight's observations?'

'How did you obtain them?'

'I went to the Records Chamber,' said Faltriste, nonplussed. 'That is where they are kept.'

'What purpose did they serve?'

Faltriste thought quickly. 'I thought it wise to learn as much about the general as I could, before we met. Although battleshock is generally caused by the accumulation of bad experiences, it can be induced by specific events. I wondered if the root of Standaire's, ah, *difficulties* lay within a certain incident. The more I knew, the better equipped I was to deal with that poor man.'

'Ah, yes,' said Rymise, smiling. 'That makes perfect sense. Do you have any pressing duties?'

'I will have to speak with my aide to be certain, but I do not believe so.'

'Then I advise you to rest. I cannot imagine how deeply this sorry affair must have struck you.'

'Oh, I have weathered worse storms,' said Faltriste, philosophically.

Leaving the hall, he set off for his bed chamber. He was grateful Rymise had led proceedings. In his younger days, the Master had had a reputation for incisiveness and determination. Now age had eroded his talents, extinguished his fire. He did not continue living because he loved life; he lived because it had become a habit. His passion was gone. He had not entered dotage, in the medical sense. But he had slipped into something similar. He was intellectually listless; his curiosity was non-existent. He had turned from a man into a scarecrow, with a head full of straw, watching the world drift by.

In his chamber, Faltriste sat by the window. Dawn was breaking. As the light poured through the window, he took stock.

He had wondered whether Standaire would eventually discover the *real* purpose of the mission to rescue Helligraine. Although unlikely, he had never ruled it out. And it had never troubled him. He had foreseen that if the general learned the truth, he would disclose it to the Masters – and they would not believe a word of it. The general had no idea how easily manipulated they were, those scarlet-clad geriatrics, how effortlessly Faltriste could bend them to his will.

It changed nothing. As he had always planned, Faltriste would leave the Sacros in two days' time, and set sail for Vohoria. There, he would journey to the Solrepta. Would Toros be resurrected by then? Certainly. Perhaps he had already been released from his millennia-long confinement in the Forest.

And then?

His loyalty to Toros would be repaid. He could not say exactly how. But this was a trifling point: those who had power, or were faithful to the powerful, always stood to gain. And those who opposed the powerful – they perished.

And Toros was – would be – powerful . . .

He yawned, baring his teeth like a cat. Fatigue washed over him; it had been a long night. He allowed himself the luxury of slipping into a doze.

He was woken by a knock on the door.

Groggily, he crossed the chamber and answered. A guard named Furrien stood outside, a large fellow, whose thick-featured face always reminded Faltriste of a donkey. A pale scar indented his forehead. A war wound, no doubt.

'Is it true, your holiness? About Heron and Dexler?' asked Furrien.

Furrien was one of Faltriste's corrupt guards. Every week, he was paid a small, secret salary to run errands on the Master's behalf. Like Heron, Dexler and numerous others, he was a venal, self-serving idiot. 'So what if it is? Do you intend to mourn them?'

Furrien swallowed. 'I am fearful, your holiness.'

'Of what?'

'That our secret . . . arrangement will be discovered.'

Faltriste laughed, disdainfully. 'There is no danger – as long as you keep your mouth shut.' He started to close the door. Incredibly, Furrien wedged it open with his foot.

'I overheard . . . I listened when you were in the Seventh Hall. I heard it all.'

Faltriste frowned. 'Playing the cunning fox were you, Furrien?'

'I do not think Rymise believed you,' said Furrien, unperturbed. 'I saw him heading to the cells. I think . . . I believe he intends to speak in private with Standaire. He and an aide discussed summoning a Law Sage. What use would a Sage be, but to extricate Standaire from the charges laid against him? Then the aide departed, and Rymise carried on toward the cells.'

'When was this?' Faltriste's face grew hot.

'Not long ago,' replied Furrien. 'I came here straight away. I did not—'

Ignoring him, Faltriste left his chamber and strode along the corridor, fighting the urge to run.

Standaire sat on the floor of a cell, far beneath the Sacros. He felt the bulk of the ancient edifice above him, as heavy as tradition; he wondered if the cell's usual inhabitants felt it too – the heretics, apostates and magickers who normally occupied the lightless, stone-walled space. If any were present, he could have asked them. But he was alone.

He had passed beyond rage, frustration, the bitterness of betrayal. In body and mind, he was numb. He sat in the darkness like a limpet at low tide, sentient yet unmoving.

A key twisted in a lock; a bar was lifted.

The door opened, and Blessed Master Rymise stepped through. He carried a lantern, its light falling on the filth-crusted walls and floor. Cockroaches scattered, pouring into cracks between the stones. A rat scritched, scampering into a corner.

'General,' said Rymise, closing the door.

'Your holiness.' Standaire squinted; although painful, the light roused him from his inertia. He wondered if he should kneel before the holy man. He decided against it. 'I did not expect a visitor.'

'I expect you did not expect to be diagnosed with battleshock, either.'

'No more than a bull expects to be told it is carrying a calf,' replied Standaire. A hint of sourness in his voice. 'Forgive me. I intended no disrespect.'

'You are only human. But the question is, are you also a *sick* human? The battleshock – speak honestly: are you afflicted?'

'Would you have come here unaccompanied if you thought I was?'

'If I was seeking excitement, perhaps.'

Standaire smiled, thinly. 'You are perfectly safe.'

'I thought as much.' Bending, Rymise put the lantern on the floor. 'I am in a quandary, General. I must decide between two competing accounts of the same event. Neither, if I am honest, is terribly plausible.'

'Travel to Brellerin Fell,' said Standaire. 'You will see the Origin. Go to Prendle House, and you will find it burned to the ground.'

'Yes, yes,' said Rymise. 'And then what? It proves nothing. Faltriste will say you set light to the house whilst affected by battleshock. You were pursuing one of your delusions. As for the Origin – he will not deny it exists. How could he? But he will claim he had nothing to do with its discovery.'

'Faltriste spoke of Daylight,' said Standaire. 'Does this hidden aspect of the Church exist?'

'It does,' said Rymise.

'Send them to Sliptere. And the village we called Whitelock. Instruct them to discover what came to pass.'

'Again, Faltriste will devise a story that will clear him of involvement,' said Rymise, 'whilst placing responsibility on your shoulders. One thing you must understand about the Church, General: affairs between the Masters are conducted like a game of chess. There are certain moves we may use, particular tactics we can employ. Like any game, there are rules; if those rules are ignored, the game collapses. If I am to act against Faltriste, I require evidence – evidence that cannot be refuted.'

'Blessed Master Rymise,' said Standaire, 'are you—?'

'Taking your side?' A hollow laugh. 'No, General. It is not a question of taking sides, but discovering the truth. If what you say is true, we may soon be at war with Vohoria. A Vohoria led by a sorcerer of immeasurable power. Thus, it would be to our benefit if we were to pre-empt their attack. Our warships could be sailing by noon; within a week, we could be fighting the Vohorin on their home soil. If Faltriste is telling the truth, however, we have nothing to worry about.'

'I understand,' said Standaire. 'Your burdens are heavy—'

'On the contrary, our burdens are light, once they are upon our shoulders,' replied Rymise. 'When we know the correct course of action, no matter how bloody, we proceed with a clean conscience. But what is the right course? Therein lies the problem.' He stared at his hands. 'In the Church's employ, there is a Scythe named Cordis. Day after day, he extracts truth from our prisoners. As an interrogator, he is unrivalled. He has served us nearly thirty years and during that time has given considerable thought to the nature of truth. Early on in his career, he recognised that truth does not exist. It is not something that can be touched, smelled, or captured; it is a perception, existing nowhere except in the mind. He observed – and this is vital to his craft – that these perceptions alter a man's behaviour. An expression of guilt, a nervous twitch – these betray truths one wishes to keep hidden. This principle extends to one's behaviour. We—'

He was interrupted by a light knock at the door.

'Enter,' he said.

A guard stepped through, a balding, heavyset man with a scarred forehead. His face was flushed pink and he was sweating. 'It is done, your holiness,' he said, nervously. 'The Master is going to the Room.'

'Good. Return to your station,' said Rymise, a trace of distaste in his voice. 'Speak of this to no one.'

'Yes, your holiness,' bowed the guard. 'It shall be so, in this as in all things.'

'Begone,' muttered Rymise, and the guard departed.

Standaire stared quizzically at Rymise.

'There is no time for explanations.' He pulled a folded parchment from behind his belt. 'Cordis says that if you pour strong liquor on pork, any worms hidden within the meat are forced to the surface. They emerge, wriggling and writhing, trying to escape the astringent fluid. So it is with truth. With secrets. They emerge when stimulated by something unpleasant, be it hot irons, or the fear of discovery.' He handed the parchment to Standaire. Written on it was what appeared to be a play actor's script. Moving close to the lantern, Standaire saw the dialogue was little more than a series of prompts, mere guides as to what should be said, rather than the words themselves.

'It is not by chance you are incarcerated in this nineteenth cell,' said Rymise, pointing upwards. 'In the ceiling, there is a small stone chute, designed to amplify every word uttered by a prisoner. The faintest whisper can be heard overhead, in the Eavesdropper's Room. In a few moments Faltriste will arrive, and listen.' He flicked a finger toward the script. 'It is hardly a work of genius; I am no Sharrakas, or Marraine. But it will suffice.'

Standaire gazed at the script. 'And then?'

'We shall see,' said Rymise.

Faltriste entered the Eavesdropping Room. A brass tube protruded from the wall, flaring like a trumpet. It was connected to a pipe of the same alloy that burrowed through the stonework, designed to catch and magnify noises in the nineteenth cell. It was a magnificent device; over the years, it had enabled the Church's servants to overhear the conversations of countless prisoners, effectively acquiring confessions – and information – without the effort of interrogation.

As he settled on a stool near the earpiece, he heard Rymise's voice, whispering out of the tube. Rasping and echoing, it had an unsettling effect; it sounded like a dead man speaking across the veil.

The first words were nonsensical – some blather about Druine's most famous playwrights. Then, 'You do not seem battleshocked, General. But then, I am not an expert.'

Faltriste leaned close to the earpiece.

'I am as sane as you are, Blessed Master Rymise,' came Standaire's voice.

'I am sure every asylum inmate would give the same reply. You must understand my position, General. You have made incredible claims without providing proof. This thing you call the Origin, the torching of Prendle House—'

'Send riders,' said Standaire. 'They will report that all is as I say.'

'The matter is in hand,' replied Rymise.

A long pause. Faltriste bent so close to the earpiece, the brass touched his cheek.

'You are trembling, General. Are you fearful? If you have spoken the truth, you need not fear. You will be dealt with according to the proper procedures.'

'And what of the *improper* ones? Those arising not from the Church, but its servants.'

'What are you speaking of?'

'Do you not consider it strange,' said Standaire, 'that a pair of Papal Guards should wake a Blessed Master hours before dawn, to solicit help? That they should bang on his door and tear him from sleep?'

'They understood the delicacy of the situation,' replied Rymise. 'They acted as they thought best.'

Standaire laughed, bitterly; the sound rose from the earpiece like a serpent's hiss. 'Surely you can see this is not normal? Surely you can see it suggests . . .'

'Yes?'

'Dexler and Heron did not wake Faltriste because the situation was *delicate*, but because it was *serious*. They knew my return would cause Faltriste problems. That he would *want* to be woken, so *he* could deal with me.'

'This speculation—'

'If Dexler and Heron were corrupt, there will be others.'

'Others?'

'Other guards,' said Standaire. 'Those men outside my cell – what is to say they are not secretly allied to Faltriste? And when the moment comes, they will slip in and kill me. You do not know whether I or Faltriste is telling the truth. I can understand your predicament, your holiness. But if I am the honest one, I could be in grave peril. You must do something. Station your own guards outside the cell. Men you can trust, if not with your own life, but mine.'

'Very well,' said Rymise. 'I shall do as you ask, if only to prove that I am keeping an open mind. But we shall know, soon enough, whether or not you are, as you say, the honest one.'

Another bitter laugh. 'It will take days for your riders to travel to and from the Origin, and the House.'

'That is so,' replied Rymise. 'But there are no riders. An aide reminded me that we have agents close to both locations. We have dispatched messenger birds, instructing them to visit the places you mentioned. They will notify us of their discoveries by bird, too. Which means we will have an answer by this afternoon, or dusk at the latest.'

Faltriste jerked away from the earpiece.

This afternoon? It was too soon. He rose, or tried to: his

body had grown heavy. Bracing a hand against the wall, he forced himself onto his feet. For the first time in years, he felt every one of his eighty-three years. Despair rushed through him like a flash flood. He half stumbled to the door, then leaned against the frame.

Be calm, he told himself. All is not lost. He stood motionless, breathing heavily, yet shallowly. He wondered if he might suffer a heart attack. Wouldn't that be an inglorious end to his plans? Undone not by fate, or his enemies, but panic so severe it gripped his internal workings, and broke them? He would only have himself to blame. Did he not pride himself on his cool-headedness? His ability to be ice in a world of fire? To lose those traits, acquired through effort, maintained by habit, would be an act of will – the willing abandonment of the very qualities he needed most.

In a matter of hours, his secrets would be discovered. Certainly, they would not be fully exposed: he was confident he could convincingly feign ignorance of the Origin, and the blaze at Prendle House. But it would not be enough. The mere existence of the Origin would cause suspicion amongst the Masters; even straw-headed Rymise would raise an eyebrow. Is the general's story so implausible after all? they would wonder. And then, like dogs seeking buried bones, they would start to *dig* . . .

Damn it! Maybe the digging had already started. What if Rymise, spurred on by Standaire's words, was questioning the Papal Guards, trying to ascertain which were loyal to the Church, and which had a secret allegiance with a certain Master who, at this instant, stood in the Eavesdropping Room, trembling, tasting bile?

Faltriste hastened to his chamber.

Furrien stood sentry, his mule's face pale, his gaze lowered. Was he ill? Tired? Hiding something?

'Have you been spoken to?' demanded Faltriste, seizing his shoulders.

'Spoken to?'

'By Rymise, or any of the others?'

'Others?'

'The Masters!'

'No,' replied Furrien, baffled.

'Then why has the blood gone from your face? Why are you staring abjectly at the floor? You look *guilty*.'

'I look *sad*,' said Furrien, with a hint of defiance. 'Heron and Dexler were my friends. Now, they are gone. They were good men yet they died . . . they died in a bloody sewer, as if they were rats. It isn't right. What will their families be told? Heron had a boy-child, six years old. He will—'

Leaving Furrien mid-sentence, Faltriste went into his chamber. Shutting the door, he paced to the window and looked out, hoping the sight of the blue sky and bright sun would ease his tension. It did not. Nor should it, Faltriste realised. Although this was not a time for panic, it was not a time for meditative slowness, either. He had to act, and act quickly.

He opened a drawer in his writing desk. Removing the false bottom, he drew out several bags of gold and silver. With these, he would purchase a horse and ride to Bluecurl Harbour, on the eastern side of Druine. There, he would bribe a fisherman to ferry him to Vohoria. Most fishermen would be reluctant to enter foreign waters, he knew. But a gold piece would change that, and within days, he would be out of the Church's reach.

Stripping, he laid his scarlet robes on the bed. From a clothes chest he took a pair of leggings, a vest and tabard, which he donned swiftly, hanging the bags of money from his belt. Then he dressed into the robes, pulling the heavy scarlet garments over the ordinary attire beneath.

Leaving the chamber, he hurried through the Sacros corridors and descended a flight of steps into a courtyard. The sun clashed into his vision; he squinted, dazzled. Although it was early, the day was barbarously hot, and he wished he had brought a flask of water.

I will survive, he thought, pacing toward the Sacros's private chapel.

Inside, the holy building was deserted. His footsteps echoed as he strode past the chancel, opened a small door, picked up a lantern left burning overnight, and descended into the ossuary. He moved between stone caskets containing the bones of several hundred years' worth of Masters – and, of course, an unidentified vagrant who had been murdered, clad in Helligraine's robes, and dumped in the Blackstyre River.

At the far wall, he shifted a heap of sackcloth, exposing another door. He opened it. A gust of stagnant air rolled into his face; he coughed.

How long since this tunnel was used? Or even inspected? One century? Two? Longer, perhaps. Unlike the other tunnels, including the one he had used to meet Standaire at the war memorial, this tunnel was deemed structurally unsound. If some cataclysm befell the Sacros and the Masters needed to escape, other tunnels would be used. Nonetheless, it suited Faltriste's purposes. The longest of the tunnels, it emerged *outside* the city walls, on moorland three miles from Barrowdown Town. It was there Faltriste would buy a horse and within three days he would be at Bluecurl.

Removing his robes, dumping them just inside the tunnel mouth, he stepped through and got moving.

Some men were born corrupt, Rymise knew. Others were driven toward it, for various reasons. Guard Furrien belonged to the latter category. He did not strike Rymise as innately evil, or wicked. Somehow, though, he had fallen under Faltriste's control. Why? Money? A childish desire to be trusted by someone of power and status? Maybe he had merely copied his fellow guards, joining in out of feelings of camaraderie. Perhaps he imagined it was wiser to be Faltriste's accomplice than enemy.

Whatever; listening in on the proceedings in the Seventh Hall, he had undergone a change of heart. No doubt, this at least was self-serving: fearing that Faltriste was cornered, his secret plots and schemes poised to come crashing down, he had told Rymise of his involvement, meagre though it was: he had been an errand boy, delivering messages, nothing more; he knew nothing of the Origin, or Helligraine, or Vohoria. He had begged for clemency, even if it meant being stripped of his position; he vowed, even, to become a monk in exchange for mercy.

Rymise told him he had to *earn* forgiveness; a few frightened promises were not enough.

If you were a dog, Rymise had said, *I might be beguiled by your subservient gestures. But you are a man, who has broken his oath, and I do not care if you roll on your back and show your belly to the world.*

To his credit, Furrien had done everything asked of him, although it did not amount to much: he had told Faltriste that he, Rymise, was heading to the nineteenth cell for a secret discussion with Standaire.

Had the Master taken the bait? Had he eavesdropped, and gulped Rymise's lies about agents and messenger birds?

Rymise shuffled along the corridor to Faltriste's chamber. As he approached, Furrien stood to attention. His long, pack animal's face wore an expression of excess reverence, as if to prove he had truly seen the error of his ways, and would never again tread the path of evil.

'Well?' asked Rymise, plainly.

'It worked, your holiness,' said Furrien. 'Blessed Master Faltriste went to the Eavesdropping Room, as you predicted.'

'And then?'

'He returned to his chamber for a short time, then departed. I followed him to the chapel, then into the ossuary. He changed into ordinary clothes then slipped out through a hole in the wall . . . A tunnel, I think.'

Rymise nodded. 'Is it not better to serve the Church than its enemies?'

'Infinitely so, your holiness,' said Furrien.

Before they learned of the Forest, various ancient cultures had their own, differing versions of a hellish afterlife. The M'urathi imagined it was a gigantic cobweb, populated by tiny spiders, who chewed the flesh of a sinner's body for all eternity; the Luranthe considered it to be a colossal throat, down which a sinner was being swallowed in perpetuity, forever travelling onward, yet making no progress.

As far as Faltriste was concerned, the tunnel manifested the defining features of both these faulty renderings of the ever-after. From the M'urathi, it took the cobwebs, hanging in thick sticky drapes from the ceiling, and spreading like veils from one side to the other. Faltriste could not take a step without crackling through the gathered strands; with every footfall, he seemed to wind himself into a ragged, suffocating cocoon. As for the Luranthe – what was the tunnel but a kind of throat? One seeming to go on for ever?

Countless times, Faltriste thought, I could die here, and no one would ever know . . .

No one except for the spiders.

Yet he pressed on. When his lantern expired, he did not curse; when blisters formed inside his boots, he did not flinch. As heat gathered in the tunnel, turning the air into barely breathable syrup, he plodded on, telling himself, Soon this will be over. Within an hour or two, I will be breathing

583

fresh moorland air and after that, the tingling salt air of the ocean . . .

He thought of the moors. Of flowing springwater. He was thirstier than he had ever been, thirstier – he imagined – than Helligraine must have been when wandering the Skravian Desert.

He gave a thin, dry-lipped smile.

Cavielle Shaelus – would he know that he had been tricked by now? That his quest was not entirely as he believed? What about Quarvis? It would not surprise him if the sickly, and sickening, runt had not survived the sea crossing to Vohoria.

Through the dense heat came a coolness, a grass-fragranced breeze. Ahead, Faltriste discerned a speck of light.

'Praise the Four,' he murmured, then laughed. *That* was a habit he would have to break.

He picked up his pace. The speck of light grew into a blot, then a clear view of sky, grass and grey boulders.

He wanted to run. With freedom so near, the tunnel grew a hundred times more claustrophobic. He had walked ten miles, maybe more. How had he endured it for so long? How had he survived a distillation of two distinct, primitive hells, without losing his mind?

He sped up, the money bags clinking softly—

—and he was out, in the cheerful glare of the sun, surrounded by rolling moorland. In the distance, sheep grazed, oblivious to everything except the grass blades beneath their soft-lipped mouths. A solitary buzzard glided overhead and, not far away, three riderless horses were tied to a rowan tree.

Horses? thought Faltriste, surprised.

'Some people consider it perverse,' came a voice, 'but on a hot day, I find nothing refreshes me more than a drop of whisky. Would you have any to spare?'

Faltriste whirled. Two men stood a few yards back from the tunnel, hands on hips, grinning.

584

Bandits? thought Faltriste, stupidly.

Then he recognised them as the Hawks who had killed Dexler and Heron.

'Three horses,' said one, pointing toward the mounts. 'Two for us, one for you. I hope you've enjoyed your stroll. Now it is time to return to the Sacros.'

Chapter Twenty-one

Dear friends,

I do not believe our journey will last much longer; at most, our destination is several days away.

We encountered a group of huntsmen, who are also Erethin. They greeted Lujaek warmly, in the manner of old friends. They spoke for a while, and when they referred to Selindak, they used his proper name and not Maritus, the pseudonym he adopted in the desert, and by which he is known throughout Vohoria. This led me to believe there is a hierarchy within the Torosian faith. At the highest point, there is Selindak. Then there is his inner circle, who share much of his knowledge. Lower down, there are High Erethin, granted access to the Doctrines, and beneath them, Erethin of ordinary rank. Lujaek, clearly, is part of the inner circle; I suspect he was sent to the Origin not only to break the stones, but to keep an eye on his fellow labourers, and me.

Believe it or not, I have found a use for Leptus Quarvis. The vainglorious little fool is so puffed up with pride he cannot resist showing off his knowledge. This knowledge is virtually non-existent but, when I ask a question, he scuttles off to Lujaek and asks it as if it is his own. Then he returns, and tells me what I wanted to know.

When I asked about our destination, he spoke to Lujaek, then revealed the following: it is a temple, of sorts, populated by Erethin. It resides in the forest's heart, which is vital, for woodland is the habitat Toros has grown accustomed to, and if he were reborn into somewhere different, a city say, the shock may be deleterious to his health, possibly fatal.

This latter point turned my thoughts to Shalfrazen. No doubt you have read his works, Ekkerlin: he wrote extensively about the perils of necromancy. His *Treacherous Returns* is the finest book on the subject. I think – or fear – it may have a bearing on the events which await us.

I must go now. It is late, I need to sleep, and the longer I write the greater the chances of my subterfuge being discovered.

It is the sixth day of the seventh month.

CS.

'We are gaining ground,' said Ballas. 'Shaelus was here yesterday.'

It was late afternoon. Beyond the forest, the sun blazed with fierce intensity. Despite the shade provided by the leaf canopy, Ballas was sweltering. He was also exhausted. Ekkerlin had intellectual matters to keep her lively. What did he have? Nothing. Despite its seriousness, the journey had grown boring. And with boredom came fatigue.

'Shalfrazen,' said Ekkerlin. 'I have read his book. He studied necromancy, not as a practitioner, but a scholar. His works are forbidden by the Church, although I understand they very nearly *weren't*: he paints a dark picture of the practice, and dwells at length on the dangers. He claimed the chances of a necromancer being successful were vanishingly small – the same, he said, as surviving an avalanche only to be struck by a lightning bolt.'

'What are you saying? There isn't a hope of Toros being resurrected? And everything Shaelus and Kraike have striven for was doomed from the start?'

'Shalfrazen said successes were rare,' replied Ekkerlin. 'But not unknown. When the process went wrong, though, the consequences were . . . interesting.'

'You've got a corpse, you say some spells, and at the end you've still got a corpse,' said Ballas. '*Ordinary* folk wouldn't consider that interesting. Just disappointing.'

'That is true,' countered Ekkerlin. 'But there are different types of failure associated with necromancy. Sometimes, as you say, nothing happens at all, because the necromancer lacks magical abilities. On other occasions, when the necromancer *does* have some talent, the outcome can be wildly unexpected.

'Consider what necromancy consists of,' she went on, as they started walking. 'There is a corpse in this world and a soul in the next. The objective is to transport the soul back into the body, reanimating it. To do so, a gateway must be opened, however fleetingly, between this realm and the afterlife – namely, the Forest. But there are difficulties.

'First, there is a danger that the soul which enters the body is not the one you were expecting. Think of it, Anhaga: if you are trapped in the afterlife, tormented by demons, and an exit appears . . . What would you do, but rush through?' She laughed, softly. 'Do you recall that time we passed a bakery in Thrilmuster, and you were hungry? Through the window you saw that there was only one pie left, resting on a shelf, and you hurtled through the front door, knocking folk aside, as if your life depended on it. It is the same principle.'

Ballas grunted.

'Then, there is another problem. What if the right soul finds its way into the correct body, but has been transformed by its time in the afterlife? What if its personality has been altered? It might have become a pious soul, grateful to be alive, and seeing wonder in all things. Equally, the goodness may have been ripped out of it by the demons, and all that remains is a cruel, corrupted individual, intent on doing others harm.

'These are the lesser problems,' said Ekkerlin. 'There is one other, which Shalfrazen considered much more serious.

'Human souls are not the only entities that want to escape the Forest; the demons are also keen to get out. Thus, when the gateway opens, they too attempt to rush through – and the consequences are even worse than you barging into a pie shop. Sometimes, they emerge as immaterial entities, visible only in glimpses, yet capable of great harm. Other times, they enter the corpse of whoever was to be necromanced – and it needs not be that one demon occupies one body; rather, a host of demons can find a home in a single person, and there ensues a struggle for supremacy. Asylums are full of people who appear to have numerous personalities, and switch from one to another without rhyme or reason.

'Lastly, a demon, freshly arrived, may occupy the flesh of someone wholly unconnected with the necromantic ritual. It may wander our world, looking for a suitable host. And when it finds one . . . In or out of the Forest, a demon is a demon. Its impulses are the same, and its behaviour.'

'So Kraike's scheme could end in failure?' asked Ballas.

'*Anything* can end in failure,' said Ekkerlin. 'But I can't believe that Kraike won't have taken the dangers into account. Remember, he has acquired his powers from the Origin – and therefore, Toros himself.' She took the letter from Ballas, looked it over. 'This is an unusual situation, for two reasons. First, it is rare for one sorcerer to resurrect another. Second, it is rarer still for the dead soul to know exactly what the resurrection will entail. As he devised the spell, Toros will know what to expect. This will limit the possibilities of the process going wrong.'

They carried on walking. The day lengthened.

CHAPTER TWENTY-TWO

'Have you ever observed a Scythe at work?' asked Blessed Master Rymise.

Standaire peered through an iron grille. Beyond, there was a circular chamber, the walls red stone. Braziers burned, filling the enclosed space with warm, smoky air. Implements of various kinds lay upon shelves and tables, and nestled inside cabinets. A long table teemed with jars of assorted liquids, some colourless, others as garish as the plumage of an exotic bird. A wooden bench, similar to a surgeon's, stood in the centre of the floor. Upon it lay an old man, held in place by leather straps encircling his wrists, ankles, throat and waist.

Faltriste.

He was naked, his decrepitude clearly visible. His skin was yellowish white, like bacon rind on the turn. His ribs jutted like a famine victim's; veins traced his arms and legs, pale and sunken, as if dry of blood. His exposed genitals were small and shrivelled; they made Standaire think of some unwholesome mollusc prised from its shell. The Master stared at the ceiling, eyes blank. He appeared to be in a world of his own. But this could not be the case. He had a rough idea of what lay ahead, and was trying not to think about it.

'No,' said Standaire, answering Rymise's question.

'You will have seen dreadful things on the battlefield,' said Rymise. 'None shall compare to this.'

The door opened. A little man scuttered through, garbed in black. He had a chubby, cheerful face, rosy cheeked and smiling. He looked like a friendly local butcher.

'This will be a novel experience,' he told Faltriste, as he closed the door. 'I have never interrogated a Master before. If you speak willingly, I promise your suffering will be minimal.' He took a leather apron from a hook. 'Do not attempt to deceive me,' he said, donning the garment. 'I have plied this trade since I was a young man. Started, yes, nearly thirty years ago. I know a lie when I hear it.'

He tied the apron strings behind his back then cracked his knuckles.

'Normally, I like to take my time. But I am told that on this occasion, I must hurry. If you care to turn your head sideways, you will – if your eyesight is good – be able to see the general on the other side of the grille. Aided by Master Rymise, he will guide the interrogation; the questions I ask will be his, not mine.' He patted Faltriste's shoulder. 'Understand that everything that follows is not personal. Not on my part, at least. We all have our jobs to do, is that not so?' A warm-hearted chuckle. 'Mine is not to reason why; mine is but to do or . . . Well, do whatever I must, to extract the truth. Oh – do not think that, as an old man, you can avoid confessing by dropping dead on me. Not a chance! I am very, *very* good at keeping my patients alive. Only in the rarest of cases does a fellow perish with his secrets intact; almost always, he dies as a betrayer.'

'Patients? You talk as if you were a doctor,' said Faltriste, voice a croak.

'I was once, as are many in my profession,' said the cheerful little man. 'In foreign countries, any cack-handed bumbler can become an interrogator; they think that all it takes is enthusiasm and a strong stomach. They are wrong. A *true* interrogator

591

is a man of science. He understands how the body and mind work. We have textbooks, printed manuals . . . But you will know all this.'

'I know more than you think,' said Faltriste.

'Oh?'

'Scythe Cordis,' said Faltriste. 'I know you have lied to me. I know my suffering will not be minimal, even if I confess. I know that whatever I say will not satisfy those men behind the grille, and you will torment me with hot irons and acids until you are certain you've wrung out every last drop of information.' A pause; his breath rustled. 'I have seen many interrogations. I know your methods. I find it peculiar that a truth-seeker such as yourself should lie so easily.'

Cordis beamed, his smile as guileless as a puppy's. 'Are you trying to delay the inevitable by engaging me in a debate? Are you trying to stir up a philosophical discussion, so I forget about my duties for a while, and you enjoy a few moments more free of pain? Yes you are, you crafty rascal!' He patted Faltriste's wrist, affectionately. 'I will have to keep an eye on you! As for my lies – well, this is the thing: not long ago, I called you by your proper title. I said, "I have never interrogated a Master before." Do you remember? Now – and this will make you laugh – as soon as I spoke those words, I completely forgot that you are a fellow of high ecclesiastical standing, one who had, indeed, overseen countless interrogations, and knew my techniques like the back of his hand. Whoosh – the notion just fled from my mind! Can you believe it? Gone was the idea that you wear the scarlet and shuffle through the Sacros, doing holy business. I looked at you and saw just another prisoner, strapped to my bench, trying to put on a brave face whilst inside,' he laid a hand flat on Faltriste's chest, 'his heart is going *bop-bop-bop*.' He stepped back from the bench. 'But that is all you are, Faltriste.

592

Another prisoner, with secrets to tell. And I must treat you as such.'

Another chuckle.

'See? You *did* get me talking after all!' He turned his round, red-cheeked face to the grille. 'My apologies, gentlemen. I shall begin forthwith. The Scythe, yes, shall go a-harvesting!'

CHAPTER TWENTY-THREE

My friends,

I have reached a conclusion. In hindsight, it seems glaringly obvious but, given my weariness and anxiety, it would take me a month to notice if you set me on fire.

I have deduced that my mysterious purpose is connected with my past. Namely, it must pertain to something I have done, or seen, or learned.

But what? That is the question, and a tricky one.

As you know, Ekkerlin, I have travelled further than most men, and laid eyes on many wonders, ancient and modern. My brain is stuffed with too much learning, too much knowledge. Admittedly, a certain amount of it is draining away, like wine from a broken pot; this is one of the perils of age. But a good proportion of my memories are intact. And that is the root of the problem: I am finding it impossible to separate what is relevant from what is merely incidental.

Since my last letter, I have pondered the matter deeply. What do I know that could be of use to Toros's resurrection? What do I know, yes, which Kraike is unwilling to ask about? The sorcerer trusts me. A born liar – as well you know – I have concealed my duplicity from him, and he believes that I am entirely loyal to his cause. He knows he merely has to utter the question, and I will reply truthfully. Yet he remains silent.

I have brooded on this matter, and I offer a hypothesis,

Ekkerlin: if you consider it absurd, please do not laugh, for it is the only idea which makes any sense.

I know something without knowing that I know it.

That is to say, I have absorbed knowledge which, although lodged in my memory, I am unable to access.

This is not such a peculiar notion. There are hypnotists who, though often decried as charlatans, can cause their subjects to reveal information they did not know they possessed. Also, certain narcotics have been shown to elicit similar effects.

As Platirus wrote, 'The memory is an attic whose darkness is pierced by a slender shaft of sunlight; most of what we know lies hidden in the gloom beyond that streak of radiance, like a lifetime's accumulated clutter, a neglected horde of childhood toys, mementoes and moth-eaten clothes; but if that light shifted an inch, swathes of our past would be revealed, and we would marvel that they should have ever been forgotten at all.'

I believe that when the time comes, Kraike will shift the light, by some means or other, and I will reveal what he needs to know. Worryingly, as Platirus also observes, this shift involves submitting to an exterior force, such as a hypnotist, or drug, or – yes – a sorcerer.

I ask – no: beg – that you make haste and put an end to this nonsense.

It is the seventh day of the seventh month.

CS.

'He tells us to make haste,' muttered Ballas, 'as if the idea had not occurred to us.'

'He is frightened,' said Ekkerlin, a note of sorrow in her voice.

'And full of self-pity,' said Ballas, sourly. 'He has brought this on himself. He's a spider trapped on its own web.'

'He realises his errors,' said Ekkerlin. Taking the letter from

Ballas, she read it a second time. 'He knows something without knowing that he knows it . . . Strange. Shaelus is astonishingly perceptive. And he remembers – *consciously* remembers – more than most. When he went on his adventures, he never made notes; he always composed his texts from memory alone, once he returned home. So . . .' She frowned. 'You have a good memory, Anhaga. You can glance at a diagram of, say, a building's layout, and it is there, locked away in your head, waiting to be used.'

Momentarily, Ballas was transported back to Silver Hoof, Mallakos's mansion, poring over the map provided by the horse-breeder's cook.

Ekkerlin continued, 'In other ways, though, you are quite forgetful. So, why can you remember some things and not others? Do you remember when you were bed-ridden after a mission? You were bored, so I brought you some philosophy books to read. You absorbed them within a week, and you *understood* them. We discussed them, yes? I confess that you surprised me; I hadn't marked you for a scholar in the making. Yet you forgot every word, every concept, as soon as you were back on your feet. Why was that?'

Ballas shrugged. 'I see no point in philosophy. But a map, if it is needed for a mission—'

'Exactly,' said Ekkerlin. 'You remember only what is useful. And I expect it is the same for Shaelus, to a degree. He primarily paid attention to things that were useful – useful, that is, for a writer of forbidden texts. Now, some text-writers are obsessed with details; their works are little more than catalogues of facts and observations; consequently, they are quite dull. Shaelus's works, however, were incredibly lively. He had the common touch; he sought not only to educate, but entertain. That is why he was derided by many of his more po-faced peers.' She tapped a knuckle against her lips. 'I'd wager that Shaelus's mysterious knowledge is something he did not consider suitable for publication. Not because it was obscene or scandalous – as if that would stop him! – but because it was neither interesting nor exciting.' She nodded. 'If he *had* written it down, maybe Kraike would have no use for him.'

'Any ideas what it could be?'

'Not yet. But I will think on it.'

CHAPTER TWENTY-FOUR

Report by Scythe Ganlain Cordis, concerning the questioning of Blessed Master (as was) Gallaston Rilture Faltriste.

Under extreme coercion, the subject revealed a wealth of information, which is to be found in the nine supplementary documents pertaining to this case.

A crude précis is as follows:

For several years following the Scourge, before rising to the level of Scholar of Outrage, the subject worked in the Unblinking Eye, the intelligence-gathering department of the Church, and forerunner to Daylight, the unit which now tends to such affairs. His role was not that of spy, but spymaster, and analyst of such information as was gathered by those 'in the field'. During this period he was privy to many secrets, including those connected with the Vohorin invasion. He disclosed that he has always been attracted to power and understandably, the plague spell wielded by Jurel Kraike caught his attention. He deduced that the possession of such a spell, even though it failed to serve its ultimate purpose (the conquest of Druine) on this occasion, would in the long term bear fruit, and the Vohorin, though exiled in the Skravian Desert, would eventually become a governing force whose power encompassed much, if not all, of the globe.

Using the spies at his disposal, he communicated with Kraike, then living in the desert under the false name of Rirriel Klaine.

Secrets passed back and forth between these two men, and the subject swore allegiance to Vohoria and, by extension, to Toros, a long-dead visionary whom Kraike claimed was the source of his gifts.

As an organisation, the Unblinking Eye was riddled with corruption. Thus, it was reformed, and became Daylight; those who formed the Eye were assigned new duties. The subject (whose misdemeanours in the Eye remained undiscovered until now) became a Scholar of Outrage. With a legion of willing spies no longer at his service, he sought someone new to deliver messages to Klaine. He chose Cavielle Shaelus, for assorted reasons, and the scheme described by General Standaire (as far as he knows it) commenced.

The subject states that Toros's return is imminent. Once this is accomplished, the visionary will not only possess extraordinary powers (it is theorised) but will have the capability to 'activate' similar abilities – that is to say, a heightened capacity for magical acts – in his descendants, who comprise as many as one in every ten Vohorin. Thus, claims the subject, Vohoria will become a force to be reckoned with.

When asked why he threw in his lot with Toros, the subject spoke at length, possibly because he had learned that when he talked, the torments would – temporarily – abate. It was then that he admitted his impious attraction to power, as both a concept and a reality, and confessed that this was a sizeable source of his dedication to Toros. But there were subtleties, he maintained, of a metaphysical nature. He was a polytheist, happy to entertain notions of the divinities belonging to other cultures; nonetheless, most disgusted him, for they never made their presence felt in this world, at this time. Through familiarity alone, the Four earned a special opprobrium: what miracles did they perform nowadays? What direct part did they play in human affairs? Yes, they served a purpose in the afterlife – but what of the here and now? Was that of no import? Apparently passive, they were starkly at odds with Toros, who did not influence mortal affairs, but intervened; it was he who had enabled the creation of Kraike's plague spell, a miracle of sorts; and it will be he, the subject claimed, who will reshape the world upon his resurrection. The subject went on to say that he found it impossible not to admire a man, divine or half-divine, who had not forgotten his mortal nature, and wished to benefit those of us who remain of flesh and bone.

As a personal observation, it is my humble opinion that for all this high talk of ideals, it was his admitted infatuation with power that primarily drove the subject along his chosen path. Simply, he struck me as greedy and venal, and desired nothing more than to be on the 'winning side', regardless of ethics, morality or the stain it would leave upon his soul.

'As you can see,' said Rymise, into the dead silence of the Seventh Hall, 'my actions were justified. Whilst it is not considered *proper* for one Master to play tricks on another, there are occasions when it is necessary. If any amongst you objects—'

'*I* object,' said Thralinge, a Master who had always been fond of Faltriste. The revelations had struck him like a hammer-blow; he could absorb them no more than a dog could digest a pebble. Although his tone was angry, his gaunt face betrayed shame. He had been made a fool of. But so had many others.

'About my methods or the outcome?' asked Rymise. Although he sympathised with Thralinge, he was in a combative mood. He did not want to waste time with petty disputes and points of order. 'If it is the latter, you are – at best – claiming that Cordis has obtained a defective confession. At worst, you know

600

the confession is true, but seek to deny it, possibly for some ulterior motive. Do you have something to hide, Blessed Master Thralinge? I should point out that Faltriste is still alive – in a fashion. Whilst unlikely, it is not *inconceivable* that Cordis failed to squeeze every drop of information out of him. For instance, the names of any fellow conspirators—'

'That is a vile allegation!' retorted Thralinge, banging a fist on the table.

'It is not an allegation, but an *insinuation*,' countered Rymise, smoothly. 'Your outburst has, quite naturally, kindled certain suspicions. Is it not the habit of a miscreant, if he cannot deny the evidence, to cry foul of the manner in which it was obtained?' Softening, he raised a hand. 'I acted as I did – alone, without the knowledge of the brethren – because I saw no other way. We may discuss this issue at a later juncture, if you wish. Now, we must decide what to do with the knowledge we have acquired. My thoughts – like those of many, I expect – are turning toward warfare.'

'Warfare?' said Master Dunis. Despite his considerable age, he was barrel-chested, and his expansive white beard made him resemble an arctic bear. 'I would go further. Extinction is called for!'

'Of the Vohorin people?'

'We should finish what the Scourge began, complete what it failed to do,' said Dunis, forcefully. 'Thirty years ago, we should've followed those rats into the sands and fed every last one of them to the vultures.'

'You propose genocide?'

'I propose *caution*,' said Dunis. 'Genocide is merely the form it shall take.'

'Let us not forget the Four's teachings,' came another voice – that of Ellef, whose gentle spirit was at odds with his high rank. 'Is it holy to wipe out an entire people, for the sake of caution? A people who have already suffered enough? No, I do not believe so. I propose that Vohoria becomes a province of Druine. Yes, we shall go there with soldiers and steel – but to tame, not annihilate.'

'Tame,' said Rymise, quietly. 'An interesting choice of word.' Gazing at Ellef, he reminded himself that beneath the old man's softness, there was a pragmatic hardness, like a pit hidden in the middle of a peach.

Ellef nodded, thoughtfully. 'A nation of sorcerers, pledged to serve the Church . . . Can you imagine it?' He lifted a finger. 'I am not suggesting anything unwholesome, or perilous. I am merely saying that if such talents exist, they should be harnessed and . . .' – a shrug – 'exploited.'

The debate continued nearly an hour. In the end, Ellef's proposal was deemed the wisest course. Invade Vohoria, instate it as a province, and if its inhabitants truly possessed untapped magical abilities – so much the better.

No sooner had agreement been reached than there was a knock on the door. A clerk entered, then bowed.

'Blessed Master Faltriste—' he began.

'He is no longer a Master,' interrupted Rymise.

'He is no longer *anything*,' said the clerk. 'He passed away several minutes ago. Cordis endeavoured to keep him alive, to no avail.'

Rymise nodded; perhaps it was for the best.

'I assume there will not be a sanctified burial? Or a funeral in the cathedral?' asked the clerk.

'No, there will not,' replied Rymise.

'What, then, is to be done with the corpse?'

'Do you keep dogs?'

'Dogs? No, your holiness.'

'A pity,' said Rymise. 'Take the corpse to the Third Enclosure and burn it.'

'And the remains?'

'Do what you will,' replied Rymise, not without satisfaction. 'Faltriste is no longer the Church's concern.'

CHAPTER TWENTY-FIVE

Sitting on a fallen oak, a parchment resting on a board on his lap, Shaelus considered what he should write. Illuminated by a shaft of moonlight piercing the forest roof, the parchment was blank – which was to be expected, for his mind was also blank. Nothing stirred within his skull; nothing interesting, at least.

He looked around the camp.

Five High Erethin lay on blankets, sleeping. Quarvis slept too, curled up like a dormouse. Further off there was a tent, in which Kraike slumbered; outside, the remaining five High Erethin stood guard, gazes probing the tree-crowded gloom.

Several times that evening, Shaelus had contemplated rushing into Kraike's tent and thrusting his quill through the sorcerer's eyeball, driving the tip deeply, *fatally*, into his brain. But it was an idle fantasy; there was no way he could get past the Erethin.

He gazed at the blank page. The Erethin believed he was writing a chronicle of Toros's resurrection, and the events that preceded it. To maintain the pretence that this was why he needed writing materials, he had written several chapters. And what dismal, uninspired chapters they were. Every word was a tooth wrenched from a rotten mouth, a flake of stone chipped from a granite block. Such effort, for no reward – in his many years as a scribe, he had experienced nothing like it.

But that was to be expected, he realised. He had always chosen themes that attracted rather than repelled him. And one way or another, he had always written about himself.

He smiled, bitterly.

That is the truth, is it not? No matter where I was, what I was doing, I placed myself centre stage. I could be wading through the Keltuskan swamps, or seeking the Clarrigean Hoard, or exploring the ancient diamond mines of Nem-peris – it made no difference: somehow, I always yelled, 'Look at me! Look at me!' Consciously or not, I made certain that I shone brighter than any heap of golden relics. I was loathsome . . .

Loathsome, yes. And often disbelieved.

His fatigue peeled away like a suffocating membrane; he felt the tingle of inspiration.

He had struggled to write his chronicle because, for once, he had stopped writing about himself. Repulsed by his role in Kraike's scheme, he had adopted a coldly objective tone, referring to himself in the third person rather than the first; and the Shaelus he described was less a living man than an unfeeling, bloodless replica, with no more personality than a broom handle.

And *this* was a mistake.

In part, Shaelus was writing his chronicle in the hope it would cast light on his 'secondary purpose'. By recounting his involvement from the start, he believed he could work out why Kraike still needed him. Engage fully with his past, he thought, and he would find answers. But that, he now realised, required a subjective approach.

Come forth, the Shaelus-as-was, he thought, dipping his quill in an inkpot perching on the oak. You are needed, you reprehensible shit.

Let us begin at the beginning . . .

For me, it started in a printing house, on a night when a storm crashed and lightning danced across the sky.

I had gone to deliver a manuscript – a minor work, but one I was sure would be enthusiastically received – to be set and printed. I had used this particular establishment many times, because the printmaster was trustworthy and discreet. Also, he was no lover of the Church and in my experience, shared animosity toward a common nuisance engenders a greater loyalty than friendship or, indeed, allegiance to one's country.

However, he was not there. As I went inside, I was greeted by seven or eight roughs, who administered a beating which, though not overly savage, was enough to subdue my spirits. Next, they manhandled me into the printmaster's office, where a familiar figure was waiting.

I had made it my business to recognise every Scholar of Outrage by sight and name, for it is always wise for the prey to know its predators. The man's name was Faltriste, and one day, he would attain the rank of Blessed Master; but at the time, as I say, he was but a lowly Scholar. However, he was not wearing the sinister blacks of his position and, as I would soon discover, he was not engaged in Church business (I would also learn that my attackers were not Papal Wardens, but common-or-garden thugs, willing to heavy-hand a stranger for money).

Faltriste and I exchanged greetings. Faltriste was visibly pleased to have apprehended me, the prize pike in the pond of blasphemy. For my part, I acted as if I had expected it all along, and my capture was all part of some enigmatic plan of my own (ah, the silly poses we strike for the sake of pride!).

As if he was an admirer of my work, but also cautiously sceptical, he asked many questions about my books. Had I done everything that I claimed? Had I been where I said, seen the sights, found the treasures? In an understanding and conspira-torial tone, he said that he would understand if I had embellished the truth. 'The most nourishing meals require seasoning, after all,' he said. I assured him that neither salt nor spices were added to my tales. Every word was the truth and, if I were a religious man, I would swear upon *The Book of the Pilgrims* that it was so.

Then, Faltriste initiated a type of brisk catechism, in which he questioned and I answered. It ran as follows:

Faltriste: You found the Sleeping Rubies on the plains of Caldrimmar?

I: Yes; I counted them too: there were fifty-seven, and I returned them to their hiding place when I was done. Although, not the entire amount: when I departed, there were fifty-four, because I needed to pay for my passage home.

F: You found the ruined Boros Temple in the jungles of Southern Keltuska?

I: After a year and a half of searching. In that humid place, the insects are unimaginable; they could drain a cow of blood in a single night.

F: You sailed the Green Vortex, and reached the Isle of Wretched Eyes?

I: I did; although, as I pointed out in my book, time, weather and geological disturbances had erased the landmarks, and I could not be sure it was the Isle at all.

F: Did you have such doubts when you walked the Dalzerte Gardens?

I. None. I knew exactly where I was.

F: And the Ice Caves of Thralise? One ice cave looks much like another . . .

I: True. But there was no mistaking the hot river flowing through their heart, and the strange fish that swam its waters.

607

Here, the catechism ended. Satisfied, Faltriste made a proposition, which caught me off guard: would I carry a letter to Rirriel Klaine, an exiled Vohorin dwelling in the Skravian Desert . . .

Shaelus stopped writing. How effortlessly the Shaelus-as-was had arisen, how natural *his* resurrection had been. Had it served a purpose?

Shaelus did not know. As soon as he lifted his quill from the page, he was overcome with weariness. He wanted only to sleep.

Would it not be wonderful, he thought, to perish during my repose? A natural death, to prevent an unnatural rebirth – I wonder if Kraike would chuckle at the irony.

He picked up the quill. At the bottom of the page he wrote:

Ekkerlin – the above is an experiment, designed to jog my memory. Has it led anywhere? I cannot say. Nonetheless, it must suffice for today's missive. In truth, nothing else has occurred. From dawn till dusk, we walk, and that is it.

I am sick of this forest. If I survive this, I shall dedicate the rest of my life to avoiding greenery.

It is the eighth day of the seventh month.

CS.

Rising, he wandered amongst the trees, seeking somewhere to hide the letter.

Quarvis waited until Shaelus was asleep. Then, getting to his feet, he walked from the camp, his tiny body fizzing with an excitement so intense it made him nauseous.

You are up to something, he thought, glancing back at Shaelus, slumbering fitfully on his blanket.

Since leaving Glavven City, he had noticed a change in Shaelus's demeanour. No, he realised. That was not true. Rather, he had noticed no change *at all*, and that struck him as strange, unnatural even. He knew he was on the final stretch of a momentous journey, and soon, Toros would be resurrected. He, Quarvis, was practically exploding with anticipation. Even the High Erethin, oblivious to the details, were infected by the sense that something marvellous was afoot. But Shaelus? He remained exactly the same — distant, reflective and impassive.

Ostensibly, there was a logical explanation. He was writing a chronicle, describing the events leading to Toros's return. It was understandable he should be preoccupied . . . but *so* preoccupied he was not moved by the prospect of bringing a long-dead visionary back into the world? A visionary endowed with unimaginable knowledge? Shaelus had spent his entire life trying to understand the universe. Could he truly be so *uninterested*?

No; it was impossible.

And then there were his odd nocturnal habits. He worked on the chronicle at night, whilst everyone slept. Always, when he finished, he laid down his quill and trooped off into the trees, out of sight of the camp. At first, Quarvis thought he was relieving himself before turning in. Indeed, he always took a sheet of parchment with him; a makeshift arsewipe, Quarvis had assumed. Certainly, he never had the sheet when he returned.

But this evening, Quarvis noticed he had written on the sheet that he took away. In fact, it contained the last thing he had written; and he had worked hard at it, his quill scratching furiously back and forth, his face rapt with concentration. Would he really clean his backside on the result of so much effort?

Inconceivable, Quarvis thought.

He followed the path, lit by slashes of moonlight. After a hundred yards or so, he stopped. Unease washed over him. He did not like being far from the camp. A city-dweller since birth, he found the forest unnerving – particularly at night. Oh yes, during the dark hours it came alive. Everything rustled, scuffled, rasped and whispered; unseen creatures prowled, lurked and scratched. And although he knew most were harmless, Quarvis found the overall effect disturbing.

A dry chuckle rose in his throat.

How would I fare in the real forest? he wondered, ruefully. There would be no need for demons. Only a few mice, or a fox or two. Yes, they would be enough!

Turning, he started back to the camp—

—and froze.

A snake's triangular head poked out of a thornbush; the creature was watching him. With a muffled yelp, Quarvis stepped back and raised empty hands, as if to prove he was unarmed. He stared at the snake; the snake stared back. Quarvis's tiny body solidified with fear. And the snake – its stillness was surely that which preceded an attack.

It is sizing me up, thought Quarvis, petrified. It is pinpointing my vulnerable areas, the soft bits easily pierced by a pair of sharp fangs . . . Oh grief, he added. Mister Snake, you are wasting your time. My entire body is a vulnerable region! From head to toe, I am as soft as a goosedown pillow!

The snake stirred slightly, the movement coinciding with a soft breeze murmuring through the trees. When the breeze dropped, the snake grew still.

Squinting, Quarvis took a step closer – and laughed.

His tormentor was naught but a scrap of cloth, snagged on a thorn. Chuckling, he tugged the tatter from the bush. He turned it between his fingers, thoughtfully. Then he lowered his gaze to the bush, growing around the base of an oak. Several stalks were crushed, leaking sap.

Has Shaelus been here? he wondered.

He raised the tatter into the moonlight. It was made of coarse brown wool – the same material as Shaelus's tabard.

He looked again at the bush. Then the tree around which it grew. Cut into the bark was a crude X.

Intriguing, he thought.

And then he saw it – the parchment, weighted down by a stone.

Knocking the stone aside, he grabbed the parchment. Unfolding it, he read line after line of Shaelus's neat quillscript. Disbelief flooded upwards from his feet to his scalp. Moments later, it was delight he felt.

I have you, you bastard! he thought. I've got you by the balls, you traitorous shit!

He hurried back to the camp. Shaelus still slept, happily oblivious.

Just past Kraike's tent, he found Lujaek. He was fast asleep, his strong features silvered by moonlight. Kneeling, Quarvis shook his shoulder.

'Wake up!' he hissed.

Lujaek opened his eyes. He peered blearily at Quarvis.

'This,' Quarvis waved the parchment, 'changes everything!'

Lujaek sat up, rubbing his eyes. 'What are you speaking of?'

'Look. Just look. Every word is a drop of venom, every phrase a blast of betrayal.'

Lujaek read. Quarvis watched his face closely. The Erethin's eyes narrowed, his mouth tightened. A tiny vein swelled in his temple.

'Very well,' he said. 'Very well . . .'

Something nudged Shaelus's chest. Groggily, he opened his eyes.

'Sit up,' came a voice. Lujaek's.

'It cannot be morning already,' said Shaelus. He was right:

the sky above the trees was dark. Stars shone; the moon glowed. 'What – are we to walk through the night, now? What is the urgency?' His body aching, he sat up. 'I need to rest. I will be no good to anyone if . . .' He trailed off.

Lujaek was flanked by two grim-faced High Erethin. Beside them was Quarvis, clutching a parchment.

'Look what I found.' The former Scholar held up the document, covered with Shaelus's handwriting. 'I have never trusted you, Cavielle Shaelus. Your brilliance conceals a rotten core. You are loyal to no one but yourself.'

Shaelus stared. What now? he wondered. Can I lie my way out of this? Does the trickster have anything up his sleeve?

No, he realised. He did not. An effective lie almost always exploited the ignorance, partial or complete, of its victim. But Quarvis held in his pallid hand irrefutable proof of his guilt.

Surely there is something I can say. A few clever words to hoist me out of this bear trap . . .

Oddly, he did not feel like lying. Certain rhythms moved through life, peculiar tides that bore a fellow this way and that, and Shaelus sensed this was the moment he was destined to be flung ashore on a bleak and barren beach. Simply, the game was up; there was no point in struggling.

Nonetheless, he said, 'Would it make any difference if I offered the adulterer's defence?' Lujaek frowned; Shaelus gestured to the letter. 'This really isn't what it looks like.'

'Come with me.' Lujaek led Shaelus to Kraike's tent. Outside, the sorcerer was waiting, leaning on his walking branch.

'Why?' he asked, without anger. 'After such loyalty, betrayal . . .'

'My loyalty was built on lies – yours, not mine,' said Shaelus. 'In Glavven, I was enlightened. I learned much about Toros, you, and this entire venture. I know that *you* wrote the *Doctrines*, under the influence of *lecterscrix*, in the days after a failed suicide attempt; I know that the tawdry little book's rules and prohibitions pertain not to the present day, as you claim, but the time after Toros's resurrection. I know that Selindak – and you, presumably – despise non-Erethin, and they shall not profit from Toros's return. Moreover, it is Toros's intention, for reasons I cannot fathom, to *selectively breed* more and more Erethin, as if they were prizewinning racehorses.'

If Kraike was surprised by Shaelus's words, it did not show. He simply nodded, glanced at the sky, nodded again. 'I suspected you would discover the truth sooner or later. You are famed for it, after all. Cavielle Shaelus: the bloodhound sniffing out the past. Rest assured: I do not care that you know. It is of no consequence. We shall carry on as before – with a few alterations. As we travel, you will be observed, constantly, and you will not be permitted to continue writing your chronicle. These privations aside, you will be fed, watered and treated well.'

'You will not punish me?'

'What good would it do? I have read your letter. Your powers of deduction are impressive. I *do* have, as you put it, a secondary purpose for you. Thus, it is in my interests to ensure that you arrive at the Solrepta in good health.'

'The Solrepta?' The word was unfamiliar. 'I assume this is Toros's resurrection site? The temple that is hidden amongst trees, so when he returns, he will not – how shall I phrase this? – die from surprise, like a spinster startled by a mouse?'

'How do you know of this?'

Shaelus pointed beyond the tent to Quarvis. 'For a feeble man, he has a mighty mouth.'

'Yes, the Solrepta is where Toros will be reborn, and the world will change,' said Kraike.

'Would you care to tell me what my secondary purpose is?'

'You will find out soon enough,' replied Kraike.

Shaelus narrowed his eyes. As always, Kraike's face was

expressionless. 'Hm,' he said thoughtfully. 'You put me in a quandary. *Why* will you not tell me, I wonder? Is it because you want to surprise me? No, I think not. I am not some smitten girl, to be startled by her paramour's offer of marriage. Is modesty behind your silence? Is the scheme so grand, so *spectacular*, you would appear boastful if you described it? Again, I do not believe that. So what, then?' He snapped his fingers. 'You fear that if I know what it is in advance, I may be able to resist it. Is that correct?'

Something flickered in Kraike's eyes.

Shaelus smiled. 'Mystery after mystery,' he said. 'Well, what do we do now? Retire to bed until dawn? Despite everything, I still feel sleepy.'

'Jurel Kraike,' piped up Quarvis, pacing over. He looked doubly guilty – guilty that he had done something foolish, and guilty that he had been eavesdropping. 'It is true that I spoke of the Solrepta. But I saw no harm in it! I had no inkling Shaelus was engaged in . . .' he clutched for the right words, 'acts of reprehensible epistolary.'

Kraike tilted his head; a nod not of forgiveness, but acceptance.

'It does not matter, Leptus Quarvis. By noon on the morrow, we will have arrived at the Solrepta.'

'But it *does* matter,' protested Quarvis. 'Not that I told Shaelus about the temple, but that the Hawks are following us. Those people – forgive me, but you have no idea what they are capable of.' Gabbling, Quarvis told Kraike about the raid on Prendle House – which the sorcerer was already aware of – and the various adventures leading up to the Hawks' appearance at his home, as they had been recounted by Ekkerlin, in the lounge, on the evening of their arrival. He spoke with a near superstitious awe, his pale face reddening, his hands gesturing crazily. When he finished, he was exhausted. 'They could be out there, even now,' he said, pointing at the darkness between the trees.

'Were they not imprisoned in Glavven?' It was Lujaek who asked the question.

'They escaped, somehow.' Quarvis looked venomously at Shaelus. 'You played a part, didn't you?'

Shaelus said nothing, just smiled.

'And you have been leaving letters ever since?' Lujaek asked.

Shaelus shrugged. 'You know that I have.'

Kraike stared at the ground, thinking. 'We cannot afford to take chances,' he said. 'Assemble the men.' He raised a finger. 'The eight *strongest* men.'

Accompanied by Lujaek, Kraike led the chosen High Erethin out of the camp.

Shaelus watched them disappear along the path, heading south, back the way they had come. None of the men knew what lay ahead. But Shaelus had an inkling. Quarvis, too: his vengeful high spirits were gone, replaced by uneasiness.

'Tell me,' said Shaelus, leaning close. 'How does it feel?'

'How does what feel?' Quarvis stared along the path.

'To know that you are not as important as me.'

'I am Erethin.'

'And Erethin are disposable,' said Shaelus. 'Your gift is commonplace; Vohoria is teeming with your kind. What does it matter, if a few are sacrificed for the cause?'

'For once, you have chosen the right word,' said Quarvis. 'Those brave men *are* making a sacrifice. And what is a sacrifice, but the proof of one's loyalty? One's dedication?'

'Those poor fellows do not know what awaits them,' said Shaelus. 'They are not martyrs, but victims of their own ignorance.' He nudged Quarvis with his elbow. 'Would you have gone, if asked? Knowing what you know?'

'Of course.'

'I shall rephrase the question: would you have gone *willingly*?'

'My answer is the same.'

Pursing his lips, Shaelus nodded. 'You could have volunteered. You could have demanded you take part. When your blood is up, you can be quite insistent – a little terrier tugging at a trouser-leg.'

'What would have been the point? I am not strong enough to survive the transformation.'

'True,' conceded Shaelus. 'I cannot imagine you turning into the Curlew. You would probably end up as . . . I know not . . . a duck, perhaps, a sickly pigeon . . .'

'You are trying to provoke me. It will not work.'

'Provoke you? Far from it. I am merely impressing upon you your lack of significance. You are Erethin, yes, but one too useless even to be sacrificed. I, however, am not Erethin, and I have betrayed Kraike in the starkest conceivable way, short of cutting his throat. Yet I have received no punishment. Why? *Because I am needed* – needed more than you, the other Erethin, even Lujaek. Quite a thought, isn't it?'

Quarvis did not reply; if he had, Shaelus would not have noticed. It seemed, suddenly, as if the whole forest was moving, shaken by a gently forceful wind. Branches swayed, creaking. The long grasses shimmered, rustling. Shaelus wondered if Kraike's magic was surging outwards, like ripples from a stone dropped in a pond, disturbing everything that lay in its path. But it was not so. Hearing wingbeats, Shaelus looked up. Overhead, birds abandoned their nests, rattling and cawing in alarm, rising in a dark mass, flashing black through the moonlight. Through the undergrowth came a succession of rats, mice, foxes and snakes, escaping something they could not understand, but knew instinctively to fear. Larger animals, deer and wild pigs, crashed through the vegetation, and the sweet smell of

616

sap touched Shaelus's nostrils. For a few baffling moments, it appeared the trees were moving, their trunks flexing in and out, like the breathing oaks of the Forest; but this too was not so. The grubs and insects inhabiting the moist gloom behind the bark were escaping, *flowing* from cracks and fissures, streaming away over the forest floor. In the branches, spiders abandoned their webs, and wasps forsook their nests.

Through the trees a blue light blossomed, feebly, but with gathering intensity. As it grew in strength, the shadows of the oaks lengthened, sprawling through the camp; on the vegetation, every speck of moisture gleamed emerald blue.

Shaelus remembered the cries of the young Erethin in the ruined town, as he warped into the Curlew. He heard the same cries now, multiplied eightfold. He knew the Erethin in the trees wanted to run, that their desire to serve Toros had been overpowered by their self-preservation instincts; he knew, too, that their bodies were under Kraike's control, and no matter how hard they tried, they could not budge an inch. He pitied them.

The blue light did not fade, but vanished. The forest slammed dark. And there came different cries, rolling through the trees. It was said that an unbroken and unbreakable silence hung over the Forest; if it were not so, it would surely sound as Brawlsnare did at that moment. There was a child's manic laughter, the hoarse screeching of an aged woman, the roaring of an indeterminate beast, a frantic clattering hiss, the rapid tap-tap-tap of spindly legs scuttling over dry leaves, and groans that, whilst agonised, were exuberant, even joyful, as if the pain was a pleasure. And there were other noises that, echoing, were impossible to identify . . .

One thing was certain: Kraike had not transformed the Erethin into a single type of demon. No; he had engendered a variety of abominations, who were already crashing deep into the forest, seeking prey.

Kraike returned, Lujaek walking alongside him. After the Curlew, the sorceror had been exhausted. Not now. He was a little tired, perhaps, but his eyes were bright, his movements brisk.

'It is easier the second time around,' he told Lujaek, as they paced over to Shaelus and Quarvis. 'It feels . . . natural.'

Natural, thought Shaelus. You commit an act that spits in nature's face – and you call it natural?

'Will they not . . .' Quarvis glanced at Kraike, then gazed into the trees, swallowing. 'Will they not come for *us*?'

'No,' replied Kraike, halting. 'Their instincts are not wholly those of demons. Some vague memories remain; they recognise us as friends. But the Hawks . . .' He looked at Shaelus. 'You have signed their death warrant.'

He turned to Lujaek.

'Dawn is approaching,' he said. 'Let us walk. I see no reason to delay.'

618

CHAPTER TWENTY-SIX

It was early morning. The Hawks walked on, keeping a brisk pace.

The forest seemed designed to induce lethargy, as all forests were. The unchanging landscape, tree after near-identical tree, had a mesmerising effect, and the sunlight pouring in strips through the leaf canopy flashed across Ballas's eyes, forcing him to squint, and inhabit an ill-lit world more suited to meditation than action. The heat was smothering, even at this early hour, and although the constant murmuring of flies was easy to ignore, it had a subconscious sedative effect, lulling the Hawk like some monotonous lullaby.

Of a sudden, a chill swept through him, followed by the crawling unease he had experienced by the woodland near the tumbledown town, where the Curlew was said to have originated. He looked at Ekkerlin. She felt it too, her skin growing pale, her eyes narrowing.

'Anhaga,' she murmured, nodding along the path.

An old woman was approaching. Clad in an off-white leather dress, her age-tanned face was cleaved by a wide, gummy grin. Her eyes sparkled with the uneasy light of senility. White hair exploded from her scalp and unless Ballas's eyes were playing tricks, the pale strands were home to a scattering of dark, beetle-like insects, scuttling this way and that, moving like ink drops flowing over marble. She carried a small hatchet, the

619

lightweight sort used for chopping wood. She advanced in slow, steady steps; her feet were bare, the toenails as yellow as sour butter. Something about her clothing struck him as strange. It hung from her scrawny body at an odd angle, as if it was a little too large or slightly the wrong shape. But that was not it. Squinting, he saw the garment was not fashioned from a single leather sheet, but a dozen or so smaller pieces. And each of these pieces, bordered by thick stitching, was perforated by five holes: two small, two medium-sized and one bigger than the others.

Skin, thought Ballas, peeled from human skulls.

'Dotage,' murmured Ekkerlin.

Thirty paces away, the woman raised the hatchet; the dull grey blade flared red-hot.

'What'd you say?' muttered Ballas, reaching for his sword.

'She is a demon,' replied Ekkerlin. 'They call her Dotage—'

Dotage sprinted at Ballas. Unsheathing his sword, he ran to meet her. When he was several yards away, Dotage dived aside, rolled onto her feet and slashed at Ballas. Ballas recoiled, but not quickly enough, the glowing blade slicing a shallow flap of skin from his forearm. There was barely any pain, and practically no blood: even as it created the wound, the superheated iron cauterised it. Dotage advanced, the toothless grin gaping blackly. She jolted as a white-fletched arrow punched into her shoulder. Taking advantage of the distraction, Ballas stepped in, hacking the sword into her throat. Dotage reeled, blood pouring from the clumsy incision, gathering in the recess of her collarbone. A second arrow *thunked* into her skull. She staggered. Hacking again, Ballas decapitated the demon, her head dropping to the ground, the smile growing slack.

Breathless, shaking, Ballas sagged against an oak. 'Piss on that,' he muttered. The hatchet lay next to the corpse; the blade was grey once more. 'Kraike's handiwork, you reckon?'

'Obviously,' said Ekkerlin. 'He used the Curlew to fight off the *virulin*. Now, he's sent Dotage after us.' She knelt by the demon. 'She is found in many accounts of the afterlife; her existence has been noted by visionaries from most cultures. She is ubiquitous.' She looked up suddenly. 'Listen.'

Ballas listened. Something half laugh, half groan drifted through the forest, accompanied by a dull *thwak-thwak* noise.

'There.' Ekkerlin pointed along the path.

A hundred yards away, a figure approached. A man, seemingly attired in tight reddish-pink tabard and leggings. He held in his hand a long rope, which he lashed against his back, again and again, like a self-scourging sinner. As he grew closer, Ballas saw that he was not garbed in brightly coloured clothing. Rather, he was naked, his body covered in scar tissue and smeared with freshly leaking blood. The rope was not a rope either, but a thick strand of some variety of black-barbed thornbush. Scarred, his face was a rigid mask, devoid of expression.

'Repentance,' said Ekkerlin. 'That is what he is called in Druinese culture. But he has other names. Self-Loathing, the Flagellant . . .'

Spotting the Hawks, Repentance stopped walking. Slowly, he closed his fist around the makeshift whip and drew it through, the thorns slicing his skin. Then he broke into a run, moving at incredible speed. His groaning laughter grew shrill, laden with a type of desperate hunger. Grabbing his bow, Ballas nocked an arrow and took aim. Ekkerlin did the same; simultaneously, two bolts thudded into Repentance's chest, without any effect: the scar tissue was as impenetrable as a leather breastplate. Cursing, Ballas nocked a second arrow. This time, he aimed for the only vulnerable part of the demon: its opened mouth. The arrow flew, but struck the demon's cheek then skittered harmlessly into the undergrowth.

Casting the bow aside, Ballas reached for a knife—

—but was too late. Ten paces away, the demon unfurled the whip to its full length and lashed out. The thorns pierced Ballas's cheek and lips, then jerked away, ripping flesh.

Roaring, Ballas pulled the knife out of its sheath and charged, slamming the blade into the demon's belly. The sharpened steel penetrated only a couple of inches of scar-hardened flesh. The demon raised the whip, looped it around Ballas's body then pulled, yanking him close. Countless thorns sank into Ballas's back. Grunting, he jammed his hand underneath the demon's jaw and pushed, forcing back its head. Rushing in, Ekkerlin sank a knife hilt-deep into its eye-socket. The whip slackened; the demon fell. Stumbling, Ballas grabbed a rock and struck the demon's skull again, and again.

A high-pitched laugh rang out. A little boy, five or six years old, scampered along the path, swinging a pair of long-bladed knives. His skin was unblemished, as white as fresh-fallen snow; golden curls bobbed upon his head. His eyes were blue and bright, gleaming with innocent joy. And his mouth . . . Bent into a grin of absolute delight, his mouth changed size constantly, one moment proportioned like that of any child, the next stretching the entire width of his face. His lips were obscenely red, as if he had been chewing raw meat. He hurtled at Ekkerlin, his tiny feet pattering on the ground, then leapt, the knives slashing at her face. Yelling, Ekkerlin flung herself out of the way, but a blade carved a long gash into her forehead. Approaching from behind, Ballas grabbed the child-demon's head and wrenched it around; tiny bones crackled in its neck. Releasing the child, he stepped back. Incredibly, the demon did not fall. It turned, slowly, its head hanging sideways, resting on its shoulder. It started to cry, its face puckering grotesquely, its forehead creasing, its eyes bundling into a squint. It ran at Ballas—

—but fell as Ekkerlin, sprawled on the ground, grabbed its ankle.

Pacing over, Ballas stamped on its head. Over and over, until it lay still.

Drawing a breath, Ballas spat out a mouthful of bile. Demon or not, it felt bad to kill the child.

Wiping blood from her face, Ekkerlin sat up. 'Innocence,' she said, gazing at the child. 'Innocence, Repentance, Dotage . . . and near the town, the Curlew . . .'

'Never mind that,' said Ballas, pacing over. 'Are you hurt—'

'Hateful Embrace.' Gazing past Ballas, Ekkerlin rose. Ballas turned.

Striding through the undergrowth came a skinny man, naked, with sharp-tipped spikes of bone jabbing out through his flesh. Retrieving his sword, Ballas did not wait for the demon to attack. Sprinting over, he dropped low, chopping the weapon into the demon's lower leg, just above the ankle. The steel blade crunched into bone. Toppling sideways, Embrace crashed to the ground. Rising, Ballas swung the blade into the demon's head, sundering its skull. Embrace writhed, its spikes carving thin channels into the soil. Ballas swung again, and the demon grew still.

'It is all starting to make sense,' said Ekkerlin, hoarsely.

'What are you talking about, woman?'

'Gluttony,' said Ekkerlin, distractedly. 'Yes, I suspected that it would be amongst them . . .'

Another demon approached. Measuring ten paces from tip to tail, this one resembled an outsized slug. Its skin was translucent, revealing a jumble of intestines and a bulging stomach, in which the shadowed outline of a still-living rabbit was visible. It dragged itself ponderously along the path, its toothless maw opening and closing, a pair of tiny ink-dot eyes glistening. Of a sudden it reared up; a tiny orifice opened above its mouth, and a jet of some clear fluid spurted out, missing Ballas by inches. It splashed on the ground; the grasses hissed and fizzed, dissolving.

Ekkerlin loosed several arrows into the demon. Squirming, its entire body pulsing like a colossal heart, it released more fluid. A spatter alighted on Ballas's hand; his skin blistered. Cursing, he ran to Repentance's corpse and, carefully, picked up the whip. Swinging it around his head, he took aim, then swept it out and downwards at Gluttony. The long barbs plunged into the demon's back, sinking as deeply as they could go, and Ballas heaved, drawing the whip back, as if he were reeling in a fish. Despite its soft, rubbery appearance, Gluttony's flesh was strangely resilient, and Ballas strained, feeling as if he was dragging a plough through clay-thick soil. Blood rushed to his head; his vision darkened, minuscule sparks glittered in front of his eyes, and for several hallucinatory moments he believed that this was the *true* Forest, and he was a damned soul, fighting not for survival, but to escape indescribable pain. He struggled on, wrenching the whip, its thorns slicing long incisions into Gluttony's slick rind; from the thin wounds, a thick oily fluid spilled out, like pus from a lanced boil, and the demon sagged into itself, as if deflating. Ballas swung the whip again, and this time the thorns dug into a red-coloured gland, as plump as a spider's egg sac; as it ripped open, the same fluid that had scalded Ballas's hand spilled out, corroding the demon from within. Gradually, Gluttony disintegrated into a sizzling, gelatinous lump.

Ballas staggered, pole-axed with exertion. His vision remained dark, the little lights continued to swim before his eyes, and he once again wondered if this was the Forest, and whether he would be trapped here for the rest of time. Then, something moved briskly inside Gluttony's heaped remains, something small and dark, scrabbling through the layers of corroded matter. With a hard, squirming wriggle, it broke free, and Ballas saw it was the rabbit, previously lodged in Gluttony's stomach. Fur sizzling from the acidic fluid, it lolloped toward the under-growth, its ears sticking straight up, its tail bouncing.

Ballas's head cleared. This was not the Forest. The land of the damned contained many things, but rabbits were not amongst them.

'Anhaga!' yelled Ekkerlin. As one, three demons crashed out of the trees. The first had the long body, crooked legs and curved sting-topped tail of a scorpion but, at the front, arching upward like a ship's figurehead, was the torso and head of shirtless man. Like the scorpion, the second demon was a hybrid, a man with the body and legs of a bull; but there was something taurine about the head, too: a pair of horns curved from its forehead, and its skull bones were so thick they deformed its face, contorting its features into a ponderous glare. The third demon was the strangest of the three, a life-sized effigy of a man woven from willow branches. Each branch was edged by a fine strip of metal, a razor blade as thin as cotton, yet insanely sharp: around the demon's legs, grass stalks tumbled as if scythed, and the low-hanging twigs that brushed its narrow head dropped neatly, as if cropped by a gardener's shears.

The demons paused, as though surprised to find human prey in this woodland populated only by animals. Then, their instincts flared, and they rushed at the Hawks, the bull-demon's hooves thudding on the soft earth, the scorpion's legs chittering, the effigy accompanied by the constant *shh-shh-shh* of falling grass.

Snatching up his sword, Ballas charged at the bull. As he went, the scorpion revolved on the spot, its legs working in tight snapping movements, then skittered to intercept him. Leaping, Ballas hacked the sword into the scorpion's human neck, the blade sinking deep through pale flesh. As the Hawk landed, the scorpion's tale lashed out, knocking the sword from his hand and slicing a shallow gash in his shoulder. Before he could retrieve the sword, the bull hurtled at Ballas, its head low, its horns aimed at his chest. Grabbing the horns, Ballas twisted, trying to wrench the demon onto the ground. But it was too heavy, too solid, too perfectly balanced. Angry now, snorting furiously, the bull swung its head from side to side, thrashing madly, Ballas clinging onto its horns, knowing that if he lost his grip and fell, all was lost: as soon as he hit the ground, the bull would be upon him, goring him from groin to guts to sternum.

Out of his eye-corner, he saw Ekkerlin fighting the effigy. Lacking a sword, axe or knife, the demon was its own weapon, springing at Ekkerlin and swiping its razor-riddled hands, the fingers spread wide, whilst Ekkerlin parried crazily, her face red and eyes wide with a mixture of panic, incredulity and helplessness. The effigy was ridiculously fast – so much so, it was visible less as a solid entity than a succession of glitters and gleams, where the sunlight bounced off sharpened steel.

Ekkerlin could not win, Ballas knew.

But he had an idea.

Opening his mouth, he tried to shout, but his voice was strangely feeble. His throat felt numb, he realised. And the numbness was seeping through his body, softening his muscles, rendering his limbs as heavy as lead. He could not feel his fingers; he had to glance down to make sure they still gripped the bull's horns. The scorpion was to blame, he knew. The sting had caught him only a glancing blow, but it was sufficient to inject at least a small measure of poison into his bloodstream. His vision grew blurred. A low murmuring hum filled his ears.

Steeling himself, he shouted, 'Gluttony . . . remains . . . acid . . .' The cry was barely louder than a whisper, but Ekkerlin heard it. Immediately, she stopped parrying and attacked the effigy with the ferocity of any doomed creature seizing the slenderest hope of survival. She forced the effigy back toward the glistening slurry that had been the sluglike demon. Stepping into the glutinous mass, the effigy contorted, as if every muscle in its muscleless body had flown into a spasm. Its lower legs blackened, wisps of steams curling from the wood—

And Ballas saw no more. Suddenly, he was flying through empty air, his grip on the bull's horn gone. He dimly observed that his limbs did not flail, but flopped, nerveless and limp; he slammed into something hard – a tree trunk perhaps – then slid into blackness.

Ballas awoke. His limbs were heavy, his head felt like a lump of stone. He assumed the scorpion-thing's venom was designed to paralyse, rather than kill, and its effects were temporary. He sat up, his body as weighty as a sack of pebbles. Looking through the trees, he saw the scorpion-thing itself, lying dead in the grass and, further off, the remnants of the effigy demon smouldering in what remained of Gluttony.

'Ekkerlin?' he mumbled, getting to his feet. Swaying, he leaned against an oak. 'Where are you—?' He fell silent: he saw her, sitting upright against a tree, her face pale. He lumbered over, moving as slowly as a warship passing through shallow water. 'You hurt?'

A feeble smile. 'Not at all, Anhaga. Merely exhausted. You?'

'A dose of demonic scorpion venom,' said Ballas. 'Reckon I'll be able to walk it off.'

'The Scorpion is called Bitterness,' said Ekkerlin. She swallowed. 'As for the other two – the bull is called Revenge, the twiglike creature Famine: its razors represent the bite of hunger. Do you know what? Those demons . . . they were a blessing in disguise.'

'You reckon?' Ballas nearly laughed.

Ekkerlin struggled to her feet. 'Every individual is formed by their culture,' she said. 'We carry around with us a jumble of ideas, images and perspectives; certain scholars refer to it as the "apperceptive mass". When we perceive the world, we do so *through* this mass: in other words, we look at things a particular way. To give a staggeringly crude example: when you think of tranquillity, what do you see?'

'A meadow,' replied Ballas, without thinking. 'Aye, a meadow on a hot day.'

'Would someone who had dwelled in, say, a tundra since birth think of the same thing? No, of course not. How could they? They have never seen a meadow. Instead, they would have their own ideas of tranquillity, created by their upbringing, their environment. Do you understand?'

Ballas nodded.

'The same principle applies to the afterlife,' continued Ekkerlin. 'It is true that visionaries of *all* cultures perceive it as an oak forest; metaphysicians believe this is because in mankind's early history, we were scarcely more intelligent than animals. As our minds grew, so did our sense of our mortality – and from this, sprang the notion of the afterlife. During this period, it is thought we dwelled in forests, hunting, gathering berries, living as savages. As our habitat was intrinsically dangerous, it was natural that the afterlife – the unpleasant version, at least – should be a similar, if somewhat corrupted facsimile. Even when our species developed, and we abandoned our forest homes, this idea of the afterlife persisted, as if it was woven into our minds. What *does* change, however, are the demons themselves. Every culture has its own bestiary of abominations.' She drew a breath. 'Do you remember the teeth-and-sun sigil? And how it could belong to any number of cultures?'

Ballas said that he did.

'Now, I have the answer,' she said. 'Those demons all belong to the mythology of the Dalzerte people. Not *one* of them has a presence in the Vohorin view of the afterlife.'

'So?'

Ekkerlin's fingertips rose from her shoulder to her forehead,

628

as if to feel the thoughts moving within her skull. 'There are different types of magic,' she said. 'Different *approaches*. These too vary by culture. The Keltuskans employ one method, those of Druinese stock another – just as, say, they have differing types of music, differing senses of harmony and melody.' She flinched. 'If we assume Kraike created those demons by transforming his fellow travellers – and I see no alternative – he will have modelled them on the demons he had grown familiar with during his nocturnal trips to the Forest. And as I say, those demons are those of the Dalzerte – not the Vohorin. And the teeth-and-sun symbols? They too were used by the Dalzerte. This is so strange . . .' She looked at Ballas. 'Kraike is using Dalzerte magic. And this solves an important riddle.' She nodded. 'Kraike wants to know something Shaelus knows – but Shaelus does not know what. But I think that I have a rough – *very* rough – idea.' She looked at Ballas. 'Shaelus's first book was an account of his visit to the ruined Gardens of Dalzerte. Before he found them, they had existed only as a myth, a rumour . . . None of this makes sense,' she said, breathlessly. 'Why is Kraike, a Vohorin, using Dalzertian magical systems? There is no connection between the Vohorin and the people of Dalzerte; they share no common ancestors, and they hailed from different parts of the globe. There is nothing to suggest that they ever came into contact with one another.' Suddenly, she gestured to Ballas's face. 'You are bleeding.'

He fingered a flap of loose flesh, lolling from his cheek. 'It is naught to worry about,' he shrugged. 'You ready to get moving?'

'Always ready, Anhaga,' she said, and they walked, treading past the fallen demons, venturing deeper into Brawlsnare.

Hours later, they reached an area of flattened grass and crushed thornbushes. Although it was midday, a strange, sticky dew clung to the trees, and the overhanging branches were warped and twisted, as if cultivated that way, over decades, by an arborealist with a peculiar sense of taste.

It was here the demons were created, Ekkerlin announced. By way of proof, she pointed to the soil path, gouged with the familiar but unsettling prints: the neat holes left by Bitterness, the long dragging swathes of Gluttony, and the tiny little prints of Innocence's hopping, prancing feet.

Further on, they found an oak with an X cut into the bark. Despite rummaging in the vegetation around the base, Ekkerlin did not find a letter.

Straightening, she said, 'Shaelus has been discovered. Somehow, Kraike and the rest found out about the letters.' A flicked gesture toward the trampled grass and warped branches. 'Hence the demons.'

Ballas felt neither sorrow nor disappointment. He did not give a streak of gull-shit whether the old man was alive or dead; and as for the letters themselves – despite Ekkerlin's excitement upon receiving them, they had served no practical purpose. Nonetheless, he sniffed the air.

'Maybe he is still alive. I can't smell rotting meat.'

Ekkerlin looked at him, nonplussed.

'If they killed him as soon as they learned about the letters, he would've started to decay by now.' He tilted his head, listening. 'Can't hear many flies, either.' A shrug. 'This secondary purpose he banged on about – they'll need him alive for that, aye?'

'Probably, yes,' said Ekkerlin, quietly. She looked worried. 'Come on. We'd better get moving.'

CHAPTER TWENTY-SEVEN

Solrepta – like many archaic Vohorin words, it encompassed several meanings. 'Rebirth' was one; so was 'enduring', and 'glory'.

But words were clumsy, Shaelus knew. They were means by which concepts inhabited the mind, and often had little bearing on reality.

So it was with the temple where Toros was to be resurrected.

The Solrepta was not a grand building. A low square structure, crafted from black stone, it resembled an outsized barn – or a shithouse. Windowless, lacking ornamentation, it was crudely functional. If it had lain on a city street, it would have garnered no attention, except from aesthetes, who would comment on how unremarkable it was.

As they approached through a clearing in the trees, Shaelus glanced at Quarvis. The little man's disappointment was obvious.

This is . . . is this . . . it? he mouthed to himself.

'You seem crestfallen,' said Shaelus. 'Expecting something glorious, were you? Something bursting with iconography? Crowded with statues? Guarded by peacocks and panthers?' He understood Quarvis's unhappiness. To a degree, he shared it. According to Crenfriste, the Solrepta had existed in Brawlsnare for nearly seven hundred years. For much of its history it had been a secret; whilst emperors came and went, generations were born and died, it quietly maintained the Torosian faith, untouched by the changes of the outside world. It had been Kraike's home; here, he had been raised, his talents cultivated, until the time came for him to infiltrate Grivillus's palace. By rights, it should have *vibrated* with historical significance, radiating importance as the sun radiated light. Yet it was just an ugly lump, an ignominiously functional stack of stone.

'Can you feel it?' Shaelus asked Quarvis, goadingly. 'Can you sense the history locked in these stones? Does it not make you feverish with delight?'

Quarvis ignored him.

'Such things these oaks must have seen,' continued Shaelus. 'These stout sentinels, ever-watchful—'

'Learn some respect, *revriek*,' spat Quarvis.

Revriek – the word was unfamiliar. Shaelus looked quizzically at Quarvis.

'It means sinner, outcast, one who is not Erethin,' said Quarvis, lifting his chin. 'You may mock me. You may hold the Solrepta in low regard. But you are *revriek*, and Toros has no plans for you. You are exiled – not from your homeland, as is the fate of some. But from *the future*. Besides,' he huffed, 'the bulk of the Solrepta lies underground. What you have seen is merely its surface embodiment.' A raspy little chuckle. 'But is that not the story of your life? You have never been able to look beyond the obvious. How could you? You are not Erethin. Unable to perceive the world of magic, you are consigned to perceiving only the superficial.'

Lujaek led them through a low doorway. Descending some stone steps, they entered a long corridor, lit by lanterns. The walls were bare, the corners cobwebbed. A pair of figures appeared at the far end of the corridor. Erethin, garbed in white robes, waists encircled by the blood-and-leaves belt.

'Lujaek?' said one, squinting through the poor light. His gaze darted to Jurel Kraike. 'Sir, you are here.' Dropping to one knee, he bowed his head; his companion followed suit. Ignoring them, Kraike limped past, his staff clacking on the floor stones. The men straightened.

'Take him to a sleeping room,' ordered Lujaek, pushing Shaelus forward a step. 'Ensure he comes to no harm. He is valuable, but there is a danger he may take his own life. He is to be watched at all times.'

'Fare thee well,' said Quarvis, mockingly, as the Erethin led Shaelus away.

He was taken to a small room. A lantern was lit, revealing a bed, a chair, and nothing else.

'This will do,' said Shaelus, sitting on the bed. 'I trust you will bring wine? Lujaek is right: there is a danger I will commit self-murder. Thus, it is essential you keep my spirits up. And what brightens one's mood more than a cup of something red and potent?'

Neither Erethin responded.

Stretching out his legs, Shaelus lay back, fingers interlaced upon his chest.

He dozed. When he woke, Lujaek was in the doorway.

'Come with me,' he said.

'Where to?'

'Selindak wishes to speak with you.'

'Tell him I am taking a catnap,' said Shaelus. 'He must wait until I am fully restored.'

Lujaek did not speak, only stared.

Feigning a sigh, Shaelus got to his feet. 'Very well. I suppose I have little choice.'

Leading him through a succession of winding corridors, and up a flight of steps, Lujaek took Shaelus to a large circular chamber. Sitting in a high-backed chair was Selindak – or what remained of him. Time had not treated him kindly. His hairless head was mushroom-pale, his ears sticking out like a mouse's. His face was tangled with wrinkles and creases; his lips shrank back over toothless gums. His white robes hung loosely from his emaciated body; his hands, resting on the chair arms, were vein-grappled and painfully thin. By rights, he should have died years ago. He looked as if he would crumble to dust at the gentlest breeze.

Yet his eyes were sharp.

'Cavielle Shaelus,' he rasped. 'Our servant, our betrayer. Lujaek has informed me of your change of heart.'

'That is a poor greeting,' observed Shaelus. 'How long since we last spoke? Fifteen years? I expected a "hail fellow" at the very least. But no, it seems you are intent on getting straight to business.' He swallowed, licked his lips. 'You look dreadful. So brittle, so flimsy – you remind me of a deserted hornets' nest.'

A faint smile touched Selindak's lips. 'But I am *alive*, Shaelus. For me, that is enough.'

'And Toros? Does he live? Is he amongst us?' Shaelus gestured to encompass the Solrepta.

'Not yet. But the process has begun. Lujaek, if you would . . .' He pointed a crooked finger to a curtained window. Walking over, Lujaek drew the curtains apart by a slender inch. Green light washed through the gap, pulsing steadily. Shaelus saw silhouetted oak trees – and the outline of Kraike, bending over something hidden from view. Lujaek shut the curtains; the light vanished.

'The Phosphorescence of Return,' said Shaelus, quietly.

'You are familiar with the principles of necromancy?'

Shaelus shrugged. 'I am familiar with the principles of almost everything,' he said. 'I have devoted my life to knowledge. And knowledge is the reason I am here, is it not? Locked away up here,' he tapped his head, 'is something that you need.

Need so badly, in fact, that Lujaek was forced to spare my life.'

A nod. 'Lujaek told me of your letters. And your supposed "secondary purpose".'

'*Supposed*, Selindak?'

'Actual,' corrected Selindak. 'Your deductions are correct. You have knowledge that Toros requires.'

'Would you care to tell me what it is?'

'Alas, that is not possible.'

'Not possible? Or *desirable*?'

'Both,' said Selindak. 'The knowledge in question is very detailed. As you rightly say, it is locked in your memory. However, there is a gulf between what you *believe* you remember, and the memory itself. If you were to describe the memory, it would become corrupted: inevitably, your imagination would reshape it, albeit to a small degree. And language – be it Vohorin or Druinese – cannot adequately express what Toros needs to know.' Another nod. 'Toros must see what you saw. To do so, he will enter your mind and access the memory directly. I should warn you: the process is painful. It is much less picking a lock than kicking open a door. Damage will be done; the only question is whether you recover afterwards. And that, Shaelus, is up to you.' He lifted the goblet to his lips. When he drank, a trickle of water escaped the corner of his mouth. 'The more you resist, the more forceful Toros will need to be. Thus, the more greatly you will suffer, and the more severe the after-effects. I suggest you make it as easy for him as possible. It is for your own benefit that I do not tell you which memory Toros will be seeking. If you knew, you would be better equipped to fight back – which would do you no good. Make no mistake: Toros *will* get the information he requires. That is a certainty.'

'And if I do not resist?'

'Toros will undo the damage he has wrought.' Selindak

returned the goblet to the table. 'You will recover completely. And you will continue to play a part in Toros's plans.'

'But I am not Erethin.'

'Does that matter?'

Shaelus frowned. 'I have spoken to someone who knew you in the desert. She told me that you revile non-Erethin. You called them cattle, cockroaches. You made it clear that Toros has no use for them.'

'I uttered those words,' said Selindak. 'As you would have done, in my circumstances. I needed to convince the Erethin that they were special. *Superior*, even. How better to elevate a group of people than by deriding everyone else? It was rhetoric, nothing more.'

'There are others who are convinced that only the Erethin will benefit from Toros's return,' said Shaelus.

'Then they have much to learn. Do you think that your ally, Faltriste, would serve Toros if he did not stand to gain?'

'Faltriste is not Erethin?'

'Did he ever say that he was?'

'No. But I assumed—'

'Do you know what makes an Erethin?'

'They carry Toros's blood in their veins,' said Shaelus.

'And that blood grants them certain innate abilities, yes?'

'Yes.'

'All true,' said Selindak. 'But it is a truth coexisting with other, similar truths. Namely, other bloodlines – *all* bloodlines in fact – have similar properties. Most of us – Vohorin, Druinese, Keltuskan, whoever – are descended from tribal leaders of the distant past. And those leaders were generally shamans. Their blood flows in the veins of most of the globe's populace. Thus, most have some magical capacity. Strictly speaking, the word *Erethin* denotes those descended from Toros. But if you take it to mean sorcerer, then it can be fairly applied to nine-tenths of the world's population. Naturally, few suspect they have this talent. And those who do seldom cultivate their gift. Have you read the *Doctrines*?'

'I have. It sickened me.'

'It provides rules by which sorcerers must live,' said Selindak, unperturbed, 'if they are to utilise their talents. These rules are universal: they apply not only to Erethin, but magic-workers of every ancestry. Discipline, focus, freedom from distractions – these principles are to be found in metaphysical texts the world over.

'However, such rigours are not always necessary. With Toros's intervention, a man such as yourself can become a sorcerer instantly. You will be able to harness whatever strain of magic exists in your blood.' The water-trickle reached his jaw; he wiped it away. 'There are different varieties of magic. Different wells, from which one may drink.'

'You are offering me the chance to become a sorcerer?'

'You claim to value knowledge,' said Selindak. 'Who knows more about the world, the *universe*, in its most intimate, unseen workings, than a magicker?'

'I assume I will be a sorcerer in servitude. I will – what – pledge loyalty to Toros?'

'There can be no greater sorcerer than he,' said Selindak. 'It is natural that he should reside at the top of the hierarchy. That he will, if you like, play the role of emperor.'

'And Toros's ultimate plans? I assume he has not spent millennia in the Forest solely to improve his magical abilities. He must have a goal, an objective—'

'That is not your concern,' said Selindak.

'Surprisingly enough, I must disagree,' said Shaelus. 'I cannot promise loyalty to one whose intentions I do not know.'

Selindak leaned forward. 'By nightfall, Toros will live. That is not in doubt. The question you must ask yourself is this: when he returns, shall I be an ally, or an enemy? Keep in mind that the former will lead to wondrous things. Whilst the latter . . . I do not need to elaborate. Consider the matter,' he concluded. 'But do not take too long. As soon as he returns, Toros will not delay in pursuing his plans.'

CHAPTER TWENTY-EIGHT

Dusk lay on the forest, the light golden and dull.

Ahead, the ground plunged into a deep recess. A green light flooded up from this concavity, its source hidden behind the dense oaks. This light had an unwholesome, grimy look, like the scaled flank of some reptile; it extended hazily toward the darkening sky, as bright as a bonfire.

'The Phosphorescence of Return,' said Ekkerlin. 'That is the term Shalfrazen used. Certain energies are discharged during necromancy; they *glow*, he said, like seafood rotting in a cellar.'

'Wait here.' Passing Ekkerlin his bow, Ballas climbed an oak. From the higher branches he obtained a slightly better view of the recess. There was a low, square building, single-floored; in the centre, a circular space, open to the sky, crowded with oak trees. From here, the light rushed upward. Squinting, Ballas discerned dark shapes floating amongst the green, fluttering and fading like scraps of ash.

Climbing down, he told Ekkerlin what he had seen. Then they descended into the recess. As they went, he looked at Ekkerlin. She wore a familiar look of concentration – frowning, gaze abstracted, lips moving silently. He envied her, he realised. Her life dedicated to obscure knowledge, she had an inkling of what was happening. Perhaps she did not know the exact details. But she had at least a loose idea; at least she knew enough to hazard a guess.

But Ballas — he had nothing of the sort. And it frightened him.

He thought of Mallakos in Olech's cell, as they waited for the Peacekeepers to arrive. The horse-breeder had not committed a violent act in his life; he did not have the faintest idea how to fight. Ballas had done his best to make him understand. He told him there was no mystery, no secret; you simply plunged in and fought. And it had worked. Although not exactly confident, Mallakos felt he was on steady ground; he acquitted himself surprisingly well.

But Ballas — he was not on steady ground. Far from it.

A day ago, he had fought demons. Or men granted demonic form. It had not been disturbing; he had not experienced fear beyond that which was natural when confronting a physical threat. And that was the thing: somehow, he treated the man-demon hybrids as physical threats, nothing more. To him, they were just exotic types of animal. He might as well have been fighting boars, wild dogs, grizzly bears.

But this business with Toros . . . with the throbbing black-flecked green light . . .

He could not comprehend it. It was too strange; it lay far beyond both his experience and knowledge.

They reached the bottom of the recess.

'What do we do?' Ballas asked, as they strode through the trees.

Sweat sparkled on Ekkerlin's face. 'First things first,' she said. 'You cast off your frustration.'

'Meaning?'

Ekkerlin laughed, softly. 'I know what you think of me,' she said. 'I can see it on that blunt instrument of a face of yours. Every time I open my mouth, you grimace like a pig with its tail trapped in the sty door. *She talks too much. Her head is in the clouds. She's learned so many useless things . . .*'

'But those things are useful now,' said Ballas, as they reached the temple.

Ekkerlin propped her bow against the black stonework. 'You are mistaken,' she said. Crouching, she began unlacing her boots. 'You've always believed all this could end with a single act of murder. Well, so it shall be.' She slapped the wall. 'We climb; we kill.' She pulled off her boot. 'Unless you have a better plan.'

'No,' said Ballas, shaking his head. He too started unlacing his boots. His hands were shaking. His mouth was dry.

Shaelus lay on the bed, thinking – or trying to.

His mind drifted, unfocused, from one topic to the next, and only one theme presented itself with any clarity: his own foolishness.

Throughout his life, he had believed he was special. With his blistering intellect and physical fearlessness – a rare combination – imagined he was *above* the rest of the human race. Ordinary men wallowed in gutters, whilst he breathed the rarefied air of mountaintops. They hungered for normal things – food, shelter, someone to love – whilst he was greedy for grander things: fame, knowledge, adventure.

We are practically a different species, he had thought. We have nothing in common.

Now he understood it was not so.

He was prey to folly as much as the next man. True, his mistakes had been grander, more complex. But they were mistakes nonetheless.

He should have known better. Mythology was littered with men who had erred in the same way, and had been undone by hubris. He had read these stories, of course – but what had he learned? Nothing. Those tales were contrived for lesser men, he had thought. They could teach him nothing.

He supposed it had started innocently enough.

When Faltriste approached him in the printing shop, asking him to carry a letter to the Skravian Desert, he had accepted because he was *curious*, nothing more. And was not curiosity one of the nobler traits? Something to be praised? But once the scheme had started properly, and he learned of the plans to resurrect Toros, a type of madness had descended. He became *obsessed*. Posing as a Scholar of Outrage, he had worked tirelessly in the Black Archives, trying to deduce the Origin's location. During those ten years, he doubted that a single thought unconnected to the task passed through his mind. And that was the problem: he lost perspective. He had ceased to consider what Toros would do once he returned; he even stopped wondering if the resurrection was possible. His work became *everything*; nothing else existed.

He smiled, grimly.

Faltriste had *known* it would be so. For all his flaws, the Master was an excellent judge of character. He saw Shaelus's compulsive streak. He knew that once he started, he could not be stopped.

The door opened. Quarvis stepped through, bearing a plate of bread, cheese and cooked boar meat.

'I assume you intend to put your boot on my throat?' said Shaelus. 'To hoist your flag, so its shadow falls upon my soul?'

'I am beyond all that,' said Quarvis. 'Not for me, sneering and gloating.'

'Truly? Then you have undergone a transformation of miraculous proportions. One equal, I would say, to the restoration of Toros to life.'

'Eat.' Quarvis proffered the plate. 'You must keep your strength up.'

Ignoring the food, Shaelus said, 'Is the resurrection over?'

'Not yet,' replied Quarvis, placing the plate on the bed. 'It will not be long now.'

'And then?'

'Then?'

Shaelus sighed. 'What will follow?'

'I am not allowed to tell you.' Smiling, Quarvis shrugged. 'I am sorry, Shaelus. But that is how it is.'

'Would you care to give me a hint? A clue that I can mull over? Life in this little room is very boring. I need something to occupy my mind.'

'Enjoy your inactivity while you can,' said Quarvis. 'I fear you will look back upon the tedium as . . . well, blissful.' He turned to go.

'Wait,' said Shaelus. Quarvis halted, turned back. 'You intrigue me, Quarvis.'

'Really? I am a simple man. There is little to understand.'

'That is not true,' said Shaelus. 'Faltriste told me about your troubled past. When you served as a Scholar, you suffered a crisis of faith. Overwhelmed, you took to drinking, whoring and gambling. When you ran out of money, you stole forbidden texts from the Black Archives and sold them on the Dark Market. Your crimes were on the verge of being discovered when Faltriste intervened. He saved your life, did he not? Were it not for him, you would have been hanged.'

'The Master spotted my true worth,' said Quarvis, with pride. 'He understood that I would be an asset to the Torosians.'

'You were a penniless, thieving drunk, riddled with a hundred different poxes, yet he perceived some merit in you?'

'Unlike you,' said Quarvis, 'he does not judge a man by a first, second or third glance. He sees beyond the obvious. He knows what is hidden.'

'And how to draw out one's untapped talents?'

'A man never knows how strong he is, until he has something to fight *for*.'

'What are *you* fighting for?'

'Toros, of course.'

Shaelus shook his head. 'He is a means to an end. Why else does anyone worship a god, or a visionary? You served as a priest for a time. Surely you must have noticed the selfishness of the faithful. In many prayers, they are asking for something. *Give me this, give me that* . . . And when they pray for others – well, that is scarcely any better. For they care about these others, and feel their joys and sorrows as their own. Toros must be offering you something. Not personally,' he added, 'but as an Erethin.'

'The truth is not mine to tell,' said Quarvis.

'I understand,' said Shaelus. 'But I am curious. What does it take to drag a man out of the depths? Your depths, Quarvis, were deeper than most. Amongst such darkness, the reviving light must be very bright indeed.' He gazed at his hands. 'Goodness knows, I crave such light myself.'

'You are not Erethin,' said Quarvis. 'For you, there can be no light.'

Shaelus nodded, sadly. 'Since we came here, I have sought consolation. I always imagined . . . always *believed* that philosophy would be the answer. How many treatises I have read on how to weather life's storms! How to take heart, regardless of the circumstances! I believed those ancient writers were wise. I was wrong. Their words are useless. It is one thing to ponder sorrow when one is in a well-balanced humour. But when one is stricken, once can be solaced by neither platitudes nor noble sentiments. When you were trapped in your own mire, did you turn to the ancients? Or were you content to indulge in sensual distractions? The whores, the alcohol . . .'

'They were hollow comforts,' said Quarvis. 'I knew they could do no good in the long run. They were, shall we say, temporary palliatives.'

'But what palliative is not temporary?' Shaelus sat up a little straighter on the bed. 'For a time, I thought Toros had offered you immortality.' He nodded, lips pursed, as if the theory caused him embarrassment. 'Then I realised it was not so, for, if that was the bargain, you would have refused it. You are not without intelligence, Quarvis. Or erudition. You know that eternal life is more a bane than a blessing. As a Churchman, you will have read the sanctioned texts on the subject. As a Scholar, you will have perused those which are forbidden. You know that, first, immortality is a sham. Sooner or later, the flesh breaks down. Yes, the body can be maintained by magic. But eventually, something will go wrong. Death can be delayed, not avoided.

'So my thoughts took a different course,' he went on. 'Maybe you were offered immortality – of the soul, not the flesh. But then I laughed, for I was wrong in this too.' A faint smile. 'Can you spot my error?'

'All souls are immortal,' replied Quarvis. 'They cannot be destroyed – except in extraordinary circumstances.'

'Exactly,' said Shaelus. 'I had made a mistake simple enough it would make a schoolboy blush. Our souls are immortal, whether we like it or not! And those trapped in the Forest do *not* like it. They crave annihilation; they beg for oblivion.'

'It is never granted,' said Quarvis, in the cold tone of a clergyman.

'As I will soon discover,' said Shaelus. 'My time in this world is short, I fear. But that is by the by. I asked myself, What can Toros offer, if not immortality of the soul? Then it came to me: a happy afterlife. That is, an afterlife untroubled by demons. An afterlife, yes, in Paradise.' He watched Quarvis closely. 'But then I saw a flaw in that theory as well. One cannot simply stride into Paradise. One must be escorted there, by a divine spirit. In our culture, we refer to it as the Four. But other lands have their own equivalents. Of course, Toros might – eventually – take over the role himself. He could become the Vohorin version of the Four. But I do not think so. No; it is beyond even his talents. So—'

'I am weary of this,' interrupted Quarvis. 'I shall depart before I fall asleep.'

'Have you presented Selindak with your gift?'

Quarvis frowned. 'My gift?'

'The animal skin found inside the Origin,' said Shaelus. 'Decorated with hunting scenes and procreative symbols on one side, and a map of the realms beyond the Forest on the other. You brought it here from Druine, did you not?'

'It is an interesting relic, nothing more.'

Shaelus chuckled. 'Ah, Quarvis! Maybe you are not as bright as I thought. Have you forgotten that the map was crossed out? That Toros drew a line through it as if to say, *I give up; I cannot get this right*. The skin is a sign of the visionary's limits; it marks the boundary of his knowledge. Then as now, I think. Oh, do not misunderstand me. I am certain Toros entered the Forest to gain magical knowledge. And in that, he has clearly triumphed: for it was that knowledge, passed onto Kraike, that enabled men to take the form of demons. But I think he was seeking something else, too.

'Those realms beyond the Forest – they are believed to be discarnate. There, all is magic, all is *soul*; there is no physical matter. Entry-points – portals, if you prefer – are hidden throughout the Forest. Find them, and you can travel from one realm to another. Why would one want to do so? Several reasons, I suppose. One is to escape the demons. Another, to experience the realms themselves – to wander through them, like a mortal man visiting foreign countries. Would either of these satisfy Toros? Perhaps. At present, this is all hypothetical. For Toros has not found these portals. And whatever you have been told, he *has* been able to search unhindered. The demons do him no harm.'

646

Quarvis blinked. 'That is nonsense. We know that he has suffered—'

'You have been *told* that he suffered,' said Shaelus. 'But he has an amulet which holds the demons at bay.'

'How – how do you know this?'

'Kraike confessed it to a friend of mine,' said Shaelus. He glanced at the two Erethin who stood guard. 'From your faces, I see this is news to you as well.'

'You are lying,' spat Quarvis.

'If so, why do you seem so *flustered*? But, to regress: Toros has not found these portals. If he had, he would have communicated their location to Kraike. And our limping, sour-faced friend would have created some accurate maps. Yet he has not done so, has he? No. And that, I think, is why I am here.'

His gaze tightened on Quarvis.

'I know how the portals can be found. Where they reside in the Forest. I,' he pressed a hand to his chest, 'have the knowledge that Toros craves.'

Quarvis grew very still. Then he broke out in laughter. 'Is *that* what you believe? No, no, no – preposterous! I will hear no more of it. What a fool you are! How could *you* know where the portals are? It makes no sense!' He pointed at Shaelus. 'You believe you succeeded where Toros failed? Nonsense!'

'I did not succeed,' said Shaelus. 'But nor did I try. During my travels, I have seen something that holds the key. What it is, I do not know. But I will work it out in time.'

'You are . . . are *deluded*.' As Quarvis turned to go, Shaelus caught him by the wrist. Quarvis whirled; the guards advanced. 'What have I seen? *Where* did I see it? The Boros Temple of Southern Keltuska? The Ice Caves of Thralise? What about—'

'Enough!' Jerking free, Quarvis stumbled to the door. 'You are an idiot, Shaelus! First you bore me with misguided theories then you—'

'Misguided? Far from it. *You* guided me, Quarvis. As I spoke, I watched your face. I observed every flicker in your eyes, every twitch of the muscles around your mouth. And I adjusted my theories accordingly.' Shaelus chuckled. 'It was like that game when a child seeks a hidden object, and its mother says, "You are getting warmer, now you are getting colder . . ." Did you forget I have that talent? When Faltriste and I first met, he asked about my writings. Which were true? Which were lies? He went through a list, and I answered honestly. I realise, now, that he was not questioning me out of idle curiosity. He wanted to know, *for certain*, whether I had visited particular places. And one of those places contained the knowledge Toros needs. But which one? From your ever-shifting face, I can see it was neither the Boros Temple nor the Ice Caves. So that leaves several possibilities . . .'

Frowning fiercely, baring his teeth, Quarvis looked as if he wanted to attack Shaelus. A guard placed a hand against the little man's chest.

'Go,' he said, tersely. 'You have done enough damage as it is.'

A flush rose through Quarvis's snarling face. 'There is no damage,' said Quarvis, turning away. 'He knows – so what? What difference does it make?' He shot a fiery glance over his shoulder. 'What lies ahead, Shaelus – you will not survive it. You have not benefited from—'

'From tricking you?' finished Shaelus. 'Maybe not. But your rage, Quarvis, your idiotic after-the-fact anger – it gladdens my heart. Oh, and think on this: if Toros is successful, and you find yourself wandering the realms beyond life, you will always, *always* know that at your moment of triumph, you were bested by Cavielle Shaelus.'

Quarvis yanked open the door. 'You are wrong, damn it all.'

'In those realms,' continued Shaelus, 'nothing will have

changed. In this world, you bemoaned your blighted body, twisted and gnarled like a dog turd frozen by a spring frost. But that was never your problem. Your spirit, your *soul*, is the taproot of your inferiority. And that is something you cannot cast off. You are condemned to be Leptus Quarvis for eternity. No judge has ever passed a harsher sentence.'

CHAPTER TWENTY-NINE

Too much, thought Ballas. This is too much.

They stood atop the temple wall. Ahead, green light poured from the circular, oak-crowded enclosure. The light itself was disturbing; it seemed strangely akin to a liquid, reminding Ballas of molten glass pouring into a glassworker's mould, except it flowed upward to the sky. The black flecks were still visible, fluttering and twisting in its depths. Surprisingly, there was no heat, not even the faintest hint of warmth. Ballas was no natural scientist, but even he knew this was not possible.

'*None* of this is possible,' he murmured, wiping sweat from his forehead.

'Oh, it is possible all right,' said Ekkerlin. '*The impossibility of something is no argument against its existence; it is merely one of the conditions under which it exists.*' She clapped him on the shoulder. 'Do not let it worry you. Just accept it for what it is.' Withdrawing her hand, she plucked an arrow from her quiver. 'Besides, you are not usually bothered by tiny details.'

Ballas turned to her. She was smiling; green light reflected from her hazel eyes. She seemed calm. For a heartbeat, he resented her. She understood what was happening. She was not unnerved by the mysteriousness of the situation. For most of her life, she had read books about arcane matters. In a fundamental way, she was prepared; Ballas, however, was not.

If only we had travelled faster once we entered Vohoria, he

thought. Damn it all – if I had not been arrested in Glavven, we could have caught up with Kraike long before now.

Inching to the edge of the wall, he gazed into the enclosure. Through the branches, he saw Kraike; swathed in light, he was a glowing silhouette, stooping over a stone bier. From his posture, it was clear his hands were resting on something; but this something – Toros, assumed Ballas – was completely lost in the light.

No, realised Ballas. It *was* the light – or the light's source.

Do not think about it, he urged himself. This is no moment to develop a sense of curiosity.

He took the bow from his shoulder. The oak branches were thick and tangled; finding a clear path through for an arrow would be difficult.

'Which one do you want?' he asked Ekkerlin.

'Your aim is better than mine,' she said. 'I will take Toros; I suspect he is a bigger target. And he is not the one we truly need to kill.'

'No?'

'Kraike is the necromancer,' said Ekkerlin. 'Once he is dead, the spell will break, and Toros will perish. Imagine that, Anhaga: you've spent millennia in the Forest then, just when you think you are coming home, you find yourself back amongst the demons – for eternity, this time.'

'Reckon he'll be teaching the demons a few ripe curse words,' said Ballas, nocking an arrow to his bowstring. 'Ready?'

'Not quite.' Ekkerlin squinted through the branches. 'I cannot find a gap to aim through. As usual, you've hogged the best spot. No matter; I'll go elsewhere. When you are ready, give a signal.'

Ballas nodded. 'Try not to bugger it up,' he said as Ekkerlin departed, pacing swiftly along the wall.

* * *

651

She had never seen Ballas so frightened. So *overwhelmed*. He reminded her, in essence if not appearance, of a fish on a river-bank: he was stranded in a situation beyond his comprehension, and a wild, baffled terror flashed in his eyes.

Yet she would gladly trade places with him.

Is it best, wise men asked, to face an ordeal in a state of ignorance, or to know fully what it entails?

To Ekkerlin, the answer was clear: in instances such as this, it was better not to know. Were it possible, she would happily forget everything she had learned about necromancy, metaphysics and countless other esoteric matters. As she told Ballas, the green light was the Phosphorescence of Return. She had not told him it contained inconceivable energies which, if uncon-tained, could wreak havoc; rolling out like a tide, it could warp living nature into unspeakable forms, and draw the dead out of the earth for miles around. But the black tatters floating in the light were more troubling. These were tiny scraps of the Forest, passing into this world; Shalfrazen had written, *These are akin to snowflakes blowing through an opened door, when a fellow retreats into a tavern to escape a blizzard*. In themselves, they were not dangerous. But they showed that a doorway had indeed been opened, and the natural partition between the living and dead was temporarily sundered.

If Ekkerlin knew none of this, she would be calmer. When the time came to draw her bowstring, her hands would be steady, her focus unbroken.

Now, though, she felt as if her very bones trembled with fear.

She halted. Peering, she spotted a straight path between the branches. From here, a true-flying arrow could strike Toros.

She gazed through the light at the bier. She could not see the visionary; he was merely the fountainhead from which the light spilled.

She nocked an arrow. Looked across the enclosure to Ballas.

The big man raised a hand, five fingers extended. She raised her own hand in confirmation. Then, lifting the bow, she took aim.

And counted.

Five, four, three, two, one . . .

She hesitated a split instant. Out of her eye-corner, she saw Kraike pitch sideways, an arrow jutting from his neck.

She released the bow string. The arrow swept cleanly through the branches, plunging into the heart of the light.

She lowered the bow.

It is done, she thought.

The light dimming, she saw the shape of a man on the bier. Arching backward, he flung up his arms, his hands clenched into fists – a posture of pain, frustration, despair. The light faded several degrees more—

—then flared, as bright as a dozen pyres.

Yelling, Ekkerlin staggered a step back.

Once again, Toros vanished from sight, lost within the light. And the light, it was changing, Ekkerlin realised. *Darkening.*

No, she realised. The light was staying the same. But the black flecks, those thin shreds of the Forest, were rising in greater profusion, twisting and folding in on themselves, whirling crazily as if trapped in an eddy. Of a sudden, they ebbed, fluttering back into the light. In their stead, a dozen red orbs appeared, each the size of an apple, hovering above the bier. They lingered a moment, as if getting their bearings; then, as one, they swept through the wall-stones into the building.

A sick feeling curdled Ekkerlin's guts. She knew what the red lights were. She knew what they meant, and what would follow.

Numbly, she took another step back – and felt the wall

653

vanish from beneath her. She fell, barely aware that she was falling; all she could see, all she could consider, were those lights that had spilled from the depths of the Forest and invaded the temple.

There was a library beneath the Solrepta, candlelit, furnished with several pockmarked desks and numerous bookcases so crudely constructed they would not have been out of place in a child's nursery. It was a dreary place, the ceiling oppressively low, the windowless stone walls brightened by neither tapestries nor drapes. The only good thing to be said about it was that it matched Quarvis's mood perfectly.

Sitting on an uncushioned settle, the little man was in the lowest of low humours. And he hated himself for it.

He ought to have been happy. More, he ought to have been *ecstatic*. Not far away, Toros was re-entering the world and he, Quarvis, had played a pivotal role in his return. He was Erethin; he was amongst the chosen.

Yet his heart was heavy. He gazed at the other Erethin, thirty or so men, scattered through the library. Their excitement crackled in the air like a type of gentle lightning storm. They kept a tight bridle on it, that was true; they did not chatter like gossiping washerwomen, or fidget, or pace restlessly back and forth, like expectant fathers outside a birthing room. But tiny gestures betrayed their happy agitation: the impatient tapping of a foot, the cracking of knuckles, the chewing of a lip – in these and other small ways, their high emotions leaked out. Even if it were not so, their joy was visible in their eyes – so bright, so ceaselessly shifting – their slightly too-fast breathing, the sweat-drops winking in the candlelight.

What would they have seen, if they paid Quarvis any attention?

A pale little man, face clenched as if suffering a gastric upset.

His stomach *did* ache. But the source was not any genuine malady. It was anger, directed primarily at himself.

Shaelus had tricked him. And that hurt. With his clever face-reading talent, he had weaselled the truth out of Quarvis. Why? Because, ultimately, he, Quarvis, allowed it to happen. He knew better than to trust Shaelus. He knew he was dangerous, cunning, and intelligent. He knew – yes – it had been folly to engage him in a conversation. Even taking him his food had been a bad step; even as he carried the plate into his room, he had known he was entering treacherous territory. But he had wanted to tip salt into Shaelus's wounds. To let the scholar know he was well and truly bested. To jab the knife in, and twist it, until it squealed against bone.

He had failed to show the proper self-restraint.

But even this was not the crux of Quarvis's woes.

Before Quarvis left, Shaelus had uttered some cruel words. And those words had struck home.

You are condemned to be Leptus Quarvis for all eternity. No judge has ever passed a harsher sentence.

Oh yes, thought Quarvis, bitterly. How very clever of you, to put the maggot of self-doubt in my mind. To strike at me where I am weakest.

It was an obvious ploy. Every bullying child employed the same tactic. And yet, Quarvis could not reverse its effect. And that was his own fault. If he was stronger, more mentally disciplined, he could forget about those words. If Eastern mystics could hold their palms over a lighted candle flame without wincing, surely he could muster a similar level of resolve and, simply, *stop thinking about what Shaelus had said.*

But it was impossible. He was like a fish with a hook embedded in its mouth; struggle as he might, he could not break free.

And Shaelus, that atrocious bastard – even though all was

655

lost, he had gained a consolation victory: he had ruined the moment for Quarvis.

Quarvis gritted his jaw so tightly his teeth ached.

He would get his revenge. Yes, he would ask Selindak if he could watch Toros extract the information from Shaelus's mind. It would be an excruciating process; he gathered it was akin to being turned inside out.

He smiled at the thought.

I will have the last laugh, Shaelus. I—

A sudden chill swept through the library. Gooseflesh rose on Quarvis's arms; an involuntary shiver shook his body. He looked up, wondering if he alone had detected the drop in temperature. The other Erethin stood stock-still, staring at one another. Yes, they had felt it too – a coarse tingling in the air, as if a thousand frost particles had blown through. The light dropped a little, too. Blinking, Quarvis saw that the candle flames were shrinking. The cold intensified; Quarvis's teeth chattered, just once. Then warmth returned, and the candle flames glowed once more.

Peculiar, he thought. But then, the Solrepta was an ancient structure, riddled with holes through which an inclement breeze could encroach . . .

He swallowed. Who was he fooling?

Not himself. He had read many texts on necromancy; the room beneath the bell tower had been full of them. He knew what the abrupt cold signified.

Assuming the books are correct, he thought. *Even the finest scholars make mistakes, and so much of metaphysics is mere conjecture . . .*

A barely suppressed panic rippled amongst the Erethin. Perhaps they had read the same texts. Maybe they knew what was happening.

No, Quarvis told himself. *Nothing is happening. Nothing*

at all. It is just a fluke, a weird but innocuous occurrence that—

Crying out, an Erethin pointed to the library door. Twelve or so red orbs floated through the wood. Several feet above the ground, they wavered from side to side, like bumblebees over a flower. One darted at an Erethin, sinking through his chest, entering his body. Shrieking, the Erethin staggered, his eyes rolling white. The remaining orbs surged into other Erethin, each a swift, glassy bubble, plunging into its prey.

Quarvis got to his feet. In his mind's eye, he saw an ancient woodcut; it had graced the pages of a book he had stolen from the Archives. With the unsettling vividness of such simple pictures, it showed men rampaging through a narrow street, ripping passers-by apart. Women stumbled, their arms torn from their sockets, blood spraying in dark thick droplets; babies lay scattered, their tender skulls bitten open; dogs, cats and horses were not spared, their soft-furred bodies chewed and gashed . . . And floating amongst the horrors were a number of spheres, which he had given little consideration, believing them to be strange symbolic embellishments, the kind of idiosyncratic flourishes whose meaning was known only to the artist. How wrong he had been.

With surprising presence of mind, Quarvis got to his feet. Already, it had begun: the orb-tainted Erethin were mauling their unaffected brethren, biting open throats, gouging eyes, snapping necks. They did so silently, as if they had come from a world where cries, yowls and snarls had no significance – a world where noise itself was a stranger . . .

Quarvis strode to the door; in an effort to remain inconspicuous, he neither walked nor ran, but moved at a brisk-but-faltering gait somewhere in between.

He grasped the ring-handle, opened the door, stepped through.

He closed the door. A strong urge to vomit bubbled into his throat.

Ignoring it, he broke into a full-blooded sprint.

When the sudden cold manifested itself, Shaelus, who had been lying down, sat up and swung his legs over the edge of the bed. The two Erethin guards felt it too, the abrupt frostiness. Shaelus glanced at the lantern, glowing on a wall-hook; behind the glass panel, the flame contracted, shrinking to the wick. Then, as the chill departed, the flame rose, burning at full strength.

Well, Shalfrazen, he thought. I wish you could be here to see this. Your knowledge was theoretical; mine, I fear, will soon be practical.

'What was that?' one Erethin guard asked the other.

Warily, the second guard opened the door and looked out. 'I cannot see anything. I think—' With a muffled grunt, he stumbled against the doorframe.

Drawing a breath, Shaelus rose. Swiftly, he unsheathed the dagger hanging from the first Erethin's belt. The man turned, incredulous.

'Aiy! Give that back—'

Pushing the man aside, Shaelus strode to the second Erethin. As he got close, the Erethin turned. The change was astonishing: his eye-whites were vivid red, the veins had burst in his face, granting his skin a scaled, reptilian look, and blood trickled from his nose and ears. His lips peeled back from his teeth; the discoloured eyes narrowed. Shaelus thrust the knife toward his throat, but the Erethin swiped out, knocking the weapon from his hand. Overbalancing, Shaelus fell against the transformed man; an unnatural heat radiated from his body: he sizzled like a hot stone. Frantically, Shaelus pushed the man away and doing so, staggered back into the room. The Erethin lunged, and Shaelus flung himself backward onto the bed.

Ducking low, the Erethin stooped, sinking his teeth into Shaelus's calf muscle. Shaelus gave a hoarse cry of pain. The second Erethin stared, goggle-eyed. Then he sprinted out into the corridor. Perhaps sensing there was more fun to be had with a livelier prey, the demon-possessed Erethin swung round and gave chase.

Shaelus's leggings were awash with blood. Carefully, he stood. Mercifully, he was too shocked to feel pain; his damaged leg was as numb as a gammon shank on a butcher's slab. But how long would it last? How long before his nerves yowled and screeched?

Best make hay while the sun shines, thought Shaelus, picking up the knife.

In the corridor, the possessed Erethin knelt atop the fallen body of the first; head low, shoulders quivering, he chewed through his former companion's spine, wrenching out the vertebrae with his teeth. Then, delving a hook-fingered hand into his lower back, he tugged out organ after dripping organ. Already, the air had the rich salty tang of an abattoir.

Turning left, Shaelus followed a different corridor, then another, recalling the route by which he had entered the Solrepta.

Clear air blew against his face. Ahead, the staircase rose into the gloomy haze of dusk.

Quarvis plunged into the circular chamber, where Selindak resided. Somewhere during his frantic run through the Solrepta, he must have climbed some steps – though he could not recall doing so – for he was now on the ground floor. There was a window, covered by a pair of curtains; green light spilled through a gap in the fabric, pulsing horribly. Within the nauseating glow, oak trees were visible, shadowy and twisted, like the salt-stiffened hair of a drowned mariner. Selindak was on his feet. Beside him, Lujaek glanced at Quarvis, then drew a knife.

'No, no!' yelled Quarvis, raising empty hands. 'It is me, Quarvis!' Then he understood. 'I am me, all the way through! From top to toe, I am unchanged! I am not . . . *inhabited* by anything that should not be there.'

Narrowing his eyes, Lujaek sheathed the blade. Quarvis closed the heavy wooden door, locking it. 'Something has gone awry,' he said. 'Terribly, *monstrously* awry! My fellow Erethin – there were these red lights, you see, and—'

'We know,' said Lujaek, taking Selindak's elbow.

'What is happening? I mean, I have read texts and . . .' Realising he was being ignored, he fell silent. Then, after a pause, 'What must we do? There is a way of reversing these effects, yes? Of restoring my brethren to their former selves?' As he spoke, he heard many feet pounding in the corridor. Then, a booming thud, as something struck the door. Startled, he scampered closer to Selindak. 'You are a sorcerer,' he said. 'You created *The Chronicle*. Surely you have a spell for occasions such as this?' He heard the wretched hopefulness in his voice. He sounded like a condemned man begging for clemency whilst knowing none would be given.

'Keep your mouth shut,' Lujaek ordered Quarvis. Strangely, the Erethin's words alarmed Quarvis more than the demon-possessed men; they were uttered in a hard, dismissive tone, they meant only one thing: Lujaek did not give an owl's hoot if Quarvis lived or died.

No, thought Quarvis. That cannot be. His voice – it reflects his terror. He sounded harsher than he intended . . .

'A knife,' said Quarvis, pacing closer. 'Do you have a spare knife? I will fight those . . .' He flapped a hand toward the door. 'I will fight—'

It was as if he had not spoken. Thud after thud resounded from the door. Hinges screeched within the frame.

Panicking, Quarvis ran to the window, praying it was the

sort that opened. If it wasn't, he decided, he would shatter the glass and climb through. So what if Kraike was outside, resurrecting Toros? So what if escaping meant plunging into that awful green light? If Lujaek would not help him, he would help himself.

He opened the curtains. Green light swept over him. Despite its brightness, it did not hurt his eyes. He looked through—

— and cried out in alarm.

The bier on which Toros lay was shrouded in light so intense it seemed almost solid; nothing could be seen through it. But the rest of the enclosure was relatively visible. And Kraike sat slumped against a tree trunk, an arrow protruding from the side of his neck, his gaze fixed on the bier.

'Kraike!' yelped Quarvis. 'He is wounded—'

Movement caught his eye. A huge figure appeared from the higher reaches of an oak. Climbing down, it hung from a low branch then dropped. Even before it turned and its face became visible, Quarvis recognised it: Anhaga Ballas, the Hawk.

'Someone – a killer – is with Toros! He will—' He swung around to Lujaek. Maybe the Erethin had ignored him until now. Maybe he thought he was irrelevant, a speck of dust. But Quarvis would *force* him to listen, whether he liked it or not. 'Out there,' he began, jabbing a finger at the window, 'there is a man named—' He fell silent.

Selindak stood in the middle of the chamber. Lujaek was close behind him. Together, they watched the door, as if waiting for it to break open. In his right hand, Selindak held a grey disc-like object, the size of a wren's nest. Both men seemed tense, yet calm. The door quaked, pounded by impact after impact. Wood splintered, suddenly; the door burst from its hinges. Eight or nine Erethin, red-eyed, faces mottled with

661

burst veins, jaws slubbered with fresh blood, scraps of flesh hanging from their fingernails, plunged over the threshold. They hurtled toward Selindak, shrieking—

—then stumbled to a halt. They stood, staring at the disc-like object – an amulet, Quarvis realised – uncertain what to do next. Then their predatory instincts took hold; as one, they turned to Quarvis.

A biting cold swept over Quarvis. This was not a supernatural chill, an icy gust arising from magic. It was the freezing blast of fear.

Quarvis backed away against the wall.

It cannot end like this, he thought.

His life darted past his eyes. He saw himself as a child, sickly and withered since birth, friendless, unloved and, he supposed, unlovable; he saw himself as an adolescent, enrolling at a seminary, believing a priest's robes would grant him the status, authority and power he craved; he saw himself four years later, stammering through his first sermon, losing his way several times, confusing one theological detail with another, feeling as if he was drowning in the baffled contempt of the congregation; he saw himself abandoning the priesthood, and acquiring the position of a Scholar, where his talents might be better used; he saw himself raiding countless homes, printing shops and market stalls, confiscating texts and sending sinners to the gallows; he saw himself weeping in his room in the Sacros, torn by a crisis of faith; he saw Faltriste rescuing him, and converting him to the Torosian cause; he saw Prendle House, with its bell tower and sprawling garden . . . He had been happy there . . .

When the Erethin arrived, swarming over him like locusts, he barely noticed; as his throat was ripped out, his ribs shattered, and entrails torn out, he saw only one thing – a memory, blazing bright in his mind's eye:

Cavielle Shaelus, uttering those words:

You are condemned to be Leptus Quarvis for all eternity . . .

And that eternity was just beginning.

CHAPTER THIRTY

Ballas stood, staring at the bier.

He could not see Toros. The light emanating from what he assumed was the visionary's body was too intense; it was like staring into the sun, except the glare did not hurt his eyes. And this was no ordinary light. It still had the glassy, half-liquid nature Ballas had noticed whilst perched upon the wall; close to, he discerned faint ripples crawling through its surface, like wavelets sprawling over a beach. The black flecks continued to flutter and dance—

Ballas twisted, vomiting.

The light, he realised. It induced a vicious type of sea-sickness . . .

The world tilted, Ballas's guts clenched, and he spilled his gorge a second time.

Small wonder there were no Erethin standing guard over Toros. Small wonder he was absolutely alone with the shaman.

He drew back his shoulders – then hesitated.

Climbing down through the trees, he had been overtaken by a hard, angry determination. He had vowed to destroy Toros where he lay; but most of all, he was determined to annihilate the sick, nerve-numbing fear that seemed to possess every atom in his body.

I will not be beaten, he had told himself. I will not be broken.

Now, suddenly, this resolve disintegrated, shattering like a dropped vase. He was out of his depth; he had waded out into waters where the currents were too strong. His limbs trembled. His eyes prickled, as if tears were approaching. And he felt weak, absurdly frail, as if he had ingested some paralysing poison.

He could retreat, if he wanted to. Just grab a low-hanging branch and climb, scrambling up through the trees and out of the enclosure. Then, he would do what? Flee Vohoria. Abandon the Hawks. Take refuge in some quiet corner of the world . . .

Or he could take a step closer to the bier.

Just one, to see what happened.

To see, at least, if he could *force* himself to move.

He did so. The sky did not fall; nothing dangerous emerged from the bier light.

And unexpectedly, it felt easy. *Natural*.

He took another step. Then another.

His fear increased. But he accepted that this too was natural; he assimilated it, absorbed it, as if swallowing a foul-tasting medicine.

Another step, and another, and another . . .

He arrived at the bier.

Now, he could see Toros. Upon the slab lay a man, slender, not gaunt, his naked body crammed with the lean, stone-hard muscles that arose from a tough life lived outdoors. His face was heavy-browed, with a strong, pugnacious jaw; his eyes were closed. The resurrection was nearly complete; a thin, dew-like sheen of moisture slicked his body – the first sweat, perhaps, of a man who for millennia had been discarnate.

He was not an imposing figure; he was the sort of man to be passed unnoticed in the street.

A haggard grin touched Ballas's lips.

This is all that you are, he thought. A man, nothing more.

Yes, you may have accomplished something strange, remarkable even. But you remain a man, when all is said and done. And I have killed many men, some who deserved it, one or two who did not. But you have earned a swift return to the Forest.

He drew a knife.

How to kill this visionary, this sorcerer?

By the usual method, Ballas decided, raising the knife.

He slammed the blade through Toros's ribcage. The weapon scraped through bone, slid through soft tissues, until it was lodged hilt-deep.

Ballas gazed at Toros's face. The mouth did not move, the eyelids did not flicker.

The green light did not diminish.

Bracing a hand against Toros's chest, Ballas wrenched out the knife. An inch-wide wound gaped where the blade had been, a grim slit, soft-edged, like the mouth of a fish. It puckered, this incision, then sealed over perfectly, as if it had never existed.

Ballas struck again at the same spot; again, the wound healed as soon as the knife was removed.

Adopting a different tactic, Ballas cut Toros's throat, carving deeply through the damp flesh.

Once more, the wound repaired itself seamlessly, like water after a pebble has pierced its surface and sunk beneath.

Shaelus emerged from the Solrepta.

Free, he thought, relieved. Then, But to what ends? If Toros survives, who will ever know true freedom? Who will—

Something caught his eye. A figure, tangled in a thornbush, eyes closed, unmoving.

Ekkerlin.

Blinking, Shaelus looked up at the top of the Solrepta, then back to the Hawk.

Fallen?

'Ekkerlin,' he murmured, hurrying over, moving quickly despite his injured calf. Kneeling, he slapped the Hawk's face, lightly. 'Girl, wake up – if you can.' Feeling beneath her jaw, he detected a pulse.

Alive, he thought. That is something.

Stirring, Ekkerlin opened her eyes. Her gaze was unfocused, and when she spoke, she slurred, as though drunk. 'Shaelus?'

Concussed? wondered Shaelus. *Or merely stunned?*

'We have little time,' said Shaelus, watching her, closely. 'Where is Anhaga?'

'I do not know.' Wincing, Ekkerlin got to her feet, tearing free of the thornbush; her movements were clumsy. 'We were up there,' she pointed to the top of the Solrepta. 'We launched arrows at Kraike and Toros. Kraike was hit; I am sure Toros was, too. Yet the . . .' she groped for the right word 'the Phosphorescence continues. A day ago, we were attacked by demons. I assume Kraike conjured them?'

'He did,' confirmed Shaelus.

'Did you see them?'

'No. I heard them, though. I am surprised that you survived.'

'I believe Kraike is not employing Vohorin magic,' said Ekkerlin. 'The demons belonged to the . . . the . . .'

'Come, my girl,' urged Shaelus. 'Concentrate. Clear your head. *What* did the demons belong to? Think.'

'The Dalzertian pantheon,' said Ekkerlin, blinking.

'As I described in my book?'

'The Scorpion, Innocence, the Hateful Embrace . . . I suspect Kraike drew inspiration from his nightly glimpses of the Forest.'

'And a visionary sees the region of the Forest related to the type of magic he is using—' A revelation coursed through Shaelus like a lightning bolt. 'Oh, damn it, damn it, *damn it*! Why did I not guess? Why did I not *see*?'

Ekkerlin swayed; Shaelus seized her shoulders. She was in no condition to return to action. Not yet. He had to bring her back to her senses.

'Pay attention, girl,' he said, staring into her eyes. 'Not long ago, I conversed with Selindak. He told me that, contrary to most thinking, a sorcerer is not limited to using magic of one particular type, as determined by his blood, his ancestry. He can, if sufficiently talented – and disciplined – adopt the practices of other cultures. So it must be, if Kraike is using Dalzertian magic. And Toros . . . if he is situated in the Dalzerte region of the Forest, he too must be using Dalzertian magic. Curse it all, yes!

'At the Origin, we found an animal skin marked with a failed attempt to map the connections between the various realms. I did not perceive its importance at the time; I imagined it was idle speculation on Toros's part. Now, I know it was not so. I believe Toros entered the Forest not merely to gain magical knowledge in general, but an understanding of the connections *in particular*. The Dalzerte had greater knowledge of the subject than almost any other culture. Do you remember what I wrote about the Gardens of Dalzerte?'

'That they had fallen into decay.'

'Good, good,' said Shaelus. By degrees, Ekkerlin's mind was growing clear. 'And the pathways?'

'You said they were convoluted, random.' Ekkerlin's eyes widened; a flash of returning cognisance. 'You think . . .'

'Yes, it is possible,' said Shaelus. 'that the pathways constitute a map of the connections. And those little stone monoliths—'

'Inscribed with pictures of plants?' She spoke quickly.

'Rare, strange plants, yes – those monoliths each symbolised a different realm. Or rather, the portals through which one must pass to enter the realms. Now, my girl: why is sorcery so dependent on self-discipline? What does self-discipline enable the conjuror to do?'

'It allows him to enter the correct state of mind,' said Ekkerlin. 'Spell words and gestures serve the same purpose. They are designed to make the sorcerer's mind operate in the correct fashion.'

'Those plants were psychotropic,' said Shaelus. 'Like *lecterscrix*, they transformed the user's thoughts and perceptions in such a way they could pass through the portals. Each portal requires a different mental state; and to *simulate* that state, the appropriate plants could be ingested. Then the prospective realm-wandering sorcerer would learn to induce those states without the plant's help, through force of will alone. Thus, when they were in the Forest, where the plants did not grow, they could access the portals.'

'You speak of the Gardens as if they were a training ground,' said Ekkerlin.

'That is *exactly* what they were,' replied Shaelus. 'And I have wandered that training ground; I know its layout and, therefore, I know how the realms are joined to one another.' He shook her shoulders, urgently. 'That is what I know without knowing it! But I cannot recall the exact details. And *that* is why Toros wants to extract the memories directly from my mind; everything that is seen is recorded, even if one cannot bring it to the surface. Toros needs to understand the pathways. And when – if – he does . . .'

'Yes?'

'It would – could – be bad,' said Shaelus, darkly. 'Very bad indeed. You have seen the black flakes fluttering in the Phosphorescence? And understand their significance?'

Ekkerlin said that she did.

'Did you spot any red orbs? About so large?' Shaelus cupped his hands.

'They spilled from the light,' confirmed Ekkerlin, her voice clear now, 'then raced into the Solrepta. I understand their significance, too. They were demons . . . The non-corporeal essence of demons, at least, seeking carnate hosts.'

'And they have found them,' said Shaelus, gesturing to the Solrepta. 'In my book, I repeated the idea that the Dalzertians destroyed themselves through cannibalism. I stressed that I had certain doubts, for the process did not take months, or years, but seemed to occur in a single night. Now, I realise that my scepticism was misplaced. The Dalzertians *did* devour one another but, at the same time, they did not. I believe they ventured into the Forest, as Toros has; maybe they even went further. On one occasion they left the door open, so to speak; orb-demons rushed through, occupied the Dalzertians' mortal bodies and, acting in accord with their base natures, set to consuming the populace.'

He exhaled.

'In the Solrepta, the same phenomenon is occurring. It is a dreadful sight, microcosmic though it is. To witness it on a grander scale though . . . which we will, Ekkerlin, if we do not stop Toros.

'Vohoria is full of Erethin, men and women whose talents are similar to the shaman's. I fear that if he returns, and gains the knowledge locked away in my head, he will ensure every Erethin is capable of navigating the pathways, of drifting from realm to realm as they please. And what is to say that they, like the Dalzertians, will not leave the door open? What is to say that Toros will even *care*, if they do?'

Unease flickered in Ekkerlin's eyes. A good sign, thought Shaelus. Her wits had returned almost completely.

'An orb here and there would not make much difference,' he continued. 'As fearsome as they might be, a handful of demons cannot cause too much damage. But if they arrived in large numbers . . . Imagine this: Toros and his fellow Erethin form an army of travellers determined to wander the various realms. To depart this world, they would open the door so wide, countless orbs could come through. And then? Literally, we would be left with a hell on earth.

'I am not certain that Toros would give a whispered damn. Our world is an aberration; every other world, as far as we know, is discarnate; only we are creatures of flesh, rather than pure soul. Despite our rarity value, our disappearance would not count for much. We are freaks, two-headed lambs to be drowned at birth.'

'You do not *know* that these are Toros's plans,' countered Ekkerlin, quietly. Inwardly, Shaelus smiled. The fog had completely lifted; Ekkerlin's mind, precise and gently combative, had returned to its proper state.

'It is not a question of knowing,' said Shaelus. 'But of a willingness to take the risk. And the more I consider Toros, the more I believe that he and I share some traits. I speak not out of vanity, but ice-cold analysis. Our determination, our lust for knowledge – these are commendable. But we both possess darker sides. For most of my life, I would have gladly watched Druine burn; I had no regard for my homeland. I fear it is the same with Toros – only he, with his extraordinary mind and abilities, considers the entire globe to be his homeland. He reviles its limitations, its restrictions. *This* is why he wants to explore other realms – and why he cares not if he destroys this realm as he does so.'

He spotted Ekkerlin's short-bow in the thornbush. Stooping, he pulled it free, disentagling it from the stems.

'Yes, there is a chance that I am mistaken,' he went on. 'But does it matter if if I am? Is it generally wise to allow a single man, such as Toros, to possess powers beyond our comprehension? Powers we could not fight against, if he misused them? The globe would become his property, his plaything, a glob of warm wax he could shape as he wished . . . You said Kraike was struck by an arrow?'

'In the throat,' confirmed Ekkerlin. 'He fell away from the bier on which Toros lay.'

'Then he is no longer performing the resurrection,' said Shaelus, thinking hard. 'Toros must be strong enough to complete the process himself. Ha! All is not lost, my girl. Do you have a knife?'

Ekkerlin patted the blade resting at her hip.

'Excellent,' said Shaelus. 'You must climb back up that wall, return to Toros and kill him. But you must do so in a particular fashion.' He grinned. 'I shall let you in on a secret. You have seen the Penance Oak?'

Ekkerlin said that she had.

'It is not just some grisly trophy case,' said Shaelus. 'The nails securing the heads to the branches, you see, are not positioned at random. Far from it! There is a part of the brain, as tiny as a kidney bean, occasionally it is referred to as the third eye. This little component enables us to communicate with the supernatural world and, by extension, perform acts of magic. Hence, the Church ensures that the nails are driven through that *precise spot*. It serves no purpose, of course, since the alleged magicians are dead. But the Church enjoys few things more than a symbolic gesture.

'For once, however, the technique will have a practical effect.' Shaelus tapped his forehead, above and between his eyebrows. 'Right there, my girl. Right there. Oh – before you go: I shall keep your bow. Naturally, I will need your arrows too . . .?' Nodding, Ekkerlin unlooped the quiver from her shoulder and passed it to him.

'My thanks,' said Shaelus. 'Now, you climb, and I shall do what I can to stop any nastiness following you. And follow you it will.'

He fingered an arrow's fletching, white as the tail-flash of a rabbit.

'I was a fine bowman once,' he said.

'You mentioned it in *Wandering through Keltuska.*'

'Every word was true,' said Shaelus. Another smile. 'I never lie, Ekkerlin.'

Approaching the wall, Ekkerlin glanced at him. '*Never*, Shaelus?'

'Sometimes never. Often, occasionally,' replied Shaelus. 'There. A nice, meaningless farewell. Now go!'

Ekkerlin climbed. Shaelus moved to the Solrepta entrance and waited.

Ballas stabbed Toros again and again. Always, the visionary healed. Ballas gashed his throat, pierced his chest and lungs, and skewered his heart a hundred times over, to no avail; he slashed open the visionary's belly, hoping to delve inside and rip out his innards – surely he could not survive such ill treatment? But the wound closed over instantly, without leaving the faintest scar. It was like attacking the ocean.

A thick fatigue congealed within Ballas's body. He had never been so tired, so bludgeoned by weariness. Yet he carried on, hoping that the next assault would leave a mark, just enough to assure him the task was not entirely futile, that there was a way to pierce Toros's defences. But there was not: in some sullen corner of his soul, Ballas knew every knife stroke, every thrust and jab, was worthless, a gesture of no significance.

But he carried on. What else could he do?

A movement at the edge of his vision. Glancing up, he saw Ekkerlin scrambling down through the trees.

'It is no good,' shouted Ballas as she dropped down. 'Nothing will—'

'You are wrong,' she said, casting about. Bending, she picked up a large stone. 'You have seen the Penance Oak?'

'I've never been to Soriterath,' said Ballas.

'But you know about the heads?'

'Aye.'

She handed him the rock. 'Hammer it through,' she said. Taking Ballas's knife, she turned it upright so it rested against Toros's forehead like a nail, the tip pressing against it. Ballas seized the handle, gripping it tightly.

'Behind!' he yelled.

Kraike was on his feet, the arrow sticking from his neck. Knife drawn, he lunged at Ekkerlin; whirling, Ekkerlin struck the sorcerer a backhanded blow across the face. As he staggered, Ekkerlin seized his wrist and twisted. The knife tumbled from his grasp. Pushing him against an oak, she launched a flurry of punches; when he slid to the ground, Ekkerlin kicked him, then stamped on him, as if he was a flame to be extinguished. Then, kneeling, she cut his throat.

She returned to the bier.

'Now, Anhaga,' she said. 'Do it *now*.'

Standing at the entrance to the Solrepta, Shaelus nocked an arrow and waited.

Well, he thought. To think that it had come to this.

In the early days, before he took holy orders, he had expected to die in the course of some adventure or other. For a fellow who took risks, it was part of the natural order. As the years wore on, however, he had anticipated a sedate death, something tranquil, preceded by a lengthy period when he could take stock of his life.

But it was not to be. And it did not matter. He felt very calm. Very focused. And weirdly content.

He was also amused by an irony. Throughout his writing career, he insisted that every word he wrote was true; his books were slabs of absolute fact. Which was accurate – except in one instance.

He was not, as he claimed in *Wandering through Keltuska,* a master bowman. He could not recall why he had included that lie. Most likely, he had jotted it down on a whim, possibly believing the book in question required a little more colour, an extra dramatic flourish. In truth, he was an absolute duffer with a bow. He knew why: in the pause between taking aim and releasing the arrow he thought too much. How strongly was the wind blowing? How much should he compensate for it? And the target – what if it were to move suddenly to the left? Or the right? Should he attempt to anticipate its next move . . . And so on. He could not suppress the analytical part of his mind; he could not trust his instincts.

A figure appeared at the far end of the corridor. Lujaek. He jolted, startled by the sight of the *acaratix*. Shaelus did not hesitate; he released the bowstring, the bow vibrated lightly, and the arrow tore toward the Erethin, slamming into his thigh.

Lujaek grunted, toppling against the wall.

'Forgive me,' said Shaelus, drawing another arrow from the quiver. 'I was aiming for your head.'

Lujaek clambered onto all fours. 'Put down the bow,' he said, rising, leaning against the wall for support, 'and I may spare your life.'

'*May?* That is hardly a guarantee.'

The second arrow flew, hitting Lujaek in the shoulder. The Erethin spun, stumbling backward along the corridor.

'Curses,' said Shaelus. 'Unlike a fine wine, my archery has not improved with age.' He nocked another arrow. 'Third time lucky, do you think?' The arrow streaked toward Lujaek. 'Evidently not,' murmured Shaelus, as the shaft flew wide, skittered off the wall then sank into Lujaek's buttock. 'Believe it or not,' he said, taking a fourth arrow, 'I am pretty sure my embarrassment is equal to your pain. I am letting myself down rather badly.' He touched the arrow to the string, drew, let go; the shaft crunched into the back of Lujaek's skull. The ginger-haired Erethin flopped lifelessly onto the floor.

'That is more like it,' said Shaelus.

More footsteps. Selindak stepped out. He held a small grey disc in his upraised right hand – an amulet, assumed Shaelus. Yes, an amulet: behind the old man, a crowd of demon-possessed Erethin bristled and teemed, torn between fear of the amulet and a desire to rip Selindak apart.

Selindak glanced at Lujaek. 'I take it you are refusing to accept my offer?'

'It would appear so,' replied Shaelus.

'Your friends are here,' said Selindak. 'I saw one preparing to attack Toros. It will do no good. By now, the visionary will be capable of self-healing. He is, I believe, the first individual in human history capable of such an act. Already, we have entered a new age. Can you not see it is time to accept—'

'—this new age? Are you going to blather about its virtues? I don't think I could stand to listen to all that again.'

'If you kill me,' said Selindak, coolly, 'do you know what will happen?'

'You will find yourself in the Forest, I assume.'

A faint smile. 'True. But so will you. Only this device,' he tilted his head toward the amulet, 'is keeping these possessed men from destroying you. If I were to die, I would drop it to the floor – and then?'

'I would die too. What of it? I am old; sooner rather than later, I shall find myself lost amongst demons.'

'It need not be so,' said Selindak. 'Have you forgotten our conversation? Have—'

'Where is my travelling companion, Leptus Quarvis?' interrupted Shaelus, abruptly.

'He is dead,' replied Selindak, frowning.

'When he died, what happened to his soul?'

Selindak frowned. 'It will have gone to the Forest, for his demise came before—'

'It did not transmute into a red sphere, and enter your body? You have not been possessed by the little pipsqueak, have you?'

Selindak's frown deepened. He did not speak.

'Because,' said Shaelus, 'you have suddenly become every bit as boring, irksome and high-minded as he. Selindak,' he took aim, 'it will be a pleasure to kill you. And as for myself – at least my death will not be blighted by some prattling fossil too stupid to realise that the game is up.'

Ballas brought the rock down on the knife handle, driving the blade into Toros's skull. There was no resistance that Ballas felt, the skull bones breaking as easily as cobwebs, the brain-tissue yielding like a tuft of cloud, and the visionary's eyes snapped open, the dark irises empty of everything except Ballas's reflection, looming twice as huge as any oak.

I am the last thing you will see of this world, thought Ballas.

Seizing the handle, he wrenched out the knife. A feeble trickle of blood, diluted with cranial fluid, crawled out of the wound, and the wound itself – it did not heal, but gaped, like an ordinary wound in an ordinary man.

The muscles slackened in Toros's face, his features slumping into the type of imbecilic death mask Ballas had seen countless times before.

The green light did not fade, but vanished, slamming into nothingness.

Good, thought Ballas—

—and a flash of silver light washed over him, flowing through his pores, flesh and muscles, as fierce as a lightning bolt, yet painless, gentle even, and then—

—darkness.

The light knocked Ekkerlin off her feet, pitching her backward amongst the trees. She yelled out incoherently; from bones to skin, she tingled; splinters of glinting light floated in her vision.

Scrambling to her feet, she stumbled through the oak-crowded enclosure to the bier, where Toros lay dead. Then she spotted Ballas, sprawled face-down on the ground.

Sweet grief, she thought, hurrying over.

Kneeling, she shook his shoulder.

'Anhaga!' she shouted. 'Come on, you outsized oaf – wake up!'

No response. Straining, she rolled him onto his back. His eyes were open, staring emptily at the sky.

Dead? she wondered.

No. He was still breathing, and the breaths were deep and strong. What was it, then? Shock? Had the silver light scrambled his wits? Leaning over the bier, he had absorbed its full force.

She slapped his face. Still nothing.

'Damn it,' she shouted. 'Rouse yourself!'

A shudder passed through the big man's body and he woke, spluttering, as if he had spent a long time underwater. Rolling onto his side, he vomited bile.

'Toros?' he asked, wiping his lips with his sleeve.

'Dead. Gone. Back in the Forest.'

'That light—'

'I do not know what it was,' replied Ekkerlin, truthfully. 'Not that it matters. Let's leave this wretched forest and go home.'

'Aye.'

It was deathly silent inside the Solrepta – except for the buzzing of flies. Already, the dark insects were laying eggs on the corpses of countless Erethin. Shaelus had spoken of a 'nastiness' occurring inside the temple, and Ekkerlin knew that the red orbs, each a demonic spirit seeking a mortal home, would

678

be to blame. But she had not expected the carnage to be so extensive. The corpses were mutilated in every manner possible, if an assailant were to use only his teeth and hands. Bones were snapped, limbs wrenched from sockets, tendons torn out like threads from a tapestry, eyes gouged, jawbones routed . . . The floor gleamed with blood and entrails; every step the Hawks took either splashed, squelched or slithered.

They wandered the holy building. In a circular room, they discovered Quarvis's remains spread across the floor, his semi-flayed skull underneath the window overlooking the enclosure, one hand crouching spiderlike under a chair, the other – finger-less – resting on a table, his intestines unspooled like a length of fishing line. Slipping on a vital organ, Ballas nearly fell.

'Even in death, the little bastard's irritating,' he said, catching his balance.

They walked on, drifting from room to room. Eventually, they found a corridor leading to the outside world. Half a dozen Erethin stood there, faces covered with blood, scraps of flesh stuck to their hair and beards. At first, Ekkerlin feared they were possessed. But their demonic inhabitants were gone, drawn back into the forest by the force of Toros's own departure, like mariners dragged underwater by the pull of a sinking vessel, and now all that remained were six ordinary men, mired in shock, wondering what had happened to them, what they had become, and what they had ceased to be.

An old man lay on his back. A circular amulet was clenched in the crooked fingers of his right hand. A white-fletched arrow jutted from his throat.

Ekkerlin felt a pang of satisfaction.

Shaelus never lied, she thought. Not in his writings, anyway . . .

They went outside. Night had fallen. Pillars of moonlight pierced the forest roof. Unseen animals scratched, rustled, sniffed, going about their business as if everything was as it ought to be.

Ekkerlin called Shaelus's name several times, but received no response.

Then she saw it – a cross carved into the wide bole of a nearby oak, illuminated by a single beam of moonlight that cut through the branches like a finger, palely bright, brightly pale, pointing as if to say, *Here is the answer.*

She approached, knelt. Parting the grasses around the tree, she did not find a letter, but another inscription, a single Vohorin symbol.

Farewell.

She lingered, then rose.

'Shall we get moving, Anhaga?' she asked the big man.

'Aye,' he replied. 'Reckon so.'

EPILOGUE

Anhaga Ballas ran over Kelledin Moor.

Autumnal frost glittered on the grass, the chill-browned ferns. The sky chimed blue, the sun was a sphere of amber ice; after the long summer, it was unimaginably cold.

Cresting the hill, Ballas sprinted down to the tarn, capped by a sheet of ice. The familiar boredom had returned, the gnawing restlessness, and he pushed himself hard, hoping to drive out the black feelings before they had a chance to flourish. Already, Toros was a distant memory – and an unextraordinary one. What had Ballas done, except that which he always did? He had killed a man, nothing more. What were the demons he encountered – Embrace, Innocence and the rest – except strange, semi-human animals, essentially no different from apes found in the tropical jungles? What was the Solrepta, but a building like any other?

He ran a circuit around the tarn then started back to the Roost. As he got close, he spotted a figure, waiting.

'Fair morning, Anhaga,' said Ekkerlin as he arrived, breathless, his sweat already cooling. 'Good news. The general wants to see us. Another mission, I believe. Nothing too demanding – just an assassination.'

A faint emphasis lay on *just*; after Brawlsnare, everything, for Ekkerlin, had become a *just*. Toros had been the high moment of her military career, possibly her life; it would never be bettered, cast into the shadow by another adventure. She would not stay as a Hawk much longer, Ballas knew. She was experiencing a restlessness of her own, one arising not from boredom exactly, but a simple yearning to explore new areas, discover new things.

Ballas spat on the ground. 'Who is it this time?'

'A silk-merchant,' said Ekkerlin. 'He has been funding rebels in the north.'

She clapped him on the shoulder.

'Let's get going. You can get your breath back later.'

General Standaire sat behind the small desk in his office at the centre of the Roost.

He was tired. But content. The grey disillusionment, the slumping of spirits he had suffered since the start of the Vohorin mission – *before*, if he remembered correctly – had dissipated. It was a phase, he assumed, that most men were destined to go through at some stage or another. But maybe – he could not be sure – it was also the effect of a guilty conscience. Things could prey on a man's mind without him realising it, sapping his energy, reducing his vigour by imperceptible degrees. After returning to the Roost, he had written a short letter to his wife and daughter; it was little more than a note, he supposed, asking after their health, their happiness. They had not responded – yet. Perhaps they never would. He could not blame them, if they wanted to keep their distance – for it was a distance *he* had created. Nonetheless, he would wait.

There was a knock on the door. He bade his visitors enter.

Ballas and Ekkerlin stepped through, the big man slathered in sweat, the woman as brightly attentive as a cat watching a starling.

Standaire described their mission, which was of no great significance. As they turned to go, he said, 'Hawk Ballas.'

Ballas halted.

'Never lie to me,' said Standaire, quietly.

'Sir?' Ballas appeared genuinely perplexed.

'You heard. Now leave.'

The door closed. Standaire stared a moment, then looked down, allowing himself a faint, fleeting smile.

'What was he on about?' Ballas asked Ekkerlin.

'I honestly don't have a clue,' replied Ekkerlin. 'Come on. We'll need horses.'

As they entered the stableyard, Ballas cupped his hands to his mouth and called, 'Two horses – now!'

'Yes, yes,' came a voice from inside a stable. 'Be patient. Hold your hor— Well, just wait. I will not be long.'

Ballas looked at the sky. 'I have not lied to the general,' he said. 'Not that I can remember, anyway. You reckon he's going senile?'

'Unlikely,' said Ekkerlin. 'He would consider it an unforgiveable lapse of self-discipline. He simply isn't . . .' Trailing off, she grunted in surprise. 'Maybe this . . . maybe *he* is the answer.'

Hooves clopped on stone. Lowering his gaze, Ballas saw a stablehand leading two mounts, saddled and ready to ride.

For a moment, the Hawk was speechless. When he found his voice, it was to curse, savagely.

'Aren't you supposed to be dead?' Ekkerlin asked the stablehand.

The stablehand laughed. 'I, Cledrun Mallakos, dead? Ha! I am too young for that sort of nonsense. No, I have many furlongs left to run before I am sent to the glue-makers. Although,' he nodded seriously, 'it is true my continuing existence is owing, in part, to the soft-heartedness of our mountainous friend. He should've cut my throat, you know. Instead, he submitted to his instinctive good nature, and spared me. How are you faring, Anhaga Ballas?'

Ballas asked the only question he could think of. 'What are you doing here?'

'I've got reins in my hands, dung on my boots and a scratchy bit of hay trapped in my undergarments. What do you think I am doing here? I have been appointed chief stablehand to the regiment.' He stuck out his chest. 'I have become a military man.'

'You were supposed to disappear,' said Ballas. 'That was our bargain.'

'Ah yes,' agreed Mallakos. 'Indeed, that was my intention. Alas, I am a sentimental fellow, and I could not flee the country without Larchfire. So I returned to Silver Hoof, hoping to grab the old girl, and head to the docks. Sadly, Wardens were waiting, trying to work out why I, Mallakos, had a stableyard full of roasted guardsmen. I was arrested, and imprisoned.'

'But all turned out well in the end?' said Ballas, eager to be away. 'Good. Give us the horses and—'

'Fearing for my life, I broke the second part of our bargain,' continued Mallakos, as if Ballas had not spoken. 'I blurted out every detail of our adventures in Sliptere. Understandably, I was treated as if I were mad. But somehow, word of my strange tale reached the Masters, who recognised its veracity; it concurred, I believe, with the general's own account of the episode—'

'The horses, Mallakos,' persisted Ballas. 'We have work to do.'

'However, a problem remained,' said Mallakos. He was in full flow; nothing could stop him. He was the sort of man, Ballas realised, who could talk for hours, with or without an audience. 'Although I was innocent, I could not be set free, lest I spread my tale about as though it was butter, and the

684

curious ears of the commonfolk were toasted crumpets. You Hawks thrive on secrecy, yes?'

'We thrive on action,' said Ballas. 'And there will be no action until you give us our hor—'

'As Standaire had decreed in Sliptere that I should be snuffed out,' Mallakos went on, deaf to all objections, 'there was a possibility his command would be carried out, albeit belatedly. Thus, the general was consulted and after, I am sure, a certain amount of wrangling, I was offered this job. Marvellous, eh? He isn't a bad sort, is the Blade. He even let me bring Larchfire. She's over there.'

He pointed to a stable. An ancient, threadbare horse peered out, its gaze fixed on Ballas.

'She is the regimental mascot,' said Mallakos. 'She must be treated with respect. No more oil-baths, understand?' He handed Ballas the reins to a black stallion. 'And my dear Bookworm,' he said, turning to Ekkerlin. 'How are you faring? Fully recovered from the snake-venom?'

'Completely,' replied Ekkerlin.

'Excellent! Well, I'll let you go on your way. Take care of these chaps, won't you?' He gave Ekkerlin the reins to an ice-white gelding. 'And yourselves, of course. Oh yes,' he added, as the Hawks moved away. 'If you could see your way to . . . if it would not be too much trouble . . . Could you bring back a few bags of sugar? For the horses? And a fresh set of grooming brushes. The ones here are rather worn out. But only if it is no bother!'

They led the horses away from the stable.

'Sugar, brushes – I *should* have killed him,' said Ballas, swinging into the saddle. 'A pox on this soft heart of mine.' He pointed to a clump of boulders on the horizon. 'Fancy a race?'

'Very well,' said Ekkerlin, mounting.

'On the count of three,' said Ballas. 'Ready? Right. One—'

And he was away, galloping through the glittering frost-light of autumn.

From the second-floor room of a small house in Glavven City, Crenfriste watched the Druinese soldiers patrolling the street outside.

Officially, Vohoria had become a province of Druine. The Druinese had arrived two months ago, and had taken over the underpopulated country with minimal effort. Fearing a second Scourge, some Vohorin fought back, true; but they were few in number, untrained and ill-equipped. Some loyal Torosians also resisted, considering it a pious necessity, unaware that their idol would never be reborn; it would take a while for their fires to be extinguished, Crenfriste knew.

These upsets aside, the conquest was largely bloodless. As expected, Churchmen had arrived in droves, attired in blue robes and gleaming Scarrendestin pendants, and had taken to preaching the faith of the Pilgrim Church. Although many Vohorin objected to their presence, few complained about their tolerance of the old Vohorin ways, abolished by the Torosians: art and music were permitted, and the vast *valrux* distilleries in the east reopened, producing the clear liquor of which the late Emperor Grivillus had been dangerously fond.

By and large, the populace was content. But it would not last, she was assured, by one who understood the Church better than most.

They are seducing you, he had said. *It is akin to courtship: at present, you are receiving scented gifts, contrived to earn your affection. Soon, you will be wed – and then what? A life of drudgery, obedience and misery.*

She turned.

Cavielle Shaelus sat in the corner, hunched over a desk,

writing. Sensing her gaze upon him, he looked up.

'You know,' he said, 'I cannot decide who will be most upset by this book.' He tapped the feather end of the quill against the manuscript. 'The Church, or those poor fools clinging to the Torosian faith.'

His book was an autobiographical account of the past fifteen years of his life, from the point he was sent to the desert by the Blessed Master named Faltriste, to his part in the destruction of Toros. He had asked Crenfriste if she thought it would prove a decent tale; she said it probably would, but advised him not to write it.

'It will destroy your reputation,' she had said.

'Why so?' he replied.

'No one will believe it. They will assume it is either untrue or the work of a lunatic. Is that how you want to be remembered?'

'It is not how I am remembered that matters,' he had said. 'It is how I choose to live. I have always — almost always — written the truth, regardless of how absurd or improbable it seems.'

'And what is at the heart of the truth?' Crenfriste countered. 'You threw your lot in with Toros for a decade and a half, and doing so, made a terrible fool of yourself.'

'Is not a man's foolishness as worthy of comment as his wisdom? Can a fellow's mistakes not be as intriguing as his triumphs?'

He could not be dissuaded, Crenfriste had realised.

'Another week,' he said now, dipping his quill, 'and I should be finished.'

'And then?'

'I'll return to Druine.' He gazed at the ink-wet quill tip. 'I think that I may take on an apprentice.'

'The girl?' Although he had told Crenfriste every detail of his adventure, Shaelus had refused to name either of the Hawks,

687

saying only that one was a large, brutish man, the other a young woman whose spirit and intellect were, in his words, a rough-hewn version of his own. He would not name them in his book either, he said; he was fond of them both, and did not want to burden them with unwanted attention.

'She would be a fitting successor,' said Shaelus. 'I would grant her access to my private library of forbidden texts, hidden away so long in a quiet corner of Druine.'

'Would she be tempted?'

'Tempted? Yes – as a fox is tempted, upon finding the hen-house door ajar.' Nodding, he bowed his head and continued writing.

ACKNOWLEDGEMENTS

It is traditional, of course, to acknowledge the various folks who assisted, directly or indirectly, in the writing of a book. So I shall do so, whether they like it or not.

My mother and father, for everything.

Rachel and Richard, for love, support and back-breaking toil.

Andy Remic, for the best sort of friendship, barbarity and mirth.

Chris Smith, for late-night jam sessions and the Rubberband Man.

Sharon Ring for casting an eye over an early version of the book, and Archie the dog for not eating it.

My editors of the past – Tim Holman, Darren Nash and Bella Pagan, who helped steer a course through choppy waters.

My current editor, Jenni Hill – who brought the ship home, then repaired the sails, killed the rats, caulked the deckboards and a host of other acts of editorial virtuosity which deserve more praise than any painfully over-extended nautical metaphor can provide.

ACKNOWLEDGEMENTS

extras

orbit

www.orbitbooks.net

about the author

Ian Graham lives in the north of England. *The Path of the Hawk* is a prequel to his first novel, *Monument*. His website can be found at iansgraham.net.

Find out more about Ian Graham and other Orbit authors by registering for the free monthly newsletter at www.orbitbooks.net.

if you enjoyed
THE WYRMLING HORDE
look out for

MONUMENT

by

Ian Graham

1

Thus it commenced, on a cloudless night,
A clothes-maker of the south
Of Meahavin
Received the word of the creator-god
And vowed to do His bidding.
Abandoning all worldly goods, he left
His home and became a Most Holy Pilgrim . . .

> *Extracted from the unexpurgated, forbidden account*
> *of the Pilgrims by Mascali, the Ninth Witness*

It was a foolish fashion, thought the big man. A mixture of vanity, bluster and juvenile stupidity.

Across the common room, a group of stonemasons sat at a long table. They were young men, sinuously muscled from long hours of labour. White dust caked their skin, hair, eyelashes – they seemed much less men than phantoms granted flesh. They were drinking ale, jesting, and waiting for the whores to arrive. The big man objected to none of these things. Alcohol, laughter and women were sensible pursuits. But he found absurd the manner in which the stonemasons wore their purses.

Each purse hung from its owner's belt on a two-inch braided leather strip. Some strips were brightly coloured, reds interwoven with greens and blues. Others were darker: a sombre plaiting of blacks, browns, and dried-blood ochre. The purses dangled from these strips as vulnerable, and as tempting, as ripe apples. The most cack-handed thief could've snatched one.

And that, supposed the big man, was precisely the point.

Like any young men with hot red blood in their veins, the stonemasons wished to appear confident, strong, dangerous . . . exactly the type of men who could fearlessly expose their valuables to theft. For no one would dare steal them. It would be akin to snatching food from a lion's jaws: an act of suicidal lunacy.

The big man lifted a wine flagon to his lips.

Since mid-morning, he had been in the tavern. He had scarcely budged from his corner table – except to use the pissing yard and purchase fresh drinks at the bar. He had imbibed enough alcohol to float a warship. Whisky, gin, rum, ale, wine . . . all had sluiced into his stomach. He had drunk enough to make most men fall violently sick. Enough, perhaps, even to kill those of an under-developed constitution. But the big man was immeasurably resilient. Effortlessly, he could drink ten times as much as most men.

And *looked* like he could.

Drink had bloated him. Over his belt sagged an ale gut – a flaccid drum of flesh, straining against his tunic. His face was swollen. And never a handsome man, he now resembled a boar. His nose had been broken so frequently in drunken brawls that it had crumpled to a snout. His beard – thick, tangled, lice-thronged – was the dull black of a tusker's pelt. His slightly hunched shoulders, barrel chest and lumbering movements added to his porcine appearance. Only his eyes looked fully human. Set in watery, bloodshot whites, the green irises were sharp, attentive. They glittered insolently.

The big man's name was Ballas.

It was time, he decided, to get himself some money.

He dropped his wine flagon deliberately and watched it shatter on the floor.

Startled by the sudden noise, the stonemasons glanced over.

'Clumsy bastard,' shouted one – a red-haired youth, his skin still blemished by childhood freckles. His brown eyes were cold and cruel; they burned with a type of habitual resentment. He gazed intently at Ballas. 'Look at the state of him,' he urged his friends, pointing. 'There is dried vomit on his shirt. His hair bristles with lice. I'd wager piss stains daub his breeches. Tell me, fat man: when did you last take a bath?'

Ballas shrugged.

'You seem untroubled by your own filth,' said the youth. 'And by your stench. Do you go whoring, eh?'

Ballas nodded.

'I take it the girls hold their breath? I take it they struggle to keep down their gorges? For you're more likely to provoke nausea than desire.'

Ballas shrugged once more.

'You have no self-respect, fat man,' said the youth. 'If I ever hit low times and live as you do, I'll kill myself. Sweet grief, I'd slit my throat. I'd slice off my balls. I'd do anything to bring about my death. No matter how painful, no matter how degrading.' He turned to the other stonemasons. 'Promise that one of you'll butcher me, if ever I take on the fat man's aspect. Go on: we are all loyal to one another. I'd do the same for you. It'd be a true act of friendship. A mercy killing. Surely you wouldn't deny me?'

The red-haired youth's purse dangled from a plain black strip. Its burden of coins strained against the fabric. Ballas eyed it for a moment like a snake eyeing a mongoose.

He stooped to pick up a shard of flagon glass.

'No, wait,' came a voice.

A serving girl hurried over. 'I shall do that. You'll only cut yourself, and then I'll have to mop up blood as well as wine.'

Kneeling, she used a short-handled brush to sweep the shards into a heap.

'You have been here since we opened,' she said, glancing up. 'It is a rare thing, to see someone drink as much as you. You have guzzled a river, sir. You are not going to turn foul, are you?'

'Foul?' murmured Ballas.

'You know: *rowdy*. This is a peaceful tavern, more or less. We don't want trouble.'

'You'd reckon it best if I left?' asked Ballas. His deep voice rolled with a Hearthfall burr.

'No,' said the girl quickly.

'A serving girl doesn't ask a man if he's going to go rotten,' said Ballas. 'Not if she wants him to stay, and keep drinking. I've spent a purseful here—'

'You misunderstand me,' interrupted the serving girl.

'I misunderstand *nothing*,' said the big man, rising. 'I'm not welcome here, right? So I'll just piss off, then. There're finer places in Soriterath – places where a man can drink, *and* be well treated.'

Edging around the table, Ballas swayed. The floor seemed to tilt like the deck of a tide-shaken ship. Gripping the table's edge, Ballas steadied himself. He was drunker than he had expected. Taking a deep breath, he started towards the doors.

He took ten paces, tripped – and crashed into the red-haired stonemason. The stonemason fumbled his tankard; the vessel clanked on to the table, and an ale pool spread over the surface. With an angry shout, the stonemason sprang to his feet.

'You bloody *oaf*!' he snapped, his eyes blazing. 'Can't you even walk properly? Look what you have done!' He pointed furiously at the spilled ale.

'Accident,' mumbled Ballas. 'I'm drunk. Every step is an adventure. Forgive me.'

The stonemason wrinkled his nose. 'Close to, your stink is even fiercer than I imagined. You reek worse than a tanner's shop!' He pushed Ballas away.

Surprised by the youth's abrupt move, Ballas stumbled over a stool and fell to the floor.

The stonemason stood over him. 'You owe me a tankard of ale.'

'I've got no money,' said Ballas, slowly. 'I've got . . . nothing.'

'No man without money can get as drunk as you are . . .'

'No man as drunk as I am,' replied Ballas, struggling to his feet, 'can possibly have any money *left*. I've supped enough to bankrupt a Blessed Master. To settle his account, he'd have to pawn the Sacros.'

'Do not lie to me,' said the stonemason. He advanced on Ballas.

'Aiy!' The serving girl glared at them from across the room. 'Do you want me to summon the tavern-master? He has a wolfhound as big and ill-tempered as a bull: would you like him to turn it loose on you?' She looked sharply at Ballas. 'Go on: do as you promised – *leave*. The first time I saw you, I knew you were bad.'

'Is that so? Then you're smarter than you look,' said Ballas. He glanced at the stonemason. He considered insulting the youth. He knew exactly what to say. The youth was embarrassed by his freckles. In every other aspect he was a man, full-grown and strong. Yet he still bore the faint leopard-markings of a child. Alternatively, Ballas could ridicule his acne: it sprawled over his chin, each spot a sore red hue, and pus-laden.

Ballas said nothing. It was wisest by far simply to leave. Turning, he shambled outdoors.

It was mid-afternoon. Bright autumnal light fell from a clear blue sky. The big man stood in a thoroughfare of half-frozen mud. On either side, there were taverns constructed from pale grey stone. Many appeared to be half-derelict: the wooden eaves were rotting, mosses and moulds blotched the brickwork, and paint had long since peeled from the doors. Ballas had been in Soriterath for only a few days, yet this particular area was one of the shabbiest he had encountered – not only in this city, he reflected, but in all of Druine. Soriterath was the Holy City, the city where the Pilgrim Church leaders dwelled. But it was not a place of splendour. In the opulent areas, there were grand buildings, true enough; but mainly the city was like many in Druine: a place of creeping squalor, of houses, taverns and shops constructed from tired stone and mouldering wood, packed tightly together, as if to confine as many souls as possible to the smallest space. And, like many such cities, it had a distinctive smell: a combination of decaying vegetation and decomposing flesh. The greengrocers dumped their unsold produce in the streets, and when any of the city's feral animals – a rabble of rats, cats and dogs – died, their carcasses were left to rot where they lay. A similar fate awaited many human corpses; others, weighted with rocks, were dumped in the Gastallen River. In an effort to control the diseases emanating from such corpses, the Pilgrim Church had erected communal pyres throughout the city. During times of plague and famine, Ballas had heard, the air over Soriterath grew black with the smoke of burning flesh.

Soriterath might have been the Holy City, but it frequently had a hellish aspect.

And when common room pessimists spoke of the country's decline, of Druine's gradual slide into moral ruin, they often held up Soriterath as an example.

When Ballas arrived here, he had felt instantly at home.

An icy breeze swirled along the thoroughfare, stinging his cold-cracked skin.

He shivered. Then he grinned.

'Let me see what I have here,' he said, unfurling the fingers of his left hand. Upon his palm crouched the stonemason's purse. It had been easily stolen. When Ballas had tripped – deliberately – into the young man, he had cut the purse from its strip with the shard of flagon glass. He had performed the operation with a conjuror's dexterity.

The purse was full.

'When night falls,' murmured Ballas, 'I shan't be dossing on the streets.'

Then he noticed that the purse felt light. *Too* light, for a purse burdened with coins.

Frowning, he rubbed it. He felt what he had previously observed: coins' hard edges, straining against the fabric.

Yet the lightness persisted.

Was the wine playing a trick on him? Could it make heavy objects seem near-weightless – just as it made ugly women appear beautiful?

He emptied the purse on to his palm. And cursed as a dozen discs of plain wood tumbled out.

He hurled them to the ground.

'Pissing eunuch,' said Ballas, as if the stonemason was present. 'Freckled, pimple-crusted eunuch. I ought to castrate you, and complete the effect.'

A door slammed open. Echoes raced along the thoroughfare.

The stonemason stepped from the tavern. Two others stood beside him.

'You idiot,' said the red-haired youth, pacing toward Ballas. His fingers probed the strip, dangling purseless from his belt. 'Did you imagine I wouldn't notice? Did you suppose that, like you, I am so insensible that I can suffer an indignity without realising?'

'What are you talking about?' said Ballas, lamely.

'Oh, come now – don't feign innocence. You stand with my purse in your hand, my coins spread about your feet. You know fully what I speak of.'

'It was a jest, nothing more—'

'As is this, my friend.' Springing forward, the stonemason swung a flagon against Ballas's head. Dazed, Ballas staggered. A second blow landed on his cheekbone. Then the stonemason kicked him in the crotch.

There was a heartbeat of terrible expectation – then a choking pain surged from Ballas's testicles to his throat.

Sinking to his knees, Ballas vomited. The stonemason ran forward and kicked him in the face. The impact knocked Ballas on to his back.

Kneeling beside him, the stonemason punched him in the mouth. Then he brought down the flagon on Ballas's head – again and again, until the vessel shattered.

Then the real violence began.

The stonemason's friends kicked Ballas in the chest, legs and stomach. They used their fists, too, and delivered blow after muscle-jarring blow. Ballas felt like a fox set upon by hounds. His body jerked this way and that. The stonemason struck him repeatedly in the face, as if determined to disfigure him . . .

Eventually, exhausted, the three men grew still.

Silence fell.

Then came a splashing noise. Something showered on to Ballas's face.

Grimacing, he cracked open his swollen eyes.

The stonemason was urinating on him.

'Is it not apt that one who belongs in a sewer should be wetted by liquid destined for a sewer? Is this fluid not your true habitat? Aren't you as at ease in piss as a fish is in water?'

The stonemason laughed; his companions laughed, too.

'A warning, fat man. If I ever set eyes on you again, or catch your stench, you are dead. Understand? I've been merciful. But next time, I'll drag down lightning, and blast you from this world into the next.' He spat at Ballas. Then, turning, he walked away.

His friends followed him, vanishing back into the tavern.

Ballas sat upright. Over his body, bruises blossomed: his skin throbbed as blood spread beneath it. Tiny spasms rippled through his muscles. Lifting his fingers, he touched his nose – and gasped: it had been broken yet again. Right now it felt like nothing more than a plug of bloody gristle.

'Bastards,' he grunted. 'Pissing bastards . . . But now, let me see.' He gave a blood-clogged laugh. 'Maybe it is not all bad news.'

Within his left hand nestled a second purse. This one also belonged – *had* belonged – to the stonemason. Like the first it was stuffed full. Unlike the first it felt heavy.

Ballas upended it. Out on to his palm tumbled twelve copper pennies. A week's wage for an apprentice stonemason.

'Well, young man,' he said, 'the purse hanging from your belt was a cheat. But this one . . . Ha! Little boys have much to learn. Treat this as a lesson.'

Getting to his feet, Ballas limped away along the thoroughfare.

Several hours later, Ballas clambered from a pallet-bed and pulled on his leggings.

From the purse he rummaged two pennies, tossing them to the plump whore beneath the blankets.

He had visited a different tavern – he could not recall its name – immediately after the beating. He had drunk a flagon of Keltuskan red. Then, his ardour roused, he had purchased a few hours of the whore's time and taken her upstairs.

She had expressed surprise that someone so recently beaten could possess carnal inclinations. In her experience, they flowed away with a victim's blood. Ballas insisted that, in his case, that was not so. The whore had believed him.

To her credit, she had treated him gently. She had performed the more strenuous motions of coupling, allowing Ballas to remain immobile, grunting like a pig happy at the trough. Contrary to the stonemason's expectations, his sweat-odour had not offended her: on the windowsill a bowl of herbs smouldered, their fragrance filling the room and masking any other smell.

Ballas put on his shirt and boots.

Opening the shutters, he observed the night-cloaked Soriterath streets. He felt drunk, satisfied, tired – and thirsty. He was a stranger in the city. But he recalled that, a few streets away, there was a tavern that sold a sweet white wine, which would provide a gentle end to a trying but satisfactory day.

He left the chamber and went down a flight of steps into the common room. There was noise here: every table was occupied, and laughter shook the rafters. Ballas crossed the floor and stepped out into the night.

Reaching back, his gaze on the darkened street, he tried to shut the tavern door. It moved a few inches – then halted.

Grunting, he tugged harder but it would not budge.

He glanced back.

And exhaled.

In the doorway stood a tall, thin figure. He had small dark eyes, a pimple-spattered chin – and freckles.

He gripped a cudgel in his right hand.

'We have hunted you all evening,' he said, very quietly. 'Your persistence amazes me. You steal from us once, and get beaten.

Then you steal from us again. Truly, I believe drink has destroyed your mind. The Four preached abstinence. I always thought that it was over-pious nonsense . . . But now, I see the hazards of the bottle.'

The stonemason's friends appeared.

Ballas opened his mouth. But the stonemason said, 'Do not speak. At the moment of his death, a man ought to tell the truth. And you utter only lies.' Leaping forward, he slammed the cudgel against Ballas's cheekbone. The big man fell. Before he could move, the stonemasons were once more upon him.

2

On the eastern coast, in Saltbrake town,
A Chandler received the creator-god's word
And became a Pilgrim, and upon a road
Of Suffering and Enlightenment, he would learn
The true natures of Good and Evil . . .

'Will he live?'

'Oh – he might.'

'You sound uncertain . . .'

'Years ago, I tended a farmer who had been stampeded by a herd of bulls, and I doubt strongly he would have traded his injuries for this fellow's.' The voice, that of an old man, paused thoughtfully.

There was a long sigh.

'Look at him,' the voice continued. 'There is scarcely a square inch of flesh unbruised. From head to toe, he is caked in dried blood. I dare say many of his bones are broken – and the Four only know what more, ah, *subtle* damage has been done.'

'Subtle damage?' echoed the other voice – that of a much younger man. He spoke softly, but with great urgency. As if fearful a moment's laxity would exact a terrible cost. 'What do you mean, Calden?'

'Damage to his innards,' replied the old man. 'To his lungs, heart, liver. They are fragile things. It isn't always obvious when they are injured. They may bleed, and no one – neither patient nor physician – will know. And there are other maladies that do not loudly proclaim their presence. A blood-taint, for instance, kills as readily as any poison. Yet it will not be detected until it strikes.'

'But you *will* treat him – as best you can?'

'Of course. But Brethrien, observe him closely. It may be necessary – despite my ministrations – to give him the Final Blessing.'

Ballas lay perfectly still. He had already attempted to open his eyes. But the surrounding flesh was too swollen. His body felt at once strange and familiar. Strange, because the beating had covered it with contusions – and, as the old man had suggested, many bones were probably broken. Familiar, for Ballas had been beaten many times. He had grown accustomed to the terrible foreignness of how his body felt when freshly thrashed.

He wondered where he was. He tried opening his mouth so that he might ask. But his lips too were swollen, and stuck together with blood.

'His Blessing,' said the younger man, 'has already been administered. I delivered it in error. I came upon him in the street, covered in blood – and *frost*: I found him at dawn, and he had been outdoors overnight. I presumed he was dead.'

'An understandable mistake,' said the old man.

'When the Papal Wardens tried to load him upon a cart, so that he might be taken to the city's pyres, his wounds bled afresh.'

'So his heart was still beating . . .'

'I could scarcely believe it. I sent for you straight away.'

Something splashed into a bowl of water.

'Well, his wounds are clean,' said the old man. 'As for the blood covering the rest of him, we shall leave it be. It will do no harm.'

There was a wet grinding noise, slow and rhythmic. A pestle pulverising something in a mortar.

'Knitbone?' queried the young man.

'Yes, and a fine thing I brought plenty of it. A meadow's-worth would be hardly sufficient.' The grinding paused.

Ballas sensed the old man leaning close.

'He has been drinking. From his breath, it seems he has downed a lively mixture: whisky, ale, wine, rum . . . He has varied tastes.'

'I found him on Vintner's Row,' explained the young man. 'A place of taverns, gambling rooms and . . . ah . . .'

'Brothels,' finished the old man. As if the younger man would have problems speaking the word. 'I know of Vintner's Row. And that urges me to ask: what do *you* know of your patient?'

'Know of him? Well, nothing. I merely found him, in a poor state. It was my duty to help him. I have sworn an oath. I cannot ignore a distressed soul.'

The old man muttered something.

'Pardon?'

'Be wary,' repeated the old man, loudly. 'No decent-minded man takes his pleasures on Vintner's Row.' The grinding noises stopped. 'Unroll that bandage, will you? My thanks.' A squelching noise followed. As of a paste being smeared.

'I will grant him the benefit of the doubt.'

The old man laughed. 'The doubt? What is there to be doubted? You find him in one of Soriterath's most disreputable quarters, stinking of liquor, beaten halfway to the Eltheryn Forest . . .'

'I must grant him shelter,' said the younger man firmly.

'For how long?'

'Until he heals. Assuming such an event . . .'

'. . . Such a minor miracle . . .'

'. . . Occurs,' finished the young man.

The squelching stopped. Something cool and sticky was draped over Ballas's chest. A poultice. For a heartbeat the sensation was nearly pleasurable. The unguent numbed Ballas's flesh, and cooled it.

Then a gentle pressure was applied, to fix the poultice.

Pain swept through Ballas's body. He felt as if a lightning bolt had struck him. He imagined white heat crackling from rib to rib, then erupting from his pores. Every sinew tightened. Every muscle clenched.

He gasped.

'Ah, a response – did you see it?' In the old man's voice there was a note of surprise. 'That is encouraging.'

If the old man spoke again, Ballas did not hear. Garish scribbles of light sizzled behind his eyes. The pain steadily increased, until Ballas thought he would burst into flame.

Then: a swirling numbness. A delicious resignation engulfed him. He found himself spinning gratefully into warm black oblivion.

After a few days – because he was constantly slipping in and out of consciousness, he was unsure how many – Ballas opened his eyes. He found himself in a small white-walled room that had a single shuttered window and a fire blazing in the grate. The floor was bare stone, and there was a table laden with an array of medicinal items: bandages, swabs, yarn and needles for stitching wounds, herbs that could be ground into poultices.

The young man was a priest. No older than twenty-five years, he glowed with pious devotion. His fair hair was short-cropped into something resembling a monk's cut. His dark blue robes hung loosely on a slender frame. This, coupled with his pale skin, lent him the appearance of someone recovering from a serious ailment.

Yet he was animated by holy urgency.

Even the smallest tasks – the bringing of food and water, the examination of Ballas's wounds – seemed of the utmost spiritual importance.

Often, while changing Ballas's dressings, he asked, *Who are you? Where are you from? Will anyone be worried about you – ought I tell someone where you are?*

Ballas never replied.

The questions irritated him; his life was his own business, not some tender-hearted priest's.

But if he *had* answered, he would have revealed only that he was a vagrant and so hailed from everywhere and nowhere. No one in Druine would be concerned about him. Not the tavern-masters who sold him wine, ale, whisky. Not the whores who caught his mouldering seed.

The small room depressed Ballas. The persistent fire-smoke, the colourless walls and unguent-scent made him restless. He wanted to breathe clean, cold air. He needed to experience sensations other than warmth.

More than anything, he needed a drink. The priest had administered many medicines – except for those he craved most strongly.

One afternoon, Ballas felt strong enough to rise. Swinging his feet from the pallet-bed, he stood. A constricting pain seized his chest. As if an iron band was bolted tightly around it. Swearing softly, he waited for the discomfort to pass.

He was naked, he realised. Except for dried blood. It covered his body like a second skin. Grunting, he flexed his left arm. Where the flesh creased, blood-flakes cracked loose, drifting to the floor. Where had the blood come from? he wondered. A stab wound? A bottle-slash? It did not seem so. Inspecting his body, he found no sharp-edge injuries. Only jagged tears, where blunt objects had struck forcefully enough to split his skin.

Bruises covered his chest; they had ripened from black to a mix of metallic greens and golds. Murmuring, he touched his face. A nose shattered still further, a grotesquely swollen jaw, lips split open like sausages left too long upon the grill – these were the things his fingertips encountered.

Grunting, Ballas spat on the floor. A gobbet of red-tinged saliva quivered on the stone.

A heap of clothes lay in the corner. A brown tunic, soft cotton vest and black leggings . . . They were not Ballas's clothes. Yet they were intended for his use. Ballas tugged on the leggings. They were a comfortable fit. But the vest was slightly too tight. And the tunic couldn't easily accommodate Ballas's ale gut, which stretched the fabric almost to breaking point.

The boots were exactly the correct size. As they should have been: for they were Ballas's own, scrubbed clean of blood and vomit. The ripped stitching had been repaired, too.

'Holy man,' murmured Ballas, 'what are you, eh? A conscientious soul? Or a meddling toe-rag?'

Ballas left the room, stepping into a long corridor. At the far end stood a door, half ajar. Beyond, there was a kitchen. On a shelf rested wooden cups and bowls. There was a fire enclave but the stacked logs were unlit.

The priest Brethrien sat at a table.

Writing on a parchment, he wore an expression of rapt concentration. An illuminated edition of *The Book of the Pilgrims* lay open in front of him. Around his neck, he wore an elongated brass triangle: a miniature of Scarrendestin, the holy mountain.

'These are not my clothes,' said Ballas, entering the kitchen. His voice was naturally loud, with a growling note.

The priest jerked, startled. A blob of ink dripped from his quill-tip, splattering the parchment. Turning his face to Ballas, he blinked.

'These are not my clothes,' repeated the big man. 'Where are the clothes you found me in? I want them back.'

'You walk very quietly,' stammered the priest. Nervously, he fingered his Scarrendestin pendant – as if it were a protective amulet. 'I did not hear your footfalls . . .'

'For the last time, where are my clothes?'

'They had to be burned,' replied the priest.

'Burned?' asked Ballas darkly.

'They were infested,' explained Brethrien. 'Every manner of crawling thing inhabited them. They were, ah, *unhealthy*: unless one were a blood-feasting parasite – a louse or a grip-worm, say. They were threadbare, too. I suspect only the wildlife held them together.' He gestured to Ballas's new apparel. 'I apologise if I have taken a liberty. But, truly, your old clothes could not be saved. And those that you presently wear – they are of better quality. The wool is soft, yes? As soft as when it lay upon the sheep's back. Your old tunic was as coarse as a hair shirt.'

He laughed uneasily. 'Saint Derethine suffered many self-imposed tortures. But I dare say even he would have shrunk from your tunic.'

Ballas stared balefully at Brethrien.

'I, ah . . . Do you hunger?'

'For days, I've eaten piss-all but soup,' grunted Ballas. 'Of course I hunger.' His gaze alighted on a shelf of wine flagons. 'But my thirst troubles me more.' Grasping a flagon, he started tugging out the cork.

Alarmed, the priest sprang to his feet. 'No!'

He seized the flagon, trying to wrest it from Ballas. 'Please – you cannot drink that! It is forbidden!'

Choderlos de Laclos

Les Liaisons dangereuses

Dossier réalisé par
Charlotte Burel

Lecture d'image par
Alain Jaubert

folioplus
classiques

Ancienne élève de l'École normale supérieure, agrégée de lettres modernes, **Charlotte Burel** a consacré une thèse à l'éloquence du corps dans la littérature française du XVIIIe siècle. Elle enseigne actuellement au lycée Condorcet de Saint-Priest (Rhône).

Alain Jaubert est écrivain et réalisateur. Après avoir été enseignant dans des écoles d'art et journaliste, il est devenu aussi documentariste. Il est l'auteur de nombreux portraits d'écrivains ou de peintres contemporains pour la télévision. Il est également l'auteur-réalisateur de *Palettes*, une série de films diffusée depuis 1990 sur la chaîne Arte et consacrée à la lecture de grands tableaux de l'histoire de la peinture.